SOUL TO FIND

THE COMPLETE SERIES

LAYLA REYNE

SOUL TO FIND

ABOUT THIS BOOK

Four lives. Four fated loves.
One unforgettable journey through the supernatural.

From mysterious vigilantes to haunted reapers and shifter betrayals, the men of the *Soul to Find* series are no strangers to danger—or desire. Bound by fate and at the center of the war between Nature and Chaos, each must face impossible odds and risk everything for the one soul who could make them whole.

Or who could kill them.

Blending heart-pounding action with tender, steamy gay romance, this complete collection delivers found family, fierce love, and the kind of magic only soulmates can spark.

ICARUS AND THE DEVIL
A SOUL TO FIND NOVEL

Icarus and the Devil

Copyright © 2023 by Layla Reyne

All rights reserved. No part of this book may be reproduced or transmitted in any form or by any means, electronic or mechanical, including photocopying, recording, or by any information storage and retrieval system without the written permission of the copyright owner, and where permitted by law. Reviewers may quote brief passages in a review.

Editing: Edits by Kristi, Adam Mongaya, Susie Selva, Lori Parks

First Edition

October, 2023

Individual E-Book ISBN: 979-8-9869229-3-5

Individual Paperback ISBN: 979-8-9869229-8-0

This is a work of fiction. Names, characters, places, and incidents are either the product of the author's imagination or are used fictitiously. Any resemblance to actual persons living or dead, business establishments, events, or locales is entirely coincidental. All person(s) depicted on the cover are model(s) used for illustrative purposes only.

Content Warnings: explicit sex; explicit language; violence; kidnapping; blackmail; off-page death of former spouses; and instances and/or discussion of depression and PTSD.

ABOUT THIS BOOK

My name is Icarus for a reason.
If there's a way to screw up a plan, I'm your man.

Case in point:
Falling for the man I'm supposed to seduce and ferry to his death.
Adam Devlin, aka the Devil.
A vigilante ex-cop and a thorn in the side of the mobster
blackmailing me.
Should be easy.
Except Adam's longing for intimacy—for submission—is
irresistible.
Seduce him, yes. Lead him to his death, world of no.

There's only one solution to save us both: kidnap the Devil.
I mentioned my name is Icarus, right?
Three guesses how this plan will go.
Bet you only need one.

Icarus and the Devil is a steamy M/M paranormal romance novel. It features two danger-magnet men trying to stay alive and failing to stay away from each other. Chaos ensues on their way to happily ever after.

ICARUS AND THE DEVIL
A SOUL TO FIND NOVEL

Icarus and the Devil

Copyright © 2023 by Layla Reyne

Editing: Edits by Kristi, Adam Mongaya, Susie Selva, Lori Parks

First Edition

October, 2023

Individual E-Book ISBN: 979-8-9869229-3-5

Individual Paperback ISBN: 979-8-9869229-8-0

This is a work of fiction. Names, characters, places, and incidents are either the product of the author's imagination or are used fictitiously. Any resemblance to actual persons living or dead, business establishments, events, or locales is entirely coincidental. All person(s) depicted on the cover are model(s) used for illustrative purposes only.

Content Warnings: explicit sex; explicit language; violence; kidnapping; blackmail; off-page death of former spouses; and instances and/or discussion of depression and PTSD.

PART ONE

ICARUS

ONE

This was the definition of fucked. And not in the good way. Not in the way Icarus liked to be fucked, and not in the well-fucked way he made sure his clients left his bed. Nope, this was just plain old five-minutes-from-being-dusted fucked.

A far cry from the good kind of fucked of five minutes ago when he'd been putting on a show for the online client who'd paid for a virtual solo session. Icarus had nestled his favorite plug in his ass, clamped the rose gold cage around his cock, and tightened the leather cuffs around his ankles and wrists, naked and spread for his client on the other end of the private live stream. With a remote in each hand, he'd been slowly ramping up the vibrating plug and tightening the cock cage, his and his client's moans escalating together. And then his remotes had stopped working. The vibrating plug had died, and the cage had gone mad, clamping down and strangling his dick.

Not mad.

Hacked.

By the client—the warlock—formerly onscreen who had materialized in his room, yanked open the curtains, and replaced Icarus's soft leather cuffs with silver-laced ones that kept Icarus bound and pliant. The warlock stood beside the bed, finger hovering over a different remote that he'd promised would ruin Icarus's dick or destroy his ass for good if pressed. In either event —or both—it would cut off Icarus's primary source of income.

Assuming he survived the next five minutes. There was a reason he was called Icarus, and it had nothing to do with his currently magenta hair.

Ignoring the shaft of sunlight that crept across the foot of his bed, ever closer to his foot, ever closer to dust, Icarus tried sexy pouting at the warlock who held his dick and ass at his mercy. "Is this any way to treat the guy who was putting on a bang-up show for you?" He eyed the tent at the front of his captor's kilt. "Now that you're here, I could put on an even better show. Suck that for you. Make you come so—"

"He's not the one calling the shots."

Icarus's attention snapped toward the voice, toward the movement at the far end of the room. A tall, broad-shouldered white man dressed in a high-dollar suit stood in the bedroom doorway. Icarus sniffed. Human. He didn't carry the rotting wood stench of dark magic like the warlock beside the bed, but that didn't make the new visitor any less frightening. The bulging impressions of pistols under each arm, likely packing lead and silver bullets, wasn't the scariest thing about him either. No, it was the cold, hard malevolence that swirled in his big brown eyes. Such a beautiful color, one only humans possessed, one Icarus loved seeing bright with cheer or dark with desire. This man's eyes were dark, but the only desire swirling in them was for power—no matter how deadly and violent the path—and that frightened Icarus to his chilly core.

He deflected the only way he knew how. "I can suck your cock too. Let you call the shots. Or you can watch while I suck his."

The stranger nodded, and hope flared, but only for a second before the warlock's open palm smacked Icarus's cheek with unchecked force.

"Ow!" Icarus howled as stinging, magic-laced pain seared across his face. He'd cradle his cheek if he could but had to settle for gritting his teeth, waiting for the worst of it to pass. Once he could see straight again, he whipped his gaze back to the human standing at the foot of his bed. "That was fucking shitty! Your warlock has my cock in a cage and could tear my ass apart with the vibrator still in there, and I'm this fucking close to being dust." He wriggled his toes enough to put the little one in the sunlight, a spark catching and a tendril of smoke pluming in the air. He yanked it back into the narrowing shadow before it fully caught fire. "You didn't have to fucking hit me."

"And you don't have to keep running your mouth. I'll have him hit you again if you persist." He eyed the encroaching sun. "You don't have time to waste."

Meaning he intended to let Icarus live.

Meaning Icarus needed to shut the fuck up.

He pressed his lips together.

"Good," the human said. "Now, at last count, you were fifteen grand in debt to me."

"To you?"

"By way of Paris Cirillo."

Icarus hung his head back and groaned. Again, not in the good way. "Of course this is about that fool."

"That fool is my son."

Icarus gasped and righted his head. Seeing the truth of the statement on the big man's face, he slammed shut his mouth again.

"You're learning." Paris's father smiled, a wicked, cruel thing, as he circled the end of the bed and came to stand beside the warlock. "I don't dispute your assessment, but the fact remains that you owe us, and I'm here to collect."

"I don't have anything. Not worth that."

"On the contrary . . ." He trailed a hand up the inside of Icarus's thigh, hitching the leg higher and wider, as much as the ankle cuff would allow. Demonstrating his power, given the circumstances. He dipped his hand into the crease of Icarus's groin, fingers skirting the edge of the cage. "You have exactly what we need."

Icarus gnashed his teeth, fighting a moan and his fangs, the natural reactions of his body as the cage clamped painfully around his cock. "I thought—"

"Not for me." He removed his hand from Icarus's groin and palmed the warlock's straining cock. The magician moaned deep in his throat, and the sharp, salty scent of precome tinged the air. "My needs are well taken care of."

"You wanna fuck and make me watch?" It would hurt like hell. Just the thought was making him harder, making the cage tighter, despite his fear, despite the pain. But right then, he feared the creeping sun more, the pain the warmth on the side of his foot was already causing. "Fine, I'll watch, but you gotta let me out of the sun first."

Paris's father shook his head. "As soon as we're done here, Mr. Magic is gonna snap us back to my car parked in the alley behind this shithole building, and I'm gonna bend over his lap, flip up that skirt, and take his uncut cock in my mouth and suck him dry." He pumped the warlock's erection, and the scent of precome intensified. "Then he'll crawl onto his hands and knees in the back seat, and I'll shove my cock into his ass, over and over, until I fill him so full he'll be sore and dripping for days. So no, we don't need your help in that department."

Icarus stared, turned on and confused all at the same time. "I don't . . ."

If he thought the man's grin was wicked and cruel before, the one he flashed then was downright deadly, so full of rank hunger —for power—that Icarus's erection waned, even as the magician's continued to strain.

"We'll let you out of the sun," the terrible man said. "Then tonight, you're gonna put on the show of your life. For the Devil." He released the trembling warlock, circled to the foot of the bed, and snapped the laptop closed. "If you fail, it'll be the last show you ever perform."

Icarus gulped. If this man wasn't the Devil, who the fuck was?

TWO

Adam Devlin, aka the Devil.

That was who Vincent—Paris's power-hungry father who'd eventually introduced himself—had commanded Icarus to seduce. To what end, Icarus hadn't asked. Not like he had a choice. Once they'd given him his "mission" and made clear what would happen to Icarus if he failed, Vincent and his warlock, Atlas, had fizzled into thin air. Five minutes later, so had the cuffs. Five seconds after that, Icarus had freed his cock from the cage, removed the plug, and chucked both toys out the open window. Shame, as they'd been personal favorites, but he could never trust them again.

Hours later, lurking in the shadows of a crowded club, Icarus thought the same about the human sitting by himself at the end of the bar. He could never trust someone that good-looking, who sat that eerily still, and who went by the moniker the Devil. Six feet, broad shoulders, fit build. Not as fit as Icarus, but not everyone was frozen in time at twenty-five. Not everyone was in peak physical condition in their twenties either. Something about Adam Devlin made Icarus think he was far more dangerous in what looked like his forties than he would've been in his younger years. Maybe it was the dark hair and beard flecked with silver, or the peaks and valleys of his long, sharp face, or his pale weathered skin, or the blue-gray eyes that never stopped surveying his surroundings, even as he lifted a glass of amber liquid to his lips.

Barrel-aged whiskey.

Icarus had tasted it once on the lips of a ridiculously wealthy, seriously buttoned-up pack leader who occasionally liked to take a walk on the wild side. Warm and spicy with hints of oak and vanilla. Flavors derived from natural resources that didn't exist in abundance anymore—precious, expensive commodities. Only the rich and powerful were able to afford vintage bottles or the sky-high price tag of a single shot in a place like Club Sutro.

Icarus bet on both about the Devil—rich and powerful. A rival of Vincent, who Icarus was beginning to understand was rich and powerful too, especially to have a warlock in his thrall. Of course the internet was scrubbed clean of their identities—Adam, Vincent, Atlas, and Paris, all of them erased persons—rich-and-powerful clue number whatever count Icarus was up to. He probably should have known better, probably should have kept an ear closer to the ground of Yerba Buena, especially where his dealers and clients were concerned, but staying oblivious was generally better in his line of work. The performance was easier when his sole focus was seducing his mark and keeping his own secrets.

Tonight's performance was going to be the opposite of easy. "The show of your life," Vincent had said. And the curtain continued to rise higher with each sip of whiskey Adam took, until the drink was all but gone and the stage lights were shining bright.

Showtime.

Icarus cinched his corset around his bare torso, tugged up his sheer black gauntlets, checked his garters were secure, and finger combed his hair, making sure his magenta strands were spiked to maximum height. He might have been a fuckup in every other aspect of his life, but in this one area, he was in control. He was the best. As if this was what he'd been born for—turned for. He relished the rare slice of confidence.

Emerging from the shadows, he sauntered across the club at human speed, his stilettos clicking on the cement floor, his lace garters and nylon stockings brushing with each step. Every paranormal in the club could hear his approach and how, after two steps, Icarus adjusted his gait so his steps were in time with the Devil's heartbeat. On the hunt, no other paranormal in the club would interrupt him. Not unless they wanted their heart torn from their chest or their jugular ripped from their throat.

Adam, however, shouldn't have been able to hear him, not over the thumping club music. Shouldn't have been able to sense him at all, Icarus approaching from his blind spot, but the human's frame stiffened with awareness. Maybe not completely human. Adam whipped his face around, glaring over his shoulder. Storm clouds gathered in his steely gaze, a back-off warning aimed squarely in Icarus's direction.

Icarus didn't falter; he didn't scare that easily. He swayed his hips as he closed the distance between them, sidling up to the bar beside Adam. "I'd offer to buy you another"—he ran a black-painted fingernail along the rim of the glass—"but even I don't have whiskey-kind-of-money, and I'm the best courtesan here."

The Devil shifted on his stool as if to leave. "Not interested."

"Yes, you are." Icarus propped a foot on the bottom rung of Adam's stool, planted a hand on his bent knee, and boxed Adam in. "If you weren't, you would have ignored my approach."

"You're new here."

"Nine months or so, up from Portola." A practiced line. Never mind the decades between when he'd left Portola the first time and arrived in Yerba Buena.

"Which is why you don't know." Adam's gaze darted past Icarus, sweeping the club again—along the wall of windows, the actual stage, the crowd, the exits—before landing back on him, impatient and unamused. "I used to be a cop. Not my instinct to ignore danger at my back."

Icarus didn't think that was Adam's only instinct at work. He went to work on another, widening his stance and giving Adam a bird's-eye view of everything being offered. The skimpy boy shorts beneath his garters did little to hide his package. Intentionally. "The only danger you're in is missing out on the best night of your life if you leave here without me."

Adam didn't take the bait. He lifted a hip, withdrew his wallet, and pulled out two bills. "I already had the best night of my life. Ten years ago." He slipped the bills under the glass, then tucked his wallet away. "Just here to commemorate it and move on. Same as every October first."

A hole opened in Icarus's chest, dark and fathomless, the sadness and loss in Adam's voice a wrecking ball like Icarus had only experienced one other time in his life: the day he'd been turned, which was why he'd never turned anyone himself. He couldn't bear to be the cause of that feeling. Couldn't bear it now for Adam either. He lifted a hand, ignoring Adam's flinch and the gun he'd glimpsed on the Devil's hip, and cupped his cheek. It was warm despite the gray clouds that hung around the man. "I can make you forget it. For a night." His own instincts—beyond mere self-preservation—demanded it.

Gray gave way to blue, a deep sad shade that reminded Icarus of Picasso's Blue Period. "I don't want to forget it," Adam said. "I can't."

"Relive it, then?"

Adam's bitter laugh made ragged the edges of the hole his earlier words had torn open in Icarus's chest. "You'd end up dead."

He already was, but Adam's instincts hadn't caught on to that detail. Hadn't caught on to the fact that the opposite of his words was doubly true. If Icarus didn't succeed in seducing him, Icarus would be dead. For good this time. He teased the corner of Adam's mouth with his thumb. "Risk I'd be willing to take."

Faster than he should have been able, Adam clasped his wrist. To yank it down and push him away, Icarus expected—but Adam did the unexpected. He pulled Icarus closer and swiped his tongue over his own bottom lip, the tip brushing the pad of Icarus's thumb. "Could I even afford you?"

Icarus bit back his gasp—surprise, victory, and lust all warring for a voice. Any of which, if spoken, would crater the mission.

The mission.

"If you can afford that whiskey"—he flicked his gaze to the glass—"you can afford me."

A shaky breath coasted over Icarus's palm, and Adam's gaze finally drifted down, taking in all of Icarus. His pulse sped, a blush streaked across his high cheekbones, and when he lifted his eyes back to Icarus's, a lake of fire stared back at him. The same fire that roared through Icarus, unlike anything he'd ever experienced. "Where—"

A phone rang, shattering the moment. A single blink and Adam disappeared, retreating into his shell, banking the heat as the storm clouds returned. The Devil tiptoed back under his skin, and he released Icarus's wrist, shifted away, and pulled out his phone. "Devlin."

The call lasted less than a minute, and when it was over, the Devil slid off his stool without another word. Without another look. Without the slightest clue that he'd just sentenced Icarus to death.

THREE

Icarus ordered a cheap shot of vodka, sulked the length of it, then got over himself. Yes, he was good at his job, but not every job was easy, and he hadn't expected this one to be. In fact, he'd been doing better than expected before that phone call had interrupted them. Success—*Adam*—had been at his fingertips. It—*he*—could be again if Icarus was in the right place at the right time when Adam finished doing whatever that call had summoned him away to do. The night wasn't over, and neither was the mission.

He paid the bartender and grabbed his trench and combat boots from the coat check. Swapping his heels for the boots, he shoved the former into his coat pockets and wrapped up tight before heading outside into the cold night. Neither the temperature nor the dark affected him, but his work attire might draw the kind of attention he didn't need at the moment. He already had a mark; he wasn't looking for another.

He sniffed the air and caught the lingering aroma of whiskey, and on its heels, the oily odor of gasoline, another thing only the rich and powerful could afford for their gas-powered automobiles. He followed the scents, keeping to the shadows as he moved at his preternatural pace, heels never touching the ground, leaping from toe to toe, block to block. The path took him down Sutro Hill and east across town toward the Canyon Lands.

Humans rarely ventured into this part of Yerba Buena, their reaction times too slow for the frequently shifting land and their eyesight too poor for an area that was shrouded in fog day and night. Magically so. It was a demented sort of fun house for paranormals—a place to hide, to trade in illicit goods, to do bad things, a playground for one's darkest fantasies—but for humans, it was a sightless, dangerous nightmare. A deadly maze that could change shape in the blink of an eye.

Icarus wasn't surprised to find a vintage Camaro parked at the end of a road in front of the barbed wire fence that ran the length of the Canyon Lands border. He was surprised, however, that Adam's scent didn't diverge left or right into one of the alleys, garages, or abandoned buildings where all sorts of shit went down. Instead, it continued straight ahead, beyond the fence and out toward the canyons of deep dark water that cut into the crumbling ruins of structures that used to stand tall and magnificent, glass and metal that had once shone in the sunlight.

Before the Rift.

Before that day thirty years ago when Nature and her allies had gone to war with Chaos and the darker forces of magic, with Yerba Buena as ground zero. When what had started as a balmy October day had turned into a dark and stormy nightmare, when the contours of the land had been irrevocably altered by earthquakes, landslides, and tsunamis, and when battle lines had been etched in stone. Skirmishes were constant in the three decades since, the push and pull between Nature and Chaos waxing and waning with the seasons and the power grabs of beings—human and paranormal—in between. But where the Canyon Lands were concerned, Nature had conceded the territory, and she hadn't left it a hospitable place.

Icarus ducked through the wire fence, cursing low when a barb snagged the lace band of his stocking. He could try to save it, but the wafting whiskey scent was growing fainter, dissipating in the heavy fog as Adam moved farther into the canyons. Cutting his losses, Icarus unclipped the garter—*that* he wasn't losing—and clawed through the thinner nylon beneath the lace top of the stocking.

Freed, he climbed the rest of the way through the fence and hustled to catch up to Adam, worrying more with each step. The ground beneath his boots was a debris-filled mess of buckled roads and sidewalks, sand and silt, and all around, in buildings and makeshift hovels, in the swirling fog that filled alleys and crevices, bright eyes glowed, their owners snarling a warning.

What the fuck was Adam doing out here? Meeting someone—or doing something—he shouldn't? In either case, was it worth risking his life?

Icarus got his answer twenty or so yards later when an explosion overhead sent him scrambling behind a rusted-out dumpster. Smoke and flames billowed from the shattered windows of a corner building, the metal fire escape rattling as another explosion wracked what was left of the crumbling structure.

"Go, go, go!" someone shouted from inside the building, and in the wake of another plume of smoke and shattering glass, a slim figure in jeans and a dark hoodie emerged from the broken window onto the fire escape. They turned back toward the building, arms outstretched, and Adam appeared at the window, leaning his torso out, a blanket-wrapped something in his arms. As Adam handed off the bundle, an arm slipped loose of the blanket, and a head fell back onto the rescuer's shoulder, exposed. Human, maybe? Dark hair, skin that was too pale and too thin, translucent almost, stretched across jutting bones. Emaciated, barely hanging on to life, a fluttering heartbeat compared to the stronger two—no, four—in its vicinity. And glowing too, a red-orange sheen the likes of which Icarus had never seen, rippling over the being's skin. A shifter, then, of some sort? Icarus sniffed, but the smoke drowned out any other scents.

"Go!" Adam shouted. "Get him to Jenn and the coven before he flames out."

Flames out?

The hooded figure wrapped their arm tight around the young man, turned, and jumped off the metal platform. Icarus muffled his shout in the crook of his arm. The jumper landed on their feet, dark hair escaping the hood, delicate features visible in profile. A woman. Definitely a shifter for how gracefully she'd landed and how fast she took off, disappearing into the fog.

The building gave another terrible shake and a groan as wood and metal scraped together, as smoke and flames gushed out of every hole, as hunks of concrete crashed to the already-splintered asphalt. Icarus whipped his gaze back to the fire escape. No sign of Adam. But three heartbeats still inside. Adam plus two other friends . . . or two other foes? *Fuck.* A tinny voice of self-preservation rang in Icarus's head. Let the building come down; let it end Adam; let Vincent blackmail Icarus to do something—anything— else. The louder voice inside Icarus's chest rebelled at the notion of leaving Adam to such a fiery fate, especially after he'd just saved a paranormal of some sort from the same.

Icarus moved to step out from behind the dumpster, to zip into the building and rescue the man he was supposed to deliver to Vincent, only to freeze midstep when a coughing Adam staggered out of a glassless window on the ground floor. The two other heartbeats emerged and rushed to Adam's side, helping to hold him up as he gulped in breaths of air. Icarus silently sank behind the dumpster and waited for Adam to recover, which happened far too quickly for Adam to be only human. Icarus didn't have long to ponder what he was, though, because the trio moved again, Adam leading them away from the burning building and deeper into the fog, stopping only when they reached the outer edge where the ground had fallen away in massive chunks, only ruins and unstable jetties left between the deep dark crevices of rushing water.

Icarus ducked inside the nearest hollowed-out ruin, inching closer to where Adam and his associates gathered on the buckled road outside. He hopped from one rusty steel pile to the next, ignoring the murder of crows perched on the broken beams overhead, the gaping holes in the slab floor around him, and the muted crash of waves somewhere far below.

"What did you find out?" Adam asked.

A growl belied the voice that answered. "He pulled the trigger on the contract. Even before that stunt tonight."

He? As in Vincent? It had to be.

"How much?" a third voice asked, solemn and dutiful, all business.

"Five million," the growly one replied.

Someone whistled. Mr. Solemn, if Icarus had to guess.

"Probably more now," Mr. Growly added. "You cost him another one." Icarus couldn't get a read on his accent. It was practiced and unnatural, like it had been pieced together from a million different dialects. Icarus crept closer, wanting to get eyes on them. Were they mostly human, like Adam? He didn't think so, at least not the growly one.

"You didn't pick the contract up?" Adam asked.

Mr. Growly laughed, and when he spoke again, some of the put-on accent was stripped away, his growl softened to an affectionate rumble. "She'd never forgive me."

She who? Someone they worked for? The Devil didn't seem the sort to work for anyone.

"She might haunt you for passing it up," Adam replied.

A dead someone. A dead and gone someone. Icarus's kind didn't "haunt." That was a term strictly reserved for ghosts. But the three men in the street didn't seem to have the same dark connotations with the word as Icarus did. They laughed, quiet and low, tender almost. Whoever *she* was, they all remembered her fondly.

Mr. Solemn's voice was gentle, beseeching when he spoke again. "Come up to the mountain."

Sneaking closer, Icarus inched into a crumbling cement corner, only rebar left on his side but still solid enough on the street-facing side to hide behind.

"I'm not running," Adam said. "I haven't run for ten years. And she—they—deserve vengeance."

They, not only *she*. And there was that ten years again.

Icarus peeked around the corner just as Mr. Growly got in Adam's face. Golden eyes glowed beneath a headful of rusty-blond hair. Definitely not human. "What good is vengeance if you're dead?" His words were full of anger and something deeper, something like brotherhood.

Icarus's own chest clenched. He batted down memories before they rose higher and instead focused on the here and now.

The present in which Adam shifted his focus, calmly rotating his face to the other man standing in the street with them. His words and expression were resigned. "Then you'll come get me and take me to them."

"Fuck." The man flinched and rotated, the tails of his long dark trench flying, and before he dipped his chin, before he raked a hand through his jet-black hair, Icarus caught the flash of violet eyes. Also not human. He spun back around the next instant, solemn long gone, anger and anxiety straining his voice. "I swear, you've had a ten-year death wish. You just ran into a burning building, for fuck's sake. Do you have any idea how hard it's been keeping you alive?"

"Can you blame me?" Adam swung his attention back to the golden-eyed man. Icarus risked a sniff, far enough away from the smoke to smell again—a canine of some sort. "If Vincent's coming after me this hard, he knows I'm close, and he can't afford that with whatever he's banking power for."

"The Rift anniversary," the dog said. "Or Samhain."

"Whatever he's planning, we have to stop him. We have to finish their work."

There was that *their* again. Mr. Solemn started to argue something, maybe about them, but his words were dampened by a wave crashing into the canyons below so thunderous the silt beneath Icarus's feet shifted, the earth giving way. Icarus bit out a low curse. "Fuck."

"Who's there?" the dog barked, and the crows above screeched an awful chorus.

Icarus debated bounding away, but he couldn't without being seen, without exposing what he was. He scooted farther into the corner instead, fingers scrabbling at rusty rebar and crumbling cement.

Voices and footsteps drew closer. "Show yourself!" Adam shouted.

Gunshots were not the answer any of them expected.

FOUR

The gunfire came from behind Icarus, from the direction of the burning building they'd fled. From the only path out of the Canyon Lands. Cliffs and dark water—all that existed the other way.

"I'll cut a path," the dark-haired man said, and in the blink of an eye, he was in the air, transformed into a crow bigger than any of the ones overhead.

No, not a crow. A raven.

The crows, though, followed his lead, taking flight and barreling through the hole in the ceiling, out past Icarus and into the street, falling into formation behind the shifter and slicing through the fog.

A hand clasped Icarus's wrist and yanked him out from his hiding place. Adam shoved him against the other side of the disintegrating wall and rammed the muzzle of a gun into the underside of his chin. "What the fuck are you doing here? Did you shoot—"

More gunfire rent the air, and birds scattered as cones of bobbing light shone through the fog. Flashlights, held by the gunmen. At least two of them. Icarus pointed their direction. "Clearly, the shots came from them."

"You heard the bird," the dog said. "Get the fuck behind me, and let's get the hell out of here." And by behind him, he meant the giant back end of a rusty-blond coyote that appeared after several bone-cracking seconds.

Icarus pretended to be shocked; it wasn't much of a stretch. While he wasn't surprised by the actual shifts—he'd known they were shifters, had witnessed shifts before—he was still struggling to grasp why Adam was working with shifters in the Canyon Lands to rescue a kid and foil Vincent's evil plans. Shifters he seemed to know well and share some history with.

"We have to get out of here!" Adam tugged him by the wrist and sprinted behind the coyote, barely stumbling over the uneven ground. "Stay behind me."

Icarus pretended to struggle, enough to be believable but not enough to slow them down. He didn't know if the bullets flying were lead or silver or both; it didn't matter. He wanted the fuck out of there too. Dark magic was closing in around them, making the hairs on his arms stand on end and the fog so heavy there was no trace of the earlier fire. "How can you see in this muck?" he asked Adam, who at no time had used a flashlight or his phone.

"Long story," he replied.

A snipe about giving the shortest answer possible was on the tip of Icarus's tongue, but then gunfire popped close enough to steal his words. The sharp, rich scent of blood spiked the air, and Adam grunted before hauling Icarus close. He slammed Icarus against the nearest wall and pressed against him, shielding him with his body, hot and thrumming with adrenaline.

Driving Icarus wild.

Instincts on hyperdrive, they threatened to tear Icarus apart, ripping him in conflicting directions. Take Adam's mouth with his; it was right there, lips parted and panting, open for the plundering, so goddamn tempting. Sink his fangs into Adam's shoulder where a bullet had sliced through fabric and skin, blood welling in the open cut. Wrench free and rip out the throat of whatever monster—human or otherwise—had harmed Adam and was trying to kill him. Icarus couldn't say where that last instinct had come from—the absolute need to protect a virtual stranger, a target he was supposed to deliver to his death—but it was there, stronger than all the rest.

He didn't get the chance to act on any of his urges. Didn't even get the chance to try and blink his senses off. Adam fired into the darkness, a curse echoed out of the fog, and the coyote launched toward the sound. A bloodcurdling wail pierced the misty air, followed by a piteous gurgling. The coyote had taken care of the threat to Adam, same as Icarus would have.

The giant raven screeched overhead again, croaking an urgent warning, and Adam peeled Icarus off the wall. "Let's go! This way."

They sprinted through the dark, the wire fence coming into sight, but then a flashlight flickered on from the other side of the border, momentarily blinding them and making Adam's steps falter.

Making a shot impossible.

Adam's pulse spiked, and his hand around Icarus's wrist tightened. Fear flooded the air, more pungent than the blood dripping down Adam's arm. Whatever the raven thought about Adam's death wish, Adam still feared it.

Which ramped Icarus's instincts higher. His vision sharpened despite the blinding beam. He saw a gun, rising next to the flashlight, aimed at them. The shooter clicked the safety off.

No time left, and no coyote or raven to save them.

No one to see him.

Moving at his preternatural speed, Icarus shoved his free hand in his coat pocket, yanked out a high heel, and chucked it at the shooter with all the might the darkness could hide.

A squelch echoed back—direct hit—and the flashlight fell to the ground, rolling away as the gunman wailed.

With the bright light gone, Adam didn't waste a second. He

tugged Icarus toward and through the fence. On the other side, he paused long enough to fire two bullets into the downed shooter—one in the chest, one in the head—before dragging Icarus the rest of the way to the Camaro.

He shoved Icarus against the passenger door, one arm braced on the car's roof, the other hand pressing the muzzle of the gun under Icarus's chin. Again. "Did you lead them to me?"

Two of the three earlier urges returned, stronger now that the danger had passed. Icarus blinked, the world going gray and odorless, and his fangs receded. One instinct suppressed. But there was no help for the other, his cock stiffening against Adam's thigh.

"Lead who?" Icarus ignored the sinking feeling in his gut that told him he knew exactly who had used him as fucking bait, assuming Vincent's thugs hadn't already been drawn by whatever diabolical plan Adam had foiled. "*If* I did," Icarus said. "If it was me and not the burning building you ran out of, I didn't mean to."

"You saw that?"

Icarus slammed shut his lips before more things escaped.

"I should leave you here."

"Fine." Icarus lifted his chin off the gun. "You killed the bad guys. We're back on this side of the border fence. I'm safe now."

Adam scoffed. "That's the furthest thing from what you are." He yanked Icarus off the side of the car and opened the passenger door. "Get in."

"Where are we going?"

"Somewhere that's actually safe." He lowered the gun and stepped back, giving Icarus the choice.

Icarus slid into the car, closing his eyes and palming the soft leather seats as Adam circled to the driver's side door. A brief reprieve before Icarus steeled himself and brought his other senses back online, focusing on the scents of leather and whiskey to distract from the blood, opening his eyes to color and sharpening his gaze instead of his fangs. He glanced out each window, checking all directions and making sure they weren't being followed.

Making sure they were safe. That was what he'd been turned for, after all. To protect. Now it seemed the Devil was his charge too.

FIVE

At the beginning of the night, if asked where he thought Adam lived, Icarus would have guessed one of the grand mansions in the Heights, or maybe a unit in one of the glitzy high-rises that rose on Sunset Hill above the Pacific cliffs. Those were the areas of Yerba Buena where most people who could afford whiskey and gas cars lived, if they lived in the city at all. He'd bet the single designer heel still in his pocket that that was where Vincent Cirillo and company lived. They probably had a whole floor or two in one of those high-rises.

After the events of the past hour, Icarus had reconsidered his guess about the Devil's habitat and had changed it to the Lost Valley, a patch of relatively stable land bound on all sides by this or that area where illegal activities of this or that variety were the norm. Property was cheap in the Valley, the weather a mix of sun and fog. Not bad if one had the means of protecting themselves from the occasional spillover violence. Icarus had thought that was where they'd been headed as Adam had sped away from the Canyon Lands toward the interior of Yerba Buena.

But then Adam had driven right past the Valley and continued across the city—to the Terrace. In no event would Icarus have guessed that Adam lived a neighborhood over from him in the foggy corridor known as the Gap. Between the max-capacity, run-down apartment buildings of Icarus's Lakeside neighborhood and the jammed-together, equally run-down rentals of the Manor, the Terrace was several blocks of single-family homes on decent-sized lots. Once affluent, the houses were now considered too modest for the wealthy and too expensive for everyone else. It was an upper-middle-class enclave for an upper-middle-class that no longer existed in YB, their numbers dwindling since the Rift, then falling precipitously since the turn of the century two decades ago. Nice middle-class folks like the ones who'd inhabited the Terrace had either been financially squeezed out or fled the epicenter of the centuries-old war between Nature and Chaos. Add to that the less stable ground—exacerbated by the Rift—and more fog than anywhere outside the Canyon Lands—naturally occurring, in this case—and the Terrace was a sort of residential graveyard where only a house every few lots was occupied.

"You live here?" Icarus asked as he stepped outside the garage where Adam had parked. From the driveway, he stared up at the two-story house, the exterior painted the same blue-gray shade as Adam's eyes. It was in better shape than any of the surrounding homes—the pitched roof whole, the chimney in one piece, the white molding peeling only a little, the yard neatly kept—and the only one occupied on the street, as far as Icarus could tell by the lack of other cars, lights, or heartbeats. "Does anyone else live here?"

Adam didn't answer either question, just slapped a button on the wall with the arm that wasn't bleeding. The garage door began to lower, and Icarus skirted back under in the nick of time and followed Adam across the garage to an interior door. Using a key, Adam opened a control panel, entered a code on a keypad, and waited for a lock to disengage before pushing open the door and flipping on the lights inside.

No biting back the gasp this time. The armory Adam ushered him into shouldn't have been a surprise. Especially not after the location of the house, the trip into the Canyon Lands, or the shifters Adam had met with, but it was still a shock. Guns, cross-bows, throwing stars, and knives hung on three walls; beneath them on workbenches were tools and explosives in progress; in the drawers under the benches were ropes, cuffs, tape, and more; and in wooden crates all about the room were rocket launchers, grenades, tranq darts, and stakes.

"You're at war," Icarus said.

"I'm trying to stop a bigger war." Adam withdrew the gun from the holster on his hip and emptied the bullets into a lined case. Silver, then, deadly to most magical creatures, including Icarus, versus lead bullets, which would have no effect on him but were deadly when fired at those on the more human end of the scale. Adam placed the weapon back in the open spot on the wall.

"And that kid you rescued tonight?"

"A weapon we couldn't let the other side have." Sadness in Adam's eyes belied the simple statement. That wasn't all the kid was, at least not to him. Before Icarus could read deeper, Adam turned to the one wall in the room that was the antithesis of violence. A utility sink stood beside a washer and dryer, fluffy gray towels piled atop the latter, and above the sink and appli-ances was a built-in cabinet from which Adam withdrew a green box with a white cross on it. "I need to clean up, then I could use your help with the cut."

Icarus slammed shut his olfactory senses and blinked the color from his vision. The entire drive across the city he'd been able to ignore the blood—mostly. But now, what Adam was asking . . . damn near impossible. Not without shutting off his triggered senses and dampening his instincts, activating the defense mecha-nism he'd been "gifted."

Maybe it was all for naught. Vincent clearly intended to kill Adam. Icarus could kill him tonight—probably, especially, once they left the armory—but that wasn't his mission. And Icarus was too damn curious for his own good. Med kit in hand, he followed Adam up the stairs to the main level of the house. "I don't think a gunshot wound is exactly a cut."

Adam went through the keypad routine again at the top of the stairs. "Relatively, this is a minor cut."

Icarus believed it, given the weapons stockpiled downstairs. The Devil was ready to do battle. For someone armed like that, tonight was merely a skirmish.

Adam pushed open the door and held it for Icarus to enter first. He closed the door behind them, rearmed it, and flicked on the lights. The same empty feeling that had first socked Icarus in the club returned, not as sharp but more encompassing. The air in the house was heavy with it. Just as the former mudroom down-stairs had been turned into an armory, the main level of what had once been a cute family home—Icarus could sense the lingering warmth of it—had been transformed into a sort of basecamp. A kitchen that looked like it hadn't been used in a decade other than as a storage area for water bottles and a receptacle for take-out containers. A dining table covered in photos and files. A living room with card tables and desk chairs for furniture, the former laden with computers and monitoring equipment, wires criss-crossing the dull wood floors.

Icarus's tiny apartment wasn't much, but it was lived in and cozy, a home. This was not. It was a lonely, tactical, sterile place.

Except for the mantel above the fireplace.

Icarus set the med kit on the kitchen island, then drifted into the living room toward the mantel. Adam drifted in the opposite direction down the hallway, turning on lights as he went. Icarus blinked color back into his vision, just for a moment, and regretted it immediately. The framed pictures on the mantel made his chest ache worse than it had in the club. A younger Adam in police blues. A dark-haired man and blond woman in military camo, holding up a sign that read We Miss You. The same man and woman in numerous other pictures with Adam. One with the man dressed in a tux, the woman in a white gown, and Adam in his dress uniform between them, the two strangers kissing either side of Adam's face. Adam's smile was sublime, bright enough to power a solar grid. Another picture of the grinning three, holding up their hands with matching wedding bands. Obviously happy, obviously in love. The family of three in front of this house, arms over each other's shoulders, standing next to a SOLD sign in the yard. Then, on either end of the mantel, triangular cases of polished wood and gleaming glass, each holding a flag and medals. Deborah Levin, a shined brass plaque read at the bottom of one. David Levin, read the plaque on the other.

Something about their names . . . Icarus squinted, concentrating, then a moment later, it clicked—anagrams were a favorite family game—and his eyes widened with another surprise. The D from their first names, plus an anagram of their last names —Devlin.

And beneath the name on each plaque was a date exactly ten years ago.

Icarus lifted a hand to touch, drawn to the contradiction of joy and misery radiating from this one spot in the otherwise emotionless environment, as if it were a giant black hole, melancholy's gravitational pull sucking him in. He caught himself at the last second, clutching the beveled edge of the mantel, then removing his hand as the wood cracked under his tense grip. He stepped back, blinked away the pain-laced color, and folded his arms over his chest.

"Who were they?" he asked when he heard Adam return from the bathroom.

"I belonged to them, and they belonged to me."

SIX

Icarus dug his fingers into his biceps, trying and failing to displace the agony from the gaping hole in his chest torn open again by Adam's words.

"What's your name?" Adam asked from behind him.

"Icarus."

Adam's sharp bark of laughter was enough to break the mantel's hold over him. He turned and focused all his attention on the bare-chested Devil moving around the kitchen, a towel around his neck, another around his injured arm. Icarus was tempted to see color again but resisted the urge, already too shaken by the emotional tides of this place.

"Okay, not really." He stood on the other side of the island from Adam. "But let's just say I have a way of fucking up and getting myself into shit. Family nicknamed me Icarus."

"King of crash and burn?"

"All my life, until I became a courtesan, but by then, the name had stuck."

Adam pulled a bottle of vodka out of the freezer and two shot glasses from a cabinet. "Your family back in Portola?"

Icarus diverted his gaze. Talk about a fuckup. "Your name?"

he asked, diverting attention from himself to a question he wasn't supposed to know the answer to.

"Adam." He nudged the med kit toward Icarus. "Could use that help now." Not waiting for a reply, he carried the vodka and glasses with him down the hallway.

Med kit in hand, Icarus followed the man supposedly called "Adam" to the bathroom at the end of the hall. He peeked into the bedroom on his way there—a lonely bare room with a cot, several books on the floor, and a single chest of drawers. There was another room to the right of the bathroom, but its door was closed. Judging by the lack of scuffs and the layer of dust on the floor beneath the door, it had been that way for a while, no traffic over its threshold.

"In here," Adam called.

Icarus shook off the melancholy he'd gotten mired in again and squeezed into the bathroom. The room was too small for two men their size, but Adam didn't give him a choice, sitting on the closed toilet and sliding the med kit from his hands. He opened it and unpacked items onto the ledge of the tub—a tube of anti-septic skin glue, a strip of butterfly bandages, and a large square of gauze. "Why did you follow me tonight?"

Icarus rolled off his gauntlets, shoved them into his coat pocket, and washed his hands in the sink. "To finish what we started."

"We didn't start anything."

"You wanted to."

Adam bobbled the vodka bottle he'd picked up, spilling a little over the side of the shot glass he'd filled for Icarus.

Icarus didn't call him on it, just accepted the shot, clinked the glass against Adam's, and tossed the alcohol back, confirming his senses were as dulled as he could make them. He set the glass aside next to Adam's empty one, then stepped between his spread knees and unknotted the makeshift tourniquet around his outer shoulder. His skin was warm, as if it burned from the inside, and the muscles under the skin were lithe and strong. Icarus removed the hastily slapped-on bandage, and dark liquid welled in the open cut, a metallic tang teasing the edges of his senses.

His fangs threatened.

Until Adam loosened the knot of his trench, pushed aside the coat's lapels, and ran a callused hand up the back of Icarus's thigh, under the lace strap of his dangling garter.

Instincts rushed in a different direction, arousal overriding the urge to bite, giving Icarus just enough headspace to treat the wound on Adam's arm quickly and efficiently.

"You're good at that," Adam said, voice low and rough.

"I was going to be a nurse."

"You still could be."

Icarus didn't answer, didn't breathe for what would be a minute too long for a human. If he did, it would be the last minute the not-quite-a-human in front of him lived. And that was the last thing Icarus wanted right then.

He finished patching the cut, tossed the capped tube back on the ledge, and snagged the matches from the windowsill above the toilet. He struck one and dropped it into the sink, the used bandage and towel catching fire. Standard operating procedure for erased persons.

Smoke filled the air, and Icarus could breathe again. He blinked and saw the world in color once more, just in time as Adam tipped forward, resting against him and exhaling a heavy breath. He inched his hand higher, rough fingertips brushing the curve of Icarus's ass.

Icarus gasped, in pleasure and desire, in chest-aching hope that he could give the same to the man nuzzling the bottom edge of his corset. He threaded his fingers through the strands of Adam's dark hair—coarse, uneven, self-cut. Icarus could happily run his hands through it all night. "What do you want?" His own voice was raspy, naturally so, not a performance.

Palming his ass, Adam nudged him closer, and his lips skirted the edge of the garter, his hot breath skating through the dips and valleys of Icarus's groin like the fog through the Gap.

Making Icarus hard, the evidence right in Adam's face.

Similar evidence making itself known behind the fly of Adam's jeans.

"What do you need?" Icarus urged.

Adam pressed his nose, then his lips against Icarus's erection. "Just this." He lowered his hand back to Icarus's thigh, holding him close. "Just for a minute. It's been so long."

Ten years, if Icarus had to guess. A guess he was sure was right this time. Ten lonely, melancholy-filled years without a caring, intimate touch from anyone. The Adam-sized hole in his chest ruptured into a canyon like the one they'd run through tonight. Ever-changing, life-threatening, terrifying and beautiful all at the same time.

A minute lasted five, and Icarus relished all three hundred seconds of them. When Adam stood, Icarus relished more the glide of Adam's hard body along the front of his. He brushed his lips over Icarus's cheek. "Thank you."

Icarus barely resisted grinding his stiff cock against the erect one nudging his hip. "You're welcome."

Adam shifted them, making enough room so he could step back and close Icarus's coat, cinching it tight and knotting the belt. "Take the cot."

Icarus shook his head. "Unnecessary." Adam needed the rest, he didn't, and the hours until dawn were dwindling. "It feels like you're running a fever already."

"Wasn't a request." Adam ducked out of the bathroom first, claimed a spot on the bedroom wall opposite the cot, and slid down to the floor. Icarus shot him a glare as he entered the room, and Adam glared a path for him to the cot. "We'll talk in the morning." He waited until Icarus was curled on his side under a blanket on the cot before shutting his eyes.

"You did good tonight, rescuing that kid," Icarus whispered, sensing Adam needed that too. A kind word, an acknowledgement of the victories in this war he was fighting.

A divot formed between Adam's brows, pain streaking across

his features. It was gone the next second, a flinch to anyone not watching as closely as Icarus. Eyes still closed, the Devil's face smoothed, his breaths evened out, and he was fast asleep in less than two minutes.

Icarus wondered if he'd picked up that skill from David and Deborah. He recalled how the soldiers in the veterans' hospital where he'd started his training could fall asleep anywhere, anytime, on a dime—in those awful plastic hallway chairs, on the too-short waiting room sofas, on the cold hard floor of a platoon mate's room. It was a talent Icarus did not possess. He stretched out his legs and his senses, keeping watch over Adam, the house, and the surrounding area.

Hours passed without incident, and when the night sky began to lighten from black to early morning blue, when Icarus's head hurt from the math he couldn't square—those happy family pictures on the mantel had to have been from before the Rift, over thirty years ago, yet Adam didn't look thirty years older now, and he'd also lost Deborah and David during that time—Icarus climbed off the cot. He left his orphaned designer heel on the folded blanket and moved with the speed and silence he hadn't dared display last night. Crouching in front of Adam, he studied the lonely man and tried to find the smiling one from those pictures under the rough yet not old enough exterior.

Icarus barely resisted the urge to run his fingers through Adam's hair again, to skate his fingertips over his cheek and drown in his warmth. Temptation, a long-forgotten drug, was riding him hard. "What are you?" he mumbled to the sleeping man, to the dawn, and to whatever twist of fate had put the Devil in his path.

SEVEN

The trip back to his apartment took Icarus less than five minutes, the morning fog heavy, the sun still shy of the horizon. Good cover for him to move through the shadows at a quickened, inhuman pace. His mind likewise operated on high speed, replaying images from last night. To say the performance—the mission—had not gone where expected was an understatement. He couldn't say he understood where it had gone at all. And that was fucking dangerous. On so many levels. He needed to excavate—Adam, David, and Deborah—and needed to sort a strategy for dealing with Vincent. Sort a way out of Yerba Buena if he had to.

At his apartment door, Icarus inserted the key in the lock, then recoiled as magic blasted through the metal, prickling his skin and lifting the hairs on his arms. Same as it had yesterday when Atlas had first appeared in his bedroom. He backed away from the door, clear across the hall, and contemplated running. To Adam and his armory? To Portola? To some place else altogether? But as sure as he'd felt the current of magic, so had its wielder felt him. He could try to run, but would he even make it out of the building?

Debatable.

Better to buy time and work on his survive-until-tomorrow to-do list. He crossed the hall and gritted his teeth, prepared for the shock this time. He grasped the key, turned it quick, and shoved open the door. His unit was dim, the blinds drawn and the lights off, but Icarus had no trouble seeing—and smelling—Atlas on the sofa in his living room. The warlock sat in the far corner, one ankle resting on the opposite knee, an arm stretched across the top of the couch, the other along the armrest, hand dangling off the end in the muted light that crept around the blinds of the sliding glass door.

How long had he been waiting there?

Icarus shut the door, undid his trench, and hung it on the metal wall hooks. He continued with his routine as if the warlock wasn't there, venturing into the tiny kitchen, laying his phone on the charger, and grabbing an express meal out of the fridge. He tipped back the vial and forced himself not to cringe. Fresh and warm was better, but convenient and safe was more valuable—and his default, absent a willing food source or an agitator who found the pointy end of his fangs.

Atlas tutted, tongue clicking behind his teeth. "Where are your manners, Icarus?"

He lowered the empty vial and licked his lips. "Oh, did you want one? I didn't think these were on your diet."

"They're not. I was thinking along the lines of vodka. You know, basic hospitality."

"I reserve hospitality, basic and otherwise, for invited guests." Icarus tossed the vial into the waste bin. "Which you are not." He crossed his arms and leaned a hip against the end of the kitchen counter. "What are you doing here?"

Atlas dropped his leg and reached between them, stroking his half chub through his slacks. "Came to finish what we started yesterday."

Icarus rolled his eyes, not the least bit tempted by the warlock's cock anymore. "World of fuck no, and aren't you supposed to be sore and dripping?"

Atlas smirked. "Who says I'm not?"

It was a shame he was a liar and an ass. He'd been filthy as fuck during their private online sessions and hands down one of the most gorgeous beings Icarus had ever seen. A toned, compact body under flawless fair skin, blond hair with an enviable wave, sinfully long lashes, and green eyes the color the forests used to be. Through computer screens, Icarus had pegged him as a white-collar professional sort. The fake profile Atlas had given him—Pierce Wilkes—confirmed as much. Perfectly groomed, expensive business casual attire that "Pierce" liked to trade for buckles and kilts, a kink or twenty that needed regular working out. He'd been Icarus's best client the past two months between solo sessions and live stream hits. The "businessman" with money and upbringing and access to resources.

Which he had, only magically.

Magic that was tied up by another.

"Where's your master?" Icarus asked.

"He sent me alone this time."

Icarus pushed off the end of the counter and peeked inside the bedroom. Sniffed. No one else that he could detect, assuming the warlock—the *lying* warlock—hadn't disguised their presence. Icarus made a swift lap around the room, checking the other side of the bed, under the bed, in the closet, and in the bathroom. All clear.

Icarus returned to the living area and rested back against the wall opposite Atlas. "You can understand how I don't trust you."

"You can understand how I can snap my fingers"—he rotated the hand hanging off the armrest, fingers at the ready—"and he'd be here."

"Hmm." Icarus caught the corner of his mouth with a fang. "I don't think so."

Their stare down lasted a good half minute before Atlas shifted forward, elbows braced on his knees. "He's overseeing a healing. There was an altercation with a coyote last night."

Icarus jolted. "That *was* you who followed me."

"Wasn't that your intent?"

The opposite was on the tip of Icarus's tongue. He bit his lip, silencing his too-truthful reply.

"That's what I thought." Grinning, Atlas pushed to his feet, brushed down his slacks, and made no effort to disguise that he was still half hard. "We'll give you another chance."

Icarus lifted his chin, defiant. "I led you to him. Not my fault he got away."

Atlas stalked the edge of the plush white rug that lay between the couch and where Icarus stood. "Maybe we found him because of that burning building and not by following you, in which case, your debts are not repaid."

"What if I could get you the money?"

"From the Devil?"

"Does it matter?"

Atlas stopped directly in front of him. "You know as well as I do that this isn't about the money."

"What does Vincent want with him?"

"He's the last thing standing in Vincent's way. Time's short. Vincent's done fucking with him."

That explained the five-million-dollar bounty on Adam's head. But if Vincent had the means to hire assassins . . . "Why do you need me?"

"Covering all our bases."

"Why would the Devil be interested in me?"

Atlas's gaze skipped over Icarus's shoulder, out of this space and time it seemed, but only for a second before returning to the present. "Everyone has a weakness."

"He doesn't know me. I can't be a weakness."

The warlock chuckled darkly, a curious mixture of condescension, amusement, and beleaguered resignation. "You've got three days, Icarus. Deliver the Devil back to the Canyon Lands by Friday night, and we'll take care of him. For good."

Atlas turned toward the door, and Icarus shot out a hand, grabbing his biceps. The warlock's green gaze snapped back to his

—anger, surprise, and something more hiding in the forest. "What does Vincent have over you? You were in his thrall last night, but he's a human. Their kind can't—"

"Not everything is about magic."

"Are you in love with him?"

If the warlock's earlier laugh had been dark, this one was well past midnight. And so cold, like the frozen tundra way up north with its thinned-out trees and utter desolation. "Do your job, Icarus." He wrenched his arm free. "Leave me to mine."

EIGHT

Once he got the stinky, horny warlock out of his apartment, Icarus helped himself to the vodka Atlas had suggested. He poured himself a generous shot and sipped it slowly, savoring the freezer-chilled liquor, letting it cool and calm him after a long, strange night and morning. He needed to be steady—focused—for the hours of work ahead of him.

He finished his drink, then changed out of his corset and garters and into his most prized possession—a pair of worn, comfy as sin blue jeans he'd rescued from a dumpster and patched a dozen times over. He yanked on a tank over his head, and over that, an equally comfy sweater he'd knitted last winter. He'd probably end up ditching the sweater, as he'd been unusually warm since last night, but until it became unbearable, his favorite soft garments would also help him focus. Grabbing his laptop out of the closet safe, he carried it into the living room, claimed the opposite end of the couch from where Atlas had stunk it up, and commenced excavation.

Hours passed with the daylight outside, the sun only coming close to his toes once, when it burned off the midafternoon fog for an hour or so and snuck in around the sides of the balcony blinds. By dusk, he'd ditched the sweater and was two seconds from ditching his laptop as well. He had little to show for his daylong efforts. Nothing about Adam Devlin—or Adam Levin, he'd checked—and only one article about Deborah and David Levin. It was in an obscure local newsletter, something the hired scrubber must have missed. They'd died in a fire in Talahalusi, the area north of Yerba Buena and the Bay. That was all Icarus could find about them or the incident. No survivors were listed, and no mention was made about whether the fire was natural, man-made, or magical. Talahalusi was a popular destination for Yerba Buena refugees. There was vegetation and agriculture, jobs and homes, and a thriving cultural scene. A different proposition than YB's dreary fog, unstable ground, and magical mayhem or the twenty-four-seven, hyper-business scene of Portola, a grimy rat race powered by drugs and money with a highly polished, highly fake veneer. And don't even get him started on the religious zealots farther south who would tie him and any other paranormal to the stake and roast them.

Talahalusi could be roasting too, though, with its increasingly long, increasingly hot summers. While much had been done in Talahalusi under the leadership of the local Indigenous communities to fight the effects of climate change, the lack of similar foresight and concern by those in the areas around them meant climate change was encroaching nonetheless, driving up Talahalusi's average daily temperature, decreasing the rainfall, and sparking wildfires.

Maybe Deborah and David had died in one of those. Or maybe they'd died because their husband was a cop? Retaliatory arson? Something to do with Vincent? Adam spoke of vengeance to the raven and coyote. Against Vincent? Were their deaths in the past connected to whatever it was Vincent was planning in the present and what he needed the Devil out of the way for? Had Adam always been the Devil—had he always been Adam—or only since his need for vengeance pushed out whatever else remained? Or because he'd survived the fire? Like he'd survived that burning building last night? He was unscathed in either instance. Icarus hadn't noticed any fresh burns or scars from old burns on him, but he'd only seen his torso; his lower half had remained covered the entire time.

He looked again at the picture accompanying the article. The Levins were slightly older in it than in the pictures on Adam's mantel, and something about Deborah looked familiar. Long blond hair, honey-colored eyes, freckles. Recalling the pictures on the mantel, something about her had looked familiar in them too, but Icarus had been too caught up in surprises to process it then. Now, he was too caught up in frustration to make a connection.

Sighing, he set his laptop on the floor, stood from the couch, and snagged his phone off the charger. Drawing back the door blinds, he found a crow on the balcony rail outside. They were frequent visitors, having overrun the old golf courses in the area, but tonight he gave his visitor a closer look. Checked its beak—narrow, its tail—fan-shaped, the scruff of its neck—smooth, the color of its eyes—black.

Just a crow, then. Not a raven.

Not *the* raven.

He slid the door open, and his visitor flew off with a parting caw. The bird didn't go far, just to one of the lonely cypress trees beside an overgrown putting green, wobbling for several seconds until it found the point of equilibrium on the branch.

Caw.

"All right, then, bravo," Icarus said, giving the bird its due.

Caw.

His chuckle eased the tightness in his chest and made it easier to punch in the numbers on his phone. He hung up after two rings, counted off thirty seconds, then dialed again.

"I was expecting your call," a woman greeted.

The smirk in her voice made Icarus smile. "I need an excavation."

"I taught you how to excavate."

"Enough to check out my clients, though apparently, I'm not even good at that."

The smirk vanished, concern coloring her words. "What happened?"

"Long story involving a stinky warlock and a hacked cock cage."

"*What?*"

"Blackmail ensued."

"What the ever-loving fuck, Icarus?"

He rolled his eyes and held the phone away from his ear as she continued her chiding. Once she'd blown out the well-placed, endearing concern, he brought the phone back to his ear. "Point is, what I need to know is beyond my capabilities."

"About the warlock?"

"No, about someone who's been erased."

A ping sounded, a request for visual. He accepted, and her face filled the screen. She looked as worried as she sounded, eyes wide and brows halfway to her dyed-green hairline. She'd been wearing it that color since they were teens. A fucking beacon, unintentionally, and then intentionally because she liked giving the world the middle finger. And she chided *him* about being reckless. He rolled his eyes.

She huffed. "Icarus . . ."

"I don't have a choice."

"You always have a choice."

He glanced away from the screen, back out at the weed-covered green and the crow still perched on the cypress branch, watching him as the evening grew darker. Reminding Icarus of the choices he'd made and the choices he'd closed off for good. Reminding him of last night. Making him wonder what choices Adam had made, what choices he had left, and how Icarus played into those. He returned his gaze to the woman onscreen. "I don't." She opened her mouth to protest, but Icarus continued before she got the chance. "But it's more with this one. I want to know. I need to. Can you help me, please?"

Expression softening, she lowered her brows and smiled, but

worry still swirled in her hazel eyes, all the colors of the earth mixed in them. "Of course, babe."

"Thank you. I'll wire payment when I can."

She shook her head, her long green curls bouncing with the motion, still none of the silver strands one would expect to see at her age. Magic had slowed her aging too—not stopped it like with him, but slowed it to as near as possible for a living being. "You'll do no such thing. You're my family."

He gulped down the lump in his throat. "You don't need—"

"Zip it, Icarus." Her voice was scratchy, like she had a lump in her throat too, but the tone brooked no argument.

He'd learned decades ago not to argue with her when she'd made up her mind. "All right," he said. "Thank you."

"Now, who is it?"

"He goes by the name Adam Devlin, aka the Devil."

NINE

Icarus felt it the second Adam entered the club, their connection a live wire electrifying the air around them. Adam's gaze seared a path across his bare back, and Icarus could hear his heartbeat over the thumping music, over the heartbeat of the client in front of him. Mike, one of his regulars, was a sweet, handsome commodities trader from out of town who always called when he was in Yerba Buena. Polite, generous, and decent in bed, he was a good, calm, and safe night's work. And as good an excuse as any to stall while excavation continued.

According to Atlas, Icarus had three days to deliver Adam back to the Canyon Lands. Three days to figure out what he was actually going to do. He could take this first one to gather his info, gather his wits, and gather extra money in case he needed to bolt. And no matter how loudly Icarus's instincts screamed at him to run Adam's direction, a night off from Mister Stranger Danger across the room was a smart decision. He needed to make more of those and less of the run-toward-danger sort.

Beside him, Mike slid some bills into the folio the bartender had left for them. "You mind if we grab a quick dinner on the way to the hotel?" He dipped his chin, and a blush reddened his dark cheeks. "I dropped off my bags and came straight here."

Icarus lifted his chin with a crooked finger. "Of course not, babe. Need you—" The rest of his words died as a hand spread across his bare back, snuck beneath the drape of his open-back halter, and inched around to clasp his side. Icarus didn't need to look to know who the hand belonged to. The heat and strength of the body that pressed against his back, the scent of whiskey that flooded his senses, and the muscled arm that draped over his shoulder, a single designer heel dangling from his fingertips, confirmed what he already knew.

As did Mike's wide eyes.

"I need a word with you," Adam said, voice deliciously rough.

Icarus shivered, and he was sure that Adam, snug as he was against Icarus's back, felt it. Adam spread his fingers over Icarus's hip, teasing the side laces of his leather shorts. Icarus would be lying if he said his dick didn't perk right up. Rude of his dick, and of Adam, seeing as Icarus was standing at the bar next to a client. "I'm busy," he said to Adam as he attempted to step forward, hand on Mike's forearm.

He failed, Adam's fingers digging into his side. "I'll outpay him."

Snatching his shoe from Adam, Icarus whipped his head to the side and glared at the too-presumptuous, too-fucking-handsome man. "That's not how it works."

One corner of the Devil's mouth hitched up. "Fine." He turned his smirk to Mike. "How much did you pay him?"

"Five hundred."

Adam removed his hand from beneath Icarus's blouse, and Icarus didn't want to admit how much he missed the touch. Adam stepped more fully beside them and withdrew a wad of bills from his wallet. He held out the cash to a slack-jawed Mike. "That's a grand. Enough for you to go away?"

Mike's gaze bounced between the cash, the two of them, and down to Icarus's erection straining the front of his shorts. "But he's the best."

Icarus chuckled. Leave it to the thirsty trader to try and negotiate.

Adam, though, had an answer for Mike's thirst: quench it with a different one. He lifted a hand, catching the attention of the bartender, who, catching sight of Adam, bobbled his shaker. He finished pouring the drink, slid it in front of the customer, then hustled in their direction. "Didn't expect to see you back so soon."

"Unfinished business," Adam replied, gaze flicking to Icarus, then to Mike. "Get . . ."

"Mike," Icarus's client supplied.

"Get Mike a barrel-aged whiskey."

"Coming right up."

"That settle us?" Adam said to Mike while the bartender accessed a secure cabinet beneath the back bar.

Mike shot Icarus a chagrined smile. "Sorry, Icarus, but I've never had the real stuff before. Rain check?"

"Of course, and I can't blame you." He leaned forward, ready to flex a bit of extra strength if Adam tried to stop him. He didn't, and Icarus gave Mike a long, lingering kiss. It was the least he could do for the money and the fleeting hope of a normal evening. He drew back, leaving the trader more than a little dazed and more than a little hard, his erection tenting his slacks and nudging Icarus's fishnet-covered thigh. Not a total waste of a night, then. A firm reminder to Mike to call again next time he was in town. "Enjoy your whiskey."

Icarus slipped out from between Mike and Adam while the latter settled the tab with the bartender. Adam caught up with him halfway across the club, slinging an arm over his shoulder again. "What happened to 'We'll talk in the morning'?"

"Somewhere else I had to be." Icarus made it one more step before his forward momentum was halted.

Adam dragged him backward instead, toward the panoramic windows that overlooked the city. "Where do you think you're going?"

"To find another client."

The speed at which they reversed accelerated, and Adam shifted their course toward a dark corner off to the side of the windows. Arm still over his shoulder, Adam slunk around to his front and planted a hand against the wall behind Icarus, caging him in. "You don't need another client tonight."

"Are you jealous?"

Adam bent his elbow, crowding closer, and Icarus backed the rest of the way up, hissing at the cold cement wall against his back. It was no match, however, for the heat that blanketed his front. "I woke up hard as a rock this morning," Adam growled in his ear. "First time in I can't remember how long."

Icarus shifted, wedging a thigh between Adam's spread legs. "Are you still hard?"

Adam took the hint, dragging his erection along Icarus's thigh, denim catching on fishnet.

Icarus pushed up against the dick and balls he'd love to get his lips around. So much for running away from danger, but when it was this goddamn tempting . . . "I can do something about that."

"You can tell me why you followed me last night."

Icarus dropped the shoe to the floor, freeing both hands to glide up Adam's chest, over the soft, worn fabric of his sweater, relishing the heat that seeped through the material to his palms, warming him to his core. "We've been over that already." He pressed his own erect cock against Adam's hip. Evidence aplenty on both their parts. "Still seems we have some—what was it you said?—unfinished business."

Adam coasted a hand over Icarus's hip, making space between the wall and his back, and snuck his fingers under the dip of the draped top, under the waistband of his shorts, inches away from where Icarus would kill to have them, spreading him open, breaching his—

"You're lying."

Icarus bit back the groan on the tip of his tongue, the fantasy interrupted, but not for long. Not if he could help it. And this right here—seduction—was what he did best. Smirking, he lifted the leg not between Adam's and hooked it over the Devil's hip, encouraging him to dip his hand lower, to grind his cock along the hard one pressed snug to his. "Am I?"

A push too far, fucking finally. Adam's hand dropped off the wall, fingers threading through the fishnet, clutching Icarus's raised leg almost painfully. But it was nothing compared to the force of the kiss he laid on Icarus—scorching in its heat and hunger, in its sheer need. Adam's lips moved over Icarus's, rough and greedy, a tongue demanding entrance, which Icarus granted without hesitation, his own desire surging to meet Adam's.

Icarus opened for him, mouth and body, hooking his leg around Adam tighter and curling his fingers in the front of his shirt, hauling him closer, rutting cock to cock. He growled down his throat as Adam shoved a hand farther down his shorts, diving into his crack, clasping a cheek and spreading him. So close to where Icarus wanted him.

Danger had never felt so fucking good. And Icarus wanted more. "Please."

As if the plea had broken a spell, Adam pulled back—lips, body, hands, the latter adorably tangled in fishnet for a few seconds before he fully separated himself. Icarus could have kept him locked tight in his hold, but not without giving away his strength, and in any event, not without Adam's consent.

Eyes half-lidded, Icarus swooned against the wall and flicked the corner of his mouth with his tongue. "You want more?"

Adam paced in front of him and roughly ran a hand over his nape, seemingly at war with himself, his angry tone confirming as much. "Of course I want more."

Icarus lifted the hem of his blouse with one hand and slid the other inside the front of his shorts, adjusting his erection, making sure Adam got a good look at how hard he'd made him. How much he wanted more too.

As good as crooking any finger, Adam's gaze went right to the intended target. Icarus could see how hard it was for the Devil to tear his gaze away. Adam stepped closer, then caught himself. "Are you in trouble?"

Icarus yanked his hand out of his shorts. "Is that what this is about? Some rescue fantasy shit? Can't get enough of playing hero after last night?"

"I am no one's fucking hero." Adam closed the distance between them and palmed Icarus's dick through the leather. "Even if I were, this isn't me trying to rescue you. This is me trying to find any excuse not to haul you into the bathroom and let you fuck me senseless with this piece."

Moaning, Icarus thrust into his hand, wishing for any other material so Adam could feel how hot and dripping he was for him already. "I fail to see the problem."

Adam curled his fingers around the ridge of Icarus's cock and slowly stroked the length of it, eliciting another moan. "You're trouble."

Icarus dropped his head back against the wall, eyelids fluttering closed. "You caught my name, right?"

Adam's lips brushed his neck, a tongue teasing in their wake. "But which of us will burn in the end?"

"Devlin."

Icarus righted his head and snarled at the intruder who'd spoken. The woman standing on the edge of the shadow they were hidden in snarled right back.

"Who's that?" Icarus spat.

Adam didn't step back or release his dick. "My second. Jennifer."

"Your second?" He aimed his next question in the intruder's direction. "Where were you last night?"

"On the receiving end of that rescue you witnessed," Adam answered for her as he licked along Icarus's collarbone, teasing the narrow halter strap.

"And after? She didn't have your back." None of them had. Not Jennifer, not the raven, not the enormous, growly coyote.

"I always spend that night alone."

Dragging his gaze away from their audience, Icarus dipped his chin and flicked the shell of Adam's ear with his tongue. "But you weren't."

Adam whimpered, and his erection dug harder into Icarus's hip. "Do you have any idea who you've decided to get into trouble with?"

"We're going to be late," Adam's second huffed.

Icarus nipped his earlobe. "Can you tell her to fuck off?"

"Unfortunately not. She's a coyote. She'll eat me." He glanced up through long dark lashes, and it was a good thing Icarus had the wall at his back. The smoldering look, the heat radiating off the man in his arms, was enough to make him swoon again. Almost enough to make him come in his shorts. "Not in the good way."

That thought didn't help Icarus's hard-on either. But as he glanced over Adam's shoulder, getting a glimpse of glowing golden eyes, Icarus came back to his cautious senses, a little. "Related to the one last night?"

"His cousin." Adam returned the earlier nip, teeth teasing Icarus's shoulder. "How do I reach you?"

Icarus dragged his leg along the outside of Adam's. "Seems you already know where to find me."

Adam kissed a path up his neck and along his jaw. "For a proper date."

Icarus laughed out loud. "Sweetheart, I am not the sort you date."

Adam drew back, smirk positively evil, positively addictive, and the fingers still around Icarus's dick tightened, bringing him back to fully erect with a single stroke. "Once I leave, I want you to go into a bathroom stall and jerk yourself off, and while you're doing that, pretend it's me on my knees in front of you, giving you the best blow job of your life." Icarus gasped, and Adam dipped his tongue inside his mouth, a parting sweep of heat and whiskey and everything Icarus wanted another taste of. "Or better yet, imagine your cock pounding my ass. It's been so long since anyone's breached me. Imagine how tight it must be, how good it'll feel." Adam dropped a final peck on his lips and stepped back. "Then decide if you want to be the sort who dates."

He turned on his heel and left without a backward glance. As soon as Adam and Jennifer cleared the exit, Icarus bolted to the bathroom, locked himself in a stall, ripped down his shorts, and yanked out his dick. He jerked himself off to the images Adam had seared onto his brain. Adam on his knees, mouth around his cock. Adam on his knees, ass in the air, taking every pounding thrust Icarus gave him. He sprayed the wall and floor in less than two minutes, coming with a shout, not the least bit ashamed if anyone heard him.

But after, forearm braced against the door, face resting in the crook of his elbow, reality set in. He hadn't been performing for anyone just now. Hell, not since he and Adam had left Mike at the bar. Icarus hadn't just fucked Adam in his imagination, he'd fucked himself in reality. A million different ways from Sunday. Living up to his name yet again.

TEN

Icarus cursed the phone vibrating on the bedside table. He wasn't ready to get up yet. Two rings, then it stopped. Didn't seem he had a choice. Thirty seconds, then, to wake the rest of the way up and activate the secure call channel. He peeled open one eye, then the other, wincing at the bright room. Midday already, judging by the ambient light that leaked in around the bedroom curtains. A longer than intended rest, but it had been a few days since he'd last slept. He snagged the phone off the charger, activated the secure channel, and was ready when she called back. He ignored the video request and lifted the phone to his ear. "I just woke up," he greeted. "You don't get to see this face."

"Eww!" she sputtered, and he could practically see her recoiling. Could imagine her curls whipping back and forth as she frantically shook her head. "As if I'd want to."

"I didn't mean it like that." Chuckling, he shifted onto his side in the bed and sank back under the cozy comforter he'd quilted. "It's my first rest in days, and I haven't eaten yet."

"So you look like death warmed over."

"Not even warm." He pulled the comforter higher, flipped the phone to speaker, and laid it on the pillow beside his head. "What'd you find out?"

"That you probably shouldn't be sharing any kind of morning face with the Devil."

He sighed and flopped onto his back.

"Wait," she squawked. "Did you already? Is he there?"

"No, but the word 'inevitable' comes to mind. I don't think I've ever wanted to fuck someone so badly in my life. It's bizarre. I hardly know the guy, I know he's dangerous, but the raging hard-on is real."

"Don't you have a whole assortment of cock cages? Have one on next time you see him. I'll hack it from here. Make sure you keep that dick locked down."

He half laughed, half groaned. "Yes, I have a whole collection. No, I don't think I'll ever use one again. They're ruined for me."

"Aww. Poor Icarus."

He pouted to no one over the loss of the toys and the inevitable bad news she was about to deliver. He retracted his jutted-out lip and ripped off the Band-Aid. "Tell me about Adam."

"Not much to tell."

"I thought—"

"The fact that he's so well-erased, his alias and his real name too, whatever that might be, and Deborah and David too, means he really doesn't want to be found. Someone who can pay for that good a scrub has something to hide. Something major."

"What *did* you find?"

She sighed, louder than his before.

"Come on," Icarus needled. "Surely you didn't think I was just going to give in?"

"A girl can dream."

"A zebra can't change its stripes."

She blew a raspberry over the line, and he covered the ache in his chest with laughter. He missed seeing and talking to her in person, missed sharing these moments together. Missed falling asleep to the sound of her rapid-fire keystrokes, the same sound that filled his room now, his phone screen lighting up with documents she pushed through.

"House is owned by a shell company, which is owned by a shell company, yada yada. Was purchased five years before the Rift." As Icarus had suspected. "The only person on the record is the attorney who set up the shell company—who set up all the shell companies—and he's dead. In the Rift."

YB had lost half its population in the Rift, most unfortunate victims in the wrong place at the wrong time, caught in the magical crossfire or pulled under the waves or into the earth that had cracked open. The number of fatalities in the Canyon Lands alone had been staggering. The half that had survived had continued to dwindle in the thirty years since.

Three decades. Icarus ran the math in his head, coming back to the same conclusion he'd reached at Adam's house the other night. The years weren't adding up. Adam wasn't adding up. And the Cirillos were mixed up in the equation too, somehow.

"Any connection to Vincent or Paris Cirillo?"

"They're just as scrubbed clean," she answered. "How'd you get mixed up with them, anyways?"

"Pretty face with a ready supply of Daylight."

"I told you that shit would get you in trouble."

"Yeah, yeah, yeah." He flapped a hand in the air, waving her off despite the fact she couldn't see him. "I don't even fucking want it. I'm fine being a hermit during the day, but it doesn't hurt to have an emergency supply."

"In case you have to rescue a certain someone during daylight hours."

"Worth it," he didn't hesitate to reply. It was the last time he'd seen her, for a few too-short hours. The time in the daylight with her was worth it, but even more worth it was keeping her safe. Worth every penny of the fifteen grand he owed to Paris—correction, Vincent—Cirillo.

"He's getting it from the warlock?" she asked.

"Probably," Icarus said. The serum that allowed Icarus's kind to withstand the sun was the sort of magic only a handful of warlocks could wield. And those that could generally wouldn't, which made Daylight exceedingly hard to come by and exceedingly expensive. Unless you had a warlock as powerful and morally bankrupt as Atlas on standby. "He's in their thrall."

"That's odd."

"No shit." Everything about the current predicament was odd.

"And you're sure the Cirillos are humans?"

"Brown eyes, and no, they're not contacts."

"Hmm." Keystrokes resumed, and a snapshot of computer gibberish appeared onscreen. "Also odd, this trace on the IP address you gave me for the warlock. It's bouncing all over the place. There's something else going on there, but I'm not sure what yet. I'm digging into it."

"Not a surprise. Atlas is all smoke and mirrors." He threw off the comforter and sat up, scrubbing a hand over his face. "Speaking of smoke, anything on the Talahalusi fire?" Another bunch of documents came through. Police and hospital records. "Summary, please," he said. "Recall, I lack blood and a shower. Not awake enough yet."

She laughed. "When you get right, start with the Tal Gen Hospital records. There was a John Doe admitted to the ER there on the day of the fire. I think it's your guy. Third degree burns all over his body per the admitting report, but then he was discharged the next day, no treatment indicated."

"No burns on him that I could see." He stood, tiptoed around the sun dappling the floor, and grabbed his robe off the back of the bedroom door. "And the police reports?"

"As thin as the news article on details. The officer from the scene died. The case was assigned to Officer Cormac Kelley, who closed it after a respectable time of doing absolutely nothing."

"Is Officer Kelley still alive?"

"Detective Kelley now, and yes, he works the cold cases for the Talahalusi Sheriff's Office."

Had he been shuttled there because he was good at his job or bad at it? "Anything else on him?" Icarus asked as he snagged the phone off the pillow and went in search of food.

"He's local. Good cop by all accounts. No complaint charges filed against him. Asked for the cold case gig. Kind of a loner. Unmarried, no kids, lives on an outparcel of the family vineyard outside of Talahalusi proper."

"Which vineyard?"

"Monte Corvo."

Icarus almost dropped the vial in his hand. "No fucking way."

"That mean something to you?"

Crow Mountain? That couldn't be a coincidence.

"Maybe. You got a picture?"

He gulped down the meal and waited for the picture to load. Once opened, he spread his fingers across the screen, examining the man in uniform. Light tan skin, black eyes, black hair. Maybe it was the raven shifter from the other night. It had been dark, and Icarus had only seen him from behind, had only gotten a glimpse of a dark eye turning violet before he'd shifted. The man in the picture could be him or just as easily someone else with tan skin, black eyes, and black hair. But still . . . Crow Mountain, plus the case, plus a cop . . . Adam's partner, maybe?

"His what?"

Shit, he hadn't meant to muse that last part out loud.

"Former partner." He tossed the vial in the bin and left his phone on the far end of the counter, farther out of earshot as he prepared for the worst. "Adam used to be a cop," he confessed with a preemptory wince.

"Icarus!"

He winced more as the banshee was unleashed on the other end of the line. He pretended not to notice. "What was that?"

She saw right through the facade. "Don't play dumb with me. That was important info."

"Which would make you panic, hence—"

"Hence you should have fucking told me." She muttered a few

curses, then the keystrokes started again, fast and furious. "What else didn't you tell me?"

Feeling like his eardrums were relatively safe from further damage, he retrieved his phone and ambled to the couch. "He drives a vintage Camaro and orders whiskey like it's tap water."

The typing stopped again, followed by a muttered, "Holy shit."

"Babe—"

"Don't fucking 'babe' me." She growled at him some more, and Icarus imagined she'd run her hands through her hair a dozen times by now, flattening the lovely curls. "I love you, you know that, but you are way out of your fucking league here."

"I'm starting to get that." He stretched out and clutched a pillow to his chest, ignoring the Adam-shaped hole that lingered there, that piqued his curiosity and hadn't dampened his desire for the man one bit, despite all the red flags.

Same as before, she saw right through his silence—saw right through him, period—and offered a tempting, impossible alternative. "Come home."

"You know I can't."

"Just meet me here, and then we'll go. I've got enough saved up. Enough for us to get settled somewhere else, then you can find work, and so can I."

He almost caved, but there was a reason he'd left Portola in the first place, a reason he only chanced seeing her when her life was in danger—at least, from someone other than him. He was powerful enough to protect her, but also dangerous enough to hurt her or those around her. "The last thing I want is to put you at risk."

"And the last thing I want is to lose you for good."

ELEVEN

Once night fell, Icarus followed his intuition from Tuesday to the cluster of glitzy high-rises on Sunset Hill. He hunkered down on a park bench across the street, keeping to the shadows and keeping an eye on the multiple entry and exit doors of the buildings, waiting for his target to emerge or arrive. The night was relatively quiet, only the occasional passing car or departing guest interrupting the crash of waves against the nearby bluffs. His head wasn't nearly so peaceful. He couldn't help but contemplate the phone call from earlier. She would chide him for coming here, for making a direct approach, but he needed more information, needed a better sense of exactly what he'd gotten himself into. And what he might get her into if he took her up on the offer to run. Was there a way to slow the chase? Avoid it altogether? To protect them both? Because after last night, he couldn't be certain he could deliver Adam to the Canyon Lands tomorrow. Hell, he couldn't be certain he could deliver Adam anywhere but to his bed.

That was a whole other scenario his imagination wouldn't stop spinning. Where would a kiss like the one from last night lead? What would it feel like to actually have Adam's mouth around his cock or to bury himself in Adam's ass? What would every inch of that hot skin taste like on his tongue, starting with the puckered rim of Adam's—

A yellow sports car screeched to a halt in front of the complex, shattering Icarus's fantasy. It didn't take a genius to guess who owned that flashy piece of trash. Paris Cirillo unfolded from the driver's side, and two women emerged from the passenger side, their doors opened by the valet. Paris rounded the front of the car and tossed the keys to the valet, then linked an arm through each of the women's. The one on Paris's right moved fluidly, like a cat of some sort. Vaguely familiar, but Icarus couldn't place her. The one on the left was like Icarus.

Paris had always insisted Icarus meet him elsewhere, at Club Sutro or at one of the other clubs or hotels where Icarus did business. So why had Paris brought these two paranormals here, to his home? Either Paris was a total fool, or the women worked for him. The latter, probably, which made Icarus's approach more precarious. Unless he wasn't the one who approached. He'd dressed for the possibility, knowing exactly what Paris liked, what would draw him in. He shrugged off his dark hoodie and slouched on the bench, legs spread, red lace panties peeking out from the top of the gray sweatpants stretched taut across his lap, nicely showing off the semi helped along by Adam-fueled fantasies. He laid one hand on his bare midriff below a cropped tee and shoved two fingers of his other hand into his mouth, amplifying his whistle.

The paranormals' heads swiveled his direction one second, their steps moved his way the next, and by the third second, they were across the street, into the park, and on him. The cat perched over him on the bench, claws around his wrists, holding his arms outstretched, while the other zipped behind him and circled his neck with her arm, putting Icarus in a chokehold.

"Wait!" Paris shouted. A car horn blew as he darted across the street, and once on the other side, he ran toward them at bumbling human speed, gravel crunching beneath his loafers. "I asked him to come here!"

Or maybe the women worked for Vincent, because that was a fucking lie.

The chokehold tightened. "You're not supposed to have visitors," Icarus's captor said to Paris. "Not here."

"I got hooked, okay?" An out-of-breath Paris arrived at their sides and made a sweeping gesture at Icarus. "I mean, look at him. Can you blame me?"

The cat cracked a sideways grin, dark eyes devilish in her tan face, as she glanced at his erection. "Not completely."

Icarus shifted to draw the fabric more taut. "I'm down to party."

The woman with her arm around his neck was not. "We already have a party to attend."

Paris grimaced, and Icarus suspected the party he was pretending to offer sounded way more fun than the party Paris was supposed to go to. "Fine," Paris huffed. "But can I have a minute with him first?"

Icarus tilted his head back as much as the chokehold allowed. "I promise not to bite."

Her blue eyes flashed, as did the white of her fangs. "You bite, it'll be the last bite you ever take." She cut her gaze to Paris. "And that would be a fucking waste of a last bite."

"Hey!" Paris protested.

She definitely worked for Vincent.

"Two minutes of his time," Icarus said. "Then I'm gone." He hoped they heard in his voice the finality he intended in the last word.

Whatever they heard, it was enough to back them off, and Paris slipped onto the bench beside him, his voice uselessly lowered. "What the fuck are you doing here?"

Icarus didn't waste time, cutting right to the chase. Or rather, how to end it. He hoped Paris had a different answer for him than Atlas had earlier. "How much will it take to get your father off my back for good?"

"There's not a number." Paris dipped his chin and laid a hand on Icarus's thigh, petting the soft fabric, petting him. His voice was rough when he spoke again. "It could have been a single dose of Daylight and it still wouldn't have mattered."

Icarus bumped off Paris's hand and crossed his legs. "You gave Atlas my number. I was the mark."

"Not you." He folded his hands and cast his gaze aside. "Not exactly."

"The Devil," Icarus reasoned, and Paris nodded. "Why me?"

"I don't know. I didn't want to know."

"So you sold me out instead?"

Paris clutched his hands in his lap, knuckles white. "They said you'd be safe."

Fool was right. But one who didn't mean to get in the trouble he did, at least not this time. Icarus knew something about being in predicaments like those. He laid a hand over Paris's fidgeting ones. "Why are you telling me this now?"

"Because you were always good to me." He lifted his eyes, and sincerity and apology swirled in their beautiful brown depths. "I know I'm not the brightest. They know it, and so do you. I don't have the head for my father's business. I act before I think, but I don't know any other way to be, to survive this as me." He shrugged. "You never made me feel less for who I am."

Icarus forced out words around the lump in his throat. "You had something I needed."

Paris smiled, a soft, sad thing. "Don't sell yourself short." He gave Icarus's hand a squeeze, then withdrew his and stood. He leaned over, dropping a kiss on Icarus's cheek. "Goodbye, Icarus."

Icarus's face heated, shame at ever thinking or calling Paris a fool. He caught the young man's chin and gave him a proper goodbye kiss, sure it would be the last they ever shared. Maybe the last Paris ever received. Leaning back, Icarus held his chin and gaze. "Don't sell yourself short either."

"Thank you."

Paris made his way back across the street, shoulders drooping more with each step. The hideous yellow car was back at the curb, and Icarus overheard the cat mention a change in plans. She took the wheel, Paris the passenger seat, the other paranormal in the back. Icarus hoped like hell Paris got out of that car alive, but he couldn't be sure of any outcome. His stomach sank. He didn't like being set up, and he didn't like being the cause of someone else's setup either.

He didn't have long to beat himself up about it. Atlas and Vincent emerged from the building less than a minute later just as a hulking black SUV pulled out of the garage and around to the curb. It was hard to hear over the rumbling engine, but Icarus flexed his powers, picking up words that made his stomach sink further.

"What's the backup plan," Vincent said, "if Icarus doesn't deliver?"

"I've got a line on the Devil's location," Atlas said. "But they want a human in return."

"Give them Paris," Vincent said without so much as a blink, not even a dollop of fatherly remorse.

Icarus had enough guilt for both of them. He'd never caused another human's death before. Tonight, it seemed he'd cursed Paris Cirillo to that fate twice over.

TWELVE

Icarus closed the computer window on his last live stream of the day, laid the remote beside it, and snagged the towel from his stash beside the bed. He wiped the come off his torso, then gently removed the massager from his ass and the cock ring from around the base of his dick. The toys were almost always a turn-on for his streaming clients, and the extra stimulation helped him too after a day packed with performances. He'd taken more appointments than usual, then an impromptu live stream, banking as much money as he could during the daylight hours so he could sneak away to Portola during the fast-approaching night.

Before Vincent or Atlas—or Adam—realized he was missing.

After what had happened with Paris last night, after hearing just how far Vincent and Atlas were willing to go to get to Adam, Icarus had decided running was his only option. He should probably also skip the stop in Portola—disappear altogether, from everyone—but this was her idea. If he left her behind, she'd keep digging, keep searching for him, and likely run afoul of the people he was trying to escape. Which would put her in danger, the very thing he was supposed to prevent, to protect her from. In Yerba Buena, he was close enough in case of emergencies but far enough away to avoid his past mistakes. Any farther, though . . . She'd be safer traveling with him than making herself a target without him.

He checked the time on his phone. Three hours until he was supposed to meet her in Portola. Enough time to finish packing, withdraw a stack of cash, and plant several false trails in case any of the aforementioned parties followed him.

Standing, he carried the toys into the shower with him, multitasking cleanup. Afterward, he snuggled in the terrycloth robe he'd treated himself to when he'd first moved to Yerba Buena, the fog-shrouded climate cooler than he was used to. He spent an indulgent few minutes sitting on the end of the bed, wrapped in the soft, cozy fabric, his last chance as the robe was too bulky to fit in his go bag.

He surveyed the room—the apartment—he'd be abandoning soon. Did he have everything? His drawers were half-open and rifled through, the bits he couldn't live without stuffed into the duffel by the door. He'd only been there nine months—not enough time to collect much more than what he'd arrived with— but enough time to get comfortable. He would miss this place and the promise Yerba Buena had held for him, including all the delicious dirty things Adam Devlin had promised him the other night. But if Icarus stayed, he couldn't be sure he or Adam would live to experience any of those delights. Misery and death were the more likely outcomes, and Adam, he sensed, had had enough of those nightmares already.

Shaking off the melancholy, he grabbed his jeans—no way he was leaving those behind—and the black lace briefs he'd left on the dresser. He pulled them on and had just grabbed a fitted tee when the phone on the bedside table vibrated. He tossed the tee on the dresser and walked around to the side of the bed, expecting a text from her. Instead, the screen was lit by a message from Mike. **Last night in town. How about that rain check?**

Icarus checked the time again and ran train schedules in his head. Less sunlight hours in the fall meant the solar-powered trains didn't run as late into the night as they did in spring and summer, but if Mike was available now, Icarus could make it work. Pocket another five hundred, dash back here for his bag, then catch the last train to Portola. The extra money wouldn't hurt, nor would a final visit with one of his favorite clients. **When were you thinking?** he texted back.

Now? I'm on the red-eye out later tonight.

Icarus could make that work. **Hotel Ellis in 20.**

See you then.

The screen went dark, and Icarus shifted into high gear. Time was tight. He retrieved the toys from the bathroom and shoved them, the remote, and a tube of lube into a sparkly satchel he snatched out of his closet. One last hurrah for another favorite item that wouldn't fit in his go bag. Next, he hauled his duffel onto the bed and dug out a little black dress, stockings, a wine-colored jockstrap and garters, and his favorite black heels. Finally, he shut down his laptop, tucked it and the necessary peripherals into a pouch, and nestled it between clothes in the duffel. He carried the satchel and the duffel to the dusk-shadowed living room and set both bags on the couch. All that was left to do when he returned was retrieve the single dose of Daylight from his freezer and pack it with the rest of his express meals in an insulated pouch. Enough food to last him a few days and an emergency safety measure if needed.

Otherwise packed and ready, Icarus turned toward the bedroom to change but only got as far as the threshold when two hard knocks rapped against his door. Not a neighbor's knock that he recognized, nor the usual delivery person's. Keeping the lights off, he stepped back into the shadowed living area and extended his hearing.

And picked up a heartbeat he did recognize. "Fuck," he cursed low.

He glanced from his bag to the balcony door to his state of relative undress—barefoot, jeans undone, robe hanging open. It was dim enough outside, the fog rolled in by now, that he could make it to the cover of the cypress trees without a burn. But a certain human outside his door would hear the commotion inside—Icarus scurrying for the last most important item in the freezer, the hanging blinds on his balcony door rattling, the door opening. Given the speed at which he'd have to move and the height from which he'd have to jump, there'd be no disguising himself anymore. And all of that assumed a coyote wasn't waiting outside, ready to pounce.

Any exposure would be for naught, assuming Adam didn't know what he was already.

The knocks sounded again. "I know you're in there, Icarus." The gruff voice confirmed the owner of the heartbeat.

The Devil knew where he lived, and Icarus had no escape.

He looked down at himself again. He could dash back into the bedroom and quickly dress, but he'd wasted enough time already. Maybe the shock factor would work for getting rid of Adam faster.

He crossed to the door and swung it open. "How do you know where I live? And how did you know I was home?"

Adam's gaze raked over him like a brand, and when he spoke again, his voice was full of gravel. "Because you haven't left all day."

"Do you have someone following me?" Like a certain coyote?

Stormy eyes flicked to his, full of lightning, enough to startle Icarus back a step. Adam took advantage, slipping past him and inside. He was in work boots, jeans, and a Henley, and had a pistol in the holster at his waist. He ambled into the living room and stood next to the couch, staring down at the bags. "This is confusing."

Icarus closed the door and took up a spot on the wall between the bedroom and living room. "So stop trying to figure it out."

"This one will be useful." He picked up the satchel, and his eyes widened, surprised either at the weight of it or what he felt inside. The shape of the items, given what Icarus did for a living, was a dead giveaway. One Adam apparently caught on to and liked given his deepening smirk. "Very useful."

Icarus darted forward, barely containing his speed, and snatched the bag away. "It wasn't for you. I'm meeting a client."

"Not anymore. You promised me a date."

"I didn't—"

"You didn't go into that bathroom and jerk off after I left you Wednesday night?" He narrowed the distance between them, less than a foot apart. "Because when I got home, I sure did. Can't remember the last time I came that hard."

Icarus flattened himself against the wall, creating as much room as he could between himself and the too-tempting man he wanted to plaster himself against instead. "I can't cancel on him again," he protested, voice breathy, not the least bit convincing.

The other corner of Adam's mouth hitched upward, a full-on devil's smile. He reached out a hand, and Icarus sucked in a breath, on the knife's edge anticipating where his warm, callused fingers might go. They slipped into Icarus's pocket, oh so close to where Icarus wanted them, but didn't venture far enough, withdrawing his phone instead.

Icarus glimpsed a message alert from Mike onscreen. As did Adam. "Mr. Whiskey from the bar?" He didn't wait for an answer. He clicked the call back option and put it on speaker.

"Icarus, hey," Mike answered, sounding winded. "I'm a little late, but on my—"

"Icarus isn't on his way," Adam replied. "But there'll be another whiskey waiting for you at . . ." Adam cut Icarus a questioning glance.

"Hotel Ellis," Icarus answered.

"Um . . . Icarus, you okay?"

"I'm fine, Mike." Icarus sighed and leaned his head against the wall, eyes closed. "But I can't be there tonight with you. I'm sorry. Enjoy your whiskey." He swallowed around the lump in his throat. "I'll see you next time."

The line went dead on whatever Mike started to say, and the phone thumped against his bags, Adam tossing it aside. Warm rough hands gently clasped Icarus's waist, inside the robe, just above the band of his jeans. "But you won't, will you?"

"Not if you keep fucking with my job."

"You know that's not what I meant." Adam ran the tip of his nose along the column of Icarus's throat. "And besides, I'm your job."

Icarus froze midshiver. Did Adam know Vincent had sent him? That his job was to act as bait? To lead Adam to his death?

"I'm trying to refocus all your attention on me."

Or maybe Adam meant "job" in Icarus's usual sense of the word, in the way that involved an intimacy Adam missed, his gestures now so like the ones Tuesday night in his bathroom. He nuzzled the crook of Icarus's neck as his warm breaths and rapid heartbeat slowed. Every second like this made whatever it was Icarus was doing with Adam feel less and less like a job and more and more like something he also wanted. And somewhere between the jumble of conflicting emotions and priorities was the one thing that mattered most: not leading Adam to his death. Maybe if he took this "job" tonight, if he gave Adam the intimacy he so clearly needed, he could find a way to warn him away from Vincent Cirillo.

Or fuck, kidnap him if he had to. Make sure he didn't run to his death.

He lifted a hand and tangled his fingers in the coarse dark strands at the back of Adam's head. "Where are we going?"

Adam smiled against his skin. "Benton's."

Finding Adam's hair too short to tug, Icarus was forced to curl his fingers around his skull instead and gently tilt his face back so Icarus could see it. "How?"

The Devil grinned. "I'm me."

Icarus didn't know whether to slap him, kiss him, or knee him in the balls for being so damn arrogant. And he sure as fuck didn't know what to wear to a joint like Benton's. Yes, he worked YB's top clubs, but courtesans didn't frequent establishments like Benton's. Only the sort of people who drank whiskey and drove gas-powered cars dined there. People like Adam Devlin. "I don't have anything to wear to a place like that."

Adam tilted his head toward the bedroom. "There's that dress in there." When the fuck had he noticed that? In the half-second glance he'd cast that direction when he'd entered? *Cop*, Icarus's brain reminded him. Then his brain short-circuited completely as Adam coasted a hand over his hip and grabbed his ass. "But I'd rather you leave these jeans on and throw on that shiny top from the other night."

Despite his full day of work, Icarus was halfway to hard already. Zero need for toys. Not when Adam's erection was shoved up against his. It was a struggle even to hold the thread of conversation. All he wanted to do was wrap his legs around Adam's hips and get fucked against the wall. Or better yet, on the bed.

Bed.

Dress.

Benton's.

The thread.

"I can't go to Benton's in patchwork jeans."

Adam used the hand not clutching Icarus's ass to gesture at his own self, dressed in jeans and a sweater.

"Yeah, but you're . . ." Icarus shoved his shoulder. "You."

"And you'll be with me." Adam grabbed his retreating wrist and pinned it to the wall, spreading the robe open more fully, exposing more of Icarus's chest to lips and teeth that scorched a path across his collarbone on their way to a nipple. "I want to take you out for a nice dinner, some whiskey. A proper date."

He flattened his tongue for a long, rough lick, and Icarus scrabbled for purchase with his free hand. Scrabbled for the thread again. "I don't—"

Adam tightened his grip on his ass. "I want to stare at your ass in these threadbare jeans." He released the cheek and glided his hand up under the robe, spreading his hand over Icarus's bare back. "I want to splay my hand here and sneak my fingers beneath the drape of that sexy top." He licked a path across Icarus's chest to the other nipple, swiped and bit. Icarus hissed. Chuckling, Adam released the sensitive nub and nuzzled the thin patch of hair between his pecs. "I want everyone to see you on my arm, then I want to take you home." The hand on Icarus's back lazily drifted around front, then, with laser-sharp precision, dove into his open jeans and roughly palmed his cock over the lace, making Icarus achingly hard in an instant. "I want to peel these jeans down your incredible fucking legs, see you in nothing but lace, then lay you out on a bed and suck your thick shaft until you're about to blow."

Fucking hell, the swings from starved for intimacy to just plain starved were making Icarus dizzy and more turned on than he'd been in his whole damn life. "I'm about to blow now."

Adam kissed up his throat and around his mouth, tongue dipping and diving between his lips, teasing, never giving Icarus the kiss he wanted. "Not yet, baby."

Groaning, Icarus chased after his mouth and missed, lips scraping scruffy cheek. "When?"

Adam shoved the lace aside and grabbed his balls. Good thing, since his next words sent Icarus soaring. "When I'm on my hands and knees and you're fucking me senseless."

THIRTEEN

Icarus tried not to focus on the heads that swiveled toward him and Adam as they crossed the restaurant to a corner booth. He wondered what was more of a shock to their audience—the fact he was wearing heels, jeans, and a slinky halter, or the fact he was walking arm in arm with Adam Devlin. Adam, who was arguably more dressed down than him in a sweater, nondescript—if well-fitting—jeans, and work boots. In one of the most exclusive restaurants in the city, where all the other patrons were dressed for a special occasion, where there were items on plates and liquids in glasses that Icarus never thought he'd see again. But the staff hadn't blinked when they'd entered. They'd greeted Adam like an old friend—definitely a frequent visitor—and led them to the table where two cut crystal glasses of whiskey were waiting.

The high-dollar liquor went a long way to helping Icarus ignore the stares they continued to catch over three courses of food the likes of which Icarus was sure he'd never taste again. He didn't need human food to survive, but he could eat and enjoy the fuck out of it. But in the moments when Icarus wasn't overwhelmed with the tastes and aromas of the food—or by the heat blanketing his side and the hand under the table nestled in his groin—he couldn't help wondering where this "date" might lead.

To Adam in his bed or to Adam dead?

That kidnap plan was sounding better and better if only Icarus had an ounce of faith he could execute it without fucking up.

He tossed back the rest of his whiskey, savoring the meld of smooth and spicy flavors and the internal warmth that rivaled the space heater beside him.

"You want another?" Adam asked.

"Lord, no, I can't—"

The rest of his words died on Adam's lips, stolen by the kiss Icarus had wanted so badly back at his apartment. Deep and slow, maddening in its intensity and its restraint. Maddening because they were in public, and Icarus couldn't crawl onto Adam's lap, grind down on him, and keep kissing like this until they came together, breathless and spent.

Adam drew back first, but only far enough to rest his forehead against Icarus's, sounding breathless already. "I've been dying to taste the whiskey on you."

Icarus ran the tip of his tongue along Adam's upper lip. "And?"

"Better than I imagined." He hummed contentedly and palmed Icarus's erection under the table. "Like I imagine this is going to be too."

"Oh, you have no idea." Icarus grinned. "How many more courses?"

"Just two." Adam kissed the hinge of Icarus's jaw while slowly stroking his length. "Should I tell you all the ways I plan to worship this tonight?"

Icarus rolled his hips with the next stroke, eager for more friction. "I think you're enjoying this a little too much, Mr. Devlin."

Like a flipped switch, Adam withdrew into himself and away from Icarus, taking his teasing lips, warm breath, and claiming hand with him. Humor and desire fled his gaze, sadness and longing taking their place, the rain clouds moving in, the sight eerily similar to the one he'd worn that first night back at his house.

An awkward silence filled the space between them. Icarus had tripped a memory wire. Something Deborah or David used to say or do? What kind of explosion had he unintentionally set off? The Adam-shaped hole in his chest made itself known again. "Fuck, Adam, I'm sorry."

Adam wiped his mouth with the cloth napkin, then folded it on the table. "I'm sorry I interrupted your work tonight."

"I think I needed to be here instead."

"Why's that?"

Finger under his chin, Icarus refocused Adam's gaze on him. "Back at my apartment, and at the club the other night, you said you wanted me to"—he lowered his voice—"fuck you senseless." He shifted his hand to cup Adam's face and tapped a finger against his temple. "What are you running from in here?" Adam tried to look away, tried to knock Icarus's hand loose, but Icarus wasn't letting him or this point go that easily. "You want a good, hard fuck, I got that, and I'm more than happy to oblige, but there are other moments when you want something else, something you miss. Whatever those memories are, whatever you're missing, I don't want to make you forget that. Lust shouldn't blot them out." He firmed his grip on Adam's face, prepared for a reaction to his next words. "Neither should vengeance."

Adam's eyes narrowed, but he didn't jerk away—yet.

"I heard you," Icarus explained, giving part of the story, hoping it would be enough. "I heard you talking to the other two in the Canyon Lands the other night once you got away from the fire."

"Stay out of it, Icarus."

"You caught my name, right?"

Adam's hardened expression faltered on a chuckle. He lifted a hand, holding Icarus's to his face. He angled his face and kissed his palm. Another of those knee-stealing intimate moments. "I'm trying to keep you safe."

Icarus gave him more of the truth, more afraid not to, more

afraid each second that Adam was headed the direction of dead instead of his bed. "Maybe I'm trying to do the same."

The grip around his hand would have crushed a human one. "What did you say?"

Icarus didn't flinch, didn't shy away from the cold, hard stare assessing his own. Adam apparently didn't like what he saw. He jerked away, yanked out his wallet, tossed a stack of bills on the table, and bolted out of the booth.

Icarus fisted his hand and thumped the seat of the leather booth. "Fuck!" He couldn't grab for Adam, couldn't block his path, and couldn't flex his speed or strength without making a scene and exposing himself. He was pretty sure Adam knew already given that grip, and he hadn't staked him for it, but Icarus couldn't be certain no other patron in this restaurant wasn't carrying. Namely the shifter two booths over who'd eyed him warily all through dinner. He just needed to get outside, into the dark, and follow the whiskey scent. He could catch up to Adam.

He slid out of the booth, calmly crossed the dining room, apologized to the waitstaff and host, then slipped outside. He sniffed the damp foggy air, caught Adam's familiar scent, and followed it around the corner into the alley where Adam had parked the Camaro.

And promptly met the business end of Adam's pistol. "What did you mean?"

Icarus held up his hands, palms out, and kept his voice as low and calm as the rising panic in his chest would allow. Not panic for his own life, but for Adam's. He argued with the only thing he thought might convince Adam to not race off. "Would Deborah and David want this for you?"

Adam shoved the gun's muzzle against Icarus's chest, backing him against the alley wall. "Stop with the fucking riddles."

"*You* stop chasing your own death." Icarus shared another truth, hoping it would convince Adam since appeals to sentiment had not. "Vincent is willing to sacrifice his own son to get to you. What do you think he'll do if he finally catches you?"

Adam's eyes flared, surprised perhaps that Icarus had given him the honest truth, but then they narrowed, and his mouth twisted into a sneer. "Nothing, if I catch him first. What exactly did Vincent say?"

"That they had a line on your location. That the source required a human in exchange for the information."

"Paris?"

Icarus closed his eyes and nodded.

"Is that source you? The location here?"

His eyes flew open. "No!" He made a slow show of moving his hands toward Adam's face. Adam remained still, his grip on the gun firm. He could pull the trigger, lodge a silver bullet in Icarus's chest, and end him just as fast as Icarus could snap his neck. But he didn't, and Icarus lightly clasped his face. "I answered the door tonight because I knew the only hope for either of us was to convince you not to run into the fire again."

"But Vincent sent you to me?"

"Yes, but I'm trying to make sure they never catch either of us again." Icarus hoped to hell and back that he'd said enough to convince Adam to let this go. That maybe for once he hadn't made a complete fucking disaster of the situation.

But his name was Icarus for a reason.

Adam lowered the pistol, wrenched his face free, and turned away. He withdrew his phone with his other hand, tapped at the screen, and brought it to his ear. "Meet me at the pier in twenty," he told whoever answered on the other end of the line.

"Adam, don't!" Icarus grabbed him by the shoulder and spun him around. "Please don't! We can leave together. We can just go."

Heartbreaking sadness and aching loneliness stared back at him. Adam hung up the phone and tucked it in his pocket. "My name isn't Adam."

Icarus skated his hand down Adam's shoulder, gripping him by the biceps and pulling him closer. "It is to me."

As gently as Icarus had held his face earlier, Adam returned the gesture, using it to draw Icarus the rest of the way in, forehead to forehead. "Go back to your apartment and wait for that man."

"Like hell."

"I can't protect both of us."

"You don't—"

"I don't know how to turn it off, Icarus. It's who I am."

He remembered back to that first night in the bar, how Adam had sensed his approach, how the cop instincts just wouldn't turn off. Was that what had happened to Deborah and David? Could Icarus bear to put more of that guilt on Adam's shoulders? "How do I know you'll come back? That it won't be someone else knocking on my door?"

Adam shoved the butt end of the gun against Icarus's chest, forcing him to take it.

Icarus flailed. He didn't need it, and he sure as fuck shouldn't handle it if those were silver bullets in the chamber. "I don't—"

"They're real bullets, not silver," Adam said. "In case it's not me at the door."

The hole in Icarus's chest grew wider, and he closed his eyes, leaning more of his weight against Adam. "My name isn't Icarus."

"You've told me that before." Adam's lips brushed his. "But you're Icarus to me."

FOURTEEN

It took every ounce of willpower Icarus had to not flash his fangs and pin Adam to the ground, to not chase after the Camaro as it disappeared into the fog, to not follow the scent of whiskey and gasoline to wherever Adam was headed. Turning the opposite direction and making his way across town, back to his apartment, was one of the hardest things Icarus had ever done.

Once inside his four walls, staying there wasn't any easier. Conflicting instincts tore at him—run after Adam or run the fuck out of town. She had lobbied hard for the latter. Icarus had called her on his way home and explained he needed to stay. She hadn't bought his explanation. She might still win. His bag was packed and ready, or rather repacked for the third time, a fruitless exercise in passing the minutes.

He considered logging on and initiating a live stream or snagging a client for a solo performance, anything to whittle away the hours, but his focus was tenuous at best, and there was a damn good chance Adam's name would fall from his lips when he came. And Icarus only wanted that to happen once Adam was there and Icarus was buried to the hilt inside him.

An express meal and a long, hot shower finally began to settle him. He settled further as he pulled on his sheer black stockings and the delicate lace jockstrap and garters he'd laid out earlier. He slid his feet into his favorite heels, wrapped himself in the terrycloth robe, and took his first steady breath since Adam had left him standing behind Benton's, gun in hand.

He leaned against the bedroom doorjamb, eyeing the weapon on the end of the kitchen counter. It was then he realized the significance he'd missed—or had been too distracted—to comprehend outside the restaurant. Adam had been packing regular bullets, not silver ones. Either Adam didn't know what he was, or more likely, given his pointed assurance that they were not silver bullets, he did and trusted him enough not to carry silver. Trusted Icarus enough to protect him if other paranormals had attacked them in public.

Icarus pushed off the doorjamb and circled the living room rug, lowering himself onto the far end of the couch. He wasn't going anywhere. Not unless a coyote or raven showed up on his doorstep and told him Adam was dead. He tossed his phone onto the cushion beside him, braced his elbows on his knees, and scrubbed his hands over his face. Fuck, he hoped that wasn't how this night ended. He peeked at the time on his phone. He could give Adam a few more hours. He just had to leave himself enough time to get to Portola on foot before the sun came up. It was doable in the dark and would be necessary, as the trains stopped running at midnight.

Hopefully the trek would be unnecessary.

But Icarus's hope waned, his stomach sank, and his steadiness faltered with each passing hour. He forced himself to stay on the couch but only by the grace of his crochet hooks, yarn, and a half-knitted sweater he'd pulled from his go bag.

The bag sat by the balcony door, taunting him. Screaming silently that he needed to run, and that he needed to run now, screaming louder and louder until hope was a whisper on the cusp of dawn. Sunrise the opposite of the widening black hole in Icarus's chest, sorrow and sadness for a man—the Devil—he would've liked to know better. Whatever fate Adam had met,

Icarus was almost certain he didn't deserve it; no one should die with that much pain and loneliness on their shoulders. It was not a fate Icarus wanted for Adam, but one he had to assume by now had likely befallen him. A similar fate would befall Icarus a second time if he didn't get the fuck out of there.

Forcing himself to his feet, he retrieved his jeans, a sweater, and his combat boots from his bag, stuffed his knitting inside the outer pocket, and was halfway to the bedroom when a knock sounded against the door.

He dropped the boots in surprise, then had to move at full speed to catch them. Not knowing whether it was friend or foe outside, he didn't want the thump of boots hitting the floor to give his presence away. And why the fuck hadn't he put on clothes before now?

A second knock, and on its heel, a familiar heartbeat.

Icarus took a lurching step toward the door, then froze as a second heartbeat joined Adam's. He traded the clothes and boots for the gun and inched toward the door. If it was Adam out there, why wasn't he saying anything like he had last night? Because he wasn't at liberty to do so? Or because he wasn't sure if Icarus was? Could this fucking night—correction, morning—be over already?

Shoulder to the door, using his speed, Icarus peeked out the peephole. Adam stood outside, Jennifer beside him. He listened once more, just two heartbeats in the immediate vicinity. Icarus opened the door but still didn't lower the gun from where it was half-raised at his side. It wouldn't do any good on the coyote, but thankfully, what Icarus saw with his eyes matched what he'd heard with his ears. Adam and his second were the only two beings in the hallway.

"You alone?" Adam asked.

Icarus opened the door wider. "Not anymore."

Adam passed his gun to Jenn, then took the one out of Icarus's hand and passed that one to her too. "Knock if it's an emergency," he told her, then, without another word or glance, he stepped over the threshold and shut the door behind him.

They reached for each other at the same time, Icarus curling his hands in Adam's sweater, Adam clasping either side of his neck, drawing him in and slamming their mouths together. Like at the club the other night, Adam kissed with a hunger Icarus was powerless to resist, his own instincts racing to keep up. He splayed his hands on Adam's chest, pushed him back against the wall, and Adam's whimper, his satisfied sigh, was the stuff Icarus's fantasies were made of. He plunged his tongue between Adam's parted lips, his thigh between his legs, and pressed their bodies close, diving deeper into the rising heat between them. Adam rocked his hips, undulating between Icarus and the wall, grinding all their hard parts together, and another wave of desire crashed over Icarus. Fuck, when was the last time he'd wanted someone this badly? But could he truly have what he wanted? And for how long?

He broke the kiss, drew in a gasping breath he didn't need, and caught Adam's hands on their way to the knot of his robe. Lacing their fingers together, he lifted their joined hands to the wall on either side of Adam's head, forcing a cease-fuck he hoped was fucking brief; he wanted a moment to catch his peace of mind. "What happened?"

Eyes closed, Adam leaned his head back against the wall, his chest rising and falling rapidly, gulping in air he did need. "It's done."

"Done?"

"We got Paris out. He's safe. You're safe."

Icarus squeezed the big, callused hands he held pinned to the wall. "And you?"

Righting his head, Adam opened his eyes, and there was a flicker of something in their blue-gray depths, something that caused a prickle at the base of Icarus's spine, but then it was gone with the next blink, burned away by the rising fire, the inferno blast caused by Adam's words. "Safe with you."

Icarus melted, inside and out, consumed by the flames.

FIFTEEN

Icarus erased the distance between them, bringing their lips and bodies back together. Releasing Adam's hands, he slid his own down Adam's sides to the hem of his sweater and shoved the garment up, exposing the lightly furred torso he'd gotten a glimpse of the other night and wanted to taste every inch of now.

Adam pushed off the wall, stripped the sweater off over his head, and used the momentum—and Icarus's admitted distraction with where his lips and hands would land—to walk them deeper into the apartment, untying Icarus's robe as they stumbled toward the couch. Adam turned them so he went down first on the cushions, and Icarus eagerly climbed onto his lap like he'd wanted to at Benton's. He shucked the robe the rest of the way off, then tilted forward, embarking on his quest to taste every inch of Adam's skin. "I'm sorry I didn't get the jeans back on," he said between kisses across Adam's collarbone.

Adam skirted his hands along Icarus's thighs, over the lace tops of his nylons and under the garters. "No, baby, this is good." He nuzzled Icarus's temple and dropped a kiss there.

The soft gesture made Icarus shiver. He moved on from Adam's collarbone to his neck, alternating nips and licks with gentle brushes of his lips and nose, returning the intimacy Adam craved, even in the heat of lust. "What do you want?"

One of Adam's hands crept higher. "Everything." Skirted Icarus's groin before palming his cock. "Anything." Icarus groaned and rocked into the tempting touch, the lace adding a dizzying degree of friction. Adam's lips brushed his ear, his breath as hot as his plea. "As long as this is inside me."

Fuck yes, Icarus wanted that. But he wanted—needed—to make this good for Adam too. Something inside him demanded it, as did Adam's dry spell leading up to now. Icarus needed to be careful with him, which meant he had to slow this down.

"We'll get there. I promise." He levered upright. "Are you inoculated?"

"I am. Annual vaccine package."

"Same," Icarus said with a nod. "Debatable if I need it, but that whole nurse thing. For the safety of my clients." He reached past Adam for the satchel he'd left on the back of the couch. "All right, then, you're going to help me get this on."

Adam eyed the bag hungrily even as he asked, "Do you need that?"

Icarus climbed off his lap, but only far enough to slide to the plush rug on the floor, tugging Adam along by the hand and the promise of what lay ahead, including himself, splayed out on his back on the rug. "I do if I'm going to make this good for you too." As Adam knelt between his legs, Icarus fished out the cock ring. His fingers brushed the massager and the remote, which gave him another idea. Another way to repay the trust Adam had shown him earlier by giving him his gun and being with him now. "And to give you control." And just that thought was making him harder. He handed the ring and lube to Adam. "You need to get this on me now while we still can."

Adam's grin was devilish, and it only continued to widen, to darken deliciously with heat and lust, as he unhooked the garters and peeled the jockstrap down Icarus's legs at a maddeningly slow speed, kissing the inside of his thigh, his knee, his ankle as he went. Then kissing back up the other leg as he reattached the garters and spread Icarus's thighs with his hands, making room so he could bury his nose in Icarus's groin, breath hot against Icarus's sack and cock, lips so fucking close.

And Icarus was going to be too if Adam didn't get a move on. "Now, Adam."

Smiling, Adam mercifully retreated, rising onto his knees and lubing up the cock ring. He eased the ring around the base of Icarus's dick and balls before clamping it closed.

"Tighter," Icarus directed.

"I'm gonna come in my jeans before you get it in me."

"No you're not."

Adam gulped, eyes flicking up to him, pleading and thankful all at the same time. Yes, this was exactly what Adam wanted. Intimacy on a whole other level.

"Tighter, Adam," Icarus directed again, and Adam did as told, eyes darkening and drinking up the sight of Icarus's rapidly plumping cock and balls. But it eased some of the strain for Icarus, reminded him of his role, except this wasn't the usual performance. It wasn't really a performance at all. Only insofar as it was needed to give Adam the pleasure, the intimacy he so desperately craved, which Icarus was craving more by the second too.

He removed the massager and remote from the bag. "We're going to lube this up too and get it inside me, then you're going to turn it on with the remote when you're ready for me to come inside you." Groaning, Adam palmed his cock through his jeans. Icarus grinned. "Now, do you want to put it in or watch me do it?"

"Watch," Adam stuttered out.

Icarus figured. "Okay, then you get out of those jeans while I get this inside me."

Adam worked quickly, jeans and boxers gone, getting his dick in his hand, stroking, while Icarus put on a show for him. He lubed up the massager, put a pillow under his ass, hole on full display, then stretched himself, fingers teasing his rim, widening his hole, so he could slide the massager inside and nestle the curved external tip against his taint. Both would vibrate and tease him to the extreme.

"Fuck," Adam grunted. "I want in there too."

"I can take you both," Icarus purred. "But that's not what you need right now, is it?"

Keening, Adam fell forward again and buried his nose under Icarus's balls, his hot breath puffing over Icarus's taint, his lips brushing the sensitive skin as he pleaded. "Fuck, Icarus. I need this. Need you." He licked a stripe up either side of the silicon tip, then around his rim at the base of the massager, and fuck if Icarus didn't worry about his own ability to hold out. Such naked, unembarrassed hunger—for him—from someone so powerful, who'd done fuck only knew what tonight to secure his safety, made Icarus's head spin, his chest ache. He'd seen a lot of clients over his working lifetime, but not a single one had ever made him so dizzy with hunger and desire.

"Let's get you what you need, then." He got his knees under him, then lured Adam upright as well, into a slow measured kiss, smoothing over the rough edges of his own need and Adam's. Letting his hands smooth over warm skin and tight ass cheeks, fingers teasing Adam's crack, getting him used to where this was going.

Their cocks brushed, and the massager turned on. He grinned against Adam's mouth. "Now who's playing dirty?"

Adam nipped at his lips. "That's only an ounce of how badly I want you right now." He nipped his jaw as he ground his cock against Icarus's. "How badly I want to drown in all this."

Icarus chuckled and slapped his ass and got a tick up in vibrations for it.

"Turn around," he told Adam. "Lean against the couch. Arms spread, face down, ass out for me."

He was pleased when the only expression that raced across Adam's face was pure, unadulterated lust. Not a hint of fear. Adam assumed the position, and Icarus rewarded him again for the trust, kneeling behind him, spreading his ass cheeks, and licking around the rim of his puckered hole.

"Fucking hell," Adam cursed.

"Need to get you ready." He speared his tongue and thrust inside, wetting and stretching Adam gently at first before adding lubed fingers and working him open more. Adam was tight, as promised, and Icarus's cock was fattened up by the ring. It was going to be a snug fit, and he didn't want to hurt Adam. Icarus wiped a hand off and tiptoed it up Adam's spine, loving the shiver that followed in its wake. "Are you sure about this?"

Adam shivered again, then ramped up the vibrator. "Icarus, inside me, now."

The gruff order sent a tremor up Icarus's spine and made the plea impossible to resist. Cock in hand, he closed the scant distance between them and lined up at Adam's hole, beginning the slow slide in. Unsurprisingly, he met resistance, and Adam groaned in frustration.

"Easy does it," Icarus coaxed, with gentle hands sweeping over Adam's ass, hips, and back and a line of kisses peppering his spine. His body blanketed Adam's, absorbing the heat and reflecting it right back on the man, reflecting back the closeness Adam—and he—needed. With the intimacy came relaxation, and Icarus stretched his arms along the backs of Adam's, wrapping his fingers around his wrists and nuzzling the nape of Adam's neck, dropping kisses there. Icarus eased the rest of the way inside Adam, cock buried to the hilt.

Adam let out a giant sigh, and Icarus smiled. He stretched enough to kiss Adam's cheek, and Adam turned his face enough so Icarus could capture the taste of satisfaction on his lips. Adam was the first to move the lower halves of their bodies, pushing gently back, rounding into the body spread across and inside his. Icarus rocked, countering Adam's movements, slowly at first, his thrusts measured, aimed at getting Adam used to his length and girth, to having anyone back inside him.

It didn't take long for Adam to adapt, for the heat and hunger to chase away gentle intentions. "More, please," he whispered against Icarus's lips.

Icarus obliged, pumping harder, deeper, faster, and Adam tore his mouth away, planting his forehead in the cushion and letting out a wanton groan. He ticked the massager's vibrations up again. "That's it," he panted. "Harder."

Icarus bit back his own groan with his fangs, chewing the inside of his lip. He desperately wanted to sink them into Adam's neck, but another part of him rebelled against the notion, rebelled at the thought of causing this man any harm. He focused instead on sinking his cock inside him, making this everything Adam wanted and more. He levered up, hands on Adam's shoulders, pressing gently down, and adjusted the angle of his thrusts. If Adam's groan before had been wanton, the next was pure ecstasy. Prostate found, Icarus continued to pound at it, continued to eat up every grunt and groan Adam belted out, barreling ever closer to his own orgasm. The sounds and sensations, the heated vise around his cock, and the massager stimulating his prostate and taint brought him right to the edge.

But he wouldn't leap without Adam. "Do you—" he started.

Adam dropped the remote and grabbed his hand, lacing their fingers and turning his head, glancing over his shoulder. Tears streaked down his blotchy face onto his swollen lips and into his ruffled scruff. Icarus faltered and lost his breath, worried at first, but looking to the source of those tears, he found no sadness in Adam's bright eyes. Only relief, only desire, only sheer worshipful appreciation. Only fire. Fuck, had anyone ever looked at Icarus like that before? He didn't think so, and he didn't think he was ever going to get the vision out of his head.

He leaned forward, licking up the tear at the corner of Adam's mouth. "I've got you. I'm right here with you. Come for me."

The mouth against his fell open on a groan, and the muscles around Icarus's dick clenched so hard Icarus closed his eyes and let himself drown. Behind his lids, all he saw was the sun as he dove off the cliff with the Devil.

SIXTEEN

Tingling fingertips nudged Icarus toward wakefulness. Searing heat and the acrid stench of smoke shoved him the rest of the way there.

"Fuck!" He yanked his dangling hand out of the sunlight that streaked through the gap in the balcony blinds. Flopping onto his back, he cradled his smoking hand against his chest and made sure none of the rest of him was singed.

Flame-free.

And Adam-free.

The realization struck like lightning, and Icarus nearly burned himself again as he hurtled to his feet, tangled in a quilt and tripping across the sunbeam.

Where the fuck was Adam?

Heart in his throat, he raced around the apartment. No sign of the other man. Last night, he'd said they were safe, but Icarus couldn't kick the sinking feeling he was missing something, that *safe* was a more flexible term in Adam's mind than in his. Why had he left without waking him? Where had he gone?

Forcing his racing mind and jittery limbs to still was a monumental feat, but his eyes weren't doing the trick. He flexed his other senses. No sounds but the usual outside his four walls, and inside, nothing but the lingering scent of sex from earlier this morning. Was it still morning? Not likely, given the brightness of the sun streaming in through his balcony door.

He went to grab his phone to check the time and to text her to see if she could pull traffic cam footage to determine which direction Adam had gone. He'd have to deal with her *I told you so*—she'd not been convinced when he'd messaged that they were safe and he wouldn't be running—but he'd eat crow if he had to for Adam's sake. Time to put the kidnap plan into action, regardless of the outcome. It had to be better than Adam dead. He lifted the phone from the charger—the screen flashing half past noon—and found a folded piece of paper under it. He snatched up the note and read the scribbled words.

You still owe me dessert. Don't go far. —AD

Icarus's panic waned, the sinking feeling muted, as a reel of devilish desserts from earlier flitted through his mind. Easing his cock out of Adam's ass and replacing it with his fingers, keeping him stuffed full, helping him come down gently. Adam likewise gently removing the cock ring and massager from his sensitive parts, light touches and lingering kisses soothing the satisfied ache. The two of them on the floor, Adam between his legs, licking up the come that had dribbled on Icarus's thighs. Moving to the couch, limbs tangled, cuddled together under the quilt, Adam's warm breath and steady snores a calming breeze over Icarus's chest, seducing him to sleep as well. Intimacy overload— the kind Adam had needed, and the kind Icarus hadn't realized he'd needed too. They'd had dessert, but apparently Adam wanted more, and Icarus didn't think he meant only the sweet kind.

Wanting to be ready for him, Icarus gathered the toys, his robe and undergarments, and his bag off the floor, careful not to catch the sun's rays. In the bedroom, he withdrew his laptop out of the bag and put it back in its safe, then dumped the rest of the bag's contents on the bed. After a quick shower, he pulled on lace briefs, jeans, and one of his off-the-shoulder knits, then put everything back where it belonged.

He got as far as the fridge in the kitchen, an express meal in hand, when a bird screeched outside his balcony door.

Panic surged, blinding in its intensity, last night's prickle at the base of his spine now sharp as a knife. He dropped the vial and it shattered, blood splattering the white tile floor.

Adam's words from last night came hurtling back at him.

Safe with you.

He hadn't actually answered Icarus's question. He was only safe last night because he was in the company of an apex predator. But now he wasn't. Adam wasn't safe, not like he'd apparently made Icarus and Paris. By doing what? "Fuck!"

Kraa! Kraa! Kraa!

Icarus didn't think it was possible, but the knife in his back twisted, all the way to his gut, making it churn. He was certain the bird outside the door wasn't like the crow from the other day. Certain it wasn't a crow at all, but a different corvid. A much bigger one.

KRAA!

Fighting the wobble of his knees, Icarus stepped over the mess in the kitchen, snagged the quilt off the sofa, and made his way to the door. Hand wrapped in the fabric, he didn't bother to hide his speed or strength as he reached through the blinds and shoved open the door, breaking the lock and rattling the glass in the metal frame. The raven outside had to know what he was, same as he knew exactly who the raven was.

The giant black bird tottered through the blinds, its violet eyes tracking every step Icarus took out of his way. "Are you here for me or for him?" Icarus asked, recalling Adam's words to the shifter—the psychopomp—the other night.

The bird jumped from the floor to the couch to the end of the kitchen counter, then spread its massive wings and flew into the bedroom. A crash of a lamp, a whoosh, and then several moments later, the black-haired man from the Canyon Lands the other night reemerged, wrapped in Icarus's robe.

Icarus leaned against the opposite wall, keeping his distance. "Well . . ."

The shifter's eyes flicked to the kitchen floor, then back to Icarus. "To be determined."

"Where's he gone?"

"The Canyon Lands."

"Fuck!" Icarus shoved off the wall. "What are you doing here?" He flung an arm toward the door. "Go help him."

"That's not my role in this."

"Bullshit! You helped him the other night."

"I owed him." Arms folded over his chest, fingers clutching his biceps, the raven—Cormac, Icarus recalled—rested on the arm of the couch. Icarus didn't think he liked that answer any more than Icarus had. The words that came next Icarus liked even less. "And I've been looking for you."

"Me?"

"Michael Rollins."

Icarus rocked back a step and froze. "What did you just say?"

"Your name. From before you went missing. Five days *before* the Rift." He withdrew Icarus's phone out of the pocket of the robe and held it out to him, a secure web page open. "You're a cold case in my stack of many."

The picture of the teen displayed onscreen was barely recognizable to Icarus. Had been then too on his first day at the shelter. "Still am."

"You're a soul I was supposed to deliver."

Icarus pocketed his phone. "Which direction?" He wasn't religious—he'd fled those people eons ago—but certain notions lingered and were reflected across ideologies. Eternal peace or eternal torment? Worth asking.

Cormac didn't answer.

Fuck whatever happened to Icarus. He was always doomed. But Adam . . . Adam had had enough loss. Icarus wouldn't let him lose his own life, and certainly not for a life and soul that was already lost. "Not until I save Adam."

Cormac's eyes flicked again to the kitchen, to the blood and glass splashed across the floor. "Saving lives isn't what your kind usually specializes in."

"I have a way of fucking up, but I think you knew that already, Detective Kelley."

Violet eyes shot to his. "You know who I am?"

"You cops aren't the only ones who can excavate."

"Your file is rather thick."

Icarus spread his arms. "I am what I am."

"So go." The raven tilted his head toward the balcony door. "I'm not ready to take his soul yet either."

"Did you miss the sun part?"

"I didn't." Standing, he crossed to the kitchen, took a long-legged step over the mess on the floor, and opened the freezer, withdrawing the single vial. "I also didn't miss the part in your file about this."

In a flash, Icarus closed the distance between them and snatched the vial of Daylight out of his hand. "Then why'd you even come here? Why didn't you just go help him?"

Cormac didn't budge, didn't back down in the face of Icarus's fury or trembling anxiousness. "I had to be sure I was right. About you." Sadness darkened his glowing eyes, and his tan face drained of color. "I owed them."

Icarus turned the vial over in his hand. How much did he owe Adam already? Could he be safe knowing that his safety was bought with Adam's life? With the lives of countless others—like the kid Adam had rescued—who wouldn't have the Devil to keep them safe anymore? Not a chance in hell. He flicked off the cap of the tube and tipped the vial up to his lips, drinking the magic down. Not the emergency he'd planned for, but the only one that mattered right then. He tossed the empty vial into the trash and cringed at the strange magical sensation coursing through his veins, lifting the hairs on his arms and making him impervious to the big ball of light in the sky. He moved into the living room and tested an arm in the sun.

No smoke.

He yanked back the blinds on the balcony door. Still no smoke. "You know where he's headed?" Icarus asked as he shoved his feet into his combat boots. He didn't figure the detective had gone through all this trouble just to sit on the sidelines.

He figured right.

Magic crackled through the air, and then the raven flew over his head and out the door. Icarus bounded over the balcony rail after him, into the sun, chasing the warmth he'd only just found and wasn't ready to lose.

SEVENTEEN

Icarus risked drawing attention in broad daylight as he leapt block by block, roof to roof, street to street. Best-case scenario, anyone he flew past wrote it off as a figment of their imagination or as a bird, like the raven that sailed above him. Worst-case scenario, he drew other paranormals to his trail and his perceived supply of Daylight that he'd completely consumed. All risks he was willing to take to make it across town and to the Canyon Lands before Adam took the ultimate risk.

Thankfully, aside from the raven, no one was on his tail as he neared the eastern edge of the city, the thickening fog blotting out the sun by the time he reached the border fence. Without slowing, he took a flying leap over the barrier and landed in a crouch, hand planted on the ground—

And immediately felt it, the perpetual give and shake these parts were known for since the Rift. Except these weren't the usual shifts that came from unstable ground, not like the shifting silt under his feet last week. No, these vibrations were bigger, rippling under the surface, a futile attempt to relieve the pressure that seemed to be pushing up against the ground.

The instability was likely the reason no other eyes glowed out of the fog at him and why no other birds joined the one that landed on a crumbling set of stone stairs across from him.

And hopped right back into the air, wings flapping.

Kraa!

"Exactly," Icarus said. "We're fucked." They had five, maybe ten minutes if he was judging the vibrations correctly. No time to waste. "Do you know where he is exactly?"

Cormac glided down onto his shoulder and gave a plaintive croak.

No, then. He probably hadn't had time to scout ahead, and with the mounting fog, flying solo would be a risk. Icarus could locate Adam instantly, but it would be another risk added to the mounting stack. If there were any paranormals hiding in the fog, it would be a flashing neon light announcing his presence, assuming they were worried about anything other than scurrying the fuck out of there.

Fuck it. What was one more risk at this point? He stilled, closed his eyes, and opened his ears, searching beyond the heart-beat on his shoulder. For the only one that mattered. Racing and strong, his own heart recognized the thump even as the world raged around them. He moved in time with the beats, rushing alongside it. As soon as he heard voices, as soon as shadowy figures appeared at the edge of the fog ten or so yards ahead, Icarus forced his steps to falter, cutting the connection.

But not before a sizzle of magic zipped toward him. If not for the fog, Icarus was sure moss green eyes would be locked on his position. He was surprised when no other spells were cast in his direction. What the fuck was the warlock playing at? Was the initial flash merely an acknowledgement, or was Atlas drawing him in and setting a trap? The obnoxious warlock didn't need to do the latter. Icarus was approaching regardless. Avoiding traps while doing so would be a bonus.

Cormac took off above him, circling, and Icarus waited. The bird returned several seconds later, banking left, and Icarus followed. As he edged closer, the voices grew louder, as did the crash of waves. They were right at the edge, the thinning fog confirming as much, spray dissipating the heavy mist. He ducked behind a crumbling pillar, then peeked around it, laying his eyes on the stomach-churning scene.

Atlas held two shifters to the ground with orbs of magic—Adam's coyote second and the cat from Paris's place the other night. She'd been a plant? *Fuck!* She'd also been the one who'd helped rescue the kid; that's why she'd seemed familiar. Surrounding them were several other shifters and paranormals, including Paris's other guard, the one like Icarus.

"Biggest mistake I ever made was letting you live that day." Vincent's voice drew Icarus's gaze to the nightmare scene unfolding on the jetty. He muffled his gasp in his elbow. Adam was on his knees, Vincent in front of him, a gun pointed at his head. "You've been a thorn in my side for ten fucking years."

Adam didn't look the least bit frightened. Chin held high, eyes steely, he glared at Vincent like he was invincible. "You thought a human wouldn't come after you."

"I thought a cop would be smart enough to know better."

"You took everything from me. I promised myself I wouldn't meet them again until I took everything from you."

Not invincible. Just had a fucking death wish. Cormac had been right the other night.

"Looks like you're going to fall short of that promise."

Not if Icarus could help it. Adam's words from earlier rang in his ears. *Safe with you.* Icarus would hold up his end of that bargain. Fangs descending, fingers stretching for maximum damage, claws growing out from under his black nails, he mentally calculated how many throats he could slash before Atlas downed him, before one of the other paranormals attacked him, before Vincent got a shot off with that gun.

That gun.

He peered through the fog and thought he recognized the weapon—and if he did, if he was right. He had an advantage only Adam realized. He just needed a fucking distraction, a few seconds to buy time, to get the jump on the enemy and put that advantage to use. He put his hand to the ground and silently begged Nature to win this skirmish, prayed she could sense him like she had since they were foster siblings. Like she had since their transformations thirty years ago. Like she had when he'd rung her on the phone the other morning.

Hearing his plea, she entered the battle, ready for a fucking war. With a kick hard enough to topple the pillar he was hiding behind, the ground buckled, and Icarus rolled with it. He came up snarling behind one shifter and broke his neck. Dashed to the next, broke his neck too. Tore out the heart of the third with his claws while tearing out the jugular of the fourth with his fangs.

Cormac shrieked overhead a second before claws tore across Icarus's back. He howled and turned, ready to return the favor, so sure it was the woman from the other night, but he was saved the hassle by Adam's two shifter guards, who took her out from behind.

"Go get him!" Jenn shouted. "The ground's not stable enough for us."

Icarus spun again, and his heart dropped upon seeing Vincent, gun arm raised, backing Adam up to the tip end of the crumbling jetty. Atlas was running in their direction, but the raven dive-bombed him, halting his progress, the delay enough for Icarus to speed ahead of him, out onto the jetty.

But Vincent fired before he could make it. The gun blast echoed, the bullet streaking out of the barrel and heading straight for Adam's head.

Icarus leapt, taking the risk, praying he was right about the gun. Spinning in the air, he landed between the mobster and the Devil, absorbing the impact of the bullet.

The lead bullet.

Vincent's brown eyes widened impossibly as Icarus snatched the gun out of his hand and turned it around on him—

And then the earth shook, more powerfully, more terrifyingly than it had a moment ago. A globe of moss green magic surrounded Vincent, and he was gone with a snap, wrapped in Atlas's magic.

Cormac screamed overhead, and then so did Adam behind him. "Icarus!"

Icarus spun only to see the jetty fall away, Adam falling with it.

"No!" Diving, he slid on his belly across the crumbling, silty earth, arm outstretched, hand reaching for the scrambling one that was fast disappearing over the edge. The waves below raged on as giant chunks of earth fell into the cold, dark water.

Icarus couldn't let Adam join them. Couldn't lose what he'd only just found.

He clasped Adam's trailing wrist, curled his fingers around bone and skin, and dug his nails in deep, holding on with everything he had. The momentum pulled at him. He spread his legs, the toes of his boots dragging the ground, the claws of his other hand shoved into a crevice of creased and buckled earth. Icarus irrationally thought about those old action movies, how this moment was always in slow motion, how the speed at which his future was falling off a cliff was the polar opposite—too fucking fast.

They caught a break. The earth shook again, pushing up the ground they were hanging from and slowing their momentum. But for how long? Seconds at most, Icarus guessed, before another shake would plunge them into the Bay below.

In such a predicament, the very fucked kind he was known for, Icarus didn't expect to look down and see the Devil grinning up at him, didn't expect the words that came out of his mouth to be just this side of gleeful. "What are you waiting for, vampire?" Adam said, confirming what Icarus had suspected all along. Adam knew exactly what he was. "Get us the fuck out of here."

Pride swelled inside him. This he could do right, after all— kidnap the Devil—and Adam trusted him to do it. He firmed up his grip, detached his claws from the earth, and using his toes for leverage, he dove off the cliff with the Devil.

PART TWO

THE DEVIL

EIGHTEEN

Free fall.

Countless seconds where Adam's only tether to reality was Icarus's hand clasped around his wrist, his nails—his vampire's claws—digging into Adam's skin.

Despite his law enforcement training, despite the sun poking through the fog, despite the "death wish" his ex-partner had correctly called, Adam couldn't stop the bile from rushing up his throat as he struggled to catch his breath and take in the crumbling landscape racing past his eyes.

Cliffs splitting in two and exposing pre-Rift foundations, rusted metal piles, and broken wires. A new canyon forming, mystical green sparks emanating from its core, a deep dark crevice the fog and water rushed into.

All of it flashed by too fast for Adam to fully comprehend.

And then he was yanked up and flung into the air. Icarus released his wrist, and the free fall from before was nothing compared to floating on fear, on the certainty that he would hit the water at any moment, break his back, and that would be the end. He'd only felt such fear once before as fiery walls had collapsed around him and his family. Loved ones he'd see again soon. And while yes, he did have a death wish and no, he didn't fear the after, he dreaded the impending moment of death. Been there. Done that. Didn't look forward to the repeat. Not like this. At least this time, death would be quick. At the rate he was falling again, he'd hit the water any—

Pink flashed by him, Icarus diving, and the next thing Adam knew, he landed in Icarus's arms just as the spray of crashing waves soaked his back.

The water never touched him again.

They were flying. There was no other way to describe it. It wasn't exactly like Cormac sailing above in raven form, but the vampire carrying him was practically walking on water, pushing off this or that shoal, leaping miles at a time. Two leaps to the peak of Pelican Island. Four leaps to the Huimen Enclave. A giant leap over the swaying light rail bridge that spanned the Bay. On and on Icarus skipped, banking right as Cormac did overhead, toward the more stable ground across the Bay, but never too far inland. He stayed to the shoreline, heading north into the giant estuary and on farther, the fog breaking over the fields of Tala-halusi, the fall colors showing off on the rows of vines and packed late harvest fields.

With the threat of death passed, Adam kicked his brain into tactical mode. They were exposed, unlikely to be perceived by human eyes, but other paranormals would notice them. They would wonder where they were headed in such a hurry and why. And if they realized Icarus was a vampire, traipsing through Tala-halusi in broad daylight, they'd either consider him a threat or consider how to steal his supply of Daylight. How large a dose had Icarus ingested? Enough to make it to Monte Corvo at the north end of the valley? Would the bullet Icarus had taken for him dampen the magic's effect? Until Adam had the answers to those questions, they needed to take cover.

He shifted in Icarus's arms, enough to survey the surrounding area. Familiar with the environs, he knew exactly where they could hide while they assessed maneuverability. He stretched an arm toward the east. "Two vineyards over, at the foot of the ridge, there's a farm. Head for the sunchoke fields. Should be tall enough to hide us."

Nodding, Icarus veered right, and Cormac screeched in protest overhead. It was clear the shifter's primary focus was getting Adam to the mountain. Adam, however, was focused on the man who'd saved his life. "Ignore the angry bird," he added, and Icarus's chuckle rumbled against his side.

Adam remembered the way that laughter had felt against his front last night, right before Icarus had slapped his ass and told him to bend over the couch. His ass still ached from how hard and rough Icarus had fucked him. He'd desperately missed that ache, the good kind.

They reached the edge of the Deere farm, and Icarus shortened his strides, slowing as they neared the plot of eight-foot-tall stalks. His last leap landed them three rows in, and Icarus covered him in a protective crouch. Cormac made two circular passes overhead to scout the area before descending several rows beyond them.

Adam patted Icarus's chest. "You can let me down now. We're safe."

Icarus lowered him to the ground feetfirst. "We're gonna have a conversation about your definition of *safe*."

Cormac came crashing through the stalks, naked as the day he was born. "Have it once we get to the mountain. Why the fuck did we stop?"

Icarus's gaze shot to Cormac's uncovered bits. Adam laughed at his savior's perfectly arched brow, louder still at his teasing. "Impressive, raven."

Cormac wasn't in the mood. "Shut it, vampire." *Angry bird* was right. Detective Kelley was usually the most levelheaded of their crew, restrained and deliberate to the point of frustrating. Unless someone he cared about was in danger . . . or on his list of souls. Both were currently in play; his patience was shot.

Adam stepped between him and Icarus. "This valley is crawling with paranormals," he said to Cormac. "If we'd kept traveling like we were, we wouldn't have made it to Monte Corvo unnoticed."

Cormac ignored him, attention fixed on Icarus. "How'd you do it?"

"You saw me take the Daylight."

"Not that."

But now that Icarus had mentioned it, Adam's most pressing questions throttled back to the front of his mind. "How long will it hold?" he asked Icarus. "Will the bullet dampen the effect?"

Icarus pulled down the collar of his sweater that was already half off his shoulder. There was a tiny pink scar the size of a quarter—a dime a blink later—where a wound should have been. "Bullet's a nonissue." He righted the collar and pushed up a sleeve, turning his hand over in the shafts of sunlight filtering through the stalks. "And the Daylight will hold at least until nightfall."

"You put that hand"—Cormac pointed at Icarus's flitting hand —"to the ground and made the earth shake."

"I can't make earthquakes happen."

"You're lying."

"Have *this* conversation once we get to the mountain," Adam said, throwing Cormac's words back at him. "We need wheels."

Cormac spread his arms. "I don't exactly have my badge on me."

"Please," Adam scoffed. "Old man Deere knows who you are."

"Not this well."

Icarus stifled a laugh behind a cough. "I hardly know you, and yet . . ."

Cormac's violet glare intensified. Adam needed to get them out of not just other paranormals' paths, but out of each other's. He dug his wallet out of his pocket and withdrew a wad of cash. "I spotted a clothesline on the other side of the bean patch," he told Cormac. "Go get what you need. I'll settle up with Deere"— he flashed the cash—"for that and some wheels."

Cormac held his gaze a long moment, then flicked it over his shoulder to Icarus. "If you hurt him—"

"One, you came to me." Feet planted shoulder-width apart, Icarus folded his arms and lifted his chin. Defensive, a low-key flex of strength. "Two, I didn't carry his ass all the way up here to bite him now." One corner of his sinful mouth ticked up, exposing a fang. "Unless he asks me to."

"Adam, we don't—"

Adam cut off the debate before it continued needlessly longer. "Go." With a huff, Cormac spun on his heel and disappeared into the stalks. Adam waited for them to stop swaying before turning back to the vamp. "You're trouble."

Icarus held his arms out, same as Cormac had. "Not hiding it."

But he had been hiding what he was, up until an hour ago. Adam wondered what Icarus's excuse was. Anything like his own? Icarus wasn't hiding now, though, at least not from Adam, who closed the distance between them and ran his hands up Icarus's torso. "Thank you for getting me out of there." He ached —the good kind—to sneak his fingers under the soft knit sweater, to glide his hands over Icarus's cool skin and firm muscles. To watch the scar disappear for good. But that wouldn't get them out of there any faster. He inched one hand higher, cupping Icarus's neck, and settled the other over his too-slowly beating heart.

Icarus curled his fingers into the hem of Adam's shirt. "You knew?"

"The second you clocked your step to *my* heartbeat at Club Sutro."

"What are you?"

Adam could tell Icarus knew he was hiding parts of himself too; that reckoning was coming for all of them. But not yet. "Add it to the list of conversations." Adam rose the couple of inches needed to press their lips together, teasing the vampire's mouth open with a swipe of his tongue, diving in and stealing a taste. He couldn't let this go on either, but on his long list of regrets was leaving Icarus's apartment earlier without a goodbye kiss. He erased that regret with his tongue, his lips, and the groan he freely surrendered.

Smiling, Icarus clasped Adam's ass and held him close, rutting through layers of denim. "So many conversations." He sighed dramatically.

Adam smiled wider, unable to contain the laughter that bubbled up and out of him. That was something else he'd missed. Something he could hardly remember doing the past ten years until a certain vampire courtesan had marked him as his own.

NINETEEN

They "rented" one of Deere's rusty old trucks that miraculously got them the rest of the way to Monte Corvo without incident. Worth the extortionate amount of money they'd paid. Once there, Adam ducked inside Cormac's villa to use the bathroom while Icarus hung back, enjoying the outside it seemed. Adam found him under the pergola, staring at the valley of vines below. Adam leaned against a column and looked his fill, eyes roving over the man he couldn't get out of his head. It had taken everything in him to suppress his reaction to the gorgeous, ballsy courtesan when he'd first approached him at Club Sutro. It had been unexpected on a night mired in grief and regret, in memories of the last anniversary Adam had shared with his husband and wife. He'd flexed his melancholy, an initial line of defense, and Icarus had crashed right through it, the first person to do so in a decade. A gentle word and a gentle hand from an apex predator, whispered promises and heated commands that didn't involve kill or be killed, all of it so different from the friends and foes that Adam usually kept.

Icarus was a tangle of juxtapositions, a mystery Adam wanted to solve. Wanted to do other things with too. Especially when he saw him like this—the sun filtering through his bright hair, reflecting off his pale, muscled shoulder, and highlighting the wide expanse of his back, his trim waist, his firm round ass in threadbare jeans . . . Resistance was futile.

He pushed off the pillar and followed the sandy path along the reflecting pool's edge, scattering the crows there. He approached behind Icarus, wound his arms around his waist, and drew him close, back against his front.

Icarus melted, hands covering Adam's where they rested at his waist. "This is the outparcel?" he asked, bemused.

"They could never get anything to grow up here for all the crows." He pressed his lips to Icarus's sun-warmed shoulder, and Icarus shivered. "Hence the name."

"Hence the name." His shiver lengthened into a roll, aligning their bodies closer but taking it no further, no doubt attuned to Cormac moving around in the house, moving in their direction. "Why does Cormac live up here alone? At least one of his parents is also a shifter."

"Both are, and as are his siblings. But once Cormac was old enough, his parents chose to create life instead of ferrying it elsewhere. The burden fell to the oldest." To the man approaching behind them, steps heavy, scuffing in the dirt, as if they needed the warning. As if his tossing peanuts on the ground for the crows didn't cause a loud enough flurry.

"I get that," Icarus said, voice full of familiar melancholy. Adam held him tighter, not loosening his embrace even as Cormac joined them under the pergola.

"Jennifer and Abigail called," he said. "They got out safely with your Camaro."

Icarus dropped his head back. "Thank fuck for that."

Adam chuckled, a cover for his own relief, not about the car, but about two of his best soldiers surviving today's shitstorm. Abigail had been instrumental in two rescues this week after months of undercover work inside the Cirillo organization. She was a wealth of information and skill they couldn't afford to lose. And Jennifer . . . well, Jenn was a professional—and family. "Tell them to go by the house and grab what they can. Weapons are the priority. What about Robin?"

"A few hours out. On his way back from a job."

Icarus righted his head and shifted in Adam's arms, enough to split a glance between him and Cormac. "The growly coyote?"

Adam nodded.

"He took a job elsewhere?" Icarus scoffed. "In the middle of all this?"

Adam appreciated the affront on his behalf, but this wasn't even the biggest shitstorm Robin had missed. Robin would carry the guilt of not being there the day his sister had died until he met the same fate. But that particular absence hadn't made him any more attentive to matters at home. If anything, his perceived failure only pushed him further into his ill-advised quest. "Robin does what Robin does."

"What the fuck does that mean?"

"Let it go," Adam gently chided.

There was nothing gentle about the strength Icarus used to shove out of his arms. No longer hiding what he was, Icarus took a giant step forward and spun on his heel. "Also, how is this hiding?" He spread his arms and circled in place. "We're in a villa on top of a bald hill." He gestured between Adam and Cormac. "And you two are ex-work partners and still tight. They've seen you"—he pointed directly at Cormac—"at both incidents. And the name of this fucking hill is *Crow* Mountain. I'm not the sharpest tool in the shed, but even I can figure this shit out. Won't Vincent and company figure out the same?"

Adam eyed the crows that had reassembled along the water's edge, none of them startled by their raised voices or Icarus's erratic movements. "Good luck getting through them to us."

"And I can have more here in an instant," Cormac added.

Icarus snapped shut his lips, but lingering doubts danced across his furrowed brow. Adam stepped forward, only to have Icarus move in the opposite direction. "I need to make a phone call," he said, then asked Cormac, "Can I use your study?"

Cormac nodded, and Icarus trudged toward the house, his combat boots kicking up enough dirt to clear a narrow path among the crows who were busy picking apart peanut shells.

"What is this?" Cormac asked as he pointed at Adam, then at the door where Icarus had disappeared into the house. "What's between you two?"

"I don't know," Adam replied. "I'm just . . ." He tore his gaze from the house. "I'm drawn to him."

"That's not you." Cormac sank sideways onto one of the loungers, elbows braced on his knees. "That's the thing inside you."

Adam had considered that, of course—his heat drawn to Icarus's cold, the promise of rebirth drawn to walking death. The thing inside him was sparked by certain situations, by certain emotions, by certain instincts, all of which Icarus fired. But Adam was practiced with keeping the Devil buried for everyone's sake, that kid the other night an example of what could happen if he ever let the thing inside him loose. But the Devil wasn't the only part of him that Icarus appealed to. There was also the cop who recognized someone in need of protection and the submissive in need of someone to handle him the way Icarus had so expertly done. Adam lowered himself onto the lounger across from Cormac. "It's some of me too. More of me than it's been in a long time."

"You've known him less than a week."

"I slept with Deb and David the night I met them. The two feds I was supposed to be working a case with. I married them a month later."

"For a cop, some of your instincts are shit."

"When you fall in love, then we'll talk." Adam instantly regretted his words, Cormac's immediate flinch as good as any punch. He'd been on the cusp of love once and had had it so cruelly snatched away that he'd sworn to never tempt that fate again. He'd only told Adam about it one night after too much bourbon, after a ferry that had hit too close to his own heartache decades before. "Shit, Mac, I'm sorry."

Cormac wiped away the pain the next second, face blank again. "You're right. I don't know. I can't risk that. But it doesn't mean I don't worry about the risks you take." He closed his eyes and hung his head, hands clasped behind his neck. "Vincent Cirillo sent Icarus after you. How do we know he's not still working for him?"

"When we were partners, what was the one instinct of mine that was always right?"

Cormac eyed him through his dark lashes, conceding. "Who to trust."

"I'm not discounting what you're saying. Vincent knew who to send to me and knew enough about Icarus to figure he wouldn't take no for an answer. But Vincent miscalculated. The connection between us was immediate, Mac. Same way it was with Deb and David. And just like with them, I knew from the start I could trust Icarus. *Me*." Adam tapped his temple. "Not the thing inside me."

Cormac lifted his face and pinned him with a glare. "You didn't see what I did out there today."

If Cormac relied on Adam's instincts about who to trust, Adam relied on Cormac's powers of observation. The raven saw everything. "Okay, tell me what you saw."

Cormac reached between his own spread knees and flattened his palm on the ground. "He put a hand to the ground like this, closed his eyes, and asked Nature to help him. And it did. I fucking felt it, Adam." He righted himself and mimicked Adam's earlier motion, except he tapped the center of his chest. "The raven felt it."

If Cormac saw it, heard it, felt it, then Adam had no reason to doubt it. But he also needed to understand the why and how of it. "I'll find out."

"Find out what?" Icarus called behind them.

Adam twisted on the lounger and was struck breathless again by the sight of him. Exiting the house, he strutted toward them, his long limbs, blue eyes, and magenta hair all glowing in the sun. Adam wanted to see more of him in the daylight, assuming Icarus had enough of the other sort in his system to last. "You sure that Daylight will hold?"

"I'm sure."

He stood and met Icarus at the edge of the pergola. "How do you feel about some time in the sun?"

"You can't—" Cormac started.

Adam silenced him with a raised hand. "I'm not planning to leave the property. Come find us when the others get here." He didn't wait for Cormac's reply. He grasped Icarus's hand and tugged him toward the steps that cut into the terraced hill and led toward the northwest sector of the property. He ignored Cormac's gasp behind them as they continued on the path he hadn't traversed in a decade.

Icarus stuttered. "Adam, what . . . where . . ."

He smiled over his shoulder at the intriguing man both he and the thing inside him wanted. "That conversation I promised you."

TWENTY

Adam stood at the bottom of the terraced hill's steps, the third time he'd had to stop and wait for Icarus to catch up. Not that he minded. Watching Icarus step to the edge of each terrace, close his eyes, and lift his face to the sun was its own kind of joy. Light filtered through his long, burnished lashes, fell across the sharp lines of his cheekbones, and kissed his full pink lips, as if the sun was as happy to spend an afternoon with him as Icarus was with it.

As Adam was with both of them. Joy had been absent from his life for so long.

Icarus lowered his chin, a smile teasing the corners of his mouth. "You're staring again."

"When's the last time you were out in the daylight?"

"A few months ago." Ignoring the rest of the steps, Icarus leapt off his present terrace and landed next to Adam.

"Around here?" Adam asked as he started them along the gravel path that bisected two of the vineyard's lots.

"Portola."

Where Icarus had lived. In a prior conversation, Icarus had diverted Adam's follow-up about whether he still had family there. Would he divert again today? "Family visit?"

"Something like that." He held up a hand, fingers spread. "I can count on one hand the number of times I've been out in the sun since I was turned. You don't realize how used to the feel of it you are until you can't bask in it any longer."

Adam let the diversion go—family clearly not a topic Icarus wanted to get into—and tried another. "How long ago were you turned?"

"Detective Kelley didn't tell you?"

"He tried multiple times. I wouldn't let him."

Icarus drew up short, gravel crunching beneath his boots. "Why's that?"

"I didn't need to know then."

"And you do now?"

Adam returned the earlier grin. "Just making conversation."

"Conversation . . ." Icarus rolled his eyes, and Adam laughed out loud. Laughed louder when Icarus put his hands on his waist and cocked a hip. "How do I know you're not going to stake me out here in the vineyards?"

Adam spread his arms and pointedly swept his gaze down his body. "You see a stake on me anywhere?" When he lifted his gaze, it was impossible to miss where Icarus's had gone. Right to his semihard cock. "Actual wood," Adam teased—and acknowledged. He closed the distance between them and took Icarus's hand in his. "Trust me."

"Why do you trust *me*?" Icarus traded his joking tone for one that was earnest and adorably confused. "I'm a vampire. I can kill you before your next breath."

Adam drew him closer, and Icarus twined an arm around his waist. Pressed together, the last thing Adam felt was threatened. Turned on, yes. Comforted, yes. Life in jeopardy, no. "You had multiple chances to kill me the past week, personally or through Vincent's hand. You didn't."

Icarus lowered his chin, gaze downcast. "I agreed to help them initially."

"How long did that agreement last?"

"Until I saw you at the club the first time."

"Exactly." Adam curled a finger under Icarus's chin and lifted his face. "And I'm guessing extortion was involved."

He tried to duck his chin again, but Adam wasn't having it, wasn't letting this point go. His tenacity was rewarded with another eye roll and a dramatic huff. "They hacked my cock cage and my vibrating plug. Threats of death and destruction. The usual."

When Adam failed to stifle his laugh, Icarus stifled it for him, capturing his lips in a scorching kiss that sorely tempted Adam to drag him off the path and into the rows. He was dying to shove his hands inside Icarus's jeans, cup his ass, and grind against him. Desperate to lower the zipper, sink to his knees, and take Icarus's cock in his mouth. Ready for Icarus to tangle his hands in his hair and use him. But he wanted all that to happen in the place he dearly missed, the place he hadn't wanted to return to until Icarus had walked into his life.

He drew back and rested his forehead against Icarus's jaw. "You didn't have a choice," he said between heavy breaths. "And even if you did, I'm not sorry. I think you're the key."

"The key to what?"

"That's a longer discussion." Fire and destiny, all of it wrapped up in the past and the future. Adam wanted to enjoy the present with Icarus, at least for today. He reluctantly extricated himself from Icarus's arms and, putting a hand in his, tugged Icarus farther along the path. "And there are some other conversations we need to have first."

Surprisingly, Icarus let it go. "Where are we going?"

"My favorite place up here. Plenty of sun for you to bask in."

Neither of them spoke for several minutes, only the rustling leaves, the crunch of gravel, and the errant *caw* disturbing the silence. This part of the property had once been a chorus of animal sounds—birds, squirrels, weasels, rats, the occasional fox or deer—but they'd all fled.

"Still not used to the quiet," Icarus said, as if reading his mind.

"Even after thirty years." Adam whipped around his gaze, surprised by the slip. "Trust nugget for a trust nugget," Icarus said with a shrug. An intentional slip, it seemed.

And if Adam's math was right . . . "The Rift?"

"Just before."

At the end of the path, Adam veered right, past the ends of the rows and into the grove of olive trees. He stopped short of the field ahead and drew Icarus close, offering another trust nugget, saying what was on the tip of his tongue the way he used to. "I haven't felt like me in ten years. Not until I met you."

Icarus swooned into him, forehead landing on his shoulder. "Fuck, Adam."

"That . . ." He ran a hand up Icarus's back and into his hair, using it to gently tilt his face, to draw his gaze again. "That's the real me. The one who doesn't hold back. But he's had to stay locked down, be Adam, the Devil, since . . ."

"Since the night they died."

"Everything changed." That man who wore his heart on his sleeve had burned with his husband and wife, leaving only Adam —and the thing inside him—behind. But pieces of their past remained. "Except this place."

Untangling, he let go of Icarus's hand and stepped the final few feet through the trees and into the field of wild mustard, wanting to get there first so he could witness the expression on Icarus's face, expecting his reaction to be even better than the one at the edge of each terrace.

Icarus didn't disappoint. He cleared the line of trees, and as their shadow receded and the sun greeted his steps, Icarus's eyes grew wider, round saucers of joyous blue, matched only by the smile that stretched across his face, as he took in the field of yellow and green. This late in the season, so much of Talahalusi was brown and dry, but protected as this property was by the mountain and the trees, blanketed with roving fog each morning, wild mustard could grow in the spring and fall, the bright yellow flowers stretching as high as Icarus's knees. Icarus flattened his hands by his sides, brushing the tops of them, laughing at the bees and butterflies that scattered. Without predators, they'd flourished and kept the vineyards, fields, and flowers pollinated. Adam strolled ahead, backward, never taking his eyes off the blissfully happy vampire playing in the sun.

He eventually came down from the high, following Adam to a thinner patch toward the far edge of the field, pulling a sexy pout as he plopped onto the ground next to him. "Do you bring all your lovers here?"

"They brought me here."

TWENTY-ONE

Icarus's pout disappeared. "Adam, I—"

He reached out and skated a thumb over Icarus's lower lip, wanting the pout back, wanting more. "I've never brought anyone else here. I haven't been here, haven't been with anyone else, since—"

Cursing, Icarus rose on his knees, and for a heart-stopping moment, Adam was terrified he was going to leave. But then he threw a leg over Adam's lap, grasped his chin, and slammed their mouths together, giving Adam the lip he wanted and more, grinding down onto his cock that had been erect since that pout had first appeared. Adam grasped his hips and rolled, pressing up against him. Icarus gasped, and Adam didn't waste the opportunity, diving inside Icarus's mouth, tongues colliding and twining, parrying until Icarus tore his mouth away long enough to rip off his sweater, giving Adam access to all the skin he hadn't had time to fully enjoy the night before.

Adam leaned forward, swirling a tongue around one pert nipple, toying with it and relishing the answering rock and grind of Icarus's hips. He traveled from one cool pec to the other, administering the same torture and receiving it right back, Icarus's glide over his cock sublime. Hands climbing Icarus's back, he felt the vampire's cool skin heat with the sun and his touch. Heat further as he trailed his fingers back down and inside Icarus's jeans, palming the cheeks he'd craved all day.

Icarus angled his ass up, forcing more separation, creating a path for where he clearly wanted Adam's fingers to go. And in case he wasn't sure, the bossy courtesan told him so. "Touch me. There."

He slid his fingers down the cleft of Icarus's ass, found his rim, and circled. Tapped. And damn near came in his pants from the wanton moan that rumbled up Icarus's throat. The spike was enough to bring his mind back online—a little. "We need to talk," he mouthed against the underside of Icarus's chin.

Icarus tilted back his head, giving him more access while at the same time shoving a hand between them and palming Adam through his jeans. "We need to celebrate the fact we're still alive." He stroked, hard and rough. "And I need to feel this inside me."

Adam was torn. Not about whether to have that talk. Fuck talking. With the gorgeous man in his lap, his hand fondling Adam's cock with maddening, wonderful strokes on the edge of too hard and too slow, there was only fucking on his mind. He was torn over whether to lie back and let Icarus torture him to death or push his finger past Icarus's rim and find out if his insides were as warm as his skin was becoming under the sun. Icarus made the decision for him, thrusting back on his finger, and fuck yes, furnace-hot muscles clenched around his finger.

He groaned, and Icarus smiled against his lips. "You want in there?"

More than anything right then, with one caveat. "Yes, but I need—"

Icarus reached behind his back, grasped Adam's wrists, and pulled them around front. He let them go only long enough to rid Adam of his Henley, then with his grip firm around Adam's far more breakable bones, he laid him out, pinned to the ground. "Don't worry. I'll still be in control while I ride you."

Relief washed through him. "Yes," he groaned. "I need that."

"You keep your hands right there."

Easier said than done, especially when Icarus stood, stripped out of his jeans, and teased a view of his erect cock, straining against his black lace underwear. Adam bit his bottom lip and fought his warring urges—shove his hand down his pants and stroke his cock or shove his hand down his pants and grab his balls to stop from coming. Either case, his hand was halfway to his fly when Icarus lightly kicked his arm back in place, tutting, "Be good now. I'll take care of that, I promise."

Step one, relieving Adam of his pants and underwear, stripping him naked. Step two, straddling his lap once more and dragging his lace-covered taint across Adam's cock in a slow, tortuous glide, making Adam bite his lip and arch his back. Step three, streaking his torso with precome as Icarus knee walked the rest of the way up his body until his knees were on either side of Adam's head, cock so close Adam could feel the heat, smell his and Icarus's precome combining to stain the lace even darker. "You're going to help me ruin these pretty panties." Knees on the insides of Adam's biceps to keep him pinned, Icarus positioned his crotch directly over his face. "Just with that gorgeous mouth of yours."

There was nothing Adam wanted to taste more. He peppered either seam of the briefs with hot breaths and long, slow licks. Twirled his tongue around one ball, then the other. Nipped along the seams until he flattened his tongue and mouthed both balls at once through the lace. Everywhere but Icarus's cock. He wanted to return some of the torture. Icarus keened above him, his broad chest beading with sweat, his head thrown back and mouth hanging open. "Get those lips on my cock. Now. I want you to taste it when I come. Then I want to taste me on you."

Adam followed orders, but not without tasting every inch of Icarus's cock, licking a slow trail up the underside, swirling a tongue around the lace-covered tip, then sealing his lips around the ridge of him. He mouthed a path to his root, then kissed every inch on the way back to his crown, lashing it with his tongue before closing his lips around the tip again, dampening the lace with his spit, wetting it further as he greedily sucked.

Icarus fell forward, stretching over him and riding his face with abandon that Adam relished. He lost himself in the scratch of rough lace, Icarus's musky scent and taste, the aching pressure building in his own balls, the breeze that wafted across his bare, heated flesh, and the pleasure of being so completely used.

Icarus tunneled a hand in his hair and forced his gaze up to meet his. "I'm going to come, but you're not. Do you understand me?"

Adam groaned, not altogether certain he could oblige.

Icarus's fingers curled in his hair. "I'll pull off. Won't give you that come you want so badly. Not if it means I can't have what I want most in the world right now. Your cock in my ass. Do you understand?"

He swirled his tongue around Icarus's crown again, and two thrusts later, Icarus came with a shout, come leaking through the lace and mesh. If Adam was greedy before, he was ravenous now, swallowing and licking up all he could, whining in protest when Icarus lifted off his face.

He slid back down him, smearing come across his chin, his chest, and then once he was straddled across Adam's hips, he smirked, fang teasing the upturned corner of his mouth. "I had to save some for myself." He reached a hand in his briefs, gathered the moisture there, and reached behind himself.

Arms freed, Adam threw one over his eyes, the sight, the pressure in his balls too much. Icarus's laugh was the definition of uninhibited and sexy, fitting here in this place where Adam last remembered being the same. The sound of fabric ripping drew Adam's gaze back to Icarus, who tossed the tattered lace aside, grasped Adam's cock with his slick hand, and guided it inside him. Adam scrabbled for mustard weeds, anything to grab hold of, to keep from reaching for Icarus so he could follow orders.

"Get your hands on me," Icarus said.

Thank fuck. Adam levered up, arms twining around the beast

in his arms, holding him tight. He thrust up as their lips met, Adam giving Icarus the moan-inducing taste he wanted while demanding Adam keep up with the frantic roll of his hips, working his cock, building him fast and furious.

"I'm gonna count us down, and you're gonna come on one."

Adam nodded.

"Five."

He grasped one of Icarus's ass cheeks.

"Four."

Clutched his shoulder.

"Three."

Licked a stripe up his neck.

"Two."

Found his lips again.

"One."

Held Icarus close, thrust up inside all that tight, hot heat, and exploded.

TWENTY-TWO

Adam couldn't say exactly how long he'd been dozing when the sun-warmed body nestled against his side tensed, Icarus instantly on alert. A second later, growling echoed from the direction of the tree line. The second after that, Icarus was crouched above him, claws digging into the ground on either side of his head, lips pulled back in a snarl around fully extended fangs.

The growls grew louder—and more familiar. Adam tilted back his head to see what Icarus had locked onto. A large honey-blond coyote prowled the edge of the field, hackles up, canines bared. No immediate danger, then, assuming two apex predators posturing didn't kill them all.

Adam reached up and patted the side of Icarus's face. "That's my second, Jenn. You know her."

The coyote snapped and gnashed its teeth. Icarus seethed through his.

"Jenn!" Adam shouted as he rolled onto his side under Icarus. "That's enough."

Abigail, in human form, strolled out from among the trees and ran her fingers through Jennifer's scruff. "Back off, baby." A little more coaxing—a scratch behind the ears, a hand flattened between her shoulder blades—and Jenn finally lowered her hackles. Abigail turned her dark eyes back to them. "You need to get to the mansion," she said, expression grim and foreboding. Granted, Yerba Buena earlier had all gone to shit, but he'd figured Abigail being back with her lover would at least take the edge off, might blunt the reality of the trouble they were in. Apparently not.

He tapped at Icarus's hip, and the vampire must have seen enough to believe the threat had passed. He moved from atop Adam, standing, then offering him a hand up. "What's happened?" Adam asked Abigail as he and Icarus dressed, the latter commando in his jeans. Not thinking about that. Not if he wanted to get his own jeans zipped. Abigail approached, and the waft of smoke that tickled Adam's nose pushed all other thoughts away. "Where's the fire?"

"Your house." Abigail reached into her back pocket, and by the size and shape of the item she withdrew, Adam knew what it was even before she unfolded the photo and held it out to him. "They torched the place. We were able to rescue some weapons from the armory, but upstairs . . . This was all that was left."

Icarus approached behind him, his hand appearing in Adam's periphery, an arm on its way to wrapping around Adam's waist, but Adam put out his own, holding Icarus off. The man in the picture, smiling on his wedding day, his husband and wife kissing his cheeks, had no business in this world, no matter how close to resurfacing he'd been with Icarus.

That man was gone, Adam was here, and the Devil was so close to getting what he'd been after the past ten years. And once vengeance was had, that man in the photo could join his husband and wife like he should have done that day ten years ago. That was the future and fate that awaited him, no matter how much he enjoyed the present escape with Icarus. "Let's get back to the house."

As if sensing Adam's mental shift, Icarus kept his physical distance the entire walk back, but he remained emotionally close, timing his steps to Adam's heartbeats, making his claim clear to Abigail and Jenn. Adam didn't tell him to do otherwise, didn't want to cut that tether completely, and besides, he was certain Abigail and Jenn could smell the come on both of them.

So could the other coyote whose head whipped their direction the second Adam and Icarus stepped through the door. Even in human form, Robin's growl shook the windows.

"Let it go," Adam said as he dropped onto the couch across from him.

"Dog," Icarus sniped from the armrest he claimed beside Adam.

"Bloodsucker," Robin sniped right back.

Cormac, in the chair at the end of the couches, was his usual droll self. "Now that introductions are out of the way."

Jenn reappeared from the bathroom in human form, dressed in jeans and a tee. "Why is he here?" She jutted her chin in Icarus's direction as she sank into the couch next to her cousin. "If you haven't noticed, shit goes sideways whenever he's involved."

"Shit is going sideways, with or without him," Adam replied. "At least with him, I'm still alive. Without him, I'd be dead."

"Vincent's unhappy you're not." Robin—a slight drawl in his voice, lingering from whatever job he'd returned from—tossed his phone onto the table between them, screen open on an encrypted app. "Raised the bounty to ten million."

"Fuck." Icarus stretched an arm behind Adam across the top of the couch cushions. "This is more than a thorn in his side. Why does he want you dead?"

Adam flicked his gaze to his concerned one. "Because I want him dead."

"That can't be the entire story."

"It's not." Cormac dropped a file onto the table beside Robin's phone. "Only file I have that's thicker than yours," he said to Icarus. "Vincent Cirillo has become a billionaire by enslaving other people's magic."

"What does that mean?" Icarus asked.

"That kid you saw me and Abigail rescue the other night?"

Adam waited for Icarus's nod, then continued. "He'd been kidnapped by Vincent's crew and nearly drained dry."

"Okay, but that's not enslaving. That's flat-out stealing."

"He was a runaway," Abigail said. "No one noticed him missing. Since I'd been inside, I knew he was stashed there and about to flame out."

Icarus opened his mouth, no doubt to ask what that meant too, which Adam was not getting into today. He picked up where Abigail left off before Icarus could. "In other cases, Vincent offers 'private security' to paranormals, and before they know it, they're doing his bidding. He takes their money, then uses their power to make more money."

"Say someone wants a soul stolen," Cormac explained, "and would pay handsomely for it. Vincent finds a soul eater or a psychopomp—like my kind—in need of protection, strikes a deal with them, then uses all that magic he's stolen from nobodies to turn his client into his tool, to convince them to steal that soul for Vincent, who turns around and sells it to the highest bidder."

"And the client can't tell anyone because now they're implicated too." Icarus lowered his chin, features pinched in sympathy. "Just like a fucking dealer."

"Only he's dealing in magic," Adam said.

Icarus jerked his head up, eyes wide. "Is that how he has a warlock in his thrall?"

Twin growls emanated from Robin and Jenn.

"Easy," Adam said, appreciating the response, not appreciating the person it was directed at. Once Abigail moved into position on the armrest next to Jenn, positioned to pounce into referee mode as was often her role, Adam turned his attention back to Icarus, explaining, "Atlas has his own agenda."

"To be even more powerful than his master," Robin said.

"That's not what it looked like to me," Icarus said.

"He's a warlock," Adam said. "You can't believe anything you see." He expected Icarus to argue, but he backed off instead, contemplative and quiet.

Robin gave them more to think about. "He's still not told Vincent what *you* are, assuming he's figured it out. If he had, Vincent would be trying to take you, not kill you."

"I still think we should take this to law enforcement," Cormac said, then when they all looked his way with raised brows, added, "Officially. With Vincent's operations escalating, there's more incentive to do something."

"There wasn't incentive enough ten years ago?" Robin barked. "He had two cops and two feds on his ass, and he still got away with murder."

Icarus rocketed back to attention beside Adam. "Wait! He's been doing this for ten years?" Then split a glance between him and Cormac. "And you haven't taken it to law enforcement yet officially?"

"We can't trust them," Adam said. "He's got moles all in law enforcement."

"Couldn't trust them then, can't now," Robin said, then with a flick of his hand in Cormac's direction, added, "Present company excluded."

"What if I had a contact?" Icarus said, the last thing Adam expected. "Someone you could trust."

Cormac scooted to the end of the chair. "How can you be sure?"

Icarus shrugged the single shoulder bared by his knit top. "He's thirsty. And I have pics of his dick."

Abigail's hand on Jenn's shoulder was the only thing that kept the coyote from leaping across the table. "Someone get him out of here before I rip his fucking throat out."

Icarus grinned, a fang snagging his lip. "I'd like to see you try."

"We don't have time for this," Cormac interrupted. "Not with a ten-million-dollar bounty on Adam's head."

A ten-million-dollar bounty and two leads. "What if we work both?" Adam said. "We continue to work our angle, Icarus works his. So long as one of them lands Vincent in jail, it'll be a success."

"Do you think jail is going to stop him?" Icarus said, equal parts doubtful and curious.

"No," Adam admitted. "But I think jail is going to put him in a single place for at least a few hours where we can get to him."

Across from them, Robin purred around a grin that was just this side of feral.

TWENTY-THREE

"Yes, I know, you were right." Icarus sighed, heavy and dramatic. "Do we have to go through this every time?"

Adam leaned against the wall outside the sunny second-floor bedroom Icarus had disappeared into and barely stifled his laugh.

Whoever was on the other end of the line was giving Icarus hell. And he loved it, judging by the affection in his voice. "Thank you for answering the call this time. You saved our lives."

Adam inched closer to the door, recalling what Cormac had described. Had there been someone else on the scene they hadn't seen? Adam didn't think so, but he hadn't been with them. Maybe this person was there? Or helped in another way?

"I'm fine, I swear, safe and sound," Icarus said, then after a pause, added, "Talahalusi." Another pause, then a chuckle. "Yes, I know it's fucking sunny up here."

Adam bit his lip. Icarus wasn't complaining, good-natured or otherwise, about the sun earlier this afternoon when he'd been naked and riding Adam's cock. He'd basked in the warm rays, same as Adam, enjoying a respite from the characters they had to play.

Which Icarus was shifting back into, same as him. "Do you want to come up here? I think you'd be safe. They're on our side."

Protective and assessing. "And if they try to hurt you, I can take them."

So someone more important than what Adam's team was planning. The family Icarus wouldn't talk about? Another vampire, another paranormal, or someone human? Adam would bet the last, given the protective streak, but then how had that person saved their lives? Certainly not the Daylight; that had come from Paris. It must have something to do with what Cormac had seen, but with Icarus's protective streak, how would Adam ever get that information?

"Fine," Icarus said, his tone indicating grudging assent. "But I want check-ins every six, and if you sense anything off, you call me. I'll get down there as fast as I can." Down there as in back to Yerba Buena or somewhere else? Portola? His bags had been packed last night when Adam had arrived at his apartment. Was this who Icarus planned to flee to? Or with?

"Love you too. Keep me posted."

A spike of jealousy kicked Adam in the gut, unwarranted. Like Cormac had said, he'd known Icarus less than a week. He had no claim over the vampire, even if Icarus was broadcasting a claim over him. For protection, because that was his role. But who else did he have to protect? What if by *family*, Icarus meant someone more than a sibling? A partner in Portola? Someone more important than him . . .

"You can come in now," Icarus said from inside the room, accompanied by the creak of bedsprings. "I can hear your heartbeat."

Adam pushed off the wall and into the bedroom, finding Icarus sprawled on the bed in the sun. He was perfectly still, not bothering to hide what he was anymore. "I thought you didn't keep in touch with your family," Adam said as he moved to sit on the windowsill.

Icarus shifted, staying in the sun. "I never said that."

"Whoever it was, they were giving you hell."

Eyes closed, he smiled, soft and fond, affection with fangs. "She always gives me hell."

"Sister?" Adam guessed, going for the option that would hurt the least and was rewarded with a nod. He crossed his arms to hide the relieved rise and fall of his chest. "Older?"

"Depends how you look at it."

"She's human, then?"

"Not exactly." He eked open one eye, pinning Adam with it. "She's something *else*, like you."

"Like me?"

"Well, I don't know what you are yet, but you're not completely human." He opened the other eye and levered up on his elbows. "There's magic in you, same as with her."

Which meant she was a target, same as him. Icarus's protective streak made even more sense now. "If she needs protection, she can come here."

"I wish she would, but she does things on her own terms." He clenched his fists. "No one else's." Forced his hands open again. He was more of a wreck about her than he was letting on.

"You care about her?"

"I promised to protect her." He lifted all the way up, crossing his legs on the bed and dropping his hands in his lap, his gaze downcast, his voice as small as Adam had ever heard it. "She's all I have left." Commiserating, Adam pushed off the window and sat on the bed next to him, hand on his knee. Icarus covered it with his and squeezed. "I'm sorry they burned down your house. It was a lovely home."

Home. It had been. A place of so many firsts, of so many hopes and dreams, of so much love. He looked out the window, looked back in time, then shut his eyes and the door on his memories. It was fitting in a way that it was gone now. It was one less thing tying him here.

Icarus removed his hand. "You know, at first, I thought Adam was the real you, and this was the Devil, but they're the same, aren't they?"

Adam returned his gaze to him and nodded. It wasn't exactly how he saw it, but close enough. Adam was both the face the Devil needed and the Devil's keeper.

"I thought so." Disappointment flashed across Icarus's face, but fast on its heels was determination. "All right, what does Adam, aka the Devil, need Icarus to do?"

"Stop picking fights with Robin."

Icarus laughed out loud. "Have you met your friend?"

Adam chuckled. "Fair, but he's set in his ways at this point. He's an asshole, but a loyal one."

"What does he do exactly?"

"He's an assassin."

Icarus startled to full attention. "How's that work with a cop and ex-cop as friends?"

Adam shrugged. "Worked even less with a twin sister and brother-in-law who were feds."

Icarus covered his gaping mouth with a hand. "Deborah was his sister?" Adam nodded, and Icarus squeezed his knee again. "Deborah and David were the feds on Vincent's trail?"

"He's responsible for their deaths." They'd had a perfect night at Club Sutro, a perfect anniversary celebration, and the next day, his spouses were dead by Vincent's hand. "They were building a case against him. Were close to shutting him down on a federal level. They had juice beyond YB."

"Vincent couldn't have that."

Adam nodded. "The federal case died with them, and the more YB was cut off by the ongoing war, the more Vincent's power grew. He thinks he's invincible. Might be trying to make himself magically so, depending on what he's planning for later this month. Either way, Robin and I can't let him get away with it."

Icarus narrowed his eyes, and his forehead creased, creating the putting-it-together expression Adam caught on his face from time to time. "So you, Robin, and Cormac have been carrying on

Deb and David's work? Building a case and disrupting his organization?"

"And rescuing those who need it," Adam said. "Destroying his stores of magic, cutting off his source of funds, interfering with his business."

"So those warehouse fires and gunfights I hear rumblings about?"

Adam pointed at himself. "Not all the time, but some of the bigger ones. Disruption to the point of destruction."

"Because that's what he's done to you." Icarus unfolded his legs, stood, and began to pace the room, hands on his hips below his sweater. "Are you stealing from him too? Is that what pays for the whiskey and meals at Benton's?"

"No. Inheritance, my pension, and the Devil pay for those things."

Icarus paused in his circuit, hip and brow cocked.

"The Devil solves problems for people," Adam clarified.

"Problems that typically involve Vincent Cirillo?"

Adam shrugged.

He rolled his eyes and resumed his pacing. "And the casework?"

"Makes Mac feel better. We've been building it for an opportunity like the one you brought us. We can use it to get Vincent where we need him."

"In jail."

"Like I said, makes him an easier target."

"For the assassin. Makes sense." He stopped in front of Adam, head tilted. "But you had him right in front of you earlier today."

"I tried to make a move without my team." Sometimes, the man Adam used to be whispered in the Devil's ear, and the thing inside him would slip its leash. Would do something impulsive, like the man Adam used to be.

"You were protecting me."

"You made *me* feel invincible. And human again." He reached out and lightly grasped one of Icarus's hands. "I don't know how to turn it off, Icarus." None of it—the lover, the cop, the gate-keeper, the fire. "It's who I am."

"Who you are . . ." Icarus threaded their fingers together and stepped closer. "Why did Vincent tell me your name was Adam Devlin if he knows who you were before?" He glanced over his shoulder toward the door. "Why do they all call you Adam?"

"Why do you call yourself Icarus? Why do you only refer to your sister as *she*?"

He pressed his lips shut.

"That's what I thought." Adam released his hand and pushed to his feet. "We all have our secrets, our reasons for keeping them and for inhabiting the skin and personas we're in."

"Okay, so back to my original question . . ." He laid a hand on Adam's forearm. Still warm, still kind, still more than Adam deserved. "What does Adam need Icarus to do?" He wrinkled his nose. "Besides play nice with the stinky, grumpy dog."

Adam took his hand in his again, not immune to the warmth and comfort, but stopping himself short of everything the old him wanted to drown in. "Get us the details on your police contact. Let us check them out. If we don't spot any immediate red flags, you can proceed."

"I've already done the excavation on him. It's solid."

"Atlas managed to fool you."

"Atlas is a warlock with skills. This is an overworked cop, married with three kids, who jerks off to me fucking myself on a dildo." He spread his arms far apart, taking Adam's arm with him. "Big difference."

Adam chuckled. "Okay, then, set it up."

"What are you going to do?"

"Shore up defenses, work with my team, and consider different angles." He rested his other hand on the strip of skin exposed between the edge of Icarus's sweater and jeans. "Get you a change of clothes."

"That would be appreciated. Little hot up here in knits, even for me. I'm surprised you're not sweating."

He'd learned to live with the heat, here and inside him, long ago. He twined his arm around Icarus, hand settling at his lower back. "We have a contact checking on your place. If it's still standing, I'll have them grab your go bag and computer. I assume you need that for work?"

Icarus nodded. "I'll get you the safe code for the laptop. Would also be nice to get my crochet stuff and my robe." He snuggled closer. "For when it gets cold here at night."

"We'll get you the crochet stuff." Adam dipped his hand below Icarus's waistband, palming his ass and imagining how good Icarus would look in that robe and nothing else. "The robe was already on my list."

Still, it wasn't the time to entertain those fantasies. He had a long list of to-do items, and Icarus wasn't on it. But when he tried to pull away, Icarus slung one arm over his shoulder and grasped his shirt with his other hand, holding him close. "Whenever you need to take a break from Adam and the Devil"—he leaned in and kissed the corner of his mouth—"I'm here."

TWENTY-FOUR

It was near nightfall when Robin's familiar tread echoed down the stairs. Icarus, who'd been relegated to the cellar when his fingers had started to smoke, must have also recognized their approaching visitor. Shoulders tense, he turned from the over-stock metal tanks he was pretending to be interested in and let his arms hang loose at his sides, at the ready, fingers spread as if preparing to flex his claws.

"Easy," Adam coaxed. "If he wasn't here in peace, you wouldn't hear him coming."

"I'd hear his heartbeat."

"Maybe." Adam tilted his head. "Maybe not."

Icarus's brows raced north. "Oh, really? How's that?"

"My secret to tell," Robin said as he cleared the bottom step. "Not his." He met them beside the retired tasting table in the middle of the cellar great room and dropped Icarus's jam-packed go bag at their feet. "Your apartment building was still standing. Too big to burn down."

Whereas a fire at Adam's house in the Terrace looked like just another arson in a dying neighborhood. A blaze caused by a squatter or a property owner trying to collect insurance. Barely a blip on the radar. It was what Adam wanted—as erased as he could make it—but memories were harder to scrub clean, the mental door on them impossible to keep shut.

He turned away, chest burning and eyes stinging.

Icarus skirted a hand across his back, a gentle sweep of comfort, enough to steady him on the edge of the abyss, to anchor him while he caught his breath. Icarus, meanwhile, interrogated the messenger. "What about the apartment itself?" he asked Robin. "Atlas broke in before."

"He'd been there, but it didn't look or smell like he stayed long."

"Computer?"

"In the bag."

"Crochet hooks?"

"Plus yarn."

Icarus smiled. "Robe too?"

Robin shook his head. "Wasn't there."

The smile died. "Stinky motherfucking warlock."

"First thing you've said I agree with."

"I get to hit him before you kill him."

"Second thing."

The shared spite forced a stuttered laugh out of Adam. An easier one followed when he caught Icarus's smirk. "Not going for a third?"

The vampire winked and hefted his bag off the floor. "I know better than to press my luck."

That absurdity deserved a full-bellied laugh. "Since when?"

"Since now," Icarus threw over his shoulder as he turned toward the vacant bunk room.

He disappeared into the shadows, and Adam, still chuckling, swung his attention back to the table. Robin eyed him with an expression that was half surprise and half . . . pity? The assassin tossed a dime-sized metal sliver—an embedded lens—onto the table. "Also found that at his place."

"A bug? Someone's been spying on him?"

"Or he's been spying on you."

Adam picked up the sophisticated piece of tech and examined it more closely, considering its other uses. "Or on his clients."

"None of the above," Icarus snapped as he zipped back into the room. He'd left on his jeans but swapped the knit sweater for a strappy tank top that left zero to the imagination, his cut biceps and ripped upper body on full display. For his benefit or Robin's, Adam couldn't say, and he didn't have time to contemplate it further. Icarus snatched the bug from his hand. "That's five grand worth of tech you ruined," he seethed at Robin.

"Who's tech?" Robin asked. "Yours?"

"Hers."

"Hers?"

"My sister's, and it wasn't active." His gaze flicked the direction of the stairs—detecting Cormac's approach, as did Adam— then back to them. "We have a signal. If I gave it, she'd know to turn it on and look around."

Robin planted his hands on the table. "There's only a handful of people with access to that kind of gear."

Icarus pocketed the tech. "My sister is one of them."

"According to your file," Cormac said as he entered the room, "your sister died in the Rift."

"Who do you think taught me how to excavate?"

"That's not an ans—"

"Enough," Adam said, cutting the volley off before it went any further, especially with Cormac-of-all-angles in the debate now. "This is all beside the point." They needed to focus on their common mission—Vincent Cirillo. Adam was done with the asshole who'd destroyed his life, and for the first time in a decade, he had the pieces to return the favor. To destroy Vincent and finish this, for good. "How do we bring this to a close? Because Vincent's clearly ready, and so am I." He gestured at the table, inviting the combatants to sit and strategize. "Help me figure this out."

The stare-off continued another few seconds before Icarus slid into the nearest chair. "I have a call with my client later tonight."

"Why not now?" Robin claimed the seat across from him. "We brought you your shit."

Icarus didn't rise to the bait, his fangs and claws tucked away, his tone carefully indifferent. "While you might prefer brute force, I usually get what I want through more persuasive means." He crossed his legs and shifted his attention to Adam. "What is it we want?"

"A meet." Adam sank into the chair beside him. "We'll try it your way first and hold brute force in our back pocket if needed."

"We'll need to meet on neutral ground," Cormac said as he took a seat beside Robin. "Extracurriculars aside, Icarus's client is still a cop. His defenses will be up. We don't want to be outgunned."

"Portola," Robin suggested.

Icarus fisted a hand beneath the table. Adam covered it with his and offered an alternative. "The Lost Valley."

Robin lurched forward and braced his forearms on the table. "You can't go back into the city."

"It's my fucking home." He tried to keep his voice even, but the unrelenting frustration darkened the already jagged edges of his words. "I'm not going to let Vincent drive me out of it."

Cormac slumped and scrubbed his hands over his face. "Fucking death wish."

Beneath the table, Icarus tangled their fingers. "So we get this meet," he said. "We convince my client to arrest Vincent and bring him in. Then what?"

Cormac dropped his arms. "Yerba Buena Building is a fortress. After the Rift, they rebuilt it to be impenetrable. Not to mention half the cops and guards inside are on Vincent's payroll."

"So we use the in we have," Adam said. "Icarus's client gets us plans and clears us a path."

"How do we separate Vincent from the warlock?"

"We give Atlas what he wants. Me."

Icarus's hand nearly crushed his, and across the table, Robin growled his disagreement. "You can't be serious."

"I don't want this thing inside me. Let him take it and then you kill him too."

"You'll die," Cormac said. "That *thing* is what's keeping you alive."

"They died to give you that *thing*," Robin rumbled.

"I didn't ask for this. I would have rather died with them, but now, all I've got left of my marriage, of my life, is a charred photo and the Devil." He shoved back from the table. Present respite over; it was time to meet fate and the future head-on. "I want it to be over, all of it."

TWENTY-FIVE

It took Adam thirty minutes and several laps around the reflecting pool to rein himself in. It took another ninety with Cormac, Robin, and the rest of his team on the main level to sort logistics and evaluate potential meet locations. By the time he returned to the cellar, Adam found the bunk room completely transformed.

With most of the winery's business in the main facility down the mountain, the villa's cellar was minimally used as storage for extra equipment and living and sleeping quarters for seasonal workers during harvest, which had ended a month ago this year. But you wouldn't know it for the lived-in coziness Icarus had created in two short hours.

The line of single beds had been pushed together in the center of the room, Cormac's mother's hand-knitted quilts thrown across them in a splash of color. More soft shades painted the walls, cast by the silk and sheer tops Icarus had draped over the room's lamps. Across from the beds, the storage trunks that normally sat at the end of each bed had been stacked and arranged so that Icarus's laptop and webcam on top were aimed directly at the now oversized bed. Everything was perfectly arranged, except for the single bed shoved in the corner nearest the door, Icarus's go bag open and spilling what was left of its contents the length of it.

Adam leaned a shoulder against the door. "Do you have everything you need?"

"Not everything," a silk-robed Icarus said. He dug through the bag once more and produced a bottle of lube. "But enough." His voice was a shade brighter than earlier but still careful, and as Icarus placed the tube of lube on the bedside table and surveyed the room's final setup, he likewise carefully avoided Adam's gaze.

Mentally replaying his earlier outburst, Adam could see how his harsh words might have bruised Icarus. They'd revealed a darkness, an inevitability, that Icarus maybe hadn't fully appreciated—or accepted. He stepped into the room, and as Icarus passed by on his way back to the spare bed, Adam lightly clasped his elbow. "Icarus, please."

He wrenched his elbow free and flicked a dismissive hand in the air. "I can't be in this headspace with you when I need to be Icarus for someone else."

The computer pinged, a guest waiting.

"I want to stay while you do this." It was a wildly inappropriate suggestion that got Adam the reaction he craved.

Stormy blues clashed with his, and Icarus gave a sharp shake of his head. "No way."

"He might say something I need to hear." A plausible enough excuse.

Icarus didn't buy it, his gaze shrewd, but he didn't outright reject it either. "Not without his consent."

"Has he been on a multifeed before?"

"Yes."

"Then it shouldn't be a problem."

Icarus pressed his lips together, and Adam bit his tongue to keep from saying more, to stifle the plea that wanted to escape. He'd become invested in the idea, tangentially for the mission, primarily for the chance to watch Icarus work.

To escape and wind down after hours of planning and debate.

Icarus heaved a sigh. "Fine. You're going to blackmail him with this in the end, anyway. But only if he consents."

Adam nodded. "Fair."

"Where's the meet?"

Adam gave him the address, and when the computer pinged again, he followed Icarus's order to take up residence on the spare bed. He shoved himself into the corner, upright, out of view of the laptop screen and camera but with an unobstructed view.

Icarus clicked the mouse, then sat on the edge of the bed, his legs crossed. "Nate, it's good to see you."

"I'm glad you pinged." There was a slight wobble in his voice, barely contained excitement tangled with I-shouldn't-be-doing-this nerves. "I hadn't heard back from you this week, so I didn't know . . ."

"I've had company in town." His gaze flicked Adam's direction, then back to the screen. "Been more exciting than I anticipated."

Adam stifled a laugh. *Exciting* was one way to put it.

Icarus smirked.

"Company?" Nate said. "Are they still there?" The cop wasn't a fool. He'd picked up on the off-camera byplay.

Icarus must have picked up on something he saw onscreen. "You dirty minx! Do you want an audience? Because yes, he's still here."

"I like knowing you have one." Nate cleared his throat, tempering the excitement he'd let slip vocally too. "But I don't want to see or hear anyone but you."

"Don't you worry. My friend's going to sit in the corner and be a good boy and just watch." Icarus's eyes pinned him to the spot. "No words and no touching. And he won't come. That's just for you and me, Nate."

Nate half hummed, half gasped his approval, the idea alone clearly turning him on. For his part, Adam nodded. He toed off his shoes and propped his feet on the bed, knees bent and legs spread. He snagged Icarus's crochet hooks, threaded them through his fingers as an extra measure of restraint, then rested his wrists on his bent knees, hands dangling where Icarus could see them and his cock already stiffening behind his zipper.

Icarus smirked and shifted his attention back to the screen. "Are you going to be a good boy too?" He crawled to the center of the bed and untied his robe.

Adam nearly swallowed his tongue.

Turquoise lace hugged Icarus's torso, a form-fitting camisole that dripped from thin silk straps, dipped low in front, and ended at the tops of his thighs. It was an inch or two shorter in the middle, balls peeking out below, owing to the stretch caused by the bulge of his erect cock that was tucked up against his pelvis.

Nate wasn't nearly so quiet, cursing and groaning.

He only got louder as Icarus ditched the robe completely. Unrestrained, Icarus ran his hands through his hair, down his long neck, over the gap in the lace, then under its edges, playing with his nipples, dipping into every ridge of his abs, tracing his V-cut to his groin, spreading his legs wider and subtly thrusting forward. Touching everywhere but his dick that swelled. All while directing Nate—how to tease himself, when to take out his cock, how to lather it up, how to stroke it.

It drove Adam crazy. His dick ached as he imagined his lips tracing a path down Icarus's neck, his hands tangled in lace, his fingers slipping inside to feel the cool heat of Icarus's skin, slipping behind to palm the ass the cami didn't cover all of.

Intentionally.

As Icarus pulled a dildo from under a pillow, his earlier words came back to Adam. *An overworked cop . . .who jerks off to me fucking myself on a dildo.* He suctioned the base of the dildo to one of the wooden headboards, grabbed the bottle of lube, and coated it. Then he hiked the cami up, exposing a plug in matching turquoise.

He'd prepared himself. He eased it out with a mewl that nearly undid Adam. But then he went down on all fours, rammed back on the dildo, and let out a relieved, shuddery sigh, and Adam was fucking gone. He closed his eyes and tilted back his head, white-knuckling the crochet hooks as his hips rocked up, aching for friction, hungry for the man he couldn't touch less than ten feet away.

"Look at me."

He wasn't sure if Icarus's sharp command was for him or Nate, but regardless, Adam whipped up his head, righting his gaze just in time to see Icarus reach down and free his cock from the lace. Stroked once, twice, then bowed like a cat, the hand in the bed fisting the sheets, Icarus coming with a deep groan that was echoed onscreen.

Adam wanted to groan too, wanted his dick in Icarus's ass instead of that dildo, wanted to be under him with his mouth around Icarus's cock, drinking up every drop of his come, wanted Icarus to flip him over and come inside him again.

Adam bit his cheek so hard he tasted blood.

Icarus's head jerked up, nostrils flared and eyes wide, his body practically vibrating. He was every inch the predator.

Adam's heart raced, but he wasn't afraid. He wanted . . . The thing inside him wanted . . . more.

Icarus blinked, and the predator was gone.

Adam closed his eyes, mind swirling, body revolting, heart on a roller coaster he didn't want to get off of.

"Wasn't that good, Nate?" Icarus said, focused again on his client. "Maybe you'd like to do this in person?"

Nate's "I can't" was wholly unconvincing, even to Adam's half-lucid brain.

"You don't have to touch," Icarus cajoled. "You can be like my friend over there watching me fuck myself, smelling the come as it drips from my dick for you, hearing every slide of the dildo into my hole."

"We've never . . ." Nate groaned, and if Adam had to bet, Nate was getting hard again just thinking about it.

"I might not be in town much longer, Nate. Last chance."

"When?" Nate panted. "Where?"

"Tomorrow night." He rattled off the address, confirmed once more, exchanged payment details, and then Icarus signed off.

The bed springs squeaked, and Adam righted his head. Icarus climbed off the show bed, left the camisole in its hiked-up state, his dripping cock and ass bare, and stalked in his direction. The blank face was gone, but the predator remained tucked away too. Adam didn't taste blood any longer, and Icarus apparently didn't smell any either.

"That turned you on," Icarus said once he reached the side of the single bed.

Adam flicked his gaze down to where his cock was at war with his fly. "Obviously."

"You weren't jealous."

"Watching you do what you do best?" He shook his head. "Not at all. Wanted to be that dildo, or between your legs sucking your cock, or getting plowed by you. But jealous? No, baby. That's your job, and you are fucking magnificent at it."

Icarus smirked, gaze drifting to Adam's erection. "Do you need me to do something about that?"

"If you want to," Adam replied, and Icarus's gaze shot back up. "I'm not your job. Only if you want to," he repeated. He didn't want an act. If he was going to be real in these moments when he put Adam and the Devil aside, when Icarus tempted him into hitting pause on the future he usually raced toward, he needed to know Icarus was being real in these moments too.

"I want to," Icarus said as he gently removed the hooks from Adam's grip. He tossed them aside, then gracefully lowered to his knees, spreading them to make the cami ride even higher. "Put your hands in my hair and come when I do." He didn't wait for a reply, Adam's "Again?" dying on the tip of his tongue. In a single blink, Adam was yanked to the end of the bed, his jeans and boxers torn down, and his legs thrown over Icarus's shoulders, his dick inside Icarus's hot mouth.

His hands shot to Icarus's head, tangling in the magenta strands, holding on for dear life as Icarus took him apart. Long licks, teasing flicks, suction that had him idly wondering if what was left of his soul was being sucked right out of him. Stolen by the predator giving him the only moments of intimacy he'd had in a decade. As his world splintered, his orgasm rushing up to meet the one Icarus groaned out around his cock, he thought it a fair deal—peace in exchange for the soul he'd already lost, claimed by the fiery beast inside him that spread its wings and flew.

TWENTY-SIX

"You know," Robin said from the passenger seat beside Adam, "he could be in there cutting his own deal with the cop."

Adam drummed his fingers on the Camaro's wheel and kept his gaze focused on the strip of retail units a short way up and across the street. To any brave—foolish—passerby on the street this late, it would look like all the units were either empty or closed, including the one on the end, a tasting room for a distillery that had gone bankrupt. Repo was scheduled for later in the week, the job assigned to one of Robin's contacts who'd been happy to lend them the keys for some extra cash. He and Robin were parked at the curb a half block away, Jenn and Abigail were prowling the nearby alleys and rooftops, and Cormac was perched on the peeling wood sign that hung by the unit's front door. It was as safe and covered as Adam could make Icarus without alerting anyone, including their target. "He could be, but I don't think he is."

Icarus had insisted on meeting Nate alone to start. He liked him well enough, wanted to do something nice for him before they blackmailed him. As he'd rightly pointed out, said blackmail would be more effective if Nate was good and compromised before they sprung their trap. But how long would that take?

When would the tasting room's outside lights flicker on, Icarus's signal that he was ready for them behind the heavy curtains that blocked the distillery's windows? How long would Cormac have to play lookout from his perch?

Truthfully, Adam was surprised they'd made it to the waiting portion of events at all. Nate was an overworked cop, but not a bad one. He'd stuttered to a stop short of the unit's steps, balking at the seemingly abandoned spot, but then Icarus had appeared in the doorway, backlit by soft candlelight and decked out in heels, nylons, and a sinfully short, sinfully tight, little black dress. Nate had caved on the spot. So would anyone with a fucking pulse.

"I'm sorry about what I said yesterday."

Robin's uncharacteristic apology drew Adam out of his thoughts. "Which part?"

"I know you never wanted to be like us."

"I'm not like you."

Robin rolled his eyes. "Your body temp isn't ninety-eight point six anymore." He propped an elbow on the open window and rested his chin in his hand, golden eyes anywhere but on Adam. "It's just…"

"Just what?"

"If you die, if what Deb and David did to keep you alive is for naught, then it makes what I didn't do even worse."

"Robin, you were halfway around the world—"

His gaze shot back to Adam, hard and angry, the emotions directed one hundred percent at himself. "She called the pack, and I didn't answer."

Adam didn't make an excuse for the truth. That same truth had taken Adam a year to come to terms with before he spoke to Robin again. It had taken Jenn longer.

"I can't imagine what it must feel like," Robin said. "To be torn from your soulmates."

Like someone with claws fiercer than Icarus's had dug into his chest, ripped out his heart, and left a raging inferno in the hollow space. The Devil moniker wasn't only about the trouble he caused

Vincent. He rubbed a hand over his chest. "Imagine if someone tore the coyote out of you. The heart of you gone. That was what it felt like. What it still feels like."

Robin gulped, the jagged swallow loud in the quiet car. "I'd want to die too." His gaze drifted back outside, and silence settled in the car, heavy and full of regret. "Tell her I'm sorry."

"She knows."

"Yes, but she'll believe it from you." Another truth, but this one made Adam chuckle. Robin smiled, and the melancholy that had filled the car lightened a measure. "How does he make your soul feel?"

Adam didn't have to ask who Robin was referring to. "I don't have one left to feel anything."

Kraa.

Robin laughed. "Even Mac knows you're lying."

The light outside the tasting room flicked on.

"Or," Adam said, "Mac heard Icarus on the move."

He grabbed the bulging folder off the dash, shoved out of the car, and hustled to the door Icarus had left unlocked, Robin close on his heels. Adam pushed aside the heavy velvet entry curtain just as Nate lurched to his feet from a nearby chaise, blinding Adam with his pale white ass.

"You didn't come," the cop said, voice plaintive. His attention was locked on Icarus, who was pulling down his dress and slipping back into his heels—until Robin forced the curtain the rest of the way back, rings clattering on the rod, a blast of cool night air gusting in around them. Nate spun in their direction. "Fuck! Who are you? What's going on?"

"This is my company," Icarus said. "From yesterday."

"But that was—"

Robin growled. "Pull your fucking pants up."

Nate scurried to comply, fumbling his belt, never taking his wide eyes off Robin. "You're not human."

"Neither is your fuck buddy."

His gaze whipped back to Icarus, who'd gone preternaturally still. "We need you to do us a favor, Nate."

Nate began backing up. Instinct, Adam presumed, as the only thing behind the cop was a corner. But with him and Robin blocking the door, Icarus the other exit, and Nate's service weapon on the floor by the chaise, back was the only option for creating more space between him and the threats to his life. Until Icarus erased that distance in half a breath, zipping across the room. Nate backed the rest of the way into the corner, trembling. "Fuck," he gasped between short, thin breaths. "You're a vampire."

"Who generally doesn't eat people." He planted a hand on the wall over Nate's shoulder, crowding into his space. "I like you, Nate. Please don't be the exception."

Adam crossed the room at a more human pace. He leaned a shoulder against the wall near Nate and waited for the cop to catch his breath. "Icarus says you're a good cop, an honest one, even if you are lying to your husband about where you are tonight." Nate looked as chastened as his fear would allow, eyes downcast before darting back up, jumping between him and Icarus. Adam gave him something else to focus on, holding the folder out to Nate. "This is everything you need to arrest and convict Vincent Cirillo."

What little color Nate had left in his cheeks fled. "He's untouchable. Fuck, that man scares me more than you three."

"He's enslaving other people's magic, not to mention murder, arson, and a dozen other crimes." Adam nodded toward the folder in Nate's hands. "All documented in there."

"Your husband is a shifter, isn't he?" Robin asked from where he'd sprawled on the chaise.

"My wife was a coyote," Adam said. "She was the twin sister of my friend over there. My husband had magic too. Magic that's in me now. They tried to stop Vincent and died for it. I almost died too."

Icarus withdrew his hand and stepped back, giving Nate room

to breathe, room to settle into the reality he hadn't chosen but was his now too, regardless. "How many other people are we gonna let die, Nate?"

"Or," Robin said, "we can tell your husband about your fang-banging fantasies."

Icarus hissed over his shoulder.

Nate, however, was oblivious to the back-and-forth. The good cop, as Icarus had promised, was flipping through the file on Vincent, taking in all the evidence assembled. He reached the end, then glanced again at Adam. "You were a cop?"

"Before I was a widower."

"I'm sorry for your loss." He glanced past Adam to Robin. "Both of you."

A good cop in more ways than one. There was a heart beneath his badge and playing to it was the right call. "We don't want Vincent to add anyone else to that list. Will you help us?"

"There's a district attorney I work with. He's good. If all this" —he lifted the file—"checks out, I think I can convince him to issue the arrest warrant. But the charges won't stick. Cirillo has all the judges in his pocket."

"We just need you to get him inside a holding cell." Adam pushed off the wall and stepped to Icarus's side. "We'll take care of the rest."

TWENTY-SEVEN

Adam found Icarus by the window in Cormac's study, the vampire's attention shifting between the early morning dark outside and the phone in his hand. No one had slept since returning from the city, Icarus included, and that phone had stayed in reach the entire time, through his change of clothes into sweats and a tee, through their debrief and an express meal, through the walk he'd taken around the reflecting pool. He hadn't taken a shower yet, but Adam bet Icarus would find a way to take the phone in there with him too. He was clutching the damn thing like a lifeline. To whom? Adam had two guesses; he started with the less likely. "Are you afraid Nate is going to change his mind?"

"No." Icarus stepped away from the window and sank into Cormac's battered office chair. "I'm afraid we put him in the line of fire."

Adam circled the desk and rested back against its edge. "You may not believe it"—he nudged Icarus's knee with his—"but you're a good person too."

He tossed the phone on the desk, then slumped back in the chair. Eyes closed, he tilted his face to the ceiling and sighed. "Keep lying to yourself."

It wasn't easy tearing his gaze from the long smooth column of

Icarus's throat, the sharp line of his jaw, the weariness beneath the vibrating tension he rarely let anyone see, but the answer to Adam's earlier question—the guess he'd figured more likely—was right beside his hip. An encrypted chat was open on the phone screen: **You're late**, from Icarus, the only message from four hours ago, and **Are you okay?** the only one within the past hour. "Is that your chat with her?"

"Should've been, but she missed check-in."

"Would you expect her to answer at midnight or four in the morning?"

"Yes."

"Do you want me to send someone?"

"If we don't hear from her by daybreak." He righted his head and opened his eyes. "Neither of us are the most reliable."

"You obviously care about her more than anyone."

Icarus shrugged, the nonchalance fake as hell.

Adam pressed, hoping Icarus's weariness would create an opening for another question that had lingered since they'd first discussed his sister. "Why did you leave her?"

Icarus leaned forward, retrieved his phone, and tapped at the screen a few times. He handed it back to Adam, open to an encrypted picture of a blue-haired Icarus in combat boots, jeans, and a leather halter, a young woman with tan skin like Cormac's, long green hair, a nose ring, and hazel eyes lined in kohl, and another young man who looked nothing like the alternakids beside him. He was white with rich chestnut hair, sky blue eyes, and everything about him—from his pressed dress shirt and khakis to his neatly trimmed hair with its perfectly coifed wave—shouted wholesome boy next door.

But the way the three of them had their arms over each other's shoulders, together with the smiles on their faces and the obvious affection in their eyes, led Adam to the obvious conclusion. "Another sibling?"

"We lost him in the Rift." And yet the pain that streaked across Icarus's face looked as fresh as any Adam had ever seen on the face of a victim's loved ones left behind. As fresh as the pain reflected in the mirror each morning.

"That was thirty years ago," Adam said. "What happened nine months ago to make you leave Portola?"

"I never said that was the first time I'd left. Or the last."

"What—"

CAW. CAW.

KRAA!

Adam locked eyes with Icarus—just half a second—before they were both in motion, Adam shoving off the desk and lunging for the window, Icarus spinning the desk chair to do the same. Both of them looked out to survey the chaos erupting below, only to have purple orbs of magic sail in their direction, slicing through the murder of crows that had taken flight, shattering the study's glass window and singeing the hair on the back of Adam's neck as a fanged, hissing Icarus dragged him to the floor. Magic pummeled the study's walls, sending books and files flying, creating divots in the centuries-old wood and stone, replacing the soft light of the shattered desk lamp with an eerie purple glow.

More glass broke a room over, followed by the howls and thundering rumble of the pack in motion. Adam needed to join them; his place was with his family. He reached toward the desk, only to have his arm slammed to the ground, Icarus pinning him in place.

"Stay the fuck down."

"Weapons!" Adam shouted. "Bottom desk drawer!"

"Well, why the fuck didn't you say so?"

Adam would've rolled his eyes if he wasn't busy scoping their surroundings and monitoring the windows and door. Icarus twisted for the weapons, grabbing the drawer handle and yanking, dislodging the entire drawer. Stakes and throwing stars, guns and ammo scattered across the wood floor, a lined box popping open from the force; silver caught Adam's eye, making his heart race as two gleaming bullets rolled toward where Icarus's bent knee was planted. Summoning his own strength, loosening the leash a careful measure, he shoved a blast of heat at Icarus, causing the vampire to teeter off-balance, giving Adam time to snatch the bullets up before they harmed Icarus.

Icarus whipped around, eyes wide. "What the fuck was that?"

Adam opened his fist, a puddle of silver evaporating in the glass-scratched palm of his hand. "Me saving a fighter we can't afford to lose right now."

Me saving the person I can't bear to lose right now.

"How?"

Robin's appearance saved Adam from answering. Still in human form, Robin, arms over his head, ducked into the room and stayed low, scurrying over to join them.

"Sitrep," Adam demanded as he wiped his hands on his jeans, then began loading the lead ammo into pistols. It was dark out; lead would be safer, would slow instead of potentially killing one of their own.

"Two warlocks, two vamps, and half a dozen shifters."

Icarus swept up the stakes and handed those to Adam too. "Atlas?" he asked Robin.

The assassin shook his head. "No sign of him. No sign of Vincent either."

"They're not letting up," Adam said. "They took a loss, but they don't want us to know it."

"They're not going to let up until you're dead."

A howl reverberated down the hall. Jenn was calling for backup.

"We need you out there," Robin said.

Adam shoved the last of the stakes in his waistband and moved to stand, only to be held down again, this time by Robin. "Not you. Him," he said with a nod to Icarus. "He's a weapon we didn't have before."

"I'm not staying here," Adam protested. He needed to be out there too, not hiding inside while everyone else fought to protect him. That was how he'd lost the loves of his life last time.

"He's right," Icarus said.

Adam turned to say thank you, but one look and he knew Icarus was agreeing with Robin, not him. "Fuck you."

"I can't let you die."

"And we can't afford to let Vincent capture you and find out what you are," Robin added. "Go to the roof and provide cover. Be the backstop." He didn't give Adam a chance to argue further, turning and moving out, joints cracking, the shift complete by the time he crossed the threshold.

Icarus's departure was even more abrupt. A rough, hard kiss, the cell phone shoved into his hand, a "Don't fucking die" mumbled against his lips, and then he was gone, disappearing after Robin.

Everything in Adam screamed to follow, a physical pull the likes of which he'd never felt before. An almost painful amplification of the tug he'd felt that night in Club Sutro when Icarus had first approached him, when confusion, desire, and betrayal had converged to spark an awareness inside him that he'd been unable to ignore. At the time, he'd glared over his shoulder, trying and failing to back fate off, but Icarus had sauntered right into his space, right into places Adam had held reserved for others. He wasn't supposed to feel this way about anyone else. He was supposed to take what Deborah and David had given him and use it to end Vincent. Burn in the process so he could join them.

None of that was going to happen if he stayed there, if those fighting for him outside, including Icarus, lost this battle. And fuck, they were too close to ending this to lose now. Adam checked his weapons were secure, then staying low, he dodged more magic on his way out of the study, down the hall, and up the stairs, emerging two flights later onto the roof and slinking across the narrow widow's walk on hands and knees. He reached the edge, hidden in a dark corner out of the moonlight, and lifted his head enough to peek between the rails, raising one pistol enough to be at the ready.

Jenn in coyote form, Abigail in mountain lion, and the rest of the pack were handling the shifters. Cormac and his corvid brethren had one of the warlocks virtually walled off, which left the two vampires and the purple-orb-wielding wizard to Robin and Icarus. Off the field of battle, they were practically enemies, but faced with a common foe, Robin and Icarus were an impressive pair. Two incredibly powerful beings, two creatures with unrivaled attack instincts and training. Adam knew Robin had it and had glimpsed a hint of Icarus's at the Canyon Lands, but seeing both in action now, Icarus held his own beside Robin, the two of them working together to dismantle one vampire, to swiftly stake the second, and to dodge and deflect the warlock's magic as they closed in on him.

Movement to their left caught Adam's eye. A bobcat broke through Jenn and Abigail's line and charged in Icarus and Robin's direction, leaping for Icarus's blind side.

Adam fired and instantly knew the lead bullet wouldn't reach the cat before the cat reached Icarus. He let more of the leash go, fire and heat licking off his fingertips, forming an invisible mire between the cat and Icarus and slowing the former's speed enough for the bullet to catch up.

The bobcat fell and howled at Icarus's feet.

The warlock ceased his spell casting long enough to see where the other had come from, zeroing in on Adam's location. He got as far as raising his arm before Cormac slammed into his face talons first. Robin crashed into his body and took him the rest of the way to the ground, and Icarus finished it, ripping the warlock's head clean off with one twist of his hands.

Victory vibrated through him, through the heated stare he shared with Icarus, until Adam realized something on his person was actually vibrating. It took a second to breach the fog of adrenaline and realize what it was. Icarus's phone in his pocket. He shoved a hand in, withdrew it, and glanced at the screen. At the picture that appeared in the encrypted chat. Vibrations of a different sort took over, and he followed his sinking heart to his knees.

TWENTY-EIGHT

"Well, this explains why Vincent didn't send Atlas."

Adam barely heard Robin's words over his thundering heart, over the flapping wings of the thing inside him desperate to beat its way out and wrap those wings of warmth around the vampire frantically pacing the length of the cellar he'd had no choice but to retreat to. The rising sun had trapped Icarus, preventing him going from after the one person Adam knew he put above all others.

Including him.

"What does he want?" Jennifer asked. "There's no ransom request, no message, just the picture."

The picture—a smug, grinning Atlas with his arm around the shoulders of a much shorter woman with long green hair and hazel eyes, only the slightest creases at the corners, far fewer than one would expect on a woman who, by Adam's math, should look closer to fifty than thirty.

Adam circled one end of the cellar table. His legs were steadier now, the battle rush of adrenaline faded, the initial shock of that picture internalized, the pain he'd felt for Icarus better tamed though no less intense. He leaned a hip against the side of the table near where Icarus was pacing. "Did they take her to leverage you?"

"I don't know." Icarus stopped in front of him, his eyes wild with fear and with self-recrimination Adam recognized all too well. "Maybe. Fuck!"

"Why else would they take her?" Adam asked, sensing that he'd finally get the whole truth now, that Icarus was either ready to share it or had no choice.

It would be the latter, judging by the frustrated twist of his lips, as if they'd sealed in the truth for so long that his body was fighting to keep it in still. "For her own power. Because I fucking showed it to them."

"You both did," Cormac said, rejoining them from upstairs where he'd been questioning two of the shifters they'd detained. The rest of Vincent's strike force, including the other warlock, had retreated. "You showed them yours tonight," he said to Adam. "And you"—he jutted his chin at Icarus—"showed them hers at the Canyon Lands that day, didn't you?"

Icarus's eyes slipped shut, a powerful cocktail of guilt and fear pinching his features, answering Cormac's question. The raven had been right.

"Which is what?" Adam asked more gently than Icarus was being with himself.

"If they don't know already, and they find out . . ." He covered his face with his hands and roared, loud enough to rattle the metal tanks and light fixtures. Everyone in the room took a step back.

Except Adam. "Icarus, what power?"

He lowered his hands and opened his eyes, locking his gaze with Adam's and drawing whatever strength he needed, everything Adam had left to give him. A slight nod, a silent thank-you, before Icarus shifted his attention to Cormac. "You weren't wrong about me putting my hand to the ground and asking for help. That's exactly what I did. And she answered."

"Your sister?" Cormac said.

"Nature." His blue gaze returned to Adam's. "Her name is Mary, and she's Mother Nature."

TWENTY-NINE

"Mary and Michael Rollins." Cormac dropped a bulging file folder onto the cellar table and flipped it open. "Crossed paths the first time at the homeless teen shelter in Portola. In 1979." He withdrew two photos and slid them to the center of the table. Teenage versions of the blue-haired man and green-haired woman from the picture on Icarus's phone, except in these older shots his hair was the color of carrots and hers was so dark brown it was almost black. "Michael was fifteen, Mary was fourteen."

Adam looked up at Icarus, who stood behind Abigail, stitching a cut she'd taken to the shoulder in the earlier skirmish. Something to steady him, he'd insisted. "I thought you said she was older."

"In every way that counts, and now technically too." He tied off the stitch and snipped it with a claw. "She's like you. She ages still, but more slowly because of the thing inside her."

"She wasn't always Mother Nature?"

"You weren't always whatever you are." He patted Abigail's shoulder. "You're good. Thank you." He quickly washed and dried his hands, then blinked as he returned to the table, and Adam sensed he was more fully in the room with them again. He slid into the chair beside Adam. "Carry on, raven."

Cormac claimed the chair at the head of the table. "Michael and Mary became inseparable. Fostered together by Brenda Rollins." He withdrew two document copies from the file and passed them to Robin's side of the table first. "Brenda filled a missing persons report for Michael and a death certificate for Mary."

"After the Rift?" Robin asked as Abigail glimpsed the docs, then slid them across the table to Adam. "I thought missing persons reports were all shoved in a corner somewhere."

"We work our way through them slowly."

"But his"—Abigail flicked a glance at Icarus—"was filed five days *before* the Rift."

"What the—" Robin started.

Adam cut him off with a raised hand. He shifted in his chair toward Icarus, toward their best avenue for answers, toward the person Adam sensed needed to give them now that he'd finally started. "Tell me about her."

Icarus smiled as he drew the photo of Mary closer. "Sharp-tongued, sass for days, and smarter than anyone I've ever met. I was at the shelter first, she sauntered in, I sauntered over, and that was that. She's the balance I need, the one who keeps me from flying too high most of the time, and who cleans up after me when I accidentally do."

"And she named you Icarus?"

"No, he did."

"He who?" Cormac asked.

Icarus shifted, withdrew his phone, and slid it in his direction. On it was the picture he'd shown Adam earlier. "Our brother, Canton. He joined us at Brenda's about eight months after we were fostered there. He fit right in and fell head over heels for her."

"Your sister?" Robin said, and at Icarus's nod, followed up with, "You didn't?"

"She's always been just a sister to me."

"I don't have any record of Canton," Cormac said as he rifled through the file again.

"Because she erased him."

"Why?"

"So no one would arrest me for almost murdering him."

Robin growled. "You sure you weren't interested?"

Icarus rolled his eyes. "He was never just a human who fell for my sister. Hell, I'm not sure if he ever really fell for *her* at all." He took the phone back and pocketed it. "Canton was in love with Nature, who was losing the war and needed to take drastic action, then hide afterward."

"Canton identified your sister," Adam said, putting it together, "as a host."

"He was a fucking spy," Icarus spat. Anger and hurt laced his words, thirty years of it that had lingered and stewed. That had kept Icarus at arm's length from everyone but her, who no doubt shared his pain. "A warlock who inserted himself into our lives, buried into our hearts, and stayed there for years. Then, ten days before the Rift, he gave me a choice."

The rest of the awful pieces slotted together, and Adam's heart ached for the selfless man beside him. "You traded your soul for hers. To protect her."

He shrugged, the most helpless gesture Adam had ever seen from the apex predator. "She's my sister. The only person who's ever given a damn about me." He glanced across the table at Robin. "Deborah was your twin?"

A begrudging nod.

"We're not blood related," Icarus carried on, "but how I feel about her is how I imagine it must feel between twins. Like she's the other half of me. I'll do anything to protect her."

Guilt and self-recrimination clouded Robin's expression, a mirror reflection of Icarus earlier. He shoved back from the table and staggered into a shadowed corner, his back to the table, a shaking hand skirting over the back of his neck as his torso heaved up and down.

While his brother-in-law gathered himself, Adam returned to his line of questioning. "Why did you leave her? The first time."

"Do you know what happens when a vampire is turned? What happens to our emotions?"

"You become a bloodsucking asshole?" Jenn chimed in.

Icarus ignored her and focused instead on Cormac. "When you shift, what's it feel like"—Icarus thumped his chest with his fist—"here?"

"Like it wants to explode out of me," the raven answered.

"No different," Icarus said. "And I died with equal parts anger and love"—he flattened his hand over his heart—"right here."

"You went after him," Adam guessed.

"He was smart enough to hide, but I found him. The only reason I didn't kill him was because she already had." He propped his elbows on the table and hung his head in his hands, fingers raking through his magenta strands. "She loved me more than Nature loved Canton, and I'll never forgive myself for putting her in that position. I made sure she survived the Rift and the transformation, and once I was sure she was safe, I left so she'd be safe from me too."

"What about your mother?" Cormac asked.

"She's never forgiven either one of us. Canton was her favorite."

"But she signed the missing persons report and death certificate?"

He lifted his head. "Do you have a pen?"

One came flying out of the shadowed corner Robin had disappeared into. Icarus caught it without missing a beat, flipped over the copy of the missing persons report, and perfectly replicated Brenda's signature. Another talent that Adam added to his mental list. "I forged them, and my sister filed them."

Robin returned to the table. "Why don't you use her name?"

"Because she's supposed to be dead. If someone found out she wasn't, found out what she is . . ."

"Someone like Atlas or Vincent," Abigail said.

"This war is older than time, bubbling up through history. The Rift was the last major eruption and the first time in ages where Chaos gained the upper hand, where it forced Nature to retreat."

Adam covered the frustrated fist Icarus had made while talking. "She hid in your sister."

Icarus flipped over his hand and laced their fingers together, squeezed, and took a deep breath before continuing. "If they find out what she is, if they harness all that power for Chaos and darkness, or worse—if they kill her while trying to manipulate all that magic, that's ball game. Humanity and what's left of this planet dies with her, and we're plunged into a dark age we'll never come out of." He slumped in his chair, as weary as Adam had ever seen him. More than just the past week on his shoulders, he shouldered thirty years of an impossible weight, of a responsibility like no other. "None of us, human or paranormal, can exist without her. She's the only thing keeping this world in balance."

THIRTY

An assassin, two detectives, and a vampire with better than average hacking skills could make quick work of excavation. Throw in a coyote and mountain lion working every contact they had between Talahalusi and Portola, and their team had an Atlas and Mary sighting by late morning. They were holed up at a motel on the coast just south of YB, and pressure applied in the right place—a source Abigail had nurtured inside Vincent's organization—yielded news of a broad daylight meet happening at Portola University later that afternoon.

That meant it was impossible for Icarus to join the extraction op they spent the rest of the morning planning. If Adam hadn't personally witnessed Icarus lock down his instincts at least twice, he would have been more worried about approaching the man pacing the cellar bunk room, the long maxi skirt and tunic he'd changed into after a shower swishing around him. Icarus had come a long way from the baby vamp who'd almost killed his brother, with no one by his side, no one to fight for him other than Mary. Well, that was over, and Adam wouldn't let him lose her too. He stepped behind Icarus, clasped his shoulders, and held his ground when Icarus whipped his head around and hissed.

Icarus's face fell the next second. "I'm sorry," he whispered.

"I'm not afraid," Adam replied, likewise speaking softly, the moment a quiet one, too much teetering on the precipice. He coasted his hands down Icarus's arms, rubbing warmth into them, before he circled his arms around the taller man's waist, embracing him from behind. "When did you realize?"

"Realize what?"

"That you could lock down your instincts."

"Senses, technically, which in turn dampens the instincts. And I'd realized too late. She showed me how after Canton. I kept my senses off until it was safe to leave her. It's saved me since a million times over." He tilted his head, back against Adam's. "Saved you a few times too."

"I can make a call," he said. "Offer to trade myself for her."

"And give Vincent exactly what he wants?" Icarus scoffed. "No, and the extraction op is good. Your team is good."

He kissed the back of Icarus's shoulder, bared by the wide neck of his tunic. "We pulled Paris out of the fire. We'll rescue her too."

"Where is Paris?"

"I don't know." He rested his cheek in the valley between Icarus's shoulder blades. "Mac hid him somewhere. The less people who know, the better."

Hands folded over Adam's, Icarus didn't speak for several long minutes. When he finally did, his voice was hoarse, struggling around a lump in his throat Adam could feel him fighting. "I failed her."

"She's still alive." He loosened his arms enough to nudge Icarus around in them. "You were going to go to her before I returned to your apartment the other night?"

Icarus closed his eyes and nodded.

Adam would have felt more guilt if this right here, Icarus in his arms, didn't feel like a fate none of them, including she, could escape. "Why did you continue to stay away?"

He rested his forehead on Adam's. "She's part of a hacker collective. I didn't want anything to happen to those around her like what happened to Canton. I couldn't put her in that situation again."

"The fact you didn't shut off your senses and still totally ignored my bleeding hands earlier tells me you wouldn't. Also the fact you haven't killed Robin yet."

Icarus's chuckle was a welcome sound. Adam leaned back to see if the smile reached his eyes. Not quite, but he was more firmly on the stable side of the precipice now. Not so close to the abyss.

Taking Icarus by the hand, Adam led him to the bed still shoved in the corner, the coziest spot that Icarus, in the short amount of time he'd been there, had made his own. "She was in trouble the last time you were in Portola?"

"Yeah, several months back," Icarus said as he lowered himself next to Adam. "Hacked the wrong person."

"Vincent?"

"No, a different job. Unrelated."

But was it? "Could that be what this is now?" he speculated aloud. "A hack gone wrong? Maybe he'd been implicated back then?" Or more likely, given the escalation of Vincent's efforts . . . "Or Vincent wants her to hack someone? No connection to us." That would be the best-case scenario. Would be more likely to result in a fast and simple meet and a fast and clean extraction.

"That makes sense, but how does Atlas figure in? We assumed he sent that picture, but what if it was her?" Icarus traced the nearly healed cuts on Adam's hand. "I'm sure it was him who told Vincent to send me to you. What else does he know? Does he know how we're all connected?"

"Did he know when you were in Portola last or why?"

He shook his head. "He'd have no reason to. He wasn't a client then, and like I said, she's good at cleaning up my messes. I'm sure she'd try to clean this up herself if she could do so without drawing undue attention to herself or me."

Utter devotion, the two of them walking a ridiculously high tightrope for three decades with virtually no safety nets.

Safety net. Fuck!

Adam's stomach roiled. "That's why you had the supply of Daylight?"

"Always kept an emergency vial on hand."

"That you wasted on me."

Icarus's reply was swift, the grip on Adam's hand almost painful. "Not a waste. No matter what happens, I do not regret that decision."

"I'll make sure of it." Adam lifted their joined hands and kissed the back of Icarus's. Then brought his lips to Icarus's, kissing those too, making a promise. "I'll bring her back to you."

THIRTY-ONE

Adam wanted to know who picked this location. Portola University's main quad was wide open, very public, and very crowded, especially at four in the afternoon. Knowing who picked the when and where would tell them a lot about how this meet would go.

Vincent was a showy motherfucker, but doing his business in this broad of daylight seemed too showy, even for him. He got away with what he did because he did it in foggy, no-rules YB. Portola was a cesspool, but it was a temperate one with a high-gloss veneer, its seedy underbelly more carefully hidden. It was maybe what Vincent aimed to be, but he wasn't there yet. Unless he'd amassed—stolen—more power than they realized. Unless he thought himself invincible already, which was a truly frightening proposition.

If that horror had not yet come to pass, and Vincent hadn't picked this location, then was it Mary? Did she think it would be safer? If Vincent had contacted her about a job, if he wanted her skills badly enough, then it would make sense for her to set the terms of a meet. But if she was being blackmailed into working for him, which was Vincent's usual MO, then Adam doubted she had the leverage to dictate the when and where.

Which left Atlas. They were so far from knowing anything about the warlock's motives that it was . . . suspect. Who was he trying to protect with this location? Vincent or himself? Or Mary? Did he know Mary was connected to Icarus? Had he told Vincent? Had Vincent then made the connection to the people who wanted to kill him? Was Atlas shoving Vincent or Mary into the open for a possible hit? While taking a shot at Vincent was sorely tempting, Adam couldn't make revenge his top priority today. He'd promised to rescue Mary. And despite how desperately he wanted to end Vincent and his operation, Adam couldn't do it here. This was not the Canyon Lands. This was a location full of people, of humans, of potential victims. Which Atlas was counting on too, if he was the one who'd picked this location.

If he was going to show at all. It was ten past four, and there was no sign of any of them.

"Anyone with eyes on?" Adam radioed the teams.

"Negative," Abigail replied from where she and Robin, both recognizable to Atlas, were posted in a parked car near the quad's south entrance.

"Negative," reported another pack pair lounging on a bench at the north end of the artificial lawn.

"Negative," Jenn radioed from where she and another pack member were pretending to be tourists, taking pictures near the west end.

"Negative," Cormac radioed from beside Adam, the two of them crouched on a rooftop at the east entrance.

They returned to silent waiting, except Cormac, whose silence didn't last a minute. His thoughts, unsurprisingly, veered in the same direction as Adam's. "If Atlas sent that picture, why? There's no demand for a ransom, no demand for a meet with Icarus or us. We don't even know if she's still alive."

"I think we'd know if she wasn't."

"If Icarus is telling the truth about what she is."

Adam side-eyed his former partner. "You're the one who kept

harping about what you saw him do at the Canyon Lands that day. Now he's told you. How else do you square that?"

"I don't know exactly what I saw, but I do know something isn't squaring. And you're a good enough detective to know that too."

He wasn't wrong; their mental gymnastics just weren't focused on the same person. Adam's gut told him to trust Icarus, but Cormac's observations couldn't be discredited either. He'd been right about that day in the Canyon Lands, even if they still didn't have all the details. "You think Icarus isn't telling us the whole truth?"

"Have *you* told him the whole truth?" Again, Cormac wasn't wrong, nor was he done examining all the angles. "I'm not sure Icarus knows the whole truth about his sister either."

Maybe not the direction Adam thought his suspicions were headed. He kept his eyes on the quad while continuing to hear the detective out. "What makes you say that?"

"I did some more digging. No record before she showed up at that shelter."

"Sealed?"

"Not that I could find." He drummed his fingers against the roof's ledge like he would his talons in raven form. "Couldn't find anything on Canton either."

"She erased all of them." That would be the safest thing to do.

"Including Atlas?"

He glanced again at the raven. "Why would you look into him? We already knew he was erased."

"Something else I saw at the Canyon Lands that day. Atlas cast an orb at me and Icarus and missed."

"It was foggy and chaotic. The earth was falling out from under us."

Cormac wasn't buying it, his lips pressed into a thin line. "He's better than that."

Jenn cut off further debate, her voice whispered over the comms. "We've got eyes on."

Adam whipped his gaze back to the quad, adrenaline spiking then heart sinking as he spotted the couple who emerged through the west entrance.

Cormac narrated the thoughts Adam didn't want but couldn't avoid. "Does that green-haired pixie look like a hostage to you?"

"We don't know what we're seeing," Adam countered to Cormac and himself. Sure, her arm was around Atlas's waist and his was casually draped over her shoulder, neither of them looking the worse for wear, but why would they want to stand out in a crowded location full of people? They looked like any other couple out for an afternoon stroll. But what did they sound like? What words were escaping their moving lips? "B team, move to second position."

"Copy that." The pack pair on the quad stood, frisbee in hand, ready to extend their reach as needed. Jenn's team also wandered closer, picking a spot just inside the lawn's edge well within their hearing distance, but far enough back from where Atlas and Mary had stopped near the center of the oval, arms around each other.

"If she's betrayed him . . ." Adam mumbled, fear and anger slipping out, even as his training coached him otherwise. Coached him to look deeper, beneath what Mary and Atlas wanted everyone to see.

"She's playing along to protect herself," Jenn said. "I can hear her heart racing from here."

"Look at her posture," Cormac added. "She's playing casual, but her back and shoulders are stiff as a board and her fist is clenched behind Atlas's back."

"Vincent entering from the south," Abigail radioed.

If Adam hadn't been so focused on that fist, if he'd shifted his gaze a split second sooner, he would have missed it. Atlas clasped her shoulder, and a shimmer of green sluiced over her, the outward signs of her distress disappearing.

Masked.

Whose side was the fucking warlock on?

"Three plainclothes trailing Vincent," Robin relayed. "The one in a jacket is human and wearing a shoulder harness. The other two are shifters. I can see an outline of a weapon beneath the one's black shirt. I'm guessing the other is armed too."

A strike was definitely out. Too much firepower and too many people. "Extraction only," Adam confirmed to the teams. They would have to wait and rely on Nate to help deliver Vincent.

If Mary didn't kill him first. Scowling, she snatched back the hand Vincent had made a show of kissing the back of.

"C team, can you hear?" Adam asked.

"Pleasantries with a side of snark," Jenn replied. "She's feistier than her brother."

Adam smiled, brief and fleeting because Jenn soon relayed Vincent's true purpose. It was enough to turn Adam's stomach. Vincent had heard from associates about Mary's hacking prowess, and he wanted to hire her to hack the location of one of the most powerful local covens. Ever since the Rift, covens stayed on the move, no one covenstead for this very reason.

Beside Adam, Cormac stiffened, his eyes flashing violet. Over the comm, Abigail growled. "More power he can suck."

"And yet," Jenn said, "he doesn't realize the ultimate power is right in front of him."

But Atlas hadn't told him either. Because Atlas didn't know? Or because Atlas was a double agent?

But that wasn't all Vincent wanted. He wanted her to dig further into Adam, into Deborah and David, because word had gotten back about last night's attack, about the power he'd flexed. Vincent was finally starting to put the pieces together, which meant their timeline had been accelerated, again.

Mary protested, Vincent threatened, Atlas cajoled, and eventually an agreement—if it could be called that—was reached. Adam suspected it was similar to how they'd muscled Icarus into their employ. Regardless, with the deal made, Vincent departed the way he came, and Atlas, arm back over Mary's shoulder, turned her not west but east, toward the entrance where Adam and

Cormac hid. The warlock's eyes flicked up as if he knew exactly where they were perched.

"What the fuck is that asshole up to?" Adam muttered.

"It could be a trap," Robin warned. "Lure us out for his own purpose."

"He could call Vincent back," Cormac said. "Turn you over himself."

"He would have done that already," Adam said. "And she won't let that happen." He was confident of that much. But if Atlas didn't know what she was, other than someone who was important to Icarus, Adam didn't want to expose her more. "Let's spring our trap first," he said. "We've got him outnumbered. Converge behind our location."

Cormac shifted between one breath and took flight the next, and the flock of ravens that had congregated around them the past hour flitted off the roof, falling into formation behind him. Eyes in the sky while the rest of the pack on human feet drew closer. Adam sensed them on either side of the building as he descended the stairs, then stepped out the back door into the small bricked-over courtyard between buildings. They fanned out on either side of him, and the handful of humans in the courtyard scattered, instincts keyed in enough to know better. By the time Atlas and Mary stepped through the opening between the buildings, they were surrounded. And yet neither of them veered off course or missed a step, Atlas leading her to stand directly in front of Adam.

"I believe this"—he nudged Mary forward—"belongs to a mutual acquaintance of ours."

"Why?" Adam asked.

"Because," Mary said, as she sauntered to Adam's side, all her previous nerves gone, her swagger so reminiscent of Icarus's that Adam almost laughed. "I threatened to flood the internet with pictures of him on a leash."

Robin snickered. "I'd like to see those."

And then a seemingly peaceful exchange went up in smoke.

Atlas summoned an orb, and Robin shifted and collided with his chest, making the orb fly off course and barely miss the dive-bombing ravens. Cormac screeched as he sailed low enough to ruffle Adam's hair, forcing him to spin. He spied Mary in a crouch, her glowing green hand an inch from the ground. Adam shot out his own hand—power channeled into it, no idea if it would be enough—and wrapped his fingers around her wrist. "No! We can't. Not yet."

She stared up at him, eyes wide, and then a slow, satisfied smile stretched across her face. "He said you were different, but he has no idea you're one of mine, does he?"

One of hers?

"Adam!" Abigail shouted behind him, and he whipped back around. She was the only shifter still in human form, the rest of the pack having shifted to defend Robin and help him pin Atlas to the ground. Robin stood over his chest, snarling in his face.

"You promised Icarus a punch," Adam reminded his brother-in-law. "And you do not get to kill him until I kill Vincent."

Robin gnashed his teeth, and Atlas snarled right back at him. "Now who's on a leash, dog?"

Golden eyes flashed, murder glowing bright, and Adam was sure Icarus wouldn't get his punch, but all Robin's teeth sank into was green mist, Atlas disappearing with a single snap of his fingers.

"Huh," Mary said, hands on her hips. "And I thought I had Atlas's number."

Speaking of numbers. Adam dug his phone out of his pocket and opened the encrypted chat app Icarus had installed. He handed the device to Mary. "Worry about them later. Text your brother now or there won't be a base camp for us to get back to."

THIRTY-TWO

He should have known better. One touch and she'd immediately sensed what he was. Why hadn't David or Deborah ever told him the creature sharing David's soul and now Adam's was a force of nature? Did they know? Deb had always been a shifter, and Adam had assumed the same of David, but thinking back, there were pictures and fleeting moments from before their deployment when David had seemed lighter, when all of his soul shined from his eyes. Before it had been dimmed by the fire inside him.

Inside Adam now.

Magic.

The same magic—the source of it—bound inside the green-haired woman beside him in the passenger seat. She'd been silently working her phone the entire drive from Portola to Tala-halusi, fingers flying, switching between chat boxes and transfer-ring files between cloud-based drives. Anyone passing them on the freeway, if they could catch a glimpse of the Camaro through the caravan of other cars surrounding them, would probably assume she was just another person who spent too much time on their phone. Maybe some would wonder if she was a hacker. But how many would guess she was the life force holding their world together? It wouldn't cross Adam's mind if she were a stranger, but she wasn't, and the questions filling his head were too many to count.

"What do you want to know?" she asked, as if reading his mind. Could she?

He chuffed. "I don't even know where to start."

A small smile turned up the corners of her mouth. "I thought I'd lost you."

"You've lost others?

"Too many."

"How did it happen?" Adam asked. "How did the magic inside David come to be inside me?" He'd been in the safe house when David had come stumbling in, his skin rippling orange and red, Deborah in coyote form in his arms. She had been too still, not breathing, a sizzling, gaping wound on her side. He'd told Adam to run, but there'd been nowhere to run, the battle raging outside, the loves of his life dying in the room with him. He wasn't leaving them; he'd promised until death do they part, and he'd planned on keeping that promise. He'd wrapped his arms around David, holding them both, and withstood the searing heat that burst from their husband and brought the walls down around them. That was the last thing he remembered before waking in a hospital bed with no burns on him. But in him . . . "Why am I still here?"

"He loved you. He made a choice to save you. And in doing so, he also saved the magic."

But how? No one had ever been able to answer him that. "It doesn't normally happen this way?"

"Too many can't control the magic. They flame out and die alone."

"They can't use it to bring themselves back again?" He'd sensed that himself; that the magic inside him was a one-shot deal, at least where he was concerned. It was another reason he'd flexed it so rarely—that and the fear a flame out would sear those around him. Contrary to what he'd told Icarus, it was the primary reason why he hadn't flexed his power when facing Vincent at the

Canyon Lands. Icarus, Cormac, Jenn, and Abigail had all been in the blast radius.

"The magic can only bring a being back once." She finished on her phone and set it on the seat between them. "It's why Chaos is winning. Every one of you that's extinguished, whose energy isn't properly channeled, is a black hole that feeds the darkness. Without the power of rebirth, of second chances, there's not enough energy to drive the living."

Again, how the hell did Adam unpack all that? But as he turned onto the narrow road that led to Monte Corvo, his thoughts likewise narrowed, catching on something she'd said and considering it more personally, considering it in terms of the man they had in common.

"Is that what I am to Icarus?" Had Icarus figured out what he was? Or even if he hadn't, had the vampire? Was the thing inside Adam a life force—rebirth—the vampire couldn't resist?

"It's what he is to you, isn't it?" she shot back, then cast her gaze out the window at the rising vineyards. "Irony, fate, call it what you will, it twists like a vine around all of us."

Adam frowned. "So it's not really us?" His awareness of Icarus before he'd even laid eyes on him, the attraction that had ridden him hard since he had, the affection that had grown steadily alongside it. Was it merely rebirth reaching for an outlet? For death? Was Icarus the death wish Cormac so often warned of? Adam the man recoiled at the idea, but Adam the detective couldn't discount the possibility. "It's just fate or the monsters inside us?"

"Not monsters," she said, those two words filled with such sorrow, such exhaustion, it stole Adam's breath. But then her voice, her whole being, brightened as they pulled into the villa's circular drive and the front door was flung open, Icarus barely holding himself back from running into the setting sun to reach her. She glanced back over her shoulder at him. "Don't sell yourselves short. I know monsters. They don't have half the love in their hearts as you and Icarus do."

She smiled, then shoved the car door open, leaving a sparkle of green in her wake as she sprinted across the drive, up the steps, and into her brother's arms. Icarus held her tight, lifting her off the ground and twirling her around, radiating relief that Adam felt in every part of his soul, the parts that belonged to him and the parts he shared with the Devil. Felt it settle deeper as he stepped out of the car and met Icarus's gaze over the roof. Read the silent thank-you on his lips.

Was she right? Was it love filling up Adam's heart and carrying him step by step closer to the person he'd been unable to shake from his life since he'd first sauntered into it? Not because of any mission or any blackmail or any forces other than attraction and affection, other than appreciation for what Icarus had brought to his life for the first time in a decade. He'd known love before, real and true, and fuck if the fullness of his heart, the peace in his soul, all of it, didn't feel the same now as it had then.

Adam climbed the steps, never taking his eyes off Icarus, sliding his hand into Icarus's outstretched one while Icarus kept his other arm wrapped around his sister. "I thought I'd lost you," he whispered into her green curls.

"I told you I'd find my way here when I was ready."

Icarus gasped and jerked back. Adam, however, found his words first. "Repeat that."

"I found a way to you," she said to Icarus, then to Adam, "And a way for you to take down Vincent Cirillo, once and for all."

THIRTY-THREE

Mary was petite, Cormac's description of her as a green-haired pixie spot on, but as she stood at the head of the cellar table, her presence loomed larger than anyone else's in the room. A power, a threat, a responsibility most of them were still trying to wrap their heads around. The only people in the room who seemed relatively comfortable in her presence were Icarus, which was a given, and Abigail, which was a surprise. They were strangers who gravitated around each other like old friends. Even more curious, Jenn hadn't raised her hackles about it, unlike her cousin, who was still seething from being deprived his taste of warlock. Robin stood against the opposite wall beside Cormac, who predictably kicked off the interrogation. "Explain what you meant outside."

"Icarus told you I'm part of a hacker collective?" When everyone around the table nodded, she continued. "A job came over the wire. Someone wanted a hack on the Redwood Coven's location."

Robin growled and Cormac stiffened, neither of them dealing with the news a second time better than they had the first.

"It's consistent," Adam said, as alarmed as the others but striving to hold it together, Icarus's hand on his thigh under the table helping him do so. "Steal all the power he can."

"I knew it was Vincent," Mary said. "I wasn't going to let anyone else put themselves in the middle of this shitstorm."

Cormac pushed off the wall. "So you put yourself in his path." He rested his forearms on the top of the chair next to Adam's. "The biggest battery Vincent could ever want."

"He doesn't know."

"Does Atlas?"

"Atlas doesn't work for Vincent."

"He works for you?"

"Not exactly."

Robin growled again. "You didn't answer his question."

She flicked her hazel gaze to where Robin remained by the wall. "Atlas isn't your concern."

He didn't stay there long, charging the table. "The fuck he's not!" He would have shouted in her face if not for Icarus and Abigail standing from their chairs to form a wall in front of her that Robin couldn't breach. "He killed my sister," he snarled over their shoulders.

Adam's chest clenched at the mention of Deb and at his friend's naked frustration, his grief boiling over. He hadn't been there that day, not that it would have mattered, and now someone else was keeping him from the retribution he so desperately needed to move on, to maybe forgive himself.

Mary seemed to sense Robin's turmoil, pushing through Icarus and Abigail to stand in front of Robin and clasp one of his balled-up fists. "Everything isn't what it seems, coyote."

"Fucking riddles." He rolled his eyes and tried to snatch his hand away.

Mary held on tight. "You'll get your revenge, I promise, but it's not your turn yet." She held Robin's gaze for several long seconds until Robin deflated and stepped back, slumping into the chair Cormac spun out for him.

Cormac, however, remained standing. "The coven."

"I don't have their location yet. But I do have evidence for you." She tapped at her phone, and the one in Mac's pocket pinged. "Phone records from the collective, along with an audio recording of today's meet. Everything Icarus's cop client needs to hand over to the DA. To get Vincent where you need him."

"Why wait?" Adam said, swinging toward Robin's position. "We can hit him when he goes after the coven."

"That's your choice, but it's a risky play on multiple levels." Her knowing gaze cut to Cormac, and Adam's stomach churned when his former partner sank into a chair and propped his elbows on the table, hands covering his face.

Adam clasped one of Cormac's wrists and pulled it far enough away to see the color leach from his friend's face. "Why are you so concerned about the coven?"

"Because I hid Paris with them."

"Fuck." Icarus spoke for the first time, succinct and what they were all thinking. "Is that why Vincent wants their location?"

Mary shook her head. "No, Vincent is just a human who wants to be a giant in the coming war. Adam's right. He wants the coven for their power, which is rising as we approach Samhain."

Adam leaned forward. "Then we should keep him away from sources of power, including you."

She pinned him with a stern look. "And you."

She wasn't wrong. Him, her, and a coven of powerful magicians, all in one location, was too much juice to ever let Vincent near. He spun toward Icarus. "Call Nate. Tell him we have more evidence. That it's time to move."

Time to get Vincent in a place where they could get the upper hand and get the revenge and retribution—the peace—they all deserved.

THIRTY-FOUR

If Icarus's phone had been a lifeline earlier, it was as good as a grenade now. Arm hitched back, he was ready to chuck it at the nearest wall, and with his full strength behind it, Adam had no doubt it would blow a hole clean through. He rushed into the bunk room and grasped Icarus's elbow. "You may still need that."

"For what?" He wrenched his arm loose and spun, gesturing wildly. "Everyone I love is here, and the best chance I had to keep you and her safe just fucking bailed." He resumed his pacing and continued his ranting, cursing the DA who'd refused to hear Nate's evidence against Vincent.

Adam, however, was stuck a few words back . . . *Everyone I love.*

Love.

Had it been a careless slip? Did Icarus mean love generally, as in care for, like he meant about Mary? Or did he mean something more when it came to Adam? Something closer to what Adam was struggling with himself? Had Icarus fallen as hard and fast too—beyond what the magic inside each of them wanted?

Did Michael want him? Because Adam—no, Gabriel—wanted Michael, Icarus, the entire package. More than he wanted his next breath right then. Maybe even more than he wanted death. That thought fucking terrified him.

But not enough to walk away. He stepped into Icarus's path. "You need to calm down."

Icarus cocked a brow. "Why aren't *you* more upset?"

"The choice is easy now."

"Easy? What planet are you living on?"

Adam closed the distance between them and laid his hands on Icarus's chest. "The one with you."

Icarus's expression was a riot of confused emotions—soft surprise, harsh incredulity, stark worry—that eventually distilled into frustrated exhaustion. He covered Adam's hands with his. "The one where I might lose you and her in one fell swoop." He leaned in, forehead resting against Adam's, eyelids fluttering closed. "And let's not even talk about how I almost got Paris killed once already."

Adam pressed their foreheads together, then shifted. Kissed a path from Icarus's temple to one corner of his mouth. "No one's getting killed except Vincent."

"You want to go in there."

He kissed the other corner and up Icarus's opposite cheek to his other temple. "I want him to pay for what he did to Deb and David. I want this to be over."

Icarus sighed and leaned more of his body into Adam's. "Fucking death wish."

Adam snaked an arm around Icarus's waist and lifted his other hand to cup his cheek. "Icarus, look at me."

He shook his head and kept his eyes screwed closed. "What am I to you?" His voice was thick, a lump in his throat that he audibly swallowed around. "A last hurrah?"

"No, baby." Adam swiped a thumb across his cheek, did it again, and Icarus opened his eyes, the blues wary and bruised. Adam wanted to see them bright again, full of fire and hope and desire. "You're the person making me doubt how much I really want to die."

He swallowed Icarus's gasp, crushing their mouths together and pushing his tongue between Icarus's lips, sweeping inside and stoking the missing fire back to life. Chasing that life himself.

Icarus groaned, a surrender and then more, arms winding around Adam, holding him tight, picking him up and moving him with preternatural speed. Adam's back hit the corner bed, Icarus stretched above him, the space narrow and perfect for the closeness they both craved. Icarus's hands were everywhere, fisting Adam's hair, creeping under his sweater, pushing it up and off, his own shirt close behind. He hitched Adam's leg over his hip and held him closer, rutting their stiff cocks together.

Content to be manhandled, Adam landed his lips anywhere he could reach, brushing them against Icarus's neck, parting them around his Adam's apple, sealing them over a nipple and sucking hard, eliciting a breathy groan and full-body shiver that rippled through both of them. He rucked up the back of Icarus's skirt and found his ass deliciously cool and bare, only a thin slice of fabric parting them. He clutched the smooth globes, and Icarus canted forward, forearms in the mattress on either side of Adam's head, lips where Adam could reach them again. He rolled his hips as he thrust his tongue between Icarus's lips, and Icarus punched back with his own hips, with fangs that descended in the midst of the messy, claiming kiss.

And nicked Adam's lip.

Icarus jerked back, nostrils flaring, eyes zeroing in on the drop of blood Adam could feel welling. He started to blink, to lock down his senses. He hadn't needed to do that last night, and Adam didn't want him to do that now. He trusted him. But more than that, he wanted Icarus with him fully, all of his senses firing, same as Adam's. He grasped Icarus's chin. "Don't. Stay here with me. All of you."

Icarus's gaze remained locked with Adam's, not once straying back to the blood. Not even when their pulses synched like they had that night a week ago in the club. "I need all of you too."

Letting some of the heat flow from his core, trusting himself and the Devil with Icarus, Adam coasted his hands up Icarus's flanks, warming the cool skin. Icarus groaned and sank down onto him, burying his face in the crook of his neck. "Fuck, that feels good."

Adam wrapped his other leg around Icarus, their cocks snug, and they rocked together, Adam touching every part of Icarus he could reach, Icarus nuzzling his neck, the ridges of his forehead, his cool breath, the press of his lips and the tips of his fangs teasing.

But never a bite.

And yet not a single muscle Adam coasted his hands over was rigid. Icarus had melted under his touch, the predator's body fully relaxed. Everything but his stiff cock rutting against Adam's. The care—the trust—in Adam, in himself, fired all of Adam's senses, stoking the fire and his desire higher.

His heart tumbled head over heels.

Icarus kissed a trail along his jaw. "I can't hurt you."

With his fangs, no, Adam believed it, but this had gone past physical, past instincts, since that first night in his Terrace bathroom, when Icarus had run his fingers through his hair and wrapped safety and intimacy around him for the first time in a decade. Had re-awoken Gabriel from where Adam had buried him deep inside. He didn't think he could go without it again. He drew back enough to meet Icarus's gaze, not hiding anything from him, putting it all out there like he used to. "I think maybe you can hurt me more than anyone."

Icarus wiped away a tear Adam hadn't realized he'd shed. "I won't let anyone hurt you. Especially me."

Adam smiled, a forgotten reflex a week ago, same as joking, which he felt compelled to do then to lighten the suddenly heavy mood. "Unless I ask you to," he said with a slow roll of his hips.

Icarus smirked. "Not right now." He canted sidewise, reached into the bag beside the bed, and retrieved a bottle of lube. Righting himself, he tossed it on the bed, then clasped each of Adam's wrists and spread his arms, pinning him to the bed. "Just let me worship you." He coasted his own hands down Adam's torso and rose on his knees. "Let me drown in this heat, in everything I feel for you, before you run off and do something foolish and heroic."

Adam chuckled. "How about you be heroic and give me your dick?"

Icarus was in his face faster than Adam could inhale. "I'll give you my dick when I'm good and ready." He drew back enough to splay his palms on Adam's chest, nails lightly scratching. "And if all this heat is any indication, I'm not gonna last that long once I'm inside you, so I'm going to make sure you're good and ready first."

Adam keened, tried to bow, then shuddered with need as Icarus used his strength to keep his back flat to the bed. Keeping one palm at the center of his chest, Icarus retracted the claws on the other and deftly flipped open Adam's fly. He shifted enough to shove Adam's jeans and boxers down, and Adam kicked them the rest of the way off. Then, in a sight Adam would never forget for the rest of his life, Icarus hitched up his skirt and shoved aside the strappy front of his black thong to free his erection. He clasped it in his hand with Adam's, stroked them together, and that was all Adam saw, his eyes rolling back in his head from sensation overload.

He wanted to writhe, but Icarus wouldn't let him, holding him firmly to the bed with his hand, forcing all of Adam's pleasure, all of his heat into one point. He slapped the bed with his outstretched hand. "Fucking hell, Icarus." He fisted the sheets. "I'm ready, I'm fucking ready."

"I don't know." He rolled his hips, slowed his strokes, and circled a thumb over their heads, smearing precome. "I could edge you like this for hours." Icarus's shadow darkened the light filtering through his lids, his breath floated over Adam's lips, and the palm on his chest trailed out the length of his arm, clawed fingers weaving over Adam's clenched fist. He continued to stroke with the other. "You would lie here for me like this, all day and night, wouldn't you? Let me take you apart piece by piece?"

"Yes," he said without hesitation.

"I'll give that to you, I promise," Icarus murmured against his lips. "But I want you too bad for that tonight. But I promise, Adam."

He forced his eyes open, gaze snaring the blue one less than an inch away. "Gabriel. My name is Gabriel." If he wasn't already in love with the vampire stretched above him, Icarus's smile, bright and fiery and full of desire, would have pushed Gabriel the rest of the way over. He let more of the leash go. And love tasted fucking divine. Icarus brought their lips together in a plundering kiss, and Gabriel lost himself in the heat that freely flowed, everything he felt for this man rushing to the surface, folded together in fire's wings, in life.

Icarus shuddered, losing his rhythm, face buried in the crook of Gabriel's neck again, and Gabriel held him close until Icarus regained his composure and lifted onto his forearms. He stroked Gabriel's temples in time with their heartbeats, and Gabriel laid himself bare, hiding nothing, same as Icarus who looked every bit the predator except for the love swirling in his eyes. He lightly brushed their lips together once more. "I promise, Gabriel."

And fuck if Gabriel didn't want to live long enough for Icarus to fulfill that promise. He smiled again. "I'll hold you to that."

Another big smile from Icarus, free and uninhibited, then fast on joy's heels, a tsunami of desire. And in a flash, Gabriel was on his stomach, his hips hitched, ass in the air, lube trickling down his crack and into his hole. Icarus pushed in a slick finger and worked him open. Fabric ripped behind him, and then all of Icarus's bare flesh covered his backside, dick making a sticky mess of his ass cheek, fingers making a slippery mess of his hole, lips down his spine making a gooey mess of his insides. Gabriel hung his head, panting, so tempted to reach down and clasp his own dick, but not until Icarus was inside him. "Now, baby, please."

He whimpered as Icarus withdrew his fingers, but the emptiness only lasted a second before Icarus slid in, whimpering himself. "Fuck, Gabriel, you feel so good." He slid them both down onto their sides, joined, a knee under Gabriel's to keep it lifted, to keep him open for the slow, long thrusts, while every other part of Icarus wrapped around him. Gabriel returned the hug, letting the leash go completely, letting the fire wrap them up and carry them into oblivion together.

THIRTY-FIVE

Gabriel woke slowly, at peace with the fire inside him for the first time in ten years. Sharing it with someone, basking in it, not fighting it as he gave all of himself to Icarus had made him feel whole. He was left with a comforting warmth inside him instead of the crater that had smoldered for a decade. It had made him consider what he and Mary had talked about yesterday. Maybe the magic inside him wasn't the fiery death sentence he'd always assumed was his fate. At least not yet. Not with Icarus by his side.

"Gabriel."

Gabriel flipped over under the sheets, planted a hand in the mattress, and vaulted his torso up. Mary stood in the doorway, a folded piece of paper dangling from her fingertips.

Wait . . . "Where's Icarus?"

She crossed the bunk room and handed him the folded paper. *Gabriel* was scribbled on the front, and though he'd never seen Icarus's handwriting before, Gabriel knew the note was from him.

His stomach sank and his pulse pounded in his ears as he shifted on the bed, legs hanging off the side under the sheet. He flipped open the paper. *My name is Icarus for a reason.*

"He flew too close to the sun," Mary said.

But Gabriel's mind had rewound to last night, to Icarus straddling his hips, gliding his hands over him. *Let me drown in this heat, in everything I feel for you, before you run off and do something foolish and heroic.*

Except it hadn't been Gabriel who'd run off to do something foolish and heroic.

I won't let anyone hurt you.

His name was Icarus for a reason.

"He left this for me."

Gabriel looked up and found Mary close with another note she held out to him.

Protect him.

The notes slipped from his fingers, and he curled over his knees, fighting back fear, tears, and the fire that licked across his skin, that raged in his core.

"Stop fighting it." Her voice was close, her presence washing over him as she laid a hand on his knee. "Use it. Use the fire. Help me protect *him.*"

Gabriel lifted his head but continued to keep the core of him buried, the fire scorching his throat as he croaked, "How?"

She crouched in front of him. "Icarus has gone inside. He'll do the job the DA wouldn't. Put Vincent in a place where we—you—can end him. We have to be ready."

"Vincent will see right through him."

"Give my brother more credit." She smirked. "Sure, the plan will go sideways because he's Icarus, but he'll get us ninety percent of the way there."

"I can't let anything happen to him. I just . . ." He gulped, floundering helplessly in this sea of emotions. "I lo—"

"Nope," she cut him off. "Save it for him. Save *Gabriel* for him. I need Adam. I need the Devil. I need the phoenix."

Gabriel closed his eyes once more and rested his head on his knees. One breath, two breaths. He let the memories of Icarus in his arms wash over him and tucked Gabriel into a warm safe space with them. Then he let the phoenix inside him stretch its wings, harnessed the fire, and honed it into an arrow.

The Devil straightened and opened his eyes. "Let's end this. Once and for all."

PART THREE

ICARUS

THIRTY-SIX

Icarus stood beside the same bench where he'd waited for Paris last week, tugging at the sleeves of his too-small suit jacket. The whole damn suit was too small, the Italian threads snug across his biceps, back, and thighs, and good fucking luck buttoning the jacket, even wearing Adam's favorite slinky top underneath. But at two in the morning, Icarus's only option had been Cormac's closet, and he hadn't had time for sartorial debate. He'd zipped in, grabbed a laundry bag, and zipped out before the raven woke.

If he was going to get past the porter of the glitzy high-rise across the street, he needed to look the part. Sure, the pink hair might give him away, but it was all about confidence, right? And he had that.

Confidence that he'd done the right thing, leaving Gabriel sleeping peacefully in his bed.

Confidence that he had the love of a good man he'd do anything to protect and keep in this world with him.

Confidence that this was the only way to do that.

Was he confident this would go as planned? Hell no, but he was confident it would buy time for her and Adam, because the Devil was who he needed right now. Enough time for them, together with Cormac and Robin, to secure Paris and to be ready for when Icarus delivered them Vincent on a silver platter.

Granted, it was tempting to scale the high-rise's facade, sneak in a window, and rip Vincent's head off himself, but there were three problems with that plan: one, Icarus didn't know which window; two, he doubted he could get past who knew how many guards; and three, it wouldn't give the people he loved the closure they needed. Also, information. Vincent had it; they could always use more of it.

He glanced up and judged the location of the constellations. He had two or so hours left before sunup, before she and Adam would wake, read his notes, and realize he was gone. He didn't have time to waste.

He crossed the street and made it as far as the sidewalk before running into an invisible wall. A magical shield. "Fuck!" He contemplated vamping out and trying to slice through it, but that would stop this party before it even started.

The willowy woman beside the door glared his direction. "May I help you?"

Snotty with a side of static, as if the wall of magic acted like a speaker. Lovely. Icarus barely resisted rolling his eyes. "I have a meeting with Atlas." He doubted saying Vincent would get him anywhere. Vincent would put his guests on the books, and as a human, no matter how criminal, he was less likely to have visitors at four in the morning. But the kinky warlock, Vincent's right hand—that tracked. And if Cormac was correct, if Atlas had missed landing kill strikes at the Canyon Lands, if he'd really turned her over yesterday without caveats and conditions, said kinky warlock was their best bet.

"Your name?"

"Icarus."

Minutes later, the elevator doors inside the lobby opened and Atlas strode out, looking morning fresh in a crisp navy suit that fit him like a glove. He smiled at the receptionist inside, said something, then with a wave of his hand, a shimmering soft spot appeared in the shield. Icarus walked through it, the magic prickling across his skin like it did sometimes in her presence.

The porter, a shifter of some sort Icarus could smell, approached. "I have orders to search you."

Icarus didn't give her any hassle, just spread his legs and held out his arms. He had no phone on him and no weapons other than those magic had bestowed, which he assumed the porter knew, given her watchful approach. "I won't bite, promise."

The porter remained alert as she patted him down then, satisfied with finding nothing, rose and held the physical door open for him. "He's clean," she reported to a waiting Atlas.

"Thank you, gorgeous," Icarus replied, tone sweet as honey, as he stepped over the threshold.

Atlas's tone wasn't nearly as saccharine. "You're late," he snapped.

Icarus smirked and gave a showy little shimmy. "For a very important date."

Atlas rolled his eyes. "Follow me." He nodded at the receptionist, another shifter, then led Icarus to the elevator, murmuring under his breath, "Not a word."

Easy enough as Icarus was too busy holding his breath, avoiding warlock stench the entire ride to the top floor. He followed a stalking Atlas out of the cab, across the hall, and into a pitifully bland condo. All metal, glass, and black leather, ultramodern with no color, barely lived in with zero personality. The appearance Atlas portrayed ninety-nine percent of the time. The warlock stopped in front of the living room's giant floor-to-ceiling windows and spun to face him, the vivid forest in his eyes giving away the other one percent. "What the fuck are you doing here?"

"My job," Icarus said as he stepped past him to look out the windows, the view of the ocean and coastline to die for, even at this dark hour. If he had to guess, Vincent occupied the end unit next door, the family and guards the other two units on the floor. He drew the map in his head while continuing to speak to Atlas.

"I may be a few days late, but I can deliver the Devil. I'm here to tell Vincent where he is."

"We know where he is. Monte Corvo."

"Which we proved your forces can't infiltrate."

"We," Atlas scoffed.

Ignoring the slither of truth, Icarus turned and leaned back against the window casing. "And that was before the entire pack and every fucking corvid in Talahalusi descended on that knobby hill."

Atlas closed the distance between them and grasped Icarus's chin, holding it between his thumb and forefinger. "Fuck me first."

"No."

"That's what I thought."

Icarus wrenched his chin free. "Last time we did that, it ended with you threatening to strangle my cock and tear my ass apart. I wouldn't fuck you again if you were the last person on earth."

"You're lying."

"I most certainly am not."

"About why you're here."

He firmed his jaw and lifted his chin. Confidence. "I will deliver the Devil to your boss. I think he'd want to hear that."

"We have other priorities now." Atlas brushed past him, crossing the cavernous space to the kitchen, his loafers thunking with each step.

Icarus's heels were louder, pinging the marble as he followed. He leaned a hip against the marble island. "*We* who?"

Atlas opened the freezer and withdrew a bottle of vodka and two frosty shot glasses. "*We* as in everyone but you," he said as he filled the glasses to the brim.

Icarus laughed. "I have more at stake than all of you." He held up his glass, and Atlas clicked his against the rim. "Two teams," he said after a sip. "One goes after the coven, the other after Adam Devlin."

"And which one would Vincent and I be on?"

"The latter, of course. I assume Vincent wants to be as done with Adam as Adam wants to be with him, and that after the last time, Vincent wouldn't trust anyone else to do the job."

"Your assumptions are correct." The evil bastard himself stepped out from a shadowed hallway. Vincent wasn't as put together as Atlas, dressed in wrinkled slacks and an undershirt, but the way he carried himself, and the leather shoulder harness packing two revolvers, put off strong I-do-evil vibes. As did the terrifying thirst for power that still swirled in his lovely brown eyes. Such a fucking waste. "Why should I trust you?" Vincent asked as he joined them at the island. "You fought with Devlin at the Canyon Lands and at Monte Corvo."

"You sent me to him for a reason. To Adam Devlin, knowing I'd be the one who could draw out Gabriel Levin." Vincent's eyes widened, a flash of surprise, then one corner of his mouth ticked up, the hint of a victorious smile. Icarus tossed back the rest of his shot. "Do you care if you lost a few soldiers in the process?"

"You cost me power."

"You stop the Devil, and no one will ever stop you from gaining power again."

Vincent claimed Atlas's empty glass and held it out for Atlas to pour a shot. He eyed Icarus over the rim as he sipped the cold liquid. "I may have misjudged you."

"Most people do, and I wasn't exactly on equal footing last time we met." He cut a glare at Atlas, then snapped his gaze back to Vincent when the boss man slammed his empty glass on the counter.

"Don't mistake this for equal footing now." He jammed a finger in Icarus's chest. "You're bait, plain and simple, and I won't hesitate to throw you to the coyotes."

Confidence waning, Icarus averted his gaze and gulped. Vincent took it as the sign of obedience he wanted. He threw the glass back at Atlas, who deftly caught it, then turned on his heel, heading for what Icarus guessed was an internal door with direct access to Atlas's unit. "Ping the hacker bitch," he tossed over his shoulder to Atlas. The only thing that stopped Icarus from snarling was Atlas's heel digging into his foot. "Get us that coven location. We hit them first, bank the power, then there's no way the Devil escapes. But come fuck me first."

Icarus waited for the door to slam, sniffed to make sure the human was gone, only warlock stench remaining, then shook off Atlas's foot. He shot out a hand for the vodka, then cursed because he was shaking too badly to actually hold the fucking bottle.

Cool as the liquid itself, Atlas refilled both glasses. He handed one to Icarus and held his out for a toast.

Icarus clinked rims, then tossed his back in one go. He needed confidence from somewhere else now because his own was fucking shot, every drop of it spent staring down the real devil. "I don't know what you're playing at, Mr. Magic, but if you hurt her, I will help the coyote rip you limb from limb."

Atlas threw back his shot, then pitched the glass in the porcelain sink, shattering it. "You're not the only one doing what he must to save the ones he loves." On the heels of that truth bomb, Atlas stepped around him, and with the kind of uncharacteristic abandon Icarus was more used to seeing when he was in buckles and kilts, Atlas ripped off his jacket and tie, slung them in the direction of the couch, and snapped his fingers, disappearing to Icarus figured he knew where. He also figured, for the first time, that Atlas wasn't happy about it. That maybe he had the warlock all wrong.

THIRTY-SEVEN

Atlas returned several hours later through whatever internal passage Icarus hadn't bothered to investigate since Vincent and the warlock had vanished. The shower kicked on, and Icarus kicked into gear, putting into action the plan he'd concocted while watching the sky lighten and the moon descend toward the ocean. The eggs were almost done, the bacon sizzling, the leftover naan resuscitating in the oven, when Atlas emerged from his shower twenty minutes later in a fresh charcoal suit, looking like his usual wound-too-tight self. "I like you better in buckles and kilts," Icarus said as he turned the heat off the eggs.

"So do I," Atlas replied, and Icarus nearly lost his spatula, the truth unexpected. "But that's neither here nor there." The dejection in Atlas's voice was even more startling, but he didn't give Icarus time to dwell, shuffling to a stop beside him. "What're you doing?"

"Well," Icarus said with a flourish of the wily spatula, "once I realized all your windows are tinted and that you may not be as evil as you want everyone to think, I cooked breakfast. Also masks the warlock smell."

"There's an express meal in the fridge."

"Yes, which I already ate. You also have eggs and cheese"—he pointed at the skillet on the stove—"and bacon"—at the sheet pan of greasy goodness—"and naan"—at the toaster oven.

"We don't have time for breakfast."

By the time Atlas had retrieved one of those disgustingly bland protein shakes from the fridge, Icarus had, at full speed, retrieved the naan and filled two folded pieces with eggs and bacon. He knocked the still unopened drink from Atlas's hand and shoved a breakfast wrap into it instead. "Eat it while we go wherever it is we need to go in a hurry."

Atlas warily eyed the food. "Is it poisoned?"

Icarus picked up his own and munched through it.

"You're a vampire. Even if it was, you wouldn't die."

"Oh, for fuck's sake, Atlas, just eat the damn food."

Atlas grudgingly took a bite, then turned for the door and took a few more, his satisfied little hum making Icarus smile. They made their way to the unit at the opposite end of the floor from Vincent's. Atlas knocked twice, then entered. Icarus followed him inside to what could only be described as a command center. Most of the unit's walls had been blown out, the space a true cavern, with only a kitchen and bathroom for dedicated areas. Two cots were shoved in the corner furthest from the windows, while the rest of the open space was occupied by desks, computers, and monitoring equipment.

And paranormals. No other humans. Vampires, shifters, and the warlock from the strike on Monte Corvo. Still pissed off it seemed, magic shimmering in the air when he spied Icarus. Atlas moved between them, facing Icarus, as he popped the last bite of breakfast sandwich into his mouth. "Tell us where you'll deliver Devlin."

Icarus cocked a brow. "You're licking your fucking fingers, and I don't even get a thank you?"

"Icarus."

Cocked a hip too.

"Fine, thank you, now"—he gestured at the giant map on one wall—"where will you deliver Devlin?"

Icarus stepped around the angry, angry warlocks and studied the map, assuming that was what Atlas-the-not-so-evil wanted. It took a minute for the picture to resolve—to understand that each pin color meant a different source of paranormal power, to realize Vincent was sucking that power from covens, packs, and loners all over the area, creating a vortex at the center right over YB—and less than a second to determine they had to kill Vincent Cirillo.

ASAP.

"Where, Icarus?"

He composed his face, turned, and shrugged, flip as he could seem. "The Canyon Lands, of course."

Atlas raked a hand through his hair, disrupting the blond coif. "Fucking vampire."

Icarus wrinkled his nose. "Not right now, baby." Sparring with him was almost as fun as sparring with Robin. Come to think of it, watching the two of them spar would be epic, assuming they didn't kill each other first. But first, they had to kill Vincent, which maybe Atlas was keen to help them do, which meant maybe Icarus shouldn't piss him off. He dropped the teasing act and channeled a little Adam. "And not there, really. Devlin would suspect something. Club Sutro, where we met."

Atlas stepped closer to one of the other shifters in the room. "Buy the place out for tomorrow night."

While they coordinated, Icarus continued to take everything in before they wised up and threw him out. He drifted toward the vampire who had multiple books open on her desk and a smaller area map with green dots—same as the green pins on the larger map. "Is this what you have on the covens so far?"

"*She* sent us locations this morning," Atlas answered him. Icarus didn't miss the emphasis he'd put on the first word; he knew. But how much? Before Icarus could contemplate further, Atlas held a sheet of paper out to him. "She also sent us this."

It was an email from an alias account he recognized. One that would ping an IP address in Portola, making it seem like she was still there. No subject line. Only one line of text in the message.

tsaEehtnIyL enoloSebotho

"We're working it as a cypher," Atlas said. "To get an exact location."

Icarus laughed. "Stop trying so hard."

The other vampire twisted in her chair. "What's that supposed to mean?"

"I had this client once. Also a hacker." Not really. It was his sister who loved these games, always had. For her protection, he shifted the facts a bit as he explained. "Everything was a fucking riddle. Like the fact he dealt in code all day meant he had to make everyone else work for it too. But with words. He'd give me these rhymes about what he wanted—"

"Icarus!" Atlas snapped, his green eyes practically glowing.

"Reverse it, then read it. 'Oh, to be so lonely in the east.' Then take out the extra space. Ohlone in the East. The Ohlone shell-mound in Encinal," Icarus said as he gestured at a location near the concentration of green dots on the other side of the Bay. "Everyone knows it's haunted."

"Recon," Atlas ordered the other warlock. "Go, and take a few shifters with you," he added with a jut of his chin to the dog of some sort that was working the Sutro angle. "Take over for her," he told the vampire.

"Are we sure—" the other magician started.

"No, which is the point of recon, and we're burning daylight, so go." The second of hesitation among the soldiers was enough to blow Atlas's gaskets. "Move!"

Everyone jumped, including Icarus. While the rest of the room scurried into action, Atlas spun back to him and snatched the email from his hand. "We hit the coven tonight, and you're coming with us."

"Wouldn't miss it for the world."

Especially the part where Adam and company intercepted

Vincent on the Huchiun Enclave, the Ohlone Island halfway between Yerba Buena and Encinal.

Isle in the Middle.

The message in the message she'd sent. The message meant for him.

THIRTY-EIGHT

Icarus's bones rattled as the gas-guzzling SUV he rode in with Vincent and Atlas and the grumpy warlock whose name he'd learned was Brock rumbled onto the decrepit auto bridge that spanned the Bay between YB and Encinal. Most folks who traveled from one side of the Bay to the other took the light rail. Several miles north, it crossed the Bay at an angle, covering more distance and connecting more stable areas of land. Their caravan, by contrast, was going from one iffy piece of land to another iffy piece of land over the iffiest of iffiest auto bridges left. No other cars dared travel on it, but what choice did they have? Vincent had insisted they roll out with a fleet of gas-powered SUVs, one in front of theirs, two behind them, so there they were, traversing a crumbling metal and cement mass that was one good shake from annihilation.

Icarus was tempted to extend his arm out the window, dig his claws into one of the pylons, and scream through the pain for her to take it all down. Impossible, unfortunately, with his wrists in Atlas's favorite pair of silver cuffs, looped through the passenger door handle to further restrict his movement. At least the asshole had divested him of the too-tight suit coat and wrapped it around his wrists, preventing the cuffs from burning through Icarus's pants where his hands rested in his lap. Trapped, Icarus waited and watched, keeping his ears on Vincent and Atlas behind him, one eye on Brock the Rock beside him, and the rest of his attention on the road ahead.

On the island in the middle of the bridge's span from which Adam and his team would launch their surprise attack.

"You seem tense," Vincent said.

Icarus twisted as much as the cuffs would allow. "I'm in a tank, in a line of tanks, on a bridge that could fall into the Bay at any second. Of course I'm fucking tense."

"But I heard you could fly."

Three days ago. No time at all, and yet it felt like a lifetime had passed since he'd taken the biggest—best—gamble of his life. He'd stared down at a smiling Adam, borrowed some of his confidence, and leapt, skipping across the water with the Devil in his arms, all the way across the Bay and north. He'd used the last of his Daylight and had risked exposure and death because Adam was worth it. Had proven as much every day since. Unlike the power-hungry murderer in the back seat. "You're not worth flying for."

Vincent laughed, and Icarus slumped in his seat, focused instead on appearing calm as they approached the quarter-mile tunnel that cut through the rocky outcrop that had survived the Rift. The neighboring isle had not, but Huchiun's bedrock—its spirit and ghosts—had held firm, prickling as they drove beneath the tunnel's arch and lifting the hairs on Icarus's arms. Atlas stopped speaking midsentence, Brock clutched the wheel so tight it creaked, and Icarus straightened in his seat. Not appearing tense flew out the window.

Vincent noticed. "What's going on?" he asked, a rare quiver to his voice. "What's that smell?"

"Hush," Atlas ordered his master in a rare show of defiance.

"Consecrated ground," Icarus said. "It doesn't like you."

"Wha—"

The tunnel lights flickered.

A flash of green.

The car slowed.

Icarus steeled himself for the pain that would come from yanking against the cuffs.

The van behind them blew its horn, and Brock hit the gas. Icarus slammed back against his seat, and in the back, Vincent cursed. "Dammit, Brock!"

Atlas slapped the back of Brock's headrest. "Go!"

Brock kept his foot on the gas, hurtling them through the short tunnel, so close to the lead van that Icarus couldn't see the other SUV's tires. Adam would have to time the attack just right. As the end of the tunnel neared, Icarus mentally ran through the possibilities.

A road blockade.

An assault from above.

An explosion, man- or magic-made.

Flickering median lamps outside the tunnel reflected off the roof of the lead car, then on the hood of their SUV, climbing the windshield.

They cleared the tunnel.

The cuffs around his wrists disappeared.

And then . . . nothing.

Their SUV continued charging forward, and it took everything in Icarus to not whip around in his seat and glance back, to confirm with his own eyes, what his mind was telling him. That Adam had deserted him. That he'd read her message wrong.

His heart rebelled.

His heart.

He closed his eyes and blocked out the other voices and heartbeats in the car, the rumble of tires over uneven concrete, the waves crashing below, and searched for Adam's heartbeat.

Nothing.

He opened his eyes and shifted enough to see in the rearview mirror, the most he could do without being obvious.

Nothing still.

Just Vincent in the back seat, turned the way Icarus wanted to be, staring back at the now-deserted tunnel. "What the fuck was that?"

Bright green eyes clashed with Icarus's in the mirror. Atlas was as confused as him as to why they were still moving forward without incident. His calm and even voice, however, didn't give his shock away. "Like Icarus said, consecrated ground. Prepare for more of the same at the shellmound."

Would the attack happen there? Icarus didn't think so. He didn't think she would risk the coven or the remains of the Indigenous people buried there either. What the fuck was going on?

Twenty minutes later, Vincent was screaming the same in his face, Icarus shoved against the side of the SUV, all of Vincent's soldiers in a line behind their boss, ready to tear Icarus apart as soon as Vincent gave the order. "I told Atlas you were a spy. That you were still working with Devlin."

"How do you get that?" Icarus shouted back. "Do you see him anywhere?" He would have spread his arms if he could, but the cuffs had rematerialized as soon as they'd reached the end of the bridge.

"I don't see *anyone*!" Vincent roared as he did what Icarus couldn't, spreading his arms and gesturing at the deserted mound of earth behind them. The grass had grown over the layers and layers of shells and bones; this was one of the Ohlone tribe's largest ancient burial sites, seemingly undisturbed by witches or otherwise. "You lied to us about the message, about the coven being here."

Icarus glared over his shoulder at Brock. "You and your recon team detected activity here earlier today, didn't you?"

Vincent wasn't hearing any of it. "You told them to leave."

"When?" Icarus shrieked. He glanced at Brock again, then at Atlas. "When was I alone today?"

Vincent held a hand out behind him. "Stake."

"Vincent," Atlas started.

"Mind your place."

Atlas promptly shut his mouth, back under his master's thrall.

Fuck!

"Someone give me a fucking stake!" Vincent roared again.

The vampire from earlier slapped one into his palm. Fucking traitor. Vincent firmed his grip on the thicker end and drew back his arm.

Icarus closed his eyes and recalled the warmth that had enveloped him last night. Thanked whatever fate had put Adam —Gabriel—in his path and prayed the Devil would keep his sister safe when he was gone.

"Boss," Brock spoke up. "I don't think we're alone."

Icarus popped open his eyes and scanned their dark surroundings. No one in sight.

Caw.

He looked up and gasped. Crows were perched on every roof and eave of the buildings bordering the streets that surrounded the shellmound.

Watching. Waiting.

"Remember what you said this morning," Atlas spoke evenly, as if any inflection would shatter the eerie stillness, would turn whatever was going on here into the battle they'd all anticipated. "He's bait. They're watching him. For the Devil." Vincent's raised arm wavered. Atlas continued to press. "We can regroup and use him like we always intended. We can end this, and then no one will stop you from sucking the coven dry."

Vincent lowered his arm but didn't step back. Didn't give an inch as he seethed in Icarus's face. "Club Sutro, tomorrow night." His brown eyes hardened, and Icarus didn't think he'd ever consider the color lovely again. "You'll die beside him if it's the last thing I do."

THIRTY-NINE

Icarus felt marginally safer on the return trip to YB. Yes, his life was more in danger than ever, but with two fewer tanks in their caravan, crossing the auto bridge didn't feel like the same death sentence it had the first time. Vincent had left one van of shifters behind to monitor the shellmound, had ordered one north to monitor Monte Corvo, and had taken the wheel of their van headed back to YB. They were in the middle, Vincent riding the bumper of the lead van driven by Brock. Vincent was paying little attention to the van behind them, unlike Atlas, who had spent extra time securing it before they'd left Encinal and was spending extra energy guarding it still, if the raised hairs on Icarus's arms and the weakened cuffs around his wrists were any indication.

Maybe that was why Atlas missed it.

Or maybe it was Vincent, in all his awful alphaness, cursing the lead car for driving too slow.

Or maybe it was just the shitty, buckled road beneath their wheels.

Whatever it was, the other two beings in the car with Icarus missed the shimmer of green as they entered the tunnel, the water stains on the cement roof that had been dry less than an hour ago, the sway of the island itself. Warning signs that would have cautioned against swerving out from behind the lead car and charging ahead.

Right into a wall of water that crashed over their SUV, that blanketed the windshield and sent them fishtailing across the bridge.

"Fuck!" Vincent cursed as he fought the wheel for control. "Hold on!"

But he was no match for her strength, for the coven she'd spared, for the spirits and ghosts who'd heeded her call and whipped the Bay around them into a frenzy. Walls of water hundreds of feet high splashed onto the already uneven surface, the entire decaying structure swaying. What had been a dark quiet night when they'd entered the tunnel had, a quarter mile later, turned into a maelstrom.

"We can't make it across the span to the other side!" Atlas shouted. "Reverse! Go back!"

"Make this stop!" Vincent countered as he continued to fight the skid. "Do something!"

"Take your foot off the gas and your hands off the wheel!"

"Why would I do that?"

When Vincent didn't comply, Atlas cut a look at Icarus in the back seat, and the next instant, the cuffs around Icarus's wrists were gone. Springing into action, Icarus reached both arms around the driver's seat from behind and clutched Vincent's biceps, yanking his hands off the wheel.

Vincent tried to wrestle free. "Let me go!"

Icarus wrapped his arms fully around Vincent and jerked him higher in the seat, pulling his feet off the pedals too, the car decelerating but still spinning out of control. "I've got him! Stop the car!"

Atlas splayed a hand on the inside of the SUV's roof and cast a spell that created a sparkling green dome over the vehicle. With his other hand, he yanked up the parking brake lever, and finally, fucking finally, the car slowed its skid—until a blast of power pummeled Atlas's shield, shoving their vehicle back toward the tunnel and the two other SUVs who'd wisely stopped before hitting the storm.

"Who's doing that?" Vincent yelled, fear creeping beneath the shock and anger. "I can't see!"

Atlas put a hand to the windshield, and a gap in the wall of water appeared.

So did the Devil.

Icarus had never seen a sexier sight.

Adam stood at the head of the pack, wind-whipped and rain-soaked, his arms extended, his hands flexed. Despite the water, an aura of glowing orange and red swirled around him and over his skin. Like the kid he'd rescued a week ago, but controlled, and at max power. Another blast of that power rocked the SUV, stronger this time without the water filtering it. Strong enough to slam their SUV back into the lead one Vincent had so foolishly passed, all three cars in the caravan piling up inside the tunnel.

"What's he doing?" Vincent said, fighting against Icarus's hold. "How's he doing this?"

"You never wondered how he survived that fire?" Atlas said, voice deathly calm. "The ultimate power was right under your nose for ten fucking years, and you never figured it out." But Atlas had. Same as he'd apparently figured out how to thwart his master's thrall, if he'd ever been under it at all. With one snap, he was gone, only green mist floating where he'd been a blink ago in the passenger seat.

Icarus twisted in his seat, leaving one arm around Vincent. Sure enough, green light appeared in the rear car, and a second later, it was gone again—with someone else, Icarus suspected—but he didn't have long to contemplate. With Atlas and the myste-rious person off the scene, the dome over their SUV shattered, and with it, Icarus's temporary view of Adam, water and rain obscuring the tunnel entrance once again. He reached out with his senses, found the heartbeat he'd know anywhere, and latched on.

A guide for Adam, a constant for Icarus, and a silent, shouted warning for any paranormal on the scene who dared lay a hand on his mate.

Vincent fought harder in his arms. "Let me go!"

Icarus did no such thing. He leaned forward and whispered in his ear, "You underestimated him too."

Glass shattered, metal crunched, and the driver's side door was wrenched open. Vincent yelped. "It's me, boss," Brock shouted over the thundering storm. "We gotta go." He summoned a blue orb and flung it in Icarus's direction. Icarus released Vincent and ducked, barely avoiding the sizzling ball of magic, and foolishly turning his back on the door, which was yanked open by someone else. Strong arms banded around Icarus and dragged him out of the car.

Icarus sniffed. One of Vincent's shifters, a horse of some sort. As soon as his feet hit the ground, Icarus bent at the waist, trying to leverage the shifter over him, but the horse had at least fifty pounds on him. Icarus was also fighting at half attention, the other half on Vincent and Brock still arguing beside them.

"We stay!" Vincent wrestled out of Brock's hold and lunged for his shoulder harness tucked in the side door compartment. "We can fight them."

"We don't have the power anymore." Brock pointed toward the third car. "Atlas took him."

What power? Whoever Atlas disappeared with? Was that the juice Vincent was using to keep Atlas and the rest of the paranormals under his thrall? How had Atlas broken through? Had the others? Was it just blind loyalty keeping Brock and the others by his side?

"We don't need him," Vincent countered, the awful lust for power back in his voice. "Not if we can get the Devil. I want his power." He finished readying his pistols and swung his gaze in Icarus's direction. Nope, nothing lovely about those brown eyes anymore. "And we use him as bait."

Icarus kicked and clawed to no avail.

"We need to go back the way we came!" Brock urged. "It's the only way out."

"Cirillo!" The Devil's shout echoed through the tunnel.

Vincent stiffened, and so did Brock and the shifter holding Icarus, all of them turning toward Adam's voice. Toward the army bearing down on them. Adam stood at the center, a gun in one hand, a throwing star in the other, with Robin and Jenn in their massive coyote forms on either side of him and flanked by Abigail and Cormac in human form. Ten more of the pack were behind them, some shifted, some not, the latter heavily armed. Jenn and Abigail had salvaged a lot from Adam's armory—guns, cross-bows, knives, and more.

Compared to Vincent and his army of eight, the odds favored Adam. Icarus smiled, and Adam grinned right back before shifting his burning blue-gray gaze to Vincent. "You have someone I belong to. I need him back."

"So trade yourself," Vincent postured. "I'll let him go if you come with us."

"Not a chance, and not a chance you're going anywhere either." He lifted the throwing star and twirled it between his fingers. Icarus counted at least three bone-cracking shifts and as many guns cocking behind him, all aimed at Adam. But Adam only had eyes for him. "Hey, baby, someone's waiting for your SOS." He flicked his gaze to the ground a half second before the throwing star came hurtling the direction of Icarus's captor. In that same half second, Icarus blinked off his senses and prepared for the splatter of blood that coated the side of his face, avoiding the instinctive distraction so that as soon as the shifter's arms fell away, Icarus could drop to a knee, flatten his palm on the ground, and ask his sister for help.

She delivered, shaking the ground so hard the rest of the bridge behind Vincent's caravan collapsed into the Bay, the thunderous booms of cement and metal crashing into the water echoing through the tunnel and driving the waves over the remaining half of the bridge higher. The span behind Adam stretching to YB swayed in an unsteady, disquieting fashion. They didn't have long to end this. Icarus spun, claws and fangs out, and hissed in Vincent's direction. "Fuck being your bait."

Vincent raised one pistol, but before he could pull the trigger, a bullet zipped past his nose. Following the path of his shot, Adam and the pack charged. With no way out, Vincent's soldiers did the same, the two groups colliding just inside the tunnel opening. Icarus rolled and came up slashing beside Adam, engaged in hand-to-hand combat with the other vampire from Vincent's crew. Growls and snarls bounced off the cement walls, joined by grunts and shouts as soldiers fought in human form, and the occasional sizzle and pop of magic as Brock hurled orbs of magic from beside Vincent.

Icarus landed a roundhouse that caught the other vampire by surprise. She fell to her knees, and a ready Abigail swung her sword, slicing the vampire's head off, while Cormac shoved a stake into her chest for good measure. The explosion of dust settled just as Robin and Adam neutralized the horse shifter. With Adam in arm's reach, Icarus blinked his senses back on and grabbed him by the coat collar, dragging him in for a quick, hard kiss, the hit of fire and whiskey intoxicating. "How mad at me are you?"

Adam smirked. "It wasn't your worst plan ever."

Robin butted his head between them, and Icarus could have sworn the massive coyote rolled his eyes. He jutted his muzzle Vincent and Brock's direction. Message received. "How do you want to do this?" Icarus asked as Cormac joined their group.

"You two"—Adam gestured at him and Cormac—"distract the wizard long enough for us to get to Vincent."

"Vincent's thrall over them is broken," Icarus said. "Atlas stole the power source on scene. The warlock with Vincent wants to leave. I don't think it'll be hard to separate them."

"You don't know what else Vincent may have over him," Cormac said.

"I doubt it's Armageddon."

And fuck if the coyote didn't grin. So did Adam as he dragged Icarus in for another too brief, drugging kiss. "Go be a fucking hero."

Using the van as a shield, Icarus and Cormac crept behind it while Adam and Robin charged back into the melee, making steady progress toward Vincent and Brock.

"I can blind him," Cormac said. "But with the wind whipping through here the way it is, it'll only be for a couple seconds."

Icarus nodded. "That's all I need."

They waited for Adam and Robin to be in striking distance before rounding the back of the car, putting them a few feet from Brock and Vincent while still covered on two sides. Icarus protected Cormac's other two while the raven closed his violet eyes and lifted his arms, murmuring in a mishmash of what sounded to Icarus like Gaelic and Wappo, words he didn't understand but that had their intended effect.

A powerful gust of wind howled down the tunnel and on its heels a chorus of *CAWs* and *KRAAs*. A wave of black undulated through the tunnel and spread like a blanket, unfurling more as the birds neared the intended targets. Focused on taking shots at Adam and Robin, Vincent and Brock were too late in noticing the attack at their back. The corvids swooped in between them and around Brock, disorienting the warlock and giving Icarus time to spring through the narrow opening they'd left him.

He wrapped his arms around the warlock and dragged him away from Vincent. "I will give you one chance to run."

The warlock trembled. "He'll come after me. After my family."

Icarus should have known. Blackmail, thy name is Vincent Cirillo. But those days would be over soon. "He won't live past tonight. Go!"

One snap—small yet sharp in the booming chaos—and all that was left in Icarus's arms was blue mist.

Followed by two gunshots—louder and more deafening than any other noise—and all that was left of Icarus's future crumpled to the ground.

FORTY

Moving at full speed, Icarus reached Adam before his head hit the ground, cradling the precious weight in his hands. He sank behind him and gathered the rest of Adam's torso into his arms. "No, no, no, no, no," he chanted as his hands moved on autopilot, pushing layers of clothes out of the way, searching and finding the gunshot wound to Adam's chest.

Blood and heat flowed through his fingers. Out of Adam. Too much. Too fast. No sign of healing.

Fuck!

He began snatching back the layers of fabric he'd pushed away, pressing them to the wound. He tore off his shirt sleeves and added those to the compress too, plus all the pressure he could exert without breaking Adam's ribs. "Come on, baby. Stay with me."

A dog whined, and Icarus jerked up his gaze, instinctively hissing, warning back any threats. Robin wasn't one, despite his appearance, his fur matted and muzzle bloodied from ripping out Vincent's throat. Deferring, he lowered to his belly at Adam's feet and stared at Icarus with pleading golden eyes.

"Come," Icarus ordered as gently as the panic coursing through him allowed. "Help keep him stable."

Robin carefully stretched alongside Adam's body, gentle but snug. Jennifer mirrored his position on Adam's other side, bumpering him in blond fur. In his pack. "What do you need me to do?" Abigail asked as she crouched beside Icarus.

"I need to get a better look at the wound." He wasn't optimistic, but keeping his mind engaged, his hands working, was the only thing keeping his heart from breaking and the vampire from rampaging. "Apply pressure on the compress," he told her. "I'm going to lift him, check for an exit wound, and if there isn't one, then I need you to slide into my place." He carefully lifted Adam's neck and head and swiped an arm under him, feeling for a tear in the fabric, or viscous blood, or an output of heat. Finding nothing, he scooted the rest of the way out from behind Adam, and Abigail moved into position, cradling his shoulders and head.

He stepped over Robin, who didn't growl or flinch, a testament to how worried he was for his brother-in-law. Kneeling between Adam's legs, Icarus checked him over for any other injuries. The movement was enough to rouse Adam, his blue-gray eyes fluttering open. Hazy with pain, they bounced around, unfocused, before finally landing on Icarus. "Hey, baby." The gurgling roughness of his voice didn't help Icarus's rising panic.

"Don't—" His voice cracked, forcing him to start over, betraying his attempt to play stern. "Don't fucking 'baby' me right now."

"Michael." So soft yet as sharp as any stake to Icarus's heart. "I love you."

Anger flared, Icarus grasping at any emotion other than the soul-crushing despair nipping at his heels. "No!" he snapped. "You do not get to say that to me as you bleed out on a fucking piece of rock in the middle of the fucking Bay. You do not get to quit on me at all. I belong to you too." He moved with every bit of speed magic had gifted him, peeking under the compress and probing the wound. "Fuck, the bullet's still in there." And there was no way he was getting it out without doing more damage. He grabbed the torn shirt sleeves, packed the wound as best he could, then piled the rest of the compress back on and exerted pressure.

Adam grunted, wincing as he lifted a hand to rest on Robin's head. "You need to go." He ran his fingers through the fur between Robin's perked ears. "Get everyone out of here before I flame out."

Icarus understood those words now and hated the inevitably staring him down, the fire that would steal the man he loved and Icarus along with him because in no scenario was Icarus leaving him alone to die. But did he have to? "Is there a way . . ." He cleared his throat. "Like the kid?"

Adam shook his head. "No time." He petted Robin again. "Go, please."

Robin shuffled closer and laid his chin on Adam's shoulder. His woeful, high-pitched whine was the straw that broke the vampire's back. Leaving one hand on the wound, Icarus turned his face away, giving the brothers a moment and giving himself a moment to choke back the threatening sobs.

"I'll tell her," Adam said to Robin. "I promise."

Robin barked, and Icarus righted his gaze. It was too soon; the sight was no less painful as Robin rose on all fours, leaned over Adam, and licked his face. A final goodbye. Icarus closed his eyes, fighting the wretched misery tearing apart his insides, the scream of hopelessness rumbling up his throat that escaped on a gasp when the coyote's tongue swiped his cheek, licking away the tears he'd shed for their friend. Icarus opened his eyes, meeting the same grief and despair in glowing gold ones. But he also met a promise. "You'll protect her?" Icarus asked.

Robin nodded his big rusty-gold head.

"Thank you."

He backed away slowly, Jenn and Abigail on his heels. Icarus reclaimed his spot behind Adam, cradling his body as he continued to press the soaked pile of clothes to his chest. Adam turned into him, face buried in his neck, the rising heat of his breath carving open that Adam-sized hole in Icarus's chest again. Adam's words, as usual, tore it wider. "You should go too."

"Not a chance," Icarus managed through his tears. "I've never seen a phoenix before."

"You knew?"

He lifted a hand and cupped Adam's cheek, thumb skating his temple, the corner of his eye. "It burned here when we made love." His voice wobbled. "Like it's burning now."

"We burn together."

Icarus leaned over and brushed his lips against Adam's. "I love you too. Thank you for believing in me."

"Thank you for giving me a second chance."

He pressed his forehead against Adam's and braced for the final, searing burst of heat, expecting it to come from the man in his arms. He didn't expect it to come from their sides. Magic popped and sizzled, green mist coalescing into a dome that formed over them, and inside it with them, Atlas, Mary, and Cormac.

Icarus clasped his sister's outstretched hand. "What are you doing here?" He then cut a glare at Atlas. "Why are you with him?"

She laid her other hand atop Icarus's on Adam's chest. "I need you to give him back to me."

He swung his gaze back at her. "What?"

"He either flames out or you give him back to me."

"What are you saying?"

"You are the balance Nature wants," Atlas interjected, explaining. "Life"—he nodded at Adam's prone form in his arms, then at Icarus—"and death. Phoenix and vampire. *That's* why I sent you to him. *You* have to be the one that kills him."

She squeezed his hand. "You're the one who saves him."

"You want me to bite him? To feed?" They nodded, and Icarus's head spun, but not nearly as fast as his heart tumbled. How did the pieces fit together? Were they a sacrifice or something more? Was this hope or a fucking curse? Did any of it matter beyond the love and life of the man in his arms?

"We can't lose another phoenix," she said. "His is the power we need in the coming war."

"We?" he croaked as he gathered Adam closer, protecting him from all possible threats.

She flattened a hand on the green dome, and the magical shield shone so bright Icarus had to slam shut his eyes, stars sparkling behind his lids. "He'll help me channel the power. Back into the life force, back into Nature."

A gentle hand on Icarus's shoulder urged his eyes back open and drew his gaze to the violet one by his side. Sanity in the swirling storm, an ally like he'd been that day in the Canyon Lands. The man in Icarus's arms was his only concern too. "I'll stay with his soul," Cormac said. "Whichever way he chooses."

Fear gripped Icarus's insides and twisted his gut in a stark reminder of that awful feeling from the day he was turned, that awful, heavy emptiness that had invaded his soul and that had only begun to lighten when Adam Devlin crossed his path. No, not only Adam—the Devil and Gabriel too. Especially Gabriel, who had already lost so much. Icarus would not curse that man or any part of the man he loved to more emptiness. Not when it was the antithesis of what he wanted. "What if I turn him?" He'd never bitten anyone before. He didn't know how this fucking worked. Never wanted to. "This, me, eternal life, it's not what he wants. You know that as well as I do. He wants peace. He fucking deserves it."

"So do you." Cormac squeezed his shoulder. "I'll stay with yours too."

Icarus gulped. "Which direction?" The same question he'd posed just days ago. He hadn't imagined they'd be revisiting it so soon.

"Whichever direction the two of you choose."

He flicked his gaze to Mary. Nature was driving the show, but misery shone from his sister's hazel eyes. "I love you," she whispered.

"I love you too, always." He turned his eyes back to the raven, the too-gentle reaper. "Is back here an option?"

Adam shifted in his arms, his lips moving against the underside of Icarus's jaw. "Icarus, it's okay. I'm not afraid anymore. Not with you. Never with you."

"I can't," he choked out on a sob. "I can't hurt you." He pressed their foreheads together again. "Your soul has hurt enough already."

"Not hurt. Free." He pressed a kiss to the corner of his mouth. "Wherever you are, that's free."

Icarus drew back enough to meet his eyes, the phoenix there glowing red, only a thin ring of blue-gray left at the edge of his fiery irises. Enough of him left for Icarus to beg and plead with, to confess the only truth that mattered. "I love you. I need you to come back to me."

"You come back to me too." One final kiss, his breath searing hot, the phoenix rising, before he leaned his head back and bared his throat, his Adam's apple bobbing around a last whispered "I love you."

Instincts Icarus had ignored the past however many minutes, the past week, the past thirty years rushed to the surface. And for the first time since he'd been turned, he gave in to them. Gave in to the hope of love. Of peace and a place that was free of emptiness. A place for Michael at Gabriel's side, forever.

Icarus sank his fangs into the Devil's neck and flew into the sun.

FORTY-ONE

Michael loved fucking in the sun. Loved the heat on his skin, the sweat dripping down his spine, the slick glide of his body against Gabriel's flushed and equally sweaty one beneath him.

Correction: Michael loved fucking Gabriel in the sun.

Loved Gabriel, period.

The handsome man beneath him chuckled. "You're drifting again."

Michael smirked. "As long as I drift while riding your dick, do you care?"

"Not a damn bit." Gabriel grasped his hips and thrust up. "But I'm close."

Michael groaned and tipped back his head, savoring every degree of warmth, every inch of fullness, every racing beat of his pulse, and every second of the second chance he and Gabriel had been given.

They had earned it.

Gabriel bent his knees and bumped him forward, chest to chest as they picked up the pace, rocking their hips faster, Gabriel thrusting deeper. "I need to come, baby."

Michael pushed back on him harder, driving him deeper, as he flattened his palms on either side of his head, wild mustard under his palms and fresh dirt under his short blunt nails, the smell of earth only adding to the intoxicating moment. He buried his face in his lover's neck, adding sweat and lingering whiskey to the scent cocktail, as he kissed and sucked a path to Gabriel's ear. "We come together."

Gabriel snaked his arms around him, sliding one hand down to palm his ass and plowing the other into his hair, fingers curling in the magenta and ginger strands, holding him close from top and bottom. "We burn together."

Michael exploded, spilling hot, sticky come between them, moaning as he rode back onto Gabriel's cock and watched the body beneath his arch so beautifully. Gabriel came soon after with a shout, filling Michael up. Filling his heart and life with so much warmth and love.

Love that had held their souls connected and guided them back to this world together.

As humans.

Sated, Michael splayed out on top of Gabriel, his limbs like jelly, his entire body happy. And too heavy for his wobbly post-orgasmic arms to hold up. Probably too heavy for Gabriel too. He shifted to his side, taking Gabriel with him, one arm over his waist, a leg still thrown over his hip. Gabriel's spent cock slipped out of his ass, and Michael wasn't the least bit embarrassed by his needy little mewl.

Chuckling, Gabriel combed his fingers through his hair, something they both enjoyed almost as much as sex. "I'll give it to you again, I promise."

Michael snuggled closer, ear pressed to Gabriel's chest, listening to the strong, steady beat of his heart. "If it's not cold and rainy on Solstice, I want to spend all day here, just fucking you in the sun."

"Why Solstice?"

"Shortest day of the year. Human recovery time is a bitch."

Gabriel laughed. "Says the twenty-something-year-old with stamina for days. Me, on the other hand . . ."

"Taking you apart is the best turn-on." He propped himself on an elbow, looking down at the sexy man he was lucky enough to spend his mortal forever with. "So I'll just pin you down and rail you into the ground until you recover."

Gabriel groaned, and his dick gave an interested jerk where it lay pressed against Michael's thigh. "You're incorrigible, and I wouldn't bet on a lazy Solstice. We may not be magical anymore, but the world still is, especially on that day, and you are one of the best medics we have."

"Buzzkill," he pouted. Gabriel laughed out loud, a sound Michael would never tire of, and he laid his head against his chest again to get the full effect, smiling even as he mentally acknowledged the truth of what Gabriel had said. Yes, Vincent was dead, but the war was far from over. As Mary had said, Vincent was just a human trying to be a giant. There were real giants—and worse —and hell, their side was still just trying to sort the good from the bad.

Like a certain warlock. "Any word from Robin?"

"Still hunting."

According to Cormac, as soon as he'd landed back with their souls at the tunnel, the green dome had disappeared, Atlas with it. Robin had waited long enough for everyone to get settled back at Monte Corvo, long enough to question an uncooperative Mary, then left, searching far and wide for the enigmatic warlock. Mary had remained tight-lipped, not bending to Cormac's or Adam's interrogations, insisting that they trust her and that Atlas was not their problem any longer, that Robin would get his revenge when his time came.

In any event, they'd had other more pressing, more present problems to deal with in the past two weeks. Skirmishes had erupted as others sought to fill the void Vincent left behind, and with the anniversary of the Rift four days ago, they'd remained busy. Adam—the Devil—had been needed to fight on the side of Nature, a position staked for the coming war that continued to bubble.

Gabriel gave his ass a gentle squeeze, bringing him back to the here and now. "Do you have a stream today?"

He lifted his chin, glancing up. "Tonight. Multiparty." Business was still good for Icarus—he'd kept the name professionally, same as Adam—though that whole being-human thing meant he had limited repeat performances, making multiparty streams more valuable than ever. His toys were more valuable too, even a few resurrected ones. "I'm thinking about the silver cock cage you bought me and that vibrating plug you love so much."

Gabriel growled and hauled him up his body. "Then I am definitely going to watch."

If they even made it that long, their stiffening cocks aligning. "I don't think we have an issue with recovery time. Yet." Grinning, he grasped them together and stroked.

Gabriel captured his mouth in a searing kiss, their tongues and moans tangling, greedy—always—for each other. Lost in each other. So much so that neither of them heard the intruder until he was nearly on them, branches cracking under hasty, approaching footsteps. They moved on instinct, Adam rolling onto his belly under Icarus, reaching out a hand for his pistol that was never far away, and Icarus springing to a crouch in front of him, his body mass still greater and his reflexes still faster than the average human.

"Adam!" A familiar voice, an unfamiliar alarm. "Icarus!"

"Stand down," Adam said, recognizing it too. They scurried up, grabbing whatever they could for cover, before Cormac shoved through the last of the trees surrounding the meadow.

They hadn't needed to worry about clothes. Cormac was naked too, running to them directly from a shift. He didn't make a quip and didn't even bother to take in their state of undress, as far as Icarus could tell. He was too caught up in whatever tragedy had left his dark hair ragged, his tan skin pale, and his violet eyes bright with fear.

Adam rushed to his side. "Mac, what's wrong?"

Icarus recognized something else besides fear in the raven's eyes. He couldn't believe he hadn't realized it until that moment. Fear—and *love*—cracked Cormac's voice as he sank to his knees and buried his face in his hands. "Paris is gone."

———

Don't stop now!
Continue the *Soul to Find* series with Jason & Kai's friends-to-lovers story, *Jason and the Storm*!

Followed by Mac & Paris's soft, swoony, and suspenseful romance, *Paris and the Reaper*.

JASON AND THE STORM
A SOUL TO FIND STORY

Jason and the Storm

Copyright © 2023 by Layla Reyne

Editing: Adam Mongaya

First Edition

October, 2023

Individual E-Book ISBN: 978-1-962010-14-6

Content Warnings: explicit sex; explicit language; violence.

ABOUT THIS BOOK

Jason is a perfectly average name.
And I'm a perfectly average human struggling to survive in a
very not average world.

My best friend Kai is extraordinary.
He is the kind of good I want to be.
The person I want to spend my life loving.

But if our world learns what Kai is hiding—what he truly is—he'll
be a target.
I have to get him out of here.
I have to protect him at all cost.
Even if that cost is my life.

*Jason and the Storm is a best friends-to-lovers M/M paranormal
romance in the Soul to Find series. It can be read as a standalone story,
but for the chronologically-minded, it falls before the last chapter of
Icarus and the Devil.*

ONE

"Jason, this is not a good idea."

Kai could count on one hand the number of times his best friend had had good ideas. This was not one of them. But like always, Jason was running full tilt into the fire.

"You don't have to keep doing this," Kai pleaded. "I get paid on Friday. That'll cover the rent."

"Good," Jason said as he continued to shove items in his pack. Dark clothing, bandana, headlamp, lock pick set, and two guns, one packing silver bullets, the other lead—the familiar tools of his trade. Kai's once too, before he'd gone straight. "You pay for this month's rent," Jason carried on. "What I make on this job should cover the rest of the year."

Sitting on the end of Jason's bed, Kai glanced around the room and into the hallway of their tiny Lakeside apartment. Yellowed walls from some prior renter's smoking habit, an ever-expanding brown stain on the ceiling from a leaking pipe upstairs, windows that were so mucked over from years of fog and salt water he could barely see out them. Even with better than average sight. This sad little box they found themselves trapped in was not worth Jason risking his life.

"Can it wait, then?" Kai said. "It's two days before the

anniversary of the Rift. It's barely been a week since Paris's dad died." He pointed at the dark, dangerous night outside. "Shit is nuts out there right now."

From his place behind the bar at Club Sutro, Kai had heard rumblings of a new war between Nature and Chaos, with mages and paranormals staking positions on Yerba Buena's front lines. Word was this war could be worse than the one that had caused the Rift thirty years ago, before either him or Jason were even born. In any event, a human like Jason—or like Kai pretended to be—had no place in it.

Jason was undeterred. "All the more reason to act now." He rooted around in his closet and returned with a pickaxe, rope, and windbreaker. A water approach, then. Fuck, was he headed into the Canyon Lands? Two days before the Rift anniversary? Unstable jetties littered with crumbling buildings, the fog-shrouded Canyon Lands were the definition of shit-going-down in Yerba Buena. "Vincent's death created a power vacuum. Half his shit is sitting unguarded, including the stash Moira has a line on."

Where did Kai even start? "One, that's Paris's stash now. You're stealing from our friend." The three of them were tight, Paris the best of them, the sweet-hearted son of the nastiest moth-erfucker in town. Until Vincent had blackmailed the wrong vampire. And while Kai was on the topic of vampires . . . "And two, Moira swore to anyone who'd listen after you two broke up that she would get her revenge. Why the fuck would you trust her now?"

"Paris is in hiding, and he wouldn't want Daddy's dirty money anyway." He finished shoving everything in his pack, then stood in front of Kai, hands on his hips. "As for Moira, she gets half of what I steal. It's in her interest too."

Kai closed his eyes and inhaled deep, biting back the litany of truths he wanted to spew.

She never loved you.

She can't be trusted.

You're just a human.

The raven doesn't like this.

Neither do I.

Don't leave us.

A finger curled under his chin, lifting it. "Open your eyes, Kai."

He could never tell Jason no. Jason with his dark messy hair, his big brown eyes, and his devil-may-care smile. A thing of beauty in this otherwise sad little box.

In Kai's sad, lonely world.

"I'll be fine," he said, thumb swiping away the tear that raced down Kai's cheek. "I always am."

"We can leave. We can just get out of here."

Jason's smile fell. "With what money?"

The truth finally slipped out. "I don't need money. I just need you."

"Kai, what—"

Shoving to his feet, he forced Jason back a step but kept him close, his hands on Jason's face, framing his cheeks and angling his gaze down to his. "I . . ." He swallowed hard, then, on a giant exhale, expelled the truth he'd been holding inside for far too long. "I fucking love you. I've always loved you. And if you walk out that door, I don't think you're ever coming back."

"Always the pessimist." Jason grinned, then did the last thing Kai expected. He crushed his mouth to Kai's, tongues and years of pent-up frustration tangling, Jason's desperate desire matching his own, the kiss everything Kai had dreamed of since he'd first laid his eyes on him.

Then, just as quickly, everything Kai had ever wanted was gone. Jason stepped out of his arms, but not completely. He left a hand over Kai's heart, over another truth that he and few others in Yerba Buena knew. "If I'm not back by tomorrow night, find me. I know you will."

TWO

Jason heaved the pickaxe over the edge of the cliff and prayed it caught.

A clank. A slide. A catch.

Thank fuck.

He tugged on the attached rope, testing the hold was secure, then, scrabbling with this other hand, hauled himself the rest of the way up and onto the slippery, uneven jetty he'd spent the past hour climbing.

Fucking finally.

Wrestling out of his pack, he shoved it aside, then flopped onto his back, gasping for air and flexing his aching fingers as he stared into the foggy nothingness above. The night sky was up there somewhere, maybe even stars, but he wasn't seeing it. Not tonight, and rarely ever in the Canyon Lands. One of the reasons the area was favored by all manner of criminals for their misdeeds. Jason wasn't surprised a mobster like Vincent Cirillo had done business here.

"It's about fucking time."

Jason closed his eyes and inhaled deep, wondering how he'd ever thought Moira's voice was sultry. More like sharp as her claws, either of which could eviscerate him on a dime. He couldn't lay there defenseless, not with her and who knows what other creatures lurking in the shadows. He dragged himself up to sitting and pushed his sopping wet hair out of his eyes. He glared at the vampire standing in front of him, hands on her hips, not a blond hair out of place, not the least bit winded. "I would've made it up here sooner if someone would've helped me."

"I needed to scout the area."

He bit his tongue, stifling the *Bullshit!* that wanted to roll off it. He'd barely finished mooring the boat to the exposed rebar at the base of the jetty when Moira had begun to scale the cliff face with relative ease, her claws making her footing sure, her small stature and speed making her impact minimal. She was at the top in no time. Meanwhile, every foot Jason scaled had been a fifty-fifty shot at death.

And every second he wasted moaning about it was another second someone—or something—could kill him. He gave himself a good, hard shake, then shoved up to his feet, ignoring his tired screaming muscles and his partner in crime's sneer. After gathering his things, he tucked the climbing gear back in the pack, withdrew his headlamp, and hefted the bag onto his shoulders. "All right, lead the way." He blinked, and she was gone again. "Fucking hell, Moira."

The best he could do was use his headlamp to follow the disturbance in the fog, hoping it was the right direction. But the farther they ventured into the Canyon Lands' ruins, the more Jason believed Kai had been right.

Kai usually was.

In no world were explosions, unstable ground, glowing eyes, and rumbling snarls better than the night Kai's kiss had promised. A kiss, a declaration they had danced around for years.

For the longest time, Jason had thought it would be Paris and Kai who'd end up together, and he'd been okay with that. Two purehearted people who clawed their way out of crime to find love together was the kind of happiness their shitty world needed. But that wasn't what either of his friends had wanted, and as

Kai's gaze had strayed to him more often, as their orbits had become inextricably entwined, he'd fallen for his best friend. A man too good for him by miles.

More than a man.

Which was why Jason had to do everything in his power to keep Kai safe, namely getting them the fuck out of Yerba Buena. They couldn't do that on what Kai made as a bartender or what Jason made pouring concrete. They needed the windfall that Moira, who zipped back in front of him, promised.

"Keep the fuck up," she hissed.

"Why don't you try keeping a human pace?"

She rolled her eyes, but when she started forward again, it was at a speed Jason could maintain.

"What exactly is in this stash?" he asked.

"Gold, like I told you. Other valuable shit."

Kai's voice rang in his head. *And Vincent thought it was secure here?*

He didn't pose the question to Moira as bluntly. "If this stash was so valuable, why didn't Vincent keep it in their private vault? In the condo at Sunset Hill?" He'd seen Paris access the family vault before, usually to steal from his father's supply of Daylight so they could turn around and trade it to vamps for cash and favors, usually at a better price than Vincent offered. That was how Jason had met Moira in the first place.

She turned down an alley and stopped in front of a metal door. "This is the last place anyone would look."

Jason glanced up at the squat building. Relatively intact compared to the high-rise rubble on either side and relatively secure, the door equipped with a bolt lock.

"Work your magic," Moira said, gesturing at the lock.

"Why can't you just rip the door open? Why do you need me here at all?"

She pressed a single finger to the door, and her flesh instantly sizzled. "Silver core," she said. "And because you can break in quietly, in case there's anyone inside."

He gulped. "And if there is?"

"You'll make a good sacrifice."

He gulped again, then glanced the way they'd come.

"You think you'll survive that trek back alone?"

Kai had been right. Bad idea from the word *go*. But Moira was right too. There was little hope in turning back now. He lowered his pack and dug out his lock pick set.

The lock took less than a minute to open. The Kai in his head poked again. *How important can it really be?*

Moira kicked the door open with her booted foot, no care for the racket it made, and Jason's alarm ratcheted up another level. He dropped the lock pick set back in his bag and retrieved both pistols before reshouldering the pack. Following her deeper into the building, he kept his eyes peeled for any other signs of life. Just rats as far as he could see or hear. Was that bread they were nibbling on? A stick of jerky one was dragging? There had to have been other life here at some point—not long ago.

A door creaked open at the end of the hallway. Jason glanced up in time to see Moira's blond hair waft behind her as she entered the room, as if a breeze blew toward her. A warm one, it seemed, a wall of heat hitting Jason just outside the door. Hot like a long-forgotten day in the sun, the last thing anyone would expect in the cold, foggy Canyon Lands. As far as Jason could tell, this building had no power, no artificial heat.

He firmed his grip on his pistols and rounded the doorjamb, through the heat and into the room, expecting a fire, some sort of spell protecting the stash . . . and found a pile of blankets in the corner.

No. Not just blankets. A person, their hands sneaking out to clutch the ends of the blanket, wrapping it more tightly around them, and their bare feet scraping over the floor as they shoved farther back into the corner. Their face was still hidden, most of their body too, but their shiver was obvious. As was the wave of heat that filled the room a moment later.

"What is this?" Jason asked the vampire who warily paced in

front of the person. "Where's the stash? The gold and jewels you promised?"

She jutted her chin at the corner. "There."

"Where? Behind them? In the walls?"

"No," she said. "He's the stash."

What. The. Fuck.

"Who is he?"

"My way out," she said with haunting reverence, a tone so different from her usual indifference that Jason startled. Then startled again when she lunged toward the person, claws and fangs out.

Jason lunged after her, his height eclipsing hers, shoving her off course and into the wall to the person's right. Jason moved between them, both guns pointed toward her. "What are you doing?"

She righted herself and began to pace—no, stalk—once more. "There's a rumor going around." She juked, and Jason juked with her, blocking her attempt to get past him. "If a vampire bites a phoenix, they become human again."

"A phoenix?" He whipped his gaze over his shoulder. And gasped.

The young man had freed a hand, and in doing so, the blanket over his head had fallen back. His brown skin was pale, his features so gaunt his skin barely clung to his bones, and his eyes . . . Fuck, his eyes glowed red and orange like the ball of light —fire—hovering over his palm, even as those same eyes shone with terror.

"He doesn't want this," Jason said, righting his gaze. Just in time for Moira to barrel into him, using her full supernatural power and speed to knock him off his feet. He hit the ground, his guns jostling from his grasp.

The phoenix screamed, and a fireball singed the hair on Jason's arm as it flew toward Moira—and missed. She was on him in the next blink, Moira all hisses and bared fangs, the phoenix barely holding her off with fireballs, the two of them struggling as heat filled the room.

Jason scrambled for the pistol with the silver bullets. He grabbed the gun, spun, and leveled it at Moira. "Leave him alone!" When she didn't show any sign of backing off, he fired.

Two bullets center mass.

She rounded on him, shrieking, her eyes wide with betrayal and her claws out, arms flailing, aiming to inflict some pain on him before the silver took her for good.

She didn't get the chance. A ball of fire swallowed her from behind and hastened her decent into ashes.

When the smoke cleared, the young man in the blankets was on his hands and knees on the other side of Moira's charred remains, struggling for breath, barely holding himself up. Jason hurried to his side, squinting against the heat, against the glowing sheen that rippled over his skin. "What can I do?"

He collapsed onto his side, panting. "Get out of here." He shivered, the tremble that wracked his body and breaths sounding as painful as it looked.

Jason gathered the blankets back around him, then laid a hand on his arm, keeping it there despite the searing heat seeping through the rough, thin material. "You shouldn't be alone." No one should be in such pain and misery by themselves. This man was obviously a shifter of some sort, and fuck, so was Kai. And Jason would want someone with Kai, God forbid he ever be in this state. It was what a good person would do. The kind of thing Kai would do. The kind of person he wanted to be for Kai.

"What's your name?" he asked the phoenix.

"Theo."

"Okay, Theo, what happens now?"

Haunted eyes of fire looked up at him. "I don't know."

"I'm not leaving you," he said, clasping Theo's hand.

He stayed by Theo's side—for Theo, for Kai, hoping like hell he'd get to be by Kai's side again when this was all over, and if he didn't, that someone else would be. That he'd done enough to put karma on Kai's side.

He stayed, even as the fire grew hotter, as flames raised his hairs and licked his skin, as the hot air forced shut his eyes and burned his lungs, as the snap and crackle of burning wood and Theo's screams filled his ears.

He stayed until it burned the very last thought from his mind.

Kai.

THREE

Kai banged on the door of the little cottage at the end of the winding, limestone road, hoping like hell he had the right one. In the dark, the nondescript cabins with their moss-covered roofs and forest green walls blended in among the overgrown cypress trees and coastal redwoods. There was nothing to distinguish one remote cottage from the next—no structural variations, no house numbers, no landscaping to speak of. Just a sea of green on the fog-shrouded Calera hills overlooking the ocean.

Nothing except the lingering scent of Kai's best friend and the corvids that had roosted in the trees around the cottage at the end of the road.

He lifted his fist to knock again, but the door swung open before his knuckles met wood.

"What?" the man who wasn't Paris demanded. He stood in the barely open doorway, one hand on the jamb, the other on the door, blocking anyone's entry or view into the cottage with his tall, rangy frame. His jet-black hair was ruffled, his dress shirt untucked and unbuttoned, a rosy blush highlighting his tan torso and face. From the anger shining in his violet eyes? Or something else?

"What do you want?" the shifter barked again at Kai. Between the eyes, the familiar flutter of his heartbeat, and the trees full of corvids outside, Kai could guess at what sort. And from his own research and what his friend had told him about the events of earlier that month, he could guess which one in particular.

"I need to speak to Paris," he told Cormac Kelley, the Talahalusi detective and reaper for the Monte Corvo ravens.

"Who?" Kelley feigned surprise, but the way his vibrating energy snapped from anger to alarm, his gaze scanning the area behind Kai and his fingers white knuckling the door, gave the truth away.

Kai had come to the right place. He squared his shoulders and pretended he wasn't a half foot shorter than the other shifter. "Paris Cirillo."

"I don't know who you're talking about."

"I know he's here."

"How's that?"

Kai's "Because I can smell him" collided with Paris's "Because I told him," the only human among them ducking under one of the detective's arms. Dressed in sweatpants and an unzipped hoodie, he barreled toward Kai, engulfing him in a hug and ignoring Kelley's indignant "You what?"

Kai supposed the detective's question could be directed at him too, and he would have answered if not for his best friend's big body muffling his reply. After the past twenty-four hours of sleepless hell, Kai took a moment to savor the closeness, to take comfort in the knowledge at least one of his best friends was safe. Paris squeezed him tight, his skin fire-warmed, and when he drew back, his human eyes were a lovely, welcoming shade of brown. Nothing like Kai's colored-lens version. "I missed you," Paris said to him, then to Kelley, "He's a friend. One of my best."

"No one is supposed to know you're here," Kelley said, strain in his voice. "Not after the last time."

Paris slid from Kai's arms to Kelley's side and gently patted his chest. "It's fine. We can trust him." He petted the shifter's chest in more than his usual tactile manner, and the detective seemed to settle a measure. "Now can we let him in before the witches get even more curious. The crows are audience enough."

Swayed, at least for the moment, the detective stepped back enough for Paris to drag Kai inside by the wrist. The cabin was cozy, a single room except for the enclosed space in the back corner that Kai assumed was the bathroom. To their right was a large, rumpled bed; in the middle of the space, where they stood, an oversize couch and chair; and in the other corners, a rustic kitchen and a table in front of a hearth. By the look of it, Paris had been here awhile. The jazz music he preferred played quietly from a device somewhere, the walls were splashed with vibrant colors, and vases of wildflowers dotted every surface, spilling their own color into the space. Paris spilling his colorful personality all over, something his overbearing, toxic father had never let him do. Kelley, who had also been here awhile judging by the case files strewn on the table, clearly didn't mind.

"What are you doing here?" Paris asked, drawing Kai's attention back to him.

"Better question," Kelley said as he crossed his arms. "Why didn't the crows alert me that you were here in the first place?"

Kai shifted his grip, clasping Paris's hand and giving it a squeeze. "You gotta promise not to be mad at me. This wasn't about you."

He looked confused, but in typical Paris fashion, his heart outweighed his head. "I missed you too much to be mad."

Kai wasn't sure that would hold, but he could practically feel the tension rolling off Kelley. He was protective of Paris, and for that, Kai was grateful and owed him the truth. He dropped Paris's hand and held his own out to the detective. "Because I'm one of you," he finally answered. "Kai Finley."

Paris's gasp was beat by Kelley's; as soon as he'd slipped his hand into Kai's, he'd known what he was. Or rather, his raven had. "What's your real name?" he asked.

"Kaimus. Finley was my father's surname. My mother's was Kasta."

"Haida?"

He nodded.

"I thought your kind were gone."

"Not gone. Just hiding."

"Cormac Kelley. It's an honor. And please, call me Mac."

Paris slid in between them, and his dark brows furrowed as his confused glare bounced between them. "I'm lost. Can someone please explain?"

"You didn't know he was a raven?" Mac said.

"Clearly not." He pointed at Kai's face. "And his eyes are brown."

"Not really," Kai said. He stepped away, withdrawing a case out of his pocket and, after setting it on the table, popped out his lenses and placed them inside. When he turned back around and met Paris's gaze, his friend's eyes grew wide. Then whipped to Mac's.

"They're not purple like yours."

"No, because he's a different kind of raven. He's special, Paris."

"Well, the *special* part I knew," Paris said, but the easy affection in his voice dwindled when he glanced back at Kai, and the hurt Kai hadn't wanted to see before dimmed his friend's lovely brown eyes. "But the other . . ."

Kai caught his hand again between both of his. "I'm sorry. With your dad, I couldn't risk him finding out what I was."

Beside them, Mac raked a hand through his hair. "Does anyone in YB know?"

"Our other best friend, Jason. He's the only person I told."

Paris's hand jerked in his. "Where is he?"

"That's why I'm here. I think he's in trouble." He shifted his gaze to Mac. "The raven knows he is."

"Jason's always in trouble," Paris said.

Truth, but this time it was different. So different that it had driven Kai the opposite direction from where his raven wanted to be. Had driven him to take desperate measures, to use the safe house address Paris had given him in case of emergencies, because this was one. And between what Paris had told him and what he'd looked up about Detective Kelley and his connections, there was no better group of people to understand that he needed to find his heart. He glanced back at Mac and lifted his free hand, splaying it over his chest. "It burns."

FOUR

"What is this place?" Kai asked as he waited for Mac to unlock the alley door of what looked like an out-of-business tasting room from the front. The street-facing windows were boarded up, the stoop was littered, and a pair of crows had perched on the peeling over-door sign. Not an unusual sight here in the Lost Valley. Most retail establishments had closed shop, and the handful that remained had been boarded up, no doubt in anticipation of the Rift anniversary and Samhain. If the howling wind and slanting rain that had picked up tonight on their way into the city were any indication, the next couple of weeks were going to be a nightmare.

"Base of operations," Mac answered. The complicated lock finally disengaged, and he pushed open the door. Kai followed him inside and down a hallway, Mac flicking on lights as they dripped their way into a larger area. The speakeasy vestiges remained—a bar and stools, some glasses and half-empty bottles on the backbar, a chaise pushed against one long wall, and a heavy curtain on a metal arch around the front door—but the tables in the open middle space had been pushed together to make workstations for computers, keyboards, and monitors, their wires snaking across the wood floors. The booths along the other long wall were ladened with weaponry—knives, crossbows, stakes, guns, and ammunition, lead bullets in marked boxes, silver ones in the stacks of lined and locked cases. A command center and armory in one.

He swiveled back to the bar where Mac was pouring a shot of vodka from a frosty bottle he must've pulled from an under-cabinet cooler. "I'll take one too." Mac shot him a violet glare but filled a second shot glass nonetheless. "I thought you were based in Talahalusi, at Monte Corvo."

"Exactly how much did Paris tell you?"

He tossed his soaked hoodie on top of Mac's trench and stood between two stools. "I knew that much from my own research. I had to know the lay of the land when I got here. The fact that you and Paris crossed paths . . ."

Mac pushed the shot glass across the bar. "Lucky coincidence?"

"I don't think so." He sipped the chilled liquor, surprised at its quality. But really, given the stockpile of weapons and other gear, he shouldn't have been. A good sign in more ways than one. "I'm glad he has you."

"Who?"

"Paris. He—" Approaching heartbeats, of both humans and shifters, stole Kai's words. Electronic beeps from the back door echoed down the hallway, then the scrape of the heavy metal door opening. A second of the storm raging outside, and then it was blocked out again by the door closing once more.

Despite the tension rippling through Kai, he took his cues from Mac, who didn't seem the least bit surprised. He didn't startle nor go on alert like he had at the cabin at Kai's arrival. Friendlies, then. As approaching footsteps grew louder, Mac tossed back the rest of his shot. "For the record, I don't have Paris."

Before Kai could press for an explanation, a ragtag group of people joined them in the tasting room, two of whom were famil-iar . . . yet not.

"Kai!" Icarus said as he led the rest of the group closer. "Mac didn't say it was you we were meeting."

Kai knew the courtesan from Club Sutro, where Kai officially worked the bar slinging drinks and Icarus unofficially worked the room slinging his own brand of escape. But this wasn't the same pink-haired, lace-wearing vampire from the last time Kai had seen him at the club. There was more actual red among the strands of pink, his favored lace, garters, and heels had been traded for an electric blue maxi skirt, a black leather coat, and combat boots, and his heart beat at a distinctly different rhythm. "You're not a vampire anymore?" he asked suddenly.

Icarus stopped short, his skirt swishing at the abrupt halt. "How'd you know that?"

"Because he's a shifter," Mac said from behind the bar before tossing back his shot of vodka.

A petite woman stepped past Icarus and right up to Kai. She had tan skin like his and Mac's and green hair styled in barrel curls that seemed impervious to the rain that had soaked everyone else. She lifted her hand to his cheek, and her mouth formed an O. Dazzling hazel eyes stared up at him. "Well, aren't you a pleasant surprise?"

Icarus tapped her shoulder. "Share with the class, babe."

"Not my secret to share," she said without looking away.

"Getting tired of that," grumbled the other man who had entered with them. Kai recognized him from Club Sutro too. How could he forget one of the few people who had, over the past few years, ordered barrel-aged whiskey, a rare and pricey commodity? And in Adam Devlin's case, on the same day each year, until this past year when he'd shown up again two days later looking for Icarus.

Adam was different too. The sadness that had hung over him was lessened, and the heat that had mysteriously warmed the air around him was gone. He hadn't exactly been a shifter before, but whatever had traveled with his soul, maybe what he sensed was traveling with Jason's now, was gone. He was human again. But no less gruff in the delivery of his words, even as he sidled to Icarus's side and slung an arm around his waist. "We're a day from the Rift anniversary. Time's ticking." His gaze bounced from Kai to Mac. "What's going on?"

Mac moved out from behind the bar, two more shot glasses in hand. One for Adam, the other for the mountain lion shifter who had been the last of the party. She'd hung back, surveying the scene. "I'd like to know that too," she said.

Mac jutted his chin in Kai's direction. "Tell them."

Kai swept his gaze over the group again. No, he didn't think Paris crossing these people's paths was a coincidence at all. "My —" He paused, unsure what to call Jason, how much to give away. While Paris seemed to know these people well, Kai was only really acquainted with one. He hedged. "My friend, Jason, he's human. And a smuggler."

"In legal terms, he's a thief and a fence." Mac handed Adam his phone. "I didn't have time to pull together a physical file."

"Why are we wasting our time, then?" Adam said, handing it back. "We've got a mile-long to-do list before tomorrow night, and petty criminals aren't on it."

The pixie, still closest to Kai, placed a hand on his chest. "Because this raven thinks his friend's a phoenix now. Jason was human before?"

Kai nodded as Adam, suddenly interested, untangled from Icarus and stepped closer. He recalled one night Club Sutro when Adam had told Icarus he used to be a cop. His sharp gaze and sharper "Explain" now were one hundred percent interrogator.

"He got a lead from a source on a 'stash' of Vincent Cirillo's somewhere in the Canyon Lands. 'Gold and jewels,' he was told. Enough money to get us out of—" Kai paused, then hedged again. "The situation we're in now. It didn't make sense to me."

"We know what kind of stash Vincent hid out there," the mountain lion said.

"Who was the source?" Adam asked him.

"A vampire he knew."

"Shit, another one."

"Word's getting around," Icarus said.

Adam raked a hand through his short brown and gray hair. "Without the entire story."

"Now I need an explanation," Kai said. He was losing the thread here while the one that tied him to Jason was stretching thin. He was running out of time.

"Adam was a phoenix," Icarus said. "I was a vamp." Lips pulled back, he clanked his teeth together in a simulated bite sans fangs.

"But you're both human now."

"Because their souls had a connection," the green-haired woman said. "And because I channeled the phoenix where it needed to go."

"Are you a witch?" Kai asked her.

"Not exactly," she said with an enigmatic grin. "I had help."

"Who's still gone," Adam said. "Any word from Robin?" he asked the woman shifter.

She shook her head.

"We may not need them," the green-haired woman said. "Not with you. Your souls have a connection?"

"Yes." He laid his hand over hers where it still rested on his chest. "It burns."

"I know." She gave him a pat, then slid her hand out from under his and glanced around at the others in the room. "We need to find him before someone else does. Before tomorrow night."

Mac withdrew his phone again, thumbed at the screen, then set it on a nearby table and waved everyone over. "These are the locations in the Canyon Lands that Paris remembered hearing his father mention."

The mountain lion tapped at three of the different X marks. "We've cleared those out already."

Adam gestured at the other two remaining. "Which leaves these, then."

Kai pointed at the more southern of the two. "That one," he

said, a flare of heat in his chest confirming his gut's instinct. "The raven knows it."

FIVE

Everything burned.

His eyes, his skin, his breath, his insides. And it burned even worse every time someone sneaked into the shell of a building he'd woken up in, every time he had to send a blast of heat in their direction to keep them back—the only defense mechanism he had with all his gear burned or buried beneath rubble.

The only relief was the wind and rain that whipped around him, the storm that called to him. He would close his burning eyes and turn his face up to the rain, to the cool water that reminded him of the blue-green of Kai's eyes behind his contacts.

Kai.

He would be frantic by now. Jason had tried half a dozen times to stand, to crawl, to move somewhere else—anywhere else— where he might be able to get his hands on a phone and call his friend, but he was so weak. His head spun, his insides boiled, and his outsides glowed. With no clothes or other coverings in sight, he would be exposed. He'd tried to call out to one of the earlier intruders and make a trade for a phone, but when the intruder had flashed his fangs, Jason hadn't had any choice but to crisp him like he'd done the other vampires who'd tried to attack.

Fucking Moira. What had she gotten him into?

Another gust of wind blew through the cavernous ruin, and Jason closed his eyes, savoring the cool blanket that surrounded him, imagining it was Kai's arms. Or the wings Kai had only ever told him about. White and cold like the snow he'd never seen before either.

Was Kai up there somewhere now? Sailing and scouting to find him? Putting himself in danger because he'd fallen for another bad idea? Fuck, Jason would never forgive himself if Kai got hurt or captured because of him. But at the rate he was going —burning—he didn't think there'd be much time left.

A *crack* to his left.

He righted his head and opened his eyes, peering into the darkness. He was disoriented, the distance and sharpness still new.

A glint of white, a hiss, a flash of movement.

Fuck, another one.

He shifted back behind the rubble he'd leaned against and balled his fists, willing the fire inside him to gather inside them. He peeked over the pile of cement, metal, and wood, searching for this target. The vampire was closer, stalking with its fangs and claws out. He raised one fist, preparing to fire, when a cacophony of *caws* and *kraas* cut through the silence, and in the next blink, the crows and ravens were there, sailing through the gaps in the building where walls and windows used to be, creating a barrier between him and the vampire.

And on the other side of the wall of black birds, growls.

There was a scuffle, more growls, then the vampire's scream and an unfamiliar voice calling, "First vamp down."

First? There was more than one? *Fuck!*

And were these rescuers, or was someone else after him?

Was Kai with them? The birds were corvids, after all, but he didn't see any white feathers among the black. Still, hope swelled —until gunfire popped off. Jason readied the fireballs again. "Second vamp down," called a voice he did vaguely recognize but couldn't place.

A chorus of "Clears" followed, and then so did the birds, flying up to perch on the various outcrops and rebar from the decimated building. All except one, the largest raven with purple eyes, that lighted on the top of the rubble pile Jason was crouched behind.

His voice wobbled as he asked, "Are you here for me?" He'd heard about certain raven shifters in these parts—the reapers.

The big black bird let out a loud *Kraa*, and Jason's heart tumbled.

"Jason!"

Then soared. He whipped his gaze back in the direction of the previous scuffle and saw Kai running in his direction. Jason struggled to try to stand, wanting—needing—to wrap his arms around his world.

But someone wrapped theirs around Kai first, halting him from falling to Jason's side at the last minute. Someone Jason recognized from Club Sutro and dealings with Paris.

Icarus. A vampire.

He fisted another fireball.

"Stop!" shouted a deep voice, an older white man running between them. "He's not a vampire anymore."

Not a—

"They're friendlies, Jason," Kai said. "Friends of Paris's." Then to Icarus, "Let me go!"

"Let her assess things first."

"Her?" Jason croaked.

"Me." From behind the group appeared a shorter woman. Her nose was pierced, her ears too, and her hazel eyes were kind as she kneeled beside him. She laid a hand on his arm and didn't recoil or react to the heat at all. "I'm here to help you."

The thing inside him flapped its wings, and *Mother* rattled around in his head, though this person was definitely not the woman who had abandoned him as a kid.

"Is he about to flame out?" the older man asked, now guarded by a mountain lion on one side and a coyote on the other.

"No, he's in recovery," the woman answered.

Recovery? "But it hurts," Jason blew out on a breath of hot air.

"I know. The phoenix is still digging in, healing you. There was a fire?"

He nodded. "The building came down on top of us."

The older man inhaled sharply and turned away, but not before Jason caught the terror and heartache in his blue-gray eyes. Icarus went to his side, releasing Kai to slide in beside the woman. "Can I touch him?"

"I think so."

He reached out a hand, cupping Jason's cheek, and the cool relief that swept through him was a million times better than the rain. Kai slumped toward him, giving him more relief, and wrapped his arms around him. "I'm here," Kai muttered into his hair. "I've got you. I've got you."

The watchful raven hopped down on their level, and the stranger with Icarus joined them. "We need to get him out of here," he said.

"Adam," Icarus said, "give her a minute."

"We don't have a minute. There'll be more, and now she's exposed too."

She, whatever her name, paid them no mind, her hazel gaze still on him. "You have a choice, but you need to make it now." She glanced at Kai. "Both of you."

"What choice?" Jason asked from where he was nestled under Kai's chin.

"One day," she said to Kai, "if you stay by his side, you will have to wrap your wings around him and deliver the fire back to me. And on that day, he will be human again, and you will become a raven like him." She nodded toward the black one by their side.

"A reaper?"

She nodded. "That day can be today. The phoenix and your magic will heal him, and you will save him from flaming out without you by his side in the future."

Jason glanced between the black raven and Kai. "You don't want to be a reaper?"

"My tribe . . . We turned away from it generations ago because . . ."

"Because your kind brought down the first phoenix for me," the woman said.

"And burned an entire village in the process."

"What happens if we don't do it today?" Jason said.

"Adam trains you to live with the phoenix and harness it for us."

"I thought you needed them back," Icarus said to her.

"The ones who are about to flame out," she said. "But we caught Jason at the beginning. You could use the firepower *and* a smuggler."

"For the phoenixes you do need," Adam said.

"Exactly, and I can use Kai's magic to channel those back."

"Without him turning to a reaper?" Jason said.

She turned her gaze back to them. "Yes, because it's your soul, your phoenix that his raven is connected with. Your souls will travel together. Your choice. Make it now."

Kai shifted and opened his mouth to speak, to no doubt try to save Jason more pain, but Jason spoke first. "I want to do good. I want to be good for you. I can do this. We can do this."

"Are you sure?"

"Sure that I want more time with you? That I don't want you to become something you aren't just for my sake?"

"But I would. I would do anything to save you."

"I know, baby, but I can finally make this life good for us." He smiled. "So long as you promise to be there by my side."

Kai lowered his forehead to his, his cool breath a balm to fiery storm inside him. "Always," he promised.

SIX

They waited out his recovery and the Rift anniversary on an outparcel of Monte Corvo, on the banks of the vineyard's reservoir, close to water and far from any people or structures. If the phoenix got away from him, minimal damage would ensue before Kai could work his magic.

But Kai hadn't needed to, and for the first time since that fateful night, Jason woke feeling like himself. A little warmer than usual, his senses more attuned than they had been before, but he didn't feel any aches and pains, and he felt in control of his mind and body.

He only remembered bits and pieces of the past few days—his head in Kai's lap on the harrowing drive out of YB in a vintage Camaro; witches, Adam, and the green-haired woman named Mary fussing over him; corvids circling overhead and coyotes roaming the fields around them; Kai snuggled against his side.

Kai wasn't by his side now, but Jason could feel him close. Eking open his eyes, he squinted against the daylight, adjusting to the bright Talahalusi sunshine before opening them fully.

And gasping at the sight above him. Against the clear blue sky, a snow-white raven soared. Kai, more beautiful than Jason had imagined. His wings spread wide, his spade-shaped tail feathers fluttering with the breeze, his blue-green eyes shining bright. There was freedom and peace in the way he glided and joy in the way he barrel-rolled with the two black ravens flying with him. Playing. Jason laughed out loud, the joy contagious. *This* was what he had wanted for his friend. For the man he'd spent years falling in love with, who had bound his soul to Jason's for good.

His laughter drew Kai's attention. The white raven circled once more with the others, then broke off and flew in Jason's direction, diving low before leveling out and gliding over him. Close enough for Jason to skate his fingertips over Kai's soft underside as he flew over. He sailed into the nearby trees, and by the time Jason flipped onto his side to look in that direction, Kai emerged in human form sans clothes.

Jason whistled low as he looked his fill. Kai wasn't a large man —average height, lean muscles, unruly dark curls—but he moved with a confident, attractive grace that put everything about him in perfect proportion. Freedom in the way he walked, same as the way he flew.

"Don't know when I'm going to get used to that," Kai said as he folded onto the ground beside him.

"Me ogling you?"

"No, you've been doing that for years." He placed his hand just above Jason's chest. "The waves of heat radiating off you."

He rotated onto his back and lifted the end of the blanket covering him. "Get under here with me, and I'll share."

Kai didn't hesitate to slide in beside him, the length of him fitted against Jason's side, arm over his belly, head on his shoulder. It was the way they'd occasionally snuggled when the heat went out in their crappy apartment, the way they snuggled nonstop the past few days.

No lack of heat now, but a delightful lack of clothing. He skated his fingertips up and down Kai's spine, relishing the closeness, the softness of his skin, all of it *more* than it had ever been before. "You look so happy up there, in the air."

"I am."

"It's safe here?"

He nodded. "They reinforced the boundaries after a recent breach."

"When's the last time you flew?"

"When I first flew down to YB. It feels like a lifetime ago."

He trailed a hand over Kai's shoulder blades, imagining the wings there. "But it feels good now?"

Kai's smile tickled his skin. "Better than I remember. How about you?"

"Good today. The phoenix isn't trying to claw in or out of me for a change. I feel like me, mostly."

"Any—" He stopped, voice a momentary wobble, but at Jason's squeeze, started again. "Any regrets?"

He glanced down, meeting the cautious blue-green ones staring up at him. "Only that I haven't kissed you yet." He hauled Kai closer and up but stopped short of claiming Kai's mouth. "But only if you still want me. I love you, but I don't want you to ever feel trapped, like I made this decision for—"

He brushed his lips across Jason's, so gentle Jason's words died on a shiver. "I love you too, and I've always wanted you. I will *always* want you." Then not gentle at all as he crushed their mouths together, freedom flowing between them, both of them taking what they'd wanted for so long.

Kai kissing him deep and thorough, then yanking the blanket under Jason to roll him on top.

Jason taking the cue and trailing kisses down Kai's neck, over his chest, throwing off the blanket and taking Kai's stiff cock in his mouth, sucking and fondling until Kai was writhing beneath him, at the edge, his fingers curled in Jason's hair, his pants and moans filling his ears.

Crawling back up the beautiful, quaking length of him, rolling onto his side and bringing Kai with him, front to front so Jason could wrap his hand around both their cocks, stroking long and slow, building their pleasure together.

Kai's hand covering his, ramping up the pace, their hips

rocking in time, the heat flowing between them, balanced and in check even as their careened toward their climax.

Their kisses growing wild, and their *I love yous* colliding with the peace they'd finally found together, the freedom, their future on the other side of the storm.

———

Mac & Paris, up next!
Want to know what sweet Paris and grumpy Mac were up to before Kai interrupted? Carry on to *Paris and the Reaper*!

PARIS AND THE REAPER

A SOUL TO FIND NOVEL

ABOUT THIS BOOK

I was given the name Paris at birth.
So far, I've lived up to it; or rather, down to it.
Too pretty, too unfocused, too easy a target.
My father even tried to sacrifice me.

And then I was saved by a beautiful, haunted man.

Mac is a reaper; he delivers lost souls.
But when he came for mine, I wouldn't let go.
And now I can hear other souls too.
I can help him. Love him, if he'll let me.

Assuming we survive a conspiracy to bring Chaos through the veil.

Mac says souls get what they deserve.
If I do enough good, then maybe I can be worthy of his.
Maybe I can hold on to him and our bond—forever.

Paris and the Reaper is a soft, swoony, and suspenseful M/M paranormal romance. It features a grumpy raven shifter afraid to love and lose again and the sweet, cursed human who makes him want to risk it all.

PART ONE

PARIS

ONE

Paris and pain were old friends.

His first memory was of pain, his lungs burning as his mouth and nose filled with water, as he struggled against the hands that held him under. That was the first time his father had tried to kill him.

Pain had accompanied every encounter with his father since.

The force of his closed fist, the sting of his open palm, the pointy tips of his loafers that pummeled him when he was down.

The sharper sting of his words that buried him deeper.

Why are you such a fool?

You're too soft.

Put away those stupid brushes.

I can't believe she gave her life for you.

The last was his father's favorite, a constant reminder of the guilt Paris lived with every day and that his father never let him forget.

They were also the last words Vincent had uttered when he'd shoved him into the seemingly frail arms of the small, bearded man in a waist apron. Paris tried to run but barely made it two steps before the stranger had stopped him in his tracks with nothing but his glowing red eyes.

Paris had known then that this was another of Vincent's attempts to kill him. And as he lay spread eagle on a cold hard altar, his hands and feet bound, blood seeping from searing cuts along the insides of his arms and thighs, Paris thought maybe his father had finally succeeded.

Beside the altar, the once small man stood taller than any person Paris had ever seen. No, not a person. A monster—a giant—with those same glowing red eyes, but where he'd had a coarse, curly beard before, he now had a nest of writhing snakes that feasted on Paris's open wounds. As they sank their fangs into his muscles and sucked his blood, their master sucked more of his life—his soul—to feed the shimmering orbs of magic that grew bigger and brighter in the air above his hands.

He spoke in tongues Paris didn't recognize, but as his voice escalated into louder more urgent chants, the pain escalated too, the snakes biting harder. Paris's soul cried out in his ears, joined by other souls crying out too. Each new one like a knife carving up through the altar beneath him, into his skin, creating a path for the souls to burrow inside and chilling him to his core. Magnifying the pain. All those souls being ripped through him. It was torture beyond anything his father had ever inflicted on him.

I can't believe she gave her life for you.

Except that.

He opened his eyes and blinked through the pain and tears that clouded his vision. He searched for the stars above, for that place a nanny had once told him his mother had gone to the day he'd been born. Bright, shining hope was there for one brief instant, the fog breaking long enough for him to glimpse the only love he'd ever known, the love he'd finally get to meet soon, before the dense gray clouds rolled back in and took the light away.

And brought something dark with them.

Something darker even than his father's hands holding him under the water. Something that intended to take his soul and all the other souls screaming with his. Something that intended to wreak chaos on Yerba Buena and beyond.

The orbs in the monster's hands burned so bright that Paris had to squint against their blinding glare.

New voices—words he recognized—cut through the chants.

"Does anyone see him?"

"He's on the altar!"

KRAA.

Roaring, the monster hurled the relatively dimmer of the two balls of fire the direction of the voices.

And then another, different kind of darkness flew at the altar—an undulating mass of black, the fluttering of wings sending a cool breeze wafting across Paris's prone body. The flock of black birds dive-bombed the monster, plucking away his snakes one by one. Paris shouted with each painful yank of their fangs out of his skin; the giant shouted louder with each subject ripped from his body and cast aside until none were left.

Until the biggest black bird of all, a giant raven, flew talons-first at the monster's eyes.

He howled and staggered beside the altar, trying to swat the raven away with the hand not holding the magical orb, but the raven wasn't backing down. He came at the giant, again and again, while other voices shouted in the background.

"Mac, watch the globe."

"We need to neutralize it."

"Adam, take the shot!"

KRAA.

The familiar sound of gunfire rent the air and fear rocketed up Paris's spine. He didn't want the raven to be hit. But the bullet, it turned out, was the least of their worries. Before it reached the monster, the fireball in his hand exploded, engulfing him and singeing Paris's skin.

"No!" Paris shouted, his voice rough, barely a whisper, but no less urgent, no less filled with fear for the fate of his rescuer.

He scrunched closed his eyes and screamed through the pain

and fear until the heat began to recede, until cool air wafted over him once more.

A gentle weight landed on his chest, and for a moment it felt like freedom, like his soul could breathe knowing the raven had lived and would carry him to the love waiting for him above.

But then another voice called to him. *Help me.*

And another, then another, more and more until the cacophony of pleas were as loud as the thunderous waves that crashed against the cliffs beneath the condo he called home.

He shook his head, trying and failing to block out the noise.

KRAA!

He opened his eyes and locked his gaze with the violet one staring down at him. The sense of freedom was gone, but in its place was a lifeline Paris's soul grabbed onto with both hands.

The raven jumped, its giant wings fluttering.

KRAA!

Paris didn't let go, even as pain ricocheted through his head and darkness clouded the edge of his vision. The riot in his ears coalesced into those same two words, over and over, the only two he could manage before his own world went dark.

"Help me."

———

Paris liked soft things.

In a world that was sharp and brutal, soft was the sensory antithesis of violence. The buttery leather of his car seats, the silky bristles of fresh paint brushes, the plush warmth of cotton jersey, the delicate threads of satin and lace.

The gentle brush of skin on skin. His best friends' arms hooked through his. A courtesan's tender touch. The backs of someone's fingers stroking his temple, oh so softly, and ruffling his hair.

He moved to tilt his head, to chase after the feather-light

touch, but barely managed to angle his chin before pain lanced through him. His head, his arms, his legs were all on fire.

Fire.

Like the globes that had hovered above the monster's hands.

As the horrific, terrifying past came rushing back, so did nausea and bile, rocketing up his throat. He shifted, needing to sit up before he choked on the sick, but fucking hell, the pain.

Far beyond anything his father had ever inflicted on him.

But his father had done this, hadn't he? Had offered him as some kind of sacrifice. Had almost succeeded in killing him this time.

"Fuck," he cursed, and even that hurt.

"I've got you," someone said, their voice deep and calm, soft in its own way. Like their fingers had been. "Let's get you on your side."

Gritting his teeth, Paris let the person help roll him. Just in time, the pain and his roiling stomach conspiring to expel what little was in it. He couldn't remember the last time he'd eaten. Couldn't fathom it now, the thought of food sending another wave of bile up and out and into a bucket.

Shuddering, he struggled for breath, for some relief from the anvils in his head and the needles in his limbs.

"You get it all out?" the voice asked.

He nodded weakly and—sweet mercy—was rolled onto his back again. A wet cloth was swiped over his lips then laid across his forehead, and with the soft, cool dampness came the needed respite, enough for him to breathe, to open his eyes and look up into the dark ones above him. Gone were the violet eyes, gone were the black feathers and hooked beak, gone were the talons that had scratched out the monster's eyes. But Paris was certain the man above him, with his tan skin, sharp nose, and black hair was the same as the raven who'd saved him.

"It hurts," he told the stranger.

"Where?"

Paris chuckled at the inane question, then winced when the motion brought more daggers, in his head worst of all.

"Hold on," the raven said, then, leaving the cloth on his forehead, covered his ears with his hands. "Need some help in here!" he called, his raised voice thankfully muffled.

So too was the voice of someone else who entered the room, the two of them conversing in what to Paris were nothing more than murmurs. But at least they were the only voices, the ones in his head from before blissfully quiet. Gone for good, he hoped. Now if the raven could just get rid of his pain too. More hands were laid on him, more voices in the room, then a chant began and memories of the monster returned.

He struggled where he lay, and the hands on him pressed harder, hotter, a wave of heat rolling from the tips of his toes up his body. Higher and hotter. "Help me," he pleaded with the raven.

The hand over his right ear shifted. "That's what they're trying to do. They're burning out the poison. Just hold on a little longer."

He stared up at the shifter asking for his trust. "Who are you?"

"Icarus sent us."

Guilt tore at his insides, sharper than any pain that tore at the rest of his body. "Is he—"

"Safe," the raven said with a wry grin. "You are too."

"My father?"

"Doesn't know where you are."

He'd look around if he could, but the raven's hands held his head steady, held him just out of the lake of fire that threatened, that inched higher with each chanted syllable. "Where am I?"

"With the Redwood Coven."

"Where? How far—"

"You're in Encinal. Near the shellmound."

Clear across Yerba Buena from the family compound of condos. Clear across the Bay too. On consecrated ground that surely his father was smart enough to avoid. He let out a relieved breath, and the ironic twist of the raven's lips smoothed into a soft curve Paris ached to paint.

Soft like the fingers that took up stroking his temples again. "Now, let the witches do their work."

"Don't leave me."

"I've got you."

As the heat rose, Paris closed his eyes and focused on the soft sheets beneath him, on the cool rag across his forehead, on the gentle fingers caressing his temples. Let the sensory anthesis carry his mind away while his body fought what he didn't fully understand yet.

The raven said he was safe.

He believed him. For now.

<h1 style="text-align:center">TWO</h1>

Paris was lost.

Wherever he was, it didn't look like any part of Yerba Buena he knew. Not Sunset Hill where he lived, not the Lakeside apartments where his best friends, Kai and Jason, stayed. Not Sutro Hill, the Lost Valley, the Manor, the Canyon Lands or anywhere in between. He'd been raised in YB, was familiar with every nook and cranny of his hometown. He was as much a child of YB's mist and hills as he was the only son of Vincent Cirillo.

This tree-lined street of single-family cottages did not exist in YB. And nowhere in his world was the sky above, the buildings around him, and the ground beneath his feet varying shades of violet.

Violet.

Something clicked. Like that instant in his favorite jazz tune when the first instrument on stage made itself known. A single spotlight on the piano, its notes high and lilting, calling to him.

For what, he wasn't sure yet.

He followed the street to the next intersection and glanced right—more houses—then left, spying what looked like a strip mall just up the street. They had those—and houses like those around him—in the suburban areas outside of YB, especially south in Portola.

Was that where he was?

He picked up the pace as he approached the shopping center. It was brighter than on the tree-lined street, but the violet hues persisted. They gave the pale bearded man in the grocery store apron a pale eerie glow as he shagged carts in the parking lot.

A shiver raced up Paris's spine. Another instrument joined the piano, a bass guitar with its deep, dark rhythm—a counterpoint.

A warning.

Paris hung back at the corner of the building, watching as the bearded man initiated a conversation with one man, then another who passed him in the parking lot. When a young woman approached the car he was closest to, he didn't speak. He just glared at her, his blue eyes burning with thinly veiled malice.

Worried for the woman's safety, Paris moved to step forward.

She whipped her gaze in his direction, and the boom of drums on Paris's mental stage drowned out his gasp.

Blond hair fell around the woman's bruised and battered face —her nose broken, her lip split, one eye bloody around a brown iris.

Human, then.

Her lips moved, but no sound came out.

That didn't matter; Paris could hear her in his head. Her two words like the final instrument joining a quartet—the trumpet wailing.

Help me.

Paris woke with a start, in full-on panic mode, choking for breath, ears ringing, scrambling to push himself upright. His hand landed on something wet. Slipped. Then he slipped too, his limbs failing to hold him, the pain that shot through them too much to fight the tangled sheets and the gravity dragging him off the side of a padded table to the floor.

His elbow hit something metal on the way—a bucket that went skidding across the wooden floor—and Paris howled. Clutching his elbow, he flopped onto his back, unable to do anything else, and stared up through tears at a ceiling that wasn't his, the plain white drop tiles a far cry from the dark and starry night he'd painted above his own bed.

Footsteps rushed toward him, their vibration and sound finally cutting through the ringing in his ears. He twisted his head, found the door, and scurried as fast as he could on his back the opposite direction, grabbing the metal bucket as he went. He rammed against the far wall and twisted onto his side, clutching the bucket in front of him, the only protection he had against the bearded monster coming for him.

Only it wasn't the monster of his nightmares that appeared in the doorway. "Oh, hey!" said a stranger with tan skin and black hair. His wide eyes were black too. "You're awake." Something about him seemed familiar, the sharp nose, the thin-lipped smile, the long lanky limbs. If not for his height and black eyes, Paris might have mistaken him for Kai, but that wasn't right either. He approached cautiously, hands up, palms out. "I'm a friendly," he said as he kneeled in front of him. "How'd you get all the way over there?"

"Where am I?" Paris gritted through clenched teeth as he tried to use the wall to lever his torso upright.

The other man clasped his shoulder, steadying him and helping him the rest of the way to sitting. "I've got you."

I've got you.

"The raven," Paris croaked, the similarity clicking into place, the words reminding him of his rescuer. "Where is he?"

"He had somewhere else he needed to be." The stranger eased the bucket from Paris's white-knuckled grip. "He asked me to stay with you."

Hands free, Paris crossed his arms over his chest and came

into contact with the bandages covering his arms. He glanced down at his legs peeking out from the sheets still tangled around his waist. Bandaged too.

All of it rough.

Like the woman's face from his dream.

Like the past however many hours of his life.

He wished he had the bucket back, nausea threatening. He tugged at the bandages instead, a distraction and an end to the immediate violence against his skin.

Long-fingered hands covered his. "You need to leave those on," the stranger said. "Your wounds are still healing."

He shuddered at the reminder of the searing heat. A sharp contrast to the cold floor beneath him and the cool wall at his back. He gathered more of the sheet around him, the chilly shock working its way inside.

"You're cold?"

He nodded.

The man stood and crossed the room to the cabinet that was near the door. When he returned, he carried a stack of gray clothing. "Icarus said to bring you these." He handed the soft sweats to Paris. "He said they would make you feel better."

His eyes watered again, and he clutched the clothing to his chest. The courtesan was always so good to him. Despite being a vampire, Icarus had never scared him, had never committed a single violent act against him. Unlike Paris, who had given his father's warlock Icarus's contact info, knowing nothing good could come of it, knowing their promises to keep Icarus safe were probably a lie, but having no choice, his father's knee on his neck at the time. He should've let him end it then.

A mug appeared in his periphery. "How about some tea?"

Paris accepted the cup, sniffed the drink inside, and, relatively confident it was just an herbal blend, sipped it slowly. It coated his throat and made it easier to get the words out. "Who are you?"

"Liam Kelley." He shifted out of his crouch and onto his ass, sitting cross-legged across from him. "Mac's brother."

"Mac?"

"Cormac. The raven."

The raven. The witches. More of it was coming back to him. "We're in Encinal?"

Liam nodded. "With the coven."

Paris could hear muffled voices, other movement in whatever building they were hiding in. "What are they doing?"

"Packing. They tend to stay on the move."

Paris had heard that about the witches. He recalled the map in his father's command center, little green pins identifying each coven's location. Had there been one in Encinal? He couldn't say. Everyone knew the nearby shellmound was haunted. That the area was consecrated. But did Vincent know the witches hid nearby too? Would he find him here? "Where will I go?" he asked Liam.

"With them, for now."

He held the sweats closer, his whole immediate world. But what of the rest? "Can I get a phone?"

"'Fraid not. Mac's orders."

"I need to check on my friends. If my father—"

"Your father has his hands full right now. He probably hasn't even realized you're missing."

"But I was supposed to meet them. They'll be worried."

"It's the week before the Rift anniversary. I doubt they'll blink."

Harsh. "I like your brother better."

Liam's laugh filled the room. "You might be the first person who's ever said that." He stood and offered Paris a hand. "Think you might be able to eat something? Mac said it's probably been a while. You're human; magic will only get you so far."

The thought of food didn't turn his stomach the way it had earlier. Maybe the tea was helping. "I can try." He held the sweats in one hand and took Liam's in the other. It was warmer than Paris expected. "You're a shifter too?"

"The whole family is." Liam helped him to his feet and, once

Paris was relatively steady, left him leaning against the wall. "Get changed, then give me a shout. I'll be right outside. Is there anything else you need?"

He shook his head, but just before Liam reached the door, an idea occurred to him. A distraction—an outlet—he'd welcome. "Liam," he called, and when the raven's brother turned, he added, "Paintbrushes."

Liam paused over the threshold, dark brow furrowed. "What?"

"Can I get some paintbrushes? And some paints, please. Any colors will do."

"Yeah," he said, smiling. "We can do that."

He disappeared out the door, and Paris exhaled, eyes closed, until the bruised and battered face of the woman from his dream appeared behind his eyelids again. "Purple!" he shouted, hoping it wasn't too late to amend his request. "I need purple paints."

THREE

Paris glanced at the phone in his hand and thought Jason would be proud. Maybe even Kai a little too. Kai had worked smuggling jobs with Jason before he'd gone straight and become the best bartender in town. Paris doubted Jason would ever give up the life. Despite the danger, and despite Kai's frequent objections, the thrill of the steal kept Jason going.

Paris understood that feeling, today especially. A bolt of excitement had raced up his spine as he'd successfully picked the pocket of the witch who'd been fussing over him. It was a smaller device, ultra lightweight, not the heavy sort you'd immediately notice missing. Nevertheless, Paris figured he didn't have long.

He slipped around the corner of the building they were hiding in and checked the location of the sun. Close to the western horizon; it would be sunset before long. Kai would already be at work. Good, he wouldn't be there to talk Jason out of the favor Paris hated to ask. He flipped open the phone and punched in his friend's number.

"Hello?" Jason answered, sounding half asleep. "Who is this?" he asked, no doubt confused by the unfamiliar number.

"Jason, it's Paris. I had to borrow a phone."

"Paris?" Bed springs squeaked, and Paris imagined his friend wiping the sleep from his big brown eyes. "Where are you? We were worried when you didn't show at the club last night."

"Dad tried to kill me again."

"He *what*?"

"Monster, snakes, altar, it was a whole thing." He'd spent the better part of the day painting out his trauma on the walls of the makeshift infirmary where he'd been treated, which was the only reason he could mention the ordeal now without throwing up. "I'm fine," he added before Jason could work himself into a fury on his behalf. He'd stepped into the fray between Paris and his father before; he didn't have to this time. "Some of Icarus's . . . friends . . . rescued me. Are you and Kai okay? Did Dad or anyone come after you?"

"We're fine too," Jason said. "And no, we haven't seen your dad or any of his crew. But Paris, should we be worried? Do I need to go get Kai from work? Do we need to come get you?" His voice escalated in volume with each sentence, uncharacteristic anxiety pushing his devil-may-care friend fully awake. "What's going on?"

Paris rested back against the wall. "Dad probably thinks I'm dead. You should be fine too. I just needed to be sure."

"Where are you?"

"Encinal, for now, but I think we're moving soon."

"Shit feels weird, Paris. Something's going down."

"It's just the Rift anniversary," he lied to himself and his friend.

If the whole sacrifice thing didn't give away the weirdness, the ramp up in his father's operations would have. He'd spent most of his days in the command center, barking orders Paris could hear through the walls, usually at his pet warlock, Atlas, who Paris was beginning to believe didn't sleep given all his comings and goings.

"When will you be back?" Jason asked.

"I don't know. Dad needs to keep thinking I'm dead. Which is why I need to ask for a favor."

"What do you need?" Jason replied without hesitation.

"You know Maxine Hill?"

"The vampire who works the door at Club Sutro?"

"That's her. Her dad's human. He's in hospice at YB Gen. He doesn't have long, and she needs Daylight to visit him."

After the Rift, that day thirty years ago before he, Jason, or Kai were born, that Paris had only read about in the books his tutors brought him, when Nature and Chaos had gone to war with YB as the epicenter, hospice had become the most locked-down ward at any hospital. Too many nearly dead bodies that could be used for evil. Vampires were at the top of the list of excluded visitors, which was why hospice visiting hours were only during the day when vampires couldn't be out. Unless they'd ingested Daylight, a magic-brewed potion that Vincent kept on hand for his own army of vamps. And that Paris had pilfered small amounts of whenever the opportunity presented itself. Never enough for Vincent to notice, but enough for those who needed it, like Icarus had in order to protect someone he loved and like Maxine did to visit her dying father.

"And you've been supplying her," Jason said.

"I was supposed to deliver her next batch last night."

"Where is it?"

"In my private wine locker at Benton's."

Jason laughed. "You think they're gonna let me into a place like that? Breaking into your condo would've been easier."

He maybe had a point. Paris couldn't recall a single pair of jeans Jason owned that weren't ripped, and ripped denim was not the recommended attire for one of the nicest restaurants in town. But he also couldn't recall Jason ever meeting a lock he couldn't pick. "Jason."

His friend's laughter subsided. "What?"

"You're the best smuggler in Yerba Buena."

"Charmer." Paris could hear the smile in his voice. "How much does she owe you?"

"Tell her it's on the house for being late."

"You're a damn softie, Cirillo."

You're too soft.

"So I've been told." More times than Paris could count.

"That wasn't meant as an insult," Jason said, his voice gentle and sincere. "It's what makes you one of the best people I know. You help others, you protect them in your own way. You do the thing your dad promises and never delivers."

His friend's words chased away some of the chill that had wound back into his soul. Made him believe what he'd been doing was right. That he was right. Maybe he was soft, but that softness, in himself and the things around him, was how he survived the violence. Violence he was asking his best friend to step into.

"Jason, if it's too risky—"

"Didn't you just say I was the best smuggler in YB?"

"Thank you," Paris said with a small, relieved smile. "Give my love to Kai."

"Will do," Jason said. "And in case it's not obvious, I'm glad your dad didn't succeed. Love you, buddy."

"Love you too."

He flipped shut the phone just as the door behind him swung open, the witch from earlier poking her head out. "Oh, there you are."

"Sorry, just needed some air," he lied. "Paint fumes and all," he said, flashing his stained fingers on one hand while he clutched the phone with the other behind his back.

She knitted her brow, no doubt wondering about those non-existent paint fumes, but a call from inside saved Paris from having to lie his way out of his lie. "It's safer inside," she said, holding the door open for him. "Our protections don't extend beyond the walls."

"What about the crows?" he asked as he stepped inside. "They're all over the roof."

"Well, not all the protections," she amended before shutting and locking the door behind him. "Have you seen my phone?"

He shook his head, playing the fool everyone thought he was. She scurried past him, muttering to herself about always leaving things behind, completely missing the moment he slipped it back in her pocket to find again soon.

FOUR

"You need to move. Now."

Paris recognized that deep, serious voice, though it was more strained than the calmer, softer version of several days ago. Hurried footsteps punctuated each word, the raven charging down the hall toward the room at the end Paris had claimed. And painted one whole wall of, from floor-to-ceiling, even the jamb around the door.

But before Mac could reach him, he was waylaid by Liam outside the room. "Where's the fire, brother?"

"Vincent hired someone to hack the coven's location. We're trying to slow him down, but someone made a call out from here. The witch whose phone was used said it wasn't her."

"Shit," Paris cursed as his brush slipped, smearing his guilt across the chin of the young woman from the grocery store parking lot.

A blink later, Mac appeared in the doorway, and Paris stumbled back against the wall behind him.

Eyes glowing violet, color high on his cheeks, wrapped in nothing but a clearly borrowed trench that barely reached his knees, the raven was even more stunning than in Paris's hazy memories. He was tall and rangy like his brother, but bigger somehow. From the added definition of his lean muscles to the authority he carried himself with to the blue, black, and violet aura that pulsed around him—duty, loyalty, and regret, a terrible tangle, inside a barely there ring of red, pushed to the very edge.

Wait . . . He could sense auras? Since when? He hadn't noticed Liam's or any of the witches' before now.

"It was you?" Mac's bark snapped him out of his thoughts. "You risked all these people." He threw an arm out the direction he'd come. "Witches who brought you back to life. My brother who watched over you. I saved your s—"

"Thank you," Paris said, finding his voice and legs as he pushed off the wall.

Mac jerked upright and blinked, the violet of his eyes fading to black. "What?"

"Thank you for saving my life. I don't think I said that before."

Mac just stared, his mouth opening and closing several times before he pressed his lips together, seemingly stymied.

Chuckling, Liam stepped to his side and clapped his shoulder. "The appropriate response is *you're welcome.*"

"Get packed up" was no less appropriate, given the circumstances he'd described. Paris didn't hold it against him, especially as he'd hastened things along. Mac rotated back to the door, then wobbled to a stop, inhaling sharply. "What is this?"

Paris flashed his stained hands, the brush woven through his fingers. "It's how I deal."

Mac moved closer to the wall, his gaze roving over the violet-tinged murals. The small, bearded man in the apron to the left of the doorway. The monster with snakes dripping from his chin to the right. "This was the giant?" Mac said. "Before and after?"

"That's right," Paris said, fighting and failing to keep the shiver out of his voice.

Another step right, and Mac stood before the mural of the altar where Paris had almost died. His fingers hovered in the air, just above the wall, tracing the knives that jutted up from the altar into the painted Paris's back, then the wispy swirls around his head. "What are these?"

"The voices," Paris said, whisper-quiet, afraid that if he spoke of them any louder they might come back. "It felt like they were carving into me, then screaming in my head."

He paused only briefly in front of the raven with its wings spread and talons extended before stopping in front of the last figure. "Who's this?"

"After the witches did their thing," Paris said, then to Liam, "Right before I woke up yesterday and you found me on the floor"—he waited for Liam's nod—"I had a dream about her. But I think it was just me projecting so my brain could work it all out."

Mac jutted his chin at the painting of the clerk, then the one of the woman. "Take pictures," he said to Liam.

"Why?" Paris asked.

"Something about her is familiar," Mac answered, his gaze still fixed on her. "Why is it all in purple?"

"That's how I saw it in my dream."

Mac's head whirled around so fast, so like a bird's, that Paris almost laughed. The shock—and alarm—in the raven's once again violet eyes stopped him. Made him gulp instead. He was thankful a witch leaned her head in the door and released him from Mac's assessing stare.

"We'll be ready to go in ten," she said.

"Where are we going?" Paris asked.

"You'll find out when we get there."

He shifted his grip on the paint brush, holding it in his fist like a weapon. Nothing the ravens or witches had done so far indicated they meant to harm him—quite the opposite—but still . . . "No offense, but unknown destinations have not worked out so well for me this week."

"He has a point," Liam said.

"You'll go with the witches to Calera," Mac conceded.

"And what about you?"

His face fell—that terrible tangled aura from earlier knocking

Paris back a step. And if his aura hadn't, the wretched pain in Mac's voice would have. "I have to do something I've put off for too long."

Liam stepped in front of him, expression sympathetic. "Is there any way around it?"

"We're about to find out."

Liam drew his brother into a tight embrace and mumbled words Paris couldn't understand. "Ní hiasc é go dtí go bhfuil sé ar an mbanc."

Mac's gaze flicked over his brother's shoulder, catching on Paris's, and when he said, "I hope you're right," Paris didn't think it was only about whatever miserable duty was directly in front of him.

FIVE

Twinkling orbs of light led their caravan down a winding limestone road and through a dense grove of towering trees. The last car in front of Liam's turned off at another cabin, this one the same as the handful of others they'd passed—four green walls, a stone chimney, a shingled roof covered in moss.

"Is there another one back there?" Paris asked, peering into the darkness.

"One more," Liam said. "If memory serves . . ."

He drove them under a stand of trees whose branches had woven together over the road, and darkness swallowed them whole for an endless few seconds. And then they were out the other side, moonlight filtering through the branches to reveal a single cabin at the end of the road, barely visible among the tangle of green that stretched as far as Paris's human eyes could see.

Liam pulled the car into the gravel drive, and Paris stared out the windshield. "What is this place?"

He'd been born in the city, had rarely traveled outside it, and never to any place like this. His world consisted of concrete, fog, and waves that crashed against sheer cliffs. The only thing remotely similar about this place were the breakers he could hear in the distance, from the direction they'd come along the ocean road. He'd thought they were going to the roadside motel by the coast, but they'd driven right past it and down the road that led to this forest. Or was it a jungle? Paris couldn't say, all of it new to him.

"Well," Liam said as he shoved his car door open, "when I was a kid, it was a campground." He waited for Paris to exit the car before continuing. "Then it was a resort property. Little cabins in the woods that the rich folk in YB and Portola could run away to."

"And then what?" Paris said as he grabbed his bag of borrowed clothes, bandages, and paint supplies from the trunk. "The moss won?"

Liam chuckled as he shouldered his duffel. "More like the Rift won, but yes, when people stopped coming out this way, Nature took over. Call it her anti–Canyon Lands."

Paris couldn't think of a better description. He rotated where he stood, inhaling deep and taking it all in. "It's beautiful."

"It's so dark out here you can hardly see."

"But it smells like life and the ocean, all rolled into one."

"Don't forget the rotting wood."

Paris glared in his direction, certain the shifter could see his rueful expression, even in the dark. "I'll amend. It smells like life and death, the *natural* kind. Nothing smells like this in YB."

"Fair enough." He fished a key out of his pocket and opened the door, holding it for Paris to enter first.

Into total darkness.

Paris extended an arm, searching cautiously for the nearest wall and, once found, backed himself against it, staying out of Liam's way. He moved around in the dark, seemingly undeterred, removing what sounded like sheets on furniture and stacking logs in a fireplace.

"You've never been to Talahalusi?" he asked from Paris's left.

"Dad forbade it." Shot him down every time he'd mentioned visiting the vineyards and farmlands north of Yerba Buena. But others had told him about the region. About the more temperate climate, the changes the governing Indigenous tribes had made to preserve their lands, the wash of colors so absent from YB, from the vegetation to the wine to the artwork. Jason had brought him sunflowers from there once, and Paris had spent months painting them in secret.

"It's like this," Liam said, drawing Paris out of his thoughts, with his words and the strike of a match. "But without the mustiness." Fire flickered to life in a corner fireplace, the flames casting enough light to make Liam visible again.

"That's where you and Mac are from?" Paris asked him as he continued to survey their surroundings. A stone hearth, a table, a rustic kitchen, and a couch and oversize chair. And if Paris squinted hard enough, a bed on the far wall and an enclosure in the far dim corner that he guessed was the bathroom. "Talahalusi?"

"Our family owns a vineyard up there. Monte Corvo."

"Mac works a vineyard?" Even if Liam weren't able see his face, Paris's voice—and the bag he dropped—would have given away his wide-eyed surprise. In no universe could he imagine the intense raven tending vines. "What's he do? Stomp the grapes?"

Liam laughed out loud, that same carefree guffaw from earlier that couldn't be more different than his brother's small, soft smiles. By the time his hilarity subsided, the flames had grown healthy, casting a warm glow about the cabin. But before Paris could get a better look, Liam's answer to his joking question stopped him cold. "No, Mac's a cop." Then sent him scrambling for the door. Liam beat him to it, blocking his path. "We know who you are, Paris. We know what you do."

"And what's that?" He hated the wobble in his voice, but there was no help for it. He was at a disadvantage—trapped in a strange place with a shifter, at the mercy of others who would use him against his father. Sure, they might have rescued him, but now that they had him, how far would they go to get information about his father's operations? His dad was right; he was a fool. He'd spent the past few days painting pictures when he should have been learning everything he could about his captors and plotting his escape.

"You're a dealer," Liam said. "You work small jobs for Vincent."

Paris whipped his gaze back to him. "I don't work for my father."

Liam stepped back, hands raised, palms out. "I believe you. Icarus vouched for you. And your dad tried to kill you. Evidence is in your favor."

"You talk like a cop too."

"I would be, if Mac let me." There was a resigned tilt to his smile, a wistfulness in his voice that Paris recognized. Dreams that someone else had quashed, though he suspected Mac's motives were more altruistic than his father's. Before Paris could question him further, Liam opened the door and left it that way while he gathered a stack of clothes from his duffel.

He was giving Paris an out. To who the hell knew where, but the gesture, the intention was loud and clear. Paris was free to go.

He stayed instead, sensing his chances were better with his rescuers than the man who'd repeatedly tried to kill him. "For what it's worth, I've never been on my father's side."

Nodding, Liam passed him on the way out the door. He didn't go far, just over the threshold to the outside bin on the tiny porch, stashing the stack of clothes inside it.

"Who are those for?" Paris asked.

"Me, after a shift." He glanced over his shoulder, a devilish smirk turning up one corner of his mouth. "Unless you want to see me naked."

"I'd rather see your brother naked—" Paris slapped a hand over his mouth, as if he could somehow hold in the words that had already escaped.

Liam rolled his eyes as he stood, but his smile gave away his amusement. "Is it the dark and broody of it all?"

"You've got dark hair and dark eyes too."

"But not the broody."

Paris shrugged as he followed Liam back inside. He hadn't known Liam long, but he didn't think the good-natured man had a broody bone in his body. And broody, for better or worse, was Paris's type, hence why he'd never fallen for Jason, whose ease and carefree attitude reminded him of Liam. And he'd never made a move on Kai because anyone with half a brain could see Jason and Kai were destined for each other.

"Tell me about him," Paris said as he sank onto the couch in the middle of the cottage. "Why is he all dark and broody?"

Liam claimed the oversize chair to Paris's left and propped his socked feet on the coffee table. "He's the oldest."

"That can't be all of it."

His gaze drifted past Paris to the fire and in the serious expression that crossed his face, Paris saw the resemblance to his brother beyond just their similar features. "He's the reaper for our clan."

"What does that mean?"

His dark gaze swung back to him, and in it was a hint of the violet Paris had seen in Mac's. "He carries souls to their ends."

Paris had read about ravens and other psychopomps who ferried souls. Had heard his father talk and brag about manipulating them to do his bidding. But Mac seemed to be heaping the torture on himself. "And he's a cop? That's misery on top of misery."

"You're not wrong, especially when it's the lost ones that keep him up at night."

Paris quirked his head, not quite following. "Lost ones?"

"Cold cases, that's his specialty. Souls he can't find. Icarus was one."

"Well, he found him now."

"And he may have to deliver him soon." Unmistakable sadness streaked through Liam's eyes before he averted his gaze again. "And a family friend too. It's almost as bad—" He cut himself off and swallowed hard. "Mac's not in a good place right now."

And yet he'd rescued him and seen him to safety. Had made

sure his brother looked after him, even after Paris had compromised their safety. "Is there anything we can do? To help?"

"What he asks." Liam pushed to his feet, then around the coffee table, headed toward the kitchen. "We stay here, safe and sound, until the coast is clear."

Paris twisted on the sofa. "What's happening to Icarus . . . to Mac's friend . . . it's because of my father, isn't it?"

"In part, but there's a lot more going on than just one evil man."

One evil man who was his father. Who Paris had unwittingly helped by giving him Icarus's contact info. Under duress, granted, but part of this was his fault. He'd find a way to do more; he had his own wrongs to rectify.

SIX

Hushed, clipped voices teased the edge of Paris's consciousness.

He didn't try too hard to listen, didn't let them pull him out from under the flannel sheets and heavy quilt that chased away the forest's nighttime chill. Besides, convos he couldn't hear had become the norm. The witches had frequently visited the cabin, regularly checking in with Liam. They were always careful to talk in low, whispered tones, too quiet for Paris's human ears to discern.

He didn't take it personally. He was Vincent Cirillo's son. Why would anyone trust him? Liam had agreed to tell him if anything happened to Icarus or Mac, and in return, Paris had agreed to do what Liam asked, what Mac needed. Stay safe and out of whatever mess was going on in YB.

He thought maybe something major had gone down last night. He'd been outside behind the cabin, picking wildflowers for the vases he'd found under the kitchen sink, when the waves in the distance thundered so loudly it was like being back home, in his condo right on top of the cliffs. And there'd been a weird energy to the forest around him, almost like it was vibrating.

He'd returned to the cabin and found Liam pacing from one end to the other, his typically relaxed manner vanished. But Liam had had no answers, just nervous energy, so Paris had put him to work kneading dough for the bread he'd wanted to make, the fireplace hearth too tempting to pass up. Then, after the dough had set the requisite time, he'd tasked Liam with babysitting it in the Dutch oven while he slept.

Which couldn't have been long, judging by the dim light behind his eyelids. Early morning, he guessed; definitely not time to get up yet. He yanked the quilt higher, aiming to pull it over his head, but then Liam's hand landed on his ankle, shaking it lightly.

"More sleep," Paris mumbled into his pillow. "Icarus and Mac okay?"

"It's me, Paris."

Sleep fled in an instant, Paris rolling onto his back and looking up into dark, haunted eyes. Mac's face was drawn, his shoulders slumped, the tan of his skin pale and his dark hair unruly. And his aura was an absolute train wreck. A speck of lighter relief, the red edge a tiny measure brighter, but darkness clawed at it—exhaustion, regret, sadness dominating.

Untangling an arm from the sheets, Paris reached up and palmed his cheek. It was so much colder than Liam's. "Are you okay?"

"I'm fine." Mac covered his hand but not to pull it away, as Paris expected. He nuzzled into it instead, as if he were searching for warmth, and Paris barely managed to swallow his surprise.

"What about Icarus and your friend?" Paris asked once he could make words again. "Liam said—"

A small smile teased the corners of his lips. "Also fine." He lowered Paris's hand, squeezed it, then stood. Paris recognized his clothes—dark jeans and a black sweater—from the stack Liam had put in the bin outside. "I have some news for you," Mac said. "Get dressed, and I'll meet you on the couch."

Paris wrestled free of the sheets and quilt and pulled on the sweats and hoodie he'd left by the bed. As he straightened, he noticed Liam was no longer in the cabin. He made a quick pit stop in the bathroom—no Liam there either—then ventured past the table to lay a hand on the loaf of bread wrapped in a towel, exactly the way he'd shown Liam to do it. The loaf was cool, taken out of the fire hours ago, the Dutch oven washed and drying upside down by the sink. "Was that you and Liam talking before? Did he leave?"

"He was needed at home."

"At Monte Corvo?" Paris said, and Mac cocked a dark, questioning brow. "He told me that's the name of the vineyard your family owns." Paris circled the chair and lowered himself onto the opposite end of the couch. "In Talahalusi."

"What other secrets did my brother spill?"

"He told me you were a reaper. Is that why you look so wrung out? Why you're cold? What happened last night? It felt . . . weird," he said, recalling his friend's too-accurate description.

Mac made a harsh sound, somewhere between a laugh and a groan, and drove a hand through his hair, disheveling it further. His gaze lighted on the waning fire and stayed there. "There was a battle," he said, tone as haunted as his eyes. "The first of many, likely."

"Right," Paris said. "As we get closer to the date of the Rift." It had happened that way every year for as long as Paris could remember. As mid-October approached, skirmishes between magical forces would escalate and most humans would plan their vacations out of YB accordingly. Well, most humans, except those like his father trying to profiteer from the madness. Sometimes the increased activity subsided after the Rift anniversary, sometimes it carried through to Samhain, and on several occasions, it had lasted all the way to winter solstice.

"It's different this time," Mac said. "Nature is back in the war."

Paris gasped aloud, no help for it. In all his tutors' lessons about the Rift, and in all the other books he'd read about it and the decades that followed, Nature hadn't been directly active in YB since that fateful October seventeenth thirty years ago. Her cause was still championed, otherwise places like this forest, like Talahalusi, like certain other parts of YB wouldn't exist. All of it would be like the Canyon Lands, which she'd ceded in the Rift, but in the battles and years since, she hadn't directly played a role. Until now. The weirdness both he and Jason had sensed.

"Last night," Paris started, "I was outside picking flowers, and there was this *energy* in the forest." He splayed his hands and wriggled his fingers, hoping Mac understood what he was trying to convey. "And the waves were so loud, even through the woods. It was like being back on Sunset Hill."

"She needed to pull the energy for what we had to do."

He shifted on the couch, angling toward Mac and pulling up a knee, intrigued to the edge of his seat. "Which was what?"

"Save a phoenix from your father."

Paris jolted. "They exist? For real?" Phoenixes were mentioned in some texts, but they were so rare, so few and far between, their identities closely guarded secrets, that the stories and reports about them were a patchwork of myth and magic. No one was quite sure how they began or even how many remained alive.

"They do, and they belong to Nature, but your father and Chaos were hunting them."

Paris's wonder crashed in despair, his father ruining another joyful moment in his life. Not to mention all the lives he must have ruined in his quest for power. Paris gathered the nearest blanket around him, needing the softness to counter such violence. "You may not believe me," he said, "but I don't work for my father. I don't support his cause or Chaos. I never have."

"But you are his heir. And you told him how to contact Icarus."

"I didn't know what for. Just something to do with someone called the Devil, and they promised to keep Icarus safe." Paris leaned his forehead against his knee, eyes slipping shut as defeat and regret swirled in his gut. "And not that it matters, because I know I shouldn't have believed them and should have just kept my mouth shut, but they got that info with my father's knee on my neck. I didn't give it up voluntarily."

Mac's sharp inhale drew Paris's attention back to him, to the person who'd clearly been through hell the past few days but had still made sure he was safe and secreted away. Paris lowered his knee and inched out a hand, covering Mac's where it rested on the cushion between them. "I'm sorry for what he's put you through. And I'm sorry he tried to hurt your friend and for whatever he did to Icarus. I don't want anything to do with him or his empire. He can keep it."

"You may not want it, but it's yours now."

Mac's gaze held his, the intensity of it momentarily distracting Paris from his words, but once they sank in, his breath caught. Made getting the most important question of his life out difficult. "Are you saying—"

Mac flipped his hand over under Paris's and gently held his. "Your father died in the battle last night."

Paris couldn't describe exactly what sound jumped out of his throat—a gulp, a shout, a gasp—it was the last news he expected. Tears welled in his eyes and raced down his cheeks, his chin wobbling so hard he had to wedge it against his chest.

Mac squeezed his hand. "I'm sorry."

"No!" Paris said, jerking his face back up. More than anything, he wanted this man, his rescuer, to know what he truly felt. "This isn't grief. It's joy, it's fucking relief I feel in my soul." The same sense of freedom he'd felt when Mac in raven form had landed on his chest on the altar. "For the first time in my entire life, I don't have to be afraid anymore."

He barely got the last word out when his sobs broke loose, twenty-plus years of pain and terror working their way up and out. Mac used the hand still in his to draw him into his arms, gathering the blanket around them both. Paris leaned against him, grateful for the steadiness, for the comfort while the awful world he knew fell away.

For his second chance at life to become a reality. Vincent would never hold him under the water again.

He could breathe, free and easy, and with that hopeful

thought, the sobs began to subside until there were only sniffles and sizzling embers left. "He's really gone?"

Mac held him tighter, chin resting on the crown of his head. "I delivered his soul myself. Watched it get extinguished. I had to be sure. He won't hurt you or anyone else ever again."

"Thank you," Paris said, and yet the words didn't seem nearly enough. As he snuggled deeper into the raven's embrace, he silently vowed to spend the rest of his life earning his second chance. And to bring warmth and color into the life of the man who had given it to him.

SEVEN

Paris wasn't lost this time.

He'd been here before. Would never forget sitting in the back seat of his father's SUV and crying over a future he'd never have. In retrospect, he'd probably been brought as a sacrifice that day, but it didn't make the day any less of a milestone in his past of painful losses.

Today looked much the same. The giant oval lawn full of people—a couple sharing a picnic, a group of friends tossing a frisbee, classmates chatting over books. The plaster and glass buildings with their echoes of mission-style architecture, the farthest north the trend had reached before magic and greed had chased the religious fanatics back south. Bright sun overhead, making the veneer of normalcy shimmer bright.

Portola University.

Paris would've liked to attend college, but erased persons, like Vincent had paid for him to be, couldn't enroll in school. Granted, he probably wouldn't have survived four years here. He would've been killed by a rival dealer or kidnapped by a tech oligarch to leverage against his father, but at least he would have been out from under Vincent's fist. Instead, Atlas had arranged for private tutors, all of them excellent and paid enough to get over their fear of working for the Cirillos. But that was as far as their connection had gone, none of them becoming friends. Paris only had Kai and Jason for that, and Icarus, whose company he'd paid for.

As a young man crossed in front of him on the oval, the glide of his steps too measured, the shift of his blue eyes too fast, the rise and fall of his chest nonexistent, Paris thought he must be a vampire like Icarus.

One with access to Daylight. Out here in the violet midday.

Violet.

Paris looked the direction the vampire had come just as the vamp glanced over his shoulder, both of them spying the small, bearded man on the oval's stone wall. Dressed in overalls, he sat munching on an apple, taking a break outside in the sun like everyone else.

But as the vampire moved to take another step and couldn't, Paris knew that wasn't what the man was doing at all. The vampire's claws extended, and he slashed at the monster's invisible hold. No one noticed his struggle except Paris. No one noticed the small man's red eyes or the snakes that slithered out from under his pant legs and sped through the grass in the vampire's direction.

No one noticed the world turn a deep, dark violet, or the oval lawn narrow into a deserted alley, or the vampire lying on the wet, grimy pavers with deep cuts in his arms and legs. No one heard him scream "Help me!" into the night.

No one except Paris.

———

"How, Paris? Tell me how to help you!"

Paris jolted awake, the dark, violet night resolving into a pair of dark, violet eyes. "Mac?" The raven's strained voice had echoed around the alley walls, pulling Paris out of Portola and back to . . . ?

A place that smelled of wildflowers, wood, and fresh-baked bread—as far away from home as Portola had been.

Tearing his gaze from Mac's, he planted a hand in the cushions and levered up to look around. A quilt-covered bed on the far wall, a half-eaten loaf on the kitchen table, a corner hearth blazing bright, a dusky green hue outside the windows. "We're still in Calera?" he asked, swinging his gaze back to Mac. "At the cabin?"

Mac nodded. "About ten hours later, but yeah, still here." He rocked onto his haunches beside the couch. "Where were you?"

"Portola." Paris hauled himself the rest of the way up and raked a hand through his hair, pushing it back off his forehead. "I can't believe I passed out like that. I'm sorry."

He gently patted his biceps, bandaged beneath the hoodie's sleeves. "You're still recovering."

Paris had removed the bandages on his forearms last night. Those wounds had mostly healed, but the deeper cuts in his biceps and thighs, the witches had warned, would take longer.

"And you got some big news this morning," Mac added.

"That you delivered, after I don't even want to know how long a night."

"It's not a competition, Paris." He stood and made his way to the kitchen. Out of the jeans and sweater and dressed in slacks and a dress shirt, barefoot and with his sleeves rolled up, he looked a hundred times more comfortable than he had in more casual clothes. "Coffee or tea?"

"Tea," Paris answered. "The olallieberry one, please." Mac threw a dark-eyed glare over his shoulder, and it took everything in Paris not to flip him the bird. Bird, heh. He settled for sass instead. "Don't judge. And *you* offered it."

"Only to be polite." One corner of his mouth twitched, fighting a smile, before he turned back to the kettle. "I'll let it slide since you make good bread."

Paris's insides warmed at the compliment, at the idea he'd been able to give Mac some comfort too. But it wasn't all his doing. "The starter for it was the witches', and your brother kneaded it, then babysat it while I slept," Paris said, as he pushed off the couch and headed toward the bathroom. "They deserve some of the credit."

A quick leak and bandage check later, Paris reemerged to two steaming mugs, bread and butter, and Mac waiting for him at the table. Also on the table was a stack of file folders Paris didn't remember from that morning. And come to think of it, those slacks and shirt Mac was wearing had not been in the stack Liam had put in the bin outside. "Did you go out when I was asleep?"

"Briefly. I met an associate at the motel down by the coast. She had some wheels and other supplies for us and the coven."

Paris peeked out the front window, to check out said wheels—a nondescript sedan—and to hide his grin that threatened, more of that earlier warmth intensifying and spreading out to his limbs. Mac had trusted him not to run.

"Where were you in Portola, in your dream?"

His grin died as he turned back to the table and slid into the other chair. "You don't need to worry about those." The last thing he wanted was to burden Mac with more concerns—he had enough on his plate already—and especially for what would amount to nothing. "Like I said before, it's just me processing."

"I'm not sure it is." Coffee in hand, Mac leaned back in his chair, legs crossed, and repeated his earlier question. "Where were you in Portola?"

"The university."

And straightened in his seat.

"That's relevant?" Paris asked.

"Maybe. The monster from last week was there?"

Paris fought off his shiver with another sip of hot tea. "He was after a vampire."

"Icarus?"

Paris shook his head. "It wasn't him or any of my other clients. I didn't recognize him."

"Can you describe him for me?"

Knowing Mac was a cop, Paris recognized the interrogation

for what it was, but if he hadn't known, he might not have made the connection, Mac gently drawing the answers out of him. More like a conversation between friends, but the raven never let a question go, circling back for the answer he needed. Paris would bet he was good with suspects and also with families of missing victims.

"He'd been turned at about my age. Midtwenties. Average height, slimmer build, dark brown skin, short, clipped hair, blue eyes, freckles over the bridge of his nose." Paris's gaze drifted out the window, summoning up the dream for anything else he'd noticed. "He knew he was being watched. And he didn't care. He was more concerned with getting out of there."

"Why do you say that?"

"He wasn't hiding what he was as he crossed the oval. It was full of people, and he was gliding too smoothly and not breathing."

"This was in broad daylight?"

Paris nodded. "As if he'd taken Daylight. I can paint him for you." His fingers itched to get to work, the walls of the cabin a blank canvas calling to him.

"And if you were to paint the giant, what would he look like this time?"

"Giant," Paris said with a harsh chuckle. "He looks nothing like that in his human form." He held his mug in both hands, close to his chest, guarding against the threatening chill. "In my dreams, he looks like he did when Dad handed me over to him. Incredibly average. You wouldn't notice him on the street. Short, skinny, frail almost, like his arms would shatter in a strong enough wind. Brown hair and beard, blue eyes that turned red when he froze the vampire, like he did to me when I tried to run. He's so small, the opposite of the giant he becomes."

"He was wearing a grocery apron when you painted him before. Was he wearing the same apron when he took you?"

"Not the same one, and he wasn't wearing any apron in this dream. He had on generic overalls, like a janitor or professional painter would wear." He lowered his mug and cupped his warm hands over his nape, head bowed. "The exact opposite of my father's suits. It's my brain, swapping one monster for another, one victim for another, but they're all me." Abused, chased, denied the bright, promising future he wanted and damned to dark, hopeless alleyways instead. "The scene changed," he told Mac. "From the oval to a dark alley where the vamp was cut open." He pushed his sleeves up and turned over his arms, the scars on his forearms fading but still visible. "Exactly like I was. He asked me to help him. It was just—"

"He's still alive, Paris."

His gaze shot up, along with his heart rate. "What?"

"The giant. He disappeared in that ball of magic he conjured." Mac pulled the top file off the stack, opened it, and pushed it in front of Paris.

The blond-haired, brown-eyed woman from the Portola parking lot stared up at him from a graduation photo. "Who is she?"

"Lola Duvall. She graduated Portola University, then went to work there as a systems engineer. She's from my stack."

"Your stack?"

"Of cold cases. She's been missing for over three years."

Paris's pulse galloped as his mind likewise raced, tying the pieces of his dreams to the pieces of the new reality around him.

To the raven sitting across from him.

"She's one of the souls you still have to deliver."

"Among others." Mac's gaze cut to the remaining folders beside him; Paris didn't think that was even close to the entirety of his stack. "You mentioned hearing other voices when you were on the altar. You painted them carving into you and swirling around your head."

"They were souls," he said, recalling more from that awful night, realizing now that that was how he'd thought of the voices then too.

Mac nodded. "I don't think you were the first being that giant sacrificed on his altar to Chaos. I want to know who he is and how many more souls he's taken. How many more humans like you and Lola he used to channel those souls through. I want to stop him from taking more. There's not much I can control in this war, but this—*this*—I can do. I need to do it. Will you help me, Paris? Will you help them?"

Help me, the vampire had begged him in that alleyway. *Help me*, Lola had pleaded in the parking lot. *Help me*, all those voices—souls—had screamed with him on that altar.

And now he had an opportunity to do just that. To make some good out of what had been the worst night of his life. To help those lost souls and to save others from being taken.

To help ease the burden of the man who'd saved him.

"Yes," Paris answered.

EIGHT

Paris stepped back from his latest mural of the monster and tapped his paint brush against his hip. "I'm missing something."

He'd been working on the painting for hours, after the hours he'd spent painting both scenes of the vampire victim, from the oval and the alley. By now, it had to be the wee hours of the morning, nothing but pitch-black darkness outside, made more so by the roaring fire inside. Mac had kept the flames going while they'd worked—Paris painting, Mac searching his case files for clues and identities. They'd taken a break hours ago to eat the lentil soup a witch had brought over and the cheese sandwiches they'd grilled on the hearth, but Paris hadn't lingered long. Every minute away from his dream was a minute he risked losing details. Like whatever detail it was now that he couldn't put his paint brush on.

"Trick I learned for investigating crime scenes," Mac said as he stood. "Close your eyes and put yourself there but in the victim's shoes. Look at it from their perspective."

Paris recoiled at the thought. He'd lived it once himself already, had been a bystander each of the other times. Watching it from the sidelines, there'd been a veil between his fear and the victims', between him and the giant. He didn't want to be in his path again, imaginary or otherwise.

"I'm right here," Mac said as he slid a hand into the groove at the small of his back, resting it lightly there. "I won't let him hurt you."

Inhaling a shaky breath, centering himself with Mac's hand and the paintbrush in his own, Paris closed his eyes and put himself back on the grassy oval, ten or so yards from where he'd first stood in his dream.

When he glanced over his shoulder, he was directly in the giant's line of sight, and as his gaze locked with the monster's blue one, he realized it lacked the malice it had in the parking lot dream. When the giant looked at the vampire, he was hungry— for power. Paris recognized the look: it was the same hunger that had been ever-present in his father's eyes.

Instinct drove Paris to move the opposite direction, away from the threat, but the now red-eyed giant stopped him in his tracks, invisible bindings digging into his thighs and arms, into his existing injuries. Pain and fear spiked, and Paris struggled to breathe.

Until Mac's hand pressing gently at his back reminded him this was just a memory, a mental scouting mission like the real ones he used to go on with Jason. Turning fully around, he studied the giant, looking for anything he hadn't already captured with his brush. Finding nothing at this scene, he took another deep breath and moved on to the next one, putting himself on the ground in the dark alley.

Only he arrived sooner than when he'd been there the last time, the vampire's soul dragging him a few terrifying moments earlier. To when the monster leaned over him, so close Paris could smell rosewater, elderflower, and quinine on his breath and could see the scar beneath his beard. He'd been so out of it with fear when he'd been on the altar himself, he'd missed those clues before. Like he'd also missed the gilded knife with its topaz stone that the giant used to slice into the vampire's barely healed scars, the nick on the blade's edge causing Paris to scream right along with him, remembering the way his own skin had torn and shredded, the awful, hopeless—

A sharp tug at the center of his chest, his name repeated in calm, soothing tones, warm hands cupping his cheeks and soft fingers against his temples, drew him out of the alley and back to violet eyes. "There you are," Mac said from right in front of him, continuing to gently stroke his temples. His breath smelled of earth and cheese and the wine they'd drunk with dinner; not the terrible cocktail of his nightmare. "Just breathe for me."

"He took me back further," Paris said between gulps, his eyes filling with tears, the unexpected terror overwhelming, the crash landing back to relief jarring. "How? What's happening to me?"

Mac drew him into his arms, chin on his crown, holding him like he had yesterday, loose enough Paris didn't feel trapped but solid enough to feel safe. "We need to talk to the witches," he said. "But those knives you painted carving into your back, the voices in your head, I think whatever happened to you on that altar opened you up. He was channeling souls through you; he made you a medium."

Forehead against Mac's shoulder, Paris gasped for breath and tried to wrap his head around the most sensible explanation for the nonsensical. And worried who would come knocking next.

Next.

Two souls had already knocked, and he had new clues that could help them. He just had to pull himself together and share those with the detective standing right in front of him. Another deep breath, then he straightened and wiped the wetness from under his eyes. "He's toying with them for the hunt," he told Mac. "He captures them, then lets them go to chase them again. Lola's face was bruised and beaten, and the vampire had barely healed scars the giant ripped open again. But they were different too. He hated Lola. I don't know if it was personal or because she was a woman or because she was human, but there was malice there.

With the vamp, he was after his power, plain and simple. He was hungry."

"That's good, Paris." Mac kept a hand lightly cupped around the side of his neck. "Means we need to look for prior connections and earlier abductions. Was there anything else?"

"He had a knife, gilded with a topaz stone. I can paint it. And his breath smelled like an elderflower tonic. The kind with rosewater."

"Only a few places to get that still."

"And he had a scar." He moved back in front of the monster's picture, grabbed the straight razor from his palette, and dipped the tip of his brush into the paint. He carefully dabbed a little onto the side of the monster's chin, swirled some to match the texture of the beard hair in that area, then, with the razor, thinned out the rest of the dab into a raised line, keeping it perfectly straight like the scar he'd seen. "Right there."

Mac moved closer, snapping pictures with his phone. "Oral or jaw surgery wouldn't leave a scar like that. Those surgeries are done inside the mouth. That scar is from an external injury, and with it being that straight, it was professionally treated. This is good, Paris," he repeated. "Real good."

"Assuming he's not erased, like I am."

Mac patted his shoulder on his way back to the kitchen table, opening his laptop and connecting his phone to various cables. "That's why multiple leads are important. There may not be surgical records, but someone sold him that tonic. I'll get the searches running."

"How do you even get a signal out here?" Paris asked as he dabbed his brush into more paint to get started on the knife. A small generator behind the cabin provided enough electricity for hot water, plumbing, a fridge, and a few other appliances, but Paris found it hard to believe Mac's computer transmitted with any reliability from these woods.

"Boosters and other tech." He gestured at the various attachments connecting the devices. "Icarus's sister is a hacker."

Paris bobbled his brush, flinging paint farther afield than he intended. "Icarus has a sister?"

"Adopted. They were in the same foster home."

"Huh, I knew he needed the Daylight to protect someone, but I never knew who." He swept his paintbrush so as to hook the tip of the knife's blade, then used his razor to shadow its peaks and valleys and create a nick in the straight edge. He winced, but shook off the thought before the remembered pain drowned him again. "Did my list of Daylight clients turn up anything? I didn't know the vamp from my dream, but maybe someone else did. Sometimes who I sold to wasn't the end user."

"Nothing in the hard files, but I have searches running against the digital." After a final flurry of keystrokes, he slumped back in his chair. "Why did you deal?"

Do deal, Paris almost corrected, but bit his tongue instead. He lifted his brush long enough to shrug, then after another swipe through the paint, continued to work on the knife's handle. "Folks needed it. Folks like Icarus. They all had good reasons."

"They could've been lying."

"I'm sure some were. Everyone knows I'm gullible, but if I was able to help one person, then I did what I could."

"While stealing from your father."

He dipped his brush in the yellow paint, added the touch of purple that tinted all his dreams still, then filled the hole he'd left for the stone in the middle of the handle. He used his razor again to clean up and define the edges, depicting a slight filigree to the border around the stone. "He promised to protect them, and he didn't." Paranormals would hire his father for protection, and the next thing the shifter or vampire or warlock knew, they were doing Vincent's dirty work for him. He was human, yes, but a monster in his own terrifying way. It was a business model, a hoard of stolen power and riches that Paris wanted nothing to do with. "What does it mean to be his heir?"

"I don't know yet. That's what I sent Liam to find out. He'll recon with Adam and Icarus and the rest of the team, then report back."

Paris turned to ask who exactly was the rest of the team, but Mac's mouth stretching wide in a silent yawn made him yawn too since he, unlike his father, wasn't a sociopath. "When's the last time you slept?" he asked the raven, who tipped back his head and laughed, a tired, resigned thing that Paris felt all the way to his bones. "Go to bed, Mac."

He righted his head, a challenging, devastating smirk turning up one corner of his mouth. "Only if you do."

"Deal." He tossed his razor on the palette, capped his paints, and rinsed his brush in another mug he'd claimed for paint water, before ducking into the bathroom to wash his hands and check his bandages. When he reemerged in his tee and boxers, Mac was spreading a blanket on the couch.

"I said *bed*. You're way too tall for that sofa, and this bed is big enough for you and me and two more people."

Mac eyed the couch, looking anywhere but at Paris. "I'll be fine here."

Paris pressed his lips together and waited, hands on his hips, for Mac to glance up and meet his no-you're-not glare. He caved almost immediately, chuckling as he snatched up the blanket and headed for the other side of the bed. "I see why you and Icarus are friends."

"We're nothing alike," Paris said as he crawled under the sheets and quilt. "He's all strong and bossy and sexy."

"There's more than one interpretation of those words." Mac stretched out on top of the quilt, fully dressed, the blanket tossed over his feet. Paris let him have that distance, counting it a win that he was beside him at all, that he would get the good night's sleep he deserved. Counted it a bonus when Mac turned on his side to face him, his dark hair falling across his forehead and making him look years younger. Sweet, almost. His words were even sweeter. "You're both good people. I didn't believe it about either of you at first, but like him, you keep proving me wrong."

Paris would have liked to stay in that gooey good place, but the ache in his heart wouldn't allow it. "Is Icarus really okay? He was always good to me. I'll never forgive—"

Mac's hand covered his where it rested between them. "He's fine. So is Adam. For what it's worth, you helped bring them together."

"Adam's the Devil, right? He's a phoenix?"

"Was. Like Icarus was a vampire."

Shock sent Paris levering up on his elbow. "He's not anymore? How did that work?"

Chuckling, Mac tugged him back down. "They were counter-balances—walking rebirth and walking death—whose souls became entwined. Mated, for lack of a better word. Nature released them both, channeling the magic back to her, and giving them a second chance. Their souls chose to come back together."

That did not sound like an easy task for the reaper who had to guide them. "And how did that work for you?"

Mac closed his eyes, but not fast enough to hide the wretched melancholy that streaked through them. He rolled onto his back and folded his hands over his middle. "We do what the souls deserve. Adam and Icarus deserved that second chance."

Paris started to reach out, but stopped himself short. "Do you want to talk about it?"

"I told—"

"What *you* felt?"

His Adam's apple bobbed, a hard swallow, then a single tear escaped the corner of his eye and raced toward the dark hair at his temple.

Fuck it.

Paris was a tactile person, and it was killing him not to try to soothe the obviously upset man—friend—beside him. He scooted closer and laid a hand on his shoulder. No words, just contact, letting Mac know he wasn't alone.

He found his words again after another swallow. "When you know the person on your list, when you love them"—he tapped his chest with his fingers—"it's a special kind of hell. What I want to happen and what must happen aren't always the same."

"Your aura was a wreck that day in Encinal and when you first showed up here."

He whipped his face Paris's direction, glassy eyes wide. "You can see auras?"

He withdrew his hand, tucking it back with the other beneath his pillow. "I couldn't before. I don't know why I do now, and I don't know how I know what they mean, but I do. Assuming I'm doing it right."

"What did you read in mine?"

"Loyalty, duty, regret."

He returned his gaze to the ceiling. "You were reading it right."

"What do you regret, Mac?"

"So much."

The words were faint, barely audible, but no less a wrecking ball for their hushed volume. They might as well have been a shouted cry for help, and it was everything Paris could do not to close the scant distance between them and to wrap himself around Mac like he'd done for him twice now, but he sensed even this was more truth than Mac let most people see. Balling his fist under the pillow, he forced his instincts back and waited Mac out, doing what he could to comfort with his presence and breaths. Eventually, Mac's slowed to match his, and after another minute, he turned back onto his side, facing Paris, hands tucked under his own pillow.

"We'll ask the witches to help you with the auras."

"I don't want to get rid of them. I think I'm supposed to see them."

"To help you understand them. Read them." He smiled softly. "For when they're not as obvious as mine."

"Thank you."

His eyelids seemed to grow heavy, slipping closed as he muttered "Welcome," and a moment later a light snore slipped out from between his lips. He shifted onto his stomach, close enough Paris could feel the puffs of his snores across his own face, could watch as the tension flowed out of his muscles. Finally, at rest.

But Paris was more awake than ever. His gaze wandered past Mac to the murals on the wall. They came to life in the dancing firelight, as did all the questions Paris still had about the people in them. Who was the monster? Who was the vampire? Why were he and Lola targeted? How could he help Mac deliver them? And why did he always see them in purple?

"The auras?" Mac mumbled, eyelids fluttering, and Paris realized he must have asked that last question aloud. And that Mac wasn't completely asleep yet.

"No, the souls."

That sweet, soft smile flitted over the raven's lips again. "Because I do." Then disappeared into the pillow as he nuzzled down, surrendering fully to sleep.

And if Paris hadn't already started surrendering some of himself to this man, the tug he felt between them told him it was only a matter of time before he was ready to surrender it all.

NINE

The rising sun had just begun to filter through the forest canopy when Liam's car pulled beside the sedan in the cabin's gravel drive.

"Didn't expect to see you up so early," Liam said as he shoved open the car door.

Paris stood from where he sat on the front stoop and zipped his hoodie against the morning chill. "Couldn't sleep." It had been a fitful few hours for him, his mind never fully slowing, his heart more tangled than it had any right to be, his body wising up to the fact there was an unfairly attractive one beside it. By contrast, Mac had slept like a rock. Paris would have worried him dead if not for the steady rumble of snores. "Your brother is still asleep."

"Thank fuck." Liam rested back against the hood, hands shoved into the pockets of his parka. "We were worried about him. No one could remember the last time he'd slept."

"Can you take me to the coast? I haven't seen the water in days."

Liam took his non sequitur in stride, waving a hand toward the sound of crashing waves in the distance. "You can hear it."

Not good enough for Paris, for multiple reasons. He gave Liam the simplest, most persuasive one. "I was born and raised in YB. I looked out my window and saw water every day. I don't know how to be away from it."

"Mac will freak if he wakes and you're gone."

"I left a note." Two of them, in fact. In case he missed the one on the pillow beside his, there was another one under the edge of the kettle, next to the leftover bread. "But I don't think he'll be waking anytime soon. We only went to bed a few hours ago."

Liam cocked a brow.

Paris rolled his eyes and hoped it distracted from the blush heating his cheeks. "I was up painting, and he was working. Once we started competition yawning, it was all downhill from there."

Laughing, Liam pushed off the car. "All right, but let's make it quick."

The cabin was a short ten-minute drive to the water, owing largely to the twists and turns of the forest road. Paris didn't mind; the forest was magical in the light of day. He counted five cabins in addition to his, and an endless variety of trees, though redwoods and cypresses dominated. He also spied a knee-high patch of wildflowers in a sunny gap between the trees that he made a mental note to revisit, the meadow so unlike anything back home.

Or what was left of it. "What's it like back there? In YB?" he asked once they turned onto the coast road.

"More unstable than I've seen it since the Rift."

"You were alive for that?" Liam didn't look much older than thirty, Mac like he'd be in his early forties, but it was impossible to tell with shifters.

"I was in college," Liam said, proving Paris's point. "Mac was already a cop and the reaper for the clan."

So however old they'd been, plus thirty years, longer than Paris had been alive. He suddenly felt very, very young. And very, very in over his head.

"It's a good thing you're out. Any humans should be."

Like his best friends, who had also claimed a spot in his worried heart last night. They were the other reason he'd asked

Liam to bring him out to the coast. As his unwitting accomplice found out as soon as they stepped onto the ocean cliffs, the waves pounding below. "I need to borrow your phone," Paris said, his hand out.

"You know the rules."

"Look, you and Mac have this whole network to keep us protected, to watch our backs. My friends only have me, and for years, they were the only ones who had mine. They don't have the means or money to just get out of YB. Not everyone has the privilege to flee a war zone." Paris intended to flex his privilege, to offer Jason and Kai a means out, assuming he could get his hands on his trust fund still. And assuming his friends would take the offered help, unlike every other time he'd offered in the past. But he still had to try, especially with the stakes so high now.

Liam looked back the direction of the cabin, up and down the deserted beach, at the crashing waves below, before finally turning his knowing gaze back to Paris. "That's why we came out here, isn't it? So Mac wouldn't hear you."

"In part, though I really did need to see the water."

"Fuck," Liam said as he slapped the phone into his hand. "He's got his hands full with you."

Paris didn't think too hard on what Liam meant, instead turning on his heel and punching in Kai's number.

"Hello?" his friend answered.

"Kai, it's me, Paris."

"Paris—fuck," he cursed, voice lowered. If Paris had to guess, his friends had fallen asleep cuddled together, as was their way. The snick of a closing door, Kai's voice back to normal volume when he spoke again, confirmed as much. "We've been worried."

"I'm fine. Are you and Jason—"

"We're good, but Paris, there's something I need to tell you."

By the appropriately somber tone of his words, Paris knew where this was going. He spared Kai the trouble. "My father's dead, I know."

"I'm sorry."

"It's weird." He spoke freely with his friend who knew as much about him and his circumstances, about the abuse his father had regularly doled out, as anyone. "I appreciate it, because I know you mean that condolence for me, not because he's actually gone, but . . . I'm not sorry, Kai. I don't know where I go from here, what it means to be the only one of my family left . . ." The heir, another thread that had kept him awake, a convo he needed to have with Mac and Liam. But it didn't change the basic premise, the underlying relief he felt, the same kind of calm he got from staring out at the wide expanse of the ocean. "I'm not sorry he's gone. I'm not sorry that we're all safer for it."

"Are you?" Kai asked. "Safe? Wherever you are . . ."

He glanced over his shoulder, catching sight of Liam strategically positioned to watch his back. "I'm safe, and I want you and Jason to be too."

"We'll be fine. I'm keeping an ear out at the club, and I get paid middle of the month. Jason was talking about some job too. We'll get enough money to get out before the seventeenth if we need to."

"I can send you money now."

"Thank you, but we'll manage."

As he'd expected. And he apparently didn't have time to argue either, Liam making a wrap it up gesture. Another car was pulling into the lot where theirs was parked, and them being seen out here probably defeated the point of being in hiding. "Fuck, I need to go. Listen, if you or Jason need me, I'm in Calera. About a mile past the ocean road motel, there's a road that leads up the hill, away from the beach and into the forest. We're the last cabin on the road. If you need backup, if you need anything, you come to me."

"You do too much for us." Kai's voice was as gentle and earnest as he was. He really was the best of them.

"I wish you'd let me do more. Love you both."

"Love you too."

He hung up and returned the phone to Liam. "Thank you.

That was important to me. They're important to me. I needed to make that call."

"You're welcome. Now let's go before my brother sends out a search party."

One last, longing stare at the water, one giant inhale of salty ocean air, then Paris turned on his heel and followed Liam back to the car so he could get back to the forest and the soul waiting for him there.

TEN

Mac was sitting on the front stoop when Liam pulled the car into the driveway. Barefoot, in the same wrinkled slacks and shirt he'd fallen asleep in, Mac clearly hadn't changed, and judging by the wild state of his black hair, he'd spent every minute since waking plowing his hands through it.

"Good luck with that," Liam said, and no sooner had he turned off the car than did Mac vault off the step, charging their direction.

Paris barely got his car door shut before Mac was there in front of him, backing him up against it. "Where'd you go?"

For all the bluster and violet swirling in the raven's eyes, Paris didn't feel an ounce of fear, not like when his father used to loom over him. His dad's posturing had been about power, control, and cutting him down; Mac's was the polar opposite, his aura pulsing with genuine concern and palpable relief. He was overreacting because he cared—about Paris.

Who stood taller for it, squaring his shoulders and lifting his chin, no fear of a backhand greeting his response. "The coast, like my notes said. Did you find them?"

"Both of them." He erased the scant distance between them and cupped the side of his neck like he had last night, but this time, Paris sensed, for his own comfort, Mac's thumb pressed against his pulse point. "But I didn't have a sample of your handwriting. I couldn't be sure it was you. That you hadn't been taken."

"I texted you," Liam called from behind the open car trunk.

Mac whipped his head to the side, frustration bubbling over in a growl. "Which could have also been faked."

Paris covered Mac's hand with his, holding his palm against his throat, making sure he could feel his heat, his heartbeat. "I'm right here."

Mac's gaze shot back to his, and Paris startled at the naked emotion in his dark eyes. The earlier concern and relief were still there, duty like always, but there was also a depth of loss Paris recognized all too well, the same sort of gaping hole in his chest where his mother lived. His absence this morning had tiptoed too close to that hole for Mac, whomever it was who'd torn it open.

"I'm sorry," Paris said, squeezing his hand. "I won't scare you like that again."

"Could use some help back here with these paint cans?" Liam called, and Mac spun on his heel with another growl that sent heat spiraling down Paris's spine. The last thing Mac needed to deal with was his bubbling crush, but if the raven kept giving him such raw glimpses and sexy growls, there'd be no stopping it from going supernova.

Shoving that distinct possibility aside for now, Paris followed his curiosity to the back of the car. "Why are there paint cans?"

"To paint over the murals when you're done," Mac said. "I assume you don't want to relive those nightmares any longer than you have to."

What was that about an impending supernova? At this rate, it would arrive by nightfall. Paris closed his eyes, took a deep breath, and willed his libido back under control. He waited until Mac's tread hit the front step, putting him far enough out of visual range, before opening his eyes again and grabbing the remaining bag of groceries out of the trunk.

Inside, Liam was already peppering Mac with updates. "She's got a line on two more phoenixes. One that's in hiding, another that Vincent was bleeding dry."

"Is she following the vamps' internet chatter?"

Liam nodded. "They think it's an out, after what happened with Adam and Icarus. Bite a phoenix, be reborn."

"They missed that whole soulmate thing."

"Not to mention a reaper willing to risk his life to pull them back."

Paris dropped the bag of foodstuffs on the kitchen counter, his head spinning like the acorn squash that went rolling. His many hours spent dribbling a soccer ball indoors saved it from splattering on the floor. "Rewind," Paris said as he flipped the squash up into his hands. "My father was bleeding phoenixes dry? That's why he was hunting them?"

"For their power," Liam said as he claimed one of the table chairs.

"We think that may have been who Atlas disappeared with," Mac said, adding more insensibility to the pile.

"Atlas is alive? And gone where? He didn't take over?"

"He vanished from the scene where your father was killed."

"And Adam said none of the captured are talking," Liam relayed. "About who he disappeared with or anything."

Paris continued to put away groceries as his mind raced. Atlas had been his father's number two and his lover, the blond-haired, green-eyed warlock rarely far from his father's side. His father even had a door that led from his bedroom into Atlas's. Most people, including Vincent, had assumed Atlas was in his thrall, but Paris had never believed that. Atlas hadn't struck him as inherently evil nor weak enough of mind or magic for any human to exert such power over. A climber, yes; a monster, no. He'd always made sure Paris was taken care of, from tutors to nurses, and Paris had worked with him on more than one occasion to do the same for those Vincent had manipulated into working for him, cleaning up broken morale and broken noses. Paris had always thought the warlock was just biding his time until Vincent fucked up and got killed, and then he would take over because no one expected Paris to.

Had he actually stayed at Vincent's side all those years because of the person he'd escaped with? They may never know, but Paris did know he wouldn't let all the groundwork, all the connections Atlas—and he—had made go to waste. He folded up the empty grocery bag and rested back against the kitchen counter. "What if I could turn some of them to our side?"

Liam's "Them?" collided with Mac's "Our side?"

"The captured," Paris clarified. "What if I could sway them to Nature's cause? Convince them to give you whatever info about my father's organization you need?"

"It's not safe for you out there," Liam said. "With your father and Atlas both gone, there's a power vacuum in YB. He left behind a lot of money and a lot of banked power and resources that a lot of nasty people are after, human and otherwise."

Paris pushed off the counter, arms spread wide. "But I'm the idiot son. Everyone knows I'm worthless. My own father tried to sacrifice me. Why don't they just take it? They can't seriously think I'm a threat."

"A second ago you implied you weren't worthless," Mac said as he peered at him with shrewd investigator's eyes. "That you have some sway over the people in your father's organization. Someone out there"—he pointed at the window, at the world outside their bubble—"will also want to play that angle. And not for Nature's cause."

"You are the heir," Liam said. "You are target number one for those people trying to climb to the top."

"I can give you a list," Paris said, approaching the table. "Set up a meet." Mac opened his mouth to no doubt object, and Paris held up a hand, pleading his case. "They're not all bad people. Vet them first if you need to. You'll find out my father had a knee to their necks too."

"I can take the idea back to her and Adam," Liam said. "See if it's something they'll entertain."

Paris didn't know who *her* was, but she wasn't the one he needed to convince right now. He circled the table and kneeled beside Mac. "Whatever we're in the middle of didn't end with my father's death. We've got the Rift anniversary, Samhain too, and possibly solstice." He laid a hand on Mac's knee and waited for him to lay his own over it. "You asked me to help you. Let me."

ELEVEN

"Should you be here?" Paris asked as he dotted sea foam onto the sandy shore he'd spent all morning painting. It had been two days since his outing to the coast, and as much as he loved the earthy forest and colorful wildflowers he'd plucked from the meadow, he missed the water more. He'd needed to see it today, even if only on the cabin walls.

Mac's furious pen strokes at the table behind him stopped. "What?"

"I get the sense you're kind of a big deal." He lowered his brush and glanced over his shoulder. "Should you be here babysitting me and working this case when there's clearly bigger things going on?"

"You're kind of a big deal too," Mac said with a wry grin.

Paris couldn't decide whether to paint him with that crooked smile, the one that reminded him of the raven, or with the soft smile that Paris had woken up to in Encinal, the same one that would flit across Mac's face in the split second before he fell asleep.

Paris turned back to his mural. "Yeah, for being a sitting duck." And because he felt on the edge of hilarity and insanity, restless to the point of ridiculous, he swiped his brush through the yellow paint and added a rubber ducky on top of the breakers. "I'm just out here in the woods, painting pretty pictures and making you listen to music you probably don't even like." The quiet had been a peaceful respite the first few days here, but he was used to constant comings and goings, the sounds of the city, and the crashing waves below his condo. He'd cracked yesterday and asked Mac if one of his devices had enough juice to stream his favorite jazz channel. It had also been the music playing right before he'd been taken by the giant. He thought maybe it would jog his subconscious. Would help him put some of the channeling techniques he'd been working on with the witches to good use. No such luck. "I haven't even had another dream."

"One, I like the music. Two, finding Icarus was a cold case you helped solve."

"Not on purpose," Paris said as he gave the ducky two beady, black eyes and an orange beak.

"You still did. Three, we're following up on your list of potential informants in your father's organization. And four, as to the case we've been working, we've identified ten missing persons who may be connected to the giant who took you."

He tossed aside his brush and wiped his hands on the sweats he'd sacrificed to the paint gods days ago. "But we still don't know who or where he is." He slid into the chair beside Mac and gestured at the spread folders. "Or where all these poor people are buried."

"If they're buried at all. The vampire in your dream was eviscerated. The altar you were on was incinerated. You would have been ash if we hadn't rescued you."

"So there was nothing else in the area? No clues, no souls, no other evidence of the mystic or mundane?"

"Nothing. Just you and your dreams."

Propping his elbows on the table, Paris scrubbed his hands over his face and groaned. "Make it make sense, Mac."

"Okay, let's start from the top," he said, and Paris was glad his hands were still over his face. They muffled his chuckle at the very detective-like opener. "He was a giant," Mac continued. "Going by your dreams and my case files, he hunted from Portola all the way up to Talahalusi. He and the three other giants we know of in that range are allied with Chaos, and history indicates they are most active in the run-up to Samhain, when they make a coordinated offering in an attempt to open the veil and bring Chaos all the way through."

Paris shivered. "It was there that night. The darkness had already started to push through over the altar."

"Meaning the veil is particularly weak there."

"In the Canyon Lands? No shit, Mac, I could've told you that, and I'm just a human."

Mac's answering laugh was cut short by some realization, his brows snapping together as he yanked the files closer. "We know he needs a human to channel the souls through for his offering." He tossed aside three folders, reducing the number to seven. "These are the missing humans." After a flurry of keystrokes on his laptop, a map appeared, seven dots stretching from Talahalusi to Yerba Buena to Portola. "And where each lived when they were taken."

"Can you add dates?" Paris asked. "Each time they were taken. And add mine." The earlier deduction about the giant hunting and toying with his victims had significantly narrowed their pool. "Color them by year. I need the painting to come together."

And it did, Paris recognizing the pattern. "He hunts a few years in one place, then moves," he said. He pointed at the cluster in the south. "Lola and two others in Portola three to five years ago." Then to the group up north. "Two potential victims in Talahalusi seven to ten years ago." Then to his home. "Three in YB the last two years."

"But we don't know for certain that's the only place he's hunting," Mac said. "We rarely have more than one per year in my files, and we know the giants make sacrifices all through the month."

"But if the pattern holds," Paris argued, "he's in YB this October. He took me from YB."

"But he didn't hunt you. What if . . ."

Paris gestured with a rolling hand for him to spit it out.

"What if you were a substitute? What if someone got away . . ."

"They're still out there, then. And he's still hunting them."

"In YB, if you're right." Mac's fingers flew across the keyboard. "We need to see who else has gone missing recently. Whoever it is, they haven't hit my pile or my list yet."

An arching flame in the hearth brought another question to mind. "If he catches them," Paris said, "where would he take them? You said the altar I was on is gone. Are there other ones?"

"Rumored," Mac said, as he opened another map on screen. "In other places where the veil is thin."

Paris pointed at the one closest to the coast, not far from where they were now. "That one's close by."

Mac nodded. "Along the fault ridge between Portola and the ocean."

"We need to go there. See if there's any activity."

Mac's "Paris" reminded him of Kai's reply to some of his and Jason's more adventurous schemes. But in those cases, he and his friend were two humans getting into trouble way above their heads. This time, Paris had a well-connected raven at his side.

"Would I be in danger down there?" he said, pointing at that spot along the ridge. "Like I would be in YB?"

The dark-eyed glare cast his way was epic. "You're asking to go to a giant's altar."

"Okay, dumb question," Paris conceded. "Better one, how fast can you get someone from the team down here to go with us?"

The wry grin reappeared, and Paris decided that was the one

he wanted to paint. "Liam, of course, and there's a shifter on our team from around these parts. And if I know her girlfriend, she'll come too." He raised a hand, quelling Paris's rising hope. "*If* Adam can spare them."

Fair enough. Bigger things and all that. "Deal."

TWELVE

The next morning, Paris stood in the middle of a deserted parking lot, zero gravel left underfoot, just knotty roots and rambling weeds covering the small unmarked area at the edge of the woods. He strolled across the similarly deserted road to the vista overlook on the other side. He glanced right toward where the ocean should be in the distance, then left toward where Portola should be, and saw nothing in either direction but the soupy gray mist that had made their drive up this mountain a terror Paris had no desire to ever relive. "Is it always this foggy up here?" he asked Mac, who was unloading gear from the car. "This is as bad as the Canyon Lands."

"Along the ridge here, yes," Mac said, as he shut the trunk. "Especially this spot. When I was a kid, there were rumors these woods were haunted." He crossed the road to stand beside Paris and pointed down the mountain toward Portola. "There's a lake down there you can't see for the fog, but before it was a lake, it was a bustling village. It flooded in one of the wars long before the Rift, when Chaos sent fire over the mountains and Nature countered it with waves. No one survived."

"Is it actually haunted here?" Before Mac could answer, a *Kraa* sounded overhead, a raven soaring out of the fog and onto a nearby branch. "Liam?"

Mac nodded as more black-feathered birds filled the trees, their *Kraas* and *Caws* joining the chorus, until their song was drowned out by the roar of a motorcycle cresting the ridge, dislodging loose pavement from the edge of the road as it swung into the lot beside Mac's car. Paris was so distracted by the stunning vintage bike—gas-powered, a rarity—that he didn't think too hard about the familiar movements of the backseat rider as she dismounted. It wasn't until she pulled off her helmet, dark hair falling around her tan face and delicate features, that Paris recognized her.

"Shit!" He turned to run and cursed again at the cliff blocking his escape. Which one was more likely to kill him—the fall or the mountain lion shifter?

Mac grabbed him by the back of the jacket, yanking him away from the edge. "It's okay, Paris. They're family."

"She worked for my dad." He kept an eye on the woman he knew as Gail and the second woman who dismounted the bike, another shifter, he guessed, given her golden eyes and the way she moved. Some sort of canine, the power in her actions more blunt, more restrained than Gail's feline power and grace.

"No," Mac said. "She works with us and is a big reason you're still alive. She helped find you that night."

Paris didn't have to ask what night he was referring to.

"I was also on that list you gave him," Gail said as she and the other shifter approached. "You must not think I'm all bad."

"You didn't seem to want to kill me on the daily like Roni." The vampire who'd been his other keeper barely tolerated him, regularly threatening to rip his throat out with her fangs.

"She was terrible. She's also dead." Gail held out a hand to him. "Real name's Abigail."

Paris returned the shake. "Thank you for helping me."

"I wish I could have stopped him from turning you over at all."

"He didn't give you much choice, and if you had, your cover would've been blown. I get it."

"What are we doing out here?" the other shifter asked.

Abigail threw an arm over the blond's shoulders. "This is my girlfriend, Jenn. Excuse her crankiness. It runs in her family."

Jenn swatted her stomach, then turned her attention back to Mac, brow raised, expecting an answer to her earlier question. "Well . . ."

"We're looking for a giant's altar," Mac answered.

Faster than Paris could blink, Jenn spun out from under her girlfriend's arm and hauled ass back across the road toward the bike. "That's a nope."

Abigail flexed all that speed and grace Paris had witnessed on occasion, beating Jenn back to the bike and snatching the helmet out of her hands. "Did you never wonder why I left my pack? Why I came home with you from the bar that night and never left? Why I volunteered for the Cirillo gig?"

The longing in her voice, the sorrow in her dark eyes, made Paris's gut clench. Then his eyes widened and his breath stuttered as he realized what he was sensing, the sadness and loss in her aura—purple and indigo, black around the edges—but a center of pure green that anchored her to this place.

To Nature.

"Babe," Jenn said, likewise sensing her girlfriend's distress. She slid the helmet from her grasp, set it back on the bike, then curled an arm around her.

"One of the giants infiltrated our pack," Abigail told them. "Manipulated them into doing his and Chaos's bidding. Helping him hunt. I couldn't stay."

"And my father," Paris said, "had connections to a giant."

Abigail nodded. "At least one. Maybe the others. Maybe the one who turned my pack against who and what we are. I was determined to find out who he was. This is my fight too."

Paris approached cautiously, sensing Jenn on the protective edge and not fully trusting him yet. Fair. He raised his hands, palms out, then slowly stretched one out toward Abigail. She placed her hand in his, and he gave it a gentle squeeze. "Thank you again."

She squeezed back, the green in her aura pulsing brighter, then, swapping his hand for Jenn's, turned toward the woods. "Let's go. I know where the altar is."

Paris shouldered his backpack, stepped to the edge of the woods, then paused. "Um, as the only human here, I have to ask . . . Should we be worried about being attacked?"

"We've got sentries," Mac said, pointing at the corvids overhead.

"And I don't feel them here," Abigail said. "They hunt with him. They must be out of range."

Except five minutes into their trek, Paris started to hear voices. In his head. Beside him, Mac's back snapped straight and he tilted his head, an ear to the woods. "You hear that too?" Paris asked him.

He glanced over, eyes violet, and nodded. Above them, Liam croaked a plaintive call; even he sensed something amiss. Mac flashed him a two-fingered gesture, and the raven went scouting ahead. "He'll check it out," Mac said, moving closer as they followed Abigail deeper into the woods.

The voices getting louder with each step.

If he closed his eyes and opened his mind the way he had with Mac in front of the mural that day, the way the witches had been teaching him, Paris was sure he'd land in a world of violet the same color as Mac's eyes.

He reached out and tangled his fingers with Mac's, giving them a squeeze to get his attention. *Are you sure she's on our side?* he mouthed, asking a question he knew the answer to but hoped he was wrong.

Mac didn't hesitate to nod, and Paris swallowed hard, dreading what the voices meant, what they were going to find at the altar. Even more certain of it when Liam came sailing back through the woods to perch on Mac's shoulder, his glossy black head bowed.

A scout was no longer needed; a reaper was.

"Abigail," Mac called. "Why don't you let us go ahead?"

She spun on her heel, asking "Why?" at the same time Jenn said, "I smell smoke."

Abigail sniffed the air once, and then she was off and running, Jenn on her heels, Liam darting after them.

"Fucking coyotes," Mac said, shoving a hand through his hair. "Zero tact."

"They're dead, aren't they?" Paris said. "Abigail's pack? That's who I'm hearing."

Mac dropped his arm, then his shoulders, and all of him looked tired already. Answer enough. "Let's get you back to the car," he said. "I'll send Liam back to drive you to the cabin. I'm going to be here a while."

Paris lowered his bag and withdrew the canteen of water, taking a slug as he debated how to ask what he wanted and get the answer he wanted too. Because contrary to what he was sure Mac was going to say, he wasn't taking no for an answer. "You can help them? Even if they're not on your list?"

He offered the bottle to Mac who took a longer swallow. "It's harder to make the connection, but it's doable. I have to try. Their souls deserve peace."

"Can I help make that connection?" He took the bottle back from Mac and tucked it in the bag. "Direct the souls your way?"

"Paris, I can't ask—"

"You're not asking." An even better approach. "I can help you, and I can maybe learn more about what happened to me and the giants' plans. This is my fight too," he said, repeating Abigail's words. He shouldered his bag and started moving again, the way Abigail and Jenn had disappeared. "Let's go."

Mac drew even with him but didn't try to stop his forward momentum. "This isn't going to be pretty."

"I know. I lived through it."

Famous last words.

Smoke was thankfully all that lingered in the air, the magical fire having reduced everything to ash, but the utter devastation had Paris falling to his knees. He hadn't been there to witness the aftermath of his own near death, and destruction was par for the course in the Canyon Lands, but the black hole that dark magic had left here—in a place of otherworldly beauty, the altar in a meadow like the one near the cabin, its view of the sky unobstructed and above the fog line—took his breath away.

And on the heels of that blow came the one in his head, all of the voices crashing into him at once, a cacophony like the one that had assaulted him on the altar in YB.

"Breathe, Paris." Mac's hand on his nape, the tug in his chest, quieted the souls a measure. "Breathe through it, tell them to hold on while I check on Abigail, and then we'll get to work. But wait for me, okay?"

Paris nodded, not about to undertake this without an anchor, not even about to argue when Mac made a flicking motion with his hand, and Liam flitted down onto Paris's shoulder. He needed the backup, but Abigail needed Mac more at the moment. "Go, I'll wait."

As he did, he tried to ignore the horror and survey the scene, like Mac the investigator would, having observed him walk through his murals the same way. The higher mound of ash that was likely where the altar had been, the smaller mounds that dotted the clearing in a semicircle, witnesses to the monster's sacrifice. Questions roiled in Paris's head along with the voices.

What had this giant done to sway these shifters to his side?

Had he died in the blast too, or was he still out there?

Were any of the pack?

Who was the human sacrifice? How many others had been sacrificed on the altar? How much power had Chaos gained as a result? How much trouble were they truly in?

THIRTEEN

By the time Mac left to ferry the last soul, the sky was full of stars above. Paris wondered again if one of those bright, twinkling lights was his mother, if she'd heard his plea to take good care of the innocents Mac had delivered today.

And there had been innocents, more than a few. Pack children who hadn't chosen Chaos, other members of the pack who'd been held against their will, the human—Dylan—who had been hunted in these woods for days. He'd been lured here by his best friend, a mountain lion from the pack. Paris had lost his breath when he'd first delved into his memories, nearly drowning from the tidal wave of betrayal Dylan had felt. He couldn't imagine Kai or Jason ever doing such a thing, but Dylan hadn't imagined his best friend would either. They'd been closer than blood, but then his friend's blind allegiance to Chaos, his fear of Nature's evolving world, had turned him against Dylan. Through Dylan's unbelieving human eyes, Paris had watched as his friend had stood next to the giant by the altar and, with his own claws, torn Dylan's heart from his chest. As Dylan's last breath escaped, as the bond he'd shared with his friend well and truly severed, the giant had lost control of the magic and burned everything and everyone to the ground. Paris didn't think the timing was a coincidence.

Nor did he think it a coincidence that Mac's violet eyes were dim and his flying off-kilter when he eventually returned. Liam took up position on his wing and guided him to Paris's shoulder. He landed, and it was like a blast chiller flipping on beside Paris, frigid air blanketing his cheek. The raven was shivering too, cold all the way to his talons. Paris needed to get him back to the cabin, ASAP.

Kneeling, he dug two sets of clothes out of his pack, placing the jeans and sweater on the ground next to Liam and the extra sweats in a pile for Mac. He'd intended them for himself, but Mac needed them more right now. "Shift and change," he told the giant black bird on his shoulder. "I'll tell Jenn and Abigail we're finished."

It was a testament to Mac's exhaustion that he didn't argue, that he simply hopped off Paris's shoulder and onto the pile of jersey material without protest. Paris crossed the large singed circle to where Jenn stood sentry over Abigail, who was scooping ashes into bowls they'd fashioned from pieces of tree bark outside the burn zone.

"I need to get Mac back to the cabin."

Abigail twisted to glance up at him. "Are all the souls gone?"

Paris nodded, suddenly feeling the weight of exhaustion in his own bones, in his head that had been a virtual drive-thru the past twelve hours as they'd sorted who and which direction souls would travel, what each soul deserved. "That's all of them."

"I couldn't feel them," Abigail said as she stood. "But you and Mac and Liam could." She handed the bowl to Jenn then pulled him into her arms. "Thank you."

He hugged her back. "Thank you for keeping me alive all those months. And we will catch the giant who did this to your people." He had a mural to paint, as soon as he got back to the cabin and got Mac buried under a mountain of blankets. "You're good here?" he asked. "Safe?"

"I can stay," Liam said, rejoining them in human form.

Jenn shook her head. "You need to rest too, but you also need to get this one"—she tilted her head toward Paris—"and Mac back down the mountain in one piece. Leave the rest of the birds. We'll text when we get home."

Paris was still learning about the team Mac spoke of often, still sorting out the hierarchy, but he surmised Adam was at the top and Jenn close by, given how easily she issued orders and how quickly Liam acquiesced. She was all business. Was she the *her* they spoke of? In any event, Paris was caught off guard when the gruff leader likewise drew him into a hug. "Thank you for doing this for her." The embrace was stiff and awkward but the words sincere, and despite the awful day, Paris couldn't hide his smile. He liked Abigail a lot, and Jenn clearly loved her and would do anything for her.

The coyote had another message for him. "Adam needs Mac," she said. "And she's not done with him yet either. We're trusting you."

So *she* wasn't Jenn, and Paris didn't think Jenn was referring to Abigail either. Nor did he think he'd ever been trusted with something so important. It scared him but also filled him with pride, something that had been in short supply during his relatively short life. He intended to keep earning it.

"I've got him."

———

"What do you need?" Mac asked, even as Paris, shoulder under his, hauled him through the cabin door.

Between the full-body shivers, chattering teeth, and cold, clammy skin, Mac had deteriorated more with each passing mile on the drive back to the cabin. Concern for him at fever pitch, Paris guided the raven across the room and lowered him onto the end of the bed. "I need you to lie down and go to sleep."

"Paris—"

"And leave your clothes on," he ordered, borrowing some of Jenn's authority. "You're freezing."

"It's normal."

"I don't think it is." He held up the sheets and blankets for Mac. "You're overworked, like you were that morning after guiding Icarus and Adam."

"He's not wrong," Liam said as he closed the cabin door behind them. "About any of it. Go to sleep, brother. I'll keep an eye on Paris."

Mac's answering glare gave Paris a measure of comfort, as did his acquiescence, the exhausted reaper finally crawling under the covers. By the time Paris was back with another blanket to throw over him, he was snoring. With Mac tucked in and warm, Paris closed his eyes to recenter himself, breathing in the scents of life in the cabin—the vases full of wildflowers, the bread he'd made yesterday, the lingering scent of fresh paint.

"You should sleep too," Liam said from where he was crouched in front of the fire, stoking it back to life.

Paris righted his head and flexed his fingers. "I need to paint while the giant is fresh in my head. I don't want to forget any details." This giant looked nothing like the one who'd taken him. He was big, bulky, and bald, and there were more things to distinguish him. Hazel eyes that weren't quite the same size, eyelashes so thick they looked kohl-lined, a birthmark in front of one ear, a tattoo inside one wrist.

He grabbed his paints and brushes and the wooden platter he'd repurposed as a palette and stood in front of the freshly repainted wall, close to the light of the fire.

Liam appeared at his side a couple minutes later. "Here," he said, offering Paris a mug of steaming tea. "For your stomach. I know that drive wasn't easy on you." Liam, bless him, had sped down the mountain so fast Paris's stomach was left somewhere back there on the winding road.

"I wouldn't have told you to slow down, no matter how sick I felt."

"I know." He glanced Mac's direction as he lowered onto the couch, the concern in his gaze the same that thrummed through Paris. "Thank you for that and for helping him. He couldn't have done that today without you."

"Or without you."

"I wish he'd let me do more."

"I know," Paris said, parroting Liam's earlier response. He swiped his brush through the brown and green paint and started the mural with the giant's eyes. "Your aura is pure indigo. Empathy, according to the witches."

"You can read auras?" Back to Liam, Paris couldn't see his eyes, but by the tone of his voice, he bet they were wide.

"It started with Mac's, then today I could see Abigail's, and now yours. I've been working with the witches to understand what I'm seeing. Still not sure on the who or the why yet."

He worked more on the outline of the giant's face—a larger than average forehead, a square, clean-shaven jaw, a crooked nose that had been broken multiple times. The silence was comfortable, Liam's presence familiar, but conversation helped keep the fear at bay. "Can there be two reapers at once?" Paris asked.

"Everyone in our family can sense the souls."

Paris glanced over his shoulder. "About five minutes into the trek, I started hearing the voices and a split second later, you *Kraa*'ed." His attempt to mimic their call drew a welcome chuckle out of Liam.

"I heard them too," he said, but then sobered, gaze straying again to where Mac was curled on his side in bed. "We can all sense them because both our parents were reapers. Our mother was the reaper for her tribe, our father from his Celtic ancestors' clan, but when they mated, the lines were joined, and there can only be one reaper from a line who crosses between the planes. I watch and learn and do what I can to help on this one whenever he'll let me."

"It'll be you next?" Paris asked as he turned back to the wall.

"If he doesn't outlive me."

"He can't give it up?"

"He can. Our parents did. But he won't."

Paris wasn't sure that was quite right. Not with the regret and duty that colored so much of Mac's aura. "Or he doesn't know how."

Liam hummed in reply, contemplating it seemed. His silence stretched on so long that Paris assumed he'd fallen asleep, until the couch cushions squeaked again sometime later, Liam rising to stoke the fire. "Is he okay?"

"He's exhausted—and exhausting," Paris said with a smile as he tinkered with the almost leaf-like collection of freckles behind the giant's ear. "But I don't think he knows any other way to be." Liam's answering laugh was warm and affectionate. "Am I wrong?"

"You're not, but he's different with you. Since you."

"If I can use that to make him sleep, then let's count it a win."

"It's going to get tougher," Liam said as he stood beside Paris in front of the wall. "Especially with the Rift anniversary in a few days. I need you—*we* need you—to keep helping him. He lets you, more than he lets any of us." The urgency in his voice made Paris pause mid-brushstroke and glance in his direction. And was nearly blinded by the pure indigo aura that radiated out of him. "Keep making him sleep. Make him talk too, when he needs that. Too many people, too many souls depend on him."

Paris nodded, for all their sakes and his own, because if the tugging in his chest today each time he dove into a vision, each time Mac came and went between the planes was any indication, Paris's soul depended on Mac too.

FOURTEEN

Paris surrendered his brush at sunrise, every detail he could muster about the giant out of his head and onto the wall. Mind and body tired, all he wanted to do was shut his eyes and forget the world for a while. He stoked the fire, made sure Liam's blankets were snug around him on the couch, then crawled into bed with a relieved sigh.

Only for worry to spike when Mac's shivers rippled across the mattress. Not as severe as earlier, and for a good long while there, he'd slept peacefully, but Paris didn't like that the tremors were back. He considered more covers, but all of them in the cabin were already in use, and he sure as hell wasn't going for a walk in the morning cold to fetch one from the witches. Taking the only action left to him, Paris scooted closer and spooned the taller man from behind. Mac didn't wake, didn't even move but for the tremors that continued to ripple through his body. Paris held him close and distracted himself from the mounting worry by counting Liam's snores from across the room. Fifty-six later, Mac's shivers finally subsided, his breaths evening out again, and before Paris reached sixty, he nodded off himself, forehead pressed against the soft fabric between Mac's shoulder blades.

When he woke sometime later, Paris detected no snores, no

voices, and no keystrokes, just the sizzling crackle of a waning fire. Opening his eyes, Paris let them adjust to the dim lighting, the late afternoon sun cutting across the cabin. And catching the note on the pillow beside his. Unfolding it, he recognized Mac's handwriting from his case files. *Thank you*, it read. *We're needed in YB. Coven is here for anything you need. Back soon.* —M

Two days later, Paris was raring for an argument over the definition of soon, if soon ever came to pass. There'd been no sign of Mac or Liam, no word from any of Paris's own contacts in YB, and no calls that the witches told him about during their lessons or over the dinner Paris made for them last night. While Paris appreciated Mac's trust in leaving him out here alone, while he appreciated the peace and protection of this forest by the sea, not knowing what was going on outside it, not knowing if he could help like he had on the ridge, was driving him crazy. The only things that kept him sane, that kept him from hot-wiring one of the witch's cars like Jason had taught him, were his paints and the unwavering connection he shared with Mac. Mac was out there, doing what his team needed, and the last thing he needed was Paris distracting him. He'd all but resigned himself to not seeing Mac or Liam until after the Rift anniversary tomorrow, so when tires crunched over the gravel outside, he nearly dropped his paintbrush.

Righting his grip on the brush, he flipped it so the pointy end was at the ready. Mac had told him only friendlies could get through the witches' protections and the crows in the trees. He wasn't expecting any witchy visitors, so . . . He moved to peek out the window, but before he reached it, the door swung open, Mac's tall, rangy frame stepping through, his face shadowed by the setting sun outside.

Paris opened his mouth to have that argument about *soon*, but then the light shifted and Mac's face came into full view. His tan skin was pale, dark circles underlined his eyes, and his hair was a tousled mess. Add the slumped shoulders under his wrinkled shirt and the tie hanging loose around his neck, and Paris didn't want to know the last time Mac had slept. In his arms two days ago, if Paris had to guess. At least he wasn't shivering this time. In any event, he was here now, and Paris needed to get him fed and to bed.

"How about some potato fennel soup and cheese sandwiches?"

"That sounds great."

"Go take a shower while I get it ready."

Mac didn't argue, just grabbed fresh clothes from the pile Paris had cleaned and headed for the bathroom. By the time he reappeared, Paris had bowls of soup on the table and was cutting the hearth-grilled sandwiches in half.

And nearly sawed his finger in half too.

Barefoot and hair wet, Mac crossed the room in his low-slung pants and unbuttoned dress shirt, more of that long, lean body on display than Paris had ever seen. And more striking than he'd ever dreamed. He took a moment to appreciate the rosy warmth the shower had returned to his skin, then took a longer few moments to appreciate Mac's broad shoulders and solid chest, abs that were toned but not overly ripped, the sprinkling of dark curls on his torso and the thicker line of dark hairs that trailed beneath his waistband.

Paris's mouth went dry, the inevitable supernova finally crashing into him and his dick responding in kind, hardening inside his sweats. Thank fuck he was standing behind a counter where Mac couldn't see.

"I'm sorry I couldn't send word," the raven said, and Paris struggled to focus on his words and not the tempting figure he cut in the firelight. "I meant to make it back last night, but then one of the names on your list flipped, and he led us to one of your father's stash houses."

Mention of Vincent quelled Paris's libido, for now. He finished slicing the sandwiches without injury and carried the plates to the table. "What does that mean?" he asked as he and Mac took their seats.

"Money, weapons, magical beings he used as power sources."

"Alive?"

He stirred his soup, a faraway look flitting across his dark eyes. "Some."

"But not as bad as the ridge?" Paris said, if he was reading the reaper's vitals correctly. "You weren't shivering when you came in."

Mac returned to the present and his food, slurping a spoonful of still steaming soup. Paris was glad he'd leaned toward over-warm. "No, thankfully, and we had another reaper helping."

"I wish I could've been there to help you."

"Me too." He aimed one of his soft smiles in Paris's direction, and Paris flip-flopped again on which expression to paint. He had time to decide, the rest of the picture still coming together in his head, the rest of the world still on fire. He wanted to paint Mac when it wasn't a necessity; when instead it was simply a matter of joy and appreciation.

They finished their soup and sandwiches in silence, jazz music playing in the background, and when Paris rose and carried the dishes to the sink, Mac joined him. "We took the physical weapons," he said. "But the money is yours. We've secured it."

"Use what you need for Nature's cause."

"Paris."

He flung a soapy hand in the air, gesturing at their surroundings. "How much have you spent on paints, on clothes, on food, on taking care of me?"

"That's not even a blip on the radar of what you've inherited."

Paris gulped. He'd known his father—their family—was rich, but he'd purposely looked the other way, ignored the how and why and stayed in his privileged golden cage. No more. "I don't want that money."

"If you don't claim it, someone else will, and not for good."

"Fine," he gritted out, fists balled under the soapy water. "Use what you need for the cause, then I'll find more good uses for the rest. Deal?"

"Deal." Mac bumped his shoulder and warmth rippled out from the simple contact, easing Paris back down from his momentary fuss. Unclenching his fists, he got back to washing dishes, and Mac grabbed the closest dishtowel to dry. "Dinner was delicious," he said.

"The witches have been good to me." Checking up on him, teaching him about auras, joining him in the meadow to pick flowers and other herbs they'd discovered among the weeds. "I wanted to do something nice for them. More than just regular bread deliveries."

Mac gifted him another soft smile, then, once they were finished, wandered out of the kitchen area. "You stayed painting while I was gone. They're so bright," he said from in front of the wall of flowers bursting with color, pretty things his father would never let him have. Belittled him for painting. "You left this, though," Mac said with a nod toward the mural of the giant from the ridge.

"I didn't know if you had enough light or enough time to take a picture before you left."

"I did, and we got a positive ID on him."

Pride swelled inside Paris's chest. He'd done something right, had turned the worst moment of his life into something good, into something he could use to help Mac and the team. He'd been told his entire life he was a fool, that he was worthless, but in this case he'd remembered enough, painted well enough to give Mac a lead. Maybe Icarus had been right when he'd told Paris not to sell himself short. "Have you found him yet?"

"Not yet, but Icarus's sister is digging into his financials and internet history. We're trying to pinpoint where he might set up for Samhain."

"One of the other altars?"

"That's the thinking, but we have to find them first."

"Are there other thin spots like the one on the ridge?"

"More than a few," Mac answered. "But we don't have an insider like we did with Abigail and the last one. We'll have to approach the rest with caution." He gestured again at the wall. "Let's paint over this one."

"In the morning," Paris replied. "You need to go to bed."

"I do," he conceded. "But if I have any hope of sleeping, I need to get out of my head first. Mindlessly rolling paint onto a wall should do the trick."

"Fair enough," Paris said with a chuckle. "You get the paint ready. I'm going to turn up the music and swap these sweats for the paint-stained ones."

A quick trip to the bathroom, then Paris returned just as one of his favorite tunes began to fill the cabin, its cresting and breaking melodies reminding him of the waves he'd gone too many days without again.

The ocean . . .

"Wait!" he called out to Mac who was running the roller brush through the tray of white paint. Mac paused, gaze straying over his shoulder. "I want to start from a different base color," Paris explained. He snagged his tubes of blue and indigo and added several dollops of the former and a single dollop of the latter to the tray. He swirled them into the white, mixing the colors, but it still wasn't quite the shade in his head. He snatched his tube of green off the nearby table, added a dollop of that too, and after several more stirs, the tray of paint finally transformed into the lovely blue-green shade he missed so much.

"The ocean," Mac said, catching on.

"Not just the shore this time." Grinning, Paris made a giant sweeping gesture. "I want a whole wall of ocean."

Mac's answering laugh was worth the dramatics.

Paris grabbed the other roller, and they worked together to cover the nightmare mural with cool blue-green, the rhythmic roll of the brushes, the smooth jazz notes filling the cabin, and the crackling fire creating the cocoon of calm they'd both needed. Paris might even go so far as to say an uplift in Mac's mood, the typically restrained raven swaying his hips to the tune as he ran the roller through the paint tray again. "He dances," Paris gasped, playing dramatic again, hoping for a similar reaction.

Mac rolled his eyes and swiped at the hair that had fallen across his forehead. "He sways because he can barely stay upright."

"I don't believe you." Leaving his roller propped against the wall, Paris gently removed Mac's from his hand and rested it beside his, then just as gently drew Mac by the wrist into his arms.

Around a smile, Mac grumbled, "What are you doing?"

"Dancing." And taking his chance, Mac's walls and defenses down, his limbs loose and body warm. Paris shifted closer, soaking up the energy that vibrated between them.

"Paris," Mac whispered, voice trembling. "I can't—"

Yes, you can was on the tip of his tongue, but when Paris looked into Mac's eyes, when he saw the desire and terror swirling in the dark depths, he altered course, desperate not to drive whatever had put that fear in his gaze higher. That was the last thing Mac needed. He laid a hand on Mac's chest and ignored his own desire to drag his fingers through the curls there. "I'm not asking for anything, Mac. Just dancing with a friend and helping you get out of your head."

The sound that slipped from Mac's lips was somewhere between a laugh and a groan, and he tilted forward, forehead pressed against Paris's. "You're doing more than that." He cupped the side of Paris's neck, and Paris's heart leapt. Jumped all the way into his throat as Mac angled his face, breath coasting over his lips.

And then gone the next instant, and it took Paris a disorienting second to realize why. Someone was banging on the cabin door, and every muscle in Mac's frame had snapped tight, gone battle-ready, his gaze fixed on the door.

"It's probably just Liam or one of the witches," Paris said, even as his own pulse raced faster, adrenaline kicking in to help him fight or flee.

"If it was Liam, I would have sensed him. And the witches

know to signal." He stepped out of Paris's arms and peeked out the side window into the trees. "Why didn't the crows alert me?"

Had someone found them? Someone who wanted to kidnap him for his inheritance? Or someone who worked for Chaos? Was it the giant coming back for him? "Mac . . ." he whispered, his voice trembling now.

Mac grabbed the bread knife off the counter and slapped the handle into Paris's hand. "Take this and go hide in the bathroom."

"*What?*"

"Paris, *please*." When he lifted his gaze, his eyes were glowing violet, all trace of desire gone, nothing but terror now. He had no idea who was on the other side of that door, and he feared the worst. Paris grabbed hold of that imaginary rope inside his chest and tugged. Mac tugged right back. "Go."

FIFTEEN

When a minute passed without the pop of gunfire or the crack of furniture, Paris nudged open the bathroom door. Hearing no raised voices or other sounds of a fight, he opened the door wider and peeked out. Mac was standing over the front door threshold, puffed up and growly, blocking Paris's view of their visitor and their visitor's view of him. He fed his crush that protective nugget, wallowing in it, until his name—"Paris Cirillo"—reached his ears.

"I don't know who you're talking about," Mac lied.

"I know he's here," said the voice Paris would recognize anywhere. Out of any danger, Paris set aside his makeshift weapons and hustled across the cabin.

"How's that?" Mac practically barked.

"Because I told him," Paris said, talking over his best friend's "Because I can smell him." Strange reply, but whatever . . . Kai was *here*. Paris ducked under Mac's arm and swallowed the smaller man in a crushing hug.

"You *what*?" Mac barked at him now, and Paris would get to that truth in just a moment.

For now, he wanted to revel in the familiar, in his first taste of home in over a week, and it warmed his heart that Kai hugged him back just as fiercely. The three of them—Kai, Jason, and Paris —were family, the real kind, and Paris had missed them, dearly. He drew back, checking his friend over, from his dark tousled curls to his tan skin to his big brown eyes. "I missed you," Paris said to him, then glancing over his shoulder at a simmering Mac, color high in his cheeks, fingers white-knuckling the door, added, "He's a friend. One of my best."

"No one is supposed to know you're here," Mac said, voice strained. "Not after the last time."

Okay, he had a point, and a right to be angry—no contact was one of the rules—but if it had been a hard and fast one, Liam wouldn't have let him use his phone that day. And Paris's position from that day hadn't changed. He wasn't going to leave his human friends stranded in the middle of a magical shitstorm without some kind of backup.

Was that why Kai was here now? Were he and Jason in trouble? Where was Jason? All questions he wanted answers to— inside the cabin. "It's fine," he told Mac. "We can trust him." He shifted from Kai's arms to Mac's side and patted his chest, seeking to assure the raven in the same place Paris felt his reassurance whenever he needed it. "Now, can we let him in before the witches get even more curious? The crows are audience enough."

With a combination glare and growl that would turn Paris on at any other time, Mac begrudgingly opened the door wide enough for Paris to slip back through with Kai in tow.

"What are you doing here?" he asked as Kai glanced around the cabin.

Mac closed the door, then stood beside them, arms crossed. "Better question. Why didn't the crows alert me that you were here in the first place?"

Kai shifted Paris's grip, flipping it so he was the one squeezing Paris's hand. The apology in his eyes nearly startled a gasp out of Paris. "You gotta promise not to be mad at me. This wasn't about you."

Not about him? Mad at Kai? For what? Showing up here? Not possible. "I missed you too much to be mad."

Kai released his hand, then held his own out to Mac. "Because I'm one of you. Kai Finley."

Paris did gasp at that. One of you, as in a raven? A shifter?

Eyes wide, Mac seemed as surprised as him for once. "What's your real name?"

"Kaimus. Finley was my father's surname. My mother's was Kasta."

"Haida?" Mac asked, and Kai nodded. When Mac spoke again, his tone did a complete one-eighty from suspicious to almost . . . reverent. "I thought your kind were gone."

His kind? So he wasn't a raven? And what was Haida? Kai rarely spoke about his parents or where he'd come from before landing in YB, but he had mentioned his mother was from an Indigenous tribe up north. Was Haida that tribe? Of shifters?

"Not gone," Kai said. "Just hiding."

"Cormac Kelley. It's an honor. And please, call me Mac."

Head spinning, Paris slid between the two men, glancing back and forth between them. "I'm lost. Can someone please explain?"

"You didn't know he was a raven?" Mac said.

"Clearly." He pointed at Kai's face. "And his eyes are brown." Only humans had brown eyes.

"Not really," Kai said, apology in his gaze once more. Standing beside the table, he removed a case from his pocket and removed contacts Paris had never suspected, had never seen him put in or take out before. When Kai lifted his gaze back to them, his blue-green irises were again not what Paris expected.

"They're not purple like yours," he said to Mac.

"No, because he's a different kind of raven. He's special, Paris."

"Well, the *special* part I knew." Kai was the best of them, the one who'd gone straight and earned an honest living tending bar. He was calm, he was caring, he kept him and Jason in line as much as he could. Paris trusted him completely, but not the other way around, it seemed? He couldn't keep the hurt from his voice. "But the other . . ."

Kai captured his flailing hand. "I'm sorry. With your dad, I couldn't risk him finding out what I was."

"Does anyone in YB know?" Mac asked.

"Our other best friend, Jason. He's the only person here I've told."

That stung, not because Kai hadn't told him, but because Paris's father had stolen something else from him, had put a wall between Paris and his best friends. One of whom was conspicuously absent, and with everything Paris had learned about ravens lately, Paris's worry ratcheted higher. "Where is he?"

"That's why I'm here. I think he's in trouble." He shifted his gaze to Mac. "The raven knows he is."

"Jason's always in trouble," Paris said, though he sensed something was different this time. It had to be for Kai to risk coming here, to expose his identity. Paris squeezed his hand in solidarity, letting him know he didn't hold anything against him, that he still had his back.

Kai nodded, then turned his attention back to Mac and lifted his other hand, splaying it over his chest. "It burns."

The resemblance to the motion Paris had just shared with Mac was unmistakable. He wasn't surprised his best friends were connected in a similar way. But what did he mean by *it burns*? "What's happened?" he asked as he led them to the seating area, Mac buttoning his shirt along the way.

Kai lowered himself on one end of the couch. "Moira."

Because *of course* it would be her. Paris flopped next to Kai and hung his head back on a groan. "Fucking hell."

"Who's Moira?" Mac asked from the chair.

"Asshole vampire of the highest order." He righted his gaze and flicked a hand in the air. "She and Jason were a thing for a hot minute."

"She told him there was a stash." Kai cleared his throat and glanced guiltily at Paris. "One of your father's in the Canyon Lands. She needed a lock pick."

"And Jason needed a payday," Paris surmised.

"To get us out before tomorrow."

Paris looped an arm around Kai's shoulders and pulled him into a sideways hug. Why wouldn't his friends just let him help? Jason didn't have to put himself in danger; Kai wouldn't have to worry about him. Granted, it was more complicated when Vincent had been alive, especially if Kai hadn't wanted to expose himself, but now . . . Now, when whatever this was was all over, they were going to have a serious conversation about how to stay alive, all of them, because Paris needed his family.

"I didn't know where else to go," Kai said.

"This is why I told you where I was, in case of emergency." It gave him some hope they could work out an arrangement in the future. Now he just needed Mac's help in the present. "I'm sorry, but I needed them to have some backup."

Mac's gaze held his for a long moment, understanding passing between them, before he leaned forward and rested his forearms on his knees. "You said it burns. What did you mean?"

"That they're connected," Paris said, and barely bit back the *like us* he wanted to add. Would Mac want that shared with Kai? Did Mac feel the same way?

"There's connected," Mac said. "And then there's 'it burns.' Very different."

"You know what my people did?" Kai asked, and at Mac's nod, he continued. "I think—" He cut himself off, swallowed hard, then started again. "I *know* Jason's a phoenix. And he's in danger."

"But Jason's human," Paris said, voice rising with panic, the world starting to spin again.

"Not anymore."

Mac rested a hand on his knee. "Breathe, Paris." Squeezed. "You did the right thing. We'll try to help him." He left his hand there as he glanced back to Kai. "I need to know everything."

For all of Atlas's efforts to make sure he was well-read and educated, Paris had gotten a crash course in the supernatural the past twelve days. And as Mac and Kai talked, as Kai divulged more details, Paris tried to suppress how overwhelmed he felt and focus instead on the mundane because that was the only way he could help in this situation.

He zeroed in on certain words from their conversation.

Stash.

Phoenix.

Power.

Staring at the calming blue-green wall, the same color as his friend's real eyes, Paris put himself in the shoes of the person he had the misfortune to know best in the world.

Vincent Cirillo.

The human who had hunted phoenixes, held them captive in stash houses, and bled them dry in order to replenish his own stolen power.

Fuel stations, his father used to say. *I need to visit a fuel station.*

Fuel stations that were marked on a map he kept in his private study, a room only he and Atlas had ever been inside. That Paris regularly broke into to steal from his father's supply of Daylight.

Rocketing off the couch, he grabbed the closest paint brush and the tubes of black and red paint. He squeezed a dollop of each onto the back of his hand, swiped his brush through the black one first, then on the blue-green wall, he began to sketch the outlines of the Canyon Lands. Crumbling stone jetties and canyons of deep, dark water, broken buildings and disintegrating streets, the barbed wire fence that separated what amounted to YB's haunted house from the rest of the city.

He was so deep in his memories, so focused on translating them correctly onto the wall, that he didn't notice the conversation behind him quiet or Mac move to stand behind him. He startled when he rocked back on one heel to evaluate his work and ran into him.

"What's this?" Mac asked, steadying him by the shoulders.

"My father had maps. Lots of them." He rinsed his brush in the paint water mug, flicked off the excess, then swiped it through the red. "There was this one in his private office. It had red dots on it." He marked the five spots on the map he'd replicated. "When I asked him what the dots were, he told me they were fuel stations."

Mac stepped beside him, stared a long moment at the wall, and then a satisfied smirk stretched across his face, the sexiest thing Paris had ever seen. "You're amazing," he said, clasping the back of Paris's head and hauling it closer to press his lips to his temple, searing Paris with the affectionate touch. "Go pack."

Wait . . . what? Paris jerked his head back, meeting the raven's dark eyes. "We're leaving?"

"I need to go into the city with Kai, but I'll send Liam for you. If your friend is a phoenix, if he survives, we'll need to bring him back to the mountain after. I assume you'll want to be with him."

"Yes, of course," Paris said as he tossed aside his brush and wiped his hands on his sweats. "But why are we going back to the ridge?"

"Not the ridge," Mac said. "We're going to Monte Corvo. In Talahalusi."

SIXTEEN

Liam turned off Talahalusi's main road and onto a paved drive blocked by iron gates, each adorned with a giant raven, their wings spread wide, and in the middle where the gates met, the letters MC molded in ornate script.

"Not hiding, are you?" Paris said.

"It was called Crow Mountain before our mother's people settled it." Liam reached out the window and pressed his thumb to a keypad. "No matter the language, that's what it means." The gates swung open, and Liam drove through. "In the light of day, you'll understand why."

In the light of the car's high beams, Paris counted row after row of vines as the road snaked higher. Around one bend, a pair of long barn-like facilities appeared on either side of the road, stretching as far as Paris could see in the dark. Around the next one, a massive mansion—correction, castle—stood majestically on a clearing.

But they weren't done climbing yet. Liam circled behind the castle and veered off the paved road onto a gravel one, and up, up, up they went, all the way to where the vegetation and trees thinned out and a smaller version of the mansion below set atop the bluff. "This is the reaper's perch," Liam said as he parked in front of the stone steps that led to the front door.

Paris climbed out of the car and wandered to the edge of the bluff. Nothing but darkness below and starlight above. He rotated back to Liam and gestured at the relatively miniature castle. "If Mac lives in this monster, who lives in the bigger one down the hill?" The Cirillos were rich by YB standards, but the kind of wealth that built these structures, that cultivated this land was generational, far eclipsing Paris's father's ill-gotten gains. Hell, the real estate value alone dwarfed their compound of penthouse condos.

Liam chuckled. "Me and the rest of the family."

"Are you sure they're not all here?" Every light in Mac's place was on, several other cars were parked in the circular drive, and music played from somewhere inside.

"This is also the team's main base of operations." Starting for the front door, his foot had barely hit the bottom step when the door swung open and two children came screaming through, yelling "Daddy!" at the top of their lungs.

"Daddy?" Paris squawked.

"Not that kind," Liam said with a wink over his shoulder before he kneeled with his arms open for . . . his kids? "Hello, my tiny terrors."

They barreled into him, all giggles, and Liam laughed along with them, that full-bellied one Paris had heard before. Now he understood where Liam's wealth of happiness came from—these two children with the same sharp Kelley nose and black eyes, with skin that was several shades darker, and with brown hair that was coarse and curly. Close in age, if Paris had to guess, around five or six, and the both of them chatty, talking over each other as they told their father what all they'd been up to. Paris caught Icarus's name several times, the mention of crocheting, and then as fast as they'd appeared, the siblings raced back inside.

Standing, Liam wiped the gravel off his knees, and without the cute distracting chatterboxes, Paris's confusion retook center stage. "I had no idea you were a dad. Do you single parent, or do you have a partner?"

"That would be me," came a new voice from the doorway, and Paris swung his gaze her direction. Tall, curvy, with dark skin, black eyes, and brown hair, and ripped biceps that gave away the fact she could probably kick both his and Liam's asses.

That knowledge, unfortunately, did not reach Paris's mouth before he said to Liam, "But you flirt with—"

"Everyone," Liam's partner said, her smile belying her beleaguered groan. She sashayed down the steps, hands in the pockets of her patterned dress. "Thankfully, I married him first."

"Because you've known since we were toddlers that I was yours." He held out an arm, and the woman slid under it, nestled against his side. "Paris, my wife, Rena. Rena, this is Paris."

"And those rug rats are our kids," Rena said. "Cherry and Abernathy."

Paris raised a brow, the contrast between the names stark.

"We let them choose," Liam said. "And after some back-and-forth, that's where we've landed."

"For now," Rena said, and by her tone, Paris fully expected the kids to have different names by tomorrow. Their prerogative.

"I'm sorry I've kept Liam away from you all lately," Paris said as he followed the happy couple inside.

"My parents are winemakers," Rena explained. "They came here to run the blending operation when I was a baby. I grew up with this one." She elbowed Liam's side. "I knew what I was signing up for."

Liam hugged her close and plastered a sloppy, wet kiss on her cheek that they all laughed over. "The kids should be asleep," he said as he drew back.

"You tell that to Icarus when he gets back. He bet them a cupcake each they couldn't out-stitch him. Pretty sure he let them win."

"That sounds like Icarus," Paris said, the vampire one of the more mischievous beings he'd ever met. But he was also inherently good-natured; of course he'd let the kids beat him.

"You know him?" Rena asked.

"Quite well," he replied, heat hitting his cheeks. Impossible for it not to given the very mischievous things, usually involving lace and blindfolds, he and Icarus had gotten up to since the courtesan had arrived in town nine months ago.

"Uh-oh," Rena said, brow lifted. "Are we going to have to referee a match between him and Adam?" she asked Liam.

Paris opened his mouth to reply, but Liam beat him to it. "No, honey, he's bonded to Mac."

Her assessing gaze shot back to him, even as she directed her question at Liam. "That's still possible? After—"

"Apparently."

Paris shook his head, losing the thread back around the word *bond*. "I'm sorry, what—"

Before he could finish his question, Cherry and Abernathy came racing back toward them, each waving what looked like pot holders at Liam. "Dad! Look it!"

"Amazing!" Liam oohed and aahed like a good parent should, until Rena eventually nipped the too late party in the bud. "We need to get them home and to bed."

The kids booed, but Liam gamely lifted one on each hip, advising, "Your mom is the smartest person on Earth. We have to do what she says. She's always right."

"I thought that was Mary," Abernathy said.

"Smartest," Liam said. "Mary's the most powerful."

Mary? Who was that? Paris was lost again.

"Can you show him to Mac's quarters?" Liam said to Rena, then said to Paris, "I'll be back to unpack once I get them to sleep."

Paris shook his head and held out his hand. "Give me the keys and I'll take care of it." He counted it a win that Liam didn't hesitate.

"Are Monte and Chaz here?" Liam asked Rena as he kissed her cheek once more.

"Down by the lake preparing for containment. Two of the coyotes are on guard."

"Good," Liam said with a nod, then readjusted the kids on his hips and shot Paris a smile. "Make yourself at home."

Once Liam carried the children out the front door, Rena closed it behind him, then waved Paris deeper into the house. "There's a lake here?" he asked, and they made conversation while he stared agape at the vaulted ceilings, at the artwork from prominent Indigenous artists, at the recently repaired sections of the walls and floor, the paints and stains not an exact match, not as aged as sections around them. Those repaired places increased in frequency as they made their way to the back of the house, then into a suite of rooms at one end, a bedroom, sitting room, and office, the latter nothing like the cabin but exactly like it. Laptops open, files scattered across an oversize desk, a notepad with the chicken scratch Paris recognized.

"You can hang out here." Rena pointed at another door on the other side of the office. "There's a guest bedroom over there." He didn't mention that he and Mac had been sharing a bed for days. Rena's ringing phone saved him from the lie. "I need to take this."

"Sure thing," Paris said. While she took her call in the hallway, he circled behind the desk, figuring he could distract himself from what might be happening with Jason and Kai, with the only family he had left, by continuing his and Mac's work. Grabbing the stack of files he recognized as the detective's cold cases, he sank into the chair and pulled them closer, flipping through to see if any jogged a memory or rattled loose another soul. Nothing in the first few.

He shuttled the third case file to the no luck stack, then turned back to start on the fourth, only to be stopped cold by the black-and-white photo that had been wedged between the folders. Two men, their clothes from a time Paris had only read about in history books, the environs behind them unrecognizable, but he'd recognize the taller of the two men anywhere. Long, rangy body, dark hair and eyes, a sharp nose and that soft smile Paris couldn't get out of his head. Only in the photo it was directed at the man standing in his arms. Shorter, broader, laughing with his head thrown back, his light hair caught in the breeze. What had Mac said to make him do that? Who was he to Mac? When he'd finished laughing, had Mac drawn him back upright and kissed him? It was a simple picture, and yet one of the most romantic Paris had ever seen.

A gasp from the doorway crashed through Paris's spiraling thoughts, and for a panicked second, he thought it would be Mac standing there, but it was Rena, her eyes wide as she clutched her phone to her chest. "I've only seen that picture out of the safe once since Mac moved in here."

"It was between these file folders," he said, gesturing at the two stacks he'd made before staring again at the photo. "Who is he?"

"The reason Mac will push you away. Don't let him."

"What did Liam mean that Mac and I are bonded?"

"You need to talk to Mac about that."

He set the photo aside and splayed a hand over his chest. "It's why I can feel him here, isn't it?" Her eyes widened impossibly further, mouth rounding into an *O*. She must not have believed Liam when he'd said it, but she believed now. "I grabbed hold of him that night I almost died. I didn't know what else to do, but if he's already bonded to someone, if he didn't want to be bonded to me—"

"Have you felt him tug back?" Rena asked.

He held her gaze and nodded.

"Trust that," she said. "And trust yourself."

SEVENTEEN

Paris was dreaming about the ocean again. He was sitting on his favorite bench outside their condo building, watching the sun sink toward the horizon and the fog roll in. Below him, waves crashed against the cliffs, misting his face with sea spray and shaking the earth beneath his feet.

Shaking him.

"Come on, Paris. Wake up."

He opened his eyes to reality. No ocean, but an equally beautiful sight.

"There he is," Mac said as he kneeled beside him.

The morning sun streamed in through the window over his shoulder, and Paris squinted. "What time is it?"

"Early. Sorry about the sun," he said with a flick of his fingers at the glowing ball of light behind him. Brighter than Paris could ever remember seeing in his life. "This side of the house faces east."

Peeling himself off the folders and papers, scattering some onto the floor, Paris propped an elbow on the desk to hold up his tired head and eked his eyes open wider, taking in the man before him. "You haven't slept." By now, Paris recognized the signs of a sleepless raven. "Long night?"

Hand on his knee, Mac lifted his dark gaze, and it swam with empathy, his aura pulsing indigo, brighter even than Liam's had that day at the cabin.

The rest of Paris's reality clicked into place, his heart drowning with it. "Is he—"

"Kai was right. Jason became a phoenix."

"How?"

"We don't know that yet. We'll ask him when he's conscious again. Kai's with him until then."

Reality shifted again, and Paris spun the chair to face Mac, sending more folders and papers to the floor. "Wait, Jason's alive? And Kai?"

"They're both alive," Mac said with a wide smile. "Was touch and go with Jason for a bit, but he should make—" Paris launched himself out of the chair and into Mac's arms. "Oof!"

Paris couldn't hold in the tears; with Mac, he thankfully didn't have to. He'd cried in his arms before, overcome with relief the morning he'd learned of his father's death. Relief racked his body again, but today, relief felt completely different. Before, his relief had been from fear, from his tormentor; a freedom Paris had never experienced, living under his abusive father's fist for twenty plus years. Today's relief was the opposite, steeped in love for the chosen family still with him and in gratitude for Mac and his team who'd rescued them. There weren't enough *thank you*s in the world, but Paris tried to give them all to Mac, a litany between broken breaths, as Mac leaned them against the desk and ran a hand up and down his spine, gentling him with soothing words.

But fast on the heels of relief came the overwhelming, shifting realities of the past two weeks. One of his best friends was a raven, the other was a phoenix, and he was just a human—in a world, a life, that was barely recognizable. In the arms of a different raven he wanted to get to know better. Where was his place anymore? With Kai and Jason, or with Mac and his team, or without any of them? How could he be anything but a burden to them all?

The questions, the doubts, stole his breath and left him gasping for air.

"Hey, hey, hey," Mac soothed as he held his face in his hands, his dark gaze inviting and calm, same as his words. "Breathe, Paris. Just breathe." A little gulp in. "They're fine." A slightly bigger gulp. "They're still your best friends." A full inhale. "And you can see them when it's safe." And finally, a deep one as Mac's thumbs swiped the tears from under his eyes.

"But Kai is safe with him?" he asked, voice wobbly.

"More than you can possibly know," he said, the same awe in his voice that had been there when Kai had arrived at the cabin. Tears pooled at the corners of his dark eyes, and when he hid them behind closed lids, a tear streaked down one cheek. He tilted forward, pressing their foreheads together. "That's how it's supposed to go."

Paris returned the earlier gesture, cupping his cheeks and offering comfort, whatever this man who'd saved him and his family needed. "What can I do? How can I help you?"

Mac's lower lip brushed against his. It was such a light touch, so soft and fleeting that Paris thought it incidental, but then Mac's lips pressed against his, firmer and longer, not an accidental brush. Paris was thrown into a tailspin, the desire that had been banked for days roaring to the surface. He hazarded a kiss back, and when Mac angled his face in Paris's hands so he could deepen it, Paris groaned and slid his hands into Mac's hair, clutching the dark strands when the tip of Mac's tongue teased his lips, asking for entrance. Paris didn't hesitate to open, to moan as Mac licked inside his mouth, tentative at first, but then growing in demand that fired every one of Paris's senses, that made him want to lie back and surrender all of himself.

Chasing that reality, he shifted in Mac's lap and tipped backward, taking Mac with him by the mouth, neither of them wanting to interrupt their greedy kisses. Mac threw out a hand to brace them on the way down—and planted on something that caused them to slip. He threw out the other hand, catching them before they hit the floor, laughter breaking their lips apart. Laughter Paris wanted to taste. But then Mac's gaze shifted to the side, catching on the thing that had caused them to slip.

The black-and-white photo of Mac and the other man.

Mac's laughter died, his skin paled, and he hastily untangled from Paris, scurrying to his feet so fast Paris nearly did hit the floor, only Mac's unerring manners saving him. "I'm sorry," he said as he helped Paris to his feet.

"Mac, wait."

"I need to get back to the team." He eyed the door like a man on fire. "We've got a lot to do before leaving for YB tonight."

He turned for the door, but Paris caught his wrist, halting his escape. "Thank you for bringing them back to me. They're the only real family I've ever had." *Before you* wanted to roll off his tongue, but he bit it back, letting the tug he made on their connection—their bond?—speak for him.

Mac's gaze snapped to his, then skittered away again. "They're valuable assets."

As Paris glanced again at the photo, he remembered Rena's advice—to trust what he felt and not let Mac push him away. No matter how their kiss had ended, it had been a breakthrough, especially for Mac who'd kept himself locked down—alone—for far too long. Taking Rena's advice, Paris pressed, a little. "That's not why you saved them, though, is it? You saved them for me." Paris lifted his hand and kissed the back of it. "Thank you."

"You're welcome," he replied, voice barely a whisper, but the tug Paris felt in his own chest as Mac left the room was louder than the thunderous waves back home.

———

Paris woke from his nap to the sense of someone watching him. He was on his side in the guest bed in Mac's quarters, the busy late night and tumultuous early morning having caught up with him by midday. He couldn't say when someone had joined him, but he was certain he wasn't alone. And given the pattern of that someone's breaths, the pine and earthy scent he'd come to associate with him, and the warmth spreading through his chest, Paris had a pretty good idea who it was beside him. No idea why, though, after the way he and Mac had left things that morning.

Instead of jumping in there, Paris led with something easier, a joke to break the ice he hated around them. "Are you sure you're not a cat?" he said, not opening his eyes.

Mac chuckled. "Why would you think that?"

"You're like one of those domestic breeds. You know, the ones that wake their people up first thing in the morning by staring and pawing at them."

"Definitely not a cat. And it's definitely not morning."

Paris opened his eyes, meeting the dark ones across from him, then glanced past Mac and out the window, the waning sun casting the sky in hues of pink and purple.

"We're getting ready to head out," Mac said, drawing Paris's gaze back to him. "I didn't want to leave without saying goodbye. And without apologizing for earlier."

He hadn't had long to wallow after Mac had bolted that morning. Spying their uncle leave his office, Cherry and Abernathy had snuck in, apparently looking to raid the stash of candies Mac kept on top of his file cabinet. Finding Paris instead, they'd enlisted him in Operation Morning Sugar, first with the candies, then with the pancakes Liam was cooking in the kitchen. Paris had pitched in to help, the distraction welcome, as was Icarus when he'd appeared midmorning.

They hadn't needed to say anything, each of them swallowing the other in a hug. Holding tight. Theirs had initially been a transactional relationship, Icarus helping him feel not so lonely, Paris giving him what he'd needed to protect his sister, but friendship had grown between them. Icarus had been one of only a few people he'd been able to be himself around, and Paris had broken that trust, a betrayal—a mistake—that no matter what Mac said, he'd always feel guilty about. He'd tried to apologize, and Icarus had slapped a hand over his mouth and told him to "Shut it." Paris had been so shocked by the warmth and pulse he'd felt in his friend's hand that words had deserted him.

They'd deserted him again when a smiling Adam Devlin had joined them. He'd brought Kai with him, and if Paris had hugged Icarus hard, he hugged his best friend harder. He'd wanted to visit Jason too, but it wasn't safe for Paris to see him yet. He took their word for it but wanted a full accounting of the night's events, which Icarus had given in dramatic fashion, as was his way.

All of that activity and there'd been no Mac sightings. Had he eaten? Had he slept? When had he joined Paris in bed? And what did he have to be sorry for? "You don't have to apologize for anything," Paris said.

"I'm the one who initiated that kiss." His gaze strayed to Paris's lips a fleeting second before he flopped onto his back and stared at the ceiling. "I wanted it, even knowing it couldn't go anywhere."

He wanted it still if that ring of red bleeding into his usual aura of guilt and regret, empathy and grief was any indication. "Why can't it?" Paris asked, hoping for more of the story he'd only gotten glimpses of.

"I was in love once before."

"The man from the photo?"

"Hank," Mac said, his voice catching on the name. "He was my best friend." Pain streaked across his face, his brows furrowing and eyes slipping closed. "And I never told him."

Regret blew out every other emotion in his aura, and Paris reached across the inches between them, clasping Mac's hand. "I'm so sorry."

Mac swallowed hard and pressed on, like he needed to get the words out. "When my parents told us they were retiring, Hank told me I could do this. That I could be our clan's reaper."

"I'm sure he knew how strong you were, like I—"

"He was the first name on my list."

"Oh shit."

Paris regretted the curse as soon as it escaped his lips, but then Mac chuckled, the sound watery but amused, and some of the tension in his grip eased. "Yeah, oh shit." He turned on his side to face Paris again, their hands still joined. "I can't go into YB tonight not knowing if either of us will make it out alive."

"Do you think it'll be that bad?"

"In Yerba Buena, it already is. Up here, I don't know. So far just some skirmishes along the Bay's north edge, but there are no guarantees the violence from YB won't spill over. It already did earlier this month with Icarus and Adam. They'll be with me in YB, but Liam and Rena and all of my family will stay here, Kai and Jason too, and some of Jenn's pack. We have to be prepared for anything."

"I'll be fine," Paris said, squeezing his hand.

And then Mac practically squeezed his heart, pulling their hands to his lips and kissing the back of Paris's, repeating his gesture from earlier. "I can't be the one who has to deliver you. I can't go through that again."

Did that mean he couldn't—wouldn't—ever go through love again either? Because it would be a shame for someone who loved others so completely, who risked and tortured his own soul and body to make sure others' were at peace, to keep himself from experiencing total love and devotion in return.

To never let Paris try to be that person because Paris was already sure Mac was that person for him. Paris wanted that shot, wanted to give Mac everything he deserved, including a second chance at love. But short of putting that declaration out into the world, which would not do Mac any good on a day he clearly already dreaded, Paris settled for putting another out there, the only one that truly mattered. "We're all getting through this day —alive."

EIGHTEEN

Paris had just finished shading in some of the vine leaves he'd painted, adding yellow, brown, and red among the green, the valley of vineyards below awash with hues the likes of which he'd never seen in YB, when a voice came from behind him.

"How long have you been painting?"

He turned from the easel he'd set up under the pergola behind Mac's villa, as Adam called it, and found a new person approaching, someone he hadn't met since arriving at Monte Corvo. Not unusual—Liam was right, Mac's place really was a base of operations—but this was a person he'd remember. Dressed in ripped jeans, a faded black tee, and combat boots, the woman was pixie petite, with tan skin, hazel eyes, and a septum ring through her nose. Her long green hair was styled in barrel curls that bounced as she made her way along the edge of the reflecting pool between the house and pergola, tossing peanuts to the crows as she approached.

"All my life," he answered, once she stepped under the wooden trellis with him. "Even when I wasn't supposed to."

"No one should tell you not to do this," she said with a jut of her chin at his painting. "It's beautiful."

"It's beautiful here."

Smiling, she stepped to the end of the pergola and turned her face up to the sun. "It is, isn't it?"

"Did you grow up here? Are you part of Mac's family?" She was on the shorter side for a Kelley and lacked the dark eyes and straight noses they all seemed to have, but she shared his tan skin, a certain aesthetic in the dark clothing she wore, and the familiar signs of outward exhaustion, though with each second she stood in the sun, she seemed to brighten.

She lowered her face and turned back to him, hand extended. "I'm Mary, Icarus's sister."

"Oh!" The dyed hair and edgy aesthetic suddenly made sense. "I've heard a lot—" He slipped his hand into hers and lost his words, his eyes going wide and mouth rounding into an *O*. The energy that flowed from her, from her pure green aura, was blinding in its intensity. "What are you?"

"What do you think I am?"

Nature was on the tip of his tongue—he was sure of it—and on the heels of that realization, so many others fell into place. Mac and team fighting against Chaos, seemingly at the heart of Nature's cause, the sheer power of the magic around them, the way no one on the team referred to Mary by name or to what she so obviously was. "You're *her*."

One corner of her mouth kicked up, her smirk reminiscent of her brother's, as were her words. "People have always underestimated you, haven't they? He said you were smart."

"Icarus is too kind," he replied, and Mary hummed as she strolled back to the edge of the pergola, taking in another shot of sunshine before she claimed one of the loungers. "In fairness," Paris added as he finished dotting in the road that snaked between the rows of vines, "I didn't always lead with my head."

"The world would be an awfully sad place if that's all anyone did."

Reminded of his other friend who typically led with his heart, Paris set aside his brush and sank into the chaise opposite her. "Do you know how Jason is doing?"

"Good," she told him. "He's taken well to the phoenix. Much better than others we've rescued. Having Kai bonded with him helps."

"When can I see him?"

"In the next day or so, I think. We have to be sure he has control of the fire."

"And Adam and Icarus, and the rest of the team? We didn't need the infirmary, so that's a good sign, right?" After the team had left yesterday, he'd helped Monte and Chaz ferry additional supplies down to the overflow barrel room beneath the villa according to Icarus's instructions. A nursing student before he was turned, and still acquainted with those skills after becoming human again, Icarus was the unofficial team medic, thankfully not overseeing an infirmary full of injured this morning.

"No major injuries, so yes, that's a good sign, but it's been a long month already," she said. "And we're only halfway through it." Exhaustion leaked into her voice again, but after a deep inhale, she seemed to shake it off, to settle back into her world. "There's still work to be done in YB. They'll come back as their jobs are done." She shifted her gaze and smirk back to him. "Ask about who you want, Paris."

He splayed a hand over his chest, over where he'd periodically tugged the past twenty-four hours and always received one in return. And done the same when he'd felt Mac tug from his end. The connection still vibrated there, warm and alive. "I know he's fine."

"Doesn't make you not worried." Her smirk smoothed into a gentle smile. "He's fine, but it may take him longer. He's working with the other reapers in the city."

"Was it bad there?"

"Not as bad as it could have been if your father had still been alive. Or if you hadn't given us that list of potential allies. It put us ahead, on a lot of fronts."

"I'm glad it was helpful."

"I have some other questions." She stood and withdrew her phone, gesturing with it. "If you don't mind taking a look?"

"Of course not." He patted the spot on the chaise next to him, and she sat close so he could see the screen.

"You told Mac your father had maps. Do you remember these locations or any discussion of them?" She spread her fingers on the screen, zooming in, then moving the map to show him each spot in YB that had been marked with a red X.

"That one," he said, when she got to the marked spot at the southern edge of YB, a fog-shrouded stick of land that jutted into the Bay. He'd been there once with his father and even just standing by the car while his father met with a suited man near the shore, he couldn't remember a time in his life when he'd been so cold. Wind-whipped and fog-dampened, he'd crawled back into the car before his dad had returned. "He called it a 'transfer point.' I assumed he moved illegal goods through there. But I also didn't realize 'fuel stations' meant phoenixes."

"You had no reason to."

"So what is this transfer point?"

"Possibly an altar."

"For souls," he surmised, and she nodded. "The veil is thin there?"

"There," she said, "and these other spots." She swiped a finger across the screen and a different map appeared, this one showing areas outside of YB too. He recognized the spot on the ridge where Abigail's pack had been decimated, the spot in YB's Canyon Lands where he'd been nearly sacrificed, but there was another marked spot on the north edge of the Bay. "This is technically in Talahalusi, isn't it?" he asked.

"Yes, that's the Huimen Enclave. The areas along the water are tribal lands, mostly undeveloped coastal woods, but the outer portions have been settled and commercialized. Do you remember something there?"

"I heard my father on the phone once talking about potential investments there. But I don't know exactly where or what for, I'm sorry."

"It's still a lead, Paris." She patted his knee. "Good job."

"Is there a thin spot in the east? The shellmound, maybe?" Two in YB, one at the edge of Talahalusi on the Bay, and one on the ridge near Portola. It stood to reason there would be more spots around the Bay.

She smiled wider. "Two, actually, relatively close together, similar to the Stick and the area where we found you. One is near the Huchiun Enclave in the middle of the Bay and the other near the shellmound in Encinal. We control those, not Chaos."

"And in the south?"

Pain flickered across her delicate features, pinching the corners of her eyes and mouth, drawing attention to the wrinkles there Paris hadn't noticed before. She was older than she looked; magic at work. "La Purisima," she said, the pain likewise reflected in her voice.

"All the way down there?" There went the circle picture in his head and any connection to his dad. "My father wouldn't dare go there." The religious cultist would burn them all at the stake for believing in the supernatural, even as they worshipped their own sort. And they were too pious to consort with the likes of Vincent Cirillo.

But even if his circle theory was a bust, another picture formed in his head. "There's still a pattern," he told her, and gestured for the device. She handed it to him, and with a few taps on the device, he drew a sort of zigzag line on the map, connecting the dots. A hunting range. "Maybe we can use it to predict where the giants will strike next?"

"Good work, Paris," she said with a smile. "He was right." She took the device back and stood. "I'm going to run these locations and any in the path against your father's assets. See if we find anything close by."

Paris rose beside her. "You think he might have been funding the giants?"

"We know he was. We connected transfers from one of Vincent's bank accounts to the ridge giant we identified."

He raked a hand through his hair and sighed. "So it's not over today, is it?"

She shook her head, the barrel curls bouncing. "We think they're working toward a Samhain sacrifice. An attempt to open the veil so Chaos can come through." Another couple clicks on her device, and she turned the screen back to him. Multiple dots were clustered around several of the locations they'd already identified. "Missing persons reports, in and around the areas where the thin spots are."

"How does no one notice?"

"Because the culprit is the cart guy at the grocery store, or a doctor killing his patients, or"—another couple taps, and a photo of the giant he'd painted appeared—"the mechanic who worked on a pack member's bike."

"How do we beat this?" It all seemed so heavy and endless, one evil after another.

She looped an arm around his waist and gave him a sideways hug, quieting some of his unrest. "We work together as a team."

"And you're part of that team now," came Kai's voice from the edge of the pergola.

"I'll leave you to it," Mary said, drawing back and smiling up at Paris, sending him another wave of green comfort. "It was lovely to meet you, Paris."

She clomped off, headed back to the villa, tossing peanuts in her wake, and Paris gladly accepted the hug Kai offered in her place. "How's Jason?" Paris asked.

"Recovering. He'll be fine, thanks to you." He drew back, and they lowered onto one of the chaises beside each other. "How are you? With all this?"

"It's a lot. I mean that was just"—he gestured the direction Mary had disappeared into the house—"*her.*"

"She's something else," Kai said with a chuckle. "Don't piss her off. She's more fiery than Icarus."

"I know they're not blood related, but the vibe is definitely siblings."

"Oh yeah, one hundred percent. Some folks are just on the same wavelength, you know? Connected, like they're destined to be in each other's lives."

Sounded familiar, especially about Paris's two best friends. He squeezed his friend's hand. "I'm so happy you and Jason are official now." Kai's cheeks heated, a shy smile turning up the corners of his lips. In all the ups and downs of the past two weeks, their happily ever after was a highlight. "I was getting tired of living in a constant state of would-you-two-just-kiss."

Kai laughed out loud, until he turned a mischievous, Jason-like smile on him. "Is that what you and Mac were doing before I showed up at the cabin?"

Paris's own cheeks heated. "We were just dancing." Close in each other's arms, the warmth of Mac's skin against his own, Mac's hand cupped around the side of his neck, the kiss that had almost happened then.

"But you want to be kissing?"

The kiss that had happened yesterday morning, that had lived rent-free in his head the past day and a half, replayed again, and Paris covered his face with his hands, groaning in frustration. "More than anything," he admitted, through his fingers. "But it's complicated. He's a reaper, and I'm just a human."

Kai rubbed a hand over his back. "You're not *just* anything, Paris."

He dropped his hands and spread one over his chest, over where his own heart beat for someone, truly, for the first time. But it wasn't the first time for Mac. "He's got a hole here, Kai, and I don't know if I or anyone can ever fill it."

"Maybe you're not supposed to. Maybe you're supposed to make your own place there."

NINETEEN

It was a good thing Mac's kitchen was huge because everyone was in it this evening. Some of the team had returned last night, more had trickled in throughout the day, and the remainder were expected back any time now, including Mac and Liam. Rena and the kids were up from the mansion, Jason and Kai were up from the lake where Jason had been recovering, and Mary and Icarus had emerged from the barrel room where a handful of returning pack members had needed medical attention. All in all, a full house, with Cherry and Abernathy—and Jason, especially—making the meal Paris was attempting to prepare a challenge. Mostly the good kind, until Jason conjured up a ball of fire to "put a little char" on the homemade garlic bread Paris had just pulled from the oven, at which point the chef put his foot down.

Paris swatted his friend's big biceps and hip checked him toward the end of the massive island. "I love you, buddy, but you have got to get out from behind here, or Mac's not gonna have a mansion to come home to."

"Aww, come on, Paris," he whined. "Let me flamethrower it." He draped his massive body over the back of Paris's, his long arms dangling over his shoulders, glowing hands palms up in front of them.

"What's a flamethrower?" Cherry asked from where she sat on the other side of the island beside Kai.

Paris could feel Jason's grin against his cheek. "Me!"

"Jason!" he, Kai, and Rena all chided . . . to absolutely no avail.

If Mac reminded him of a domestic cat sometimes, then Jason was the epitome of a puppy, one of those big blond breeds that liked to throw itself into walls while endlessly chasing a ball. Good natured, carefree fun until said wall gave way. Or until Jason lit the pot holders on Paris's hands on fire, and Paris had to fling them to the floor and stomp the flames out.

"Oops," Jason said, grinning as he unwound from around Paris and stole the charred heel of the bread.

Paris hung his head back on a heavy sigh, dramatics turned up to Icarus levels, and everyone laughed, as he'd intended; the antics were good for lifting spirits, including his own. Food would do the same. He wisely waited until Jason was safely across the room before pulling the bubbling vegetable and cheese lasagna out of the oven. He'd just gotten the pans on the trivets and recovered in foil, holding ready until the rest of the team arrived, when Mary called from the hallway opening. "Hey, Paris, can I borrow you for a second?"

"Sure." He untied his apron, tossed it on the island, and wagged a finger at Jason as he crossed the room. "No more touching."

"No promises," he said with a wink from between a giggling Cherry and Abernathy.

"That's the trio of trouble right there," he said to Kai and Rena.

"We'll keep them in line," Rena assured him as she slid off her stool and took up kitchen guard duty. "That lasagna looks too good to end up on the floor."

Paris had to agree, the sweet potatoes, beets, and butternut squash creating layers that reminded him of the sunset he'd painted the other day. He hoped it tasted as good as it looked, once they got a chance to dig in. For now, he followed Mary into the parlor at the front of the house where Icarus, in combat boots, patchwork jeans, and a strappy tank, waited at the poker table by the corner window, his blue gaze fixed on the driveway out front. She slid into the chair behind the open laptop, beside her brother, and Paris claimed the one across from them. "Did you find something?" he asked.

"Prepare yourself," she said, then turned the laptop to face him. The warning should have been enough—he knew to expect the worst at this point—but the worst still took his breath away. Like at the ridge, the altar in the silent video had been reduced to rubble, though not as charred as the other crime scene. Fresher when the video had been taken. Blood still soaked the ground, witness corpses smoldered, and a pile of bones smoked atop the broken altar. Bones that could have been Paris at a different altar if not for Adam, Mac, and the rest of the team that had rescued him. He glanced away and swallowed hard, forcing the words out. "That's definitely a giant's altar," he said. "The Stick?"

"Yes," Mary replied. "Likely from the seventeenth. A source sent me this video."

He shifted his gaze to Icarus, whose brows had furrowed. "Not your team on the scene?"

"No," Mary answered for him. "I didn't want to add this to their plate. Or this . . ." She rotated the laptop back around, then after a few keystrokes, turned it back to Paris. "This is aerial footage of the Huimen Enclave."

"One of the thin spots we talked about the other day."

She nodded, then, reaching around the side of the screen, clicked the right arrow key, and three dots appeared near the road that ran along the western edge of the enclave. "These are cold storage properties your father recently purchased in the area." Another click, and the map changed, showing a series of pathways that snaked through the peninsular territory. "These," Mary said, "are river-forged tunnels that run beneath the surface. The rivers are long gone, but the tidewater still comes and goes in the ones close to the water. The tunnels remain."

The horrible picture came together in Paris's head, and he

covered his gaping mouth with a hand. "To chase the victims through."

"That's what we think." She met his gaze and cringed, apology in her hazel eyes. "There's more."

"Do I want to hear it?"

"Not really," Icarus answered, never taking his eyes off the driveway out the window.

"Tell me anyway."

"I cross-checked the localized missing persons cases for any known associations with your father." Mary clicked the forward arrow once more and three pictures appeared, name and descriptions in the captions underneath. "All paranormals. One who was also on Mac's list."

Paris didn't recognize any of them by appearance or by name, but he recognized his father's MO. Three powerful paranormals—a shifter, a warlock, and a vamp—and one power-hungry human. "Dad used them up, then turned them over."

"Or he lured them to the giant," Icarus said.

"Or they betrayed him, and Dad turned them over." He snagged one of the poker chips from its center holder and flipped it through his fingers the way Atlas had taught him. Like his painting, the repetitive motion provided an outlet for his fear and anxiety so his mind could work. "This must be him. The same giant who took me."

"Maybe," Mary said. "Or maybe it's the ridge giant, who we know Vincent transferred funds to. It's likely your father had connections to multiple of them."

Paris tossed the chip aside and propped his elbows on the table, head in his hands. "Ugh. Could he be any more of an asshole?"

Icarus chuckled. "Go easy on him, babe." He pushed back from the table and circled it to Paris's side, giving his shoulder a squeeze. "Not sure he's used to the data dumps."

"I can handle it," Paris said, as he and Mary likewise rose. "I've been with Mac for two weeks."

Icarus's ginger brows raced north. "Have you now?"

"I didn't mean it like—"

His protest was interrupted by the roar of engines and gravel crunching under tires, but before he could lean to the side and peek out the window, Icarus grasped his chin. "Don't do anything heroic," he said, gaze fiery. "It usually ends in death."

"The way I hear it, you ran off and did something heroic, and you lived. Were reborn, in fact."

Icarus rolled his eyes. "What are we going to do with you?" He leaned forward and planted a smacking kiss on his cheek, and when he stepped back, Adam and Mac were waiting at the parlor door, while Liam, Jenn, and Abigail continued on to the kitchen, screaming children greeting their arrival.

Icarus greeted Adam by running across the room and jumping into his arms, the older man somehow not stumbling under Icarus's jacked body. "Fuck or food, baby?"

In answer, Adam turned on his heel and carried his lover toward the stairs, disappearing up them much to Mary's amusement, her laughter carrying her all the way to the kitchen, leaving only Mac and Paris in the parlor. Paris didn't run and jump at Mac; he didn't have to, Mac meeting him midstride, colliding in the middle of the room and wrapping their arms around each other, the bond between them solid. And singing.

"Welcome home," Paris said as he held Mac close, the raven seeming to want to burrow into him, hiding his face in the crook of his neck.

"I'm sorry," he mumbled against his skin, the words more felt than heard. "I didn't know it was going to take so long."

Paris cupped his cheek and tilted his face, catching his fading violet gaze. "Please quit apologizing for doing the thing that makes you you. You don't have to, not with me." A long exhale later, Mac let go of the remaining tension in his body and went practically limp in Paris's arms. In his care, right where Paris wanted him to stay. "You're here now, and that's all that matters. I've got you."

TWENTY

Paris woke to sun on his face and heat at his back, to soft skin and softer kisses along his shoulder blades, to pine and earth and Mac's breath on his nape. A dream, then, one he wanted to stay in for a change. An alternate reality in which, after Paris had finished cleaning up after dinner and returned to his room, he'd found Mac asleep in the guest bed he'd used since arriving at Monte Corvo. He'd crawled in with him, and sometime during the night, the man he was falling for had wrapped around him, was touching him, kissing him, hard for him.

Paris rutted back against Mac's erection, and the dream Mac grunted. Then glided a hand down Paris's side, from his shoulder, along the curve of his flank, over his hip, and held him there as he rocked closer, dick notching along Paris's crack, leaking through the damnable fabric between them. And fucking hell if Paris didn't want their boxers gone so Mac could shove inside him to the hilt. Fill him full. He leaned his head back on Mac's shoulder, groaning. "Fuck, I need you."

Mac's hand on his hip shifted forward, and for a fleeting second Paris thought it was on the way to where he wanted it most, to give his aching cock the relief he craved, but then Mac coasted it up his torso instead. Up, up, up, until he clasped his chin and angled his face to look over his shoulder. "Open your eyes, Paris."

He obeyed—and jolted. Not a dream. So not a dream. Mac's hair was a mess, a thin ring of violet circled his blown wide pupils, and the color was high on his cheeks, a dark pink like the spider web of desire splintering his aura, cracking through the usual black and blue.

"You brought me home," Mac said, and Paris felt the pull in his chest. "Every time I crossed the plane, I had a reason to come back. I've never had that before. Some part of me always felt adrift, the worst on the day of the Rift and each anniversary since. Like I might just drift away too, into the cold, but that didn't happen this time. I came back, because of you."

"Because we're bonded," Paris said, as he sent a pulse of understanding—of acceptance—along the connection between them.

Gasping, Mac released his chin and splayed his hand over Paris's chest, right where Paris felt their connection. "You grabbed hold, and now I can't let go either." Forehead to his temple, he nuzzled the side of Paris's face, lips brushing the corner of his mouth. "I'm terrified, Paris, but I can't fight this. I don't want to."

"I don't want you to fight it." He turned over in Mac's arms so he could hold his face, so Mac could see—would believe—the conviction in his gaze as he repeated his promise from last night. "It's my turn now. I've got you."

Mac groaned, relief made audible, that same emotion Paris was getting used to thanks to him, and then his lips were on Paris's, hard and greedy, forcing Paris's apart so he could spear his tongue inside his mouth. Paris sucked him in deeper, threw a leg over his hip, and hauled his body closer, their cocks bumping. The needy whine that rumbled up from Mac's chest was a sound Paris wanted to wallow in, wanted to hear over and over again. Better to be had with Mac on top, grinding down on him. Using his leg over Mac's hip, he moved to roll him, but Mac caught himself before falling through Paris's open legs, his features pinched. "Paris, I—"

"What is it?"

"I don't know how to do this."

"Stop overthinking." It was a habit of Mac's, consideration from all angles. Good for a detective, less so for a lover. Paris wanted him to let go and just feel this, feel them.

"No." He shook his head and bit his bottom lip as red climbed his cheeks again. "I don't know how to do *this*," he said with a pointed glance down to where their cocks were straining between them.

Oh, fuck . . . "Are you saying you're a virgin?"

He hid his flaming face in the crook of Paris's neck. "I've only been attracted to one other person, and I didn't tell him. We didn't get this far."

"Hank?"

He nodded, and by the hitch of his torso, by the grief and regret that flared in his aura, the mention had brought his former loss to the surface again.

Paris carded his fingers through his hair and kissed his temple. "One, you have nothing to be embarrassed about, and two, I'm sorry, for both your sakes. I could see in that picture how much you loved each other. You should have gotten this chance with him."

Mac lifted his face from his neck, eyes glassy, and for a split second, Paris thought he was going to pull away, that he might leave the bed altogether, but then he shifted and sank between his thighs, fully on top of Paris, his elbows braced on either side of his head, fingertips soft at his temples, like that first time Paris had woken to his gaze. "I don't know how to do any of this. I swore I never would again. But I want to, with you. Just please . . ." He lowered his forehead against Paris's, their noses bumping, lips brushing. "Please be patient with me."

"I've got you," Paris vowed a final time before acting on his words, closing the distance between their lips and sending a wave of comfort and care down the bond between them.

Pink and red cracked through Mac's aura again, brightening as Mac deepened their kiss, as he began to explore, a hand roving down Paris's side and under his thigh, hitching it higher and bringing their cocks back into contact. And when Paris rocked up this time, Mac countered, rutting with a hungry growl that lifted goose bumps along Paris's skin and made his dick ache.

"Fuck, yes," Paris groaned.

"Show me what you like."

He encouraged Mac to keep rutting, to keep questing, a hand in Mac's hair guiding his lips down his throat and to all the places he loved being teased. Behind his ear, the divot at the base of his throat, along his collar bones and around his nipples. He was writhing beneath him in no time, his dick a sticky mess in his boxers. Desperate to get them the rest of the way undressed, he skated a hand down Mac's back and inside the waistband of his boxers. "Let's get these off."

Mac helped shove his own off, then Paris's, and when they came back together, bare, Mac trembled. Then damn near jolted off the bed when Paris wrapped a hand around both their cocks. "Oh, fuck."

"Not there yet." Paris smirked as he stroked them together, smearing precome between them. He wasn't usually such a bossy bottom, but he was the more experienced one here, and the less Mac thought, the more he just felt, the better this would be for both of them. "Soon," he promised. "And just to be clear, once you get inside me, I fully expect you to blow in two seconds flat. And that's a compliment to me; it says nothing about you."

"But what about *you*?" Mac gritted out as he tunneled into Paris's fist, dragging his cock along Paris's. "I have no idea what I'm doing, but it feels good. And I want it to feel good for you too."

"Oh, it will." He captured Mac's lips again, dragging him into a plundering kiss, only coming for air when the pace of Mac's thrusts came too fast, too close. "I'm going to make you come, and then after, you're going to suck me off while you play with the come you leave in my ass."

Mac's eyes grew wide. "Fuck, you're amazing."

Pride swelled, Mac always so good at doing that for him, at making him feel like he was more than the fool he'd always been led to believe was his fate. In this man's life, in his arms, he could be so much more. "I'm about to show you how amazing." Grinning, he planted an elbow in the bed beneath him and flipped them so Mac was on his back, Paris straddling his hips.

And fuck, as much as Paris wanted to sink onto his dick, all that rosy tan skin on display had him leaning forward and kissing a similar path to the one he'd led Mac on earlier. From the sensitive spot behind his ear, down either side of his neck to the dip where his sharp collar bones met, then across every inch of his chest, giving each nipple extra attention, Mac seeming to especially enjoy it when Paris alternated between nipping the sensitive nub and running the flat of his tongue around it. He shivered and moaned under Paris's touch, begging for more among a litany of curses.

He'd begun a trek south, covering more of Mac's torso with kisses, when the raven grasped his shoulders and hauled him up, panting "About to come" against his lips. "Need to be inside, please."

"Grit your teeth," Paris said, before spitting in his hand, then reaching behind himself to stroke Mac's length, smearing it with the precome there before shoving his own slick fingers into his hole, hastily working himself open. They'd do more prep next time, he'd let Mac have all day exploring his hole if he wanted, but if the tightness in Mac's jaw was any indication, two seconds was being generous.

"Okay, breathe with me," he coached, waiting for Mac to

match his inhale, his exhale before he took Mac in hand and slid down onto him, inch by glorious inch, until he was buried to the hilt.

Mac's hands clutched his thighs. "Fucking hell, Paris," he cursed as he closed his eyes and arched his neck, head jammed into the pillow.

Paris took advantage of the opportunity, leaning forward and licking a stripe up the column of his throat. "No, baby, this is you fucking me, and it's far from hell."

"So far," Mac keened as Paris lifted up, then slammed back down on his dick.

Three more times, an admirable couple of seconds longer than Paris had estimated, before all of Mac arched, his back bowing off the bed as his warmth flooded inside Paris.

As the bond between them flooded with so much more.

Desire. Gratitude. Hope. Love.

The last one making Paris gasp, making him wobble off balance.

And in the next blink, he was on his back, the shifter previously beneath him flexing his speed, hovering over him with burning violet eyes. "Let me know if I do something wrong." And then he was kissing a path down Paris's torso, making a beeline for his dick. He didn't take long getting there, didn't approach with the same caution he had their first kiss. No, he swiped his tongue around the head once, then swallowed him until he gagged. A quick readjustment later, and he was sucking his cock like he was made for it. And then his fingers entered the picture, pushing into his dripping hole, and Paris was lost.

To the hot mouth greedily taking his cock, to the demanding fingers that found the sensitive spot inside him and worked it relentlessly, drawing pleas of "harder" and "faster" out of him, to the bond that sang between them, knitting their souls together tighter, spinning the threads of pink and red throughout Mac's aura.

And as Paris's orgasm barreled into him, as he squeezed shut his eyes and gave himself over to the explosion of pleasure, he was sure if he looked into a mirror, if he could see his own aura, it would be the color of the sunsets he loved to paint so much. Red and pink, his feelings for Mac, orange for the power and momentum he'd put in Paris's hands, and yellow for the confidence and hope he would have never found without him.

TWENTY-ONE

Paris was cold.

Not as cold as he had been locked in that awful freezer, but down here in the violet dark, it wasn't much better.

Violet.

He froze and reevaluated his surroundings. Not pitch-black, a purple hue coloring the edges. A dream—or memory—he had fallen into. Whose was it? And where was it?

He inhaled and smelled earth and brine, shifted his feet and felt water lap at his ankles, and when he stretched his arms out wide, his fingertips brushed walls of dirt and mud, tree roots and rock.

The tunnels beneath the Huimen Enclave. While he'd never been there before, he was sure that was where he was now, in the network of underground tunnels Mary had shown him.

Splashing echoed from somewhere in the tunnels, growing louder, coming closer. Paris flattened himself against one side of the tunnel and inched along the wall, careful not to splash, until he found the next junction and rounded the corner, plastering himself to a different cold dirt wall.

And waiting.

The splashing grew louder, accompanied by that horrible voice

Paris would never forget. "You can't save her, warlock!" bellowed the giant who'd tortured and tried to sacrifice him. Who couldn't see him now, Paris reminded himself as the splashing footsteps stopped right outside the tunnel where he hid. He was here for a reason; he had to keep his eyes and ears open for clues.

He peered around the corner and spied two people in the main tunnel, the warlock's green magic faint but bright enough to light his and the woman's face. He recognized Quinn Paxton from the photo Mary had shown him—tan skin, dark hair, green eyes, compact body—but he was all skin and bones, his hair limp, his eyes dull, and his clothes too big for his emaciated frame.

Paris didn't recognize the woman with him. She wasn't much older than him, with tan skin and big brown eyes, and like the victim from the Portola parking lot, her face was bloodied and bruised. But unlike that woman, this stranger was pregnant, one arm in a makeshift sling, the other wrapped protectively over her round belly.

"Go," Quinn said, with a nod toward the tunnel where Paris hid. "I'll hold him off."

"How?" she said. "You're weak already. Vincent made sure of that."

"I'm strong enough to give you a head start."

"You're mine," the giant shouted, ever closer. "Both of you."

"Please, Pati, go," Quinn urged the woman.

Pati, Pati, Pati, Paris repeated to himself, committing her name to memory.

She clasped Quinn's hand in hers. "I'll name him Pax, after you."

He laid his other hand on her belly, a mist of green shimmering around them. "It would be my honor. Now go!" With a final sideways hug, he directed her into the tunnel, and she splashed past Paris, into the dark.

Just in time as the giant sent a barrage of fireballs down the tunnel. They exploded against a shield of green, one after another until the giant was right in front of Quinn. The worst night of Paris's life, his nightmares since, come to life again.

"Paris."

He whipped his gaze to the warlock who was staring straight at him, his mouth moving, forming urgent words. "Help her," he pleaded, a second before a fireball sizzled through the shield of magic and swallowed him whole.

———

Paris would have lurched to sitting in bed if not for the man draped over him, Mac's thigh thrown over his and an arm slung across his middle. Mac's breaths blew steadily over his chest, his familiar snores the first thing that penetrated the blood whooshing in Paris's ears as he returned to this reality, only a few hours since he and Mac had fallen back asleep after making love. His mind—and body—wanted to go back there, to that perfect place of warmth and connection, but he didn't have time. He needed to get the details down before they flitted away.

He scooted out from under Mac, a testament to the raven's exhaustion that he didn't wake, then slipped the rest of the way out of bed, pulling on his sweats and sneaking out of the room, closing the door behind him. He hustled through Mac's office to the sitting room where he kept his painting supplies and gathered what he needed, setting up an easel in the corner and getting to work, painting the faces and places of his nightmare.

Once every detail had made it to canvas, Paris laid down his brush and returned to the bedroom. He'd been planning while painting, a means to rescue Pati coming together in his head. But he stalled over the threshold, watching Mac's beautiful body rise and fall, his tan skin warm and rosy in the late morning sun. The aura around him flowing blue and violet, red bleeding through from the rim, and at the very center, a new green orb. The man who'd helped everyone else first the past two weeks, who'd done everything Nature had asked of him, was finally taking a much-needed rest.

How could Paris wake him? How could he burden him with more? How could he ever convince Mac to let him do what he had to? Paris could take it from here, thanks in no small part to the confidence Mac had instilled in him. *I've got this*, he'd told Mac. Now he had to prove it—to Mac, to himself, to everyone who'd ever thought him a fool.

PART TWO

MAC

TWENTY-TWO

Mac was hot, a long-lost sensation, so much of his reaper's existence spent in the cold ether between planes. He wrestled with the tangled sheets, kicking them down so he could roll onto his back, the other side of the bed blissfully cool.

He bolted upright.

Paris wasn't here. Hadn't been for some time, judging by the coolness of the sheets under his hand.

Paris, who had grabbed hold of his soul that night on the altar and hadn't let go.

Paris, who had spent the past two weeks surprising him, impressing him, understanding him.

Paris, who had held him, cared for him, offered him something he'd thought lost forever.

Mac closed his eyes, felt for the bond between their souls, and tugged.

And got no tug in return.

He shot out of the bed.

Suppressing the panic that threatened, he surveyed the room through a detective's eyes. Paris's sweats were gone, his bag of clothes too, and outside the window, the sun shone bright. Two in the afternoon, according to the bedside clock.

Spinning on his heel, he ran into the office. Nothing out of place.

He ran farther, into the sitting room, and skidded to a halt. Two easels stood by the window, and on them, canvases in violet.

On one, an earthen tunnel, a face from his list, a crumbling shield of green magic between the warlock and the giant who'd almost murdered Paris.

On the other, a pregnant woman Mac had never seen before, and in the corner of the canvas, where Paris usually signed his paintings, two words: Help her.

———

A full house last night and nary a one of them to be found today. Monte and Chaz were in the infirmary monitoring the several injured they'd brought to the mountain yesterday, but otherwise, Mac found no one on the main floor or in the upstairs rooms.

And no sign of Paris.

He stood in the parlor where Paris had held him last night and wondered if this was all a bad dream. But even in those the past two weeks, in every trip he took across the veil, Paris was with him, in that place he'd carved for himself at the center of Mac's world. Where Mac had sworn he'd never let anyone in again.

Especially someone on his list, which Paris had been since the night they'd rescued him. Mac hadn't told anyone, hadn't wanted to explain why he didn't take Paris's soul through the veil. He'd known Paris didn't deserve the same fate as his father, but at the time, he hadn't known why. Hadn't known how to explain his certainty to anyone else. So instead, he'd secreted Paris away in Encinal, then Calera, as far from death as possible and as far from him and the fate Mac had barely survived before. But he hadn't been able to stay away, drawn by the man and the bond between them, and now the same fate was chasing him again, closer each day he fell a little more in love with Paris Cirillo.

"Fuck!" How had he let this happen? Any of it, all of it. He knew better. He'd pushed everyone away for decades, keeping only a handful of trusted friends, a stack of cases no one else wanted, and the memory of a love that had never had a chance to bloom. But then the fool son of a mobster had grabbed hold of his soul, had proved he was anything but a fool, and now . . . "Fuck!" he cursed again as he plowed his hands through his hair.

"We need to find the woman in the tunnels."

Mac spun the direction of Mary's voice, finding the green-haired pixie in the doorway. "Where's Paris?"

"Where he needs to be."

Fuck her riddles.

He tore off past her and out the front door, took to wing, and scoured the grounds for any sign of Paris or the team he needed to help find him.

A flash of pale skin and red hair caught Mac's eye, and he sailed to the edge of the woods near Adam's favorite meadow. Needing his words, he shifted right into a dead sprint toward where he'd glimpsed Icarus, heedless of the noise he was making, footfalls heavy and words louder. "Adam!" he shouted. "Icarus!"

He crashed into the meadow, into what must have been an intimate moment, the two of them clutching clothes to their fronts, but then Adam took one look at him, handed his pistol to Icarus, and rushed to his side, hand on his arm. "Mac, what's wrong?"

The warmth of his hand—the kind of warmth Mac had felt when he woke, that he'd fallen asleep to in Paris's arms, that he might never feel again—brought reality crashing down, and Mac with it, falling to his knees and burying his face in his hands. "Paris is gone."

Adam kneeled beside him. "What do you mean Paris is gone?"

"Babe." Icarus *tsk*ed. "Give him a minute to breathe. And give me my skirt."

Mac snarled at the blue-eyed former vampire. "Your sister."

Icarus rolled his eyes as he and Adam dressed. "What about her?"

"She knows where he is, and she wants us to rescue someone else."

"Maybe Paris doesn't need rescuing."

"Mac," Adam said as he shoved his gun in the waistband of his jeans, then crouched in front of him again. "Start from the top."

"You're in love with him," Icarus said from behind his mate, and Mac's snarl escalated to a full-on growl.

"Babe," Adam said, returning the earlier *tsk*. "Not helping."

Icarus just shrugged, insolent as ever. "Wait until Robin hears this."

Robin—that was who they needed, on multiple fronts. The time for revenge and wild goose chases was over. "Get him back here," Mac said to Adam. "We need a tracker."

Adam didn't argue. They'd been partners on the force for years; yes, emotions were running high, but tactically, they could read each other like a book. "Call Jenn," he said, handing Icarus his phone. "Tell her to call the pack. Robin won't ignore it. Not after last time." The last time Robin had ignored the pack call, his twin sister, Adam's late wife, had been killed along with their husband. As Icarus stepped a few feet away, phone to his ear, Adam turned back to him. "What happened?"

Mac rocked back on his ass and accepted the shirt Adam handed him, spreading it over his lap. "He must have had a dream. I woke up and he was gone, but there were paintings. One was of the giant who took him, faced off with a warlock from my list in some kind of underground tunnel. The other was—"

"Pati Miwra," Mary said, walking toward them under Icarus's arm. "She's the daughter of one of the Huimen tribe's leaders. She carries an eagle. She'll name them Pax, after her savior."

"An eagle?" Adam gasped. "I thought they were gone."

The reappearance of eagles was significant. Perhaps more so, though, was this one's name. "Pax, as in *peace*?" Mac asked.

Mary nodded, and Mac propped his elbows on his knees, head

in his hands. She was right; they had to rescue this woman. But fuck, where was Paris, and why couldn't he feel his soul?

Mary laid a hand on his shoulder, and a wave of warmth washed through him, holding back the threatening chill. "Kai and Jason are with him. He's going to help us find Pati. You need to believe in him."

He hung back his head and stared at the woman with all the answers, the deity who held his fate, his heart, in her hands. "Why didn't he wake me?"

"Because you wouldn't have let him do what he needs to do."

"Which is what?"

"Be Vincent Cirillo's son."

TWENTY-THREE

Robin rose from his crouch, wiping his muddy fingers on his denim-clad thigh. "Tracks are fresh," he said, voice low. "She's still in here."

"And the giant?" Mac asked, likewise whispering.

"Him too." He lifted his headful of rusty-blond hair, sniffed the air, then veered into a narrow tunnel to the right, barely wide enough for the coyote shifter's shoulders. Only Icarus was a match for Robin's size, which made him a brick wall when he halted on a dime, Adam crashing into the back of him with a curse.

"Fuck, Robin, a little warning."

"Sorry," he said, not sounding sorry at all. "Forgot you were human again."

He'd come when called, exactly as Adam had predicted, and when he'd found out why, he'd bitched the entire afternoon and evening they'd had to wait for low tide and the cover of darkness. Never mind the lives and lasting peace on the line; he'd heard *Paris Cirillo* and had been ready to bolt right back out the door, back to chasing the warlock he blamed for his sister's death. From Mary's and Paris's comments about Atlas, from what Mac had witnessed with his own eyes the night they'd battled Vincent, Mac was beginning to think there was more to Atlas than they realized, but Robin was a dog with a bone and on one side of that bone was the warlock's name and on the other was Robin's own guilt. Good luck stopping him; they only had him for a blink and then he'd be gone again. They just had to deal with his surliness in the meantime because they needed their best hunter.

"What is it?" Mac said.

Robin extended a hand to the wall, then jerked it away like he'd been burned. He glanced over his shoulder, golden eyes skipping past Adam to him. "Your precious human's been here too."

"How?" Mac said, surprise amplifying his voice louder than intended. He lowered it again and asked quietly, "When?" According to Mary, Paris had gone to the Cirillo compound in YB. He hadn't actually been here in the tunnels beneath the Huimen Enclave.

"I don't know," Robin sniped. "This is your kind of magic. Not mine."

Mac put his hand to the wall, in the same spot Robin had, and felt the soul that had been hidden from his for the past six hours. He yanked on the soul bond—and Paris yanked back. Mac nearly fell to his knees, only the wall he leaned against holding him up. Paris had been here; Paris was still on this plane. Thank fuck.

And just as Mac recognized Paris's soul, he also recognized the viewpoint of the paintings he'd left behind. "This is where he watched from." And given how he'd painted Pati, looking back over her shoulder, she'd run right past him. "Pati went this way," he said, shoving off the wall and charging ahead, keeping his footfalls light, the mud further dampening the sound of their movements.

The next tunnel junction was a three-way, and above it, a chute in the ground that had metal rebar rungs leading up to a hatch door, the lights on the keypad beside it glowing purple. The way she'd programmed it. "Paris installed the hack," Mac said, pride tipping up the corners of his lips. He'd gotten into the compound and into Vincent's office, then into the safe he'd broken into countless times before to steal from his father's supply of Daylight. The same safe where Vincent stored his laptop that Mary now had control of.

"So," Adam said. "That's one cold storage facility cleared. Stands to reason, the door that leads to the second one, which should be farther down that tunnel"—he pointed to the far-right one—"should also be cleared." Jenn and Abigail were each leading surface teams, rescuing any victims still held in the facilities Vincent had owned on the eastern side of the border road.

"Meaning the third," Mac said, referring to the facility on the other side of the road, down the far-left tunnel, "is waiting and ready." For them to herd a giant into so they could capture him on the surface. Liam and Icarus were standing by to lead that charge, *after* their trio got Pati out of here alive.

"And the woman is down that one," Robin said, pointing straight ahead.

"The giant?" Adam said.

Robin shook his head. "I lose him here. Must have turned back."

"They hunt their victims," Mac said. "He'll be back."

"Let's go, then," Adam said, poorly disguising the shiver in the detective-turned-vigilante's voice.

Robin led them down the middle tunnel, Mac following behind Adam, somewhat less careful now, Mac also sensing another presence, smelling her and the unborn shifter as they snaked farther into the earth, coming to another junction.

And meeting a wall of fire.

Mac shifted on instinct and so did Robin, the crack of bones one second, a giant rust-blond body on all fours the next. Beneath him, Adam drew his pistol and leveled it at the knees of the large bald man they knew as the giant from the ridge, in human form no doubt to disguise his scent or to give the pregnant woman behind him the illusion of a chance. Not the giant they were expecting but no less dangerous, balls of fire hovering over his hands.

Backed into a dead end, hunted to within an inch of her life, Pati was still in jeopardy. A shot fired in the giant's direction could hit her too, and while the silver bullets in Adam's gun might not kill her, they would kill the eagle she carried. Mac needed to create more space between the giant and Pati if they had any hope of saving her and themselves.

Adam realized it too, gesturing up with his gun and rolling out from under Robin, staying between the coyote's big body and the tunnel wall, eyeing a path to get behind the giant with Pati, if Mac could carve out that extra space for him.

He flew high, wings spread wide, but rather than attack the giant's eyes and possibly push him backward, closer to Pati, he flew over and behind him, then dug his talons into his neck and wrapped his wings around his head, blinding him with feathers and pain, hoping like hell the fireballs he flung as he staggered forward missed his friends. And gave them the room they needed to maneuver—fast—because Mac felt the energy inside the giant sizzling. At any moment, he would transform into the nightmare of Paris's paintings, and none of them would survive.

Two shots fired and the giant lurched, sank, and Mac released him, flying back and up, out of Robin's way as the coyote slammed into the giant from behind and took him to the ground, pinned him there long enough for Adam to run past with Pati under his arm. The giant roared, the tunnel walls trembling, and while the plan had been to herd him out, at the rate the earth around them was crumbling, they just needed to get out alive.

Mac sounded the alarm, a shrill *KRAA* his team knew well. Robin banged the giant into the ground one more time, enough to momentarily daze him, then took off after Adam and Pati, Mac flying overhead. Watching as the coyote shifted midstride so that when they reached Adam and Pati beneath the exit chute, he could help Adam lift her high enough to reach the rungs and start to climb toward the hatch. Adam stayed right behind her, reaching a long arm around her to key in the code Mary had given them. They shoved open the hatch door and cold air rushed into the tunnel, just as hot air began to build beneath Mac's wings, orange light and thundering steps closing in.

Mac cried again, as much a "GO!" as he could manage in raven form. Robin got the message, quickly scaling the rungs next, Mac providing cover behind him as the giant, in full monstrous form, charged their direction, hands of fireballs out, ready to defend himself. Mac did the unexpected—swooping low, talons digging into the bullet wounds behind the giant's knees, driving the silver bullets deeper, speeding along what the rush of magic had temporarily slowed. The giant staggered into the fragmenting wall, his weight dislodging chunks of mud and limestone.

"Mac, let's go!" Adam called from overhead. "She's gonna blow it."

He dodged the giant's flailing arms and sailed up and out the chute, Robin slamming shut the hatch door just as the earth heaved, Nature answering the call like Mac had seen her do weeks ago at the Canyon Lands.

KRAA!

"Run!" Robin shoved a shoulder under Pati's armpit, Adam under her other, and they sprinted out of the cold storage unit, out of the building, and toward the road, Mac sailing above them with a flock of corvids, their group reaching stable ground not a moment too soon.

Nature gave a final, powerful jolt and the land on the other side of the road sank, the tunnel walls collapsing into a massive sinkhole and, with any luck, swallowing the giant for good.

TWENTY-FOUR

Twenty-four agonizing hours later, Mac sailed toward the Sunset Hill condo building that earlier that month had been impenetrable to their team. Only Icarus had been able to get through then, and only after baiting Atlas into letting him in. But thanks to Paris's list of potential allies in Vincent's ranks, thanks to his intelligence and courage, Mac was able to slice through the shimmer of blue magic that shielded the building, wielded by a warlock who had previously used that very magic against Mac and his team. Paris had been right; Vincent had had his knee to more necks than just his own son's.

As soon as he was inside the shield, he felt it—Paris's soul woven with his. Whatever magic was in the shield had temporarily masked it, but it was still there, stronger than ever. He circled the building inside the shield, surveying with his own eyes what communications from inside had told him. Paris was safe; he'd declared himself the heir and taken control of his father's empire.

For now.

He'd no doubt be contested, but not from the inside by the look of it. From the outside, yes, that was already happening, but it appeared he'd made more friends inside than he'd let on given how quickly Vincent's remaining operatives had fallen in line. The detective part of Mac had a long list of questions, but the raven, the soul that had improbably found a second mate, just wanted Paris back in his arms.

On his second lap around the building, he spied Kai waiting in a halo of light on the rooftop, a folded stack of clothes under one arm. Mac coasted to a landing at his feet, shifting in the space between one breath and the next. "Where's Paris?"

"Waiting for you," Kai said. He held out the clothes and a pair of athletic flops. "Did everyone get back okay last night?"

"All in one piece." Mac donned the charcoal pants and lavender dress shirt, leftovers from Atlas judging by the lingering warlock stench and the too-short inseam and sleeves, Atlas a good half foot shorter than him. Whatever, he only needed clothes long enough to reach Paris's condo a floor below. He slid his feet into the flops, then glanced back up at Kai. "Take me to him."

He opened the rooftop door and led them into the stairwell. "Did they find anyone else at the cold storage facilities?"

"One was empty," Mac told him as they descended. "The missing vampire and shifter were in the other."

"It's a good thing Paris is here, then."

"How do you mean?"

"Who knows how many more victims Vincent has squirreled away. Now we have an inside line."

Mac opened his mouth to argue—there were less dangerous ways to gather intel—but then Kai opened the door to the penthouse floor and all of Mac's arguments vanished, his gaze landing on the man waiting at the end of the hall.

Paris had traded his sweats for an impeccably tailored suit, the dark fabric tucked in all the right places, the black dress shirt open at the collar, accentuating the long column of his throat. The whole ensemble showed off the tall, toned figure that would be walking runways in a different era, in a different place, if Paris hadn't been born into YB's ongoing war between Nature and Chaos. And to a cruel man who'd overshadowed him, abused him, and held him down his entire life. With the weight of Vincent gone, Paris was a different man than earlier surveillance photos had let on, pictures in which he was always in a suit and tie, his smile tight, his hair slicked back, his brown eyes dull. *A pretty face,* Icarus had once said.

The Paris in front of Mac now was more than just a pretty face. He was vibrant, his smile wide, his dark hair in waves around his face, his brown eyes swirling with warmth and affection—desire —that pulsed along the bond between them. He was everything Mac wanted.

A different door opened, and Mac smelled shifter, felt heat, and was a blink away from shifting himself when Paris's "Mac, no!" collided with the "Jason, no!" from behind him.

"It's just me!" Jason let go of the door and lifted his hands, palms out. "Sorry, man, I heard voices."

Kai slid between them, shoving Jason back into the condo that would've been Atlas's, if Mac recalled Icarus's hand-drawn blue-prints correctly. "For a smuggler, you have the absolute worst timing." He glanced over his shoulder at Mac, then Paris. "Let us know if you need anything." Then slipped into the condo, closing the door behind him and Jason.

Swinging his gaze back to Paris, Mac opened his mouth again, only to be cut off by Paris's raised hand. "I know you're mad, and I'll explain and apologize, but I'd rather we not argue and do all that in the hall where folks can hear us."

Mac nodded; he didn't want to stay in the hallway either, but not for the reasons Paris thought. As soon as they were inside Paris's condo, as soon as Paris turned the lock on the door, Mac spun and shoved him against it, claiming the mouth he'd gone too long without. Paris groaned, tipping back his head as he rocked his hips, and Mac's lips slipped lower, to his jaw, then his throat, tasting skin and sucking on the pulse point that hammered in his neck, a sign of the blood that still flowed through his veins, the life that for a time yesterday Mac had feared taken.

Life he needed to be connected to again. "We'll argue about it later," he panted, tearing Paris's gaping shirt wider and splaying his hands over his chest, over warm skin reddening more as a blush climbed toward his neck. Mac nuzzled into all that heat, kissing and licking to the melody of Paris's groans, to the insistent rock of his hips, his cock hard against Mac's thigh, Mac's own straining inside his pants. "Right now, I just need to be inside you. To be . . ."

Paris grasped his chin and lifted Mac's gaze to his burning brown one. "To be what, Mac?"

"Where I belong, with you."

He had his work, his friends, his family, but he'd only truly belonged once before. He didn't think he'd ever find that feeling again, had actively avoided it, afraid the loss that came after would well and truly destroy him a second time, and then this beautiful, surprising man had demanded a chance, first grabbing onto his soul in desperation, then nursing it back to health in his soft and patient ways. He was a comfort, and Mac hadn't realized how much he'd needed that, how dark his life had become until color had stumbled into it. Had given him a place to belong again.

Paris lifted his lips the rest of the way to his, the kiss he offered achingly soft and gentle, even as he yanked open the borrowed shirt, buttons flying, then shoved his hands into the back of Mac's pants, fingers clutching at his cheeks, forcing Mac to rut harder against him.

And fuck if inexperience wasn't about to bite him in the ass again, the build too good, too fast. He wasn't practiced at this, didn't know how not to go off in four seconds flat when Paris was grinding all of his hard body against him.

He ripped himself out of Paris's arms and staggered back a step, breaths heavy, climax a hair trigger from exploding. Paris's devilish grin as he lounged back against the wall wasn't helping. Neither was his hand trailing a path down his rosy red torso and into his pants, stroking his erection. With his other hand, he unbuttoned and lowered the zipper, and with no underwear on, his pants fell open to reveal his erect cock, glistening with precome.

Mac licked his lips and stumbled back a few more steps, into the corner of the table. He spread his legs as he rested back on the edge, and fuck, if his hand didn't find its way to his own cock, gliding up and down the length over the material. "Fuck, Paris, what are you doing to me?"

Paris shoved off the wall, letting his pants fall the rest of the way to floor as he sauntered toward him in nothing but a shredded shirt and suit jacket, stopping only when he was between Mac's legs, lips on his again. "Loving you." And then he was gone the next instant, before Mac could wrap his arms and legs around him, before he could show Paris how fast and hard he was falling in love with him too. As if reading his mind, Paris braced one hand on the tabletop and flipped up the tails of his shirt and coat with the other, his bare ass canted out and up. "Show me."

Mac clasped his balls and groaned. All that pale skin on display. That perfect ass that had been barely concealed in sweats the past two weeks, that as their bond had strengthened, had awakened Mac's body in ways it hadn't known for decades, waiting for him.

"Get inside me, Mac. Where you belong."

He pushed off the table and let his own pants fall. "What do I need to do? To get you ready?"

"Nothing," Paris said with a wink. "I planned ahead."

Mac cocked a brow, much to Paris's amusement, his infectious laughter filling the condo, then turning into a shivering groan as Mac skated his fingertips over the curve of his bare hip, lifting goose bumps as Mac circled behind him.

And froze.

"Fuck." The purple flared end of a plug was nestled between Paris's cheeks. The only reason Mac knew what the toy was, despite his very limited experience, was because Icarus had a habit of leaving his assortment just sitting out in the villa rooms he shared with Adam.

"You okay back there?" Paris teased.

Mac jerked his gaze up, meeting the brown one staring back at him, smoldering but also dancing with more than a little pride and mirth. The combination was as good as any dare, and while Mac usually stayed away from those, he had no intention of staying away from Paris tonight.

Stepping close, he left one hand splayed on Paris's ass while he clasped the end of the toy with the other. But as he started to pull it out, Paris shuddered and lost the tension in his arms, sinking to his elbows with a moan. Wanting more of that reaction, Mac wriggled the toy, and Paris hung his head, keening. "You like this don't you?" Same as he'd liked it the other night when Mac had stuffed him full of his fingers and made him come. He circled a fingertip around the neck of the toy, teasing Paris's rim, and Paris tried to curl his fingers into the wooden tabletop. Mac did it again, loving the way Paris's body quaked in response. "What would happen if this was my tongue instead of my finger?"

Paris shoved an arm between his body and the table, grabbing his balls as Mac had had to do earlier. When he glared back at him, his pupils were blown wide, nothing left but lust. "We can play later," he gritted out. "Please, Mac, just get inside me. I don't want to wait."

Neither did Mac; twenty-four hours was more than enough.

He shuttled his hand down his own stiff cock, spreading precome and coating his fingers, making it easier to remove the toy while still leaving a part of himself inside Paris, fascinated as Paris's hole seemed eager for more. Then losing all thought, giving himself over to sensation, as he lined up and plunged into Paris's hot and ready body.

Paris slapped the table. "Fuck, that feels good."

Even better when Mac clasped his hips and hauled Paris closer, using his grip to steady them both as he began to pound into him, over and over, his grunts twining with Paris's pleas for more, even as his arms gave the rest of the way out and he flattened himself on the table, surrendering completely to Mac.

It was the sexiest thing Mac had ever seen. Paris splayed out in that perfect suit jacket that hugged his arms and shoulders, that accentuated his tapered back, that was flipped up so Mac could witness Paris's ass greedily taking his cock.

But Mac was greedy too, for all the things he'd never had. More pleasure, more passion, and more Paris. Bending over Paris's back, he slid his arms under his front and lifted his torso off the table, enough so he could capture Paris's lips, enough so that he sank impossibly deeper inside him, enough to taste the scream on Paris's lips as he came.

Enough to whisper "I'm loving you too" as he followed Paris over the edge.

TWENTY-FIVE

Mac stood in front of the floor-to-ceiling windows of Paris's bedroom, watching as the waves crested under the moonlight, listening as they broke against the sheer cliffs below. He'd been born and raised in Talahalusi; his family lived in the trees and cultivated the land. He'd spent his fair share of time in YB, but Crow Mountain with its tangled limbs and knotty roots, its trailing vines and blooming meadows was home. That said, he couldn't deny the swell of the waves, the thunder as they crashed to shore was peaceful and centering in its own way.

The bathroom light behind him flickered off, plunging the room and condo back into moonlight.

Paris's footsteps approached, then his heat wrapped around him, skin to skin, his arms circling Mac's waist as he slid in under his arm and nestled against his side, his soft cock pressed against Mac's hip. Desire tempted, but after the fast and furious release in the kitchen, then a much slower, languid one in bed, the sated want he felt for Paris was more like a warm blanket on a cold morning, a comfort. Like the ocean was to Paris. "I understand now why you keep painting it," Mac said. "Why you need it. This view is something else."

"It was the only good thing about living here." He nuzzled his pec and held him tighter. "When this is over, I don't know if I can stay in Talahalusi with you."

Mac's heart crashed like the waves below, but he couldn't say he was surprised. Someone so full of life, so bright was bound to come to his senses eventually. Of course Paris wouldn't want to be tied to him, to the duty that came with him. "I understand."

Paris's answering chuckle was a surprise, as were his words. "I don't think you do." Circling the rest of the way in front of him, Paris pushed him up against the nearest casement and cupped his cheek. "I just meant the lake isn't the same as the ocean. We may need a place near the coast too. Maybe the cabin, so long as I can drive out to the beach whenever I want."

Mac angled his face to kiss his palm. "We make it out of this . . ." Alive, together, in one piece. "I'll take you there myself. Every day."

Paris stretched up to brush their lips together, more of that soft comfort Mac had realized he liked, that Paris gave so effortlessly. He settled against his chest, fingers playing with the smattering of hair there. "I'm sorry I worried you."

"I woke up, and you weren't there." He covered Paris's hand with his, holding it over the spot where their bond hummed. "I couldn't feel you here."

"I couldn't risk it. Not until I firmed up control. And I couldn't risk Pati and her child either." He glanced away from the ocean and up at him, brown eyes searching. "They're okay? She told Kai when they were on the phone, but I—"

"Safe and sound," Mac reassured him, carding his fingers through his hair. "And two other victims as well. You did good, Paris."

"I can do more good."

Sighing, Mac closed his eyes and leaned his forehead against the same of the too good man in his arms.

"I'm here because of you, Mac," Paris gently pressed. "You helped me find the confidence to own this, to use it for good."

"You're a target, Paris. For everyone who wants this, and for the giant who knows exactly where you are now."

Paris shivered and lowered his head, resting back against Mac's chest and looking out at the calming ocean. "It really wasn't him?"

Mac coasted a hand up and down his spine. "It was the one from the ridge."

"Why did I see the other one then?"

"He'd likely been there too. Maybe it was him when you saw them."

A beat of comfortable silence later, Paris inhaled deep and straightened in his arms, lifting his chin and meeting his gaze. "Let me do this, Mac. There's a wealth of information and connections here. We can use this for good, against the giants and Chaos."

Like Mac could argue him anything when he blazed with such confidence and conviction. But he could lay down some ground rules for the sake of safety and the bond between them. "No running off without telling me the plan."

"I'll try." Mac opened his mouth to object, but Paris's raised hand stalled him again. "I act before I think sometimes. My heart gets ahead of my head, but that's me, Mac. I'll try to be better, but I can't say I won't ever do it again. And for the record, I did have a plan yesterday morning, hours to think about it as I painted, but then I saw you asleep so soundly, and you needed it so much. I couldn't bear to wake you."

Mac lightly grasped his chin, drawing him in for a kiss, to whisper against his lips, "Next time, wake me." He drew back and brushed wavy brown strands off the pretty face that had become the center of his world. A world he had no choice but to bring Paris all the way into now. "All right, then," he said. "But if we're going to do this, we need to discuss it as part of the bigger plan, with everyone."

TWENTY-SIX

Mac was surprised it took Paris until they were halfway down the hall to ask, "What is this place?" Between the corner unit's boarded-up windows, the steel back door they'd entered through, and the old barrels and stacked weapons crates that crowded the hallway, it was a confusing place for any uninitiated.

Mac chuckled. "Kai asked the same thing when he first came here. It used to be a distillery tasting room. We acquired it from the lender who was going to foreclose. It serves as our base of operations here in YB since—"

"Since your father torched my house," Adam said, and Mac cut a glare his direction. He sat beside Jenn at the bar, Icarus behind it pouring vodka into shot glasses.

"No," Paris said, hand on his forearm. "That's fair. I'll make you whole," he said to Adam. "As soon as I get access to the necessary accounts."

"Don't do that," Icarus said. "Your father took a lot, from a lot of people. You'll be broke before you know it."

"Yes, but I betrayed *you*," Paris said to him, voice earnest. "One of the few people who was good to me, so when this is done, let me help you."

The courtesan slid two shot glasses onto the bar for Adam and

Jenn, then brought a third out from behind the bar and handed it to Paris. "He's loaded," he said with a head tilt toward Adam. "Being the Devil pays well. So you don't need to help us but thank you. And you were always good to me too." He pecked Paris's cheek, then flitted over to sit on the corner of the table where his sister worked on her laptop, oblivious to the mounting tension of her surroundings.

Most pointedly coming from the coyote across the room, one booted foot propped against the wall, his flannel-covered arms crossed over his broad chest. "Can we get down to business?" Robin said. "I want to know how much longer I have to be here."

"Atlas has outrun you this long," Icarus said. "How much longer are you going to keep chasing him?"

"Until I catch him."

"I told you," Mary said, not looking up from her laptop. "You'll get your turn."

"Clocks tickin', sweetheart."

Mac cleared his throat. "I don't believe you two have formally met. Robin, this is Paris. Paris, this is Robin."

Paris stepped to the center of the room, hand outstretched, and Robin, predictably, didn't move from his post on the wall. "Exactly how did you take control of your father's operation in less than twenty-four hours?"

Paris squared his shoulders and lifted his chin. "I made them an offer. I'd actually do for them what my father promised. Protection. And if they didn't want to take my offer, they could leave without retribution."

"Without even holding them? We could have questioned them."

Mac moved forward, sliding a hand into the groove of Paris's lower back, ready to intervene if he needed, but Paris seemed keen to spar with Robin.

"As I understand it from Mac," he said, "half of them were questioned already, and correct me if I'm wrong"—he split a glance between Mac and Adam—"but technically you have no authority to hold them. In fact," he leveled his gaze on Mac, "I haven't seen or heard you once mention going into the station or wherever it is you're supposed to work since you rescued me from that altar."

"They know to leave me alone this time of year."

"Sheriff's a pack member," Jenn added. "It's why he and Adam left the YB force to join the Talahalusi department."

Paris nodded, then cut a glance through all of them, eventually landing back on Robin. "I won't be my father. I won't have people working for me out of fear."

"We're all afraid right now," Robin admitted in a rare display of truth and vulnerability.

"And that's more than enough. They don't need to fear me too."

"Can we move on?" Adam said from his barstool.

"I want to know why he's after Atlas," Paris insisted, and Mac barely bit back his curse. They'd been so close to a break in hostilities, and then Paris had to go and throw a grenade into the mix.

"Because he killed my sister and brother-in-law." Robin nodded toward Adam. "His spouses."

Paris's response was immediate. "No, he didn't."

And so was Robin's, flying off the wall at him. Mac shot between them and flexed every bit of magic in him, every bit of growl in his own voice. "I love you like a brother, but if you lay a fucking paw on him, I will end you."

His eyes flashed gold, and for a second Mac feared he'd have to follow through on his promise, but then Robin thankfully backed off, his gaze sliding past Mac to Paris. "You're playing a game you don't understand, kid."

"I understand I can help," Paris said. "And that's what I intend to do."

"We have just over a week until Samhain," Mary said, reentering the conversation. She snapped shut her laptop and stood, rounding the table to prop herself next to Icarus. "The giants need to be our focus. They're the ones trying to bring through Chaos, not Atlas."

"So you say," Robin bit back.

"So I know."

"One day you're gonna spill."

"You'll be the first to know."

Robin huffed off to reclaim his spot on the wall, while brother and sister rolled their eyes. Mac almost laughed out loud. Behind him, Paris did, trying and failing to muffle it against the back of his shoulder. He didn't need to, the moment of levity easing some of the tension in the room, Mary smiling widest of all.

Mac directed Paris to the open chaise by the wall, the two of them sitting side by side, as Mary brought them up to speed. "We talked to Pati. Both giants, the one from the ridge and the one who chased you," she said to Paris, "chased her and Quinn through those tunnels."

"What about the other two giants?" Mac asked.

"No sign of them."

"I need to go to the Stick," Paris said. "If I can get one of the souls to talk, then maybe they can show me which giant was there."

"We have to be careful," Adam said. "Outside of the Canyon Lands, it's the only remaining altar site not under our control."

"And the one in La Purisima," Paris said, tossing another grenade. "I checked," he hurried on, peppering the playing field with landmines. "Dad wouldn't dare go down there himself, but he did make investments there. The only three people who can safely travel there are me and you two"—he gestured at Adam and Icarus, the only other two humans in the room—"but you both got the same look on your faces just now as Icarus's sister when I first brought it up, so I'm assuming that's a no. And I know he"—he jutted a thumb at Mac—"won't let me go, so let me send someone on Dad's—sorry, my team to check them out. "

"There's unlikely to be any Samhain activity there," Mac said. "The religious cultist won't allow it."

"Send your people," Adam said to Paris. "Assuming no activity there, then that leaves us two giants here to deal with. The one who took Paris, and one other, possibly responsible for the Stick massacre."

Paris leaned forward and propped his elbows on his knees, fully engaged in the conversation, actively participating in the planning. "If we completely destroy the altar at the Stick, what happens?"

"They build a new one in its place," Adam replied. "If we don't also cleanse and secure the territory."

"And like you said, if we do that at the Stick, we'll control all of them in and around YB, other than the Canyon Lands, which I assume we'll never control?"

"Maybe the kid's not so useless," Robin said, straightening off the wall. "We could trap them."

Icarus scoffed. "Why would they be stupid enough to do that?"

"Because we have the one who got away," Robin said, his smirk bordering on feral. "The ultimate soul channeler. With Paris, they can rip the veil wide open."

"Exactly," Paris said, nodding. "I can do—"

"Absolutely not," Mac dissented, at the same time Icarus and Mary likewise expressed their objections.

"We have a week," Adam said, stepping into the fray and cutting short the debate. "Let's continue to work the case. We've got two serial killers, access to their backer's records, and a crime scene with potential witnesses." He raised his brows in question at Paris.

"I can reach them," he confirmed with a nod.

"Then let's see how far we get."

TWENTY-SEVEN

The rising sun did little to cut through the naturally occurring fog at the Stick. It painted Mac's windshield with a heavy, windswept mist that would've required wipers if they'd been moving instead of parked. As it were, he could barely make out Liam's raven-shaped form standing sentry on the car's hood as they waited for Jenn's advance team to confirm the giant was nowhere near the altar.

"Tell me why Robin hates Atlas so much." Paris shifted in the passenger seat, angling toward him and pulling up a leg, propping his chin on his knee. "Did Atlas really kill his sister?"

"His *twin* sister. And her husband."

"I don't follow."

Of course he didn't; he'd only heard bits and pieces of the story, usually in the midst of a heated argument. "Deborah and David were feds," Mac explained. "Adam and I were assigned as their local department contacts. Adam fell in love with them at first sight and married them a month later, conflict of interest be damned." He couldn't help but smile, remembering the Adam— then, Gabriel—of those days. Lighter, hopeful, his heart on his sleeve; a lot like Paris. After their deaths, he'd adopted the name Adam as a cover and drawn into himself, using the phoenix—his

Devil—as a boogeyman against Vincent and as a shield to keep others at bay too. Until Icarus had bullied his way past the Devil and into his heart, bringing out a little more of Gabriel every day.

"Was David a coyote too?"

Mac shook his head. "David was a phoenix."

"Fuck." Paris lowered his chin, forehead on his knee, correctly anticipating the worst. "What did my father do?"

"We were building a case against him, were close to nailing him, when he sent an army after us, including Atlas. Deborah got hit with a blast of his magic." Staring out the windshield into the gray mist, Mac recalled that sunny morning ten years ago like it was yesterday. "David overtaxed himself. He was about to flame out, and he carried his wife back to the safe house where they'd left Adam. But Adam wouldn't leave them. David's flameout brought the entire structure down and started a fire that took weeks to put out. Adam was the only survivor."

Paris laid a hand on his shoulder. "I'm sorry for your loss." The warmth of his touch dissolved the knot of emotion in his throat, allowing him to tell the most critical part of the story, at least where Robin was concerned.

"Robin wasn't there when it happened. He's a merc, and he was halfway around the world on a job when Deb called the pack. He didn't answer."

"Oh shit."

Mac nodded, the sentiment spot-on. "Robin's as angry at himself as he is at Atlas."

Paris laced his hands around the front of his shin, then rested his temple on his knee, staring out the windshield. "So, if Robin wasn't there, who saw Atlas? You? Adam or Jenn? Someone else?"

"We all saw him."

"And you saw him kill Deb?"

"Me, no," Mac said. "But plenty of others did."

"I don't buy it."

"He was your father's henchman. He was in Vincent's thrall."

Paris righted his gaze, chin propped on his knee. "Then why did he make sure I had the best tutors? Why did he make sure I had the history lessons to understand the context of what's happened to me? Why did he help me help others that worked for my father? Why did he save me from my father's wrath more times than I can count?"

"Why didn't he save you that night we did?"

Paris lowered his knee and raked a hand through his hair, tugging at the ends, frustration bubbling over. "It doesn't add up, Mac."

Mac knew the feeling well. "For the record," he said, "I don't disagree with you." Paris whipped his gaze back to him. "He helped us save Adam and Icarus the night your father was killed. And she knows something she's not telling anyone, about Atlas and all this."

"Maybe you should trust her."

Blind trust didn't come easy, though. Not for a cop and not for someone who'd witnessed allegiances shift and sway through the years. She was Nature, the highest power in their world, but to what end she used that power, and how she moved them all around her chessboard in her game with Chaos, was still a mystery. As someone who solved those for a living, Mac didn't like being kept in the dark. And as someone who found himself miraculously bonded again, falling more in love with the person —the human—in the car beside him each day, he liked it even less. He had too much at stake now; he needed to know the rules and the players, all of them.

His phone beeped with a text, interrupting his darkening thoughts. He read the text from Jenn aloud. "All clear." Paris inhaled deep and straightened in his seat, steeling himself, but the fear in his eyes was unmistakable. Mac cupped the side of his neck. "You don't have to do this."

"I want to," he replied with zero hesitation.

Fuck, he was amazing. Mac hadn't been bluffing when he'd told Robin he'd end him if he laid a hand on Paris. He would go to war for this man, against anyone. He drew Paris closer and kissed him deep, pouring all his affection into the kiss and their bond. "Then I'm with you every step of the way." Exiting the car, they met at the edge of the sandy path that snaked through the sea grass. Mac laced their fingers together, giving Paris's a squeeze. "I didn't get to say it before, but I'm proud of you. For making a stand, for the way you handled your father's assets, and for the way you handled Robin."

"I could do that because of you. My father snuffed it out all my life, but you helped bring it back. Bring me back." Paris returned the earlier kiss, and then they followed Liam's lead through the fog, wind whipping the sea grass and fog around them, soaking them through by the time they reached the clearing where Jenn and Abigail waited. The pack had spread out along the peninsula's land edges, while Liam and the flock of corvids were scattered along the rocky beach behind the remnants of the giant's altar.

As Paris gravitated toward the altar, Mac surveyed the rest of the scene. The charred mounds of flesh and bone in a semicircle, the burnt sea grass around the edges of the scene, the deep stains in the earth. All familiar, reminding him of the ridge, except for the silence.

He joined Paris by the altar, a broken mess of rock and driftwood, the pile of bones from the picture Mary had received gone. "A reaper's been here already," Mac said, and Paris nodded.

But as Paris stepped around the altar, he froze midstride and swung his wide-eyed gaze back to Mac. "Out there," he said with a nod toward the Bay, and as Mac drew closer, he heard it too, a whisper on the edge of the waves.

Paris took off running, scattering crows and ravens as he tripped and slipped over slick rocks. Mac grabbed the back of his jacket, helping him stay upright, but as they hit the edge of the water, there was no stopping Paris from sinking to his knees and plunging his hands into the cold, dark water.

Liam jumped into the air, squawking in alarm.

"I know," Mac said. "I know." His worry ratcheted higher with each passing second, the water lapping at their knees too cold for Paris to withstand, but he was gone from his plane, lost in whatever vision the voice on the waves was sharing with him. In human form, the best Mac could do was curl around his body and keep him warm, then be there for him when he returned.

Which he did after another minute, shivering and pale, and with a purple hue to his brown eyes. Mac gasped. What was happening to him? But before that question could occupy more of his thoughts, Paris stuttered through chattering teeth, "I saw him. The giant who did this."

Mac bundled him in his arms and lifted him out of the water, Jenn and Abigail steadying him as he crossed the rocks back to stable ground. "Can you paint him?"

"I don't need to," Paris said, voice fraught with agony—and terror. "I know who he is."

Mac stumbled. Would've hit the dirt if not for Jenn and Abigail holding them up. "How?"

"He worked for my father."

TWENTY-EIGHT

Mac stood at the end of the island in his parents' bustling, chaotic kitchen, unsure if he'd made the right decision fleeing his place for the evening to come here. But he'd been shooed out of the infirmary by Monte and Chaz, and he hadn't wanted to stay on the main floor either, listening through the ceiling as Icarus streamed a scene, Adam watched him, and the inevitable ensued. Maybe Mary could tune that out with her headphones and hacking, but he'd nearly died of embarrassment the first time, no doubt would for sure now that he had a better idea of what exactly was going on upstairs. Pati likewise wasn't there to distract him, the elders and midwives from her tribe having made the journey to the mountain and set up camp on one of the outparcels. Not far from where Robin and Jenn were meeting with the rest of the pack to organize the hunt for Wallace Boyle, the giant Paris had identified from his vision at the Stick.

"No Paris tonight?" Rena asked, as if reading his mind. She sat between Cherry and Abernathy at the kitchen's eat-in table, helping the children ice a cake.

"He's in YB with Abigail, Jason, and Kai. Recon for her." Once they'd had a face and name to go with another giant on their map, the search was on. Mac had held Paris through the rest of the day and night, made sure he'd recovered from his dip in the cold Bay, and then reluctantly seen him off yesterday morning to the condo in YB. He would have liked to keep him at home another day, to wallow in the bond between them before it disappeared again, but Paris's drive to do something was irrepressible. "They'll be back later tonight."

"Yay!" Cherry and Abernathy cheered, spatulas in the air, icing more of the table than the cake.

"When do we get to meet this man?" his mom asked as she slid the foil-covered skillet of ratatouille he'd helped assemble into the oven. Normally, he stayed out of the way, but he'd gotten used to cooking with Paris. "The kids can't stop talking about him." She wiped her hands on the front of her apron, then slipped it off over her head, her silver and black braid resettling over her shoulder. "I didn't think anyone could top Icarus as their favorite."

"You should bring him to the Samhain festival," his dad said from where he and Liam were slathering loaves of bread with garlic butter.

"I wanted to talk to you about that," Mac started, only to be cut off by his youngest brother, Declan, who joined Rena and the kids at the table, taking a swipe of icing for himself.

"It's dangerous, thin veil, we know the drill, brother."

"This is different," Mac insisted. "The giants are going to try and open it this year. All the way."

"They try every year."

"This is *different*." His family took their role as stewards of the land and souls seriously, but he needed them to understand that it was beyond serious this time. That Chaos was pressing harder and was closer than ever.

"He's not exaggerating," Liam said. "What we've seen this past month . . ." He shook his head. "We haven't had a fight like this on our hands since the Rift."

"Which we lost ground in," Mac said. "We're more powerful

this time, but so is Chaos."

His mother came around the island and pushed between them, her arms around their waists, hugging them both. "We'll keep it small, then. Only family and folks who work with us here."

"Mom."

"It's tradition." Mostly from his father's Gaelic roots, but his mother's people also celebrated, giving thanks for the harvest and honoring the souls they'd delivered. "But we will also stand guard, over our harvest, our plane, and our family."

Mac could live with that compromise. He dropped a kiss on the crown of her head. "Thank you," he said. "I can't go into this worrying about you and also having to protect him."

She tipped her head back, her dark brows waggling. He'd opened the door with a slip of his words, and she wasn't going to let it go this time.

"You might as well tell them," Rena said. "They know."

"Know what?" Declan said.

"That you've bonded again," his father replied as he tucked the garlic bread into the other oven. "We know."

"How?" Mac gasped.

"One, you're in the kitchen cooking," Rena said.

"I missed—"

"Cooking with him?" Liam said with a knowing smile.

His mother grinned up at him. "Just because we no longer deliver the souls doesn't mean we can't hear them. Especially when they sing."

"I didn't want to tell you, in case—"

"In case what happens with Hank happens again." She let go of Liam so she could turn fully to him, hugging him tight. "I'm happy for you, son."

"But I don't think I'll survive it when my other half is torn away again." Paris was still on his list; there was no erasing or taking that back. And he'd gone and made himself seen, a blinking target for the giants and for anyone who wanted a piece of his father's empire. He was the center of the storm—and of Mac's world.

His mother patted his chest, over the spot where his bond with Paris lived. "When the time comes, your soul will get what it deserves."

"What does that mean?"

"We didn't just retire, son," his father said. "My name appeared on your mother's list."

Mac jolted, having to use his mother to catch his wavering weight. "What?" He'd been told his parents chose to retire, that they'd handed him the reaper title because they'd decided to create life rather than ferry it elsewhere.

Not this.

How had they even survived?

His mother shuffled him to the stool beside his father, the two of them making sure he was steady. Good thing as she continued to deliver blow after blow. "Nature came to us and gave us a choice. We'd done enough. She'll give you the same choice."

"Why didn't I get a choice last time?" he asked, voice cracking with pain and regret, all of it washing back up, a tsunami of memories. Hank's name appearing, the bond between them fraying, then later that same night, a phone call asking him to come identify a body. Hank's lifeless frame in the morgue, in his arms, the bond between them severed for good as he'd taken Hank's soul across the veil, delivering it to the peace it deserved. He'd never known pain like that day before or since. Had cast love aside, never wanting to feel that sort of agony again, until Paris Cirillo had grabbed hold and made him his.

"Because the last time it wasn't about you," his father said. "Your aura then versus now . . ." His dark eyes glittered, a sprinkling of the green magic from his mother's maternal line, some of their coven's gifts passing to him too. "It's completely changed. Before, it was red in the center, with blue and violet around the outside, but now . . . Now you feel everything, blue and violet, the red bleeding through from the outside, and at the center, green. Your connection to Nature wasn't there before. You've changed."

"He's right," Liam said. "And not just because of Paris."

"Nature needed you," his mom said. "You've delivered her two phoenixes, a white raven, an eagle, and now a medium. You're her warrior, and for that loyalty, she'll give you and Paris what your souls deserve, same as she did ours."

———

It was past midnight when Mac returned to his thankfully quiet house, only the muffled beep of monitors drifting up from the infirmary below.

Dinner at the main house had been good, the dessert a sticky delicious mess and the Samhain planning afterward reassuring. His family had heard what he and Liam had said and were taking the situation seriously, even Declan. They'd have their celebration, but by keeping it small, they could better protect the gathered people, including Pati and her tribe, and once they were secure, provide support to neighboring farms as needed. Mac didn't want them stretched too thin, especially if he, Adam, and the rest of the pack leaders were dealing with the giants elsewhere.

Especially if Paris remained in his family's protection here. Paris would no doubt object, and if he and Adam needed him on the scene, then that was where he'd be. But if not, if he stayed behind here, Mac wanted him safe. Because after what his parents had told him, for the first time since Paris had grabbed hold of his soul—hell, since he'd lost Hank—he saw an alternative to heartache and loneliness in his future. A spark of hope—of love— that might grow into the kind of roaring blaze Paris had loved to build in the hearth back at the cabin.

Granted, part of him was still angry that he'd been denied the chance with Hank, but Nature's mysteries had been coming hard and fast lately, and as he stood in the doorway of his bedroom, taking in a slumbering Paris in the moonlight, he couldn't deny he was thankful for the opportunity to get to know this amazing man.

To love him.

He also couldn't deny that in this moment he understood Paris's instinct the other morning to leave him asleep in the bed. He looked so peaceful, the steady rise and fall of his tapered back, his dark hair tousled against the white sheets. After two very long days of digging into his father's dealings, Paris had left his precious ocean to come back to Monte Corvo, back to him. He should let him sleep.

Turning for his office, he barely made it a step when "Come to bed, Mac," rumbled from behind him.

He glanced over his shoulder. Paris was still on his stomach, the sheets tangled around his waist, but his breaths weren't as long and steady as before. Mac felt guilty for disturbing his rest. "I can let you—"

"You need to sleep too," Paris mumbled into the pillow. "Get in bed."

Smiling at the gentle, muffled order, Mac undressed and crawled in beside him, soaking in the warmth and trailing a hand down his spine, savoring the goose bumps that rose in his wake. "Everything good in YB?"

"Got what we needed." Paris scooted more fully into the curve of him, hitching up a leg so Mac could line his up behind it, nestling them closer. "What'd you have for dinner?"

"Ratatouille."

Mac couldn't see his smile, Paris's face angled away, but he could hear it in his sleepy voice. "Can never spell that right on the first try."

Mac muffled his laughter, his love in Paris's shoulder. What had he done without this light, this warmth in his life for so long?

"You had a good night?" Paris asked once Mac's laughter subsided.

"I learned a lot." That maybe he could keep this light, this warmth, this incredible man for longer than his list prescribed. He trailed his fingers along his back, telling Paris exactly how he felt, Paris's breaths evening out more with each letter Mac brushed over his skin, from the I to the L-O-V-E to the U. Mac stretched an arm across his back, rested his cheek against his shoulder, and closed his eyes. "I learned that maybe I can keep you. Forever."

Paris's reply reached him on the edge of sleep, on the terrifying, wonderful edge of hope. "I love you too."

TWENTY-NINE

The peaceful reprieve lasted barely a day. Paris's momentum inside his father's organization was halted by a freeze on the Cirillo funds. Mary had traced the action to Charlotte Taylor, Vincent's human accountant. Mac had a file on her already; she'd been cooking the books for Vincent for years, moving his money around to keep it sheltered. If anyone had the inside track on where Vincent's money was and how to tie it up, it was Charlotte.

It had taken another day to arrange a meet. Mac was against it, suspecting a trap. Mary would eventually hack through the wall. But Adam, the traitor, had sided with Paris in the no-time-to-waste camp. Which was how they found themselves in a back office at Club Sutro, a relatively neutral site, and thanks to Kai's and Icarus's connections, one they were able to access in the middle of the afternoon, limiting collateral damage if things went sideways. Which they always did.

Paris seemed to sense that, his loafers wearing a hole in the carpet at the far end of the room where he paced. Adam, Icarus, and Robin were more comfortable with the inevitable chaos, lounging around a table in the corner, topping up their caffeine, while Mary sat behind the desk, furiously typing on her laptop.

Mac pushed off the front of the desk and crossed the room, making a barrier of himself in Paris's pacing circle. "You don't have to do this," he told him, as he smoothed down the lapels of his suit jacket. "We can send Adam out to negotiate."

"The Devil?" Paris scoffed. "You know that's what they still call him, right? They'll think *we're* trying to trap *them*."

Robin set aside his mug. "I fail to see the problem."

Paris's jaw clenched, and Mac bit back a laugh. Robin worked everyone's last nerve, even Paris's. "Look," he said, stepping around Mac to address the table. "Folks are on edge. They know I'm working with you. They also need to know there won't be reprisals."

"She's also holding your accounts hostage," Adam said.

"Which is the trap they won't see coming," Paris said, then asked Mary, "How long do you need?"

"Ten minutes," she replied.

"Question is," Robin mused, "do you want the money for yourself or for the cause?"

"Which is it, Robin?" Paris snapped, irritated to outburst. "You don't believe me because we thought they'd all fallen in line? Or because they didn't?"

"Hey," Mac said, stepping between them and cupping Paris's cheek, waiting for his brown gaze to settle back on his. "I know it feels like he's the enemy, but he's not."

"We've all been there," Icarus said, earning a growl from Robin. Which in turn earned a raspberry from Icarus. And like a popped balloon, the tension in the room deflated, everyone except Robin chuckling.

Paris inhaled deep, then exhaled, letting more of the tension go as he shook out his shoulders. When he righted his gaze, he was calm once more, confident, the spat with Robin doing some good it seemed. "We've seen it already. When we talk to people, when we let them be heard, we get more information out of them. We add allies. We learn how to win this." He nodded. "I can do this."

Mac was sure of it. Sure of him. And sure that if he didn't kiss him right then, he'd regret it. In front of everyone, he pulled the man he loved into his arms and kissed him deep, hoping Paris sensed all the pride and confidence Mac had in him. To pull this off, to pull anything off he set his mind to.

Paris kissed him back, his lips curving into a smile against his, the two of them parting when cat calls and whistles erupted. In his arms, Paris laughed with the joy, the warmth that had brightened Mac's world these past few weeks. And more, according to Paris. "You should see your aura right now," he whispered at his year. "I can't wait to get home so I can paint it. So you can see it too."

Mac couldn't wait either.

And neither could reality, interrupting the happy moment. "Eyes on Taylor," Mary said.

Lounging ceased. Adam and Robin shot to their feet, Icarus too, the latter coming around the table to hook his arm through Paris's. The both of them were stylishly suited, though Icarus stood several inches taller in his stilettos. "You ready to go?"

Paris would meet Charlotte with Icarus, their best fighter, at his side. Jason was already in the main room, behind the bar with Kai, and Adam, Robin and Mac would join them, fanned out to block the exit doors. Jenn and Abigail would shift from their positions on the floor to the room here with Mary, as guards and backup.

"Last line of human defense," Paris said with a sharp nod, then tucked the folders Mac handed him under his arm. Ammunition, for when he needed it. One last stolen kiss, and then their group strode down the hall to the main room, Paris and Icarus continuing to the lone table in the center of the dance floor where Charlotte Taylor waited, two men—shifters they'd already identified as her usual entourage—standing guard behind her.

"This is the company you keep now?" she said, her dainty nose turned up, her brown hair twisted in a bun at her neck.

"This was always the company I kept." Paris lowered into the chair Icarus pulled out for him and set the folders on the table. "You're holding my money hostage."

"Your money?" She scoffed. "You think you should be the heir? A worthless layabout who stole from his own father? You don't know the first thing about running a business."

"So you want the money for yourself, then?"

"We're the ones who earned it."

We, Mac noted. As in the royal we, or the we that included the two shifters behind her, or a larger we of more defectors?

Didn't matter for Paris's response, though, the strategy planned. "You're right," he said, and Charlotte reared back, her eyes wide with surprise. "I don't know how to run the finances," he said to her, then to the two shifters and whomever they were also standing in for, "And I wasn't the one my father sent into battle. So no, I don't know how to run his business, as he did. I'll need your help, *all* of you, to run it a different way."

"And how's that?" she asked, leaning slightly forward, giving away the interest she hid behind her skepticism.

"The way my father should have. By affording you the protection you came to him for in the first place." He opened one of the folders, pushing it toward her, and Charlotte paled. "You came to my father for protection for your daughter, a witch who inherited your late husband's magic. What did Vincent make her do instead?"

She hesitated, fingers splayed on the edge of the picture of her daughter.

"He's gone, Charlotte," Paris said. "My father can't hurt your family anymore. Let me help you. Let me help her."

"Potions," she said after another moment. "Killing ones. They've made her sick too."

"And you, Frankie," Paris said, as he glanced up at the blond shifter behind her. "You're a psychopomp. You should be delivering souls to peace, not to the highest bidder." He opened a different folder. "My father found you and offered you protection from a gang who sought to kill you instead of having their souls delivered. What did my father have you do instead?"

He cast his hazel gaze aside. "Deliver them to a giant." Wallace Boyle, if Mac had to guess, another reason Paris had lobbied for recruiting Charlotte and her guards.

"I won't do that," Paris said, conviction and earnestness in his voice. "I'll give you the protection he promised."

"And if we disagree?" the other shifter asked.

"You leave here unharmed."

"And your money?" Charlotte said.

"Is mine now, regardless."

She cursed, then snatched her phone out of her purse, tapping the screen a few times before glancing back at him with an incredulous glare. "This was a trap."

"To free my money, yes, but the offer to free you is also very real."

Through it all, Paris had kept his voice even, calm, gentle almost. No smirk, no victory smile, just the caring, empathetic human who was offering a lifeline, and Charlotte, Mac was sure, was ready to take it, but then Frankie said, "It's too late."

She whirled around in her chair. "What do you mean it's too late? This is a good deal. Better than the other one."

Icarus had shifted forward, muscles coiled. "What other one?"

"I thought it was a trap." Frankie's hazel eyes shifted from Icarus to where Jason had hopped the bar, then to each of Robin's, Adam's, and Mac's positions, all of them moving closer. "I already said yes."

"You were supposed to wait!" Charlotte yelled.

But her bellow was barely audible over the sound of metal ripping apart above, an opening torn in the roof, followed by a rain of fireballs.

Paris yanked on the bond, and Mac's gaze collided with his frightened one. Only a second before Icarus covered his head and hauled him out of the chair, dragging him back toward the bar where Jason stood churning out fireballs of his own.

Mac mentally calculated how fast he could reach them, by foot or wing, but then his math was rearranged by Wallace Boyle falling through the hole in the roof, the giant's feet hitting the floor with a massive rumble. A firefight ensued, cutting off Mac's path, as Jason and Wallace exchanged shots, the latter's height and breadth growing by the second, the tattoos on his skin coming to life, weapons and beasts on the cusp of materializing into this reality.

"Where's the medium?" he bellowed.

A shifted Robin launched at the giant, aiming for his knees, while Adam aimed a shot at his head. Neither attack landed, Wallace deftly maneuvering out of the way—toward where Icarus stood over Kai, Paris, and Charlotte behind a wall of fire Jason had erected. A wall the giant would likely walk right through if Mac didn't do something.

He didn't have a clear path himself, not one that wouldn't push the giant closer to the vulnerable, but he did have a clear path to call in reinforcements so that he, Robin, and Adam could get a better shot at Wallace.

Arms raised, tapping into the two ancient magics that ran through his veins, he recited the words of his ancestors, calling down the wind. And on the next gust that blew through the opening in the roof, Liam led a wave of ravens and crows, all of them flying at the giant's head, disorienting him and causing him to stagger back a step.

Almost enough for Robin to take him down, for Adam to take another shot.

"Seasamh síos!"

Mac went down on one knee, the order issued with power, with magic greater than his own, and the rest of the corvids obeyed too, falling away from the giant, whose gaze locked once more on Paris.

Mac swung his own gaze the direction of the call, to the top of the bar where a certain missing warlock stood wielding a crossbow.

"Stay down!" Atlas yelled for everyone else's benefit.

Right before he unleashed a bronze arrow that sailed through the air and into Wallace Boyle's chest, putting an end to another giant.

THIRTY

"Is this really necessary?" Paris gestured at the caged corner of the basement barrel room where Mac's family kept a collection of library wines . . . and today, a warlock of dubious intent.

"It's for his protection more than ours," Mac said with a pointed look across the room to Robin seething in a club chair, thinly veiled hate swirling in his golden eyes. The only reason they'd made it back to Talahalusi with Atlas in one piece was because Adam had forced Robin to make the trip on paw to "run the murderous impulses out." Mac didn't think it had worked.

For his part, Atlas didn't seem the least bit fazed, resting back against a barrel and magically stitching together a tear in his kilt. Otherwise, the warlock looked his usual put-together self, not a blond hair out of place, his green eyes bright, his thin black tee hugging his fit, compact torso. Sounded like his usual acerbic self too. "One, I can snap my fingers and be out of here whenever I want." He finished with his kilt and straightened, perusing the shelves of wine behind him. "And two," he said as he withdrew a bottle Mac recognized well, "if memory serves, this vintage had a perfect rating and trades in the high six figures." He was right on both counts, and when he sizzled through the wax and cork and drank straight from the bottle, Mac had to tamp down his own murderous impulses.

Paris did his part to calm him too, turning his back on Atlas and patting Mac's chest, those big brown eyes gazing up at him. "He's an ass, but he saved my life."

"About that . . ." Robin said. "You two been working together the entire time?"

Atlas laughed out loud. "No, and truth be told, I'm amazed he's managed to stay alive this long."

Paris spun around so fast he almost stumbled, Mac's arm around his waist the only thing that held him upright. The loss of balance didn't stop his "Hey!" from sounding any less indignant. "What about all those tutors? All those books you made me read? You prepared me for this. If I'd failed, it would've been your fucking fault."

Atlas shrugged and took another slug from the bottle before wiping his mouth on his leather gauntlet. "I did what I could, but you still made some questionable choices." His green gaze slid toward Icarus, who, sitting on Adam's lap at the table across from Robin, flipped him the middle finger.

Mac was on the verge of screaming *Children!* when Paris laid a hand over his on his waist, refocusing Mac on the matter at hand —what role had Atlas played in another giant coming after Paris today? More than timely savior? Robin was right to question.

"Why are you here?" Mac asked.

"Because I got wind you"—he nodded at Paris—"had sent some of Vincent's soldiers to look for the giant in La Purisima."

Robin pushed out of his chair and strolled closer to the cage. "You buddies?"

"Don't think so, seeing as I put a bolt in his chest too."

Adam bumped Icarus off his lap and stood too, joining Robin in front of the cage. "So it's just the one who tried to kill Paris left?"

"Like he wants it to be. He wants to do it himself. Your father," he said to Paris, "wanted to be Chaos's right hand. The giant wanted to be Chaos's champion."

Mac instinctively drew Paris closer, tightening his hold. "Then why did you hand Paris over to him?"

"Because I was trying to find out who he is. He's erased. Vincent always talked about him as a partner but never by name. I would have found out that night, tracked him down and killed him, if all of you hadn't interfered."

Paris shivered in his arms. "I could have died."

"The sacrifice would've been worth it."

Only Paris in his arms kept Mac from flying at the cage. Icarus, though, did it for him, growling as he wrapped his hands around the iron bars. Atlas lifted a hand, like he was about to snap himself out of near death, but then Mary stepped out of the shadows and laid a hand on her brother's shoulder, backing him off while her gaze remained locked on the warlock. "That wouldn't have made me happy," she said to Atlas.

He sneered . . . but tellingly rocked back a step on his leather knee-high boots. "Unlike others, *I* don't take orders from you." He tipped back the bottle and took an even healthier gulp.

"But you sent me that footage from the Stick, didn't you? Were they both there?"

"Only Wallace. I needed to try to draw him out again."

Paris's shivers turned to vibrations, a rare flash of anger riding a wave of hurt. He pushed out of Mac's hold, shoved himself between Icarus and Mary, and stared Atlas down through the bars. "So you used me as bait. Again."

"I won't say I'm sorry. That's one less giant we have to deal with."

"I defended you to them."

He tipped back the bottle one last time, then tossed the empty aside, the glass shattering against the concrete floor. "Don't bother." And with a snap, he was gone.

———

Mac found Paris upstairs in the kitchen, head in the fridge, yanking out ingredients and tossing them onto the island behind him. Seemingly at random: mushrooms, yogurt, onion, cilantro. Afraid of what might come next, Mac hustled across the room and pushed the fridge door closed, forcing Paris out, but not before he'd snatched another carton of mushrooms.

"I'm gonna cook," he sniffled, spinning toward the island as he swiped at the tears on his cheeks.

"No," Mac said, curling an arm around his waist and drawing him into his arms. "You're gonna breathe." He gently tugged at the carton of mushrooms in Paris's hand. "And you're going to let these go because in no world do they belong with the rest of those ingredients."

"I was going to make dill sauce," he said as he released his hostage mushrooms.

"With cilantro?"

His gaze shot to the island, eyes widening. "Fuck, that's gross."

"Very." Mac chuckled, tossed the extra mushrooms aside, and pulled Paris the rest of the way into his arms, gliding a hand up and down his back until his breathing calmed and his tears subsided. "You good?"

"Debatable." A heavy sigh later, he took a half step out of his arms, resting back against the island. "I know I volunteered to be bait a few days ago, but that was on my terms. He used me. Twice!"

"Atlas always has his own agenda."

"I just . . ."

"You just what?"

"Want to be respected," he said with a shrug, casting his gaze aside.

Mac closed the distance between them once again, physically and through their bond, sending admiration and affection through it. Finger curled under Paris's chin, he lifted his face and stared into his eyes, wanting Paris to see—to believe—the truth in his. "I respect you. You are smart, caring, and *good*."

A beautiful blush warmed his pale cheeks, heat flickering in his eyes too. "You're not exactly impartial."

He didn't take the tempting bait. Gliding his hand lower, he cupped the side of Paris's neck. "Everyone here respects you."

"Except Robin."

"Robin doesn't respect anyone."

Paris's watery laugh under his palm felt like victory. He wanted more of those laughs—Paris needed more of those laughs after the day he'd had—and Mac knew just where to get them.

"Put the stuff back in the fridge," he told Paris.

"I was going to make us dinner. I'll find not gross stuff."

Mac shook his head. "There's something else I want to do instead."

"What's that?"

"Introduce you to my parents."

———

Adam and Icarus had graciously surrendered their meadow for the family Samhain gathering. A pavilion stood in the middle of the clearing, round tables and chairs scattered underneath, a long buffet table at one end that in a few days would be overflowing with the bounty of their harvest. Mac leaned against a pole, eaves-dropping as his mother animatedly explained to Paris how every-thing would be set up, what all would be served. Paris oohed and aahed in all the right places, asking about recipes and offering some of his own. All of it genuine, his mother taking to him right away, and when the topic of bread came up, Paris won a mega fan in his father too. Just as Mac had suspected he would. Same as Paris had won Liam over from the start, then Rena and the kids; even Declan had warmed up to him over the past hour as they'd helped with the setup.

Because as Mac had told Paris in the kitchen, he was good. Caring and smart, a kind soul who was loyal to his friends, who'd made sure they were protected, who still carried guilt over the one he'd betrayed, and who'd helped save the pregnant then-stranger now laughing at a table with Mary and Kai. Even if Mac had saved Paris's soul out of some selfish instinct, it had been the right call, because he hadn't truly known then what Paris's soul deserved. Not like he did now.

"You're in love with him," Adam said, the truth not startling, nor the man, his footsteps heavier now that he was human again. He leaned against the next pole over, arms crossed, gaze tracking Icarus as he and Jason chased Cherry and Abernathy around the tables with the gingham cloths they were supposed to be spreading on each, not trying to wrap the kids up in them.

"I'm sorry I doubted you," Mac said. "When you told me how you felt about Icarus. I get it now."

"In fairness, you took a few days longer."

Mac shook his head, a small resigned smile—fate—making his lips curve. "He grabbed hold that night at the altar, and I didn't deliver him."

Gasping, Adam shot off the pole. "He's on your list?"

"Has been since that night."

Adam clasped his shoulder. "Mac—"

"There may be a way around it," he said, cutting off the sympathy that threatened in his friend's voice. He didn't need condolences. He needed a miracle, the same kind that had held his family together once before. "My father was on my mother's list. That's the real reason they retired."

Adam's gaze drifted back out under the tent, to where Paris stood chatting with his parents. "They're still here. Happy and healthy."

Mac's attention drifted elsewhere, to his brother snatching up his kids midrun, hauling them under his arms, all of them laughing, free and easy, unburdened. His gut churned. "I don't know if I can do it to him."

"Liam wants it, Mac. He's ready."

"But Rena and the kids . . ."

"Will keep him grounded. And when it's Declan's turn or one of the kids', it'll pass to them. No one expects you to do this forever, except you."

He swung his gaze back to Adam. "So Paris and I just go off to our happily ever after?"

Adam chuckled. "You two would fail at that as badly as me and Icarus. Paris has a gift, and so do you, as a detective and as a raven with acute observation skills. Those won't go away just because you give up the reaper. And we'll all help Liam because that's what family does." He squeezed his shoulder and gifted Mac one of his rare smiles, though thanks to Icarus, they were coming more frequently again these days.

Mac hated to wipe it from his face, but he had one more favor to ask, and Adam was the only person he trusted to fulfill it. "If for some reason he doesn't make it, I don't want to either. Not again."

Using the hand still on his shoulder, Adam pulled him into a crushing embrace. "I hope it doesn't come to that, but if it does, you have my word."

Mac hugged him back, blinking back tears and forcing words out around the lump in his throat. "Thank you."

"Hey, wallflowers!" Icarus shouted, yanking them out of their melancholy moment. They drew apart, eyeing the courtesan standing with Paris mid-tent, the former holding up an orange gingham, Paris a violet one. "Need your votes."

Paris's smile grew wider with each step Mac came closer, his gaze bright with happiness, with the confidence Atlas and Robin had tried unsuccessfully to chip away at, with the love that had been growing between them these past few weeks, that Mac had no intention of existing without.

"I like the violet," he said as Mac reached him.

"I should hope so." Smirking, he looped an arm around Paris's waist, trapping him in said violet and kissing him with his whole soul.

Cheers erupted and a camera clicked somewhere, capturing the second love of his life. His last. "Forever," he whispered against Paris's lips.

"Forever," his mate promised back.

THIRTY-ONE

Infirmary no longer needed, the tasting table had been moved back into the barrel room and all but one seat was occupied around it, the room full of people, including Mac with Paris sitting beside him, waiting for the last person to arrive.

To confirm the wheels had been set in motion.

Jason, on the other side of Paris, leaned across the table, asking Icarus, "What happened to Miss Types-Like-the-Wind?"

"You wouldn't want me to send these messages to the wrong people, would you?" Mary said as she cleared the bottom step.

No, they would not. With Charlotte's help decoding Vincent's books and contacts, Mac's cold case files and access to missing persons reports, the pack digging deeper into Atlas's potential whereabouts, and Mary hacking surgical records, official and not, they'd identified three possible suspects as the giant who'd attacked Paris, all of them erased persons, presumably all the names they'd associated with them aliases too.

Brett Barrett.

Samuel Thomas.

Neil Roberts.

And just now, Mary had sent encrypted emails to each, putting it out there that Paris, as Vincent's successor, wanted to meet at the Stick tomorrow, the day before Samhain, to discuss a possible partnership for future endeavors. They were counting on the giant, whichever one he was, to see an opportunity he couldn't pass up. A chance to catch the one who got away.

And Paris acting the bait on his own terms, with plenty of backup.

Mac looked again at the pictures of their three suspects—a single photo of each that Mary had managed to scrounge up. "Can you give us a more likely than not?" he asked Paris.

Paris pulled each photo closer, taking a long look then trading one for another. "All of them are the right build and appearance, perfectly average. But all of their beards are too thick for me to see if the scar is there," he said, tapping at the spot on Brett's chin where the raised slash would be. "And the photos are too grainy to see much else."

"Best I could find," Mary said. "We're lucky to get any for erased persons."

"Samuel is the most likely candidate," Robin said. "If that report he paid a surgeon for fixing his face after a bar fight is legit."

"A bar that has the ingredients for the drink you smelled on his breath," Mac said.

"Wrong eye color," Jenn countered.

"Could be contacts," Kai said, and he would know. The white raven's contacts had fooled people for years into thinking he was a human.

"Then there's the loan shark, Neil," Abigail said. "Vincent did business with him."

"He could've taken that knife Paris painted as collateral," Jason speculated. "High value." The smuggler would know.

But Icarus shook his head. "Atlas would've known him."

"That might be an apron Brett is wearing," Liam said, peering at the photo he'd snagged from in front of Paris.

"Store clerk, janitor, mechanic would make sense for an erased person," Adam said. "He bounces around, gets paid under the table."

Paris shoved back from the table with a frustrated grunt. "*If, might, could be* . . . We don't know anything for sure," he said, raking his hands through his hair as he paced away from the table.

Mac rose slowly, not cutting him off abruptly this time, but letting Paris wind down as he circled back to where Mac stood. When he was in front of him, Mac laid a hand over his stomach. "Who do you think it is *here*, in your gut?"

"It could be any of—"

He splayed his fingers. "Who, Paris?"

"Brett," he answered without hesitation. "Adam is right, and the malice in his eyes . . . Whomever he was looking at, he hated them. That was the way he looked at Lola." His whole body shivered, and Mac wrapped an arm around his shoulders while the remembered fear passed.

"Brett is priority one," he told the group over his shoulder. "But we still need to be ready for Samuel or Neil."

"If we can find them," Mary said. "I'll keep digging, but no known addresses as of yet."

"What if I'm wrong?" Paris said, quietly, as if intended only for Mac's ears, but in a room full of shifters and magical beings, everyone heard him.

And of course Robin was the one to press, the coyote strolling over to where they stood. "You can't go into this and be knocked off your game if it's not Brett who shows up at the Stick tomorrow."

He was an asshole, but he wasn't wrong. Given the geography of the location, the plan depended on Paris keeping the giant, whomever he turned out to be, talking long enough to one, incriminate himself, and two, allow the teams to converge from the water, air, and land.

The asshole, it seemed, tended to bring out the fight in Paris.

He straightened his spine and lifted his chin, glaring Robin down. "As long as you're on your game to catch the fucker."

Behind them, Icarus and Jason high-fived, and Robin even cracked a smirk. "We'll be ready," he said, then gestured to the table. "Let's go over those mission specs one more time so you'll know exactly where we're coming from."

With a nod, Paris led them back to the table, and after another hour of planning, the meeting broke up, folks scattering for the evening.

Paris moved to stand too, but Mac placed a hand on his knee, holding him seated until it was just the two of them left in the room. He rotated Paris in his chair toward him, their knees bumping. "It's just me now," he said. "I know you can do this, I believe in you, but if you have any doubt, or if you don't want to do this, you always have an out." They were asking a lot of someone who was relatively new to this war, who hadn't been fighting it for decades like him and many of the others. "You just have to tell me."

Paris shook his head, sharp and certain. "I'm the last line of human defense," he said, repeating the mantra he'd said to Icarus the other day. "We need a place in this fight. This is our home too. I intend to defend it."

"All right," Mac said, standing and offering Paris his hand. "Tomorrow we fight. But tonight, I have something else in mind."

THIRTY-TWO

Mac had been sneaking glances every so often at Paris in the passenger seat, watching his smile grow wider as he grew more certain of their destination. He was beaming by the time Mac pulled his car into the drive at the cabin in Calera.

Paris climbed out, inhaled deep, then spun, asking him over the car roof, "What are we doing here?"

"I know I've kept you away from your ocean lately. And this isn't right on it either, not like your condo, but it's close. I thought it might help center you before tomorrow. And . . ." Heat rushed to his cheeks, making him feel hot all over, the romantic sentiment on the tip of his tongue big. And telling. Not that he hadn't told Paris already about his history or how he felt about him, but this seemed different. More. Like putting it all on the line—his heart, his hopes, his forever.

"And what?" Paris said, as he rounded the front of the car and cozied up to his side, hand on his chest.

Mac covered it with his, sliding his fingers between Paris's. "And this is where I fell in love with you. I wanted to spend tonight with you here. Make love to you here." In their own little oasis, away from the rest of the world that was horribly fast and dangerous these days.

Paris shoved him against the side of the car and stole a hard, deep kiss that had Mac seriously considering whether to skip the next surprise of the evening and go straight to the finale, right here against the side of the car. But then Paris drew back, his brown eyes staring up at him. "You're a good man too," he said. "More than you give yourself credit for."

"I hope you continue to think that."

"Oh!" He drummed his fingers on Mac's chest. "You have more surprises for me, don't you?" As fast as he'd spun getting out of the car, he did so again, darting for the cabin door. Only to find it locked.

"Oh!" Mac parroted back. "You need a key, don't you?" He took his time, unloading their bag from the trunk and strolling to the door.

"Now you're just being mean," Paris said with an adorable pout. Which disappeared as soon as he walked through the door into the candlelit cabin. He stood in the center of the space, wide-eyed and rotating to take it all in: the wildflowers on every surface, the spread of cheeses, nuts, and fruits on the table, the jazz music playing softly in the background. "Who did all this?" he asked. "The rest of the cabins were dark when we drove in, and all the witches' cars were gone."

"They've moved on." As the covens did, never too long in one place. "Mom and Dad helped out, with Rena and the kids"—he pointed at the cake under the glass dome on the counter— "pitching in too." He dropped the duffel at the end of the bed, then wandered back to where Paris stood in a stunned daze. Wrapping his arms around him from behind, he pulled him against his chest and nuzzled the crook of his neck, swaying them to the music. "I wanted us to finish that dance that got interrupted."

Paris rested his head on Mac's shoulder, giving him more access to his throat, more skin to pepper with kisses. "And where would it have ended?"

"Right here," Mac said, holding him tight. "Where you're the center of my world."

"And you mine." Paris angled his head, and Mac didn't hesitate to claim his lips, to sweep his tongue into his mouth and taste every bit of sweetness and light Paris had brought into his life, every ounce of love and desire Mac had avoided for so long but couldn't get enough of now.

Especially with Paris twisting in his arms and grinding up against him, his cock hard against the length of Mac's. "Is there any food that won't keep?"

Mac nipped at his lips, along his jaw, the lobe of his ear. "I just need to put the cheese in the fridge," he said, loving the tremors that quaked through Paris, the short breaths panted against the side of his face.

But not for long, Paris drawing out of his arms and holding up a hand when Mac started to reach for him, not willing to let him go. "Do that," he said. "Get a fire going, and I'll meet you back at the bed. I need to get my wits about me or this will be over way too fast."

Mac chuckled as Paris practically ran to the bathroom. He enjoyed turning Paris on, liked having him on the pleasure ropes for a change. He wondered if he could do more of that this evening, if he could try what he'd thought about that day Paris had been waiting for him with the toy. Mac hadn't packed the plug, but he bet Paris would still enjoy the stimulation. Mac sure would, the thought alone—of Paris writhing under his teasing tongue—getting him harder. When he stood from in front of the hearth, there was no hiding his erection. But then Paris wasn't hiding his either, standing naked beside the bed.

"Fuck," Mac cursed as he crossed the room. "Do you have any idea how beautiful you are?" The blush that rosied his pale cheeks only added to the devastating picture. "If I had any artistic talent at all, I'd paint these eyes," he said as he cupped Paris's cheek and swiped a thumb under the molten brown. He trailed his hand down, fingers barely touching skin, lifting goose bumps. "I'd paint these collarbones too, and the dip of your throat." He leaned forward, tonguing the divot, as he continued to travel south first with his hand, then his lips, kissing a path in its wake. "This valley that cuts between your pecs and your ribs and your abs." He sank to his knees and circled Paris's length with his fist, giving it a long, slow stroke. "This cock."

Paris let his head fall back on a groan. "You do okay with words. And the touch. Fuck, I love to be touched like this. So soft." Mac continued to stroke his cock, in no hurry, while he teased Paris everywhere around it with the soft kisses he seemed to love so much—his pelvis, his thighs, his sac—until Paris begged for more.

"You want me to kiss you here?" Mac teased, dropping one on the sticky head of his cock. He caught a bead of precome with his tongue and spread it around the head, pulling off after a flick to the underside.

Paris righted his gaze and his pupils were blown so wide that only a thin ring of brown remained, the dark black reflecting the violet of Mac's own eyes. "I want you to suck me off," Paris said as he plowed a hand into his hair, possessively clenching his fingers and urging Mac forward. "Make me come."

He swallowed Paris as far as his throat would allow, until he gagged, then did it over and over again, sucking and licking, teasing the tip each time he came close to drawing off, before plunging back down, using his hand to lengthen the strokes, especially as Paris increased the pace of his thrusting hips, putting more speed and power behind the movement, fucking Mac's mouth with abandon.

It was a sight to behold, the most beautiful man Mac had ever seen panting above him, at the mercy of his mouth, trusting Mac enough to let it all go with him. It was the biggest fucking turn-on, and Mac had to spread his own knees wider, had to make room for his own aching cock inside his trousers.

Paris's needy "I'm gonna come" didn't help his situation.

Mac grunted around his cock, and that was all it took, Paris coming in his mouth, filling it with come faster than he could swallow, some of it leaking out the corners of his mouth, because he would be damned if he didn't milk every last ounce of pleasure from Paris. When he was finally, completely spent, Mac drew off his cock with a parting kiss and stood.

"You made a mess," Paris said, sounding almost drunk as he wiped the come from Mac's chin. "And I'm not sure how much longer I can stand on these orgasm-jellied legs."

"Let's go, then," Mac said, his voice rough as he shuffled them the rest of the way to the bed, the two of them side by side on the edge.

Paris rested his chin on his shoulder and slid a hand over his thigh, sliding it higher until he was cupping him through his slacks. "We need to get this inside me."

Mac rocked up into his hand, the friction tempting, but his earlier thought still lingered, a fantasy he wanted to live. He rotated his face toward Paris's, whispering against his lips. "I want to taste you there first."

"Fuck," Paris cursed on a long, tortured groan. "You're gonna make me come again."

"Would that be a problem?"

Paris kissed the upturned corner of his mouth. "I love that smirk. I don't know if I want to paint it or your smile."

"Not the raven?" Mac asked as Paris began undressing him, his shirt the first piece of clothing to go.

"I thought about that too. I want you to see all the colors in your feathers. Like they are in your aura."

"What's it look like right now?" He lifted his hips so Paris could push his pants and boxers off, freeing his cock.

"Rivers of pink and red in a sea of flowing blue, violet, and green." He trailed a hand back up his leg, inside his thigh, cradling his balls. "It's beautiful, Mac. It's the peace you're supposed to have, that you deserve." Then fisted his cock, mimicking the long, slow strokes Mac had given him.

"Need you, Paris."

"You still want—"

"Yes," Mac said, wanting it more than ever, wanting all of Paris.

He waited for Paris to arrange himself on his stomach, his ass lifted by a pillow under his hips, then crawled between his spread legs, hands sliding up the backs of his thighs and palming his ass. Paris rolled his hips. "You gonna make me fuck this pillow?"

Mac answered by pulling his cheeks apart, exposing his hole, and lashing across it with his tongue.

Paris curled his hands in the sheets. "Again."

Mac was more than happy to oblige, happy to feast, happy to learn he was right—that his tongue teasing Paris's rim, dipping inside his hole, drove them both wild. Mac rutted against the mattress while Paris lolled his head with his groans, grabbed more of the sheets with each flick of Mac's tongue, and fucked the pillow with as much abandon as he'd fucked his mouth. And when Mac pushed one, then a second finger into him, opening him wider, getting him ready, he rode those with abandon too.

Trust and love, desire and hope pulsing along their bond the entire time.

A third finger and Paris cried mercy, thank fuck. "Get inside me, please."

"I've got you," he said, drawing those soft words over Paris's back again with one hand, while with the other he lined his cock up at Paris's hole and pushed inside him. They sighed in relief together, Mac stretching the rest of the way over him, lips against Paris's nape. "I could stay here forever."

"That's fine with me," Paris said, then thrust his hips. "Less so my cock."

Mac chuckled, Paris's torso under his rumbling with laughter too, until he started to move and their amusement became a series of grunts and moans, pleas for harder and faster.

As his orgasm approached, Mac stretched out his arms, hands seeking Paris's, his fingers sliding into the spaces between his spread ones. A perfect fit. Like their bodies, like their souls, which would get what they deserve. They'd get a choice, and Mac knew his. "I choose you, Paris. Forever."

Paris turned his head, his brown eyes swirling with love and a violet hue. "And I choose you. Forever."

He rested their foreheads together, lips brushing. "I love you. My soul is yours."

"And mine yours," Paris said on a gasp, body quaking and clenching around his. "I love you too."

"What we deserve," Mac promised as he rode the wave of pleasure with forever in his arms.

THIRTY-THREE

The one thing his parents, Rena, and the kids forgot to stock the cabin with was more tea. Not surprising, given their family was a coffee one, Paris the odd-tea-drinker-out. And not surprising that Mac had caved when Paris had rolled over in bed, stuck out that adorable bottom lip, and, arm slung across the rest of his pretty face, claimed dramatically that he would never be able to get out of bed without his leaf water. Mac had considered saying no just to keep him there in bed, looking like the beautifully debauched lover he was—his brown hair rumpled, his pale skin marked from lips and teeth, his morning wood tenting the sheet over his hips—but they had *a day* ahead of them, one in which Paris would carry the heavy mantle for their team and for Nature. Grabbing him the morning beverage of his choice was the least Mac could do.

He'd paused, however, over the threshold, fear creeping up his spine at leaving Paris out here alone, no witches in the other cabins, only a half arsenal of corvids in the trees, their numbers having been needed elsewhere overnight. But then Paris had reminded him that no one except Kai had found them in the woods before, and the only reason he had was because Paris had told him exactly where to look.

"Ten minutes down to the motel and back," he'd pleaded with another pout. "I'll be fine."

Mac had relented, and thankfully, the little store had the olallieberry tea he favored.

"Anything else?" the clerk asked.

"I'm go—" he started to say, then noticed the collection of mugs behind her, one that made him think of Paris and grin. "Actually, can I get that yellow mug that says *Not Paint Water*?" The words were in black brush strokes, big and bold, on a can't miss background.

The clerk laughed as she rose on her tiptoes to reach it. "Painter in your life?"

"Yes," Mac said, smiling wider. "And he steals all the mugs for rinse buckets."

"My husband too," she said as she wrapped the ceramic mug in craft paper. "I ordered a half dozen of these and kept three for us."

"Did they work?"

She smiled, an amused, commiserative thing, as she handed him his bag of purchases. "Not one bit. Let me know how it goes with your man."

"Will do," Mac said, as he exited the shop for the car. He figured they probably would be back here, and that it would probably go about the same with Paris as it had with the store clerk's husband. And Mac wouldn't give a damn if it did, wouldn't care one bit if Paris filled any place they lived with paint mugs, as long as Paris was in his li—

The sudden, hard yank on the soul bond dropped him to his knees, the mug shattering beneath his hand on the concrete, his heart and mind racing to decipher the fear and fire—the betrayal—coursing along the bond.

The resignation.

Mac yanked back. To no response.

Fuck.

He shifted, soaring into the air, and as soon as he did, he saw the smoke billowing through the treetops of the forest. He sailed across the highway and up the hill, cutting a direct path, slicing through the trees, the heat ratcheting up the farther into the woods he flew, the closer he got to the cabin.

A wall of smoke met him at the last dense arch of foliage where the other corvids had retreated. Sailing past them and under the arch, fire and flames greeted him on the other side, stinging his eyes and singeing the ends of his wings as he sailed around the burning cabin, searching for any signs of Paris.

Then hurtling back as a blast of heat erupted from inside the cabin, shattering the glass windows, buckling the walls, and caving in the roof, the entire structure collapsing.

He wasn't in there, Mac told himself. He couldn't have been. He would've gotten out, and the corvids would've escorted him to safety, to him, except they hadn't. They'd fallen back instead. Like they'd been ordered.

He dove closer to the ground, to where the front step of the cabin once existed. And that was when he saw it, in the morning damp earth, beside the massive footprint that could only belong to a giant.

A familiar oval-shaped paw print.

Mac shifted into human form a few feet shy of the villa's front door where Liam waited, trench in hand. "I felt you coming." His brother handed him the coat, and by his pinched brows and anxious gaze, Liam had also sensed the anger and desperation warring inside him. "What's wrong?" he asked. "Where's Paris?"

Mac shoved his arms into the sleeves and belted the coat around his waist. "Robin's in the barrel room?"

Liam nodded. "With some of the others. Where's Paris?" he asked again, voice pitched higher with worry for his friend.

Mac was sure his "Gone" didn't help, but he needed to get to Robin before the coyote was gone too. As it was, he was shocked the traitor had the gall to return here, unless he wanted to be caught. Which seemed to be the case, his golden gaze locking with Mac's as soon as he cleared the bottom step. "I can explain."

Mac flew at him, shoving him two-handed against the nearest wall and snarling through clenched teeth. "What did you do?"

"What he would have."

"Mac," Adam said, his footsteps approaching beside him. "What's going on?"

"I went out this morning to get Paris some tea, and this asshole led the giant right to him."

"How do you know it was the giant?" Liam asked.

Mac splayed a hand over his chest where the soul bond should be. "Because I felt it, here. Paris's fear and the fire he associated with him, the resignation when he surrendered himself." He pressed harder with the other hand against Robin still. "The betrayal. I found your paw print next to the giant's in the dirt outside the burning cabin. Why'd you do it? Why'd you betray us?"

Robin didn't put up a fight, didn't even try to skirt out of the hold Mac had on him. He could have—Robin was bigger, more powerful—but he gave him an explanation instead, their gazes locked. "I was patrolling last night. I found Brett on the outskirts of the property. Paris was right; he was the giant who attacked him. And he was coming after Pati. I offered him a different target."

"You brought him to our doorstep."

"He was ready, Mac. You're ready."

"He's on my fucking list, Robin." One more hard shove and Mac stepped back, desperation eclipsing anger, his voice ragged as he confessed the secret he'd shared with only a few. "I was supposed to deliver his soul that night at the altar in YB. Same as I had to deliver the first person I ever loved, and now you might've just doomed me to do it again."

Startled sounds echoed around the room, while in front of Mac, Robin paled and slumped against the wall. "I'm sorry," he said. "I didn't know."

"What else did Brett offer you?" Mary asked from where she stood at the head of the table. "Information on Atlas?"

Robin lowered his chin, running a hand across the back of his neck, a guilty tell Mac had seen countless times over the years, and anger surged once more. But not as fast and fiery as Jason's, the phoenix's glowing red fist connecting with Robin's nose. He reared back for another, but Kai backed him off at the last second.

Only for Icarus to take Jason's place, seething in Robin's face. "This vendetta of yours is going to get all of us killed. Do you get that?"

Robin wiped his bloody nose on his sleeve. "I get it, okay."

"Do you, Robin?" Adam said, as he pulled his partner back. "Because your actions say otherwise, time and again. How many more good people have to die for your selfishness? How many more souls can your conscious bear?"

It was a blow that even Mac, despite his own fury at Robin, felt in his gut, empathy not something he could just turn off.

Robin's guilty gaze shifted past Adam to him. "I'm sorry," he said, and Mac believed some part of him meant it. But another part of him also knew he'd make the same choice again, evidenced by his words. "But we know who the giant is now, and we know he'll be in one of two places tomorrow."

"What if I'm at the wrong one?" Mac said, letting the anguish he felt creep into his voice, the last hour of adrenaline burning out of him, leaving only fear and the very real prospect of despair. "What if I'm not there to save him again?"

"The Canyon Lands," Adam said, shifting into tactical mode. "We don't control and couldn't cleanse that one. There'll be more lingering souls to offer to Chaos."

"Or trust Paris to sell the Stick," Icarus said. "I'm angry as fuck at the dog, but he's not wrong about Paris being ready."

"We'll cover both," Mary said as she joined their group. She laid a hand on Mac's shoulder, her warmth pushing back at the threatening cold again. "Paris will show you, and when he does, we'll be ready."

THIRTY-FOUR

Just as Mac had put a hand over Paris's gut and asked him to make a call two days ago, Mac had done the same today, trusting his gut—and Icarus's logic—that Paris would convince Brett to bring him to the altar at the Stick for tonight's sacrifice.

And even though they'd felt certain that Brett would wait until tonight, until Samhain when the veil would be at its thinnest, they'd quickly moved into position yesterday, ready in case Brett accelerated the schedule. Mac had flown back and forth between the two sites yesterday, Liam on his wing, but tonight, he'd committed to the Stick. And like Mary had said, if it turned out the sacrifice was at the other altar in the Canyon Lands, Adam's team there would fight until Mac and the rest of his team made it to them.

Paris hadn't confirmed one way or another yet, hadn't shown him anything via their bond, which still hummed oh so quietly between them, almost as if Paris was hiding it. Not like at the condo, behind a wall of magic and inaccessible to Mac, but like he didn't want someone else to notice it. Mac took the comfort for what it was—Paris was still alive and the bond was still there when they needed it.

"We've got activity in the parking lot," Icarus radioed from where he was stationed with Jenn and members of the pack for the ground assault. Close enough to be inside the bank of fog that blocked the rest of them from seeing anything, but far enough out not to trigger anyone else's notice. "Group of cars are trickling in."

"Any sign of Paris or Brett?" Mac asked.

"Negative," Jenn reported, then after a moment added, "Visitors aren't human."

"Shifters or warlocks?" Jason asked, the lap of water audible against the side of the boat where he, Kai, Mary, and several of Paris's recruits waited. Two warlocks for the field and another to stay behind and protect Mary.

"Bit of both."

"Witnesses," Liam said from beside Mac on the bluff where they were stationed with the flock. "Like at the other sites."

They'd been prepared for that. No reason to think tonight—especially tonight—would be any different.

"Fucking hell," Icarus cursed.

"What?" Mac snapped, harsher than intended, but his nerves were already fraying after twenty-four hours of waiting with no indication of when or if he'd ever see Paris again.

"Atlas just got out of one of the cars," Icarus relayed. "And he's back in his villain attire. Fully suited."

No *if*, then, just *when*.

"What the fuck is he playing at?" Jason growled, and from Mac's vantage on the bluff, he saw the light of a fireball through the fog, on the water near where their boat should be.

"Call the other team down," Mary said. "This is the site."

Mac clasped his collar, ready to yank his shirt off and shift, but Liam stopped him, hand around his biceps. "Not yet, brother. I know you want to fly, but we can't go until Paris is there."

"He's right," Jenn said. "We can't risk scaring them off. We might never find Paris, then."

He appreciated that Paris was her primary concern, not the giant, but fuck, this was killing him. And he was lashing out at any target. "Then someone tell Jason to put the fucking fireball out," he gritted between clenched teeth. "I can see it from here."

The light on the water vanished, the Bay dark again.

"What's going on?" Mac asked after another minute passed.

"The witnesses are gathering," Jenn replied. "In a semicircle like at the ridge."

"Atlas is behind the altar," Icarus added as the wind gusted around them. "That fucker, what is he doing?"

"Babe!" Mary chided before Mac could. "Details."

"It looks like he's sucking power from the other warlocks. He's got his hands raised. Why's his magic yellow? It's usually green. Fuck, he's chanting something, but I can't hear it."

"It sounds like Gaelic, Mac," Jenn said.

Kai gasped. "Is he trying to open the portal himself?"

"No," Mary said. "But he's thinning it out more." Belying her typically confident voice was an undercurrent of very real fear. Mac had only heard her sound like that once before, that day in Portola when she'd faced down Vincent, ironically under Atlas's arm. "I can feel it."

And in the next instant, Mac felt something too.

Paris.

A single pulse—agony—pushed down the bond, and then the earth groaned, as if torn apart by some awful magic, and a blast of light that Mac could see through the fog lit the Stick.

"He's here," Jenn confirmed. "With Paris."

That was all the go-ahead Mac needed, and this time, Liam didn't stop him, taking to wing beside him, the flock at their backs as they streaked toward the site.

Comm no longer in ear, Mac couldn't hear whether Jenn and Icarus were leading the pack members into the fight, nor whether Jason and Kai were powering the boat of magical reinforcements to shore, but he had to trust his team. Trust that Adam's contingent would get here too as fast as magic and motors would carry them.

He and Liam sliced through the fog, and when they emerged

on the other side, the battle was already in full swing. Jenn and other members of the pack in their big coyote bodies, tumbling with other shifters. Icarus and Jason and their warlocks engaged in combat with several other warlocks. Kai in the air, a white beacon surveying the scene, causing others to look up and gasp, giving their own fighters a chance at the upper hand.

But as Mac scanned past the battle to the altar, he wobbled in flight, the sight of Paris in pain rocking Mac to his core. Blood poured from fresh cuts on his arms and legs and his back bowed and hands fisted as souls poured through him. The scene had been gruesome the first time around, but now that was the man Mac loved on the altar, his forever being tortured, and Mac felt every ounce of his pain in his own soul.

KRAA! Liam screeched beside him and, wing under his, kept him aloft as the initial shock—the agony—ripped through him.

Then morphed into anger, into single-minded purpose.

He called back his thanks, and Paris's head on the altar lolled their direction, his eyes wide and glowing violet, tracking his and Liam's flight toward him, before they squeezed shut again and his back bowed once more, his mouth forming the same words, over and over.

Help me.

What horrible deaths was he reliving behind those eyes each time a soul traveled through him? How many could he bear before his own weakened body gave out? Before his soul joined them and the bond between him and Mac was severed? They didn't have time to waste.

Mac pushed love and strength, pride and reassurance along the bond, everything he couldn't say in raven form, then, with his brother at his side and his flock at his back, dove for the giant.

And streaked back when fireballs and magic sliced through their wave of black, searing the tips of his wings. He banked left, taking half the flock with him, Liam going right with the rest, and they spread wide, too many targets for one warlock and one giant, the rest of the witnesses otherwise occupied.

And more of Mac's forces arriving by the second, Robin's big rusty-blond body tearing onto the scene, Abigail's feline form on his heels, and Adam with his guns at the ready. More of the pack and Paris's recruits charging in and overwhelming the witnesses.

The giant hurled his fireballs, growing more distracted and disoriented by the second as souls that passed through Paris escaped to the water, toward where Nature called them away from Chaos. Atlas spun, as if sensing her there, and Robin pounced, taking a fireball hit to his pointed ear yet still sailing across the altar at the warlock and taking him down. He opened his jaws on a roar . . . and then nothing but yellow mist, Atlas snapping away from the scene.

Mac called to Kai, pointedly directing him back to the boat, to Mary in case Atlas reappeared there and sending half the flock with him. He kept the remaining corvids with him and Liam, circling the giant, the heat rolling off him in waves, no doubt scorching Paris where he lay in front of him. They needed to neutralize him before he disappeared into another fireball and charred everything, including Paris.

Mac circled back over Adam, Liam gliding to his flank, in position for them to build on their experience with the ridge giant. And Robin was already where they needed him.

"Robin!" Adam shouted, as if reading Mac's mind. "Grab him!"

The coyote reared up and snapped at the shreds of the giant's clothing, using it to pull him back, exposing his chest for Adam's silver bullets, then clamping hold of his shoulder and dragging him back further, heedless of the heat and flames. The smell of burnt fur tickled Mac's senses as he and Liam swarmed with their brethren around the giant's head, pecking and flapping their wings, drawing his fire and fists their direction and away from those on the ground below.

"Brock!" Icarus called. "Chains, now!"

The warlock they'd recruited spread his glowing blue hands, a heavy silver chain appearing out of thin air between them. Adam grabbed one end, Icarus the other, the two humans who could handle it running around the altar, then splitting off in opposite directions, circling the giant's waist. Brett howled and flailed, shaking off Robin, but Adam and Icarus, the pack at their backs, the flock harassing the giant from the front, dragged him back, back, back over the rocks and to the water's edge.

Where Mary waited, hanging off the side of the boat, her hands in the water, ripples of green cresting and crashing, circling Brett's ankles as Adam and Icarus hauled him in.

Turning him back into nothing but a small power-hungry, hate-filled man.

The silver chain dissolved, and before Brett could make a run for it, before he could transform back into the giant, Robin crashed into the waves and held his body under, the assassin doing what he did best, Nature his witness to the kill.

"Mac!" Jason yelled from behind them, and Mac wheeled in the air back toward the altar where Jason was hauling Paris down with Brock's help. "Mac! We're losing him!"

THIRTY-FIVE

Mac landed on his feet, in a dead sprint, chanting "No, no, no . . ." as he slid onto his knees beside Jason. He hauled Paris into his arms, holding his body close. He was too cold, too still. The bond between them pulsed erratically, dimming bit by bit.

"Come on, Paris, stay with me." He cupped his cheek, wiping away the tear tracks that stained his beautiful, pale face. He forced more love, more gratitude, more pride through the bond. "You did it, baby. You slayed the giant. Now come back to me. Open your eyes, *please*."

"Mac," he mumbled weakly.

"I'm right here."

His eyelids fluttered open, and hazy violet irises stared back at Mac. "Help me."

"What do you need?"

"The stars. Mom."

Mac lifted his gaze and cursed the fog.

"The ocean," Paris rasped.

"We're right by it."

"Can't hear," Paris said, shaking his head, eyes slipping closed again. "Need to, one last time."

Mac's heart stopped, then caved in on itself. "No, no, no, we said forever."

"Please," Paris whispered on a shallow breath.

Beside them, Liam kneeled and clasped Mac's shoulder. "Do you need me to help?"

He glanced at his brother, finding his face as wet as Mac's felt, his eyes swirling with shared grief.

Mac nodded, and Liam helped him to his feet, steadied him as he adjusted Paris in his arms. He turned toward the water and met Adam's stormy gaze. Asked him, without a word, if he was ready to fulfill a promise.

Adam nodded.

And with that reassurance, Mac put one foot in front of the other, Liam on one side, Jason on the other, as he carried his precious cargo across the slippery rocks to the water's edge where Mary waited.

He sank to his knees, letting it wash around them, and the smile that graced Paris's face was pure peace, the same one he wore in sleep and ecstasy, in everyday life as he brightened the world around him, the same one that had convinced Mac to love again.

Mary kneeled beside him. "Are you ready to let him go?"

"Never."

"Are you ready to take his place?"

Caught off guard by her question, Mac looked up and found Mary's gaze on Liam.

"I am," his brother answered.

"What—" Mac started, then gasped as the water around them turned green and violet, and the souls he'd seen escape came rushing back across the top of the gentle breakers, back to Paris, as if he and Mary had called them. They surrounded Paris in his arms, warming his body and caging in his soul, keeping him there.

With him.

"You've done enough," Mary said. "Both of you. Now they want to return the favor, and so do I."

A spark of hope caught, like the embers of the fireplace back at the cabin. "We can have forever?"

"You can have what you deserve," she said. "Liam is the reaper now. You'll deliver no more souls until it's time to deliver his," she said with a nod to Paris. "And you'll deliver yours with him. Many, many years in the future, if you can help it."

Mac laughed, improbably, then leaned over and pressed his forehead to Paris's warming one. "Do you still want forever with me?"

"Forever," Paris whispered back, sealing the future Mac hadn't dared hope for until the man in his arms grabbed hold of his soul and refused to let go.

PART THREE

MAC & PARIS

THIRTY-SIX

"These three missing persons cases came into the office after the Rift anniversary." Mac handed Liam copies of his department files, then nodded at the two green-hued crime scene paintings leaned against the wall of his study. "Paris was able to call two of the souls to him. Got us some more details."

Since the Stick, Paris wasn't only able to dive into souls' memories. He was also able to call souls to him, a game changer when it came to Mac's cold cases and the department's missing persons ones. It had barely been a week since the Stick, and they'd already solved multiple cases. Mac wanted him to slow down, to pace himself as he recovered, but Paris was determined to help, to make sure as many souls as possible reached their destination before winter solstice, not wanting anyone else to try and manipulate them for evil.

Liam flipped open the first file and glanced between the photo of the young woman in the file and Paris's painting of that same woman floating in a lake, a letterman jacket thrown over her. "She's on my list," Liam said, then set that file aside and opened the next. "Not on my list," he said of the second person Paris had painted, "but I'll send out word to the other reapers." He snapped a photo of the painting.

"And we'll keep investigating the third," Mac said.

Liam dropped the files on the desk, then rested back against the edge. "This doesn't seem so bad."

Mac sighed and leaned a hip next to his, raking a hand through his hair. "I should have let all of you help me sooner."

"It was a good lesson for me." He bumped their shoulders together. "And you're a good mentor too, regardless."

"He's also a good husband," Paris called from the adjoining room. "So far!"

Liam laughed out loud, one of the things Mac had always loved about his brother. Something he was trying to learn to do more of himself, smiling as he joked, "I think Mom left that tent up on purpose."

"I don't think there's any *think* about it." Liam pushed off the desk, chuckling. "You and Paris will be down for dinner tonight?"

"Are you sure you don't want to move up here?" Mac asked as he followed him into the other room. "This is the reaper's perch, and you're the reaper now."

"The big house is our home. This is yours and Paris's."

"Until we get a place by the ocean," Paris amended from behind his easel at the window. "Tell Rena I'll bring bread."

"We'll see you in a bit," Liam said with a departing wink before disappearing out the door.

"Did you have another vision?" Mac asked as he circled the couch. "Or are you painting your oce—" The rest of his question died, words caught in his throat, blocked by his heart that had suddenly lodged there. "Paris . . ." He stared in awe at the painting of himself, asleep on his stomach in their bed, a soft smile on his face, his left hand on the pillow, wedding band bright, reflecting all the colors of the aura that shimmered around him. The blue, violet, and green flowing, the rivers of red and pink a beautiful swirling design throughout. "This is what it looks like?"

"Now, yes," Paris said, as much awe in his voice as Mac felt in his soul, in the bond that sang between them.

He reached out a hand, drawn to the swirls of red and pink, but Paris stopped him short, grabbing his wrist. "It's still wet."

Using Paris's hand around his wrist, Mac turned him in his arms, his front to Paris's back, admiring the painting over his shoulder. "You went with the smile?"

Paris angled his head to look up at him, his big brown eyes warm with love and a touch of violet, their soul bond shining through. "I've got forever to paint the smirk."

"I like the sound of that," Mac said as he brushed his lips across his husband's, repeating the promise that tied their souls together until their end, as Mary said, hopefully many, many years in the future. Until then . . . "Forever."

THIRTY-SEVEN

Paris and pain were officially broken up.

His wounds were healed, his soul intact, his bond with Mac stronger than ever, singing whenever he paused to listen to it, all the chords of his favorite jazz tune the background music of a life —a forever—he couldn't have imagined a month ago. Aside from missing his ocean when he wasn't at the condo in YB, he was happy here under the Talahalusi sun, soaking up its warmth and inspiration. Free from his own painful past, committed to freeing from pain the others who'd suffered under his father, and working with Mac and Liam to free souls from the pain that kept them lingering here on this plane.

Which was what brought him here today, Mary at his side. "This is where it happened?" he asked.

She kneeled and put a hand to the earth, digging her fingers into the ground and mixing up the layers of clay, silt, and ash. A clearing in the forest, ten years after a devastating magical fire. A myriad of colors he'd have to paint when he got back home, once he helped the lingering soul here find his way.

Mary stood and saplings sprouted in the divots she left in the ground. She brushed the dirt off on her jeans and nodded. "This is it."

As if the coyote shifter sitting on the ground, back leaned against a charred mess of wood at the edge of the clearing, didn't give it away. "What are you doing here?" Robin rumbled as they approached.

He looked like hell, his golden eyes dull, his rusty-blond hair matted and overlong, his right ear scarred, the days-old dust on his sunken cheeks crisscrossed with dried tear tracks.

Paris lowered to the ground in front of him, sitting with his legs crossed, then offered Mary a hand down as well. "Do you actually stay with the pack, or are you out here every night?" she asked Robin.

"What difference does it make?"

"Because none of us should exist alone," Paris said. "Especially not someone whose aura is as wrecked as yours. And I thought Mac's when I met him was bad." He whistled low, and the coyote cracked a smirk.

"You sound like him."

"Mac?"

"Icarus."

Paris shrugged, taking it as a compliment to be compared to his sassy friend. "Maybe we're both just people who will give it to you honest."

"And what are you here to give me honest, medium?"

"For starters, forgiveness."

He snarled. "I don't need—"

"Bullshit," Paris snarled right back. "You do, and I give it to you, because you were right. We were ready; I was ready." There'd been a time when Robin had made him doubt himself, but when it had mattered most, he'd believed in him. "And now the giants are gone."

His golden gaze drifted over Paris's shoulder, the direction he and Mary had come, back toward Monte Corvo. "Do they forgive me?"

"No, and they won't for a while."

"And you're no closer to finding Atlas, are you?" Mary asked.

"What's it matter to you? You gonna 'fess up finally?"

When she didn't reply, Paris reached out and laid a hand on Robin's knee, drawing the coyote's attention back to him. "That's the other thing I'm here to give you."

His eyes grew wide. "Atlas?"

"No. The truth about the day your sister died, *if* you want it."

Robin's gulp was audible in the otherwise quiet clearing, only the buzz of late harvest bees zipping from one plot to the next breaking the silence. Until eventually Robin stuttered out a shaky "Yes."

Paris closed his eyes and felt for the souls connected to the tragedy that had occurred here ten years ago. He could call Deborah or David across the plane, anyone else who'd been here that day, but where he could help it, he didn't disrupt souls from their final resting place. And besides, he'd sensed another lingering soul here, other than Robin's living one, as soon as they'd neared the clearing—a shifter who'd been pressed into service for the other side, who'd known something they'd waited all this time to share.

Contact made, the vision shifted, Paris in his shoes on the edge of a green-tinged battle in the same clearing, only there were more trees then and a wooden structure where Robin sat.

Deborah and David were easy to spot among the other combatants, she the largest coyote on the field, he a human with orange and red magic rippling across his skin. On one knee, he was desperate to save his family but struggling to keep the phoenix in check.

A bolt of yellow magic zipped their direction, and Paris swung his gaze in the direction it had come. A suited Atlas stood wielding globes of magic, sending one after another Deborah and David's direction. Until someone grabbed his arm, sending a bolt off-kilter. Paris followed its trajectory, afraid it was the one that killed Deborah, but it missed, just barely, and he turned his attention back to Atlas.

And gasped. There were two of them. The suited one from

before and another one in a kilt and leather gauntlets. Side by side, Paris noticed the differences he'd missed the other night on the altar when he'd been consumed by pain and betrayal. The suited one's blond hair a shade darker, his green eyes shot through with yellow, a mole at the corner of his right eye that Paris knew Atlas didn't have.

"Don't do this," the kilted Atlas argued. "I can't bring you back from this."

"First, it was Canton. Now, it's you. Is Cole here too?"

"Listen to me."

"No," the stranger barked, because that was who he was to Paris—a stranger, not Atlas. "I'm done listening. I'm done falling in line. I'm done pretending we're not as powerful as we are."

"Chaos will use you."

"You'd know," the stranger sneered. "It's my turn now." Yellow and gray swirled in his eyes, blotting out the green, and he conjured two sizzling yellow globes of magic.

And Paris knew with heartbreaking certainty what came next.

"Evan, no!" Atlas shouted, but he was too late.

With one hand, Evan flung a globe at him. Atlas barely managed a magical green shield before getting slammed back into a tree, his magic no match for Evan's, which disappeared Atlas from the scene before he could throw the green globe he'd had in hand.

Before Evan, with his other hand, hurled the other yellow globe directly at Deborah.

Paris ripped himself out of the vision, nearly losing his stomach as he gasped for breath, his own fingers digging into the earth, reconnecting to this plane, waiting for the ringing in his ears to give way to the jazz notes of the bond that anchored him here. He'd come back with Liam for the lingering soul, give him the peace he deserved, but Paris had needed to get out of there, to plant his soul firmly back here before it got sucked further into tragedy and pain.

"It wasn't him, was it?" Mary asked once he finally righted

himself with Robin's help. At some point during his vision, the coyote had moved to his side, a steadying hand wrapped around his biceps.

"It wasn't," Paris said, and Robin yanked back his hand like he'd been burned. "What do you mean it wasn't him?"

"It wasn't him," he repeated. "He's after the same thing you are. The person who killed your sister. Evan."

Mary gasped.

"You didn't know?" Robin said.

"Not all of it." Sadness flashed across her hazel eyes before she shoved to her feet. "Well, we're going to find him first." She kicked Robin in the knee with her booted foot. "Let's go. We have a new mission."

"We?" Robin rose, almost as quickly as his bushy blond brows. "They'll think I took you."

"They already think you're a traitor. What's one more betrayal?"

As Paris rose, he worried how many more barbs like that Robin could take. Yes, he was a selfish ass, but beneath that front was a man ravaged by guilt, by a heart that was too big for the tragedies that continued to pummel it, by the death he doled out for a living. Darkness soaked his aura, and Paris feared he'd never escape it, that no one would ever be able to crack through his walls and find the heart that had so much to offer. So much potential for joy and good.

For love.

If he'd just believe he deserved it. Paris stepped closer and lifted a hand, cupping his dusty cheek. "They may not trust you, but I do. I see your aura. I know what haunts you, why you need to fix this. And on behalf of all of them, I'm trusting you with her."

A flicker of light in his golden eyes. "He was lucky to find you."

"I'm the lucky one," Paris said with a smile, remembering Mac's soft sleepy one as he'd left that morning. The same one he got to wake up to for the rest of their lives. Anyone with a heart as big as Robin's deserved that kind of happiness too. "We both got what we deserved. And you will too."

———

Last but not least...
Buckle up and turn the page for Atlas and Robin's steamy enemies-to-lovers romance!

ATLAS AND THE TRAITOR

A SOUL TO FIND NOVEL

ABOUT THIS BOOK

I was supposed to bring balance.
That's what my name—Atlas—means.
It feels more like being torn apart.
Between good and evil, Nature and Chaos.

Always running after or from something.
Including a certain coyote shifter who wants to rip me limb from limb.
I'd rather he shred my kilt and do other things to me.
But alas, shouldering fate keeps getting in the way.

Or maybe I've got it all wrong.
Maybe he's the only path to balance, to the future.
An end to the running.
But we'd have to trust each other first.
I'd rather tear myself apart than ever do that.

Atlas and the Traitor is a steamy, enemies-to-lovers M/M paranormal romance between a grumpy coyote shifter and an even grumpier warlock fated to run toward each other. It is book three of the Soul to Find series and is best enjoyed after the prior books in the series.

PART ONE

ATLAS

ONE

Nine days.

Nine days since Atlas had rescued his brother from Vincent Cirillo, only for Cole to run right back to danger's door.

On the Rift anniversary of all days.

Atlas flicked his fingers, and a green dome of magic descended over them. It was a risk. One of the paranormals in the clearing below might notice them up here on the bluff, but Cole wasn't exactly giving him a choice.

"You shouldn't be here," Atlas urged. "Nine days is not enough time to refill your tank." If that was even possible at this point. Vincent had been bleeding his baby brother dry for years, stealing his magic and keeping him hidden. Torturing him. And torturing Atlas with the knowledge that his brother had been caught trying to rescue him and was being held right under Atlas's nose, out of reach but never out of mind.

Vincent had kept them both leashed since he couldn't catch the most powerful Shaw brother. Atlas had finally snapped his and Cole's leashes nine days ago when Vincent had pushed his own enemies too far, bringing down Nature's wrath and giving Atlas the opening he'd needed to steal Cole away, out of the back of an SUV and to a safe house.

Only to end up here, the definition of unsafe, a magically and physically weakened Cole determined to fight a giant. "I'm not letting you face him alone," his brother insisted, all heart and earnestness. The very things that had gotten him captured in the first place. He had the will to do good, more than any of the Shaws, but realizing his limits had never been Cole's strong suit.

Atlas clasped his biceps, his fingers easily circling bone and muscles, and he worried for a moment that he might break his little brother—a once laughable notion. While Cole was younger than him, he'd always been bigger in height and build. Now, he was all skin and bones in a borrowed suit that should have been two sizes too small. Atlas wanted to see him healthy and whole again, bursting at the seams of his clothes like he used to. "I just got you back," he pleaded.

Cole laid a cool, slender hand over his. "This is what we were made for, Atlas. Four brothers, four giants. You've been hunting them, alone, all these years. Let me help you now."

"Three brothers since the Rift," Atlas corrected, that day thirty years ago when Nature and Chaos had gone to war with Yerba Buena as ground zero. "And I've been hunting our other brother who's always in their orbit."

Cole's eyes sparkled from under his shaggy chestnut hair, the color so like that of their other brother who was forever lost, the warmth in Cole's muted green gaze like the comfort that used to shine from Canton's sky blue one. "You're better than that, big bro. I see you."

Did he? Was he? Were his actions over the past decade-plus altruism or selfishness? Love or guilt? Had he saved Cole for Cole's sake or to stave off his own self-imposed loneliness? It was a thin line even in his own head, a balancing act he'd failed at more times than he could count.

In any event, there was only one choice today. "I'll snap you back to the safe house." Cole was too weak to transport himself, and Atlas did not trust him to go where directed. Left to his own devises, Cole would wind up down there on that windswept stick of land, ready and unable to fight the shifters, vampires, and warlocks gathering around the makeshift altar.

Witnesses to a sacrifice that aimed to bring Chaos through the veil.

A veil that was thinning more and more each second they wasted arguing. They were running out of time. The giant—and possibly Evan, their other brother—was close. "I can get back here in time," Atlas said.

"Maybe," Cole rightly assessed. "Or I can stay here and help you. You don't have to do this alone anymore. We promised."

Atlas's chest ached, Cole's words striking at the lonely heart of him. He was so tired of being a one-man show, maneuvering and fighting solo to keep a promise he and his brothers had made countless years ago. But Cole wasn't in any kind of shape to hold up his end of that bargain.

Atlas reached again for him and caught nothing but air, the earth heaving beneath their feet and knocking them both off balance. A blinding flash of light later, and Cole was gone, using the distraction and flicker in Atlas's shield to port himself the short distance he could—to the clearing below, standing between the witnesses and the giant who'd arrived behind the altar, sacrificial human bleeding in his arms.

Atlas didn't have time for anger, fear far outpacing it. He'd just gotten his brother back; he couldn't lose him again. With a snap, he joined Cole in the clearing, his leather boots barely hitting the ground before a sizzling bolt of blue magic came hurtling his direction. Dead aim, center mass, only missing at the last second because Cole's faded green orb knocked the magic off course.

Saving him.

Atlas nodded his thanks, then threw himself into the battle that had kicked into high gear. He jousted with the shifters nipping at his kilt while Cole and the blue bolt–wielding warlock traded spells. Until an orange fireball zipped past Atlas, singeing the hair on his arm as it barreled toward the weaker target.

"Cole!" Atlas shouted. "Seasamh síos!" he ordered in their mother's tongue, infusing the words with every bit of power that ran through his veins. His brother's magic answered, dropping Cole to his knees, the giant's fireball screaming over his head and into the other warlock.

One witness down.

Atlas took out three more with the knives hidden in his leather gauntlets, then he and Cole decapitated a pair of vampires together.

"I'm going for the human!" Cole shouted. "Cover me!" He sprinted toward the altar, not giving Atlas a chance to argue, leaving him no choice but to follow fast on his heels. But before they reached the human laid atop a makeshift pile of sticks and rocks, power seared through the atmosphere and lifted the hairs on the back of Atlas's neck.

Power Atlas recognized all too well.

Evan appeared beside the giant, dressed in a tailored suit like the ones Atlas hadn't worn again since Vincent's death.

"Cole, get back!" Atlas yelled, as he slung moss-green orbs past him at their other brother, shattering Evan's yellow ones and holding him off long enough to get an arm around Cole's waist and haul him backward.

Away from danger.

He lifted a hand to snap.

Power slammed into them, yellow and awful, a split second before his thumb and middle finger met. The second after that, Cole crumpled in his arms.

TWO

Atlas tossed a handful of dirt into the open grave and murmured the blessing his mother used to recite at these things.

"Careful," came a whispered warning above him. "Someone might hear you."

He flicked the kick pleat of his cousin's seemingly demure black dress, briefly exposing the bright pink lining. "Like you being careful in this frock?"

Green eyes dancing, Daphne lowered into a crouch beside him. "Who the fuck says frock anymore?"

He flitted a hand in the air. "Old habits."

"Like you and these things," she said, fingering a fold in his kilt. "So scratchy." She covered her mouth with her other hand and raised her brows, pretending to be scandalized. "And so much leg, Mr. Shaw."

Atlas lost the battle with his laughter, drawing a disapproving glare from his father who stood nearby chatting with the parish priest and Daphne's father.

"Whoops," Daphne said, muffling her own giggle before falling silent. When she spoke again, her voice was filled with the same warmth that reminded Atlas so much of their mothers. "I'm sorry you lost him."

He swallowed hard, staring into the distance as his mind replayed the past six weeks of hell. The gaping wound Evan's strike had left in Cole's side. The sleepless days and nights Atlas had spent by his bed, listening to the ramblings of a dying warlock whose heart wasn't ready to surrender but whose body could no longer fight. The agonizing two trips Atlas had had to make away from him, the first to dispatch a giant in La Purisima, the second to take care of another one in Yerba Buena. The endless hours he'd pretended to sit caged at Monte Corvo for the sake of intel, given and received. The crushing words Cole had spoken on Samhain, his dying wish to go home. Cole's soul had clung to his bones another agonizing three weeks, the longest of Atlas's life during which he'd been too afraid to leave again, sure Cole would be dead when he returned. He wouldn't let another brother die alone.

"Thank you for finding a reaper," Atlas said. "I know it couldn't have been easy to get someone down here." Santa Maria wasn't La Purisima, but it was close enough that the local and nearby religious fanatics made life hell for paranormals and magical beings. Unless they renounced their identity like his father had done, like Daphne's father had done too.

"It's what Cole wanted." She tossed a handful of dirt onto the casket below. Then with a tilt of her head to the grave on their other side, added, "And what your mother would've wanted." She wiped her hand on her skirt and slid her gaze to where the rest of their family stood. "Fuck what they want."

"And yet here we are," he said. "Pretending to be good little zealots. I can't believe Cole wanted to come back here."

"Are you telling me you don't want to be buried beside your mother when all is said and done?"

He raked his hands through his hair and laced his fingers behind his neck. Of course he wanted to be buried here. For as awful as life had been before he and his brothers had left, this was where his mother would wait for each of her sons on the other side of the veil, hoping they'd be delivered to her and not extinguished. Even Evan, if by some miracle he were to reject Chaos and side with Nature.

Repent was on the tip of his tongue, and he rolled his eyes at himself. Maybe he was a good little zealot after all. "We're a fucked-up bunch, you know?"

"Oh, I know." She bumped her shoulder against his. "But we're family. Hers." He didn't think she was only referring to his mother or her own. Daphne was older than him, closer in age to Canton, privy to his abject devotion to Nature. Same as their mothers'. What would Daphne think if she knew Nature was now a five-foot-nothing slip of a woman with a nose ring, bright green hair, and an attitude as fiery as her brother's red hair?

Would probably try to fuck her.

He laughed again, drawing her amused, knowing side-eye. "You heard that?" he asked, and at her nod, added, "Get out of my head."

"I can't wait to meet her," she said with a wink before standing.

Atlas shot up beside her. "Daphne, you can't tell—"

The light in her eyes hardened, revealing the battle-honed warrior her fizzy exterior hid. "I've been doing this far longer than you, cuz."

"You two aren't quarreling now, are you?"

Uncle James's question caught him off guard. He and Daphne had been so wrapped up in their own conversation that they hadn't noticed the other one winding down or their parents heading their direction.

Daphne tossed a playful smile over her shoulder. "Just reminding Atlas who's older," she told her father. "Still."

Atlas played along with her charade, bending at the waist in an exaggerated bow.

"Will you be joining us back at the house, Atlas?" His uncle's words and sympathetic smile were genuine. He was a different sort of zealot, a missionary who would rather convert the magical than banish them. Atlas's father, on the other hand, wanted nothing to do with the power that ran through their veins. Perhaps because his wife's magic had always been more powerful than his own, and beliefs aside, his father had always been, first and foremost, an asshole.

Atlas had taken enough beatings to learn his cues and to stay out of his way. Case in point, his father's expression today was as clear a *get out* as any spoken words. "Thank you," he told his uncle. "But I have somewhere I need to be."

"Your brother is dead," James said. "You need to be with family." He laid a hand on his forearm. "Come with us to church tomorrow and witness His grace."

It was all Atlas could do not to roll his eyes. Hand over his uncle's, he gave it a squeeze, then stepped back and tucked his hands in the pockets of his kilt. "I appreciate the offer, but I have to pass this time." Every time, if he could help it.

"Very well," James said, before he leaned forward and kissed his daughter's cheek. "We'll see you back at the house?"

"I'll be on my way shortly."

He nodded, wished Atlas well, then continued past them toward the cemetery exit. Atlas's father was slower to leave, giving him a disdainful up and down before turning up his nose. "Your magic won't save you."

He gestured at Cole's freshly dug grave. "Clearly."

With a disgusted huff, his father stalked off, following in James's wake.

Once they were out of earshot, Daphne bumped his shoulder again and whispered low, "Whatever hole you're going to stick your dick in tonight won't save you either."

"I'm the hole," he replied with a wink, delighting in the actual scandalized expression that raced across his cousin's face. "And at least it'll make me feel better."

THREE

Atlas hadn't exactly lied to his cousin. Sex would make him feel better. Sex with the same priest who'd officiated Cole's funeral was doubly delicious. The fact said priest also from time to time slipped him intel about Evan's whereabouts was the wicked cherry on top.

Niall's morals and nerves tangled to make him chatty, even more so if the sex was, in his mind, particularly illicit. Which was how Atlas had ended up here, in one of the private rooms of a very particular type of club on the outskirts of town, blindfolded and tied to a very different sort of cross than the one the priest usually prayed to.

"I told myself I wouldn't come back here," Niall muttered as he ran his long fingers along the edges of the leather harness that crisscrossed Atlas's bare torso.

Atlas hissed, the sensations magnified by the lack of sight. Wanting that teasing touch elsewhere, he arched his back, nudging Niall's fingers lower, over the belt that was holding open his kilt and into the crease of his groin, putting Niall on a direct path to his hardening cock.

Niall sucked in a sharp breath, and Atlas shivered. He could only imagine how high the color would be on the priest's pale cheeks. Niall wasn't an unattractive man. Mid-forties, a headful of dark brown waves, a tall, slim body he kept in shape by tending the community gardens and herding cattle at his family's ranch. And a cock he knew how to use, even if some fictional higher power made him think he shouldn't.

Niall's fingers skirted around the root of Atlas's cock. "An hour ago, I was at your father's home, witnessing His grace with your family."

Atlas angled up his face, toward the warm breath hovering close. He found the priest's stubbled chin and nibbled along it. "You witness anything else while you were there?"

"Your father was more agitated than usual." His touch drifted lower. "Then again, he's lost another son."

Atlas rolled his hips and groaned against Niall's throat. "You were barely a teenager when he lost the last one."

Niall purred as he fondled Atlas's balls. "Those were the days."

Atlas arched again, as much as his bindings would allow, body skirting the front of Niall's, heat rolling off his chest. If past experience held, the priest still had his collar on while his shirt hung open and his wet dick hung over the elastic of his briefs, his pants discarded in the corner by the door. "Were you a naughty teenager, Niall?"

His hand circled Atlas's cock. "I hadn't found my path yet."

Atlas thrust into the tight, sure grip, smearing Niall's palm and fingers with precome. "You're still naughty, aren't you?"

Niall melted into him, his lean body pressed the length of Atlas's, his fat cock digging into Atlas's hip and streaking his skin with sticky arousal.

Atlas grinned. He may have been the one tied up, but it was Niall who had surrendered. "Seems you found your path today," he rumbled low and tunneled again into Niall's fist.

"I want to help ease his pain. But with you still practicing . . ."

Atlas slammed the brakes on his surging libido. They'd somehow gotten onto him and off the path to Evan. He needed to redirect, needed to work Niall to the very edge so he would spill more of the info Atlas needed. And less of the judgment. He flicked his fingers, loosening the rope around one of his ankles enough to hitch his leg between Niall's.

Niall moaned. "Oh, fuck." Then ground down on Atlas's thigh, sliding his cotton-trapped taint and balls along the hard muscle and rutting his leaking dick against Atlas's hip. With another flick, Atlas sent a trail of magic down Niall's spine and between his ass cheeks, a virtual tongue rimming his hole the way Atlas knew he liked it.

"Oh, fuck!" Louder as the speed of Niall's strokes and ruts increased. He pressed his sweaty brow against Atlas's temple, his hot breath a heavy pant in his ear, coming unhinged with a litany of grunts and curses.

Exactly the state Atlas needed him in. He kissed up the side of Niall's face and pecked away at more of the truth. "Has my brother been practicing in these parts too?"

Evan had been a no-show in La Purisima when Atlas had slayed another giant and again at Club Sutro when the giant from the Stick had attacked Vincent's son, Paris, who'd allied himself with Nature. Atlas had killed that giant too, finally, and had made it back to the safe house in time to move Cole—and missed Evan's return to the Stick on Samhain. Evan had joined the last remaining giant in another attempt to bring Chaos through the veil, but Paris, Nature, and their team had defeated the giant and kept Chaos at bay a little longer.

And Evan had disappeared. Again.

"Not practicing," Niall said on a groan.

"But he's been here?"

"He wanted to say a prayer for your brother."

Anger caused Atlas to bite down harder than intended on Niall's ear lobe. The priest only groaned louder . . . and disclosed a nugget of useful information, finally. "He wanted me to arrange a meet at the casino."

The closest casino was located on Chumash land. The local

Indigenous tribe had steadily reclaimed more and more of the southern inland territories, same as other tribes had done north and east of Yerba Buena.

Sensing Niall was close to spilling come and more intel, Atlas hitched his leg higher and rolled his hips, jostling Niall so his erection collided with his fist stroking Atlas's. Niall was powerless to resist the offered pleasure, wrapping his hand around them both, their hard cocks slippery against each other in his grip. He wound his other arm around Atlas's neck, needing more leverage and balance for his rutting, for the climax bearing down on him.

Atlas didn't have much time. He licked into the hollow behind Niall's ear. "What did he want with the Chumash?"

"Help Cole reach peace," Niall panted. "One way or another."

Niall might have believed that; the priest always wanted to see the good in people. Atlas didn't buy it for one second. Evan was after something.

Or someone.

"Who did he want a meet with?" Atlas had a few ideas, but he needed Niall to confirm which one was right.

Instead, the priest's body tensed, practically vibrating, and with a shouted "Oh, fuck!" he erupted, soaking his fist and Atlas's cock with warm, sticky come.

And then with his next breath, he promptly panicked, his self-hatred welling up and out. "Fuck," he cursed again in a decidedly different tone. "I'm sorry, I'm sorry," the familiar litany began as he scurried off Atlas. He always did this. Every single fucking time.

Atlas was glad for the blindfold. It hid his rolling eyes as he tried to coax Niall back with a gentler tone. "Niall, it's okay," Atlas called after him, his best lead in months stumbling for the door. "You did so good. We can do more good." Sometimes the cajoling worked, but more often than not, Atlas was left hard and hanging.

Literally, this time.

The door opened and slammed shut, leaving Atlas to curse

alone. To sulk in a rare moment of exhaustion, letting the cross and bindings hold him up. No one was there to see him, to take advantage of his weakness. He could indulge in a well-earned moment of self-pity. Two months, four dead giants, a second dead brother, and his last surviving brother on the run again, each passing day another one closer to Solstice and Evan's next best opportunity to bring Chaos through the veil.

And Atlas had to stop him.

Because of a promise he'd made their mother.

He leaned back his head, his world blissfully dark beneath the blindfold, his earlier sweat and Niall's come cooling on his skin. "Did you have any idea how hard this would be?" he idly asked the keeper of his vow. "What you were asking of us? Of me?"

Times like these, he wished it had been him who'd taken Evan's hit six weeks ago—or on that day ten years ago in Talahalusi.

"But then who would champion Her cause?" his mother lilted in his head. *"Who could balance it all but you, my sweet?"*

Balance.

Sweet.

He laughed out loud, the cold, harsh sound bouncing off the cement walls. No one would ever accuse him of being sweet, and as for balanced . . . He felt more unbalanced every futile day, like he was teetering on the edge of one of those jetties in the Canyon Lands, nothing but a sheer cliff and the cold dark water below.

"It's too hard," he told her.

"There's another way. You don't have to do it alone."

Always that possibility. Always a risk he wasn't willing to take.

The door clicked open, and he stepped back from the teetering edge, pretending to be balanced once more. "Niall, I'm glad—"

The scent of dog tickled his nose.

A very particular dog.

Loathing, shame, fear, and a list of other things Atlas didn't want to name slammed into him, knocking him all the way to unbalanced for a startled second before self-preservation kicked in and he flipped over his hand, fingers poised to snap.

But that single damnable second of unsteadiness was enough for Robin to race behind him and grab his hands, holding his fingers apart. The shifter growled beside his ear. "Not so fast, you stinky bastard."

"You're one to fucking talk," Atlas spat back. "You smell like you rolled in your own shit."

"Enough," snapped a third familiar voice before the blindfold was ripped off his face. Nature stood before him in all her five-foot-nothing pissed-off glory, color high on her tan cheeks, dyed green curls piled atop her head, a new piercing in her nose. "For the record, you *both* stink." She stepped closer and shoved the blindfold between the leather straps of his harness. "But right now, you stink worse. And I want to know why."

FOUR

Atlas pointedly flicked his gaze down, then back up to Mary's hazel one. "Can I get dressed for this conversation?"

"Can you promise not to snap yourself out of here?" Robin answered, and Atlas slid his gaze to the golden one over his shoulder. The asshole coyote had the gall to laugh. "How does that even work?" he asked with a glance at Atlas's fingers still held apart by his.

Atlas scoffed. "How do you not know that?" Robin was a highly sought-after tracker. People paid handsomely for his skills —and for what the hunter did when he caught his prey. Someone you wanted found and never found again? Robin was the assassin of choice for many.

"No one's ever run from me like you do." He leaned forward, those golden eyes searing a path down Atlas's front to where his cock was still half hard. Nothing at all to do with the big, rough hands pinning his to the cross. Robin eyed him from under his long lashes, burnished gold like the rusty blond mop of shaggy hair atop his head. "Looks like you don't really want to either." His smirk was the definition of smug; Atlas wanted to punch it off his face. "I see that whole naked under the tartan thing is true."

"When I mean to have sex, yes. So, around you, never. Voluntarily."

"His snap," Mary said, interrupting their pissing contest, "creates a tear in the plane that he slips through."

"In that case," Robin said, "I am definitely not letting your hands go."

Fine, two could play at that game, especially as they were already near tied, the bulge behind Robin's fly poking Atlas's side. He shimmied his hips against the cross behind him, aiming to dislodge his kilt completely.

Mary jumped into action, covering his goods and securing the tartan around him. Removing his leverage. "If you two are done," she said with a huff, "we have three weeks until Solstice. Three weeks to find Evan."

Atlas feigned ignorance. "I have no idea what you're talking about."

"Then why can I hear your heart racing?" Robin said.

Fucking tracker. "Because I don't do *we*." *We* had gotten Cole killed, and that was just the most recent tragedy owing to that menacing two-letter word. "I don't go chasing after ghosts either."

"Then what have you been doing the past ten years?"

Atlas swiveled his gaze to the hypocrite. "You're one to talk."

Robin's deep, sinister growl would've rattled the windows if the room had any.

"Atlas," Mary chided in his head. "Don't push him."

He swung his attention back to the deity in borrowed human skin. "This again?" he mentally asked.

"It worked well for us before." When Vincent was still alive, Mary had allowed herself to be kidnapped in order to trick Vincent into hiring her to hack the location of a powerful coven. Instead, she'd hacked his network and diverted his attention. "What happened at the Stick?" she continued in his head. "I know you sent me that footage."

"I lost a brother," he told her. "I'd just gotten him back from

Vincent." He flicked his gaze to Robin, then added, "I lost him the same way he lost his sister."

Mary's eyes grew wide, at least one mystery solved for her. "I'm sorry for your loss," she said. "Robin is too, even if he'll never say it."

Atlas scoffed, seriously doubting it. "He knows it wasn't me?" For the past decade, Robin had chased him, thinking he was the one who'd thrown the orb that had killed his twin sister, Deborah.

He'd been chasing the wrong Shaw twin.

"Paris saw it through the eyes of a lingering soul. He told us it wasn't you. That it was Evan." She stepped closer once more. "We can work together," she said, her aspirations for him unrealistically high. Same as his mother's. "We're after the same thing."

"I don't think we are."

She pressed her lips together, assessing. "You think you can save him."

"Not for myself," he admitted. Honestly, he'd love nothing more than to hold Evan down while Robin ripped out his throat. But for the sake of the woman waiting on the other side of the veil for him—and his brothers, all of them—he had to try.

"I promised Robin vengeance," Mary said, as if reading his thoughts. Her telepathy, unlike Daphne's, didn't go that far, but her observational skills were just as sharp. "If we get to him first, without you, I won't stop him."

"And you think *I* can?" Her answering smirk made his own hackles rise. "Always with your games. Go home, or what Canton did, what Cole gave his life for, will be all for naught."

She gasped, eyes wide once more. Another mystery solved, most of his secrets out in the open for her now. This close to the end, why bo—

A roar shattered the connection between them and spiked claws dug into his palms, making the hairs on his arms stand up.

Making his cock take notice too.

"Do not shut me out," Robin snarled.

"Take her home," Atlas bit back. He didn't believe for one

second that Mary's brother, Icarus, had sent her off into the wild with their team's least reliable member.

"What planet are you on?"

"Hers." He nodded at Mary. "And I'm trying to fucking save it, but you and your lot are *constantly* in the way."

This autumn alone, Robin's brother-in-law, Adam, a cop turned vigilante, had gone head-to-head with Vincent, who he blamed for his late spouses' deaths. And while that chaos was ongoing, Vincent had offered Paris to a giant as a sacrifice. Paris had been rescued from near-death, but as a result of the spell, he'd become a medium and soulbound to detective Cormac Kelley, Adam's former cop partner and the then-reaper for the Monte Corvo ravens.

And Atlas, admittedly, had had a hand in all of it, which Robin rightfully called him on. "Except when you need us to be your fucking bait. First Icarus, then Paris. Why do you get to use us, and we can't use you?"

Problem was, they could never just be bait. If it could go sideways, it did when Robin and company were involved, which was why Atlas needed them as far away as possible at this late, delicate stage of the game. "Not how this works, dog."

The coyote flashed his pointed canines. "Oh, I beg to differ."

"Don't you have someone to go kill?"

Robin's hold on his hands faltered and something that looked an awful lot like guilt flashed through his gaze. But before Atlas could bring his thumb and middle finger together, Robin hardened his grip and every bit of the hunter—the assassin—shone in his glowing golden eyes. "Make no mistake, you're still on that list. Just in the two spot now."

"You have to fucking catch me first."

Robin's claws pierced his skin. "What was that?"

"You cheated."

For once, Mary defused the situation instead of stirring the pot. "Robin, let it go. He's not going to give us anything tonight."

But the shifter couldn't just let it go. Ever. He leaned close, nose behind Atlas's ear, his hot breath flooding the hollow there, his hotter words so low only Atlas could hear them. "I can smell you," he purred. "Not the dirty warlock stench. The real you. I know you're hard under that kilt." Atlas didn't bother to deny it. "Do you want to give me that load?"

He channeled the shiver racing up his spine into his voice, pitching it low and gravelly, hiding the edge of desire just on the other side of hate. "Not if your mouth was the last warm hole on earth."

A cold nose and chapped lips skated the outer shell of his ear. "It's a bet."

FIVE

A week passed with no more surprise visits from Mary or Robin. No more visits with Niall either, the holy man keeping his distance. Atlas had even gone to church with Daphne to try to steal two minutes alone with him, but all Atlas got for his trouble were two awkward hours with family. He was no closer to confirming who Evan had wanted to meet with among the Chumash, but with Niall's slip about the casino, and a week's worth of excavation, Atlas had a pretty good idea and was ready to make his own approach.

Dressed in a suit for the first time in over a month, he forced himself not to fidget as he surveyed the practically deserted casino. A few folks at the penny slots, a trio of guys around a corner poker table, dealers scattered among the other game tables, ready to move where a visitor might go. Not as busy as Atlas would have figured for the weekend.

Halfway through his second sweep, Atlas spotted his mark: Lucy Aguin, né Marin. According to the excavator he'd hired, Lucy was a recent transplant from the Huimen Enclave. She was also the dealer here with the newest license. Multiple angles he could work. He sidled up to the blackjack table she stood closest to.

"Good afternoon, sir," the young woman greeted, as she stepped behind the table. "You know the rules?"

He placed two chips in the box at his position. "Hit me."

A barely-there smile turned up one corner of her mouth before she righted her professional mask, perfectly neutral as she shuffled, then dealt two cards for him and two for herself. His two of hearts and three of diamonds gave him time to work. He tapped the table for another hit.

Seven of hearts, up to eleven, and Lucy wasn't over yet either.

He doubled down, another chip in the box, and tapped the table again, flashing her a smile. "You're new here."

A blush warmed her tan cheeks, but she otherwise kept her tone as neutral as her expression. "My second month."

Jack of diamonds; he was over.

Lucy wasn't, hitting twenty with the last card.

"Well played," he acknowledged, as she swept the table of cards and chips. He put another two in the box. "Are you from around here?" he asked, as she dealt another hand. He already knew she wasn't, but it was the question a stranger would ask on the way to the answer he needed.

"Talahalusi," she replied. "My husband's family is here, though. I moved down after the wedding."

"How's the tribe treating you?"

She cocked a brow. "What do you know about tribes?"

Very little, anyone would guess on first glance. He was a pale white man with blond hair and green eyes, dressed in an expensive designer suit. But looks, Atlas knew, could be deceiving. He flicked two fingers just above his chips and turned them over with a tendril of green magic. "I know we're on the same side."

She gasped, then hastily flipped over the next card, a queen that pushed them both over twenty-one. She cleared their cards in a single sweep, knocking his hand aside in the process. "Don't let them see you do that," she whispered with a flick of her gaze toward the nearest eye in the sky. "They'll throw you out if they think you're cheating."

"I wouldn't dare," he said with a wink, tapping the table for another round.

She dipped her chin, hiding her smile. "Are *you* from around here?"

"Santa Maria, originally, but I'm in Yerba Buena now."

"Ah!" she said, brightening. "I'm technically from the Huimen Enclave, but it's easier to tell folks down here that I'm from Talahalusi."

"I know the actual place," Atlas said with a smile he hoped didn't look too forced. He'd helped his former boss purchase cold-storage properties along the enclave's borders in order to hide hostages in them.

"What brings you back this way?" Lucy asked.

"My brother passed."

She paused mid-flip. "I'm sorry for your loss." Then laid down the card, pushing him over twenty-one again. She apologized again before clearing the table.

"Thank you," he said, chin lowered and swallowing hard, playing on her sympathy. He kept his gaze downcast as he put two more chips in the box. "I hear one of your elders here—Dyami, I think?—is particularly good at helping people with their grief."

"White people don't usually come to us seeking peace. You have churches and saints for that."

He lifted his gaze, meeting her dark one. "You mean big buildings built to false idols?"

"Some say that about Dyami too."

Her tone implied she was among the *some*. "You're not a fan?"

"I preferred our Miwok elders."

"How are they?" he asked, feigning curiosity. "I heard about the sinkhole and what happened to Pati Miwra." He'd engineered it in fact, kidnapping Pati for a giant Vincent had wanted to curry favor with. But as soon as Atlas had realized who she was—the tribe leader's daughter—and what she carried—a child that could end the war between Nature and Chaos, that could spare him from his role in it, eventually—he'd made sure Pati was stashed at one of those cold storage properties with her protector. Quinn had ultimately sacrificed himself for her, and in so doing, had bought Mary, Paris, and their team enough time to rescue Pati and kill the giant.

The story had apparently traveled far, Lucy's smile sneaking free again. "But Pati made it out, and her son . . ." Her smile broadened. "He's the real deal." A true eagle shifter, the first in generations. Unlike Dyami, who, by all excavated accounts, had only assumed the name. "He'll bring—"

"Peace," Atlas finished. He'd known it as soon as he'd touched Pati's arm. It had killed him to leave the very thing his mother had dedicated her life to bringing about in someone else's care, but he'd had no choice. And in the end, it had been the right call. Barely.

"It feels good to talk about it," Lucy said, drawing him out of his own half regrets.

"They're not celebrating here?"

"Not everyone believes," she said, as she swept the table once more.

He tossed his last two chips in the box. "Meaning Dyami?"

With his power and reputation threatened, Dyami would be Evan's ideal ally. Rich, power hungry, selfish, afraid. Everything his brother and Chaos preyed on.

Lucy finished dealing and glanced up, her brow furrowed and mouth open, as if she were about to agree, but then her gaze skated over his shoulder and her eyes grew wide. The next thing Atlas knew, he was being yanked off his stool by two giant men. "Didn't we tell you last week to get out of here?" one of them said.

Or maybe his brother hadn't been welcome, after all.

"Last week?" Lucy said, brows snapped together, but before Atlas could reply, the guards dragged him away from her table.

He waited until he was out of her earshot to continue the ruse he'd been dealt, angling for more information. "I just wanted another word with Dyami. I'm sure we can reach an agreement."

"The eagle has nothing left to say to you."

They hauled him to the nearest exit doors and tossed him outside. He spun to try to beg his way back inside—to talk with the man his brother had—but his vibrating phone stopped him short. He yanked the device out of his pocket and read the text from one of his sources in La Purisima. **SOS.**

The same source who, weeks back, had alerted him to the giant there. As much as he wanted back inside that casino, Atlas couldn't ignore the text, not after the last one had proven so pivotal. He hit dial and lifted the phone to his ear.

The call connected after one ring, and Watson launched right in, not bothering with pleasantries as a crash sounded in the background. "That green-haired woman you sent me a picture of is here."

"Where, exactly?"

"The Gathering House in La Purisima."

"Are you fucking kidding me?" The Gathering House was across the street from the town's largest church, and on a Sunday afternoon, it would be packed with people eating and shopping at the local merchant booths before evening service.

"She and the dog with her are asking questions," Watson said. "The sort that will let on what they are before long."

Atlas gazed longingly at the casino, cursing Mary and Robin for making him leave the very warm lead inside. Cursing fate that wouldn't leave him the fuck alone. "I'm on my way."

SIX

Atlas ported himself into the woods at the edge of The Gathering House parking lot, keeping his sudden appearance out of sight.

Not that anyone would have noticed. Humans dressed in their Sunday best streamed out of the long, barnlike structure, running the opposite direction of Atlas, across the four-lane road toward the church on the other side. Cars slammed on brakes, some slammed into each other, but even the squeal of tires and the crunch of metal couldn't drown out the coyote's roar from inside the building.

"Fucking hell."

Atlas sprinted across the parking lot, gravel crunching under his loafers, and for once he was glad for his suit. No one gave him a second look as he fought his way inside. He hustled down the long corridor, passing merchants hastily emptying their stalls, on his way to the mess hall in the middle of the structure.

And cursed again at the sight before him.

Mary stood atop a communal dining table, wall at her back, a knife in one hand, a ceramic mug in the other, while Robin stood on all fours in front of her, his massive jaws open as he unleashed another roar at the group of men who'd squared off against them.

"Not good," Atlas muttered.

"Not good at all." Watson scooted in beside him, as close as his duffels full of unsold baked goods allowed. "I tried to warn them, but they didn't listen."

"Trust me," Atlas said with a resigned sigh. "There's nothing you could have said that would've made them."

As if to prove his point, Mary continued to interrogate from where she stood. "We just want to know who the giant met with before he was killed. Simple question."

One of the men lunged, thrusting a chair at Robin. The coyote caught the foot rail, yanked the chair free, then flung it wide, scattering the remaining onlookers.

"Get out of here," Atlas said to Watson.

Unlike the coyote and hard-headed deity, the baker didn't need to be told twice, joining the rest of the merchants as they cleared out with their goods, only the combatants left behind.

Ten against two. Despite what the group of humans thought, the odds favored Mary and Robin. And Atlas could hasten things along. He shoved two fingers in his mouth and whistled, the high-pitched noise drawing everyone's attention. "How about we even things up a bit?" Palms up, he summoned two green orbs, and Robin yipped twice, a call that Atlas had only ever heard before in battle. And technically, that's what this was, but those yips, combined with the dancing golden eyes and stretched wide mouth, canines gleaming, registered to Atlas as laughter.

Only, he couldn't figure out who Robin was laughing at—him or the humans? Couldn't figure out whether to throw one of his orbs at Robin for being an ass even now or if he was about to have the most fun in a fight he'd had in ages.

The quandary distracted Atlas a second too long, time enough for one of the humans to draw a gun and fire. The bullet sailed wide of Robin's head, past a fluffy ear that was already missing its point. Atlas didn't hesitate to hurl his first orb at the shooter, searing the gun from his hand and leaving him howling in pain.

"Guard her," he shouted at Robin, then advanced on the remaining humans, scattering the group with his other orb before spinning up more, chucking them each time the humans tried to reassemble or attack with whatever furniture they could use. They spouted scripture the entire time, as if it would somehow magically make the warlock and shifter disappear. Even more ridiculous were their attempts to talk Mary "out from under their spell." To try and "save" her.

Atlas laughed at the irony, a series of yips echoing him, and he had the answer to his earlier question. Laughing with him, not at him. He didn't want to like that as much as he did.

"Atlas, get down!" Mary called from her perch, as she'd done through much of the fight, directing his and Robin's maneuvers. Atlas dropped into a crouch, and the coyote vaulted over him, taking down the human who'd been coming at Atlas from behind. Robin knocked his makeshift spear free and pinned the man to the floor, letting loose a thunderous growl in his face. Atlas didn't want to like that either—or the heat it sent racing down his spine.

Thankfully, he didn't have time to get caught up in the implications, Robin roaring an order Atlas had no trouble interpreting. He hurried to take up Robin's prior position, reaching Mary just as another of the humans had the dumb idea to engage her in a knife fight. The attacker got a slash across his chest for his idiocy, and the good little zealot act died on his next nasty breath. "You little bitch," he seethed, as he drew back an arm, preparing to lunge with his own knife again.

Atlas caught him by the elbow. "So much for that godliness," he seethed back, then flung the man into the nearest wall, knocking him unconscious. Robin flung another body on top of him, adding to the pile. But the five remaining attackers were reorganizing, one of them lighting a washcloth stuffed in a bottle of cleaning solution on fire.

Mary grabbed Atlas by the biceps. "I'll bring this place down if I have to. We'll walk out alive; they won't."

"Do *not* show yourself." Right now, she was just a nosy, green-haired human who was asking the wrong questions and in the wrong company. If she revealed who she truly was—

The doors at the opposite end of the mess hall slammed open and mangled furniture was tossed aside, revealing a hulking man dressed in all black, from his hooded trench to his leather boots to the crossbow propped on his shoulder. He tossed back the hood, revealing the scarred face of Atlas's nightmares.

"Change of plans," Atlas said and, with another whistle, called Robin back to them. For once, thank fuck, the coyote obeyed, leaping over two attackers to land between him and Mary. "Bring it down," he told the deity, then waited only long enough for her earthquake to shake the first ceiling beam loose before snapping them out of there.

SEVEN

Robin's "Who the fuck was that?" collided with Mary's "Where the fuck are we?" and all Atlas could do was hang back his head and exhale his exhaustion.

No *thank you*. No *are you okay*. Not even a second to get a drink or take a piss or to check if he was actually still in one piece. Just right into the interrogation.

"The ceiling didn't ask you a question," Robin mocked, and Atlas lowered his chin, ready to list the many reasons why he'd rather have a conversation with the pitched ceiling than either of them, but his words died a swift death, snuffed out by the man standing naked in the middle of his safe house.

Rays of afternoon sun streamed in through the structure's A-frame windows, painting Robin's freckled skin with warmth. Burnished, all of him, from the golden hairs on his muscular limbs, to the coppery strands mixed with the blond atop his head, to the swirls of red-gold hair on his chest and the wiry curls around the root of his thick cock.

Fuck, even soft it was impressive. Hard, it would be big enough to choke Atlas, to split him in two, to fill him full and make him scream.

"Eyes up here, sugar."

Atlas snapped his gaze to the heated gold one that was unmistakably smug. Fucker. "There are extra clothes upstairs," he bit out, as he retrieved a bottle of much-needed vodka from the freezer under the stairs.

When he didn't hear Robin move, he poured himself a double, tossed back the shot, poured a second, then turned back around, marginally more fortified to face the shifter who seemed hell-bent on driving him mad.

Robin sat propped on the arm of the leather couch, arms crossed, legs spread, semi-hard cock resting against his thigh. At least he wasn't unaffected; unfortunately, he wasn't distracted either. "Now, who or what was that nightmare that walked through the door before you snapped us out of there?"

Atlas leaned against the side of the stairs. "A hunter."

"I don't know him."

"Because he only works in the South, which you usually stay out of. So why venture this way now? To La Purisima, of all places." He shifted his attention to Mary, who stood leaned against the stone wall by the double front doors. "You, especially, know better." All the trouble Icarus had gone to to keep her out of these parts, and she was right back here. "Someone could have recognized you."

"You killed a giant in LP," she said, ignoring the parts of his logic she didn't like and substituting her own. "Stood to reason Evan had been there too."

"And witnesses reported seeing a man fitting Evan's description on or about the time the giant died," Robin added.

Atlas sipped from his glass, the only thing keeping him from throwing it. "And what description was that?"

"White, short, fit, clean-cut, blond hair, dressed in a suit."

Atlas gestured at himself. "Yes, that was me, killing said giant."

Robin cocked a bushy brow, then after an up-and-down sweep of him, finally registered the change in attire since the last time he'd seen him. "What happened to the kilt?"

"I put on a suit when I need someone to think I'm Evan." The other brow rose to match, and Atlas hung back his head on another pained sigh. When he righted it, he set his sights on the biggest liar in the room. "You didn't tell him?" he said to Mary.

Robin shot off the couch. "Tell me what?"

"Atlas, don't—"

Whatever argument she was going to make was moot at this point; Robin was so close to the truth that he'd put it together any second now. No use wasting valuable time when Atlas needed answers and needed the stinky, attractive dog out of his presence. He grabbed the single framed picture off the fireplace mantel and shoved it in Robin's direction. "That's me and my brothers, including Evan."

"Brother?" He looked down at the picture, then back up at him. "He's your twin?"

"Yes, my older brother." He lowered the hammer. "By seven minutes." Robin's eyes rounded into saucers, the connection made. "Same as you and Deborah." He and Evan weren't accidentally in their lives; they never had been. Balance and a hefty dose of fate had conspired to put the four of them in this hellscape together. But that was a conversation for a different day. He needed answers, and with Mary on her heels, she was the one to press. "That couldn't have been all there was for you to risk the South."

"Someone saw him in LP last month."

Right around the time Evan would have met with Niall. "He used Cole's death as a pretense."

"Is that one of your other brothers?"

"The youngest," he said, voice rough, words scraping over the knives in his throat as he set the frame back on the mantel.

"And the last one in the picture?"

"Canton."

A low growl rumbled from deep in Robin's chest, familiar betrayal made audible.

"Yes, it's all a very tangled web." Atlas tossed back the rest of his vodka, refilled the glass, and handed it to Robin. "Welcome to the party." Unbeknownst to the coyote, he'd been a part of it his whole life, same as his late sister, same as Atlas and Evan.

Robin didn't hesitate to gulp the shot down before turning for the stairs. "I'm gonna go change so I don't rip her head off."

"Now you're catching on." Though Atlas rather liked the view of Robin from behind, his backside as firm as the front.

"Eyes over here, sugar," Mary parroted, and Atlas jutted a finger at her. "Don't you start too." He ducked into the compact kitchen under the loft and began pulling together something to eat for himself and his unexpected visitors.

Mary drifted his direction, then veered onto the couch, putting a knee to the cushions and leaning over the back to look out the window. "Where are we?"

"Safe house."

"Who owns these vineyards?"

"Me. Or, more accurately, a shell company that owns a shell company that—"

"I get it." She pushed off the couch and took the plate of cheese, nuts, and grapes he held out to her. "Hacker, remember?"

"So, tell me, then . . ." He tossed a stale baguette on the coffee table next to the cheeseboard. "What did you hack that led you home, besides Evan's maybe whereabouts?"

"Who works these vineyards?" came a question from the opposite direction, Robin loping down the stairs in a pair of sweats he'd ripped off at the knees, probably with his claws.

Atlas forced himself not to rise, in any fashion, to the bait. "The family of humans I rent it to," he said, as he grabbed a knife to cut the baguette. "They live in the main house down by the road. I keep the cottage here."

"Risky." Robin flopped onto the couch beside Mary. "They know what you are?"

"They worship her," he said with a jut of his chin toward the green-haired pixie popping grapes into her mouth. "Now, stop stalling, and tell me why you're really here."

Mary leaned forward, like she was about to answer, only to be cut off again by the fucking dog. "If we show you our cards, you show us yours."

Atlas fetched three glasses, grabbed the bottle of vodka, and lowered into the chair on the other side of Mary.

"I'm not giving you everything we know," Robin said, as Atlas filled their glasses, "so you can just run off and save your brother."

"Who says that's what I intend to do?" He slid the glass the length of the table, vodka sloshing over the rim when Robin saved it from toppling off the edge and onto the floor. Atlas lifted his gaze, meeting Robin's intrigued gold one. "She promised you vengeance. You'll get it."

"On your terms."

Atlas lifted his glass. "Does it matter?"

EIGHT

"I knew there had to be more to the calm than just vodka."

Atlas took another puff on his joint, then glanced over his shoulder at his unwelcome visitor—who was still bare-chested despite the cool December night. "Are you allergic to shirts?"

"More like allergic to you." He approached behind Atlas's chair and plucked the joint from his fingers. "I don't trust you. I may need to shift at any moment."

"But you trust my weed?"

Robin circled the fire pit and lowered into the chair on the other side of the bistro table from Atlas. "If it's anything like your vodka, only the high-end shit for you." He took a long drag on the joint, then puffed smoke rings out of his nostrils like some kind of silly dragon. "Yep, as I expected." He handed the joint back across the table, then stretched his legs out in front of him, ankles propped on the fire pit ledge, hands folded on his abs that Atlas did not notice rippling. "I hope you weren't planning to sleep in the loft tonight. Mary's spread her shit all over the place. Never ends well."

"How long have you two been traveling together?"

"About a month."

"And Icarus hasn't come after you yet?"

Mary's brother had spent the last thirty years protecting her. That devotion, apparent even when he and Mary were simple humans, was the reason Canton had identified Mary as a vessel for Nature, why he'd infiltrated their lives to make sure the transformations happened—Mary into Nature, Icarus into her vampire protector. Why Canton had ultimately given his life for the effort, though the circumstances of his death remained a fuzzy mystery —a weighty guilt—that nagged at Atlas.

In any event, Icarus had been dutiful, staying far enough away from Mary to avoid detection but close enough to reach her in case of emergencies. Atlas had made sure Paris always had enough Daylight to sell to him for such occasions. And now, after all that effort, when Icarus was no longer a vampire but had a whole army at his back, he'd let his sister wander off . . . with Robin?

"Your pupil's doing," the coyote explained. "Paris told Mac that she's safe with me. If he'd been lying, Mac would've felt it in their soul bond. Mac told the others. That and they're probably still pissed at me for giving Paris's location to the final giant."

Atlas smiled around the joint. "He was ready."

"You raised him well."

"I didn't—"

"Did Vincent think you were Evan?"

The abrupt swerve saved Atlas from the pinch in his chest and the half-made deflection. He thanked Robin for the small mercy with a small piece of the truth. "He wanted Evan, but only Chaos would do for my brother. So I offered Vincent the next best thing, a look-alike and the second most powerful Shaw brother."

"Is that why you don't wear the suit anymore?"

"That, and I always preferred kilts." He took another long puff on the joint before handing it back across the table.

Robin accepted it with narrowed eyes. "I can't decide whether you're good or evil."

"Do you still want to kill me?"

"Yes," he answered with zero hesitation.

Balance. "Then, does it matter?"

"I suppose not." Robin sank back in his chair, joint to his lips.

"Why haven't you killed me yet?" Atlas wondered aloud after several annoyingly comfortable minutes of silence. He expected a smirking, joking response, not Robin's well-reasoned explanation.

"Because it's apparent you hold a good many of the cards on the table. You have power and information we need in this war with Chaos."

"And when you get what you need from me?"

He mimicked a slash across his throat, added a *snick* for effect, then handed back the joint.

"You're awfully serene about it all," Atlas said.

This version of Robin was not the rabid dog he'd spent the better part of ten years running from, who just two months ago had had his muzzle around Atlas's throat, ready to end him.

"I figure, I can spend the next two weeks driving myself crazy or driving you crazy . . ." His golden eyes danced. "Is it working yet?"

"You're an asshole."

"I know." He grinned, then stretched out further in the chair, all that muscled body burnished in the firelight.

Atlas tore his gaze away, staring at the rows of swaying vines instead. The grapes were long picked, only wilting leaves in shades of autumn left rustling in the breeze. A quiet song as one day slipped to the next. He didn't mind that Mary had commandeered the loft. Didn't mind spending time out here, sleeping out here even, after being cooped up inside with Cole for weeks, after being trapped in Vincent's compound for years. He idly wondered how Vincent's other captive was adjusting to life among the vineyards. "How is Paris, truly?"

"Alive, somehow, like Adam too, when they both weren't for a time."

Atlas shivered around the memory of Adam bleeding out on that bridge in YB. Then shivered again at what Paris must have gone through, being sacrificed by giants, twice. He was stronger than any of them had ever given him credit for.

"He's pretty remarkable," Robin said, words mirroring Atlas's thoughts. "Whether you had a hand in that or not, I wouldn't be here if not for him."

"He rescued you?"

"He gave me a purpose," he said, tone lightening, words lengthening, like maybe he wouldn't mind sleeping out here among the vines either. "Pushed the guilt aside, at least for a while."

It never truly went away. Atlas had decades on Robin in that regard. But at least the freshest guilt was somewhat assuaged. "I'm glad he's doing well. He deserved better than Vincent, better than me."

"You were him, weren't you? The way you grew up?"

Perceptive fucker. "In a lot of ways," he admitted. "My brothers and I had a mother, where Paris didn't, but our father . . . He was a different sort of man than Vincent but no less malicious."

"And yet Evan became the evil one?"

"Who says I wasn't too at one point?"

Robin lolled his head on his neck, face angled toward him, even as his eyelids drooped. "Is that how you faked it so well? It couldn't have just been the suit. Or the belief it was all for a higher good."

Atlas took a final drag of the joint, then snuffed it out in the dirt under his heel. "No, it was the guilt."

"Or your soul."

"Same difference."

Two sides of the same coin.

Like him and the coyote across the table whose body sank deeper into the chair, whose chest rose and fell with the steady, even breaths of sleep. Atlas added jealousy to his mental box labeled Robin Whelan.

He stood slowly, careful not to wake the slumbering shifter, careful not to hover too close as he paused at Robin's side, hand over his chest, basking in the heat that lapped against his palm. He was so warm, and Atlas would bet those whorls of red-gold hair on his chest were soft too, same as the copper and blond strands on his head.

He ached to find out.

He fisted his hand instead, capturing a fleeting tendril of warmth before walking away from roaring temptation and unproductive fantasy, from a fate that would only end in more guilt and misery.

He turned to the bleak reality of the here and now.

Inside, he climbed the stairs to the loft where Mary had, indeed, spread her shit out all over. She sat cross-legged in the middle of the bed, computer open on her lap, a half dozen other devices and countless cords scattered around her. "Did you get a location?" he asked her.

"I think so. Dyami has a meeting tomorrow at the bed and breakfast in downtown LP. Two of his guards are checked in there tonight."

"But not him?" he asked, and she shook her head. "Advance team," he speculated.

"Most likely, especially as a person fitting the hunter's description is staying there too."

"Do you have a list of all the registered guests?" Maybe he'd recognize an alias.

She held a tablet out to him. He got as far as the third name, then passed it back to her. "I'll leave tonight so I'm in position if Evan shows tomorrow. If he doesn't, I'll recon the meet."

"I can be packed and ready in twenty."

"You can't be there."

Red streaked across her tan cheeks, and she tossed her laptop aside, rising on her knees to protest. "You can't—"

"I can." He leaned forward and lowered his voice, just in case the coyote was feigning sleep. "Canton died for you. Cole died for you." He angled closer, voice hardened, as he threw an arm out the direction of where he'd left Robin. "He doesn't know it yet, but his sister and brother-in-law did too. Quinn and countless others. Your own brother, plus, Adam and Paris. Magic brought the latter few back to life, but it will run out at some point. You will exhaust the phoenixes. You are a temporary vessel, like all the vessels before this one, and the eagle is not ready yet for what he has to do." He waited for her to lower back to her haunches. "You have to quit putting yourself and others in jeopardy. Not as long as the deity is in there. Do you understand?"

The smile that tipped up her lips made him want to scream. "I was right about you."

He wasn't so sure. "We'll see."

NINE

Crouched behind the parapet wall of a building rooftop, Atlas took one look through his monocular into the bed and breakfast's corner café and knew things were about to go sideways. He hadn't wanted to believe what he'd read on that list Mary had handed him last night—an alias he knew all too well—but there was no denying the truth of what he saw with his own eyes.

No denying the calls, real and telepathic, that had gone unanswered overnight and this morning.

"What's your cousin doing cozied up with the pretender?"

Atlas nearly dropped his spyglass. Cursing, he spun from the unsettling sight of Daphne and Dyami cuddled together at a table to the equally unsettling shifter who'd somehow snuck up on him, not a footfall or heartbeat warning of his approach, not a whiff of dog. "How did you—"

"I'm good at my job." His gaze drifted over Atlas's shoulder. "Same as them."

Atlas followed his line of sight to the sidewalk outside the café. To the seemingly twenty-something redhead in a crocheted sweater and patchwork jeans and his silver fox partner in denim and leather approaching the cafe's glass door. Daphne and Dyami had probably noticed them already. Icarus, with his tall, chiseled frame, blue eyes, and fiery hair was one of the most striking men Atlas had ever met; add in Adam's rugged good looks and they were a formidable, distracting pair.

"They can't be here," Atlas seethed, his already sideways plan well on the way to upside down. He couldn't even lob an orb to stop them from entering. Daphne would instantly recognize his magic.

"They can be," Robin said, as he kneeled beside him. "Adam and Icarus are human. We're not."

"By that logic, my cousin and Dyami shouldn't be here either." He might not have been a true eagle shifter, but Dyami was an elder of not-insignificant influence. He had enough juice to make people think he was a shifter, by magical deception or otherwise. And speaking of power . . . "My brother definitely shouldn't be here, if he even shows."

"Except your cousin plays the convert, and Dyami the holy man."

Icarus and Adam entered the café, and Atlas hung his head, no help for it now. "They're going to blow the op."

"They're professionals," Robin said. "They'll watch for the hunter and neutralize him if they have to."

"Shouldn't that be your job?"

He swung his golden gaze to the side, eyeing him pointedly. "Someone has to keep eyes on you." Then eyeing his attire, added, "In a suit again, I see."

"In case I have to pretend to be Evan." Daphne would immediately know it was him, but unless Dyami had paid close attention to his twin's eye color last time or had been in the presence of Evan's magic, he likely wouldn't. No telling if Daphne would tell him; no telling whose side she was on—Chaos or Nature.

Nature, fuck.

"What about—"

"The pack has her covered," Robin said, anticipating his query.

"At my safe house? That everyone knows about now?"

Robin shrugged and shifted his gaze across the street again. "Back to your cousin . . ."

"Maybe she's playing him."

"Or she's playing you. Could she be working with Evan?"

The thought made his stomach churn. "Daphne and Canton were tight." They were the oldest siblings in each family, born only a couple of days apart. They grew up together, worked together, each other's professional partner. "I can't believe she'd betray him or Nature."

Robin was uncharacteristically quiet, as he kept a watchful eye on the café. "How much do you know about Canton's final days?"

Atlas wobbled in his crouch, caught off guard by Robin's question. He braced himself on the parapet wall and let the familiar waves of guilt crash over him. "He went off the grid," Atlas said, recalling those horrible days of nothingness until one night he'd been jarred out of sleep by the sense of imbalance, of falling, like the earth had disappeared out from under his feet. Three blinks to wakefulness later and he'd known his brother was gone. Three weeks later, Daphne had returned with confirmation of his death. He swallowed hard and shook off the ghosts of that awful time. "But Mary became Nature, and Icarus a vampire, so Canton was successful."

"And then he died."

The simple statement had the definitive tone of consequence, not chronology, and Atlas was knocked off balance once more. "What are you—"

Robin's phone dinged, cutting off Atlas's question. The coyote took one look at the screen and snarled "Fuck."

"What's going on?"

Robin tilted the phone his direction. One look and Atlas's vision went red. In the photo Adam had snapped, Daphne was handing Dyami a sheet of paper with a sketch on it—of Mary. Her hair, her outfit, and her expression were the same as in the vision Daphne had nicked from him.

Was this why Canton had gone dark at the end? Because his

best friend, his family, his partner had turned on him? How long had Daphne been working with the enemy? Had some part of Atlas always known and that was why he'd stayed away from home? Why he'd never worked as a team? He knew why when it came to the shifter beside him, why it was easier to hate him than open himself to fate's mercy. But when it came to Daphne, was this what had stopped him from taking Canton's place at her side?

He didn't hesitate, raising his hand to snap, and at the last second, Robin grabbed hold, porting them both through the tear —and into a fight already in progress. Daphne was hurling orbs, keeping Adam and Icarus trapped behind a flipped-over table, while she and Dyami scuttled for the door.

"Can you get her hands?" Atlas whispered low. "Like you did mine at the club?"

"If you can hold those orbs back long enough for me to get behind her."

Atlas couldn't recall the last time he'd seen Daphne's magic, but he was certain it hadn't been swirled green and gray like it was today. There was no yellow in it, not like in Evan's, but there was enough doubt in her mind and magic that Atlas's full-strength conviction easily deflected her orbs. Given the opening, Adam and Icarus chased a fleeing Dyami out the door, while he and Robin advanced on the real traitor in the room. One more blinding blast by Atlas, and an impressive human leap by the shifter—from a bench seat, to a table, to an overhead beam, from which he swung to a landing behind Daphne—and they had her. Robin shoved his fingers through her smaller ones, holding them apart, while Atlas pushed her back against Robin's sturdy frame, a hand circling her throat.

"When did he get to you?" he demanded.

She didn't have to ask who. Yellow flickered in her eyes, streaking through the green, before her once vivid irises faded to dull gray. "When I lost another cousin." She gulped, her words pleading and strained as she forced them out beneath his hand. "We can't keep going like this, Atlas."

His heart ached with sympathy and betrayal. He understood, better than anyone—the exhaustion and loneliness, the ups and too many downs, the never-ending fight. And she'd been fighting it longer than him. Long enough, it seemed, to consider a different path. One that led away from him, from the promises they'd made to their mothers, and from the calling they'd all once served. She'd been a beacon to him, strength and hope in a world that too often seemed hopeless. "I trusted you. I looked up to you."

"Join us." Yellow swirled in the gray. "Let's end this."

End this.

He didn't have a choice. "You know what she looks like."

If Daphne was telling the truth, she'd only just switched sides, but that sense of falling like he'd felt the day Canton had died ripped through Atlas again. Together with another tear in his chest like the day he'd lost his other brother. They'd both known, Canton and Cole. Both going it alone rather than risk the breaking point they knew Daphne had somewhere.

Yet only he was left to find it.

To end this.

"You told me, cuz," she said. "Deep down, you want this to be over too."

A final manipulation, and yet, nothing compared to Atlas's over the past decade, moving pieces around the board to fit his agenda, but today he wasn't the one in the wrong.

"No." Wetness pricked the corners of his eyes, as he pressed more firmly with his hand. "You stole it from me."

"You don't have to keep going like this," she urged him once more.

If only that were true, if only his destiny hadn't been set the day he and Evan were born and cemented for good when the man behind Daphne and his twin sister had come into this world. "I do," Atlas said, voice wavering, his vision wobbly with unshed tears.

"It's the name she gave me." He lifted his other hand and cupped her cheek, wiping away the tear that streaked down her own pale cheek, a match to the one racing down his. "I love you," he told her.

"I love you too." She closed her eyes, her final words a whisper. "And I forgive you."

"Thank you," he said, even if he didn't believe there was enough forgiveness in the world to save him. From any of this. He closed his fist around her throat and added another loved one lost to the war.

TEN

Daphne's body had barely dropped between him and Robin when Adam and Icarus came rushing back through the door—sans pretender. "Where's Dyami?" Robin barked.

"Gone," Icarus replied. "Getaway car."

"Fuck!" Atlas cursed, then because he needed to do something with the anger and resentment, the hopelessness, spiraling through him, he shoved Robin in the chest, two-handed. "Why didn't you go after him?"

He gestured at the lifeless witch between them. "Because I was holding her fucking fingers apart. Like you asked me to."

"Dyami knows what she looks like now. I have to—"

"The pack has her." The coyote's calm confidence was the only thing keeping Atlas from flying into a million magical pieces, from giving in to the awful energy raging inside him. Robin glanced past him to the other pair. "Was the hunter ever here?"

Adam flashed a keycard. "Bribed the front desk clerk for it. Let's go find out."

"Did you also tell them to stay out of here?" Atlas asked with a sweep of his hand at the death and destruction surrounding them.

"I have been doing this for a while," the ex-cop deadpanned, before following his partner down the hallway toward the internal staircase leading to the rooms upstairs.

Atlas moved to follow but was stopped by Robin's big hand splayed against his chest. "Channel it."

"I don't know what you're talking about."

"Your magic. It's bordering on chartreuse right now. It's supposed to be moss. Fix it."

"Fix it?" The magic he tried to channel to the hand in the center of his chest hit a brick wall, rebounding on Atlas and causing him to stumble back a step, gasping. "How?"

"You tell me. Later." He moved to block the hallway, arms crossed. "Channel it for now."

It was on the tip of Atlas's tongue to argue, the defensive instinct so ingrained at this point when it came to Robin, but they didn't have time for that today. Not with Dyami and the hunter on the loose, Evan too. He closed his eyes and inhaled deep, smothering the darkness with his mission, his purpose, his vow. When he was steady, his magic no longer pinging around like a reckless pinball, he opened his eyes. Whatever Robin saw there must have been enough, the shifter dropping his arms and turning for the stairs.

Atlas followed him up to the second floor, then to the open door at the end of the hallway. A half step over the threshold and Atlas had to clasp the doorframe to keep the magic he'd just chan-neled grounded.

"Doesn't look like he was ever here," Icarus said, Atlas hearing him as if in a tunnel.

"But the clerk's description matched," Adam said. "He was here, at least briefly."

"Or someone was magically pretending to be him," Robin said.

Someone like Evan, who'd definitely been here, his magic lingering.

And if Daphne had sent him a quick mental word about

Mary's best protectors all being in LP instead of at the safe house, a property Daphne knew about from Cole's final days, then Atlas knew exactly where Evan would be headed.

Fuck. "We need to get out of here."

"We'll search the surrounding area and deal with the body," Adam said, as the ringing in Atlas's ears grew louder.

"The body?" he practically shouted. "She was my cousin." Even if it had been his own hands that had taken her life. Another death in the family he was responsible for. Robin's increasingly, annoyingly familiar hand landed on his shoulder, and Atlas shrugged it off. "Don't touch me," he barked at the dog, before setting his irate sights on the hometown resident in the room. "You don't think anyone will recognize you?" he said to Icarus, same as he had to Mary.

"If they do, they won't understand why I look the same as I did thirty years ago." He flicked a hand at his ginger hair. "And it's the first time I've had my real color since I was ten."

"What about the barber who dyed it the first time?"

Icarus laughed. "The guy at Shorty's in Santa Maria? He was ancient back then. I'm sure he's dead by now."

If he knew Shorty's, then . . . "You remember the cemetery a block over from there?"

He nodded.

"Bury her between her mother and Canton."

Color drained from Icarus's face, and he gulped, his words seemingly caught in his throat. Did the nurse turned vampire turned field medic suddenly have an affliction against dead bodies and graveyards?

Before he could ask, Adam stepped in for his partner. "We'll take care of her and meet you back at the safe house."

"Fuck, Robin," Atlas said, spinning on his heel. "How many people did you tell?"

"The ones who needed to know," he replied. "Who won't try to kill her."

Fair. But dirty. "Fuck you."

Robin brought his hand down on his shoulder once more. "Be mad at me later. Right now, just get us the fuck out of here."

Also fair. And not up for debate. Atlas raised his hand and snapped.

ELEVEN

Atlas ported them to the no-longer-safe house and realized how true his words had become.

A battle was in full swing. Dyami's two casino goons were squared off with Robin's coyote cousin, Jenn, and her mountain lion partner, Abigail. Two other faces Atlas recognized from the casino were trading blows with Brock, one of Vincent's warlocks Adam had turned, and Jason, the hulking smuggler who was Paris's best friend and carried a phoenix with his soul. His skin glowed with the firebird's red and orange heat.

That battle, however, didn't frighten Atlas; he was confident Adam's team could handle Dyami's henchmen. It was the familiar magic that raised his hairs and threatened to unleash his own that caused his pulse to spike.

"Evan's here," he said, and in the space of one breath, in a flash of golden light and cracking bones, Robin shifted, the giant coyote pulling even with Atlas's steps. Together, they slunk from the edge of the vineyard to the shadows of the cottage, approaching the back steps. Then halting when Mary appeared in the loft window above.

Atlas held his breath, certain Evan would appear behind her, would snap her neck as he'd done Daphne's and then Nature would be dead for good. Chaos would reign, with Evan as his vessel, and the world would never be the same, would be over before any of them knew it.

But Evan didn't appear, and the green-haired pixie made a series of hand gestures Atlas vaguely recognized as sign language. Nothing vague about Robin's understanding, though. Golden eyes keen, he nodded his big rusty head, then nudged Atlas's hip with his muzzle, aiming him away from the cottage. "He's not in there with her?"

Robin shook his head, then made a low plaintive whine as he prodded him again, shoving him toward the walkway that led down the hill.

To the main house.

Above which corvids circled, two giant ravens among them, Mac and his younger brother Liam, the current reaper for the Monte Corvo clan.

Atlas's stomach sank.

With no time to waste, he grabbed the dog by the scruff and cut a hole in the plane to the more vulnerable. But they were too late. The green mist had barely faded from around them when Evan appeared in the doorway from the kitchen, an arm curled around the throat of the vineyard manager's preteen son.

"Stay right there, brother," he said, yellow orb hovering at his side.

"Let them go," Atlas said. "They have nothing to do with this."

"On the contrary, I showed up, and they wanted an update on the battle for Nature. Wanted to know how they could help." He cinched his arm tighter around the trembling boy's neck. "Even this one. Simon, was it?"

The boy's dark, tear-filled gaze strayed toward the kitchen before bouncing back to Atlas and the coyote beside him, Robin's teeth bared.

"Simon," Atlas said, focusing the boy's attention on him. "Are your parents in there?" he asked as gently as the anger gathering in the back of his throat would allow. Twin tears escaped Simon's eyes, streaking down his cheeks, and some of the anger escaped. "They're humans!" Atlas shouted at his brother. "You should've left them out of this."

"They're fodder."

Growling, Robin tensed, every muscle coiled, as if he were about to pounce, but as Evan's orb grew brighter, Atlas put a hand in front of Robin, pausing the impending attack. "Go check the kitchen."

Another low growl but Robin conceded, veering into the adjacent room to confirm the nightmare Simon's tears hinted at.

"Does he know?" Evan asked, and Atlas snapped his gaze back to his suited twin.

"There's been enough death today already." The last thing any of them needed was a fully informed Robin on the rampage.

"I heard you killed our dear cousin."

Simon's eyes grew wide, then wider still at Robin's thunderous howl from the kitchen, loud enough to rattle the windows in the room where they stood. The boy cut his eyes toward the front door, wisely away from the threat supernatural beings posed to humans like him. But every minute Atlas kept his brother talking was another Simon stayed alive. And another for the cavalry swirling above to answer Robin's call.

"Because you preyed on her fears," he said to Evan. "On the losses we've all suffered. Same as Chaos is preying on yours."

"You could join me too. We could share the power, like we were always meant to."

Atlas shook his head, dismissing his brother's corrupted version of fate. "Not like this." From the kitchen, a door slammed and a cacophony of *caws* and *kraas* followed, the cavalry closing in. "You're outnumbered. You can't get to her."

"Maybe I wasn't here for her," he said, then hurled his orb at Atlas.

So much for sharing power.

Atlas blocked the hit with his own orb, diverting Evan's to the cabinet of wine goblets along the wall. Between the shattering glass and the sea of corvids streaming in from the kitchen, Mac's violet-eyed raven at the point, Evan was momentarily distracted, his arm loosening around the boy's neck.

"Simon, get down!" Atlas shouted, before firing an orb of his own at Evan. Then another, buying Robin time to corral Simon. "Get him to the others!"

The coyote didn't argue, sliding across the hardwoods, scooping Simon up with his mass, and carrying him out the door that Atlas blasted open for them. Mac and his flock followed them outside, creating a shield against the enemy, leaving Atlas alone in a face-off with his brother.

"You're their prisoner," Evan said as he spun up another orb. "Nature, fate, our mother and his. You can be free, brother. You don't have to do what they say. You don't have to end up like Canton and Cole."

All the anger that had been gathering in the pit of Atlas's stomach, that had been clawing up his throat and searing through his veins, made the two glowing green orbs above his hands glow brighter, made them powerful enough to end Evan.

But then Robin charged back through the door and drew Evan's attention—and the orbs meant for Atlas.

Atlas had no choice. He didn't want the same fate to befall him that had befallen his twin.

With a final blast of power, he put everything he had into the orbs he hurled at the yellow ones, then hurled himself at Robin, grabbing the dog's tail and snapping them out of there.

TWELVE

They landed back in the crowded safe house to find Nature's army checking each other over for injuries, including Abigail tending to a still trembling Simon. Atlas moved to comfort the boy too but barely made it a step before he was spun back around by the biceps, a post-shift Robin growling in his face. "Why'd you do that?"

"He was going to kill you."

"And now he's going to come up here and kill her and the rest of us."

"He's not," Atlas said, shaking loose of Robin's hold. "Evan would have come after her already if that was his purpose."

"What was it then?" Mary asked from atop the loft stairs. She stood next to Mac, who was cinching the terrycloth robe Atlas had stolen from Icarus around him.

"You need to get somewhere safe," Atlas replied, then said to Mac, "Take her back to Monte Corvo. Non-magically."

"We're not idiots," Jenn grumbled, the bark in her tone so much like her cousin's that Atlas had to fight a smile. "We took Paris's plane down here."

Atlas's smile fought harder, making his lips twitch. He covered it with a smirk. "Take everyone back with you." When Simon stiffened, Atlas kneeled before him. "Go with them, okay?" The boy hesitated, trembling harder, and Atlas gently clasped his arm, easing some of the anxiety. "They're going to an even bigger vineyard than this one." That notion seemed to comfort him some. "They'll take care of you. And I'll be there before long too. Promise."

The boy gave a small nod and accepted Abigail's offered hand, the shifter leading him toward the front door. Once they were outside, Atlas stood, snatched the framed picture of his brothers off the mantel, then headed the opposite direction, to the back door. "And torch this place on your way out."

It was already burned; might as well make it official. Plus, it was standard operating procedure for erased persons; burn all the evidence. The stone walls would survive, as they had for generations. The rest Atlas couldn't care less about, the only important item in his hand. He let the door slam behind him and set off on the path to the main house, needing to pick up Evan's trail again, hoping there would be enough of his brother's magic left to track.

He made it as far as the corner of the main house when Mister Doesn't Make a Sound caught up with him again. Robin hauled him into the shadows and shoved him back against the stone wall, the picture falling from Atlas's grasp and clattering to the ground. Mister Also Allergic to Clothes paid it no mind, crunching the frame under his bare foot. He pinned Atlas's wrists above his head and loomed over him, invading every inch of his space. Chests pressed together, Robin shoved his thick thigh between his legs and, leaving one rough hand around his pinned wrists, circled his throat with the other.

"What are you doing?" Atlas rasped out against the painful, obnoxiously perfect hold.

"Making sure you're really you."

"What the fuck does that mean?"

"You and Evan were dressed just alike. You *look* just alike. And I left that room."

"For two minutes, at most. And as soon as you were back, you saw my magic."

"How do I know you didn't fake that?" Robin said, voice louder, body pressing impossibly closer. "Didn't make it another color?"

Atlas matched him in resistance and volume, fighting the hold and shouting, "Look at my eyes!"

"Same answer!" the coyote roared back.

With a flick of his fingers, Atlas cast a sparkling green dome around them, from the wall above their hands to the ground beneath their feet, blanketing them in the energy he balanced daily, magic that the man pressed against him could either destroy or fortify, even if he didn't realize it yet. "You know what my magic *feels* like."

Robin's deep-throated growl was a menacing almost-purr that sent goose bumps racing across Atlas's skin. Robin's voice, when he spoke again, sounded as strained as Atlas's cock felt. "What was he talking about fate?"

Atlas tossed another grenade into the conflict; what was one more explosion today? "It's what we do, me and you. We run from fate."

Robin rolled his hips, digging his own stiff cock against Atlas's hip. "Does this feel like running?"

Atlas groaned, his Adam's apple bobbing wildly against the hand still clasped around his throat. This felt like the furthest thing from running, which was what they both should be doing, for their own sakes and humanity's, but fuck if Atlas didn't want to feel more of him.

As if hearing his deepest, darkest desire, Robin released his wrists so he could shove a hand between them, palming Atlas's cock through his pants. "I know what you smell like too." He curled his fingers around his length and stroked, long and slow and hard, eliciting another groan from Atlas. "The real you. Not the decaying stench of dark warlock you put on like you do these fucking suits." He released his cock, and Atlas nearly snapped at him to put his goddamn hand back where it belonged, but caught his words when Robin ripped open his fly instead. That was more like it, and Robin's grin when he found him bare underneath only made Atlas's dick harder. But then the fucking coyote had to go and be a menace, putting impossible conditions on an already agonizing predicament. "Make the stench go away."

"No."

The grip on his throat tightened. "Drop the shield, Atlas."

He shook his head. He'd never admit it to anyone, but he'd wanted Robin's hands on him like this for longer than he could remember. He'd allow himself this much, a quick hate fuck to get their frustrations out, but nothing more. Not the other side of the coin that would destroy them both in the end, the fate he'd spent a lifetime running from. Dropping the scent shield, letting Robin all the way in, was a line Atlas wouldn't—couldn't—cross, for all their sakes.

Robin took him in hand, the rough friction of his calloused fingers making Atlas's eyes flutter closed. But then Robin shifted the hold around his neck, sliding his hand up to clasp the side of his face, fingers digging painfully against this skin. "If you're not going to drop the smell, then keep these open." He tapped his fingers at the corner of Atlas's eye. "So I know it's you."

Atlas opened his eyes and met the burning gold ones mere inches from his. "You believe me now?"

Robin stroked his length. "You're not faking this."

No, he wasn't. For all the times he had while playing this or that role, he wasn't playing any role today. He was just a needy man being expertly handled by the one person he'd wanted to handle him most. He thrust his hips, shoving his dick into Robin's fist, tunneling through the tight, rough grip.

When Robin took his hand away again, Atlas's anger flared. "Don't you dare leave me hanging again, asshole." The coyote's smirk made his anger flare hotter and the shield around them grow brighter. But then anger ignited into something else searing when Robin clasped his own cock with Atlas's in his fist, the two of them hot and hard together. "Oh, fuck."

"Tell me, Atlas . . ." He added a twist to his stroke, and Atlas thanked all the deities for the thigh holding him up. "Who did this better? Me or that priest in the club the other night?"

Fire tripped through Atlas's veins. "You were watching?"

"Fuck yes," Robin purred, his cock like steel against Atlas's. "And for the record, I like you better in the kilts."

"So do I." Fighting Robin's grip on his face, Atlas dipped his chin enough to spit on Robin's fist, adding the extra bit of slick and filthy he needed.

"Did you do that the other night?" Robin added his own, the glide of his fist easy now, the only friction each other. "Did you go home, spit in your fist, and fuck it like this?" He thrust hard against him, the stone wall behind Atlas digging against his back. "Were you thinking about me and that bet you've lost?"

Atlas glared at the irresistible menace, and Robin's answering laugh was as sexy as it was irritating. And when he released his face to brace his forearm on the wall behind Atlas, to cushion Atlas's head from the hard stone, Atlas didn't want to think about the pinch in his chest. An obnoxious ache that intensified when Robin pressed their temples together, grunting in Atlas's ear with each stroke toward their climax. That damn near exploded when they spilled together over Robin's fingers, and Robin spilled the sweetest, most terrifying words in his ear. "I'm done letting you hide from me."

Fuck, what would that mean for them, for their allies and enemies, for Nature and Chaos? Robin didn't know the half of it. And he never could. It was easier—and safer—to keep up the not altogether difficult pretense of hate.

To keep running.

Atlas dropped the magic around them and let the cool December air dissipate the heat that had built between them. Let it harden his voice and spine as he rebuilt his walls. "I still hate you."

"I know you do." Robin pushed off the wall, then had the fucking gall to lick his fingers clean. "And you still hate yourself more, same as me."

Thank fuck for the wall holding Atlas up, the sight and the verbal shot taking his already wobbly knees out completely. And thank fuck Robin had already turned back toward the cottage, tossing a dismissive "Meet us at the mountain" over his shoulder.

Atlas lowered his arms that he'd left above his head against the wall, his fingers free the entire time. Not once during that entire encounter had he ever considered snapping himself out of the coyote's hold.

They were so fucked.

THIRTEEN

Atlas didn't immediately go to Talahalusi like he'd ordered the others.

After catching his breath and cursing himself, he cleaned himself up, then bent to pick up the picture of his brothers.

And the one behind it that had jostled loose when he shook the other free of the broken glass. Two green-eyed women and a third one with golden eyes and honey blond hair, each of their faces split with a smile.

He should burn it, let their secret die here, but that seemed like a push too far, especially on a day when he'd already tempted fate to the max. Folding the photo instead, he hid it inside the other and shoved them both in his wallet, then with a last look at the blazing cottage up the hill, snapped himself to the cemetery where he'd buried another brother eight days ago. He'd been prepared to kneel alone next to the second freshly dug grave but found a familiar form sitting cross-legged between the two, like he was hanging out with friends. Souls the medium could see and hear.

"I know," Paris said with a laugh to one of them. "But I consider him a friend." He twisted half around and threw him a smile. "There you are. Took you long enough."

"Did they take your plane and leave you behind?" Atlas teased as he wove through the Shaw graves to reach his former pupil, as Robin had called him.

"I told them you'd get me home." He looked good, color in his cheeks, brown eyes lively, a wide easy smile. He seemed comfortable in his skin in a way Atlas had never seen the young man. "And I thought you might need a friend."

A knot formed in Atlas's throat, and he swallowed hard to force it down. Paris Cirillo was the one thing he'd done right in this world. Teaching him, sheltering him, believing in him. "You thought wrong."

"Cut the crap, Atlas."

"Oh," Atlas drawled, dramatically rearing back, a hand splayed on his chest. "Growing more of that backbone."

"Thanks to you."

He lowered himself onto the ground beside Paris. "I tried to sacrifice you."

"So did Robin. You both had your reasons."

"That's not—"

Paris bumped a shoulder against his. "I forgive you. Same as I forgave him." Then jutted his chin at the freshly dug grave. "Can you forgive her?"

"Some part of me understands." He propped his elbows on his knees and held his head in his hands, fingers tugging at the roots of his hair. "The things I did at Vincent's side . . ."

"The things my father *made* you do because he had your brother." Atlas whipped his gaze back up. "I saw it," Paris explained.

"I was there voluntarily, at first."

Paris shook his head. "Not voluntarily. You were doing your job. Did you forgive Cole, or Canton, or your mother, for putting all this on you?"

The kid was also growing into that big brain Atlas always knew he had. Wrap all that knowledge and intuition in a blanket of empathy, and it was a powerful combination. He was a perfect medium; Atlas only hated what he'd had to put Paris through to get him there.

He raked a hand through his hair, then let his arms hang over his knees. "I lied before. I am sorry for what I did to you."

"I know you are. I can see it in your aura. I thought Robin won the prize for aura with the most guilt but nope, you're the winner."

Atlas hung his head back and sighed, something else he and the coyote had in common.

"Not gonna tell you what I saw just now."

Atlas chuckled. "Thank you."

Several long moments of comfortable silence passed while Atlas pushed aside the matter of the coyote and searched inside himself for a well of forgiveness that was perilously close to dry. Daphne had forgiven him for what he'd had to do, same as Paris. Could he return the favor? "She could have plunged us into darkness."

"Unless she knew you'd stop that from happening."

"Maybe a part of her thought that, but a bigger part of her wanted out."

"Flip that," Paris said. "Assuming what Liam told me before he joined the others is true. And I have no reason to doubt him."

Neither did Atlas; the reaper had no reason to lie. And that truth only made Atlas feel worse. He hung his head again and wrapped his hands around his nape, the weight of it all too much to balance.

Paris clasped his shoulder, his touch and words gentle. "Come to the mountain, Atlas. You don't have to keep doing this alone."

Folks kept telling him that, and folks kept dying. For *we*. He couldn't risk the man beside him, the deity they protected, the son of the woman whose picture was in his pocket. "I can't—"

"At least hear us out. At least lay eyes on her there so you know she's safe. Then make your decision. You owe me that much."

Atlas had to laugh at the spunk that had been punched down

for so long, that suited Paris so well. "There's that backbone again. No promises."

Paris nodded. "No promises." He stood and brushed off his pants. "I'll give you a minute," he said, then wandered off among the headstones.

Worry instinctively spiked, but then Atlas remembered who the human here was and who the souls in their presence were more likely to protect. With Paris safe, he turned his attention back to the grave in front of him. "I'm sorry," he told her, then tapping that well Paris had somehow filled with just enough of what he needed, added, "I forgive you."

He shifted onto his knees and dug his fingers into the dirt, pouring all his magic into it, all of his real self that only a few people sensed beneath the stench of decay. He propelled blades of grass up through the dirt, growing high and fast enough to match the strips of green on either side of the grave, hiding it within seconds. Her father, their family would simply think Daphne had gone off on another of her "work assignments." Atlas would have Mary forge an email to sell the story. And by the time the truth came out, Atlas would be gone too. "I'll see you soon, cuz."

FOURTEEN

Atlas leaned against the bars of the library cage in the cellar of Mac and Paris's Monte Corvo villa. "I like it better on this side." Two months ago, he'd been on the other side of the bars, pretending to be held captive while trying to convince Mary's forces to stay out of his way. No such luck, seeing as he was right back here. And without a bottle in his hand this time. "Miss the wine, though."

Jenn growled from where she sat at the retired tasting table in the middle of the room.

Robin strolled around the end of the table to the empty chair beside her, resting his forearms on top of it. "He's baiting you."

She twisted in her chair, glaring up at him. "Why aren't you taking it?"

He straightened off the chair back, and for a moment, Atlas thought he was going to claim it, but he just shrugged and continued walking the length of the table, past the end of it, and to a barrel in the far corner. He hitched himself onto it and leaned his torso back against the wall, flannel-clad arms crossed over his chest.

The rest of the team made their way down the stairs and into the room, filling up all the seats except the one beside Jenn, and if

Atlas figured right, that last one was for Abigail, not Robin. His friends hadn't fully forgiven him either, especially not Mac, whose wary violet gaze bounced between them.

Abigail was the last person to enter the room.

"How's Simon?" Paris asked from his seat at Mac's side.

"Understandably upset," Abigail said, as she claimed the open chair. "But Pati and Pax are helping."

Atlas swung his gaze to Mary at the head of the table. "You shouldn't all be under one roof."

"We have less than two weeks to Solstice," she answered. "We have no time to waste. Jason and Kai have them. Put up more shields if you think it's necessary."

He pushed off the bars and slowly circled the room, testing the shields that were in place and reinforcing any weak spots, all while listening to the debrief going on at the table, Adam taking lead.

"These are the three main players on the board." He opened a folder and withdrew three photos, spreading them out on the table, one by one. "Evan Shaw, Atlas's twin brother and Chaos's right hand. Dyami, the pretender eagle, Chumash elder for the tribe in Nipomo. And the hunter."

"We know who the first two are," Robin said from his perch. "Who's the hunter?"

"A human," Adam answered.

"Erased," added Icarus, who'd been holed up excavating with his sister all evening.

"He sounds closer to the three of us," Atlas said, gesturing at himself, Mary, and Icarus, indicating the subtle shift in vocal tone that set folks from the South apart from their Northern neighbors. "From what I've gathered, he lost someone about the time of the Rift, maybe multiple someones, and he's been on the warpath ever since, targeting the magical and supernatural."

"So he's a religious zealot?" Icarus said, as he cinched his reclaimed robe around himself.

Atlas shook his head. "He blew up a church harboring paranormals. I barely got everyone out of there. Even my zealot father wouldn't go that far."

"So he wants what?" Mac asked.

"A normal life." Atlas flitted a hand in the air. "Free of all this."

"And he what?" Jenn scoffed. "Thinks if he kills her—"

"And Chaos."

"That magic will disappear, and the world will be one where his loved ones would've lived?"

"They'll still be dead," Abigail said.

"And besides," Mac picked up, "that's not how it works. There are no humans either without Nature."

"And no Nature without Chaos," Atlas finished.

"It's a balancing act," Robin said. He'd been so uncharacteristically quiet that Atlas had almost forgotten he was there, same as everyone else at the table who whipped their gazes his direction. "It always has been."

Paris was the first to twist back around in his chair toward Mary. "But you've been trying to destroy Chaos?"

"Is that what she's been doing?" Atlas challenged, and the pixie tellingly kept her lips sealed.

Everyone around that table thought he was the master manipulator, and they weren't wrong, but Nature was in a class by herself. She was also right, however; there were too few days until Solstice to get into how inconsequential they all were when the poles of their existence went to war. If he was going to balance their shit so they didn't all die, he needed the table full of people —distractions—occupied and out of his way.

He finished casting his last spell, then slid into the space between Mac and Paris, because yes, he was an asshole. And because Adam, the most strategic of the soldiers around the table, was directly across from them. He pushed the picture of the hunter back toward him. "You take the hunter. He'll be making his way north. I'll give Icarus and Mary everything I know on him. Excavate and track until you find him." He grabbed the picture of Dyami next and pulled it in front of Mac. "You're on Dyami. Use your connections with the tribes and your badge. He's power hungry. He's made other mistakes. I'll turn over what my excavator found. Investigate the licenses at the casinos and bring him down."

Robin hopped off the barrel, his heavy boots *thunk*ing as they hit the floor. "And you'll go after Evan?"

He rotated to face the coyote stalking his direction. "He thinks I'm wavering."

Robin stopped directly in front of him, his golden eyes hard and assessing. "Are you?"

"It's a balancing act," Atlas said. "Every day."

"And if you catch him, will you kill him or use him to bring Chaos through the veil?"

"What if we can do both?" Atlas realized his slip the minute it crossed his lips.

Robin didn't miss the *we* either, his stern face cracking into a victorious smirk. "She promised me revenge."

"You'll get it." Of that, Atlas was certain. Whether any of them survived was a whole other question.

FIFTEEN

Robin did him the courtesy of making noise as he approached for a change, scuffing his booted feet along the sandy path that led from the villa, along the edge of the reflecting pool, to the vista overlook where Atlas stood casting spells to shore up the property's perimeter. "Are the suits gone for good?"

"If I can help it," Atlas replied. On the way to Talahalusi, he and Paris had made a pit stop by the compound of Sunset Hill penthouse condos that now belonged to Paris. Atlas had needed to resupply on essentials, including his kilts. He hadn't brought any suits with him.

"And all is right with the world," Robin lilted, the put-on tone full of sarcasm, as he flopped onto one of the chaises under the overlook's pergola.

All was certainly not right with the world, but Atlas did feel a measure more like himself out of the suits. Reflected in his magic too, the orbs he was lobbing over the vineyards as green as the grape leaves would turn come spring, assuming they won the battle ahead.

Robin stretched his big body out on the chaise, hands pillowed behind his head, eyes closed, leaving Atlas to finish his work, his heartbeat slowing and breaths evening out such that Atlas thought he'd fallen asleep, but as soon as he lowered his arms, the inquisition he'd expected began.

"What does Mary really want?" the coyote asked.

Not the question he expected, but not a surprise either. As far as Robin knew, he was a bystander to this war, a victim who'd lost a loved one, who was trying to save his other friends and family from meeting the same fate. Who was after something far simpler —revenge. Perhaps he was starting to realize his goals and those of the person pulling the strings might not align as he'd understood.

Possibly not as Atlas understood either. "You're the one who's traveled with her the past month."

"You're the one who's been in the shit the past however many years," Robin replied, as Atlas lowered onto the chaise across from him. "How long's it actually been?"

"I can't even remember at this point."

"Were you always on Nature's side?"

He stared up through the pergola's slats at the night sky that was just beginning to lighten, from black to bruised, like he'd been when he'd lost his way. "No."

He expected Robin to want to know all about it, to prove which side he was on now, but the shifter surprised him again, skipping over both those questions to a more painful one. "What brought you back?"

"Who," he corrected, voice a cracked whisper, the truth dismally ironic after the events of yesterday. He rubbed at the center of his chest, trying and failing to make the ache go away. "Daphne."

"I'm sorry you lost her."

The surprising sincerity prompted the same from Atlas. "I'm sorry you lost your sister."

The silence that lingered was a heavy blanket of commiseration, comfortable in its familiarity, awkward to be trapped in it with Robin of all people. While fate had put them on the same side time and again—hell, from the beginning—they'd rarely put themselves there.

"This is weird," Robin said, as if reading his thoughts.

Atlas chuckled. "Don't worry, I still don't like you."

"I don't like you either."

"And no one here likes either of us," Atlas said, recalling the debrief from earlier, Robin relegated to a corner while Atlas tiptoed around folks who wanted to kill him on the regular.

Robin smirked at the sky. "Noticed that, huh?"

"If they're dumb enough to think she didn't decide who went where, then I shouldn't have given them those assignments."

He didn't argue the point. "Mac may never forgive me."

"Even though Paris has?"

"Not good enough. And Adam, well . . ." He raked a hand over his face, but not before Atlas glimpsed the tightening around the corners of his eyes and mouth. "I should have been there that day."

Atlas didn't have to ask what day. He idly wondered what Robin would do if he ever learned the full truth about the day his sister died.

"You didn't answer my question," Robin said, drawing him back to the present. "What's Mary after? What's the endgame this go-round?"

"I don't know," Atlas lied, then told a partial truth. "Pax is ultimately the answer, but he's too young to do anything about it right now."

Robin wasn't letting him get away with it, shifting on the chaise so he was upright and angled toward him, forearms braced on his knees. "So what do *you* plan to do about it?"

"Make sure Chaos stays trapped on the other side of the veil until Pax is ready." Or trapped somewhere on this side, which was a far more excruciating, far more likely outcome.

"We have to stop Evan."

"One way or another, you'll get your revenge." Either option depended on his last brother being dead by Solstice. What happened after that death, which direction his soul traveled, depended on what side Evan chose when he met his end.

Robin rose from the chaise. "Thank you."

"You're welcome."

"Not for that." He stepped closer, looming over Atlas, stirring memories of what they'd done in the shadows yesterday afternoon. Robin's mind was back then too, only slightly earlier. "For shielding me."

Atlas nodded.

"Why did you?"

The well of things he couldn't name bubbled up again, battling to roll off his tongue. Respect. Commiseration. Desire. Fate. "Because I need a hunter," he said. Also true. "And I hear you're the best."

"At least we can agree on that." He threw a smirk over his shoulder as he turned to leave, and for a brief moment, all did seem right with the world.

SIXTEEN

Three days later, Atlas was ready to murder Robin.

Or fuck him again.

It was a balancing act he was going to lose either way.

And the coyote knew it. What was it he'd said that night at the safe house? He could either drive himself crazy or drive Atlas crazy.

Well, mission fucking accomplished.

Just missing Evan outside of Nipomo, watching him disappear into the crowd at Holy Cross Pier, losing him again after a chase through Portola University, realizing the tip that had led them to Encinal was a wash was all very frustrating.

But not nearly as frustrating as being trapped in motel rooms with a still allergic-to-shirts Robin who regularly walked around with his jeans unbuttoned, no briefs or boxers on underneath. Who prowled around without making a sound, and, like Atlas, somehow disguised his scent. Who showed up the past two mornings with a perfect cup of coffee, like he'd conjured it out of thin air.

He was infuriating, he was maddening, he was everything Atlas wanted and could never fucking keep. And knowing what he sounded like when he came, how rough his voice had been when he'd vowed not to let Atlas hide, what his cock felt like trapped against his, how that big body could cover his made it damn near impossible not to let the madness drive him right back into Robin's arms.

He needed to get out of there before he did something he'd regret, something that would alter the course of the conflict and result in one or both of them dead.

Finishing that morning's perfect cup of joe, he pitched the cup in the tiny trashcan by the scuffed and scratched motel room dresser and headed for the door.

"Where are you going?" Robin asked from his casually lounged position on the bed farthest from the door.

"Out," Atlas said without another tempting look back. "Away from the smell of dog." Robin wasn't reining any of it in today, not his smell, not his heartbeat that too often clocked to his own, and definitely not his throaty chuckle that Atlas slammed the door on.

Outside, he leaned back against the cement wall and inhaled deep, struggling to center himself. *"Whose idea was this?"* he mentally asked his mother. *"Yours or hers?"*

"We decided together."

He rolled his eyes. *"Of course you did."*

"You could let him in."

"I could get him killed. Like his sister."

No reply. She never had an answer for that one.

He inhaled once more, letting the cold air and salty scent of the angry Bay tamp down the boiling frustration. A winter storm had moved through last night, bringing rain, wind, and colder temps, leaving the parking lot full of puddles.

Solstice was growing near; they were running out of time.

Refocused on his mission, he pulled out his phone to start following up with the sources he'd pinged last night after realizing Encinal was a bust. Before he dialed the first source, though, a text appeared onscreen from a North Bay number he didn't recognize. No name, no message, just an address that Atlas mapped to The Corners, a crossroads town further inland, over the ridge and at the foot of Tuyshtak. Miwok land.

Another text came through. **For Pati. —L.**

Lucy.

How had she gotten his number? What had she overheard? Questions continued to cascade, his mind racing, and he turned back for the motel room door.

And stopped short.

Did Lucy know who he really was? Or did she think he was someone else? A suited someone else? If he needed to be Evan, he couldn't go in wherever Lucy was sending him with Robin. Or wearing his kilt. They'd lose the advantage of surprise and deception.

But could he afford not to take Robin? Simon would probably be dead if not for Robin; maybe even Atlas. What if Lucy was being held hostage? What if someone had taken her phone and used it to set him up? To send him into a trap?

He needed to thread the needle, to account for both possibilities. Which meant he needed a suit and a head start, and then he'd call in backup.

SEVENTEEN

In the shadow of Tuyshtak, The Corners was a small crossroads village inhabited mostly by the indigenous Miwok. Atlas had rarely strayed this far east. Vincent's criminal doings had been largely confined to YB and Talahalusi. The one time he'd ventured east, to try and steal power from a coven in hiding, it had ultimately led to his death.

Aiming to avoid a similar fate, Atlas withdrew his phone from the pocket of the suit he'd stolen out of another guest's motel room and texted Robin the address of the single-family home he found himself standing in front of. Not the industrial warehouse, saloon, or other commercial building he'd expected. Atlas pushed gently at the aura surrounding the ranch-style home and the generous lot it stood on; no magic that he could detect. He walked up the path to the front door as casually as possible while glancing through the plate glass windows on either side of the front porch. No sign of Lucy, no sign of anyone home, as far as he could tell. No answer to his knock either. Thankful for the cover from the juniper and laurel trees that surrounded the house, he slipped around the side, checking for open doors and windows, peeking through them for any movement or motion detectors in the usual places. Seeing none, he ported himself inside.

And breathed a sigh of relief at not sensing any magic inside either. Ears and eyes open, he slowly worked his way through the home. The house was older but well kept, everything neat, no clutter, no pictures, no personal items whatsoever, the drawers and closets empty. He wouldn't have been surprised to see a For Sale sign in the front yard. It certainly didn't look like Lucy or anyone had been here in some time. Didn't feel or smell like it either, the air stale and cool, no heat on since the temps had begun to drop.

Why had Lucy—or someone—sent him this address? Who did this house belong to? What did it have to do with Pati Miwra? He shot off a text to his excavator as he made his way back to the kitchen, then exited out the back door, only the detached garage left to check.

He approached with caution, the structure behind the house similar in style but not in condition. The windows were papered over, the gutters were full of leaves, and cracks snaked through the structure's exposed foundation. He tried to lift the debris-covered roll-up door. Locked. He circled around to the side and found the single step to the side door broken. The lock on the door, however, was not. Modern and high-tech, its keypad glowed red. He wasn't getting past that in fast fashion, which meant he'd have to port inside blind. Always a risk. He circled the structure, looking and listening for any signs of life. Still nothing, and the state of the place lent itself to the same conclusion. Likely the house was for sale and the owners had shoved all their belongings in the garage, which would be torn down when sold. He contemplated waiting for Robin. The coyote would probably know how to get past the lock, and if there was someone inside, he'd have backup. But it was a small building, one car at most; there couldn't be that many people in there. Atlas could handle them, or at least hold them off long enough for Robin to reach him.

He lifted a hand and snapped.

Into darkness.

Remaining in one place, he extended his senses, listening and smelling, then tentatively poking for any other magic in the space. Finding none, he spun up his own globe as potential defense and to light his surroundings.

The interior of the space was far more akin to the door lock than the structure's exterior. A high-tech monitoring setup like the command room that had been in Vincent's compound lined one wall, a weapons cache the one perpendicular to it, and Atlas assumed the jut out in the far corner was a bathroom given the bed on the other side. The final wall, though, was the one that drew his attention, that called him closer as he tried to make sense of what he was seeing.

An entire wall covered in pictures—of the Shaw family.

Some were the same posed-type shots that Atlas had grown up seeing around the house, including the one of his brothers currently in his pocket. But more were the sort that had been taken at a distance, by someone watching. There were family shots, solo snaps, pictures of each of them at work. Atlas struggled to take it all in, heart pounding, chest tightening, as his gaze bounced from Evan in various states of evil, including standing next to the giant Atlas had killed in LP, to his own arc in photos, from good to evil to seemingly evil, to Cole sneaking into Vincent's compound, what would ultimately prove a life-altering turn of events, to Canton with an arm around a green-haired Mary, the two of them trailing a blue-haired Icarus somewhere, and then a different shot, with Mary standing in between Canton and a snarling Icarus, his fangs extended. Before he could wonder long on when exactly that photo was taken, what exactly had transpired before and after that snapshot in time, his gaze strayed to the last collection of photos, the biggest.

Of his father.

At home, in town, at church, at Cole's funeral two weeks ago.

What the fuck was this? Whose was this? Holding his globe aloft, he made another slow sweep of the space, his gaze passing then speeding back to a familiar sight on the weapons wall.

A crossbow he'd seen a week ago in La Purisima—on the hunter's shoulder.

Was that who this place belonged to? Was the hunter not after magical beings in general, but the Shaws in particular? Was his father the ultimate target?

He needed to have a much longer conversation with his excavator, and he needed another set of eyes on this. With Nature and Chaos on the brink of full-out war, a third-party variable like this was the last thing Atlas needed.

Lifting his phone, he switched the camera to video, held his globe close to the wall, and made a slow survey of the photo collage first, then standing back in the center of the room, made a slow circle to capture it all.

Finished, he clicked back to the text he'd sent Robin earlier and sent another: **ETA?** When it remained on Delivered, not switching to Read, he figured Robin was on paw. He moved to extinguish his globe and snap back outside, but stopped himself short, one photo in particular calling him back. He snatched it off the wall, pocketed it with the others, then, putting out his globe, ported himself back onto the lawn.

And into the enemy's hands.

EIGHTEEN

They were waiting for him on the lawn. Three henchmen this time, a bobcat shifter who was new to Atlas and two humans he recognized from Dyami's casino. They'd been dressed as dealers that day, but their bulging biceps and thighs had given them away as more than croupiers.

The bobcat sprang first, slamming into Atlas and taking him down face-first, his chest to the ground, the cat on his back. The relatively smaller of the other two men bagged his head and the big one tied his hands. They didn't, however, separate his fingers, and as the trio marched him around the garage toward the driveway, Atlas contemplated snapping himself free.

He stopped himself short again. This was an opportunity to learn more about Dyami's role in all this. Were they taking him to the pretender? Would he finally get a meet? Could he convince Dyami that he wanted to take Daphne's place? Were they holding Lucy hostage? Was Dyami working with the hunter?

His mind was swimming with questions, with possibilities and tactics, while the rest of him was drowning with fear. If he ported himself away, only for Robin to show up moments later, how would the coyote fare in a three-on-one battle? Atlas had no reason to think Robin couldn't hold his own, but could Atlas take that risk? He didn't have to think twice about that answer. Yet even as he committed to the action, allowing Dyami's goons to shove him into the back of what felt and sounded like a utility van, he worried about the fallout. What would Robin think when he found him gone? What the fuck would he do?

"Get in there," one of the humans said, shoving him to the van floor and using his foot to kick him to one side. Atlas shimmied away from the boot, across the grooved metal floor until his back hit shelving, the smell of paint and chemicals stinging his nose.

His nose.

Scent.

Fuck.

He'd spent a lifetime avoiding this, running from it, but what choice did he have in the current situation? Absolutely none. His best hope was that a little would be enough for Robin to lock onto but not enough to give fate the win. Not yet.

He flicked his fingers, casting a tendril of his scent, the real one, along the metal floor and out the drainage grooves beneath the van's back doors.

"This is the guy, right?" said the human who'd shoved him earlier. To make room on a bench seat by the sound of it. "The one Dyami put a bounty out on?"

"Yeah," said the other human from farther away, near where the driver should be. "That's him. Call the eagle and let him know."

A stretch of silence followed during which Atlas idly wondered how much the price on his head was up to—and did Robin know?—before the goon closest to him spoke again. "We got him," he said to Dyami, Atlas assumed. "He was at Cyrus's place. Right where Lucy sent him."

Cyrus. A name to go with the nightmare.

"You're going to let her go, right?" said a new voice from beside the first one. "She did what you asked. I'll keep her in line now, I swear."

The new husband, then—and the shifter, back in human form.

He sounded distressed, the promise one of appeasement, but Atlas would have to be convinced that—

A loud crash sounded against the van roof, and the vehicle teetered onto two wheels, sending paint cans flying off the racks and Atlas sliding into a pair of shins. He tucked his head, protecting himself from kicks or cans, just in time as the driver overcorrected, the van teetering the opposite direction, jostling the other two men in the back.

A knee landed in his back, another in his shoulder, and then fuck if one of the assholes didn't use his calf to leverage himself up.

"What the hell, Duncan?" shouted the human. "Sit this van down!"

"What's going on?" echoed the husband.

Duncan, the driver apparently, got the van back on four wheels, skidding to a stop, but before he could answer either question, a familiar roar Atlas shook the van's walls.

"It's that fucking coyote," Duncan hollered. "The bounty hunter one."

"You need to shift again," said the other human to Lucy's husband. "We need this money."

"Not unless you guarantee Lucy's safety," he bargained. "And I get half the payout." Shrewd, Atlas conceded, but maybe not the time to push his luck.

"Yes, fuck, fine!" Duncan agreed. "Just shift and get rid of the fucking dog."

Magic sizzled inside the van, bones cracked, and a moment later, the bobcat growled. The back doors flew open, claws scraped across metal, and the cat barely got out a fighting hiss before it howled in unmistakable pain.

"Fuck, Duncan!" the other human yelled. "Just leave him!"

Atlas flicked his fingers, the hood and bindings disappearing, and he hurled an orb forward, jamming the gear shift back into park before it broke out the front windshield. Robin leapt through the opening the next instant, jaws open wide for Duncan's neck.

Blood splattered across the front seats, and the other man standing astride Atlas tripped over himself and Atlas in his haste to flee the opposite direction, practically falling out the van's back door.

Atlas sent an orb slamming into his back, making sure he'd never get up again.

A bark behind him was all the warning Atlas got before Robin went rushing past him, hurtling out the open doors toward the bobcat who was trying to stagger up. Robin landed on all fours above him, batting him back down and letting out another thunderous roar, his intention clear.

"Robin, wait!" Atlas shouted, as he jumped down from the van and sprinted after him. "They're holding his wife hostage."

Under Robin, the bobcat rolled onto his back and presented his belly, and in the space of a breath, Robin shifted back into human form. He didn't release the cat, though, continuing to hold him down by the neck. Atlas had never heard his voice so menacing as when he leaned down and whispered in Lucy's husband's ear, "Tell whomever you're working for, whomever needs to hear it, that he's mine."

Heat raced down Atlas's spine and fast on its heels was dread, chilling him to his core. So much for only a little.

Robin stalked past him without so much as a look or a word, and Atlas, figuring he needed a minute to cool off, kneeled beside Lucy's husband instead. He spoke as gently as the war of emotions climbing up his throat would allow. "Get Lucy and take her back to her people. Stay there. Do you understand?"

The cat nodded with a whimper.

Straightening, Atlas followed Robin's scent around to the front of the van.

Naked in the midday sun was not a bad look on him. Atlas opened his mouth to make a snide comment to the contrary, or snipe about Robin being late, anything to build up the wall of hate he was desperately clinging to, but Robin beat him to it, hand raised and eyes burning gold. "Not a fucking word." He grabbed hold of Atlas's arm. "You know the distillery tasting room in YB we use as a base?"

Of course he did. He nodded, not saying a word, keeping to the volatile shifter's directive.

Robin tightened his grip, hard enough to bruise. "Take us there. Now."

NINETEEN

Atlas stood in the alley behind the seemingly shuttered tasting room, admiring Robin's bare ass, his firm round cheeks dusted with fine blond hairs that were afire with the midday sun. Atlas looked his fill while Robin unlocked the door, gawking far easier than dealing with what had just happened, what Robin had just said to Lucy's husband.

Mine.

Robin's muscles bunched as he pushed open the metal door and stepped inside. Then let the heavy thing swing right back in Atlas's face. "Hey!" Atlas protested, using both hands to stop the steel weight. Barely.

"Watch the door," Robin called back. "It's heavy."

"No fucking shit." Heaving the door open enough to slip inside, he cringed as the metal scraped across the floor again on its way to closed. Keeping their presence quiet from anyone in the building's other units would be impossible, though from the outside, those other units had looked as deserted as this one. When he turned around, Robin was gone, but his steps and heartbeats echoed from the front of the boarded-up shop. Orb lighting his way, Atlas followed the sounds, distracting himself by peeking into rooms—an office, a bathroom—and taking stock of the crates

—weapons, first aid supplies, electronics—and barrels—whiskey, as far as he could smell—that crowded the narrow hall. Before he reached the end, he nearly collided with Robin who, with jeans and a flannel in hand, careened around the corner without so much as an *excuse me.*

"Since when are you not just gonna prance around naked?" Atlas called after his fleeing backside.

And got no reply, Robin ducking into the bathroom and slamming the door shut behind him. When running water started a moment later, Atlas let the angry coyote be and ambled into the main tasting room instead. There was enough light sneaking in around the edges of the boarded-up windows that he didn't need his magic to get a good look at the place. There was a bar off to the right, nothing on the backbar shelves, only a smattering of bottles and glasses on the bar itself. Several square tables were pushed together along another wall, a tangle of cords beneath them, a tech setup for whomever needed it. There were several other chairs around the room, another table he tossed his suit jacket onto, and on the far wall, in the shadows, a chaise. On the floor beside it, denim and flannel spilled out of an open duffel.

Had Robin been staying here at some point? Was this a pit stop on the way to Monte Corvo so he could pick up his things?

Atlas was tempted to go poking through the bag, but as the bathroom toilet flushed, he abandoned that one-way ticket to an even angrier coyote and diverted to the bar instead. Turning over two clean glasses, he filled them with the vodka he found in the underbar fridge and held out a glass to Robin when he returned.

"Why didn't we just go to Monte Corvo?" he asked. A direct question he wanted the answer to and an indirect one to extract a possible explanation for his other observations.

Robin threw back the shot, slammed the glass on the bar, then stepped closer, trapping Atlas between the bar and the barstool behind him. "We didn't go to the mountain yet because I haven't decided whether I need to kill you and dump your body in the Canyon Lands."

Atlas raised a hand, but Robin beat him to the snap, threading his thick fingers between his and pining his hand to the bar. Atlas dropped the glass in his other one, but Robin didn't take the shattering bait. Grabbing that hand too, he twisted it up between them, fingers shoved between his, and splaying their joined hands over his chest. "Eh, eh, eh," Robin chided. "See, I can't decide if you're more dangerous to the cause or the whole fucking key to it, and that's the fucking rub."

He'd known Robin was pissed after The Corners. He'd torn that van apart, torn Duncan apart, and would have done the same to Lucy's husband if Atlas hadn't stopped him. Maybe he shouldn't have, given where the convo had gone.

Mine.

Atlas had one distraction left. He rolled his hips, his own cock half hard from the proximity, Robin's semi likewise poking Atlas's hip. "Is that the only rub?"

"We're not doing that right now," Robin gritted out.

"Oh, so now this is only on your terms?"

"Be fucking serious." Robin squeezed his fingers. "Why did you leave?" The danger and desperation in his tone warranted an answer.

Atlas gave him the bare minimum. "I got a tip."

"But you didn't tell me?"

"I sent you a text!"

"After you left! We"—he moved their clasped hands between them, Atlas's knuckles first tapping his chest, then Robin's tapping Atlas's—"are a team."

Atlas straightened his back and lifted his chin, pushing back at the glaring coyote. "I already told you, I don't do *we.*"

"Then why'd you text at all?"

"In case they were holding Lucy hostage, like they did Simon, and I needed backup."

Robin erased the last inch of space between them. "Is that the only reason?"

The answer to that question was too complicated and too

simple all at once . . . *Mine*. Atlas pressed his lips together to keep the truth from spilling out.

Robin growled. "You need to fucking convince me not to kill you right now."

Again, the bare minimum. "I know Evan better than any of you."

"And yet you haven't stopped him in how many years?"

"He knows me better than anyone too."

It didn't have to be that way; the man holding him pinned could change that, if Atlas let him.

If Robin even wanted that, and at the present juncture, he seemed far keener on violence, on the revenge he'd been seeking all these years. "You and your brothers are playing a game, using my friends and family—*innocents*—as pieces, and we keep getting killed."

"And *she* doesn't do the same thing?"

"*She* isn't my concern right now. You are the one who went off alone. To the meet in LP and to the one this morning." He clenched his fingers around his. "And fucking hell, Atlas, I think you get it." Desperation overtook the danger in his tone and words. "You understand that neither of them, Nature or Chaos, are the endgame, that it's a balancing act, and if you fucking die, this whole thing falls apart."

The same was true for him, whether he realized it yet or not.

Mine.

Robin dipped his chin and nuzzled behind Atlas's ear. "You let me smell you." A growled purr laced with agony sent a full body shiver rippling through Atlas. "You cannot risk yourself anymore."

"Why?" he asked on a stuttered breath, wanting to hear that word again in Robin's broken timbre, wanting it to drown out the cackle of fate in his head.

Releasing the hand pinning his to the bar, Robin grasped his face and held them nose to nose, his golden gaze boring into Atlas's. "Because you're mine."

He may have been angry, but Robin still wanted, as much as Atlas. Maybe more. Heat raced down Atlas's spine, from the tips of Robin's fingers digging into his cheek to his stiff cock wedged between them.

Fuck it.

Atlas had sealed their fate the second he'd cast his scent into the wind for Robin to track. To lock onto. He could keep fighting this, keep trying to balance it all himself, keep putting them both in jeopardy by keeping Robin on the outside. Or he could let Robin in and protect him from the inside.

They could both get what they wanted, fools diving headfirst into foolishness.

With his free hand, he covered Robin's on his face and increased the pressure of his hold, just on the edge of painful, just the way Atlas liked it. "Are you going to keep barking at me, or are you going to fucking kiss me like you've always wanted? Like we were always meant to."

Robin's answering growl shook the walls.

His kiss shook Atlas to his core.

TWENTY

Chapped lips, rough stubble, a demanding tongue that forced open Atlas's mouth.

Taking, claiming, devouring.

Using the grip on his face to adjust the angle then diving in for more.

Atlas groaned, caught between turned on and frustrated, melting and fighting. As was usually the case with Robin, the latter won, Atlas taking over the kiss by sucking Robin's tongue deeper into his mouth and pulling him impossibly closer, forcing that big body to stretch the length of his as he leaned back over the arm of the barstool.

They slid together—tongues, bodies, desire.

Short-circuiting reason and filling empty caverns Atlas hadn't realized existed.

When Robin withdrew his tongue for a gulp of air, Atlas let him have two before grabbing the front of his shirt and exerting more control, yanking him back close and taking his turn in Robin's mouth, tongue sweeping through. He tasted wild and hungry, as irresistible as Atlas had always feared. The sadness—the guilt—underpinning it all dreadfully familiar. Atlas wanted to erase it as much for Robin as for himself.

Fuck, this was a terrible idea, and yet Atlas had zero will to stop it, no idea how to even do that. He went back for more, over and over; the first real kiss he'd had in ages—not a show, not an act, not a hold your nose until it's over farce—was making his head spin, his insides tangle, and his cock ache.

He rolled his hips, chasing friction, and when Robin rolled his back, cocks rutting together, Atlas tore his mouth away and panted, just shy of a whine. "Robin, I need . . ." The rest of his words died on a groan, Robin clasping one of his ass cheeks and jerking him higher, a thigh between his legs for Atlas to grind down on, giving him what he needed. He let his head fall back, eyes slipping closed as he rutted. Harder as Robin licked a stripe up his throat. "Fuck yes."

Atlas threaded his fingers through Robin's rusty blond locks, and damn if they weren't softer than they looked. He palmed Robin's scalp, holding his face against his neck as he rode his leg, regretting his pants more with each thrust.

"Last time I'm going to say this," Robin rumbled against his neck, the movement of his rough lips on skin giving Atlas goose bumps and all sorts of mental images. "No more suits."

"But what if I need—"

He shoved back against Atlas's hand, righting his head and looking him dead in the eye. "Wouldn't you rather be humping my leg bare right now?"

Atlas pressed his lips together rather than tell the asshole he'd read his mind.

Robin smirked. "You can't give me anything, can you?"

"I'm about to give you my hole."

And smirk gone, replaced by pure fire in his golden eyes. The suit was practically gone a second later, Robin ripping the shirt down the middle, sending buttons flying, before he likewise ripped the pants from the waist to the middle of one leg. "This isn't even a good one," he snarled.

"I stole it from the motel room two over," Atlas said, as he ditched the remains of the shirt. "I had to make do."

Robin splayed a hand on his chest, fingers drifting across his pecs, from one nipple to the other, making Atlas quake in his arms. "The next time I fuck you—"

"Getting ahead of yourself—"

Robin's leg disappeared, Atlas lost his words in the drop back to his heels, then lost his breath when Robin spun him toward the barstool and, hand in the middle of the back, forced him to bend over the seat. "The next time I fuck you," he repeated, "I want to flip up your kilt"—he ripped the pants the rest of the way off— "suck your cock"—the sucking sound he made around what Atlas glanced over his shoulder to see were two fingers shoved in his sinful mouth—"then fill this hole"—which he then shoved into his hole, Atlas gasping with pleasure and pain—"with your own come before I fill it with mine." Atlas melted over the barstool. "And when I'm done, I'm going to tongue fuck you until you come again."

And melted some more, his mind supplying the pictures to go with Robin's words, his knees weak at the thought alone, his rock-hard cock leaking precome down the inside of his leg.

"Now, are you gonna wear a suit again?"

Atlas shook his head, words too hard to come by.

"And you better be bare under that kilt for me."

"If I mean to have sex." The reply came reflexively, as did the gasp when Robin added another finger, stuffing him full.

"You gonna turn this down?" He pumped inside him, and Atlas keened, so close to the edge, pushing back on Robin's fingers for more. But it wasn't enough, wasn't what he needed to fill all the empty caverns.

"Robin, I need . . ."

As if reading his thoughts again, Robin hauled him off the barstool and spun him around, holding him by the throat until he was steady on his feet. Only to coast his hand down, along the center line of his chest, over his abs, and along the trail of coarse hair that led to the thatch of dark blond curls around his cock. He curled his fingers around the base of Atlas's cock, then made a long, agonizing stroke down the length of him, fingers trailing off at the end, precome dripping from his fingertips. "Not helping," Atlas grumbled, knees weak again.

Robin chuckled. "Not much longer, I promise." He turned on his heel, shedding clothes as he made his way across the room. He was naked when he lowered himself onto the chaise, in that same fucking relaxed posture that had driven Atlas mad all week. Arm stretched across the chaise back, legs spread, his fat cock ready and waiting. "Come here," he rumbled, and not even fate's *I told you so* could have stopped Atlas from crossing that room, especially not when Robin spit in his hand and stroked himself, spreading moisture down his length, getting himself ready.

Atlas didn't hesitate to crawl onto his lap, knees on either side of his hips, fingers coasting through the dusting of red-gold hairs on his broad chest. He leaned forward to nip at the freckled skin that had so tempted and teased him, that was even warmer than he'd imagined. "That was mean."

Robin stopped him short, hand holding him by the face again, the pressure exactly right this time. "I'm not a nice person," he said. "Neither are you. We accept that about each other."

"So how mean are you going to be?"

"I'm not going to touch your pretty cock. You're going to sit on my dick and make yourself come." He tilted Atlas's face down, their lips brushing. "Use me."

Atlas grinned against his lips. "We may have to work on your definition of *mean*."

Robin's palm came down hard against his ass cheek. "Less talking, more riding."

His lips wanted to curl into a wider smile, but he busied his mouth with Robin's for another deep, sweeping taste before he reared back and rose on his knees. Hand around Robin's cock for position, he slowly slid down the length of him, inch by torturous inch, until he was fully seated, stuffed full of Robin.

The shifter leaned back his head, and his thunderous moan nearly made Atlas come on the spot. When he was sure the brush of the coarse hairs that bisected Robin's pelvis wouldn't make him explode, he tipped forward, arms outstretched, hands on either side of Robin's head and nibbled a path up his neck to his ear. "You ready?"

"Now, who's being mean?"

"I'll show you fucking mean." Curling his fingers around the top of the chaise for leverage, he rose to the tip end of Robin's cock, then rammed himself back onto it. Over and over, building them up, Robin's rough grunts in his ear as good as any sweet words, his fingers leaving bruises on his hip and shoulder as he slammed him down harder better than any soft touches, his growled "Mine" as they raced toward their climax almost enough to throw Atlas over the edge.

He reared up one last time and clasped Robin's face, forcing his golden gaze back to his. "It cuts both ways. You get that, right?"

Robin covered his hand, digging his fingers in harder, same as Atlas had done his earlier. "Yours."

Heat and something else exploded inside Atlas, and as he shoved back a final time, his orgasm erupting, Robin's doing the same inside him, he tipped back his head, let his eyes slip closed, and told a cackling fate to fuck right off.

TWENTY-ONE

Atlas kicked the shredded stolen suit aside as he returned from the bathroom. "You know, I have nothing to wear out of here now."

"You can borrow some jeans and a flannel," Robin said from where he stood by the bar.

Atlas made a retching sound, then promptly erased the horrific thought with the shot of vodka Robin offered him.

The coyote eyed him over the rim of his own glass, gaze heated even after round-Atlas-had-lost count. "Tie the flannel around your waist, like a kilt."

An admittedly less horrific idea, but the implications . . . "If I walk into Monte Corvo with your flannel around my hips, they'll know we fucked."

Robin shrugged, tossed back the rest of his vodka, then wound an arm around his middle. He pulled him closer, nose nuzzling behind his ear, semi nudging his hip, ramping up to go again. "Speaking of fucking . . ."

They'd get there—impossible not to with the both of them still naked—but Robin's comment had piqued Atlas's earlier curiosity again. "Have you been staying here?"

He promptly unplastered himself from Atlas's side and

poured another shot. "Between Icarus's shit and Paris's." He rotated to rest back against the bar, gaze toward the boarded-up windows as if he could somehow see outside. "We needed eyes on the city." Atlas didn't think that was all there was to it, given the tightness of his shoulders and the lines that deepened around the corners of his eyes. "And I like it better here."

"Aren't you supposed to love the wide-open range? Roaming the hills and valleys and shit?"

Robin chuckled, his shoulders loosening, and Atlas was glad for it. "It makes me antsy."

"Same," Atlas said, hiding his smile in his glass. "I loathed working for Vincent, but I enjoyed living in YB."

Robin cut him a side-eye and returned a version of his earlier question. "Aren't *you* supposed to love nature? You bought a vineyard, for fuck's sake."

His turn to laugh. "I do, when I just want to be. No mission, no to-do list, no crisis to avert. But when I need to work, I like the challenge of the city. What's more impressive than a weed fighting to grow through a crack in the concrete?"

"You mean Paris," the shifter astutely surmised. Atlas shrugged and finished his shot. "I feel the same," Robin continued. "Running comes naturally, but hunting here in the city, any city for that matter, takes more than speed and strength."

"Strategy."

"Exactly." Robin finished his drink, then angled again toward Atlas. "It's what we need to do if we're going to survive the next nine days."

He'd walked right into that one, tricky bastard. "I don't do—"

Robin's mouth stole the rest of his protest, drowned it with another of those toe-curling kisses that tangled his insides. "You lost the right to that excuse five fucks ago." Arm around his shoulders, Robin brought them front to front again and buried his nose in the divot behind his ear. "And when you let me smell the real you. Fuck, it's addictive."

He arched his neck, wanting more, Robin's rough lips and teasing touch ramping him up again too. "What do you smell?"

"Spring, in the dead of winter."

Atlas shivered for a different reason; Robin had him dead to rights.

"We have to stop running," Robin said as he withdrew his face from the crook of his neck. "We stop chasing you, you stop chasing Evan, and we work together to catch him and stop Chaos."

"Robin—"

The coyote lifted a hand to his face, palm cupping his cheek, the touch so gentle, so earnest, so unlike the rough touches of earlier, that Atlas nearly whimpered. He didn't know what to do with this Robin nor what to do with his own twisted insides. "Stop fucking running, Atlas. For the sake of all of us and for the sake of your soul."

"You can't run from yours either."

Robin shifted them so Atlas's back was against the bar, to argue more or bend him backward over it, Atlas guessed, but the shifter surprised him, making him gasp when he hoisted him onto the bar top and stood between his spread legs, hands splayed on his inner thighs. "What do you think I'm doing here?" he said, golden eyes smirking up at him. "Now, about that bet you've lost six times over. Make it seven." He didn't wait for a reply before he lowered his head and took Atlas's cock to the back of his throat, stealing Atlas's next breath and silencing any further arguments over *we*.

PART TWO

ROBIN

TWENTY-TWO

Mate was Robin's first thought when he woke.

Gone followed fast on its heels, Atlas absent from the bed they'd made on the tasting room floor.

Robin shot to his feet, pulse racing, senses on high alert. The early morning light was weak around the boarded windows, but he didn't need it, his eyesight more than capable in the dark. His sense of smell too, only a faint trace of Atlas on the air.

He grabbed his phone off the chaise, checking for texts.

Nothing.

He nearly hurled it across the room. That fucker had left.

Again.

After everything they'd said last night. After everything they'd done.

Robin wasn't one for sentiment, but he'd thought they'd reached an agreement—a truce, at the very least—where their common purpose was concerned. And an acknowledgment, acted on if not plainly spoken, as to what magic had made them to each other. What the two of them had finally given in to after months—years—of fighting it.

He sank onto the chaise, elbows propped on his knees and head held in his hands. Atlas Fucking Shaw, of all people. He'd sensed a connection the first time he'd been in the supposedly evil warlock's presence. Had written it off as instinct, his coyote recognizing a threat. And Atlas was. Just not in the way Robin had initially thought.

He'd never even considered that Atlas could be the mate his mother had told him about in her letters, the match he'd spent a lifetime running from, being tied to one person as antsy making as the hills and valleys where he'd grown up.

Hell, after Deb's death, he'd used Atlas as the boogeyman, the excuse for his long absences, his erratic behavior, his swings from angry to angrier. But pieces of the puzzle had shifted over the past two months, painting a different picture.

Atlas helping to save Adam and Icarus.

Atlas protecting Mary from Vincent.

Atlas slaying giants allied with Chaos.

Atlas practically raising Paris.

Evan—not Atlas—killing Deborah.

And when Robin had gotten a whiff of the real Atlas beneath the stench he wore like a mask, same as those fucking suits, the connection he'd always sensed, the instinct his coyote had misunderstood, came into focus. Sharpened to a vicious point yesterday when Atlas had cast a tendril of his scent into the wind for him to track.

Mate.

Gone.

Fuck.

He shot out a hand for his phone again, but before he fired off the *Where the fuck are you?* text, the lock on the back door disengaged.

He told the magic inside him to quiet, to disguise his presence from any foe who might enter. Only friendlies should know the code, but he knew enough hackers to accept that an electronic lock wasn't one hundred percent secure. He slid off the chaise into a crouch, prepared to shift if a foe walked through the door, but then coffee and spring tickled his nose and the *who* was no longer a question.

Whether to shift, however . . . Robin was tempted to let the coyote out just so he could roar in Atlas's face for fucking leaving. He was tempted to do something else entirely, though, when the infuriating fucker appeared at the opening to the tasting room, two coffees in hand, with Robin's favorite flannel tied around his waist.

Robin growled as he straightened, no part of it anger, all of it hunger for the sexy blond—his mate—wearing his clothes.

Atlas strolled casually across the room, seemingly oblivious to the fact he'd caused Robin a coronary one second and a boner the next, to the fact his high and tight ass wrapped in plaid was Robin's new favorite target. He set one cup down on the table and sipped from the other, the heat from the drink giving his pale cheeks a lovely blush. "Did you run back here the past two mornings to get us coffee?"

Busted. "How'd you find the place?"

"Followed my nose."

Robin's nose was leading him straight to Atlas's side. He tugged at the knotted sleeves holding the flannel around Atlas's hips. "This works. I like my idea."

"I can tell," Atlas said with a flick of his gaze to where Robin's erection was poking his hip. "But we don't have time for that."

Robin begged to differ. He slipped a hand beneath the flannel to fondle Atlas's gloriously bare balls. Turned out the warlock obeyed some orders. "Do you remember—"

"Yes, I fucking remember," he snapped in that haughty tone that pissed Robin the hell off ninety-nine percent of the time. But that other one percent, when Robin had his hands on him, it turned him the fuck on. "I would love nothing more than to bend over this table and let you shove that fat cock inside me again, but we have to go."

Robin huffed and withdrew his hand.

"Don't pout," Atlas said. "It's unattractive." The smile turning up the corners of his lips said otherwise.

"Liar."

Atlas didn't argue, dodging instead as he strolled with his cup to the chaise and toed the duffel on the floor there. "Get dressed."

He'd rather drink is coffee first. "Where are we going?" he asked between sips of his favorite brew from the only shop left in the Lost Valley.

"Talahalusi. I already called her. She's bringing everyone in."

Whatever Atlas wanted to discuss with the team had to be serious, if he was the one who'd reached out. Maybe what had happened between them last night, what Robin had said about running, had sunk in—for both of them. Robin drained his coffee and tossed the empty cup behind the bar. "What's going on?"

"I know how to find my brother."

"How's that?"

"After that stunt of yours at The Corners yesterday, he knows I'm yours." Tossing his own empty the same direction as Robin's, Atlas closed the distance between them, their breaths mingling as they stood chest to chest, nose to nose. "Now we have to remind him you're also a traitor."

TWENTY-THREE

Jenn propped herself against the cellar wall beside him. "He's wearing your shirt as a kilt."

And Atlas looked damn good doing so. Robin had offered to stop by his condo or to ride along on a snap to wherever else he kept a stockpile of tartans, but the warlock had refused. Robin wasn't mad about it. "I know."

His cousin lowered her voice. "You fucked him."

One corner of his mouth crept up. "I know."

Lower still. "He's the fucking enemy."

The other corner of his lips tried to tip up, but he bit the inside of his cheek to stop it. "I know."

She whipped her gaze to him, strands of honey blond hair escaping her ponytail. "Would you stop—"

"I know it's driving you nuts." His cousin was, second only to Atlas, the easiest of targets to rile up.

Her growl faltered when he let loose his smile, her own resigned chuckle following. "The way you two fight, I guess part of me always knew it was coming."

He waggled his brows. "You know who else was coming last night . . ."

She rolled her golden eyes and backhanded his gut. "Did you

get it out of your system?" she asked, as the rest of the team filled the room and claimed their seats at the tasting table.

Robin's smile faded as his gaze sought his mate across the room, the last person he ever thought he'd be tied to, the person he wanted to fuck and strangle in equal measure. "I don't think I'm ever getting him out of my system," he replied, and Jenn gasped, correctly interpreting his meaning. "Trust me," he added, "no one hates that more than me."

Not the sex he'd spent all night having. Not even the fact that he and Atlas seemed to be on the same page for a change, working together to catch Evan and defeat Chaos. But after that mission was done, was Robin ready to have a mate? He'd been a lone wolf the past thirty years. Yes, he had the team here, friends and at least one family member who hadn't shunned him completely, but he was on the outside looking in. Always had been, even before Deborah had died. She'd been his connection to the people around the table; without her, the threads still tying them together were no less heartfelt but all the more tenuous. He'd put his life on the line for any of them, he'd made Deborah that promise, and he acknowledged the world was a better place with all of them in it, even Icarus despite how much the mouthy courtesan exasperated him, but he'd rather hide out in the distillery alone than stay here and sing kumbaya. And he sensed every friend around the table and even the cousin beside him would rather he stay there too.

He deserved that for what he'd done—or rather hadn't.

And it was easier to not disappoint anyone if he kept everyone out.

But he couldn't keep his mate out. While he missed having someone in his life like Deborah, someone who had known him inside and out, he valued his independence more. Valued his free will the most. Was this magic that had tied him and Atlas together, that his mother had told him in her letters would find him when Nature needed him most, overriding that will? He meant what he'd told Atlas last night; he was tired of being a pawn in other people's games—the warlock's, Nature's, magic's. But was the draw he felt toward Atlas, even when he'd hated him most—the blood rushing in his veins, the tightening of his gut, the warmth in his chest, the stiffness of his cock—magic or something else entirely?

Robin didn't like either answer. Hated that it didn't matter even more.

He'd told Atlas to stop running. Could he ignore his own instinct to do the same?

Mac, dressed for a day at the office no matter the location, was the last team member to join them, the scrape of his chair across the floor drawing Robin out of his head and back into the room. "All right, we're all here, again," the raven said, droll as always.

Icarus wouldn't know what the word meant if it hit him in the face, his blue gaze alight with mischief as it tracked a roving Atlas around the room. "Why are you wearing Robin's shirt as a kilt?"

"They fucked," Jenn announced.

The responses were as mixed and hilarious as Robin expected.

Paris, a sighed, "Finally."

Mac, a choked, "What?"

Icarus, a maniacal cackle.

Adam, his head hung.

Abigail, a low whistle.

Mary, clapping from her position at the head of the table.

"Moving on . . ." Robin said with a carry-on gesture.

Only for Atlas to hit replay. "When Robin claimed me yesterday—"

Responses were noticeably less varied, some version of "What the fuck?" echoing around the table—except from Mary.

Of course she knew.

Atlas didn't break his stride, in steps or words, talking over the grenade he'd thrown. "It gave me an idea. The men who snatched me yesterday outside the hunter's house—"

"Wait, back up," Adam said. "We need the full story. Not the fucking one, the kidnapping one."

"Atlas got a text yesterday morning," Robin explained. "It sent him to a house in The Corners."

"The hunter's," Atlas said.

Adam pulled a sheet of paper from his jacket pocket. "That's consistent with what we found." From over his shoulder, Robin studied the regional map—LP to Talahalusi—marked with locations. "Mentions of his appearance over the past few years are concentrated in the South or near reservations. Human, like Atlas said; Indigenous, we think, at least partially so."

"I got a name too," Atlas said. "Cyrus." He held a slip of paper out to Icarus. "Contact info for my excavator. Compare notes."

Icarus opened his laptop, fingers flying, while Mac picked up the interrogation. "Did you find anything there?"

Atlas looked to be heading to the spot beside Robin until Mac's question had him abruptly changing direction. "Nope," he answered, strolling way from Robin. Too casual not to be suspect.

"How'd you know it was his place?" Mac asked.

"They said so."

His answers had become clipped; there was something he didn't want the larger group to know. Robin stepped in before Adam or Mac could press. "It was a setup. Three of Dyami's men jumped him. Took him."

"Took him?" Jenn said. "How'd they manage that?"

"It's possible," Robin said with a sly grin aimed Atlas's direction.

It wasn't enough to lure the warlock back to his side, Atlas posting up across the room from him, back and boot propped against the wall. "I let them. I wanted to get more information."

Probably why he'd stayed out of reach, knowing his motive would piss Robin off. A growl rumbled up from his chest and into his words. "When I intercepted the van, they assumed I was after the bounty on his head."

"Did you know?" Atlas asked him, and Robin nodded. It was a modest contract, not outrageous enough to attract a flood of takers, but high enough to weed out first-timers. Attractive to hunters like Robin, like Cyrus. "Why didn't you take me in? Claim it for yourself?"

"Did you miss that whole key-to-it-all conversation yesterday?"

"That's not—"

Robin cut him off with another truth. "It has never been my intention to give you up."

"Just end me yourself."

That was one solution. But first . . . "After I end your brother."

"Is there a plan in this bickering somewhere?" Mary interrupted.

"We're going to play to Robin's strengths," Atlas said. "To his reputation as a bounty hunter. I can't be the only one Evan has a bounty out on."

"You're not," Robin confirmed.

"And those bounties have other interested parties?"

Robin nodded again.

"Good." He pushed off the wall, roving again. "You're going to steal those bounties out from under him. Get his attention. Then catch me."

"But Evan's seen you two working together," Mac said.

Atlas beat him to the reply, and the vehemence in it surprised Robin, did more funny things to his insides. "Evan's also seen him shunned by all of you, and he's seen us fighting each other. He also knows me."

"What's that supposed to mean?" Icarus said.

"He knows what's at stake if Robin catches me."

"To Mac's point," Abigail said, "doesn't he think Robin caught you already?"

"I didn't take him in and claim the bounty," Robin said, then with a flit of his hand added, "He escaped."

"Not the first time." Atlas landed against the wall next to him with an irritating wink. "Evan will need to see me out in the open. Or at least get reports of it. He also needs to believe the ties here are severed. They're frayed already, so that shouldn't be a stretch."

Seething, Jenn shot off the wall on Robin's other side, and Robin had to throw out an arm to hold her back from murdering his mate. "We don't cut people off like you do."

The murder, however, came from the opposite direction. "Is that so?" Paris's raised voice from across the table drew everyone's attention, indignation unfamiliar in his soft voice, judgment unusual on his typically serene face. "When I found him, when I told him the truth about his sister, he'd been sleeping outside in the field where she died for days."

Jenn immediately retreated, gaze cast aside as she tucked her tail and slunk to Abigail's side.

Rotating on his shoulder, Atlas angled Robin's direction, and when he spoke, it was a request, not an order. For Robin's decision, irrespective of the opinion of anyone else in the room. "There needs to be another visible blowup, in case anyone is watching. Can you do it?"

His call, his will, his independence. "I can do it."

TWENTY-FOUR

It had been a decade since Robin set foot in his childhood home. Not much had changed inside since and yet his entire world outside it had been turned upside down.

The family home—a two-story stucco structure built into the side of a hill, halfway up the mountain Mac's mother's people referred to as Kanamota—was well cared for. Freshly painted a soft white, none of the roof's terracotta tiles missing, the windows sparkling clean. The home cared well for its inhabitants too, its location naturally protected from elements and enemies, its foundations strong and sturdy, surviving the earth's shifts for three generations of Whelans.

From the main floor balcony where Robin stood, the grounds around the home seemed similarly in order. Among the cultivated fields that dotted the forest clearings, half of them were beginning to show the first shoots of winter vegetables, while the other half were at rest until spring when they'd be planted with sunflowers, sage, and more.

And beyond the homestead, the peaks and valleys of the pack's range were just beginning to recover from the long hot summer. In a couple rainy months' time, the peaks would be green and the valley floor awash with yellow from the wild mustard that flourished in these parts.

Growing up, March had always been his favorite time to run, when the towering, swaying weeds made the range feel a little less huge. When the mustard reminded him of his mother. They'd laid him and his sister on her chest right after their birth, as she'd struggled for breath, the life bleeding out of her, and she'd smelled like the wild mustard did under his paws.

"Never thought I'd see you back here."

Robin rotated away from the view to the older man standing over the balcony threshold. "Uncle."

Jasper's strawberry blond hair was thinner and streaked with more white than the last time Robin had seen him, but those white hairs and the deeper wrinkles around his eyes and mouth were the only signs of age on his mother's brother, the man who'd raised him and Deborah.

Their father had died within a year of their mother. A broken heart, everyone had said. A self-inflicted gunshot wound, the police report said. Jasper had seen Robin through that and more, until the day of Deborah's funeral when he'd told Robin that he never wanted to see him again.

Toned arms folded, Jasper's stature was as imposing as Robin remembered, his golden eyes as sharp and discerning as they'd been whenever Robin had pulled explosion-worthy stunts as a teen. "What brings the prodigal son home?"

"I need Mom's letters." There'd been a stack of them waiting for him and Deborah when they'd come of age. Everything she'd wanted them to know in case she didn't survive their birth, like she'd somehow known she wouldn't. He'd read them countless times over, looking for clues and finding few, the mate bit having stuck with—frightened—him most. Now, given that the mate bit had come true, and given everything else he'd learned the past few months, plus the wealth of knowledge in said mate's head, he might connect the dots he hadn't recognized before.

"They're gone," Jasper said, as he wandered back into the great room.

Robin followed, momentarily distracted by the additional pack members who'd gathered inside, including Jenn and Abigail. Their wide-eyed expressions indicated they were just as surprised as him by Jenn's father's statement.

"Gone where?" Robin asked, trying to squash the tangle of anger and panic rising in his voice. No way Jasper would destroy those; they were all he had left of his sister. They were all Robin had left of his mother. After he'd last read them, the day of Deborah's funeral, he'd put them into the family safe like he and Deborah had always done. Jenn, who'd assumed the mantle of pack leader after Deborah's death, had assured him they'd always be there, as part of the pack's historical record.

"I burned them."

Jenn vaulted off the arm of the couch. "Why'd you do that?"

"In case this war you two"—Jasper waggled a finger between them—"are set on fighting goes the other way."

"You'd fold?" Robin scoffed. "Just like that?"

"I'm protecting our family and this pack."

Robin glanced around the room, meeting each pack member's gaze. "Do all of you feel that way?"

"We're with Jenn," said Bruce, her younger brother.

"And I'm with her, always," Jenn replied, her devotion to Nature unwavering, but when she swung her gaze to Robin, it was clear her feelings toward him were more than just an act's worth. "But where are you, cousin?"

"What's that supposed to mean?"

"You turned Paris over to a giant," Abigail said, and Robin's gaze shot to the most level-headed member of their team, the one who understood nuance better than most, abandoned by a pack who had allied themselves with a giant.

"Just like your mate did," Jenn added.

"I didn't know he was my mate, then," he barked back.

It was a risky move, bringing Atlas into this. Volatile for their pack, and if someone was leaking information to Evan, how would this change the calculus? Would he believe that Atlas, once he caught Robin, would ever turn his mate over? Was Jenn even considering that or just acting out of frustration and anger?

Regardless, the cat was out of the bag. "Wait?" Bruce said. "The same warlock who killed Deborah?"

"He didn't," Robin corrected. "It was his twin."

"Because that's so much better," another of their cousins, Olivia, said from where she'd been eyeing something out the window.

"You vanish for days on end, Robin," Jenn said, drawing his attention back to her. "You don't let anyone in on your plans." She swallowed hard. "You don't answer pack calls."

His gut roiled, familiar guilt creeping up his throat, his voice rough with it as he gritted out his response. "I have answered every one of them the past two months."

"How much of the past two months," Jasper said, "could have been avoided if you'd answered the call ten years ago?"

And as fast as the guilt had climbed, it brought him low, taking his stomach to the floor, same as it always did when the worst mistake of his life was thrown back in his face. "So, we're back to that?"

"Once a traitor, always a traitor."

Good to know where he stood. While this may have started as an act, the performance had been hijacked by the truth, which made what he came here for all the more important. He'd never get another chance. "Give me Mom's letters."

"I told you—"

"Give them to me," Robin roared, the voice he would have used to give an order if he'd taken control of the pack after Deborah. By birthright, he'd deserved it; by deed, he'd forfeited it. Instincts were instincts, though, and everyone but Jasper took a step back and lowered their heads.

While he didn't join them in physically submitting, Jasper

tempered his voice, the tone deferential, when he spoke again. "She was my sister."

"She was my mother," Robin said, letting every bit of sorrow bleed into his words. "You had a lifetime with her. I had minutes. If you don't want anything to do with me, fine. But give me that piece of her, of my history, and I'll never show my face here again."

Jenn gasped. "Robin—"

He kept his gaze locked on his uncle. "Do we have a deal?"

The older man stared him down another long minute before seeming to accept the truth of Robin's words and nodding to Bruce, who disappeared into the house.

"Robin." Jenn stepped to his side, hand on his forearm, tears glistening in her eyes. "You don't have to do this."

He covered her hand, giving it a squeeze, as he forced out words around the lump in his throat. She was a good pack leader; she didn't need the albatross that was him hanging around her neck. "I do, cuz."

Bruce returned with the stack of letters, tied together by the green and yellow ribbons of Robin's memories. He handed them to Jasper, who slapped them into Robin's outstretched hand. "Willow deserved better. So did Deborah."

Robin didn't disagree.

TWENTY-FIVE

Near the end of the half-mile gravel drive, Robin reached for the hem of his shirt to undress before shifting when Atlas stepped out of the woods. "That should do the trick."

"You were there?"

"Close enough to hear the good bits."

Robin's answering laugh sounded as cold as his insides felt.

"Come this way," Atlas said with a tip of his head toward the woods he'd just appeared out of.

A few minutes later, once the replays in Robin's head quieted enough to appreciate reality's comfortable silence, he realized where they were headed. Following Atlas, he didn't bother to hide his smile, grateful for it to chase away the chill. "I used to come here as a kid," he said, as they emerged from the trees beside a small reservoir pond. Surrounded by tall pines, the little lake had always felt like an oasis amid the vastness.

"Damn." Atlas clicked his tongue against the back of his teeth. "I was hoping to surprise you." His rolling eyes belied his words. "Maybe this will do?" he added, as he pulled out a joint.

"That'll do," Robin said. "Could use a smoke."

Atlas lit the joint with a flick of fire from his fingertip and handed it to Robin. A few puffs to get it going, then he inhaled a lungful of earthy peace before passing the joint back. He wandered out onto the short wooden dock where he and Deborah used to spend countless hours as kids, daydreaming about all the places they were going to visit one day. She'd done it as a soldier, then a federal agent; he'd done it as a tracker.

Hunting was always hardest when it was someone close to you. He shucked out of his flannel, wrapped his mother's letters in the fabric, then lowered himself onto the dock beside Atlas. "You think someone in the pack is a traitor."

"Statistically speaking, yes." He handed the joint back, then reclined on the dock, his eyes closed, the setting sun painting his blond hair and pale skin in shades of orange and violet. Everyone always talked about how pretty Paris was, and the Cirillo heir admittedly had runway model good looks. By contrast, Atlas, in suits or kilts, had an untouchable ethereal quality to his appearance that was hilariously at odds with every other acerbic side of him. "I'm sorry."

Not acerbic, and not the sentiment out of Atlas's mouth that Robin needed. The last thing he wanted was Atlas's pity. "Don't," he told him. "This is already weird as fuck."

Atlas's sexy, smart-ass laugh was more like it, and Robin caught on to the trap he'd walked into. "You did that on purpose, didn't you?"

Atlas rotated on his side toward him, dancing green eyes glancing up at him. "Worked, didn't it?" Then down to the mound of flannel and parchment between them. "What are those?"

"Letters from my mother, to me and Deborah."

"What do you hope to find in them?"

"Answers. Things I thought were cryptic before are starting to connect now. I need to reread them. You need to read them. See if there's something we can use."

Atlas righted himself, and Robin anticipated an argument over *we* just to make him feel better. Instead, Atlas dug out his phone, tapped the screen a few times, then held the device out to him. "You need to read this first."

He traded him the joint for the phone and read the posted contract. "This is the bounty you want to go after?"

"Not me, her. She thinks he's hiding a phoenix."

"Which is why Evan would want him too. But if I catch him, turn him over to the team, then all that"—he gestured back to the house—"was for naught."

He shook his head. "She just wants a meet. An alliance for when the time comes."

Robin continued reading. "This says he'll be at Club Sutro tonight."

Atlas finished the joint and snuffed it out on the dock. "We'll need to leave enough time to swing by the condo and distillery."

Leave enough, as in they didn't have to leave right away. They had time for something else. And by the blush that hit Atlas's cheeks, the warlock was thinking about the same something else as Robin. Something that would make them both feel better. Robin laid Atlas's phone atop the letters and pushed them well out of the way. "We have some time until then."

Green eyes, the color of the forest around them, heated from more than just the sun reflecting off the water. "What do you have in mind?"

Closing the distance between them, Robin propped one hand behind Atlas's back and snuck the other through the gap in his makeshift kilt, skirting his fingers over his inner thigh. "You remember what I said about the next time I fucked you?"

"Yes, but . . ." Atlas's words stuttered on a moan when Robin nuzzled behind his ear, a full body shiver rippling through him. Robin's own cock hardened, Atlas's reaction, plus the waft of his scent that tickled Robin's nose, a potent combination. Atlas found his words again, but they were breathy, uttered on a gasp as Robin trailed his hand higher. "That was ten—eleven?—fucks ago now."

The backs of his knuckles brushed his cock, his lips the shell of Atlas's ear. "Yes, but you weren't wearing a kilt then."

"I'm still not," he snapped, haughty making a comeback. Always a last line of defense, their perfect foreplay. "I'm wearing your shirt."

Robin grinned, this entire encounter, the push and pull where they both won, exactly what he needed. He adjusted his hand, fingers curling around Atlas's length and giving him a long, slow tug, his thumb circling the damp tip when he reached it. "Might be even sexier."

He was so distracted by the rising color on Atlas's cheeks, by his darkening eyes, by the rock-hard cock in his hand, that Robin missed Atlas moving his own until he closed it over his erection, palming him through his jeans. "When you fuck me with this fat cock like you promised, I want to enjoy it. I don't want to be on the clock, and I don't want to be in the fucking woods."

Robin rocked up to meet the rough handling, loving every aggressive second of it. Then rocked his entire body closer, withdrawing his hand from between Atlas's thighs and dragging his thumb over Atlas's bottom lip, smearing it with his own precome. "Sometimes the truth does come out of this mouth."

"Too often lately."

Like it had just then, but Robin was too turned on to call him on it, and the last thing he wanted to do was derail where this heated teasing was headed, the truth their bodies were seeking. "I know how to stop that, for now."

"How's that?" Atlas replied coyly, then proving he already knew the answer, sucked Robin's thumb into his mouth, swirling his tongue around the tip like Robin's finger had him, like he was making sure to lick up every drop of precome Robin had collected.

Too much, too good, not enough. "Stretch that pretty mouth around my cock."

"Will that make you forget about it?"

Another slip, a truth offered in return. "For a little while."

Their gazes locked, truths and sorrows acknowledged, commiseration accepted, before Atlas flipped open the shirt-kilt, took his cock in hand, and continued to jerk himself. Robin wasted no time unfastening his jeans and getting his own cock out, the cool air barely grazing his overheated skin before it was enveloped in scorching heat, Atlas's mouth closing around him while he continued to stroke himself.

Pleasuring them both.

Robin threaded his fingers through Atlas's thick blond waves, held on tight, and forgot about everything but the heat flooding his senses, the whisper of spring chasing away the chill he hadn't escaped in far too long.

TWENTY-SIX

It felt good to work again, even if Robin did always feel out of place at Club Sutro.

Jeans, flannel, and hair that hadn't seen a proper cut in years didn't exactly fit the mold of Yerba Buena's most exclusive club. This was more Icarus's scene, alluring courtesans winding through the crowd of wealthy patrons. It had been Paris's too, before he'd settled down, heirs like him nursing high-end booze from crystal glassware that somehow survived the thumping music. And before Paris was even old enough to frequent clubs, Sutro had been Deb's scene, a place for her to let off steam and dance with her husbands after dealing with pack business and work trips.

"You want another beer?"

Kai's question knocked Robin out of the past and back to the present. He glanced over his shoulder at Paris's other best friend, Jason's raven partner, who was working the bar tonight. Robin traded his empty for the fresh bottle Kai offered. "Thanks."

The raven disappeared to the opposite end of the bar, waiting on another customer, and Robin turned his attention back to the packed club. One would never guess that two months ago a giant had come crashing through the ceiling, the furniture and walls had been riddled with bullet holes, and a certain blond warlock had stood atop the backbar and fired a crossbow bolt into another giant.

Tonight, Robin was hunting a different blond: Glen Brewster, a six-foot-two bear shifter who led a loosely affiliated group of his kind that inhabited the coastal woods north of YB. And Robin wasn't the only one on the hunt for Mr. Brewster. In one of the large booths by the windows, a feline shifter of some sort was trying and failing to fit in with the other patrons in his booth who were drinking and laughing merrily. And on the dance floor, a pair of humans were getting all kinds of attention as they put on an amorous couple looking for a third routine, inviting others to dance with them. A clever trap for Glen, if he ever showed.

Robin was beginning to doubt he would when finally the bear shifter strode through the door—with a big beefy arm looped around Atlas's waist.

Not the plan.

So not the plan.

Atlas was on perimeter duty. He was supposed to radio when Glen was close, then stay outside, in case things inside went sideways and Robin needed an emergency escape snap while dashing out.

He was *not* supposed to let another man put his hands on him.

The only thing that kept Robin from vaulting off his barstool was the fact Atlas wasn't pretending to be Evan. He was very much in his Atlas element, blond hair perfectly coiffed, chin held high, wearing the kilt and leather harness he'd changed into at his condo.

Evan needed to see—or at least hear about—his twin being free and out in the open, no longer Robin's prisoner. And there he was, on the dance floor at Club Sutro in another man's arms. Two flashing neon targets for the three other bounty hunters in the room. "Shit."

Jason squeezed in next to him at the bar. "There was an alter-cation outside," he whispered low. The phoenix had already been at the club when Robin arrived, and because Robin still didn't fully trust his mate, he'd roped Jason into reconning the recon man.

"Who?" Robin asked.

"Another bounty hunter. We dispatched him. Glen was going to leave, but Atlas convinced him to come inside and forget about it."

Forget about it.

Robin clenched his teeth. Was that what Atlas said to all the guys? Had he just been giving him the same line earlier at the lake?

"What do you want to do here?" Jason asked as he raked a hand through his dark unruly curls.

"Kill him."

"Yes, we all know. But like, right now, what do you want to do?"

Robin jutted his chin toward the hunter in the booth. "The feline shifter on the end there is here for the same reason as us. Get Kai to give you a bottle of bourbon on Adam's tab, then go join them. Box the shifter in."

"What are you going to do?" Jason asked.

"See the flirty human couple on the dance floor?"

"The ones looking for a third?"

Robin nodded. "More like hunters looking to lure their target. I'm going to make sure neither Atlas nor Glen end up in their hands."

"On it," Jason said, then wove his way to the other end of the bar, leaning over it to whisper in his boyfriend's ear.

With the feline shifter handled, Robin focused on his targets and enacted a plan to foil theirs. He tipped back the rest of his beer, slid off the stool, and removed his flannel, stripping down to the black tank he had on underneath.

Heads swiveled his direction, including a certain blond one, the owner's green gaze furious.

Good.

Even better that the bounty hunter pair had also picked him up on his way to the dance floor. He hadn't danced in years, but he must have been convincing enough, the woman hunter crooking her finger to call him over. Robin's gaze slid back to Atlas, who was watching him over Glen's shoulder, the bear shifter oblivious to his partner's wandering eye. Robin made a deliberate sweep of his gaze, to the booth where Jason was sliding in next to the hunter there, then back to the couple who had eyes on him. Identifying the threats for Atlas before Robin returned his attention to the couple meeting him halfway on the dance floor.

The woman slung an arm over his shoulder, drawing him closer while her partner hemmed him in from behind, his tall, toned body pressed against Robin's back. "How about we make a deal?" the woman said. "The three of us take the two of them." She tipped her head toward where Atlas and Glen were dancing. "Then we split the bounties three ways?"

"I don't need your help," Robin said.

The sharp point of a blade pressed against his back, right over his kidney. "We don't need you either," the man said. "Call it professional courtesy."

"You think you can catch them?" Robin replied. "A warlock who can snap his way out of anywhere and a giant bear shifter."

"The warlock got away from you," the woman said. "You need us too."

Robin pretended to be conflicted while swaying between the bodies on either side of him.

"What'll it be?" the guy said, and Robin honestly wondered if he was asking about the bounties or the boner he notched against the seam of Robin's jeans, sliding it along his ass crack.

"All right," Robin said, playing along and rocking back his hips, distracting the already distracted. "You two take the warlock. He's smaller. I'll take the shifter."

He didn't give them a chance to argue, ducking out from between them and spinning toward Atlas and Glen. The head start gave him time to crowd behind Glen and whisper, "Did he explain to you what's going on?"

"I'm in," the bear said.

"Good, then shift!"

A giant bear appearing in the middle of a crowded club was a recipe for disaster. Add a roaring coyote and a warlock throwing orbs of green magic, and almost everyone was headed to the exits. None of the other paranormals, including Jason's mark, wanted any part of the chaos.

Only the two human hunters were dumb enough to try and battle Atlas while Robin made a show of cornering the bear. He lunged, no teeth, and Glen made it seem like he was surrendering, letting Robin hold him down by the neck. If word got back to Evan, it would be of a catch by Robin. And of another escape by his twin, Atlas using his magic to throw the hunter pair into the backbar before snapping out of there.

TWENTY-SEVEN

It was near dawn by the time everyone else cleared out of the distillery tasting room, alliances made and another phoenix in Mary's pocket.

Robin didn't care about any of that. All he cared about was setting the record straight with the warlock in a kilt sprawled on the chaise. Turning his back on the reckless fucker, he busied himself with a shot of vodka to avoid charging across the room and wringing Atlas's neck. "You want to tell me what the fuck that was?"

"*That* was a successful operation."

"*That* wasn't the plan."

"I improvised."

The absolute arrogance was enraging, the growl bleeding into his voice. "Without a word of warning."

"I told you, I don't—"

Robin slammed his glass down and rounded on him, unleashing a roared warning. "Don't you fucking say it."

Atlas's smirk would be the death of him. The warlock rose from the couch and sauntered across the room. "Don't tell me you didn't love it. Thinking on your feet, setting traps, negotiating a deal in two seconds flat."

Robin met him halfway, beside the table Atlas had leaned a hip against. "I didn't love seeing another man's hands on my mate."

Atlas's eyes flared, as if he didn't expect Robin to put the word to their connection. But then his mossy irises turned a darker shade of green, like the forest just before a summer storm, like maybe *mate* wasn't a bad thing at all. He pushed off the table, narrowing the space between them, and when he spoke, voice dangerously low, the snap of his order—"Take the flannel off"— went straight to Robin's dick. "And the undershirt."

He didn't hesitate to pull them both off over his head, even as part of him railed at how fast Atlas had turned the tables. A bigger part of him didn't give a damn, loved it even. Loved Atlas's hands on him too, the warlock gliding them up his front as he pressed close behind him. "I didn't love seeing another man's dick rutting against what's mine either. Or you rutting back."

"I was improvising," Robin said, parroting Atlas's words, then lifting his ass to rut against his mate's cock.

Atlas clasped his hip, holding him close as he rolled back. "I didn't need to know you could dance."

"I was rusty."

He nipped the back of his shoulder. "You were sexy as hell, and no one in that club could take their eyes off you."

Robin glanced over his shoulder. "Including you?"

"Including me." Atlas lifted his gaze, and the pure heat staring up at Robin was the final straw.

Using his speed, he spun and shoved Atlas against the nearest post, crowding into his space, gripping his face the way he liked and forcing that burning green gaze back to his. Atlas needed to understand the tightrope he was walking, the razor-thin patience he was playing with. "If you'd come in there in a suit, I might have killed you."

"He needed—"

"To know you were free, I got that."

"And I needed to make sure you kept your promise." He lifted a hand and snapped, leaving Robin with a handful of green mist and a gut full of boiling anger.

But only for a split second.

The sneaky bastard reappeared on the table, his legs spread and that devastating smirk back in place. "Starting with sucking my cock."

Bare, underneath the kilt he flipped up.

His erection was as stiff as Robin's, the head glistening with a bead of precome that Robin descended on. Atlas's cock wasn't as fat or as long as his, but it was perfectly proportioned to his compact frame and perfectly sized for Robin's mouth. He could swirl his tongue around it on each pull to the tip, stretch his mouth all the way around it's girth as he descended to the root again, his nose buried in the wiry hairs there, Atlas's real scent intoxicating.

He'd happily spend all day there, Atlas's cock in his mouth, his nose buried in the first breaths of spring, but the horny warlock had other ideas, his fingers curling in his hair, nails scraping across his scalp. "Fucking suck me off like you mean it."

For that sass, he got a slap to his thigh and the rough working over he obviously wanted, Robin sliding his hands under his buttocks, using them for leverage, then setting a relentless pace. Fast hard sucks that made Atlas groan, flicks of his tongue under the head that made him curse, the hint of teeth that made him hiss, Robin's fingers digging into his ass cheeks, then sliding into his crack, making him shout for more. Robin kept him right there on the edge of pleasure and torture.

Half reclined, Atlas's bare chest strained against the leather harness as he white-knuckled the edge of the table, holding on for dear life. "Now, you maddening coyote, fucking now."

Given the swell of his own cock still trapped in his jeans, Robin finally conceded, ready to claim the hole he'd been teasing just as mercilessly. A couple fast flicks under the head, then he closed his lips around Atlas's cock again, took it all the way to the back of his throat, and growled.

Atlas exploded with a shout, filling Robin's mouth with come. He swallowed some and held the rest in reserve. To do what he'd promised. Straightening, he flipped Atlas over on the table, nothing gentle about it, spread his ass cheeks, nothing gentle there either, and opened his mouth, forcing Atlas's own come into his hole with his tongue.

"Fuck," Atlas keened, slapping a hand on the table. "Please, please, please."

Robin didn't think he'd ever heard anything as sweet as a blissed-out Atlas Shaw begging.

He begged even louder once Robin shoved his cock in that come-slick hole. For "more," for "harder," for Robin to "please, come" so he'd get his tongue back on him. Gripping the harness for leverage, Robin rammed into him as hard and as fast as his body allowed.

He didn't last long after that, the sight of a writhing, sweaty Atlas, the promise of the scent of them together on his tongue too intoxicating, too erotic to withstand, his climax rushing up and claiming him like the man below him.

And as he buried his face back between Atlas's pale, round ass cheeks, his tongue swiping over his messy, quivering hole, he realized his imagination had nothing on the real thing.

This was spring, summer, fall, and winter all wrapped into one.

He'd never been more certain this man was his mate, that he'd do anything to keep him for as long as they had on this earth.

TWENTY-EIGHT

"Did you think we wouldn't find it?"

Atlas ignored Adam's question and boosted himself onto the table where Robin had done all manner of filthy things to him yesterday. They'd gone their separate ways later that morning, each of them needing to be seen in public without the other to dispel any rumors that they'd been working together at Club Sutro. Robin had spent nearly every second of the past thirty-six hours mentally replaying Atlas's shouts and groans, remembering the silky hardness of his cock and the tight heat of his hole, fantasizing about when he'd get to taste and smell him again.

Atlas's gaze drifted to where Robin stood behind the bar and one corner of his mouth hitched up, as if he knew exactly where Robin's mind had drifted. He hadn't jerked off once since they'd parted, and he was paying for it now. Atlas wasn't helping, dressed in another tight tee and kilt, the tartan riding high on his thighs. Robin flipped him the bird and the other side of the sexy fucker's mouth turned up in a sly grin.

He was so distracted he missed Icarus hurling a balled-up napkin at him, hitting him square in the forehead. "Do you mind?"

"You two called this meeting," Robin said with a shrug. "I

can't help that you put us in the same room together after a day apart. And for the record, you two are just as bad."

Icarus glanced over his shoulder at his partner. "That's true."

Adam rolled his eyes, then tossed the first of the four folders under his arm onto the other table in the middle of the room, photos scattering across the tabletop. "There's a wall of pictures in the hunter's house. Of Atlas and his family."

Fantasies forgotten, Robin shot out from behind the bar to get a better look at reality. No, not reality, a nightmare. It was a massive collage—pictures of Atlas, of his brothers, of an older man he assumed was Atlas's father, based on resemblance. Some of the photos were posed, some were surveillance, taken from afar and up close, taken as recently as Atlas's brother's funeral.

He whipped his gaze to the liar still sitting on the table. "You didn't think I needed to know about this?" Atlas had told him he'd found nothing at Cyrus's house.

"Not until I knew more."

"That's not how this works."

He hopped off the table. "That's how this has always worked."

The detachment in his words, in the tilt of his chin and the coolness of gaze, was a one-eighty from the flirty Atlas of seconds ago. Robin felt the whiplash in his chest and his balls.

"What else did you find out?" Atlas asked Adam.

"His mother was Indigenous, Bay Miwok, and the original owner of the house." He tossed a second folder onto the table, this one a mix of papers and photo. "Malila Contra."

Tan skin, short dark hair, dark eyes, tall and imposing. Robin could see where her son got his height from.

"Lila?"

Robin jerked his gaze up, not used to hearing Atlas's voice so strangled. He'd only ever heard it like that when Atlas was about to come, when his gaze was lust-clouded and his cheeks rosy. Right then, Atlas's eyes were wide with surprise and his face was pale.

He looked like he'd seen a ghost.

The ex-cop was no stranger to that look. "You knew her?" Adam asked.

"Knew," Robin said, picking up on the past tense. Same as Adam's earlier *was*. "She's dead?"

Icarus waved a hand over the pile of Shaw family pictures. "See giant wall of vengeance."

Atlas didn't take the bait, a rarity where Icarus's softballs were concerned. He wandered over to the bar instead, grabbed the bottle of vodka, and tipped it up to his lips, not bothering with a glass. Two big gulps later, he lowered the bottle and wiped his mouth with the back of his hand. "She was the human who held Chaos before it was cast to the other side of the veil."

"She was also your father's mistress," Adam said, dropping the third folder, open to a birth certificate. For Cyrus Contra. Malila Contra was listed as mother; Pierce Shaw as father. "That" —he tapped the grainy photo on the other side of the folder, Malila holding a baby, seemingly in an argument with Atlas's father—"is your half brother."

"I can't believe you used your father's name as an alias," Icarus said to Atlas.

Atlas strode to the table and mimicked Icarus's earlier gesture, hand circling over the collage of his father. "See giant wall of asshole. It fit."

"I was so robbed of a punch."

"Why is Cyrus trying to kill you?" Adam asked, righting the conversation.

"Has he actually tried to kill you?" Robin queried instead, this latest information putting a new spin on Cyrus's prior appearance. "Or is it possible he just wants to have a conversation?"

Atlas glared at him. "I know what someone looks like when they want to kill me. He does."

"What's he after, then?" Adam said. "Your father's approval?"

"Maybe," Icarus replied. "His asshole dad does hate him."

Robin couldn't make any of those deductions without more context. "When did Lila die?"

"A few years after the Rift," Adam replied.

Almost there. "How?" he asked Atlas, sensing the truth would blow things wide open.

Sure enough. "My mother and Daphne's cast Chaos behind the veil again. Lila didn't survive the spell."

Wall of vengeance was right, from multiple angles. "And he's been after your family ever since?"

"Apparently."

Robin shifted into tactical mode, requiring a plan to protect his mate. "Do we have a location on him?"

Beneath Cyrus's birth certificate was a map of Yerba Buena, dotted with red X marks, a cluster of them in the Lost Valley. "Sightings over the past three days," Adam said.

"Fucking hell," Robin cursed. "This place is burned."

Icarus groaned. "We're going to have to move all that shit again."

Robin ignored his whining, more concerned with their safety. "Get back to the mountain," he told Adam and Icarus. "Fill them in." Then to Atlas, said, "Go to the condo. No one can get past those spells."

As if the barked order had brought him back to life, Atlas straightened his spine and lifted his chin, barking back. "I'm not going to fucking hide. We're six days from Solstice. We need to keep luring Evan out."

"On that note . . ." Adam handed Robin the final file. "You look like you could kill someone."

"Please."

Robin flipped open the folder. On one side was a dossier for a witch who'd previously been a member of the Redwood Coven. On the other side was her photo. Attractive, middle-aged, white, with blue eyes, light brown hair, and a button nose.

"Your other brother," Adam said, "just doubled the bounty on this witch."

"What's she to Evan?" Robin asked.

"A potential rival. Mac talked to his contacts in the coven.

They tossed her out decades ago when they learned she was working against them to bring Chaos through the veil."

And there went the color in Atlas's face again, but he didn't shrink like he had before. Almost like he knew the answer to this mystery and was steeling himself for it. "Name?"

"Karoline Wiles," Robin read from the dossier.

His eyes slipped closed, but not before Robin recognized the guilt that streaked through his green gaze. "She's one of Chaos's devotees."

"What else?"

"She was the one who recruited me, who tempted me with the promise of Chaos for a while."

Robin saw red, imagining the worst of what all that entailed for Atlas, understanding that glimpse of guilt now, better than most. He felt it too, every time he killed, every time he remembered the day he let his sister get killed too.

"It's a trap," Atlas's words yanked him out of the familiar mire. "Evan could easily defeat her. He did defeat her already. He doesn't need to hire the job out, and he certainly doesn't need to double the bounty."

"So he wants us on her," Robin said, following the train of thought, recalling what Atlas had previously said—he knew Evan better than anyone, and vice versa, even if Robin intended to change that eventually. "While he does what?"

"Eliminates the real threat to Chaos—Pati Miwra's son."

TWENTY-NINE

Robin checked his phone for the umpteenth time over the past six hours. No word from the team at Monte Corvo, no word from the pack, no word from Atlas. He hadn't seen any of them for two days, only communicating via encrypted texts. The team had been moving Pati and Pax, Atlas had been investigating Cyrus and working with Mary to prepare for Solstice, and Robin had been hunting Karoline.

Which was how he'd ended up in the Canyon Lands, Yerba Buena's mystical equivalent of a terror-filled funhouse. Nature had conceded this area of YB during the Rift, the weather magically and naturally terrible, the land unstable, more of it falling into the Bay each day, and the carcasses of once-gleaming buildings reduced to rubble.

Robin found himself crouched in one of those broken buildings, peering through sheets of rain, ears attuned, for any sign of Karoline at the meet that was supposed to take place in the building across the crumbled street below.

He checked his phone again.

"They'll call if they need you."

He whipped around with a growl. Not because he felt threatened—he'd know that voice anywhere—but because the asshole was playing with fire, sneaking around when Robin was already on edge. When he hadn't smelled him, touched him, kissed him in two fucking days.

"Not nice, is it?" Atlas said, strolling toward him. "Someone sneaking up on you without making a sound." He flicked his fingers. "Covering their scent."

Robin didn't inhale too deeply, certain he'd jump the man with the slightest provocation. He lightly sniffed the air, just enough Atlas to settle the queasiness that had swished around in his belly since they'd parted. "You started it." He rotated back around, peering once more through the rain for any movement in the empty room across the street. Still dark, still quiet. He sank to his ass and relaxed back against the frame of the long-gone plate glass window. "And you shouldn't be here either," he said to Atlas.

He wisely lowered himself across from Robin and rested back against the opposite side of the window frame, only their feet in touching distance. "I'm here in case you get the call. You can't be in two places at once."

And fuck if Robin didn't want to crawl on his hands and knees across the floor and kiss the fuck out of the man, the enemy turned mate, who somehow seemed to understand him best.

He'd like to understand him better too so he could return the care and concern. "Why didn't you tell me about the wall at Cyrus's place?"

His gaze drifted outside, but by the faraway look in his green eyes, Atlas was somewhere—sometime—else completely. "*We* doesn't end well for folks around me," he said. "Cole, Daphne, Canton, Paris. The last thing I wanted was for my shit, another person targeting me and mine, to also target you and yours."

Except Atlas was his now, and he was Atlas's. Those lines of separation were getting blurrier every day.

"And Karoline? You're not just here in case I get the call, are you?"

"I intended to take care of things myself."

Robin knocked his foot, once, twice, until Atlas gave him his attention. "What if it's a double blind? I leave, Evan shows up instead of Karoline, and you've got no backup."

He shrugged. "Then he takes me, and you come to the rescue."

"If he doesn't kill you first."

"Last," he said, barely a whisper, and the guilt he didn't bother to hide this time made Robin's chest ache. Fuck, it was like looking in a mirror. He rested his foot against Atlas's. "I know what it feels like."

Atlas pressed back with his. "I know you do."

They stayed that way, in each other's quiet company, as the rain outside turned to a mist and the building across the street remained dark, the only movement in the vicinity the ground periodically shifting beneath them. "I hate it here," Atlas grumbled.

"It's not so bad," Robin said. He wished he'd had a camera ready to capture Atlas's aghast expression. "The ruins and fence keep it all contained and when the fog's in, it's like a blanket."

"Yeah," Atlas scoffed. "A cold, wet one."

Robin chuckled. "It's not so overwhelming here, and in a fight, it's close work, hand to hand combat, no fancy devices, just pure skill."

"And obstacles, like not being able to see a foot in front of you."

"You were here all the time for Vincent."

"I know, and I hated it."

Since Atlas seemed to be feeling truthful, Robin asked another question that had been weighing on his mind. "Your time with Karoline and Lila . . . Is that how you convinced Vincent to trust you? That you were on the same side?"

"A man like Vincent hears and sees what he wants to." He nodded at the dark, empty space across the street. "Same as her."

It was Robin's turn to gasp. "I thought she recruited you?"

"Yes, but I went in as a spy first."

"What changed?"

"I got tired, same as you, of being a pawn. She promised me freedom, independence. But if she, Evan, and Chaos get what they want—"

"There'll be no place left worth being free in."

A light flickered on across the street, Karoline entered the room, and for one terrifying, heart-stopping second, Robin thought he'd lost him, Atlas snapping right out from in front of him.

But a single beat of Robin's heart later, Atlas appeared behind him, hidden in the shadows, out of the moonlight that had broken through the clouds and shown exactly where he'd been standing.

"Fuck," Robin cursed.

Atlas clasped the outsides of his shoulders. "I needed to act fast. And so do you. You need to get to the pack."

Robin spun to face him. "What? I haven't—" The phone in his pocket buzzed.

"You need to go."

He glanced over his shoulder. Still just Karoline in the room. "Atlas . . ."

"Hey," he said softly, and just as gently grasped his chin and used it to draw his attention back to him. "She won't hurt me."

Except for the hit his soul would take when he had to kill again, like it had when he'd killed Daphne. But if Daphne hadn't known about Mary, Robin was sure now that Atlas would have . . . "You're going to give her a chance to change her mind, aren't you?"

He pressed his lips together.

And Robin jumped to the next logical conclusion. "Same as you're going to give your brother."

He slid the hand on his jaw higher, cupping his cheek. "I promise, you will still get what you deserve." Robin wanted to argue but the phone in his pocket buzzed again. Atlas firmed the grip on his face. "Go."

Robin returned the hold and drew Atlas closer, nose to nose, growling a "Yours" against his lips.

Atlas's "Mine" bled into a kiss that was wild and peaceful all at once, that made Robin's soul settle in that certain way his mother had talked about in her letters. Like Mac must have found with Paris, like Adam with Icarus, and before that with David and Deborah, like his and Deb's mother had shared with their father.

Like maybe he'd found freedom.

THIRTY

Each mile closer to the pack homestead made Robin more uneasy.

Not because he'd left his mate in the Canyon Lands. Atlas could take care of himself. The warlock had made it fuck-all-knew how long before their paths had crossed.

And not because Robin was breaking a promise returning here. Jenn had called; he answered.

And not even because Jenn had needed to call him; crisis at this point was inevitable.

No, it wasn't anything so monumental, more a sense of absence he couldn't put his finger on, a chill crawling up his spine, a smell that was unmistakable as he neared the lake where he and Atlas had shared a joint and gotten off together a few days ago.

Unlike then, it was the middle of the night, pitch black outside, the trees still dripping from the earlier rain. And someone was dead in these woods.

He wasn't surprised when a violet-eyed Liam sailed overhead, croaking a mournful *Kraa*. He circled once more, another *Kraa* to alert Jenn, Jason, and Abigail to his presence. A quick change of clothes later, Robin emerged from the woods to join them.

"Pati or one of the team?" he asked his cousin. Jenn wouldn't have called him here for just any dead pack member; he'd missed plenty of those over the years. This one had to involve one of their team or Pati and Pax, who were being moved between safe houses daily.

"Pati," she answered. "Still alive, we think, but her escorts..." She ran a hand over her head, growling when she met her pony-tail holder. "They were taking her and Pax to the handoff spot." Her voice was rough, her eyes bloodshot and puffy. "Fuck, I should have gone with them."

"Liam and I were supposed to meet them," Jason said, then cast his gaze aside. "Paris met them first. He called us, and I called Jenn."

They. Multiple souls who'd contacted the medium. Multiple deaths.

"How long ago?"

"Two hours."

"And you just called me?" he barked, frustration turning up the volume of his voice. Unjustifiably so, and Robin immediately regretted it, lifting his hands, palms out. "Sorry, that was unfair." Jenn's wide eyes made him smile, but the multiple deaths, the reaper on Abigail's shoulder, the despair that had drained all color from his cousin's face, flattened the curve of his lips. "Take me to the bodies."

Liam led the way into the woods to where three bodies lay covered by blankets. Robin kneeled beside the smallest mound and pulled back the blanket. Olivia, his youngest cousin, in human form. The ground and leaves beneath her were dark from the blood that had seeped from the gunshot wounds to her chest and head.

Execution style.

He leaned closer, sniffed, then recoiled as silver stung his nostrils.

Beside her was another body, the shape of a coyote beneath the blanket. Pulling it back, he recognized Bruce by the dark patches of fur on his shoulders. His face, though . . . Robin had to look away. Bruce must have been mid-attack, protecting his cousin, when he'd taken a bullet to the face, the silver going clean through.

Robin glanced the few feet to the last coyote-shaped mound. His chest tightened with certainty, the evidence indisputable. Jenn's heightened distress, the reason she hadn't been with Pati and Pax, the uneasiness Robin had felt the closer he got to this place. It all made horrible, devastating sense.

He bowed his head, Jenn hiccupped a sob, and he had his confirmation. He didn't need to look under that third blanket. He stood instead and drew his cousin into his arms, holding her tight as they grieved for the man who'd been a father to both of them, to their pack. "I'm so sorry," he murmured into her hair.

"I should have—"

"You are the pack leader," Robin told her. "You did exactly what you're supposed to do. Jasper knew that. They all did."

He held his cousin while she sobbed, while he struggled to get his own emotions under control. His heart ached for his pack, for his uncle and cousins who'd been slaughtered. Ached worse for Jenn, understanding all too well the depth of her grief and the weight of the survivor's guilt bearing down on her. Crushing. His gut burned with rage at the person who'd injured his family, at Jasper for not taking more backup, at himself for leaving things the way he had, at Nature and Chaos for this whole fucked-up situation. Blood churned in his veins, urging him to run, urging him to exact mighty vengeance on all the people who'd done this to him and his.

More than anything, though, his soul longed for the one person who could settle the storm inside him.

He closed his eyes and recalled Atlas sitting across from him earlier in the night, the contemplative set of his elegant features, the weight of Altas's foot against his, the spring of his gaze and scent.

The acceptance and understanding that grounded Robin.

He inhaled deep and felt his soul settle, the instinct to run stayed for a little while.

He waited for his cousin to likewise settle, for her sobs to fade to sniffles, before he drew back. It wasn't nearly enough time for them to grieve the way they should, but they were up against a ticking clock none of them could afford to ignore. Pati and her son, the key to ending this awful game that kept taking from them, were missing.

"Did anyone hear the gunshots?" Robin asked.

"Nothing," Jason said. "And I would've been the closest."

Silver, plus a silencer.

The killer—or killers—weren't taking any chances. They'd covered their tracks too, no sign of footprints in the mud. But there were other signs and smells a tracker of average skill could follow. Bent tree limbs, broken stalks of winter weeds, bad coffee. Handing a steadier Jenn to Abigail, Robin followed the trail to the service road that snaked through the property. Tire tracks in gravel gave some direction. "They went south," he told the others once they joined him. "Likely a van, given the size and spacing of the tracks."

"We think we know where they're headed," Abigail said, as Jenn dug something out of her pocket.

"We found these in Olivia's room." She dropped two game chips into his palm, branded with the name and logo of Dyami's casino in Nipomo.

Fuck, Atlas had been right; there'd been a traitor in the pack. He should have argued harder to keep Pati and Pax out of their lands, but where else could they go and still get the rest of the team there in short order? Still wasn't close enough.

He checked the time on his phone. "The kidnappers can't have made it to Nipomo yet."

"Mac was already here," Jenn said. "Came to the same conclusion. He's on the horn with other departments. They're putting up roadblocks."

"What did the van that took Atlas look like?" Abigail asked.

"Mangled metal, when I was done with it," Robin replied, but he followed her train of thought. Maybe there were more like it connected to Dyami's business or the people he employed, though Robin doubted this was the work of hired muscle like the goons who'd come after Atlas.

He doubted this was Dyami's work at all. It wasn't Evan's either. Not flashy enough, and by now, Robin would recognize Atlas's twin's scent, would never forget it. There was no trace of Evan on the air.

Nevertheless, the casino chips were the best lead they had. They dialed in Mac, Robin described the van, then also told them about Lucy. Atlas had been convinced she and her husband were forced to cooperate the last time. Lucy believed in Nature's cause, according Atlas. She believed in Pati and Pax. Perhaps she'd cooperate by choice with the other side.

All that said, even if this was Dyami, the casino seemed too obvious. They'd head to familiar territory, but not there exactly. "If they're smart, they'll stay off the main roads," Robin said.

Jenn clutched his biceps, giving his arm a squeeze. "That's why we need our best tracker on this."

THIRTY-ONE

It was midday before they found the van halfway down a ravine below the winding road from Pajaro to Matsun, the feline shifter from Club Sutro hanging dead in the front seat, pinned there not by the seat belt but by a crossbow bolt to the chest.

The occasional siren sounded from the elevated road overhead, the local sheriff's department having blocked it off a mile in either direction, but down here, it was just Robin and Mac and a hovering guard of ravens, the terrain too steep for humans.

Unless you were a warlock who could snap into the perfect position. Except Atlas's aim was off this time, his right foot landing on a clump of muddy soil that gave way under his heel. Robin tensed, ready to pounce, anything to stop Atlas from tumbling into the raging water below, but then Mac squawked an order and Robin's coyote obeyed on instinct, freezing in place.

Another snap later, Atlas reappeared a couple inches over on a more stable incline. "Thanks for the assist," he said to Mac before turning his cocky smirk on Robin.

Who was sorely tempted to pounce for an entirely different reason. While they'd exchanged texts over the past eighteen hours, Robin hadn't heard his mate's voice or seen him in the flesh since the Canyon Lands. When Robin had left him to face down a deadly, determined witch alone. To kill her, as his texts had flatly informed the team. He'd survived whatever skirmish had resulted in Karoline's death, and now there he was, uninjured as far as Robin could tell.

Safe, relatively.

Like they needed to make Pax and Pati. The reasons they were there on the side of a mud-slick cliff, poking around an upside-down vehicle.

Atlas carefully bent to peer through the busted-out front windshield. "That's definitely Cyrus's handiwork." He narrowed his eyes, head tilted. "Is that the cat from the club the other night?"

Robin nodded. In retrospect, seeing how methodically and brutally the shifter had dispatched his uncle and cousins, how he'd risked handling silver to do it, Robin regretted putting Jason in his crosshairs at the club. If he'd gotten one of Mary's phoenixes killed . . . But it seemed the shifter hadn't realized who or what Jason was. Didn't matter now.

"Did you confirm Pati and Pax were in the van?"

Very carefully, Robin crossed in front of Atlas. Offering his hackles for balance and because he desperately needed the contact, Robin led him to the open back doors of the van. Inside was a baby bottle and Pax's blanket, one of the quilted ones Mac's mother had made.

Atlas conjured an orb and sent it slowly floating around the interior of the van. "No seats, no straps, nothing to hold on to," he said, cataloguing the same observations he and Mac had made. "If they'd been in there when the van went over the rail, there'd be blood, hair . . . bodies. No one could survive that."

The same conclusions too, especially given the one other piece of evidence Robin had to show him. They continued to carefully make their way to the driver's side where Robin stuck his muzzle through the open window and pointed it down, the direction of the pedals.

To where a cinder block was wedged against the gas pedal.

Atlas took one look through the window and whistled low. "Well, I guess that answers that question."

He didn't waste time on the precarious footing, letting Robin guide him back to a relatively stable ledge of rock. He leaned back against the wall of dirt, and Robin leaned against his front, keeping him secure and taking the contact he needed.

Atlas allowed it, indulged him more by combing his fingers through his fur as he talked through the evidence. "So, Dyami puts the feline hunter and your cousin in touch. She gets word to him that they're moving Pati and Pax, and he intercepts them." Robin appreciated the detachment in Atlas's summary and the acknowledgement of loss in his actions, a slow stroke over Robin's head, a lingering moment of silence, before he picked the debrief back up. "The cat wasn't actually headed for Nipomo." Robin swung his head around, ear cocked back at this new bit of intel. "Dyami is a silent partner in another casino in Matsun."

Matsun was halfway between YB and Nipomo. Close enough to both paranormal and human populations, far enough from the dangers of YB but still close enough to get in on the action while still drawing the more adventurous, rebellious humans from the South. "The shifter took the coastal road, occasionally detouring through the forests, towns, and missions to hide his trail, before cutting back through these mountains to the interior, on the way to Matsun, when Cyrus intercepted him."

Robin barked in the direction of the last rest stop.

Atlas nodded. "That makes sense. He takes Pati and Pax at the rest stop, then takes out the cat and sets up this whole scene," he said with a wave of his hand at the upside-down vehicle. "First things first, Mac, can you get the cat's phone?"

The raven carefully glided inside the cab, then back out a moment later, device in his talons. He dropped it into Atlas's hand, and after a quick flick of the warlock's green magic over the screen, the phone was unlocked. Atlas's fingers flew over the screen, typing out something. Robin put his muzzle on the inside of Atlas's elbow, tugging the arm down so he could see.

"We're going to let Dyami know the package was intercepted," Atlas said, "By Robin. See if we can draw my brother out, once and for all." That done, he tucked the stolen phone away and glanced back the direction of the rest stop. "As for Pati and Pax, Cyrus either subdued them at the rest stop. Or . . ."

Mac's ominous croak put sound to the tingle of unease working its way up Robin's spine.

"*Or*, Pati left with him voluntarily."

Because she was afraid not to, Robin wondered, or a more concerning possibility, no doubt the cause of his and Mac's unease, because Pati had been working with Cyrus all along.

THIRTY-TWO

Finding Cyrus took the rest of the day and the better part of the night. And the only reason they'd found him was because Paris had stepped in and called Lila's soul to him.

Mac had nearly had a coronary over the idea, which had been his husband's. After a day and night of police and tracking work turned up nothing, Paris had offered an alternative. If Cyrus had gone to his mother's house last time, was there another place that held meaning to them? And would Lila tell them? Mac had delivered enough evil souls to be extinguished, including Paris's own father, that he'd refused to believe Atlas when the warlock had assured them that the Lila who Paris might reach would be different, that it had been Chaos who'd infected her soul.

Mac wouldn't hear it, refusing to put his soulmate at risk. Robin couldn't say that if it was Atlas offering to do the same, that he wouldn't put up as fierce a fight. Atlas, of course, would tell him to fuck right off, and Paris was, lest anyone forget, Atlas's pupil. His delivery, though, was much gentler than Atlas's would have been, the medium reminding his husband that the clock was ticking. Solstice was two days away, and the future of peace was missing.

The raven had finally relented, but only with Liam, Mary,

Jason, and Atlas on standby to channel the soul if it proved hostile. Unnecessary, it turned out; Atlas hadn't lied. Lila had only been doing what she thought was best for her son, what Atlas's father had encouraged her to do, what he made her. Based on the timing, Atlas had determined channeling Chaos into Lila had been the last spell his father ever cast before he'd turned to religion.

Nearly fifty years of Hail Marys to assuage his guilt.

Atlas had simmered with anger, the knowledge that his father was an even bigger asshole than he'd already thought rage-making, but he'd stashed the fury in a mental box somewhere and cooled down while Paris had finished painting the small coastal cottage Lila had shown him.

An hour later, Robin was hiding in the shadows of a cypress grove near said cottage with Atlas and Brock and Adam and Mac. "How do you want to handle this?" he asked Adam.

"Ambush," he replied. "Atlas snaps us all in together."

Atlas propped himself against the closest tree trunk. "You're assuming he doesn't already know we're out here."

"Can you put a shield around us?" Mac asked.

"As soon as we land, but not a second sooner, if we don't want to end up out there," he said with a jut of his chin toward the rough-and-tumble ocean, another storm moving in.

"Got it," Adam said. "That'll have to be soon enough."

"Smash and grab?" Brock asked.

"No," Robin said, and everyone's gaze shot to him. "He'll just keep coming. We're two days out. We can't afford another swerve like this. And if Pati's working with him—"

"She'll just try it again," Atlas finished.

"All right," Adam said. "Brock, you take perimeter. You two" —he gestured at him and Atlas—"neutralize Cyrus. Mac and I will talk to Pati." That division made sense: a warlock lookout, the two heavies on the threat, the interrogators on the unknown.

There was another variable Robin needed to know how to handle. "And if we have to kill Cyrus?" he said, gaze landing on

Atlas. They'd both lost family to this war, so many, Robin most recently, and he was still tender, no time to grieve. And now Atlas's was in the crosshairs again. Recently discovered, and an enemy, but family, nonetheless.

Not a problem for Atlas. "Then we kill him."

Robin didn't buy it. "Atlas—"

"Don't," he said with a sharp shake of his head. "We share a sperm donor. That's it."

"But after we defeat Evan—"

"There will be only one Shaw left, assuming I survive."

Robin growled. That was not an outcome he would entertain.

"We need to go," Adam said. "Brock, you're up first."

The warlock snapped to the roof, landing silently, then after a moment, signaled them all clear. They positioned themselves so Adam, the human among them, was shielded, then, each with a hand on Atlas, rode his snap into the cabin.

And froze, the sight that greeted them catching them all off guard.

Pati was asleep on the couch beneath a colorful quilt, and in the rocking chair by the fire, under a similar quilt, Cyrus sat cradling Pax against his chest. His other hand rested on his knee, gripping a pistol.

"No one fucking move," he said, voice as rough as his appearance, then with a flick of his brown gaze to Atlas, added, "And no spells either, brother."

"We're not here for you," Adam said, human to human.

"I know. You're here for Pati and this little eaglet." He gently patted the snoring baby's back.

"Do you know what you're holding?" Mac said, his voice calm and even. He had the skills of a trained investigator, combined with the empathy of a reaper. Made him a hell of a negotiator.

Usually.

Cyrus wasn't so easy a sell. "I know he's important. He has something to do with my mother's death." His gaze drifted back to Atlas. "At your mother's hands. I kill this baby, and my mother will be avenged."

"Or," Atlas said, "I can give you our father instead. A win for both of us."

Cyrus smirked, and for the first time, Robin saw the resemblance between brothers. There wasn't much else they shared in common—Atlas was a pretty pale package in a compact body; Cyrus was on the grizzled side of handsome, with dark hair and eyes and a scar that bisected his tan face, and a body that was almost too big for the rocker, Pax a small bean on his massive chest—but that twist of their lips, that shared arrogance was strikingly familiar.

Until Pax muttered a soft mewl, his little fingers curling in Cyrus's T-shirt, and the big man's smirk morphed into a soft, affectionate smile that Robin couldn't ever remember seeing on Atlas's face.

Mac saw it too. "You have no intention of harming that child, do you?"

"Of course not," Cyrus said. "He's innocent, just like his mother, like mine was too."

"Why have you been hunting Atlas?" Robin asked.

"Not just Atlas, all of them, so they couldn't do to another person what was done to my mother." His brown eyes glanced at Adam. "Your redhead saved me the trouble with the first one."

"The first one?" Atlas said, taking a step forward.

He would've taken another if Robin hadn't grabbed the back of his shirt, Cyrus's finger curling around the trigger, the truth he threatened to spill, sending twin bolts of fear through him. Now was not the time for another fucking swerve, and this one would send Atlas veering off the road. "He's baiting you," Robin said.

Atlas kept his foot on the gas. "You mean Canton? Brown hair, blue eyes, preppy clothes."

"That's the one. A few nights after he turned Icarus into a vampire and the girl with him into whatever she is."

Atlas moved again, but not forward. He dug his wallet out of his pocket and withdrew a folded photo. Two actually, another fluttering to the floor with the wallet Atlas tossed aside, too busy shoving the photo in his hand toward Cyrus. "This night?"

Robin ignored the photo on the floor, ignored his own safety, and moved between Atlas and his half brother. "He's got it wrong."

"Look at this picture." He practically shoved it in Robin's face. Canton was squared off with a snarling Icarus, Mary standing off to the side, the photo clearly taken from someplace close, a surveillance angle. Like Cyrus said, the job being done for him, but the picture failed to capture what happened next.

"Atlas, it wasn't him."

His eyes widened, a spark of yellow—betrayal—exploding in them. "You knew?" He lifted his other hand to snap, but Robin, well familiar with the action by now, stopped him short, shoving his fingers through Atlas's and threading them together. He held his mate to this awful reality, racing around the bend and off the road with him because he could no longer afford to lose him. None of them could. "She did it," he told Atlas. "So Icarus wouldn't have to."

Yellow spiraled through the green, and it fucking terrified Robin, made him fear he was about to lose Atlas to the other side, but his mate's hand gripping his back, holding on to him like a lifeline, meant Atlas was fighting to stay with him too. Robin kept hold of his hand while he lifted his other, gripping Atlas's face, keeping his focus solely on him, fighting together, just the two of them. "Think, Atlas. You would have done the same for Cole. And if that had been me, if you'd turned me into a vampire and Deborah into Nature, or vice versa, either of us would have killed to spare the other from doing so in that state. I love you, but I would have killed you for her."

Atlas's gaze held his while the green pushed back against the yellow, his better self responding to the logic. Robin fed it more. "Put it in the same box as your father. We'll deal with it later."

Another endless moment passed as the yellow faded. Atlas

jerked his face free and cut a glare Adam's direction before he stepped over to the fire and threw the picture into the roaring flames.

"That's what she is, Nature?" Cyrus said, as Atlas leaned against the hearth. "And what was my mother?"

"Chaos."

He lifted his hand off Pax's back and gestured around the room. "Does this look like Chaos?"

"No, it looks and feels like peace." Everyone's attention swung the direction of the couch to where Pati was now sitting up, awake. She didn't seem fearful, just cautious as she took in the brewing conflict around her. Getting to her feet, she wrapped her blanket around her shoulders and stepped next to Cyrus's chair, her fingers softly combing over her baby's dark hair. "Which is what my son is."

"He's too young," Cyrus said, glancing up at her. "For any of this."

"Which is why we have to protect them," Mac said in his even negotiator tone from earlier.

Cyrus chuffed. "Fat lot of good you all have done with that."

"So you give it a try," Robin said, calling an audible. "If Pati is good with that?" At her nod, he explained his reasoning to the rest of the group. "His identity is scrubbed, he's a ghost, and no one knows about this place."

"Then how'd you find it?" Cyrus asked.

"Your mother told us," Atlas replied.

Cyrus was on his feet the next second, grizzled mug snarling at Atlas, the baby in his arms waking at the tension and letting out a wail.

Mac stepped between them. "Lila is good," he said, somehow keeping that calm tone even as the situation deteriorated around them. "My husband is a medium. He spoke to her. After she told us about this place, my brother, our reaper, delivered her."

"To?"

"Peace."

The tension left Cyrus's body, and he leaned into Pati beside them, their hands together on Pax's back. There was a connection there already. "Did you two know each other, before today?" Robin asked.

"No," Pati said, shaking her head. "But I knew right away that we could trust him."

Shared experience, years apart, but both part of this world not by their choice but by fate, who had seen fit to put them together.

Adam had come to the same conclusion. "We have a guard on the roof. We'll leave him here until we can get more of the pack in the area around you."

Cyrus opened his mouth to no doubt protest, and Robin beat him to it. "Not enough to give away your location and they won't bother you. Just backup, if you need it."

Cyrus looked to Pati, and at her nod, acquiesced.

"Good," Atlas said as he pushed off the hearth. "Since we're done here . . ."

Robin was too far away this time to stop him from snapping away. "Shit." He whipped his head to Adam. "Warn them."

He lifted his phone, text thread with Icarus open onscreen. "Already done."

"We need to get back—" He lost his words as his gaze caught on the other picture still on the floor. Golden eyes he'd only ever seen in pictures stared up at him, his mother's smiling face between two other blond women who were also smiling, their green eyes dancing. One was a mirror image of Daphne, only older, and the other . . . Now he knew where Atlas got his ethereal looks from—his mother. Who, along with Daphne's mother, clearly knew his. And Atlas knew this too? Had a picture of the three of them together in his wallet?

Betrayal found a new home, burning in Robin's gut as his head spun with the implications.

"Robin."

"What?" he barked at Mac and that even fucking tone,

unhappy to be on the receiving end of it. Calm was the antithesis of everything swirling inside him.

"He bit," Mac said, holding the feline shifter's phone out to him.

"Who? Dyami?"

"No, Evan."

Robin glanced down at the screen, at the text thread open on it. The message Atlas had shot off to Dyami yesterday and a new reply. **Sunrise, Matsun casino. E will be there.**

THIRTY-THREE

On first glance, Evan looked almost exactly like Atlas. His blond hair was maybe a shade darker, there was a mole beside one eye that Atlas didn't have, and their eye color was different now, but otherwise they shared the same pale skin and elegant features. The same defiant set of their chins. And Evan was dressed in the sort of tailored suit Robin used to think Atlas preferred.

He sounded just like his twin too, haughty and smug. "So, you're my brother's mate?"

This was a mind fuck. Same as it had been earlier that month at the vineyard. Maybe even more so. That day, things had been moving a mile a minute—Daphne dead, an innocent to rescue, brothers hurling orbs at each other, and Nature hiding in the cottage up the hill. Today, it was just him and Evan in a dimly lit casino bar.

With time to consider and his coyote banked, Robin understood how, for the past ten years, they'd been chasing the wrong man. And now that he knew the real Atlas, knew him down to his scent, he also better understood how hard the performance must have been, how much of it he'd shouldered alone.

Never again.

"I am," Robin said, as he claimed the stool on the other side of the bar from Evan, who was pouring high-dollar whiskey into crystal tumblers.

"Has he told you that I was supposed to be your sister's?"

Robin clenched his jaw to keep it from hitting the bar.

Evan laughed and pushed a tumbler in front of him. "My dear brother, always keeping secrets. She picked not one but two other people over me."

The head spinning from back at Cyrus's cabin returned, but Evan's bitterness over Deborah focused the anger on the twin who well and truly deserved it. "Sore loser much?"

"I was for a while, and then I killed her."

The Robin of two months ago would have leapt across the bar. But this Robin recognized the bait for what it was. And this Robin had a mate—a lying one, albeit—he had to get back to. For the truth, about more than one thing. And because they had to work together if they were going to defeat the lookalike on the other side of the bar.

Robin tossed back the high-dollar bourbon like the low-class dog he was sure the slowly sipping warlock assumed he was.

Evan turned up his pretty nose and propped himself against the backbar. "Is he too much for you? Or not enough, like I clearly wasn't for Deborah? Is that why you're betraying him now?"

Robin laughed. "He's just right, actually." Atlas was smart, intense, arrogant, elegant, and filthy. He was wild at times, measured at others, and he was the only person in Robin's life since Deborah who had made him feel settled. He reached over the bar for the whiskey, refilled his glass, then took a long drink before mentally asking Atlas for forgiveness as he borrowed his words for a lie he needed to tell. "But I don't do we."

Evan stayed leaned against the backbar, arms crossed, cut crystal tumbler against his lips. "Tell me more."

"I don't want a mate, I don't want a team, and I lost my family the day my sister died."

"You're a lone wolf."

"There's something inside here"—he tapped at his chest with

the glass—"that makes me want to run. I want to be free. I don't want anything or anyone tying me down. I want to follow the jobs wherever they take me." The words that had come naturally before now tasted awful in his mouth.

But they did the trick, Evan polishing off his whiskey and setting his glass aside. "Your track record is impressive. Chaos could use you."

"One-time deal," Robin said with a sharp shake of his head. "You want Pati and her son, I can deliver."

"And your fee?"

He grabbed a napkin off the nearby stack, a pen from the cup by the register, and jotted down a figure and account number. He slid it across the bar to Evan.

The warlock balled it up and tossed it in the trash. "The money will be in your account when you deliver."

Robin threw back the rest of his drink, grabbed the bottle of whiskey, and slid off his stool. "No deal. Not how it works."

"How do I know you'll deliver?" Evan asked his retreating backside.

Robin spun on his heel mid-room. "You were the one who just commented on my track record." He tipped the bottle up for a healthy swallow, then wiped his lips off with the back of his hand. "Do you think I took payment afterward from any of them?"

"You drive a hard bargain, Mr. Whelan." He drew out his phone, tapped the screen a few times, and a moment later, Robin's phone vibrated in his pocket. Wire received. Evan grabbed another napkin, scribbled something on it, then strolled out from behind the bar.

Robin had another flash of cognitive dissonance, thinking he was seeing his mate approach in another damn suit. But as quick as the confusion came, it vanished with a single inhaled breath. All he could smell was the rotting stench of dark warlock, not a hint of spring.

Evan drew even with him and handed him the napkin. "Bring them there. Tomorrow night at eleven."

Robin pocketed the coordinates for the altar site in the Canyon Lands. The single weak spot in the veil, other than in La Purisima, that their team didn't control. "What are you going to do with them?"

"Use them to open the veil for Chaos to rejoin us."

Use them as sacrifice, more precisely. Robin forced his coyote not to snarl. Tough doing when Evan stepped closer. "Are you sure I can't tempt you?" He laid a hand on his chest and stared up at him with hooded yellow eyes. "One twin for the other. Maybe it was the two of us who were meant to be together."

As attracted as Robin was to Atlas, as he'd always been, he felt zero desire for the lookalike in front of him. Only hatred that he was certain would never turn into anything more. Not because he was fated to be with Atlas, but because the man in front of him was pure evil.

"Maybe our mothers got it wrong," Evan said, as he glided his hand higher.

Robin grabbed his wrist and yanked his hand off him. Not wanting his touch or the distraction. "Our mothers?"

"Ask my brother after you fuck him one last time." Evan's sly smile made the urge to strangle him harder and harder to resist. Made stealing the bottle back from his hand too easy, Evan turning on his heel and tipping the bottle up as he'd done. "Good day, Mr. Whelan."

Robin's head spun all the way to the parking lot, distracting him such that he missed the fact his car doors were unlocked. But he didn't miss the smell of intruder. He whipped around in the seat, prepared to strike, but Dyami slowly straightened with his hands raised, his palms outs.

"I'm here to help!" the pretender said.

"Since when?"

"Since I realized I was wrong." He handed Robin a folded piece of paper. "The real altar is here. Just call, and my people will be there. For peace."

THIRTY-FOUR

Robin didn't think twice about walking into Atlas's glitzy Sunset Hill high-rise. Evan had all but told him to go confront Atlas, to fuck him one last time. Robin intended to do both, and he hoped like hell it wasn't the last time for either.

He opened the door to Atlas's unit, wondering which would come first—fight or fuck. Finding Atlas in front of the floor-to-ceiling windows in nothing but a towel, water still dripping from the ends of his hair seemed to indicate a fuck was up first.

Until Atlas spoke and his voice was ice cold. "You lied to me."

Fight, then. "So did you."

Robin tossed his phone, wallet, and keys on the kitchen island where his mother's letters lay open and scattered. He'd left them at the condo when they'd swung by the other day. For safe-keeping and for Atlas to read, hoping he might connect more dots for Robin. Seeing them strewn from one end of the island to the other made him regret the ask, brought his own anger back to simmering. He withdrew the photo of Willow and the Shaw women from his pocket and crossed the living room to Atlas. "Explain this to me," he barked, shoving the picture in Atlas's line of sight.

Atlas glanced at the photo, then back to the ocean outside his tinted windows. "You first."

The asshole still wouldn't give him anything.

Fine, he'd put his cards on the table first if it meant getting to the truths he wanted sooner. "For what it's worth, I didn't know Canton was your brother until that day in the vineyard. I don't think Mary or Icarus had made the connection until then either."

"Nature doesn't always tell her everything."

"Well, as soon as I found out, I tried telling you what happened, that day and on that rooftop in La Purisima."

Atlas whipped his gaze to him, and Robin was relieved to see his irises were green, the deep mossy shade he loved, no hint of yellow. "You couldn't just tell me?"

"Would it have made a difference?" he bit back, then regretted the tone when Atlas retreated, turning his gaze back to the waves. Robin tempered his tone and added, "I didn't mean to betray you."

"They were best friends," Atlas replied.

"Who?" Robin asked, the non sequitur catching him off guard.

He nodded at the photo in Robin's hand. "My mother, your mother, and Daphne's."

Except he'd never seen the other two women in that picture. Not in the flesh and not in any photo albums at the homestead. "If they were best friends, why weren't they around after Mom died?"

"Jasper forbade it." More dots connected: his uncle's distrust of outsiders, his skepticism of witches, his reluctance to travel any farther south than YB. "They kept their distance, and then they died."

"Casting Chaos out of Lila and behind the veil?"

Atlas nodded. "It's why Canton had to be the one to channel Nature into Mary. Mom and Vanessa, Daphne's mom, couldn't know who the new vessel was, in case they lost control of the spell and Lila got the information out of them."

"And where were you?"

"Keeping Evan distracted. He was keen to use the disturbance as cover for killing the woman who'd spurned him."

"Deborah."

"I stopped him that night. I couldn't that day. I'm sorry."

Robin turned from the view of the endless horizon, too much when his world was already starting to spin, and sank onto the living room couch. It was boringly modern and not particularly comfortable but it was squarely within the walls of the condo. "He said you were meant for me, and Deborah was meant for him. That our mothers had made it that way."

Atlas leaned back his head and groaned, not the good kind.

"Make it make sense, Atlas. Neither Deb nor I could understand what Mom was trying to tell us in those letters, other than vague notions of mates and Nature, and Jasper wouldn't say a damn thing either. He took whatever he knew to the grave with him. Same as Daphne. I need you to explain it to me. Please."

Atlas turned from the windows but rather than sit on the cushion beside him, he sat on the couch arm facing the bar. "Look at the colors of the ribbons. With everything you know now, *look.*"

Green and yellow.

Green and yellow.

Robin gasped, dots connecting.

"They weren't just best friends," Atlas continued. "My mom, Sybil, and Vanessa worshiped yours. They were her disciples. Willow was the last time Nature and Chaos were joined in one vessel."

Robin had never been in a tornado, but he figured this mental and emotional whirlwind was what it felt like. "How?"

"Sheer force of will. They're not supposed to exist in one person, not until the eagle brings peace, but your mother held them as long as she could, until she ultimately succumbed to the most natural and chaotic thing on this earth, childbirth."

"She knew she wouldn't make it." That was why she'd written those letters—the uncertainty of what would happen to her and the magic inside her when she brought Deb and him into this world. And if his father had been anything like him, the guilt would have eaten him alive. Driven him to make it stop so he could be reunited with the love of his life.

Which left Deb and him.

"What happened to the magic? When Deb and I were born?" He swallowed hard and inhaled deep, the memory of wild mustard tickling his senses. "When Mom died?"

Atlas laid a hand on his shoulder. "When she died, my mom and Vanessa channeled the deities into new vessels. But some of the magic was passed on to you and Deborah."

More and more dots connected.

His mother's written words about *wild* being only one of their instincts. Her coaching on how to use the magic inside them to silence that wild. Her lessons in tracking, in tending the homestead gardens, in using everything nature had to offer, that he and Deb would be uniquely able to detect and manipulate.

"She says in one of those letters that our mates would find us when Nature needed us most. Deb thought that was David and Adam. I thought I'd run from mine, forever."

"And I thought you two were intended to ground us, a twin for a twin, if Evan and I ever had to hold the deities. There were two of us, so it would be easier to share the load, to balance the forces and keep the peace until the eagle arrived. Until we had lasting peace."

"But that doesn't work anymore," Robin said, shaking his head. "Deborah is gone and Evan's evil. I looked the devil in the face today, and we can't let him have Chaos or Nature. Nothing good will come of it, and Pax is still too young."

"I know, and until tonight, I thought it was me who would have to hold them both instead. After all, it's what my mother named me."

"Balance."

"I was wrong."

Robin jerked his gaze to his; he hadn't seen the swerve

coming. He parsed back through Atlas's words, through his mother's.

Until tonight.

Wild.

Magic.

Peace.

Balance.

More connections, the pieces coming together in a different way to form a new picture that caused Robin's chest to tighten and panic to swirl in his gut.

"No, no, no," he muttered. "Deborah was the good one. She was Nature. You don't want to give me Chaos either."

Atlas stretched out a hand, cupping Robin's cheek. "Don't think so little of yourself."

"But she was good."

"You are too. You both were, and the both of you were a little wild too, a little fearless, a little chaotic."

Robin huffed. "A little?"

"I was trying to be kind," Atlas said with a roll of his eyes that was both obnoxious and comforting. But then his face turned serious again as he pushed off the arm of the couch and came around to sit on the coffee table in front of him. "You both were primed, with a little bit of Nature and a little bit of Chaos."

"But Deborah's gone."

Atlas averted his gaze, guilt so obvious and familiar that Robin cursed himself for not recognizing it, for not making another horrifying connection sooner.

For not realizing that Atlas's high-end vodka was the same brand that was anonymously sent to him at the bar halfway around the world where he was drinking the night before Deborah's last pack call came in. When Robin had gotten so shit-faced he'd missed it. He'd blocked out everything from that night except the guilt from the consequences of his actions. But someone had helped him along.

"Are you the reason I didn't answer Deborah's call that day?"

Atlas righted his gaze and lifted his chin. "Yes."

Robin shot off the couch, nearly knocking Atlas off the arm in the process, all that simmering anger coming to a boil. "And to think, I came in here tonight thinking I'd told the bigger lie. First my mother"—he flung his arms wide, letting all the chaos hang out—"and now this!"

Atlas wasn't afraid of it, of him, in the least. He stepped directly in front of him and grasped his face. "This battle couldn't afford to lose you both. *I* couldn't afford to lose you, and I wasn't even in love with you then."

Robin's eyes grew wide, hearing those words out of Atlas's mouth.

And in the next breath, realizing he'd already said them to Atlas, earlier at Cyrus's cabin when it had been the warlock dangerously on edge.

Balance.

A fucking mirror, in more ways that Robin discovered every day.

The two of them, in this together.

"My brother was on the warpath that day," Atlas said. "He was twice jilted, and Vincent gave him the perfect cover. He wanted revenge and Chaos's attention, and he got both. By killing the woman who'd scorned him and who was also one of Nature's vessels. I wasn't going to let him have the other one. I made sure you were safe, and then I got to the scene as fast as I could, but I couldn't stop him. I tried, Robin. I promise you I tried with everything I had, but I wasn't strong enough, then."

His anger deflated as the overwhelming despair rushed back in. "What am I supposed to do with this, Atlas? Any of it, all of it?"

Atlas eased the grip on his face, gently holding his cheek as he closed the distance between them. "It was supposed to be the two of you, a shared burden, but now you have to be the strong one."

Too much, too wide, more than the peaks and valleys of the range that stretched around their homestead. He shook his head, eyes slipping closed, breaths coming short as he faltered. "That's not me, Atlas. I'm a traitor."

Atlas cupped the other side of his face and pressed their foreheads together, making Robin's world smaller, making it so he could breathe. "You made a mistake that I helped you make. That doesn't make you a traitor."

"But Paris—"

"Was not a mistake, and the team has forgiven you. They'll rally behind you."

"Atlas, I run, *that's* who I am." He'd thought he'd changed when he'd stood in that casino bar with Evan, but that was before the rug had been yanked out from under him. Before his old world had been turned upside down by back-to-back revelations that put the weight of said world on his shoulders. He was not the man for that job. Deborah could have done it, but not—

Atlas's lips brushed over his, silencing the whirlwind. Settling him. "If you run, I will run with you. I will run with you forever." He drew back far enough for Robin to see the truth in his dark green gaze. "But you can't run from your soul, Robin. And neither can I."

He held his stare another long moment, his whole world right in front of him, his mate. The world didn't seem so scary, so big in the forest. In the eyes of the man magic had put in his path but who had found his own way into Robin's heart. "You settle me," he told him.

"And you balance me," Atlas replied, thumb skating over his cheek.

Robin would do anything to keep that, to keep him, including the thing that scared him the most. He inhaled deep and nodded. "All right," he said. "We face it. We fight."

A smirk turned up one corner of Atlas's lips. He lowered a hand and loosened the knot in the towel at his hip, the damp terrycloth hitting the floor. "After we fuck."

And because Atlas hadn't given him anything earlier, Robin

resisted giving him the easy win now. One last fight, since they did it so well. "I don't answer to you."

Atlas's eyes sparkled, spring in all the shades of green. "But my soul answers to yours."

Robin brought their lips back together, bruising and soft. Balanced. "And mine to yours."

The only fight after that was over where to fuck: against the windows—too distracting; on the couch—too soft; in the bedroom —way too far away. They settled on the living room floor, with Atlas astride his lap, riding his cock, while Robin stroked Atlas's length with his spit-slick fist. Getting them off together just as the fog rolled back from the shore, giving way to the bright midday sun that streamed in through the windows and painted a sweaty head-thrown-back Atlas in shades of orange and gold.

On fire, with no shield between them to stop the smell of spring from filling the air around them, from filling their souls.

Robin would fight anyone to protect this connection, this mate he'd never wanted and now couldn't imagine his life without. And when it was all over, he couldn't wait to run with Atlas out there in the sun.

THIRTY-FIVE

"Evan wants us to think tomorrow night's spell will take place at the altar in the Canyon Lands." Robin rested his forearms against the back of the chair at the head of the cellar tasting table, next to where Atlas sat, as far away from Mary and Icarus at the other end as possible. The warlock might understand why Mary had killed his older brother, but he wasn't ready to forgive her yet. Robin couldn't blame him.

"Where's it going down for real?" Jason asked from Atlas's other side.

"La Purisima."

Icarus dropped the sweater he was panic crocheting, the metal hooks clattering to the table, his forehead following suit as he thunked it against the weathered wood. "Fuck me."

"Home sweet home," Atlas singsonged, and Robin bit the inside of his cheek, fighting a grin. It was a cheap shot, but Atlas's haughty poking at Icarus felt like the most normal thing in the world right then.

"But LP is full of humans," Paris said, dampening the admittedly ill-timed humor. The medium was no doubt already contemplating the cleanup work, assuming they survived. He, Mac, and Liam would be busy for days.

"Like picking sacrifices off a tree," Adam correctly assessed.

"It's risky," Abigail said. "The humans could turn on them."

"Or on us," Robin added.

"What happens when you don't show up with Pati and Pax?" Jenn asked from Robin's other side.

"We'll call Evan and tell him I killed them." Robin took the stack of printouts Atlas handed him and tossed them onto the table. Photos of a staged massacre. "I'll tell Evan what he thinks he already knows. That I'm a traitor."

"Why would Evan believe you?" Adam asked.

"Because Deborah betrayed him already," Atlas said. "She was supposed to be his mate, and she chose David and you over him."

A wide-eyed Adam propped his elbows on the table and held his head in his hands. Robin felt for his friend. Been there, done that, got the head spinning. Icarus coasted a hand over his shoulder while Mac picked up the interrogation.

"He'll have a backup plan," the raven said to Atlas. "It won't be as powerful as Pati and Pax would've been, but he'll be ready."

"Good thing we have the last barrier between him and Chaos."

Gazes drifted toward Mary until Robin straightened. "Not her, me."

Icarus whipped his head up, ginger brows racing north. "You?"

"Evan wants Chaos. I'm ready to take them both. Like my mother did. Like Deborah and I were supposed to do together."

Multiple gasps of "What?" echoed around the table, except from the green-haired pixie at the other end.

"I thought it was me and Evan," Atlas explained. "That we were supposed to hold Nature and Chaos together, with Robin and Deborah as our anchors, but Evan's unanchored and only interested in Chaos. If he succeeded in bringing Chaos through, I was going to channel them both into me and balance the ends, with Robin as my anchor, but it was never me." He glanced up at

Robin, the confidence in his gaze making Robin stand that much taller. "I'm the anchor, he's the vessel."

Questions erupted.

"What's that mean?" from Jason.

"What's he have to do?" from Paris.

"Will he make it?" from Jenn, her voice rough as she turned in her chair toward Atlas. "I can't lose any more family."

"He'll make it," Atlas said, reaching across the chair between them and covering her hand. "If I have anything to say about it."

"The phoenixes are ready," Mary said. "The other warlocks and witches too."

All the work Atlas had been doing with her when he wasn't with him the past two weeks. "You're ready to let it go?" Robin asked her.

Mary's hazel gaze slid to Atlas. "As he's told me multiple times, I was only a vessel."

But she was family to the man beside her. "Will she survive it?" Icarus pressed.

"Will you kill me if she doesn't?" Atlas bit back, and Robin clenched his jaw. He could give Atlas the prior dig, but this one was a push too far, especially when emotions were raw and life as they knew it was on the line.

He prepared to step in, to defuse the situation, but Mary beat him to it. "It's my choice, Icarus. I'm ready to be the old lady who complains about her little brother and his rowdy friends. I'm ready to live my life." She shifted her gaze to him. "Are you ready to give up yours?"

"I'm not giving up anything," Robin said. "I'm taking responsibility." He split a glance between Jenn and Adam. "I'm doing for her what I should have done ten years ago. I'm here now. And I'll stay here until Pax is ready."

"You'll be a target," Mac said. "Even if you kill Evan, someone will always come for you."

"They'll have to go through me first." Atlas threaded their fingers together, and Robin couldn't help but smile. All the times he'd done the same to keep Atlas from snapping away, from running, and now Atlas was tying them together. No more running. "Can he count on all of you?"

Adam rose first, walking the length of the table to where Robin stood and throwing his arms around him. "She would be so proud of you. I'm here for you, whatever you need."

Paris shot out of his chair next and practically launched himself at Robin. "Thank you for giving him a chance," he whispered, and Robin grinned through the wet in his eyes. "I'm with you."

Mac was next, a hug as calm as his husband's had been enthusiastic. "I and the rest of the flock are behind you."

One by one, the others followed, a hug and a pledge, until only Jenn was left.

When his cousin moved to lower her head in deference, Robin gently clasped her shoulder, stopping her short. "Don't," he said. "You are the pack leader, and a damn good one. Better than I ever would've been." He lowered his head to her instead, but only for a moment before Jenn yanked him into a crushing hug.

"Your pack will be there for you," his leader said. "Always."

THIRTY-SIX

"Where are you?" Evan snapped in greeting.

"If you're referring to the traitor," Atlas replied into Robin's phone that he held between them, the two of them standing on the end of the lake dock, slightly away from their gathered forces. "He's in my favorite pair of silver handcuffs."

Robin liked the sound of that—well, not the silver part—but the mention of handcuffs in Atlas's confident, haughty tone was a welcome reprieve after twenty-four hours of nonstop apocalypse prep. He and Atlas hadn't even had time for an end-of-the-world fuck, and he was pretty damn sure Adam and Mac had each gotten that courtesy when it had been their turn in the shit.

"Looks like he betrayed you too," Atlas added, and Robin tuned back in. At his mate's nod, he pressed Send on the pictures Cyrus had staged. They watched as the delivery notification beneath the text bubble changed from Sending to Delivered to Read, then waited as the silence from the other end dragged on.

No words, no sound, no reply from the other warlock.

Atlas continued to needle, tsking his brother. "I thought you would've learned your lesson by now. First Deborah, now Robin. But I guess it wasn't so bad this time. The dog just took your money and ran, not your whole reason for existing."

A low menacing snarl rumbled over the line.

"I can give you a reason again," Atlas said, tone mimicking Mac's when he was negotiating, calm and even, offering Evan the redemption Robin had been sure he would. "There's still work to do, brother. Last offer."

Evan didn't take the out. "You're an idiot if you think I don't have a backup plan."

"I fully expect it," Atlas replied, infusing his voice with equal strength, two powerful warlocks squaring off. "You won't win this. And you won't see our mother on the other side. You won't keep your promise."

Another long pause, and then, "I broke it a long time ago. She won't be surprised," before the line went dead.

Decision made, fate sealed.

Robin ended the call and handed Atlas the phone. "What did you all promise her?"

"That we'd join her in peace when peace also existed on this side of the veil."

"You'd have to make all the right choices to get there." It was a heavy ask on its own, but that wasn't all Sybil had asked of her sons.

"It's not been easy." He tucked the device in his pocket, then looked up with unguarded eyes, the first time Robin had ever seen him so open. "You were the hardest one to make."

Robin was tempted to cup his cheek, to return soft with soft, but that wasn't the balance Atlas needed, not right now. He gripped his face instead, rough, the way he needed it, and held him firm, green clashing with gold. "Thank you for making the right one."

He smashed their lips together, drowning in spring one last time before taking the dive into winter, hoping like hell they made it out the other side.

"Anytime now," Icarus snarked from the lakeshore behind them, popping the bubble around the small world he and Atlas had made for themselves on the end of the dock.

Robin didn't feel overwhelmed, though. Atlas had insisted they stage their forces here, on the lake where Robin had spent countless hours with his sister, where the range and world out there didn't feel so big. Atlas had done it for him, when he'd needed it most.

He squeezed the warlock's fingers, threaded through his own, as they returned to the shore.

"He said no?" Mary asked.

"Did you expect anything else?" Atlas replied.

"A deity can hope."

"The time for hope has passed," Adam said. "It's time for action."

"To end this," Robin agreed. "Word from recon?" he asked Mac.

"Site confirmed," he answered. "The revival field in La Purisima, like Dyami told us."

Icarus leaned his head back on a pained groaned. "Fucking irony."

His partner, however, was focused on logistics. "How many?" Adam pressed for details.

"So far, the flock reports a fieldful."

"And Evan?" Atlas asked.

"Not there yet, but the altar is ready."

For whomever he appeared there with, like he and the giant had appeared with Paris at the Stick. All the giants were gone now, though, so who would be at Evan's side tonight? Who would help him channel the souls to thin the veil? Who would be the sacrifice on the altar? Judging by the location of the moon, they were five minutes from finding out. "You're sure you can get us all there?" he asked Atlas.

The warlock glared at him through narrowed green eyes. "Fuck you for even asking."

Robin grinned; there was the Atlas he loved. "We're ready," he told Adam, and the call went down the line and through the crowd to move to their designated positions in the forest. A phoenix paired with a warlock or witch at each point of the star, the pack gathered around the arc between each point, the rest of their forces inside the circle. Adam and Icarus, Mac and Paris, and Liam, Jenn, and Abigail in a close circle around Atlas, Mary and him in the center of the giant forest pentagram.

Nature at its most powerful.

Robin barely got the "I love you" out before Mary and Paris shouted "Go," their sense of the thinning veil keener than the rest, and Atlas dropped to his knees, digging his hands in the dirt. Lines of green magic shot across the ground, bringing the pentagram to life, and Robin was powerless to resist the shift, same as every other shifter in the circle.

And when the phoenixes and magicians put their hands to the ground too, fire and magic racing back on either side of Atlas's green and colliding with Mary in the center, completing the circuit, it was as if the earth fell out from under Robin's paws.

THIRTY-SEVEN

He landed in a field, paws hitting hay, and as soon as he lifted his head, several things became clear.

While there were paranormals among the crowd they'd ported into, most of the people there were humans.

Said humans seemed to be there for a revival, led by the priest sitting shirtless on the altar of plywood and two-by-fours, railing about sin and the ultimate sacrifice to cleanse his soul. The same priest, Niall, who'd sinned with Atlas in a club earlier that month.

And behind the altar stood a sharp-dressed warlock holding a knife and on either side of him were two older men holding the priest's outstretched arms. One of the men shared the same blond hair and nose as Atlas's deceased cousin. The other wore a smirk that matched that of his son beside him . . . and of his other son, the man Robin loved.

Robin threw back his head and roared at the betrayal—of Atlas, of Sybil, of Deborah and his own mother.

Their presence announced, pandemonium erupted.

Some of the humans ran. Others revealed weapons they'd hidden under their jackets. They'd been primed, by the priest and supposed converts behind the altar with Evan. Adam gave the call to spare them when they could, Jenn echoing it to the pack, but a crossbow was a crossbow, and as their group made their way forward in the crowd, Robin didn't hesitate to bite into any human aiming at his family. Same as Atlas beside him, hurling green orbs of magic, and Mary, slinging knives at anyone who got close to their fighters.

"Atlas!" Paris shouted from where he was crouched beside one of the dead. "The altar!"

Robin slung the latest attacker aside and rounded behind Atlas, stomach sinking at the sight a half crowd away. Long bloody slashes crisscrossed Niall's chest, and deep cuts bisected the insides of his arms, blood spilling out of him. Pierce and James moved to either end of the alter, Evan remaining in the middle, and the magic that rippled over the field was awful, like it was a wind scooping up souls and sending them skyward.

It chilled Robin's insides and made his stomach churn, the dreadful dark magic stench left behind only adding to the nausea.

"We need to get to that altar!" Atlas shouted.

Robin howled for backup, and Jenn and Abigail joined him in a point, more of the pack flanking them, clearing a path forward by claw and teeth, for Jason and Atlas who were likewise hurling orbs of fire and magic at anyone who got in their way.

Adam, Icarus, and Paris, with Mary between them, were also making their way forward, while Mac, Liam, Kai, and the rest of the ravens sailed higher, maneuvering above the altar, avoiding enemy orbs while trying to intercept the souls the evil warlocks were using like a battering ram against the veil.

"I thought you two were done with magic?" Atlas shouted at his father and uncle when they were close enough to be heard. They were still fighting their way through what appeared to be the other side's best fighters at the base of the altar, other shifters and warlocks tempted Chaos's promise of power.

"He's closing the veil once and for all," Pierce called back. "Like you and Daphne, and Sybil and Vanessa would never do."

"We're finishing this!" James added.

"Is that what you think he's doing?" Atlas scoffed.

"He's thinning it, you morons," Jason shouted. "He wants to bring Chaos through."

"He's ending this!" Pierce continued to insist, but James was wavering, his hold on the altar and the magic loosening.

Adam noticed the same. "Paris!" he shouted. "Call Daphne to you." The problem with thinning the veil was that it could work in their favor too. The souls being swept up coalesced around the stately blond who appeared a moment later over her father's shoulder. "Daddy, stop," Daphne said. "He's using you like he used me."

Paris didn't stop there. Canton and Cole appeared next, and Atlas gasped beside him.

"Dad, stop this!" Canton pleaded. "Don't make our deaths for nothing."

"Evan, if you stop now," Cole begged, "I'll forgive you, Mom will forgive you."

And then Lila, adoringly wrapping herself around Pierce. "Your sons need you."

"Argh!" Pierce shouted, letting go of the altar.

For a second, as Robin and his contingent broke through the line, he thought victory was within their grasp, but then Pierce whirled on his heel, set his sights on Paris, and spun up a globe, arm reared back.

Robin tensed to jump, to vault over the altar if that was what it would take to prevent Pierce from hurling that globe at the best of them. But he didn't need to. Green magic streaked past him and collided with Pierce, sending him tumbling.

Robin whipped around in time to see pain streak across Atlas's face, to feel it in his own chest. A kill his mate hadn't wanted to make but one he'd had to—to protect his real family.

And Robin acted to protect his. Sensing a threat to Atlas, he spun back around, just in time to see Evan cast a yellow globe in their direction. Robin flattened Atlas, taking Mary down with them, the tip of his other ear taking the singe.

And fuck if that didn't piss him off more.

End this! the wild called inside him.

"Get what you deserve," Mary whispered in his ear.

He roared for his pack, and they answered, rushing to meet him at the foot of the altar, jumping after him, as he leapt the altar, sending Evan wheeling backward.

The force of Adam's bullet, Atlas's green globe, and Robin's big coyote body all hitting him at once took him to the ground.

Robin stood on the laughing warlock's chest, Jenn on one arm, Abigail on the other, as blood leaked out of his wounds. But once Adam and Atlas joined them, Evan's laughter stopped and his words, gargled through blood bubbling on his lips, turned Robin's insides even to ice. "I never intended to live." His yellow eyes, swirling with gray, drifted overhead. "You brought Chaos through the veil. Not me." Nearly all gray, they traveled back to Atlas. "My backup plan, brother."

After one last gasp, his chest stilled under Robin's paws.

And then the earth heaved, worse than any jolt he'd felt in YB since the Rift, and he was knocked off balance.

A yawning canyon opened in the ground and swallowed the altar whole. Threatened to swallow more. "Robin!" Atlas shouted. "Help me!"

He rolled back onto his feet, just in time to get a paw around Mary before the canyon took her.

"Higher ground!" Adam shouted, and everyone who could got a hand on a warlock who snapped them to the ridge at the other end of the field. But their position wouldn't last long, the canyon growing wider with each shake of the earth.

Atlas landed crouched beside him and laid a hand on his chest. "Shift!" he ordered, and Robin's magic answered, putting him back in human form. "Are you ready?" Atlas asked him.

"Do it now." The future of his pack, the lives of his family, of his mate depended on it.

Atlas pressed a kiss to his lips. "I love you too."

It was the last thing Robin remembered before magic seared through him, Atlas's and the other witches' and warlocks', the burning life fire of the phoenixes, the souls that Paris called to him, the magic some of them brought to bear, including Sybil's and Vanessa's, Daphne's, Canton's, and Cole's.

Ripping him from one end to the other.

Magnets pushing against each other.

Like he would never be put back together again.

The terrifying distance between one piece of him and the other.

The span of every wide-open space that had ever made him feel claustrophobic.

Like he'd never be able to run far enough to put it all back together.

Blood pounding in his ears and racing through his veins.

His coyote crying out.

His mother's, his twin's answering.

His pack answering, coming together around him with the rest of his family, bounding him in and making it so he couldn't be ripped so far apart.

Making it like he was back on the dock in the forest.

A whisper of spring tickled his nose, and then warm lips brushed his forehead. "I'll run with you."

Mate.

His blood calmed, the magic settled, his soul—both sides of it —planted.

He opened his eyes and gasped. Atlas's green gaze was swirled through with another color. Not yellow, but gold. Like his. And reflected in them were his own, swirling with green.

He lifted a hand, gripping his face. "Mine."

Atlas gripped his face right back. "Mine."

Their lips connected, "yours" a promise they both made, forever.

THIRTY-EIGHT

Robin was beginning to think Mac's family should just leave the festival tent up year-round. It had gone up for Samhain, stayed up for Mac and Paris's wedding, and now was playing host to Yule.

All his family under one tent, sparkling lights strung from one side to the other, making reality seem like a fairy tale.

His pack, Jenn and Abigail and others from the homestead and nearby range, joining after the funerals today and camping here for the remainder of the holidays.

The extended family Deborah had brought into his life, Icarus on Adam's lap as they debated with Mac and Paris and Jason and Kai over how long it would take to reopen Club Sutro this time.

Even the family that had recently come with Atlas, Cyrus cradling a sleeping Pax while not being shy at all about his interest in a once-again fully human Mary, who was dancing up a storm with Pati.

Robin stood on the outskirts of it all, leaned against a sturdy tent pole, sipping a beer and, for the first time in his life, not feeling like an outsider.

He'd fought for them, and they'd fought for him too, answering his call and helping to hold him together when it had felt impossible.

They were his, and he was theirs.

But there was someone else he belonged to first.

He went searching for his mate, unsurprised to find him stretched out on a chaise under the pergola, smoking a joint and watching the sunset. "Trade you?" he said, offering the beer for a hit.

Atlas wrinkled his nose. "Not if that beer was the last beverage on earth."

"Because that sort of absolute worked out so well for you the last time."

Atlas handed him the joint and flipped him off in the same motion. Sexy fucking asshole.

Robin tossed the beer bottle aside, then lowered himself onto the side of his chaise, a hand on Atlas's stomach while he smoked. It had become a habit after LP, always needing to have a hand on Atlas when he was near. Maybe it would pass, eventually, but it helped him feel settled. And Atlas didn't seem to mind.

"You doing okay?" Atlas asked, a less pleasant habit he'd picked up after LP.

Careful to keep the joint off the furniture and his mate, he stretched over Atlas. "For the last fucking time, I'm good. Better than, even. And if I'm ever not, I will tell you."

Atlas held his gaze, seeming to assess the truth of his promise, and finding it sufficient, huffed out a "Fine."

Robin chuckled. "You're grumpy today."

"I'm not grumpy, I'm horny. We saved the world, and it's been nonstop festival or family ever since. We didn't even get to fuck before—"

Robin cut off his rant with a kiss that was admittedly more laughter than passion, but the direction of Atlas's thoughts had so closely mirrored his own that he couldn't help but find the humor in their mutual frustration. He snuck a hand under his kilt and fondled his bare balls.

"That's not nice," Atlas muttered against his lips. "On either count."

"Snap us to your vineyard."

Atlas drew back, meeting his gaze. "Why?"

"Because I want to roll around in the dirt with you. I want all this"—he trailed a finger along the underside of Atlas's stiffening cock—"in its natural element."

He'd barely finished the last word when he landed on his back between the rows of vines, Atlas tearing open his flannel and attacking his chest, tongue swirling around one then the other nipple before Atlas seemed to get lost in the divot between his pecs, like he'd nuzzle there all day and night given the option.

But Robin had other ideas, starting with ridding the warlock of his shirt. He pushed the tight black tee up and off, wanting to see the oranges and reds, the yellows and pinks of sunset painting his skin like they had that day on the dock. Wanting to taste every inch of the skin he hadn't gotten to enjoy that day. The soft spot behind Robin's ear, the sharp line of his clavicle, his nipples that shriveled on contact.

Atlas held him there by the back of his head. "Harder," he moaned, as he rocked in his lap. Robin was happy to oblige, sucking his nipple hard between his lips, then nipping it with his teeth. A quick, rough lash with his tongue, then repeating it all over. Making Atlas writhe in his lap, and with his kilt rucked up between them, the tip of his cock leaking against Robin's abs.

His own cock ached, trapped in his jeans while Atlas rutted bare against him, but he'd do this all night if it was what Atlas wanted, what he needed. Atlas had given him exactly that—what he needed. Peace, family, and a place for his soul to feel settled. Acceptance of and relief from the guilt that had plagued him for so long. He wanted to do and be the same for Atlas, always.

Warm lips tickled his ear. "You can fuck me now."

Given the green light, he'd happily step on the gas.

Tipping forward, he laid his mate in the dirt, flipped his kilt up, and wasted no time taking his cock to the back of his throat and swallowing around the tip. Atlas moaned, arching his back and digging his fingers into the soil, making the scent of it all even more potent. Making Robin hungrier than he'd ever been for his mate.

Atlas too, one hand curling in his hair, flecks of dirt tickling Robin's cheek as it rained down around him. "That wasn't a request. Get your cock in my ass. Now."

One more pass over his dick, then Robin drew back to ditch the rest of his clothes. Half propped up, Atlas spit in his palm to stroke over Robin's length to help get him ready, while Robin did the same with his hole, stretching it with spit-slick fingers the way Atlas liked.

Then stretching him with his cock, pushing in hard and fast, all the way to the hilt.

Atlas sighed, the tension fading as they settled into their rhythm. Robin planted his forearms in the dirt on either side of his head, fingers playing with the tips of his hair, nose buried behind his ear so he could smell Atlas and the earth, nature in one breath, while their lower bodies chaotically drove them toward their climax.

"Tomorrow morning," Atlas panted in his ear as they raced toward the end. "I want to run with you." He arched his body, one hand plowing through his hair, the other through the dirt. "In the sun."

Robin gasped against the side of his face. So close. "It's a date, mate."

Atlas's "ugh" died on a moan as he came, cock erupting between them, painting Robin's torso with come, the heat and the smell tripping Robin the rest of the way over too.

When he came back to earth, Atlas was smirking up at him, green and gold eyes dancing. "You should be ashamed of yourself for that line."

Robin nipped at his sexy grin. "How much do you hate me for it?"

"So much," Atlas groaned dramatically, then with a snap, flipped them over and threaded his fingers through Robin's, pressing their hands into the dirt and their foreheads together, Robin's whole world right there with him. "But I love you more."

Robin's lips curved against his. "Balance."

———

For all the latest updates on new projects, sneak peeks, and more, sign up for Layla's Newsletter and join the Layla's Lushes Reader Group on Facebook.

———

Reviews are an invaluable tool when it comes to spreading the word about great reads. Please consider leaving an honest review for the *Soul to Find* series on your favorite review site.

Thank you for reading!

ALSO BY LAYLA REYNE

For the most up-to-date list of titles and a helpful reading order, please visit www.laylareyne.com.

Soul to Find:

Icarus and the Devil

Jason and the Storm

Paris and the Reaper

Atlas and the Traitor

Agents Irish and Whiskey:

Single Malt

Cask Strength

Barrel Proof

Tequila Sunrise

Blended Whiskey

Angel's Share

Trouble Brewing:

Imperial Stout

Craft Brew

Noble Hops

Final Gravity

Fog City:

Prince of Killers

King Slayer

A New Empire

Queen's Ransom

Silent Knight

What We May Be

Perfect Play:

Dead Draw

Bad Bishop

King Hunt

Best Play

Redemption Inc:

The Accidental

The Bounty

The Martyr

The Boss

Guard Duty:

High Winds

Rough Waters

Wild Type:

Variable Onset

Affinity Drift

Matched Pair

Table for Two:

The Last Drop

Dine With Me

Blue Plate Special

Over a Barrel

The Sweet Spot

Sigh of Relief

Changing Lanes:

Relay

Medley

Freestyle

Three Sticks:

Barn Burner

Dirty Dangle

ABOUT THE AUTHOR

Layla Reyne is the author of *What We May Be* and the *Agents Irish and Whiskey*, *Fog City*, and *Perfect Play* series. She writes sexy, intense LGBTQIA+ romance featuring competent adults in kitchens, sports arenas, car chases, and other high-stakes situations. Whether it's adrenaline-fueled suspense, rival athletes, vampires and shifters, or love mixed with mouth-watering foodie goodness, queer folks finding happily-ever-afters is guaranteed.

You can find Layla online at laylareyne.com and at the following sites:

- bookbub.com/authors/layla-reyne
- facebook.com/laylareyne
- instagram.com/laylareyne
- tiktok.com/@laylareyne
- bsky.app/profile/laylareyne